THE EYE OF THE STORM

THE EYE OF THE STORM

Also by Patrick White

PATRICK WHITE

The Eye of the Storm

THE VIKING PRESS   NEW YORK

Copyright © 1973 by Patrick White

Published in 1974 by The Viking Press, Inc.
625 Madison Avenue, New York, N.Y. 10022

Published simultaneously in Canada by
The Macmillan Company of Canada Limited

SBN 670-30374-7

Library of Congress catalog card number: 73-3501

Printed in U.S.A.

Third printing February 1974

TO MAIE CASEY

I was given by chance this human body so
difficult to wear.

Nō play

He felt what could have been a tremor of
heaven's own perverse love.

Kawabata

Men and boughs break;
Praise life while you walk and wake;
It is only lent.

David Campbell

One

THE OLD woman's head was barely fretting against the pillow. She could have moaned slightly.

'What is it?' asked the nurse, advancing on her out of the shadow. 'Aren't you comfortable, Mrs Hunter?'

'Not at all. I'm lying on corks. They're hurting me.'

The nurse smoothed the kidney-blanket, the macintosh, and stretched the sheet. She worked with an air which was not quite professional detachment, nor yet human tenderness; she was probably something of a ritualist. There was no need to switch on a lamp: a white light had begun spilling through the open window; there was a bloom of moonstones on the dark grove of furniture.

'Oh dear, will it never be morning?' Mrs Hunter got her head as well as she could out of the steamy pillows.

'It is,' said the nurse; 'can't you—can't you *feel* it?' While working around this almost chrysalis in her charge, her veil had grown transparent; on the other hand, the wings of her hair, escaping from beneath the lawn, could not have looked a more solid black.

'Yes. I can feel it. It is morning.' The old creature sighed; then the lips, the pale gums opened in the smile of a giant baby. 'Which one are you?' she asked.

'De Santis. But I'm sure you know. I'm the night nurse.'

'Yes. Of course.'

Sister de Santis had taken the pillows and was shaking them up, all but one; in spite of this continued support, Mrs Hunter looked pretty flat.

'I do hope it's going to be one of my good days,' she said. 'I do want to *sound* intelligent. And look—presentable.'

'You will if you want to.' Sister de Santis replaced the pillows. 'I've never known you not rise to an occasion.'

'My will is sometimes rusty.'

'Dr Gidley's coming in case. I rang him last night. We must remember to tell Sister Badgery.'

'The will doesn't depend on doctors.'

Though she might have been in agreement, it was one of the remarks Sister de Santis chose not to hear. 'Are you comfortable now, Mrs Hunter?'

The old head lay looking almost embalmed against the perfect structure of pillows; below the chin a straight line of sheet was pinning the body to the bed. 'I haven't felt comfortable for years,' said the voice. 'And why do you have to go? Why must I have Badgery?'

'Because she takes over at morning.'

A burst of pigeons' wings was fired from somewhere in the garden below.

'I hate Badgery.'

'You know you don't. She's so kind.'

'She talks too much—on and on about that husband. She's too bossy.'

'She's only practical. You have to be in the daytime.' One reason why she herself preferred night duties.

'I hate all those other women.' Mrs Hunter had mustered her complete stubbornness this morning. 'It's only you I love, Sister de Santis.' She directed at the nurse that milky stare which at times still seemed to unshutter glimpses of a terrifying mineral blue.

Sister de Santis began moving about the room with practised discretion.

'At least I can see you this morning,' Mrs Hunter announced. 'You can't escape me. You look like some kind of—big—*lily*.'

The nurse could not prevent herself ducking her veil.

'Are you listening to me?'

Of course she was: these were the moments which refreshed them both.

'I can see the window too,' Mrs Hunter meandered. 'And something—a sort of wateriness—oh yes, the looking-glass. All good signs! This is one of the days when I can see better. I shall see *them*!'

'Yes. You'll see them.' The nurse was arranging the hairbrushes; the ivory brushes with their true-lovers' knots in gold and lapis lazuli had a fascination for her.

'The worst thing about love between human beings,' the voice was directed at her from the bed, 'when you're prepared to love them they don't want it; when they do, it's you who can't bear the idea.'

'You've got an exhausting day ahead,' Sister de Santis warned; 'you'd better not excite yourself.'

'I've always excited myself if the opportunity arose. I can't stop now — for anyone.'

Again there was that moment of splintered sapphires, before the lids, dropping like scales, extinguished it.

'You're right, though. I shall need my strength.' The voice began to wheedle. 'Won't you hold my hand a little, dear Mary — isn't it? de Santis?'

Sister de Santis hesitated enough to appease the spirit of her training. Then she drew up a little mahogany tabouret upholstered in a faded sage. She settled her opulent breasts, a surprise in an otherwise austere figure, and took the skin and bone of Mrs Hunter's hand.

Thus placed they were exquisitely united. According to the light it was neither night nor day. They inhabited a world of trust, to which their bodies and minds were no more than entrance gates. Of course Sister de Santis could not answer truthfully for her patient's mind: so old and erratic, often feeble since the stroke; but there were moments such as this when they seemed to reach a peculiar pitch of empathy. The nurse might have wished to remain clinging to their state of perfection if she had not evolved, in the course of her working life, a belief — no, it was stronger: a religion — of perpetual becoming. Because she was handsome in looks and her bearing suggested authority, those of her colleagues who detected in her something odd and reprehensible would not have dared call it 'religious'; if they laughed at her, it was not to her face. Even so, it could have been the breath of scorn which had dictated her choice of the night hours in which to patrol the intenser world of her conviction, to practise not only the disciplines of her professed vocation, but the rituals of her secret faith.

Then why Mrs Hunter? those less dedicated or more rational might have suggested, and Mary de Santis failed to explain; except that this ruin of an over-indulged and beautiful youth, rustling with fretful spite when not bludgeoning with a brutality only old age is ingenious enough to use, was also a soul about to leave the body it had worn, and already able to emancipate itself so completely from human emotions, it became at times as redemptive as water, as clear as morning light.

This actual morning old Mrs Hunter opened her eyes and said to her nurse, 'Where are the dolls?'

'Where you left them, I expect.' Because her inept answer satisfied neither of them, the nurse developed a pained look.

'But that's what they always say! Why don't they bring them?' Mrs Hunter protested.

The nurse could only bite her lip; the hand had been dragged away from hers.

'Of course you know about the dolls. Don't say I didn't tell you.' The old woman was threatening to become vindictive. 'We were living beside the—oh, some—some *geographical* river. My father had given me a hundred dolls. Think of it—a hundred! Some of them I didn't look at because they didn't interest me, but some I loved to distraction.'

Suddenly Mrs Hunter turned her head with such a doll's jerk Sister de Santis held her breath.

'You know it isn't true,' the old child complained. 'It was Kate Nutley had the dolls. She was spoilt. I had two—rather battered ones. And still didn't love them equally.'

Sister de Santis was troubled by the complexities of a world she had been forced to re-enter too quickly.

'I tore the leg off one,' Mrs Hunter admitted; her recovered calm was enviable.

'Didn't they mend it?' the nurse dared inquire.

'I can't remember.' Mrs Hunter gave a little whimper. 'And have to remember everything today. People try to catch you out—accuse you—of not—not loving them enough.'

She was staring at the increasing light, if not glaring, frightfully. 'And look my best. Bring me my looking-glass, Nurse.'

Sister de Santis fetched the glass: it was of that same ivory set as the brushes with lovers' knots in gold and lapis lazuli. Holding it by its fluted handle she tilted the glass for her patient to look. The nurse was glad she could not see the reflection: reflections can be worse than faces.

Mrs Hunter was panting. 'Somebody must make me up.'

'Sister Badgery will see to that.'

'Oh, Badgery! She's awful. If only little Manhood were here—she knows how to do it properly. She's the one I like.'

'Sister Manhood won't be here till lunch.'

'Why can't somebody telephone her?'

'She'll still be asleep. And later she'll probably have some shopping to do.'

Mrs Hunter was so upset she let her head drop on the pillow: tears gushed surprisingly out of the half-closed eyes.

Sister de Santis heard her own voice sound more placid than she felt. 'If you rest your mind you'll probably look far more beautiful as your natural self. And that is how they'll want to see you.'

But the old woman fully closed her eyes. 'Not now. Why, my lashes are gone—my complexion. I can *feel* the freckles, even on my eyelids, without having to look for them.'

'I'm sure you're exaggerating, Mrs Hunter.' Small comfort; but the nurse's feet were aching, nor had her mind, her eyes, adjusted themselves to daylight: the withdrawal of darkness had left her puffy and moth-like.

When she noticed her patient staring at her too obsessively. 'I'd like you to bring me something to drink. And something else—' putting out a hand at its oldest and feeblest, 'I want you to forgive

13

me, Mary. Will you?' stroking no longer with bones, but the tips of feathers.

The sensation experienced by Sister de Santis was scarcely sensual; nor did it lift her to that state of disembodiment they sometimes enjoyed together. It was disturbing, though.

For her own protection the nurse ignored half the request, while agreeing too heartily to the other. 'All right! What do you fancy?'

'Nothing milky.' Mrs Hunter made a smacking sound with her lips, because those two glutinous strips did not release each other easily. 'Something cold and pure,' she added after rejecting pap.

Sister de Santis had to relent; she had to look; and at once added to the caress of feathers, there were the eyes, some at least of their original mineral fire burning through the film with which age and sickness had attempted to obscure it. 'I'd like a glass of water,' Mrs Hunter said.

Sister de Santis was reduced to feeling embarrassed and lumpish. 'It'll be cold,' she promised, 'from the fridge. I can't answer for its purity. It's what the Water Board provides.'

As she left the room, a glare from furniture and a bedpan scarcely covered by a towel, sprang at the high priestess, stripping her of the illusions of her office, the night thoughts, speculations of a mystical turn few had ever guessed at, and certainly, thank God, no one shared, except, perhaps, one malicious old woman. In her daytime form, Mary de Santis of thumping bust and pronounced calves, might have been headed for basket-ball.

Left alone, which after all was how she wanted to be, with due respect to poor broody faithful de Santis, Mrs Hunter lay with her eyes closed listening to her house, her thoughts, her life. All around her clocks were ticking, not to mention that muffled metronome which might have been her heart. In some ways it was an advantage to be what they refer to as 'half blind'. She had always seen too clearly, it seemed: opaque friends had been alarmed by it; a husband and lovers had resented; worst of all, the children — they could have done murder. She scrabbled after the handkerchief a nurse had

14

hidden; so she cried without it. *I've never seen you cry, Elizabeth, unless you wanted something.* Alfred would lower his chin as though riding at an armoured opponent. And she would raise hers, accepting the challenge. *It hadn't occurred to me. But must be right if you've noticed.* Opposing a husband with the weapon of her profile: she had perfect nostrils, so they told her; she had also seen for herself in the glass. Only Alfred had not told her; was it out of delicacy? His friends all referred to him as 'Bill'. Most of his life he had spent trying to disguise himself as one of the costive, crutch-heavy males who came to discuss wool and meat: so slow and ponderous, like rams dragging their sex through a stand of lucerne. There were also the would-be cuddly fe-males making up to 'Bill', unaware how immaculate he was.

Mrs Hunter laughed.

You know, Betty, you are the only one who has never called me by a friendly name. Not 'Bill': just to attempt it made her feel she was shaking her jowls like a bloodhound. *How can I? When 'Alfred' is the name you've been given. I mean it's your* NAME—*as mine is 'Elizabeth'.* She raised her voice and drew down her mouth to produce a dimple she held in reserve; but on this occasion it failed to persuade him.

Though he had never accused her of being cold, others had suggested that she was: satellite spinsters hopeful of prolonging schoolgirl crushes; wives in need of a receptacle in which to pour an accumulation of injustices; a man like Athol Shreve (she had only done it as an essay in sensuality; the hair alone disgusted her); that young Norwegian—no, or had he? (wasn't his subject fish?)— on the Warmings' island.

Not everyone is an island: they loved 'Bill', while admiring Elizabeth Hunter. It is the children who are the most forbidding, the least hospitable of islands, though you can light a fire if you know how to scrape together the wherewithal.

She sucked the corner of a pillowslip remembering the children. What were their names? Dor-o-thy? And Bsl? Bas-il! Words of love at the time, ugly and pretentious in the end.

Mrs Hunter fell into a snooze trying to remember something else she had discovered, not in any hairy embrace, or under threat by wet-kissing females, or children's butterfly-flickers alternating with denunciations. Falling into her light snooze she would have liked to experience a state of mind she knew existed, but which was too subtle to enter except by special grace.

The night nurse made her way down through what was technically her employer's house, an ugly, ostentatious one. She must remember that. It would be easier now that daylight was cracking the curtains. She must remember her framed certificate hanging beside her father's diploma; she must remember her thirty-two years of nursing (she would be fifty in a couple of months). In Mrs Hunter's house, furniture choked even the landings and the passages: presses and consoles and cabinets which could not be crammed into the rooms. Carpets, once rich and uniformly springy, were thinning in patches the owner would not see, and those who did, ignored; because what was the use? they expected her to die.

On the half-landing the nurse jerked at a curtain and let in more of the abrasive light. It fairly clashed with a vase of honesty standing in a niche: the silver medals on dry stems seemed to twitter as her hand withdrew. Dust hung in the light, like scentless incense, in spite of Mrs Cush: *with a person operatun on er own only two mornuns a week a speck of dust can be expected.*

Something walked over Sister de Santis's grave, and she shivered. That is how they explain it, she ought to remember, not let her conscience get her down for having seen herself, that instant, laying the damp pledgets on the freckly eyelids after the last tremor had subsided. Remember, rather, that a disagreeable case drains less out of you—or so some of her colleagues maintained.

The nurse continued down the stairs, holding on to the rail as though in need of support. By night she floated, unassisted, whether up or down, her stiff white skirt barely brushing the protective hedge, its tangle of iron branches loaded with Hesperian fruit. Doubts seldom arose at night, because love and usage will invest the most material house with numinous forms and purposes, from amongst which an initiate's thoughts will soar like multi-coloured invocations.

Whereas this morning, as she descended deeper into this stuffy well, Sister de Santis was unreasonably pursued by faint faecal whiffs, by the insinuating stench of urine from an aged bladder; while the light itself, or iron thorns, or old transparent fingernails, scratched at her viciously.

She would have to remember that no patient is entirely vicious or unreasonable.

It must have been fifteen years ago that Mr Wyburd gave warning, 'I ought to tell you, Miss de Santis, you're taking on what I would call a *difficult* case.'

The solicitor made a pyramid out of his hands, fingertip to fingertip, almost too conventionally legal. She tried to calculate his age: not old, but old enough (probably born with an elderly manner). His skin was beginning to dry out, leaving behind a relief of veins on the formal hands. On the little finger of one hand was a signet ring, its stone a matching blue for the veins.

'Not exactly capricious—I'd rather say "changeable",' he emphasized in his careful voice.

While eyeing the nurse, he could have been wondering whether he might trust her with his reputation as well as the care of one of his more important clients. This was only for an instant, though: he was too respectful of the professions.

Outwardly as placid as her acquaintances accused her of being, Sister de Santis had sat forward, mentally at least, to take a better look at the difficulties, the caprices, with which the solicitor was threatening her. Something about the situation made her tingle, though a wordless mumbling, and her slow, creamy smile, conveyed disbelief.

A handsome woman: sluggish, but reliable. Her references were excellent; a colonel had left her an annuity.

Mr Wyburd coughed. 'Mrs Hunter was something of a beauty in her day. Oh, she still has her looks. She is much admired. Many have depended on her—for opinions and advice.' Mr Wyburd laughed; he dismantled his hands and hid them under the desk. 'She enjoys a battle of wits, too!'

Mary de Santis smiled what was intended as appreciation. She must have looked rather stupid, she felt, but it was necessary to disguise her feelings: her excitement and expectations. Before each new case she hoped that she might prove herself afresh, but never so much as in combat with this vision of fragmented beauty. So she looked, still smiling, over the solicitor's shoulder, at the immaculately folded documents tied with identical ribbons of a disinfectant pink: she was fascinated by these too, by their mystic anonymity.

Mr Wyburd approached something which might be giving him trouble. 'As I mentioned, Mrs Hunter is suffering from—you could hardly call it a breakdown—a slight nervous upset. Her daughter recently returned to France—where she has lived since her marriage to a Frenchman.' More than ever Mr Wyburd hesitated to disgorge. 'I can hardly refer to this gentleman as her "husband". You might say he "re-married" after a *form* of divorce. Which Dorothy Hunter's adopted faith won't allow her to recognize.'

The solicitor and the nurse were united in suitable gravity over these biographical details.

It comforted him to decide that Sister de Santis was in some ways probably obtuse: no disadvantage in a relationship with Elizabeth Hunter; nor should it weaken her sense of vocation. The solicitor caught a glimpse of the veil hovering behind her timeless hat, which his daughters might have referred to as 'frumpish'.

'When am I expected, Mr Wyburd?'

In the fifteen years since first acquaintance with Elizabeth Hunter, Mary de Santis had been sent for intermittently, sometimes to fulfil the needs of friendship, on several occasions to help dramatize a minor illness, and, finally, to officiate at the great showdown. In the circumstances, Sisters Badgery and Manhood, Mrs Lippmann and Mrs Cush, accepted lesser rank in the hierarchy without damage to their self-importance. None of them questioned the efficiency of their superior, while some even sensed an authority of the spirit which gave her deeper access to the heart of the creature round whom they revolved, and to whom they were all, more or less, dedicated.

Until this morning, here was the archpriestess, a heavy woman clumping down the stairs, stumbling on the last of them. In her present condition her clumsiness was doubly irritating, and to look down and find the rod had broken free, the runner come adrift. On a day of such importance the incident made Sister de Santis perspire. She could feel a trickling down her back; the pores in her nose must be looking exaggerated; night had tossed her out, a crumpled, grubby stickiness.

If she had not been so mild, something which might have passed for rage made her snatch at curtains as she passed, unlatch fastenings, heave at windows: the air surrounding her was thick as flannel. Without real justification, she could have pounced on the house-keeper if the opportunity had occurred, but Mrs Lippmann would still be in bed: it was her one fault, her only luxury. (*Half my life, or before I am myself a servant, Miss de Santis, I am coming home while the maid is still only rising.*)

So whether you liked it or not, the house too, was in your charge a little longer, unless this great gilded mirror swallowed its once shadowy familiar, together with a crunch of Meissen, and splintering of marquetry.

Bad enough the mirrors, worse the portraits. Bound for the pantry, Sister de Santis could not resist the drawing-room. Whether the portraits were of any value she had never been able to judge, only guess they must have cost a lot of money. Beyond this, and their ephemeral elegance, their fashionable truthlessness, they had that certain pathos of the possessions of the very rich. In spite of his curving lashes, his golden cheeks, Basil might have been a nasty little boy, Dorothy a plain sour girl, without a splendour of varnish and the protection of their gilded frames. The fall of diamonds from Elizabeth Hunter's wrists and shoulders might have drowned the dutiful or innocent in a wave of admiration. But Mary de Santis was unimpressed by jewels. Only the face was real, through no virtue of the painter's, she had decided long ago, or rather, the face transcended a vulgarity of superficial, slippery paint, to reveal a correspondence, as will some of the semi-precious stones, or flowers, or phrases of music, or passages of light.

It was the children who finally routed the nurse by reminding her of a desiccated carcase, blotched with brown, streaked with yellow, scarred by knives: the body from which they had sprung to force their purposes on life. This morning the portraits of Mrs Hunter's children made Sister de Santis shudder. (*I love all kiddies; don't you love the kiddies, Sister?* At least Sister Badgery never waited for anyone else's opinion.)

Sister de Santis did not stop to draw the curtains in the dining-room, but hurried through its brown-velvet hush, past the portrait of Alfred Hunter ('Bill' to his friends). Mr Hunter's portrait was smaller than his wife's; it must have cost considerably less: even so, a lot of money, if you read the signature in the corner. For a man of wealth Mr Hunter looked rather diffident: he probably disappointed the painter, except by writing out his cheque. The nurse moderated her pace, walking with the reverence accorded to those you have not known in their lifetime, but might have. Out of respect, she endowed Mr Hunter with virtues she could remember in her father.

I wanted very badly to love my husband, Sister, even after I knew I didn't—or couldn't enough. Mrs Hunter's admissions had been embarrassing at first: you had to persuade yourself you were not overhearing.

Sister de Santis pushed the baize which would admit her to the pantry. The door sighed like a human being; it might have felt like one too, if she had allowed herself to think so.

She had half filled a little crystal jug from the pantry fridge when she heard a thumping in the kitchen beyond. She went in. It was the housekeeper throwing her arms around while getting herself into an apron. Her face hidden by the bib, her contortions looked grotesque: she was still probably stupefied by sleep.

'Early for you, isn't it?' the night nurse remarked while the housekeeper was still submerged.

'*Ach*, but I'm so—*nervös!*' As she struggled free the effect was even more grotesque: the stiffened lips in the stone face might have been designed as an escape in times of downpour. 'So nervous!' she gasped. 'It's the visitors. And Mr Wyburd expected to breakfast.'

'Mr Wyburd will cope with the visitors.'

'Yes, but it is still so very early. And I do not easily leave my bett. *Übrigens*,' it cheered Mrs Lippmann to realize, 'aren't you later than usual, Sister?'

'Out of shameful curiosity.'

The housekeeper returned at once to looking racked; the knuckles she was clenching appeared to have aged sooner than her face, mock-youthful in almost all its conscious expressions. 'Oh, this is always the frightful hour! Why you cannot stay every morning, Miss de Santis, till Sister Badgery shows herself? *Diese Badgery kann nie nie pünktlich kommen*—never! What if *she* should roll out of bett while I am all alone with her? Or what if she have another stroke?' Mrs Lippmann began a series of laments which led her to the core of tragedy, sounds which shocked Badgery and Manhood, but which Sister de Santis's foreign blood made it easier for her to accept.

Foreignness alone did not always help her comfort this small unhappy Jewess. 'Probably nothing of what you imagine will happen,' was the best she could offer this morning. 'By the way, Mrs Lippmann, we never talk about the stroke. In any case, it was only a very slight one: a blood vessel broke somewhere behind one of her eyes.'

Although corrected, Mrs Lippmann seemed elated by this hint of conspiracy over medical matters: she danced a few steps across the considerable kitchen, jiggling her buttocks, wagging her head, before coming to a standstill, every piece of her anatomy exaggeratedly taut.

'That is so! And our visitors will bring life. I am almost out of myself to see them. *Auch ein wirklicher Künstler!* I have made the betts. I have put flowers as she wishes.'

21

'You needn't have put the flowers.'

'But while she is in her chair she may ask somebody to wheel her in.'

'She wouldn't see.'

'Mrs Hunter will see through a wall if she is determined to.'

'What I should have said was: your flowers will be wasted on the visitors. They're not staying—not in the house.'

'But I have made the betts! That was her order.'

'They're not staying.'

'Somebody must tell her.'

'Mr Wyburd must. He's had plenty of practice at that sort of thing.' On realizing that she had neglected her duty, Sister de Santis frowned at the little jug she was holding.

Mrs Lippmann's eyebrows reached towards each other like glistening, palpitating caterpillars. 'I will never understand why Anglo-Saxons reject the warm of the family.'

'They're afraid of being consumed. Families can eat you.'

'Something will always consume: if not the family, then it's the incinerators,' Mrs Lippmann moaned.

All the way up the stairs the glass clinked against the jug Sister de Santis was carrying carefully on a salver. Like all the silver in the house, the salver bore someone else's arms.

When she arrived at the bedside she saw that her patient had fallen asleep: the parted lips were sucked back repeatedly against the gums; the chalky claws, hooked into the hem of the sheet, were lifted by a regular breathing.

Sister de Santis stood the salver so expertly on the bedside table there was not a single clink of crystal, not the slightest jarring of silver.

'I'm not asleep, you know, Sister,' Mrs Hunter's voice informed. 'The worst symptom of my—condition—I practically hardly ever sleep.'

Sister de Santis filled the glass. When she had raised her patient's shoulders, the neck worked; the lips reached out, and supped uglily at the water. The lips suggested some lower form of life, a sea creature perhaps, extracting more than water from water. As humanity was not what one got from Elizabeth Hunter, one should not have felt disillusioned.

By the time she had done her duty the silver sun set in the rosewood bed had started duelling with the actual one. Sister de Santis took brief refuge in what Sister Badgery liked to refer to as the Nurses' Retiring Room, but which was really a wardrobe in which were hoarded most of the dresses Mrs Hunter had bought in her lifetime. Seated in front of the mirror Mary de Santis unpinned her hair. What, she tried to remember, had she expected, ever? Her face, inside the dark, streaming hair, continued haunting the looking glass.

Whether asleep or awake — in fact her life had become one long waking sleep — Mrs Hunter slipped back into the dream she had left. She found it easy enough to resume these waking dreams of which her life was constituted; sometimes she could even manipulate the deep dreadful dreams which belonged to the sleep she would not admit to.

Now the water her dutiful, but possibly sulking nurse had brought her, helped her return to this other, shallower kind of experience or dream. They were walking, she and Kate Nutley, their arms full of dolls, beside this great river. No, it wasn't: it was the shallow and often drought-stricken stream which meandered through everybody's place, through Salkelds', Nutleys' and Hunters' that is, a brown ribbon ruffling over stones, under willows. At its best the river was all joyous motion, though in its less pleasing backwaters scum formed, and sometimes a swollen sheep floated. Elizabeth, never Kate, had to prod the bloated sheep. When they had reached a certain point where the water swirled deeper round a bend, Elizabeth Salkeld and Kate Nutley halted. Elizabeth started throwing in the dolls. Some of them bobbed on the surface of the water; the limbs of others grew soggy and dragged them under. Kate began to cry. She was a serious child, as well as a simple soul, Elizabeth sensed from the beginning.

23

Why are you crying when you've got so many? And isn't it interesting to see what happens? Kate had a habit of sniffling: *I wasn't crying for the dolls, but for what happened to my sister. Don't you know about it?* Elizabeth grunted to hide her shame; the Salkelds lowered their voices more than most parents in the district, and she hadn't yet found out what had happened to Lilian, Kate's elder sister. Kate was ready to explain, *Lilian ran away with someone, a Russian or something.* Oh, you knew about that! *And now she has been murdered.* How could they be sure? People you know don't get murdered. But Kate seemed to have grown up all of a sudden: she was even more serious than before. *They found Lilian's body on the banks of some great river — in China, or Siberia.* So there *was* this other river! *The blood was drying on her neck.* Kate could not tell any more because she was crying again. But Elizabeth Salkeld could not cry for Kate's sister Lilian galloping wildly towards her death on the banks of the great Asiatic river. By comparison, their own shallow life, their stagnant days, were becoming unbearable. Elizabeth Salkeld could have slapped her friend for not hearing the thud of hooves, or seeing the magnificence of Lilian's full gallop. Instead, she whipped the water with a willow switch.

'Horrid little girl I was!' Mrs Hunter muttered. 'Most children are horrid except in theory.'

She also knew she had no desire to die however stagnant her life became: she only hoped she would be allowed to experience again that state of pure, living bliss she was now and then allowed to enter. How, she wasn't sure. It could depend on Sister de Santis; she needed Mary to hold her hand.

When she opened her eyes, and started groping for her little handbell, to accuse her nurse of abandoning her, there was another figure, taller and thinner, standing in the doorway, but so misty she could not guess, except that, she fancied, she could smell a man.

'Is it you, darling?' she tried out. 'What a long time I've been waiting.'

A dry silence told her she had given herself away.

Then a voice, 'It is I — Wyburd.' He had hesitated from wondering

24

how to compose his reply; his grandchildren, sometimes even his daughters, laughed at his correct grammar.

'Oh, it is! I suppose I'm glad to see you, Arnold. I knew you were coming. Of course I'm glad!' She put on a bit more than the voice you use for the solicitor, because Arnold Wyburd was: a bit more than the solicitor; he couldn't very well help it after all this time.

Keemis is sending up the papers with Arnold Wyburd the junior partner, so that we make sure nobody else grabs the block you have your eye on. This was the year Elizabeth and Alfred ('Bill') Hunter had looked at each other and finally admitted. Alfred looked at her longer than she at him because he was the more honest, she granted even then: not that she was dis-honest; she only lacked his purity of heart. *The point is, Alfred, you must allow me to give our children what we owe them; here there is no life; and what about their education?* Mention of education always stirred Alfred to action. So they were buying the block in Sydney, at Centennial Park, and *the young cove* was bringing the agreement for signature. Elizabeth Hunter had found Arnold Wyburd *an agreeable young fellow, harmless anyway.* It was the evening after he had gone. They were strolling up and down the veranda. Alfred was looking at her cleavage: she was wearing a rather lovely though simple dress of white lace which collaborated in a delicious cool with a breeze sweeping down off the hills. She realized she would have to allow Alfred tonight: she could hear by his breathing he expected it; but he was so kind, and the evenings at 'Kudjeri' interminable.

And now this old man Arnold Wyburd had approached her bed —well, not old, not as old as herself, nobody else was as old as that but oldish. He smelled old. He sounded dry. He had taken her hand, and she was touching paper, delicate tissue, against her own. She might have played a little with the hand if she could have been bothered.

'Everything under control?' the solicitor inquired in a loud though slightly tremulous voice.

'Why not?'

It was the sort of thing men always ask; and Arnold in that old woman's voice. Perhaps Lal had been the man; anyway, between them, they had got a couple of girls.

'How's Lal?'

'Suffering, I'm sorry to say, from her rheumatic pains.'

'Didn't know she had any.'

'For years. Only on and off, though.'

'Then she ought to be thankful. "On and off" is nothing. I've been racked by arthritis, without pause, for years.'

'Oh?'

Remember to give him a present for Lal: the plainest woman ever; freckles. (Mrs Hunter put her hands to her face, to touch.) Lal had pouches under her eyes even as a girl.

The solicitor cleared his throat. 'I've got a disappointment for you, a very slight one however.'

'Don't—tell me.'

She had opened her eyes. Arnold Wyburd decided not to look at them.

'Basil has been delayed in Bangkok. He'll be here this evening.'

'Why—why? *Bangkok!*' Mrs Hunter's mouth was working past grief towards abuse. 'Basil knew better than anybody how to—disappoint,' she gasped. 'I wonder whether he would have disappointed me as an actor.'

'He has a great following. Lal saw him, you remember, when she took Marjorie and Heather over to London. I believe they saw him in *Macbeth*. Marjorie read somewhere that only the greatest actors can manage the part of Macbeth: the others don't have the voice for it. Very taxing, it appears.'

Arnold's snippet of information, however dry, might have fed her pride if she had not felt temporarily quenched. For the moment she loathed herself so intensely she wished Arnold Wyburd would leave.

Sensing something of her wishes, though not enough, he had moved across to one of the windows overlooking the park. Summer had left the grass yellow, the lake shrunken; only the columns had succeeded in keeping up appearances of a sort: rising out of a civic embroidery of cannas and agapanthus, they continued offering their job lot of European statuary.

Why had he never lost a sense of inferiority in his relationship with Mrs Hunter? He should have disliked; instead he had not shed his admiration, first for his client's wife, then for the widow. There was Lal of course to heal the wounds: *in so many ways a splendid woman, Mrs Hunter; we must forgive the faults, even if she won't let us forget them.*

He turned round, possibly to offer further consolation for the delay in Basil's arrival: *Dorothy will be here on time according to the last check with the airport.* But she was again lying with her mouth open, not quite snoring, sucking at air, at life.

Ohhh she was moaning deep down while standing outside one of the many envelopes of flesh she could remember wearing. She was looking at her sleeping husband. He certainly wasn't dead, only unaware of the other lives she was leading beside him in his house while engaged in the practical business of bottling fruit and pickling onions—if the cook allowed it—when she was not supervising or sacking governesses, or chivvying maids. He liked her to ride through the paddocks with him. Even when they rode out together, he was not aware that she had never been the person he thought her to be. Not even when his full calf in its leather legging brushed so close the stirrup-irons clashed. She used to wear that old velour with stains round the band, which heightened the deception. As cattle seethed past with a sound of scuffed buckram; or ewes milled or scampered; or rams plodded, coughing and panting. She was once photographed holding a ram by the horns, smoothing a ribbon on his prize shoulders. More than anything the rams helped break what should have been an interminable marriage.

Oh darling she moaned she moaned; from now on she was going to love him. Having known him as the Hunter boy, 'Bill', Alfred, kind husband, the Juggernaut of stifling nights under a mosquito net, there should have been no situation they could not embrace equally: when their mere bodies prevented that, or so it seemed, as he groped, stroked, fumbled, looking for some kind of confirmation through his hands, before thrusting up inside her to reach the secret she was keeping from him.

The wool men and cattle experts who came to ask his advice approached the presence in a spirit of blustering servility. She only realized how small he was as he lay wilted and sweating, rather fatty about the shoulders, his exhausted lungs still battering at her practically pulverized breasts. At his most masterful his toes would be gripping the sheets on either side of her long legs, as though he had found the purchase to impress her more deeply than ever before. Once, she remembered, she had felt, not his sweat, his tears trickling down the side of her neck, till he started coughing, and tore himself away from her: their skins sounded like sticking plaster. She tried to make herself, and finally did, ask what had upset him. His 'luck', in everything, was more than he deserved; however indistinct the answer, that was what it amounted to.

At least she had given him their children. She must remember that, re-create their faces: fluctuating on the dark screen, Dorothy's little mask, never quite transparent nor yet opaque, not unlike those silver medals on the dried stems of honesty; and Basil the Superb, who preferred to perform for strangers or gullible innocents like Lal Wyburd. Their children. Hardly Alfred's, except by the accident of blood.

So she must make amends. She was not ungenerous with her long cool body for which he had paid so largely: it was no fault of his he had not been in time to save her father's life. Tragedy and the elasticity of awakened flesh brought them close in those early years. So they believed. What else she could give was more than she knew. She began going out of her way to avoid him, hoping to find in solitude insight into a mystery of which she was perhaps the least part. It was easy enough to excuse herself from riding round the paddocks with him: household matters; a child ill; endless simple and convincing reasons. But she continued hemmed in, not only by the visible landscape of hills and scrub, but by the landscape of her mind. *I am superficial and frivolous*, she blurted hopelessly; *there is no evidence, least of all these children, that I am not barren.* By the light of spring the surrounding hills had glittered like jewels, in the more brutal summer blaze they were smelted into heaps of blue metal: either way they looked dead. Her own state of mind appalled her increasingly.

How much of it he guessed, let alone understood, she had not been able to decide; he could not have been so insensitively male not to be hurt. He was: hadn't she on one occasion felt his tears? Otherwise he hid his feelings with a delicacy which must have made her behaviour appear more shocking: not exactly selfish, as some no doubt had seen it, though nobody had dared accuse her, simply because she had dared them to and they were afraid of her. Maids had accused, silently: maids are more candid in the thoughts their eyes reflect, from overhearing telephone conversations and living through one's headaches and colds. Friends can be held at bay with social conventions—and by maids. In any case the women, if not too stupid, were saving you up against the necessity of a future alliance. Men friends were either too dense to see, or too honourable to comment: like Arnold Wyburd, who must have seen more than most. Arnold was an honourable man, as opposed to his wife, who was an honest woman. You hardly ever saw Lal; but when you did, the flat replies, together with a certain tension of manner, implied judgment.

Lal Wyburd would naturally have interpreted as selfishness every floundering attempt anybody made to break out of the straitjacket and recover a sanity which must have been theirs in the beginning, and might be theirs again in the end. That left the long stretch of the responsible years, when you were lunging in your madness after love, money, position, possessions, while an inkling persisted, sometimes even a certainty descended: of a calm in which the self had been stripped, if painfully, of its human imperfections.

Mrs Hunter sighed, and the solicitor at the window turned to look. The Plantagenet attitude she had preserved for so long under the sheet was breaking up.

'That is something Lal Wyburd would never understand: she's too *normal*,' she said, or moaned.

With his wife in the foreground of his thoughts, his client's uncanny intrusion started the solicitor stuttering. 'Wuh-what is it? Are you in pain? Can I do something – tuh-turn you, or something?' when he wasn't normally a stutterer, and would have liked to express, however rustily, some degree of tenderness.

As for Mrs Hunter, she did not seem to find it necessary to reply: her mouth was again firmly adapted to her gums.

So he continued standing at the window, still the junior in a firm whose senior partner had died many years ago.

In the park, morning had solidified by now. Autumn at its blandest had infused an almost convincing life into dead grass and exhausted leaves. Anonymous figures strayed along the banks of the ornamental lakes, or walked more purposefully to work. A girl on a livery stable hack just missed becoming unseated when her nag shied at a tussock.

As a young man Arnold Wyburd had fancied himself in a boater with striped band; he had started wearing, or liked to think he was 'sporting', a blue blazer with brass buttons. He had given up because, frankly, it was not what people expected of him. Suddenly he found himself head of a family, married to Lal Pennecuick, a thoroughly sensible, not pretty, but pleasing young woman, with whom he got the two little girls they had christened Marjorie and Heather. Nowadays he saw less of Lal, but that was understandable since grandchildren claimed so much of her attention, and in any case there seemed more to get through since they themselves had begun slowing up.

In spite of the encroachment of family, very satisfying in its way, and the equally satisfying, if exhausting demands of a restricted, though respectable practice, he and Lal continued meeting every night in bed. Probably both were at their happiest discussing the events of the day. He could trust Lal's discretion, and would sometimes report on the more reprehensible whims of his most respected clients; while she was equally frank in some of her disclosures, such as the symptoms of meanness she was discovering in their son-in-law Oscar Hawkins, and Heather's menopausal troubles. If he had not revealed his secret passion for Marjorie's middle daughter, Jenny, it was because a sense of being disloyal to the other grandchildren prevented him.

Arnold Wyburd hardly allowed himself to hear what could only be a slow, soft fart from the direction of his client's bed; he could not remember ever having heard a woman break wind before. Whether Mrs Hunter herself heard, it was impossible to tell: she appeared too engrossed in sleep or thought.

Actually she no longer attached much importance to her own physical behaviour, unless it hurt her. Didn't care for smells, though: those dreadfully increasing accidents. But they gave the nurses something to do.

And solicitors? What did Arnold Wyburd do? It was doubtful whether his morning consisted of much more than reading the *Herald* at that old-fashioned office. Lucky there were the nurses and Mrs Lippmann for him to pay. Otherwise she had to invent little jobs for him, like looking up retired housemaids to see whether they were in need of financial assistance, or inquiring about the arrival of aeroplanes.

Was his arrival at 'Kudjeri' with the deeds to the block of land Alfred bought for her in Sydney, and on which she was determined to die—none of those convalescent homes, and certainly not the Thingummy Village, thank you—was the occasion of the deeds her first sight of the young Arnold? She could not remember any other. He looked so thin and prissy, white too, beside the coarser, ruddier Alfred. He was everything she felt a solicitor ought to be. Because he looked so hot in his dark and incongruous city clothes, she told him to take his coat off, but he said he wouldn't.

Then, after giving the matter a reasonable amount of thought, he changed his mind. In moving the coat from the sofa to the back of a chair she detected a faint smell of moist warmth, hardly perspiration: certainly unlike the tom-cat stench of male sweat.

(Why does all this come back when I can't always remember what I've had for lunch, or if I've had it? The past has been burnt into me, I suppose—like they do with cattle.)

Was Arnold already married? Oh yes, he must have been. There was some formal talk about children at dinner that night. Yes. The worthy Lal had produced her first, and was expecting another. After dinner Dorothy and Basil came in: Dorothy still looking thin after her bronchitis that winter (the official reason why Alfred proposed to build a house in Sydney); Basil on the other hand never had an illness, and not a nerve in his body. The children had not taken to Mr Wyburd: not surprisingly he bored them. Later on, Dorothy developed a passion for his wife. On the few occasions when they all met she wouldn't leave Lal alone, putting her arms round that freckled neck, wanting to cuddle—quite laughable. Even Basil used to talk to Mrs Wyburd, at an age when he had started sulking at everybody else; wanted to drag the solicitor's wife into corners to tell her about his ambitions. One was thankful for his civility.

But Arnold was rigid in the company of children, with almost everybody. That night at 'Kudjeri' he had lit her cigarette, and his hand trembled. She held his wrist, to steady him, and was surprised at its sinewiness. Perhaps she could teach him courage. Yes, that was something she could give to them all—perhaps; she had never been afraid.

It was an excruciating evening. Alfred fell asleep after telling about the rams and the Gimcrack mare slipping her foal the night before. That young Arnold Wyburd, unhappy in his comfortable shirtsleeves, sat watching you toss your ankle as you tried to think of a topic which might break the agony. (Lal shortened her skirt only after everybody had forgotten skirts were short.) Next morning he left and you didn't see him: there was no reason why you should; Alfred's driving him into Gogong in the Bentley, to catch the train, was attention enough.

(All country evenings were boring. People only become religious about them after escaping and forgetting the details. Funny you

32

should remember that sinewiness in Arnold's smooth, hairless wrist.)

When the house was built—the spiteful, and those in any way radically inclined, liked to refer to it as a 'mansion', which it wasn't: only four reception, and as many bedrooms, not counting the maids' quarters—you decided not to give gossip a chance by moving in too enthusiastically. Besides, this was starting from scratch, unlike 'Kudjeri', with all those inherited monstrosities. At Moreton Drive there were cabinet-makers, decorators and so forth to make patience a virtue. Delay and an unfashionable address should have silenced most tongues. People still talked, however, the babbling, frivolous ones. *Why, Elizabeth, won't you be cutting yourself off living at Centennial Park? Coming from the bush to settle, practically—in the bush! We've never known anyone live in Moreton Drive.* She could only answer, *Now you will know somebody, won't you?* It was certainly very sandy, almost dune wherever houses had not been built; the branches of bottlebrush rattled when winds blew, which was permanently. Bad for the garden and the hair. But she would show the trivial members of her acquaintance.

She had faith in her own originality and taste; everybody admitted those were among her virtues. She was not interested in possessions for the sake of possessions, but could not resist beautiful and often expensive objects. To those who accused her of extravagance she used to reply, *They'll probably become more valuable*; not that she was materialistic, not for a moment. Her argument was: if I can't take your breath away, if I can't awaken you from the stupor of your ugly houses, I've failed. She did honestly want to make her acquaintances as drunk as she with sensuousness.

Oh, she would screw her eyeballs deeper into her skull today, knowing she would never again see her long drawing-room, its copper and crimson and emerald melting together behind the bronze curtains drawn against the afternoon sun.

You see, she said, *you can't say it's extravagant if it's beautiful—now can you?* Standing on the stairs. Flinging out her arms to embrace this work of art her house; not forgetting her husband, her children, and a couple of servants she had as audience. If she overdid it slightly it was because she had something of the actress in her. (They used to say of Basil later, *you can see where he gets it from*.)

Only now it is Alfred speaking, *Don't over-excite yourself, Betty, every one of us is full of admiration*. Poor dear Alfred, she could have eaten him at times, from gratitude. When gentle devotion was what he would have liked. She was always trying to include him in what she was doing. *Come and see your room—the study—which I hope you'll use—when you come down to be with us—I hope you'll make a habit of it, darling—because we'll miss you, shan't we? Dorothy?* Dragging Alfred, and Alfred alone, by the hand, its skin coarsened by joining in the work at 'Kudjeri'—to jolly the men—a square, undemonstrative hand, trying manfully to return her enthusiasm with curious little encouraging pressures. (Their whole married life they had spent trying to encourage each other's uninteresting interests.) *What am I going to study in this study?* He laughed after a fashion. *If I ever use it.*

And yet, Alfred read, she discovered: he had accumulated a whole library of unexpected books, used ones, you could tell by the stains on them and crumbs between the pages. So she had found out in the painful months at the end when they were together again at 'Kudjeri'.

Earlier, when he would come down and ask them to put him up at Moreton Drive, he took to film-going. Though what Dad saw in the pictures he sat through, Basil could not imagine. It made him laugh in his in-between voice (his lovely pure little treble had broken). Basil was at his most horrid, exploiting harshness under cover of his beauty: like a still-ripening plum, he would have shrivelled the mouth if you had bitten into him. But he was right about those crude films; after tagging along to one or two, you could only conclude that poor Alfred interpreted them to suit himself, laughing when there was nothing to laugh at, crying— you suspected—at a common actress in corkscrew curls bringing her illegitimate baby to be christened in the parish church patronized by the young man's family. Admittedly, you did sniffle slightly yourself—against your better judgment. Or because Alfred was trying to get hold of your hand and press his thigh against yours.

(Imagine if the lights went up and anyone you knew was at the 'pictures'!)

Mrs Hunter's eyelids might have been turned to walnut-shells if tears had not started oozing from beneath them: out of old, mottled, dammed-up eyes.

Even during the phase after the (unofficial) separation, she never withheld herself when he came down to Sydney from 'Kudjeri'. She was determined to show her gratitude and repay him in affection for what amounted to her freedom. (He, too, must appreciate that affection is much less bumpy going than passion.) She used to make some sign, cough a shade too dramatically, or slam a drawer, or remark in an unnaturally high voice, *Those Wyburds of yours—do you think she knows how to treat him?* and Alfred would come to her, on bare feet, from the next room, and immediately they would drop their disguises. If he had still been alive she hoped he would remember with as much delight as she the pleasures of this calmer, therapeutic relationship.

Not that the other hadn't been necessary, desirable: the purposeful is necessary. And their children were purposeful. She would still dream of the barbs he had planted in her womb.

But was Arnold Wyburd necessary?

Scarcely saw him at first after the move to Moreton Drive. Old Keemis was too possessive: an old, reputed masher, in silk hat and thin white ribbon of a necktie pushed through what looked like a wedding ring. Married to Millicent, a person you never set eyes on: an invalid, it was said. The old man was very correct in his behaviour: sucked peppermints, for instance, to disguise his breath. She would have preferred the full blast of tobacco which lingered under the peppermint. Flowers for her birthday from Keemis: yellow roses; at Christmas the box of French liqueur chocolates. Archie Keemis was a man who made life seem everlasting: then he went and died in Pitt Street, on Cup Day, on his way to the club. Her grief for this old man who hadn't meant all that much to her was as spontaneous as any she had experienced. Must have been the suddenness, the shock, the removal of something solid and dependable. An almost solidly male funeral watched her while pretending not to. She was glad she had thought to wear a veil. They were watching to see what 'Bill' Hunter's wife had meant to their solicitor. And Millicent Keemis was not there. The wife's absence, however invalid she may have been, made your presence more calculable to men who believed in their powers of calculation. (Honest affection, she had found, often appears more dubious than outright infidelity: probably no one—well, almost no one, had guessed at her consummated flings; there had been other, unconsummated ones of course, because you can be unfaithful, mentally unfaithful, with a jewel, a house, a child, a woman—couldn't have gone all the way with a woman, or not farther than a hand's flirt. Who had said—some forgotten brute—*Her only genuine adulteries are those she commits with herself?* She must try to remember.

Not Archie Keemis: whatever his reputation as a ladykiller, he had always been respectful. Too old. Too honourable. So was his junior, Arnold Wyburd. It was Archie who suggested she should make a will—only a couple of weeks before they picked him up dead in Pitt Street. (Dead: she used to shy away from the word, saw it as a stone; then it becomes an idea rather, hovering round the body like mist, straying through the skull in unravelled snatches of thought, but never frightening, or personal.) And here was Archie, incredibly, asking her to confess to a belief in her own death now that she had property to leave: the house in Moreton Drive was hers; her jewels; the stocks Alfred had settled on her after they married. She had never thought about it. Might have enjoyed a sense of importance if it had not been for a slight uneasiness in her stomach. The document itself was ludicrous: the laborious phrases he insisted on wrapping round her simple wishes. His serious courtliness made her smile as she sat twisting her rings, looking at everything there was to look at in that dusty office; she always enjoyed seeing what there was to see. To save her the trouble of a trip to the city—which she made every day in her little electric brougham, even when there was scarcely a pretext—he said he would bring out the draft for her approval.

36

Then they telephoned to say Mr Keemis was off-colour: he hadn't come to the office today; Mr Wyburd would bring the draft after lunch.

Arnold Wyburd was dressed in grey on this occasion: a great improvement on that hot black he wore for 'Kudjeri'. When she came in he was standing looking out the window. She surprised herself thinking she would like to touch the lines of this back, to slide her arms round the waist, and up, till her hands met on the other side, knotted on his chest; to fit herself closely to this splendid, slender, still unconscious, grey form.

Though he must have been conscious. If he did not turn immediately, she began to sense he was postponing their facing each other. She could feel herself flush, jaws clenching to prevent what was still only a warmth in her throat from gushing out as something more reprehensible. It was a warm, not a hot day, a scent of daphne from the bed outside. When he could no longer put off turning, it was not his eyes she was drawn to, it was the drops of perspiration lying in the saucer of a temple.

They were making sounds at each other, of welcome, of apology: social sounds, by one interpretation. He was carrying the folded will, the guarantee of her eventual death. She half noticed the stiff paper was tied with a ribbon: the ribbon gave it a coquettish air.

You mustn't be afraid, she said; it would have sounded more surprising if it had not been part of a plan or theory, she suspected, which had started evolving already at 'Kudjeri' as she held his white though sinewy wrist to steady a wavering flame. She began elaborating—Mrs Hunter laughed to remember, *You must realize I'm much older than you—that I married late: I was thirty-two—that there's nothing to be afraid of.* The irrelevance of it all made it sound strangely idiotic, even now. Must have decided in the beginning Arnold was a stupid young man. Herself doubtfully cool; but coolness prevailed: at least it must have impressed him more than Lal Pennecuick and the two little girls, Marjorie and Whatever. You hadn't forgotten your own Dorothy and Basil: they were out walking in the park with Nanny. Nora—you knew her habits—would have returned to her interrupted novelette; Gertrude, by now in her basket chair, is snoring off a lunch of scones and tea.

This was the extent of the coolness which spread also to Arnold Wyburd: never could a mouth have grown more familiar in a shorter time.

'Oh dear!' Mrs Hunter was momentarily so racked by guilt, the elderly solicitor at the bedroom window again wondered whether he should advance to the bedside and try in some way to share whatever she was suffering.

Making love by daylight: it was the first time as far as she could remember; and yes, it must certainly be the first time Arnold Wyburd had taken off his clothes in public. It appeared easier after the shoes. Her bed felt so deliciously cold it made her shiver; it had never looked so blinding. She closed her eyes, out of modesty as well, and in this way hoped to make it easier for Arnold to find the courage she had promised herself to inspire in him. Only it seemed, in the end, that Arnold was not in need of inspiration. His heavy breathing exploded her theory. So she opened her eyes to his white, practically hairless, sinewy body. As he surfaced for breath, it was Arnold's eyes which were closed. To shut her out because she wasn't Lal? At least she could say, with eyes open or shut, he wasn't Alfred; this was neither love, nor the more satisfactory affection. On her part it was only desire, and on Arnold's a kind of dissolved frustration. She was so relieved she almost laughed. But he can't have felt the least tremor: he was too deeply concentrated; and she lulled him deeper and deeper, it seemed, and deeper. At his climax, she took his head with her hands, and tried to press into his mouth the admiration with which she was running over: that he had succeeded in leaping a barrier — and with her help.

When Arnold Wyburd dashed her off, disengaged himself entirely, and stubbed his toe on a caster. *Never forgive myself Mrs Hunter a position of trust so many others involved.* Poor man. *But we don't love each other Arnold and I am the one to blame I don't love you but I loved it it is something which had to which you will forget and I shall remember with pleasure.* Too foolish of her to suggest that they were only half-absolved. She would always remember his braces, his suspenders, trying to impress an enormity on her. Men are at their most priggish managing braces or suspenders. Ah well, better a priggish solicitor than a lecherous one, she supposed.

She could not remember how Arnold Wyburd got away. Didn't telephone for a cab; must have walked to the tramstop. When she went downstairs, in time for the children's return from the park, she found the draft will. She wished it had been the final version. She drove herself in next morning, in the electric brougham, and handed over the approved draft to some young woman at Keemis & Wyburd's office: Arnold did not appear; and poor Archie was at home preparing for his fall in Pitt Street.

'Who's for brekkie?' Too much a clattering scratching clucking: too rude an interruption to thought and stillness.

'Who are you?' Mrs Hunter asked.

'I'm your nurse—Sister Badgery. And here's a nice *coddled* egg!'

'I was hoping you'd be the other one—Mary. She hasn't walked out on me—has she?'

'She's downstairs enjoying a cup of coffee. Sister's off duty now. She only stayed on this morning in hopes of catching a glimpse of the—your daughter.'

'Oh, yes. They never met. De Santis came to me that other time—just after I'd returned from some island—after Dorothy had flown back to France in one of her huffs.'

'Here's the lovely egg, dear! Open mouth, Mrs Hunter!'

Mrs Hunter pointed her chin. 'I haven't been interested in breakfast—not since I married. I like a good luncheon—"dinner" they seemed to call it nowadays—nothing heavy at night.' After which her gums closed down.

'Just a tiny spoonful!' Mrs Hunter could feel Sister Badgery's bone spoon trying to prise her lips open. 'I'm sure you don't want to disappoint me. Or Mr Wyburd here. There's no one has your interests at heart so much as Mr Wyburd.'

'Oh, my solicitor. Yes. Have you met him?'

Sister Badgery's arrival with the hateful egg had confused Mrs

Hunter: she was terrified her mind might crumble before Dorothy came, let alone Basil, who was delayed.

'Oh yes, we know each other. Don't we, Mr Wyburd?' Sister Badgery winked, and moistened her already glistening teeth.

He knew her too well. She had shaken her head at him on sidling into the room with the tray, reminding him of a white Leghorn: inquisitive, ostentatiously industrious, silly, easily outraged. She would look in at the office on Fridays after duty and he handed her her envelope. (This had been ordained by Mrs Hunter for all her staff, not as a nuisance to him, but to ensure personal relationships for them.) Sister Badgery would sit a while to air her pretensions, based on her training at the Royal Prince Alfred and a curtailed marriage to a retired tea planter from Ceylon.

Over just visibly reluctant lips Mr Wyburd murmured, 'Sister Badgery and I are old friends.'

Mrs Hunter swallowed her third mouthful of nauseating egg, some of which, she could feel, had dribbled on to her chin, and Badgery would be too flattered by Arnold to notice. 'Mr Wyburd,' she succeeded in ejecting the words, 'should be having his own breakfast. It's been arranged. I hope it's a man's breakfast, Arnold. Foreign women don't understand that a man's strength — hinges — on his breakfast.'

Sister Badgery laughed at the joke; the things on the tray clattered.

'I don't doubt it will be an adequate breakfast,' Mr Wyburd said, and Sister Badgery renewed her laughter as though he too had made a joke.

'I don't know why you didn't go sooner,' Mrs Hunter was hectoring: foolishness in a dependent would turn her lungs to leather in an instant.

'You were having such a good sleep,' he protested; 'I didn't want to disturb it.'

'I wasn't sleeping — only thinking. I hope Mrs Lippmann has cooked you a chop — or a dish of devilled kidneys. Alfred used to take *cold* chops whenever he went mustering or drafting. Horrid! But that's what the men like. Take him — show him, Sister!'

'I'm sure Mr Wyburd knows the way. I dare say he could show me corners of this house I never ever knew existed.' Sister Badgery laughed some more, and Mr Wyburd went downstairs exceedingly humiliated.

'Now you can put away that wretched egg. There are things you must do for me – urgently.'

'Really? But the coffee. You've forgotten your coffee, Mrs Hunter.'

She had too. 'Did you put the brandy in it?'

'Oh dear, yes, my life wouldn't be worth much, would it? if I forgot the brandy.'

Mrs Hunter groped for and took the cup, her lips feeling for the lip. She found, and strength returned in a delirious stream, through the funnel of her mouth, right down to her chilly toes.

Sister Badgery watched this old blind puppy with approval, even affection. She did not approve of drink, only of Mrs Hunter's brandy. She admired the rich, and enjoyed working for them because it gave her a sense of security, of connection, however vicarious. To her friends she would refer to wealthy patients always by their first names; she knew intimately strangers she had read about in gossip columns: they were no longer strangers if you read about them often enough.

Mrs Hunter was supping her brandied coffee; soon she would grow muzzy, and sleep.

'I want you to make me up, Sister,' she spluttered through a last mouthful, 'for my daughter's arrival.'

'Make you up? You know I can't. In all my life nothing but good soap and water ever touched my face.'

'I was afraid of that.' She sounded more resigned than bitter. 'If only it were little Manhood: she could do it for me.'

'I don't doubt. Sister Manhood comes of a different background.'

'So what? She came off a banana farm. And you're an engine driver's daughter.'

'My father was an engineer employed by the State Government.

41

My three brothers are public servants, and two of them elders of the Presbyterian Church.' Mrs Hunter did not care as much as Sister Badgery. 'I had a very strict upbringing. Even when I started my nurse's training at P.A., my father expected a full account of my leisure activities. As for Sister Manhood – she was out dancing around with any young resident doctor who asked her. I know that for a fact. Oh, I have nothing *against* Sister Manhood. Believe *me*! She's a charming girl – so full of vitality. I'm actually fond of Sister Manhood, and only wish she wouldn't touch up so much; it gives strangers a wrong impression.'

Mrs Hunter said, 'I like to feel I have been made up. It fills me with – an illusion – of beauty. Of course I may never have been beautiful: even in my heyday I was never absolutely sure – only of what was reflected in other people's eyes – and I can no longer see distinctly.'

'Sorry, dear, I can't be of any help when it comes to cosmetics.' Sister Badgery was slightly remorseful as she took the cup from the old thing's hands. 'Anything else I can do for you?'

The nurse stood holding her breath: bad enough if it were the bedpan, but to hoist her patient on to the commode almost always ricked her back.

'Yes. There is something,' Mrs Hunter said. 'My jewel case. Then I shan't feel completely naked.'

Sister Badgery began swishing about. The jewels played such a part in their owner's life they increased the self-importance of any member of her household assisting at the ceremony.

Mrs Lippmann had once ventured to suggest, 'She shouldn't be allowed to flash her jewels at whoever comes: at the electrician, if you please, and window cleaners!' But the housekeeper was notoriously jealous.

'Poor old soul, they're what she's got to show,' Sister Badgery replied, 'and what she loves.'

'Someone might steal – or murder her for them.'

'They mightn't dare.'

Mrs Lippmann agreed they might not.

Now when she had brought the case Sister Badgery asked, 'Hadn't I better open it for you?'

'No, thank you.' The catch responded less quickly to more agile fingers: she knew its tricks. She knew every inch of the mangy, velvet-covered box.

Her jewels.

Sister Badgery who thought she could recognize each, or almost every jewel—that was the peculiar part: not everything had been revealed—and who knew by heart the stories attached, though again not all, for the stories would breed others, was regularly entranced at the unveiling; but this morning felt provoked that Mrs Hunter should have scrabbled through the velvet trays and got herself into half-a-dozen rings behind her back.

'Aren't you *well*! Aren't you active today!' The nurse was genuinely impressed. 'It's your daughter's arrival.'

'Oh, the tale of jewels!' Mrs Hunter knew her acolytes must often have caught her out telling her once blazing, if now extinct, beads.

Whatever her own feelings Sister Badgery would never be caught out in any popish act: no one would guess how she adored, for instance, this pigeon's-blood ruby, or that she was capable of worshipping an ancient idol for its treasure.

To deflect the wrath of her forebears by a display of down-to-earth professional skill, the nurse announced, 'We'll prop you up a step or two, shall we? Whoopsy-dey, Mrs Hunter!' as she hoisted.

And there was the idol propped against the pillows, the encrusted fingers outspread as though preparing to play a complicated scale on the hem of the sheet.

To introduce a touch of warmth, the nurse inquired, 'Would you like your maribou jacket, dear? Or the woolly stole, perhaps?'

'Thank you. The stole.' Mrs Hunter barely breathed: physical exertion had exhausted her.

Sister Badgery draped the stole; she could not have treated a saint with greater reverence, though she did not believe in saints, not, at any rate, those Roman Catholic ones: ugh!

43

'Wouldn't you like me to choose you a necklace seeing as it's a great occasion?'

'Not a necklace. Not before luncheon. Not for Dorothy.'

Sister Badgery accepted reproof. 'Gordon gave me an amethyst pendant.'

'Gordon?'

'My husband. Don't you remember me telling you?'

'I ought to.'

'Well, Gordon gave me this pendant. It's in exquisite taste. I wear it still—only when I visit friends, or to the Nurses' and Residents' Ball.'

Though Mrs Hunter had never distinctly seen Sister Badgery's neck, she imagined it thin, white, and well-soaped: fitting support for the amethyst pendant.

'Perhaps I never told you—' Sister Badgery was treading familiar ground, 'I met Mr Badgery—Gordon—on my way to the Temple of the Tooth. I was visiting Ceylon for pleasure—between cases, that is. What did you say, dear? Mrs Hunter?'

Mrs Hunter was not coaxed into repeating, but they used to call them 'the Fishing Fleet': the Australian women who went up to cast their nets in Ceylon waters; instead she confessed to a weakness of her own. 'For years I kept the children's baby teeth in a bottle. Then one day, for some reason, I threw them out.'

'I was telling you about my trip to Kandy. My friends' car got a puncture, and a tea planter who happened to be passing fetched a native to do the necessary. The planter was Mr Badgery. He kindly invited us to take refreshments—which was how everything started. Shortly after, he retired from tea and followed me by P. & O. to Sydney.'

'He died, didn't he?' As if you didn't know; but his widow liked to be asked.

'Yes, he died. But not before we were married. That was when he gave me the amethyst pendant.'

Mrs Hunter wondered momentarily whether she should give Mrs Badgery something from her jewel box; it was easier to give

44

presents than to waste emotions you were storing up against some possible cataclysm: as time ran on you did not know what you might have to face.

'What is this weird ring I've never seen before?' Sister Badgery was asking. 'The one on your right thumb.'

The old girl was lolling there, her smouldering fingers scarcely part of her, and on that thumb a nest of plaited gold surrounding what might have been a cross, but out of plumb; the whole effect was thoroughly heathen.

'That is an Ethiopian ring,' Mrs Hunter explained. 'It's the only thing ever sent me by my son — apart from letters asking for money.'

Sister Badgery sucked her teeth. 'And Sir Basil a great man! That's what the papers tell us.'

'I suppose, when they're not being great, great men are as weak as the insignificant ones.'

Because of a tone of perversity and sadness, Sister Badgery changed the subject. 'I expect your daughter — Dorothy — has lots of exquisite jewels: a lady in her position.'

'She came off badly when he left her — though she was the innocent one. Still, she did manage to extract a jewel or two from her husband's atrocious family.'

Sister Badgery was delighted to hear of this material success. She brought a brush and began stroking her patient's hair.

'I don't believe you know my daughter's name.'

'Well, "Dorothy", isn't it? I'm no good at those foreign names.'

'I shall teach you,' said Mrs Hunter, her lips inflating as though she were tasting a delicious food, her nostrils filling with what could have been a subtle perfume. ' "*Princesse de Lascabanes*" '; she laid on the French pretty thick for Sister Badgery's benefit. 'Let me hear you say it.'

The nurse obliged after a fashion. 'But what shall I *call* her?' the voice whined despairingly.

'Nothing more elaborate than "Madame".'

' "Mad-damm, mad-damm," ' Sister Badgery breathed in imitation, and a more sonorous variant, ' "Ma-*darm*!" '

Mrs Hunter sensed she had got her nurse under control, which was where she wanted her; she also suspected Sister Badgery would refer to 'Princess Dorothy' to please herself and impress her friends.

'"Mad-damm, ma-*darm*"!' Happier for its new accomplishment the voice went clucking in and out the golden morning.

Mrs Hunter was so soothed by clocks and brandy it seemed unlikely that anybody would arrive; if they did, it might even be undesirable: her life was too closely charted.

'Open mouth! Mrs Hunter?' It was that Badgery again. 'Whatever happens, we must take our temp, mustn't we?'

What did they call it? Dettol? Cool, anyway. Sterilizing. Was it better this way: to be sterilized out of existence? *I don't mind dying, Dr Gidley, but I do expect my nurses to protect me against worse than death*: such as the visitants you do not conjure up for yourself, worst of all the tender ones.

'Shall I be strong enough, I wonder?'

Holding her patient's wrist, Sister Badgery found it unnecessary to answer: the pulse was remarkably strong.

When they were both shocked, if not positively alarmed, by an interruption to their celebration.

The door opened.

'Sister, can she be seen?' It was Mr Wyburd in something too loud for a whisper and less than his usual grammar. 'The princess has arrived. Her daughter.'

As if this were not enough, a second figure was pushing rustling past the one at the door: for Mrs Hunter it was sound perfume joy despair; whereas Sister Badgery saw a tall thin hatless woman, somewhere around fifty (to be on the kind side) her dress unsurprising except for its simplicity and the pearls bounding about around her neck, and on her bosom, as she half ran half staggered.

A princess shouldn't run, the nurse recovered herself enough to disapprove; and she shouldn't have a horse face.

But Dorothy floundered, imperviously, on. '*O mon Dieu, aidez-moi!*' she gasped, before assuming another of her selves, or voices, to utter, 'Mother!' and lower, 'Mum!'

46

Then, by act of special grace, a blind was drawn over the expression the intruder was wearing for this old *mummy* propped up in bed, a thermometer sticking out of its mouth; if life were present, it was the life generated by jewels with which the rigid claws were loaded.

The princess fell against the bed, groping through the scents of Dettol and baby powder, to embrace, deeper than her mother, her own childhood.

Rejecting the thermometer with her mouth—lucky it didn't break off—Mrs Hunter was smiling, whether in bliss or fright it was difficult to tell.

Till she giggled through her flux of tears, 'Too much excitement! I think I've wet myself.'

Madame de Lascabanes had felt her anxiety, together with a morbid craving for acceptance, turn to rage, as she endured the humiliations of the airport.

The man said, looking through her passport, '"Princess Dorothy de Lascabanes", eh? French subject. Born at Gogong, Australie. Waddayerknow!'

The princess glared back along the ridge of her white nose. Her rather flat breasts were heaving beneath the uncomplicated little dress she had chosen for the journey: her faithful old Chanel; how would she manage when it wore out?

'What business is it of yours where I was born?' The unaccustomed language was making her spit.

'Only reading what's in the passport.'

'I should have thought my birthplace beside the point—in the circumstances.' The rustiness of her English made it sound ruder, which was what she had intended after all.

'That's what comes of offerun friendship. But we won't hold it against yer, lady. Welcome to yer native land!' The man laughed, and handed back the passport.

'I'll report,' she began; but to whom? and for what?

She was by now more humiliated by her own ill temper than by what had been only questionable insolence in the passport official.

It might have been worse at the customs if she had not clenched her jaws, after deciding to answer any questions as briefly and coldly as she knew how: French economy in fact.

The surly youth in an official's uniform who began stirring up the two bags packed by herself with such practical ingenuity, immediately put her to the test. Again, in rummaging through the case in which she carried her make-up, her tissues and so forth, as well as a few jewels, he provoked, but failed to draw her; not even when running his hands through the jewels with a cynical air of estimating their value. (They were certainly an impressive lot: some, gently lustrous, others, by the grubby airport light, imperiously brilliant. Her spoils. If she had not been so well-informed in the details of Hubert's private life, she might have lost the battle for the jewels; but *cette créature vulgaire, cette infecte Australienne* simply knew too much for her former *belle-mère*, the old Princesse Etienne, to launch a successful offensive.)

At least the customs official's lack of respect was not expressed in words; she might not have borne it otherwise. Silently she hid her gall as he silently poured a few of her sleeping pills into his hand; and when he left his fingerprints on her books, as he scuffed up the pages, always ferreting, almost breaking the spine of her precious *Chartreuse de Parme*.

He only opened his mouth to mumble, while sticking a plastic strip on her violated luggage, 'Bet you get a good read out of some of these French books of yours.'

For a moment she regretted insisting that nobody should meet her, and that she had avoided travelling by the line she thought Basil most likely to choose. All she could do now was ignore, lower her discreetly smeared eyelids, dust down the coat she was carrying (her rather mature Persian lamb) and stalk behind the barrow on which her bags were being wheeled away. The briefest glance at her own reflection ought to restore her confidence if it were to falter. As it did. And her impeccable reflection let her down.

Dorothy Hunter's misfortune was to feel at her most French in Australia, her most Australian in France. Sometimes she wished she had been born a Finn: she might not have felt so strongly about it. She had only met a couple of Finns; but Australians—here they were, teeming around her, the older men like mattresses from which the hair was bursting out, or those younger, more disturbing ones, hipless, and over-articulated; the women, either in loud summery shifts, apparently with nothing underneath, or else imprisoned in a rigid armature of lace, shrieked at one another monotonously out of unhealed wounds. Some of the women looked as though they would expect to die in hats.

The Princesse de Lascabanes pushed her way between the bodies, using her hands united in an attitude of prayer inside the lumped-up coat she was carrying. Protected by this fur buckler, Madame de Lascabanes shoved on, to arrive beside the queue of infiltrating taxis, where she overtipped (one of the principles of 'poverty') the unsuspecting, decent man her porter—or whatever he was: she had all but forgotten her native language.

As she entered the cab she was on the verge of crying; in fact she did drop a tear or two after bumping her head and giving the address, 'The Queen Victoria Club.'

After very little correspondence the princess had been elected an honorary member of this irreproachable institution to which she now intended to drive. Go to Mother's later in the day, after resting. She was too *écoeurée* at the moment to risk being dragged under by the emotional demands of a domineering old woman. Carried along an impersonal expressway from the airport she would not allow herself to think of Mother, least of all 'Mummy'. Were you really *rapace* as your *belle-mère* had insisted? Were you a SNOB? as every second Australian seemed to accuse: the bursting mattresses, the hipless Gary Coopers of your youth, not forgetting the fe-males, blue-glaring out of their wounded leather.

Dorothy Hunter might have had a good cry if, on opening the wrong bag, she could have found her tissues. *I have never managed to escape being this thing Myself.*

Instead she addressed the driver's neck, '*Voyez—*' coughing for her lapse, 'I've changed my mind. Take me to Moreton Drive, will you?' adding, strangely, superfluously, 'To my mother's house.'

The driver did not seem to find it odd. 'Been away long?'

'Oh, years—*years*!' She heard a wheeze from deep down in her reply; and coughed again.

But felt fulfilled: it was like the sensation of settling yourself inside a cotton frock, between licks at an ice-cream horn, while voices droned on about weather, the wool clip, and the come-and-go of relatives.

'Dear dear! Aren't we unfortunate? These terrible accidents!' Sister Badgery had hurried to the bedside to disengage her patient from a too emotional embrace; intent on professional duties, her least concern was a princess.

While Mrs Hunter, curled on her side in something like a foetal position, was grinning up at her daughter. 'Don't worry, Dorothy. It's not as bad as you might imagine. There's the macintosh.' Relief drifted over her face as the water spread inside her bed: for the moment she would not have to think of what to talk about to this stranger; better disgraced by the body than by the mind.

She sighed and said, 'You'll have to go into the nursery, Kate, play with the dolls—though mine aren't as good as yours;' then listened cunningly for the sound of Kate's boots tapping across the boards.

Kate Nutley was altogether too simple. Betty Salkeld had never cared for her friend, any more than for Kate's glacé buttonboots; the Nutleys were wealthier than the Salkelds.

Dorothy Hunter was rent as the nurse dragged the sheet back too quickly and her own babyhood was exposed. Its smell of pitiful flannel and the painful prickling of a rash invaded her far more ruthlessly than the memory of that adult ordeal: the trek through a chain of icy *salons* to the *cabinets* at Lunegarde; the door which wouldn't open at first and which wouldn't shut on the screech of urine, while the *belle-mère* snored, and Oncle Amédée slit the night and the newspapers with his scissors, cutting out reports of incidents which might be interpreted as Communist conspiracy.

Confused by this collision between her still passive babyhood and some of the most painful steps she had taken in what remained a gawky-schoolgirl marriage, she was relieved to hear a man's voice. 'We'd better leave them to it. I dare say they'll fetch you when everything's in order.' She had forgotten the solicitor.

Arnold Wyburd led her out along the passage towards the landing. He was the sort of person you take for granted: a nice bore; so reasonable and honest there is no need to be on your guard against him. She felt remorseful for never having sent a New Year card to the one who had managed their affairs all these years. He appeared dry enough not to look for sentimental attentions from a client. Or so she hoped.

On the other hand, he had known her as her other self: Dorothy Hunter.

He was so kind she might have been recovering from an illness. 'I expect you'll want to potter about the house – quietly – by yourself.'

The Princesse de Lascabanes was restored to health, when it should have been Dorothy Hunter.

'Yes,' she replied, returning his kindness with a kind smile. 'Isn't it ridiculous of me – I'm dying to see my old room!' She settled her pearls with a practised hand. 'I believe rooms actually mean more to me than people.' That was not entirely true, and she hoped it had not sounded shocking to somebody as good as the solicitor.

Looking at her he suspected her of having more of her mother than they credited her with: a horse-faced version of Elizabeth Hunter.

'They got your room ready for you, if you care to change your mind.'

'Oh, no,' she said in her highest voice, 'I couldn't impose to that extent – on the housekeeper person. And besides, they have a room for me at the club. Wasn't it civil of them to make me an honorary member for my visit?'

51

They looked at each other. Perhaps he did not consider it a visit; he saw her gummed up in the web of nostalgic associations and forced to witness the great conjuring trick to which her mother must soon lend herself. A gust of renewed panic made her determined to cling to her not altogether satisfactory life in Paris: the underfurnished apartment at Passy; a pretence of meals prepared by herself over a leaking gas stove; her art of making expensive dresses continue to look expensive; the rationed sympathy of practical friends (her folly had been to value the friendship of those who respect *rentes*). All this might change of course, but how quickly? Her flight to the bedside could decide. She had never been a skilled beggar, perhaps because it was only late in life that there had been any need to beg; the alternate solution was something she must not think about, though she often did in terrifying detail.

Making a great effort, and still at a considerable distance, Madame de Lascabanes inquired, 'How is dear Mrs Wyburd?' At once she hoped her smile allied to the borrowed adjective would not strike the solicitor as fulsome; and come to think of it, she did have a genuine affection for his wife; in fact, as a child she had loved Lal.

'Thank you. She's keeping pretty well. We hope you'll come to see her.'

'That will be charming – charming.' Doubly stupid: the words she used half the time were not her own; but one skates more smoothly shod with platitudes. 'See the children – and grandchildren.'

The solicitor was so far encouraged as to launch into Wyburd history; but stopped when he saw she was not interested.

She was though, she was: she remembered a picnic smelling of trampled grass when she had stuck her face in a freckled neck and thought she would have liked Mrs Wyburd as mother; till Basil stole the solicitor's wife, as Basil stole everybody. *I've been reading Lady Windermere's Fan don't tell my mother Mrs Wyburd.* Basil always impressed and nobody ever seemed to guess when he was being dishonest. *Have you Basil and is there a particular part you think you'd like to play?* Fancy Mrs Wyburd lapping it up; or was she too, dishonest in her way? *Oh no nothing big interesting enough in*

Lady Windermere I'll only ever want the great roles Lear particularly.
Mrs Wyburd seriously saying *you'll have to wait a long time for that
but I expect you'll play it in the end if that's what you've decided.* She
hated Mrs Wyburd almost as much as she hated her brother, who
never looked in her direction unless to make faces or persuade her
she was a fool.

'There'll be a number of business matters we'll have to discuss.
Not these first days of course,' the solicitor was reminding her.
'You're not in any hurry now that you're here.'

Why did he have to take that for granted? She looked at him
suspiciously.

'Your brother's delayed—did you know? at Bangkok. He'll
arrive this evening, according to the telegram.'

'How *extraordinary*!' She adopted the tone used in social intercourse. 'Bangkok! Where I changed planes. I didn't run into him,'
she added, and giggled on realizing the inanity of her remark.

She was glad the solicitor was old enough to be her father, equally
glad he was not nearly as old as her mother. She wished she had
known her father better; probably her mother had not allowed it:
Mother was the mouthpiece through which they addressed one
another (even Basil fell for that) *all so helpless how would you manage
I wonder if I weren't here?*

Dorothy Hunter, long-legged and shy, almost of the same shoulder height as the solicitor, confessed with an abruptness which
surprised him, 'Some day I want to talk to you about my father.'

He became as abrupt, expressed the opinion that Alfred Hunter
had been a fine man, and announced that he ought to be going
along to the office to see what was happening there.

Which of them had made the break it was difficult to decide, but
the Princesse de Lascabanes was at liberty to shut herself up in
Dorothy Hunter's room.

It was very little changed, it seemed at first: a chaste, girl's room,
fairly narrow and predominantly white. There was the glass in
which she had tried massaging her face into a more desirable shape.
The cupboards opened on naphthalene and emptiness. Still arranged

on shelves, books she remembered, some of them anyway: *The Forest Lovers*; *Salammbô*; *A Man of Property*; *Winnie-the-Pooh*; *Confessions of an English Opium Eater* (a grey book when she had hoped for purple).

Across the bed was arranged a rug she could not remember from her own reign of chintz; it was made from, probably, some kind of native fur: bumpy, humble, yet soft, soothing to the cheek, seducing the body, surprisingly, through dress and two-way stretch. She wallowed in it, hardly bothering to imagine what a sight she must look sprawled on the fur cover and enjoying it with every part of her; when normally she was not a sensual woman.

Even in the early days, while her marriage was still officially considered a success, she might have dismissed sexual love if it had not been for the sense of gratitude a rare climax produced in her. So she loved a husband almost old enough to be her father; she admired while fearing the cynic and dandy in this man so expensively acquired; at times she admitted to herself she found him physically luscious, the skin tones and the whorled rosettes of the nipples faintly seen through the monogrammed shirts she bought him at Sulka. But she dreaded many of his replies, the quirk at the corner of his mouth, one eyebrow lifted noticeably higher than the other. *No, I am not laughing, my darling, only interested to find Australians can behave as perversely as anybody else.* She brooded badly. Criticism made her squint: the sun might have been striking at her as she jogged homeward on Taffy under the dusty casuarinas; when here she was in her white, actual skin, the formal helmet of her lacquered hair, and the sapphire brooch the old princess had surrendered during the engagement as a gesture towards *notre petite Australienne*.

She had never been theirs, alas. She was not *la petite Australienne*, not even, perhaps, an Australian, except on damp piercing nights at Lunegarde, or in moments of expatriate despair alone in the Paris apartment. Sometimes Dorothy Hunter suspected she existed only in the novels of Balzac and Stendhal and Flaubert, the plays of Racine.

Naturellement la littérature française est un héritage considérable. She would have liked to encounter someone whose attitude to books was passionate rather than dutifully respectful. Could it be that her French 'family', her 'husband', saw in her fossicking through their literary cupboards a form of immorality? They knew the prodigious cupboards were there, but preferred to keep them closed, anyway to foreigners.

So she too had closed, whether in the Paris apartment where she and Hubert led their more intimate life, or in their wing at Lunegarde, from which they took part in the family rituals of the Lascabanes. (So much for theory; in fact neither of them participated, though each withdrew differently.)

Mon fils adore la chasse, the belle-mère had dared her daughter-in-law to misunderstand.

Almost all evenings at Lunegarde seemed to close in mist. Wherever a fire was lit, it smoked. The old princess rattled with bronchitis laying out her patience, as you waited for the guns to return: first the sound of men's voices as logical as typewriters along the paths, then their boots in corridors of stone. Should you run to greet? The *belle-mère* at her patience did not look up, but was watching to see the wrong thing done. So you chafed your goose-flesh, till here he was, kissing the hand you offered, winking for some sacrilege he hoped to provoke you into committing, but in which he most likely would not take part, in his mother's *salon*, amongst the painted furniture, the faded tapestries, and mould. By contrast, Hubert smelled of thyme, woodsmoke, healthy exertion, and perhaps you imagined – blood. At least the bundles of bloodied feathers and dangling fur were carried into the court to be sorted, some for the vaulted kitchen, inferior stuff for the cottages.

Once Dorothy de Lascabanes had slipped on the cobbles in the dark, on a patch of what she afterwards identified as blood, and grazed her knee. She bound the knee; she would not tell – not even when she was dying, probably, of blood poisoning.

There was a lot she hid, and her secretive air was sometimes mistaken for worldliness. *Elle est admirable, vous savez — votre femme,* said the aunts, cousins, and the few friends, equally glacial and exalted, who foregathered at Lunegarde. She soon realized to what extent she was *admirable*: that money may be overlooked provided there is enough of it; and that a talking dog offers temporary social distraction. Though a few of them liked to try out their English, the majority preferred her to risk her French, which remained bad enough to pass for amusing, eccentric, even chic, along with the exotic 'Dor-rô-ti'. She had, too, the gift for entertaining aged men, which most young girls fail to discover in themselves, and prettier, more assured women do not think of squandering. Mainly by listening and applying an invisible ointment, she revived in her ancients an illusion of youth. They appreciated what they saw as kindness, when she wasn't kind, or not very. Protected by the armour of a happy marriage she might have snubbed the lot of them. Instead, after Hubert left her, she clumsily rejected the four or five creaking boars and arthritic tortoises from whom she might have chosen a lover if that had been her fancy.

The name she had acquired remained her compensation, as well as a recurring reflexion of the marriage in which she had failed to please. Most desolating were those evenings the *belle-mère* had envisaged for them: *when Dor-rô-ti and Hubert wish to be alone.* Herself in a state of sick tension, he with glittering eye and a mock flamboyance, they fled the little huggermugger *salon* the family used for comfort; while the *belle-mère* continued laying out her patience, Oncle Amédée pasting in his cuttings, Tante Eulalie (the Hon. Mrs Scrymgeour-Talbot: *he deserted me my dear during the male menopause*) devoting herself to astrological research, and Tante Daisy de Pougues to the sinuses which tortured her, but for which she lived. Every eye in the room was paying attention from beneath disinterested lids; doubtless after the door had closed the assembly would start listening instead, down reverberating corridors, through panelling in which more than the beetle ticked.

In their own quarters, a cupboard had been equipped as a kitchen. *Le Butagaz,* the old princess explained, *est si commode — et vraiment pas cher.* The will to succeed made a plausible cook of the bride, though on nights of dreadful anticipation her *omelette truffée* was inclined to stick; there was a *manque de liaison* about her sauces; there was the suicidal smell of *Butagaz.* While Hubert did not seem to care: *tu es si gentille ma chère petite de te donner tant de peine.* What should have been proof of her serious intentions he was only concerned with reducing to bed level: by lip flattery, by hand, by every dishonest means. Worse than his indifference his lechery: *ton omelette bien baveuse m'inspire — this time Dorothy we shall do things more interestingly.* When her most rigid submission was a torment, except in half languorous, half surprised, and wholly grateful retrospect. But to behave 'interestingly' was beyond her capacity: *non Hubert je ne veux je ne peux pas.*

Sometimes falling asleep her prince farted as though in disgust.

Perhaps she had never loved Hubert: that would explain everything; she had only almost drowned in admiration, for his title, his flesh tones, his insolent assurance, his French-ness, and the white sideburns rising to slicks of still black hair, in which the lights would begin to glow after he had drenched it with *eau de Portugal* and slashed rather than brushed it into shape.

Mon fils adore la chasse; if the old princess had dared her daughter-in-law to misinterpret, *la Cousine Marie-Ange* had taken it upon herself to keep his second wife informed. For there had been a first (nobody had hidden her: far from it) *la pauvre Madeleine cette fille si douce qui est morte en couches on n'a pas pu sauver l'enfant non plus.* (Classic interlude in the life of a man who happens actually to be your husband.) Hubert was desolated. (Why not? Why not?) The teeth of Marie-Ange, yellow-looking and brittle, still tasted her cousin's grief: the more touching in that Hubert was by nature such a *coureur de jupons — et pas difficile!* The cousin had a laugh to match what she saw as the less savoury peccadilloes. *But you understand Dor-rô-ti I only tell you out of frankness and — amitié. A woman can so much better hold her husband if she understands his mœurs.*

Marie-Ange herself remained unmarried. The aigrette she wore in her perennial hat was shuddering with expectation the day she brought the Australian news of the American, *une personne très commune née à Cincinnati le père a fait fortune dans le margarine.* The cousin's lips were shining, not with margarine, but the superior unctuousness of best Norman butter. *Comme je vous plains ma pauvre amie.* The hot black glove fingering your cold skin. *Mais ça ne durera peut-être pas vous savez bien qu'Hubert a toujours eu besoin de distractions on a même raconté qu'il avait tâté des garçons.* The cousin could hardly restrain her spit. *Il paraît qu'il a eu une aventure avec un gondolier l'année passée ...*

Grinding her cheek into the soft unidentifiable fur (remember to ask Mother) Dorothy Hunter tried to invoke the Spirit of Games, who might have coached her, though too late, in holding a scabrous husband's interest.

When somebody started knocking on her thoughts. 'Maddamm? Ma-*darm*?' Must be that boiled nurse.

'Yes?' Her own voice depressed her in one syllable.

'Mrs Hunter — madam — is ready to receive you in her room.' The nurse sounded as though she must be smiling the other side of the closed door she was addressing so elaborately.

'Tell her I'm coming. Thank you. I'll be there. Thank you, Nurse.' Or was it 'Sister'?

Beyond the window of her girlhood a landscape was returning: under the skyline of convents and araucarias, a geometry of concrete and brick she could not remember ever having seen before. She stood a moment wondering whether it gave her further cause for resentment.

On closing the door of her refuge behind her, Dorothy Hunter followed the beaten track, along the landing, down the passage, to her mother's bedroom. She was glad she had the de Lascabanes pearls for company. Faced with making any kind of rational comment, she could only hope for inspiration, which almost never came. In her best moments she did not act: necessity started working in her; but now a part she had learnt, after long and exacting rehearsal, possessed her as she entered the room, and she repeated automatically, 'I must hand it to you, darling! Isn't she miraculous, Sister?' In the French tongue, it might have sounded more convincing.

For the mummy's head balanced on the pillows, the structure of bones arranged beneath the sheet, denied the human miracle; though the spirit was preparing to tilt, the princess uneasily sensed.

'Miraculous what?'

'I think your daughter—Princess Dorothy—means: what a wonderful old lady we all find you.'

'Wonderful old lady—ugh!' Mrs Hunter ground her gums together. 'Wonderful old bagpipes!'

'What is it you said, darling?' Dorothy trembled in making contact with this thing: her mother's wrist.

Mrs Hunter had not decided how to reply to her poor her Dorothy daughter, when she was led—yes, positively *led*, in a direction she had not foreseen.

'That day I went with your father to see Mrs—Mrs Hewlett. She was living at—Wilberforce? Yes, there was a river which used to flood, but the Hewletts were on higher ground. Your father was drinking his cocktail, when a bird flew and settled on his shoulder. It was a—a—what was it, Dorothy?'

'A canary?' The princess had seated herself in a lopsided chair the nurse had drawn up for her.

'I don't know. I ought to remember. Today I can't. I almost can. Yesterday we had cabbage, and it was nasty: she had put something in it—cumm—coomm?'

'I don't know, Mummy. Tell me about the bird, though. Was it a songbird?' The daughter had leant forward, neck anxiously stretched, herself an expectant swan; she wanted their reunion to be a success.

'Oh—you *know*—of course—it was a *love*bird!'

The Princesse de Lascabanes exposed her teeth in a giggle, becoming the schoolgirl who was never long absent from her.

The nurse suggested sotto voce, 'May I tempt you to a drop of this?' At the same time she was pouring something opaque out of a glass jug. 'It's so refreshing. It's your mother's favourite: barley water.'

'Thank you, Nurse.'

'You know I don't. You force it on me,' the patient protested.

'Thank you. Yes, Sister, I'd adore a glass of barley water. Tell me, Mummy, about Mrs Hewlett's lovebird.'

'That's what I'm telling. It settled on Alfred's shoulder—climbed down his arm—on to a finger of the hand which was disengaged—and up again. I can see it distinctly.' Mrs Hunter was in fact looking straight ahead, intently, into and through the misted glass. 'Mrs Hewlett was so afraid for her bird she had a gardener stationed outside the window with a gun.'

'Really? Whatever for?'

'You won't let me tell you. She was afraid the bird might fly out the window into the orchard—and that a cat might be waiting in the long grass—to pounce.'

'Now who would have thought—a gardener with a gun! Can't have done too much gardening, waiting for cats to pounce on the boodgy. Can he, Miss Dorothy—*mad-dam*?'

Dorothy sipped her barley water. Nobody really expected her to give an opinion, just as they will ask, but don't expect, an opinion from a child. This, and the cool innocent stuff she was drinking, made the princess feel fulfilled rather than bored.

'All the same it's a most unusual story,' Sister Badgery allowed.

While Mrs Hunter drifted on another plane, outside her skull probably, where vision cleared, above the orchard grass.

'Mrs Hewlett loved her lovebird. That's why she went to such trouble. And was a bit jealous, I think—the bird flirting like that with Alfred.'

'And what happened, Mother? Did the bird fly out the window?'

'No.' The eyes staring, thoughts exploring even deeper into the past. 'Not on that occasion. They say it did at some—oh, later date.'

'I bet it gave Mrs Hewlett an anxious time. Did they manage to catch it, Mrs Hunter? Or did the cat?'

'No. I believe the gardener shot the bird.'

'Ohhhh!'

'Oh, ma-*darm*! Look – let me take it: you're spilling your barley water.'

'I can't – I won't believe it, Mother. Do you, really?'

'They found his body on the river bank – the blood still fresh in his neck feathers.'

Mrs Hunter thought she no longer believed in the situation herself, though Dorothy apparently did: she was appropriating the death of Mrs Hewlett's lovebird as something she might have prevented personally; that is the way all good myths are born.

Dorothy had sat forward again. 'But was the gardener – *mad*?'

'Who knows? Was the Russian lover mad who murdered Lilian Nutley in Manchuria or – wherever?'

Dorothy saw Sister Badgery had pursed up her lips till they were an only slightly pinker protuberance on her otherwise flat, colourless face; at the same time the veil was flicked so purposefully it suggested an attempt at semaphore. 'We're expecting Dr Gidley – only as a precaution – in the unusual circumstances,' she managed finally to whisper.

The person she was addressing suddenly felt most unhappy, neither the Princesse de Lascabanes, nor yet Dorothy Hunter: no more than a visitor on a chair. If she could at least have remembered Dr Gidley from out of the legion of retainers, he might have given her a sense of belonging; but she couldn't.

Mother had not heard, or had chosen to overlook her nurse's remark. 'Tell me about something, Dorothy – but *something*. Everybody flying here and there; I want to be brought news.'

Dorothy tried, but could not for the life of her think.

'That mother-in-law of yours – is she alive?'

'No, she – died. I wrote you about it.'

'I thought she was probably dead.'

'She suffered from bronchitis.'

'She hadn't the will to live.'

'Not everybody has, or there would be too many of us.'

'And that other woman – the one with the goitre – Eulalie?'

'She died too. I told you.' Madame de Lascabanes turned *in extremis* to her mother's nurse. 'That was my English aunt-by-marriage. At least, she was French, but married an Englishman who left her for the Côte d'Azur.'

Sister Badgery was entranced. 'My husband was an Englishman — a tea planter from Ceylon. We passed through Paris, once only, on our honeymoon to the Old Country. Gordon was a public-school man — Brighton College in Sussex. D'you know it?'

The princess didn't. Sister Badgery couldn't believe: such a well-known school.

'Sister Badgery, isn't it time Mrs Lippmann gave you your tea — or whatever you take — Madeira. There's an excellent Madeira in the sideboard; Alfred developed a taste for it.'

'You know I never touch a drop of anything strong.'

'I want to talk to my daughter — Mrs Hunter — privately,' Mrs Hunter said.

She knew from the sound of the knife-edged skirt that she had offended her nurse. That made two presents she would have to give: Mrs Wyburd and Mrs Badgery.

When the nurse had closed the door the princess felt imprisoned, not only in the room, but in her own body. In her state of foreboding she reached out for the glass of barley water Sister Badgery had removed, and tried to find comfort in sips of that mawkish stuff. She could see herself in one of the looking-glasses with which her blind mother still kept herself surrounded. If the princess had not been so terrified of what the next moment could hold, she might have noticed that her own eyes were deep and lustrous: beautiful in fact; but in the circumstances her mind could only flutter through imagined eventualities.

Actually Mrs Hunter was enjoying the luxury of being alone and perfectly silent with somebody she loved. (They did love each other, didn't they? You could never be sure about other people; sometimes you found they had hated you all their lives.) This state of perfect stillness was not unlike what she enjoyed in her relationship with Sister de Santis, though in essence it was different; with the night nurse she was frequently united in a worship of something too vast and selfless to describe even if your mind had been completely compos whatever it is. This other state of unity in perfect stillness, which she hoped she was beginning to enjoy with Dorothy, she had experienced finally with Alfred when she returned to 'Kudjeri' to nurse him in his last illness. There were moments when their minds were folded into each other without any trace of the cross-hatching of wilfulness or desire to possess. Yet at the same time all the comfort of touch was present in their absorption. At least that was the way *you* had felt, and believed, or hoped for the same in someone else.

Mrs Hunter coughed out of delicacy for the feelers extended in the direction of her silent daughter.

Dorothy said, after swallowing, 'I do think, darling, they ought to get you another carpet. This one is threadbare in places, particularly at the door.'

Mrs Hunter gasped and frowned. 'I haven't noticed.' Then she recovered herself. 'They haven't told me.' She began easing one or two of her encrusting rings. 'I expect they've worked it out that I'm going to die—that it wouldn't be worth while.'

Dorothy was making those pained sounds.

'But I shan't die—or anyway, not till I feel like it. I don't believe anybody dies who doesn't want to—unless by thunderbolts.'

'Nobody wants to suggest you're going to die, Mother.'

'Then why does everybody come flying from the ends of the earth?'

'Because you've been ill. Weren't you?' Dorothy was kicking at one of the legs of the bed: an awkward and useless gesture on the part of her otherwise flawless foot; she had never given up those classic Pinet shoes, and only the perverse would have denied she had been right in flouting fashion; again, only the perverse would have caught sight of the lubberly schoolgirl the Pinet shoes and her little Chanel camouflaged. 'You can't say you weren't ill,' she repeated through lips grown heavy with the sulks as she continued kicking at the bed.

Mother said, 'Stop doing it, Dorothy, please. I don't want my furniture ruined. You must learn to control your feelings.'

The Princesse de Lascabanes knew that her eyes were threatening to overflow: because the great, the constant grudge had been against her over-controlled feelings; when the showdown came, hadn't he even accused her of being 'frigid'?

'I can only — well, I'd *like* to explain your flying out here as lack of emotional control,' Mother was still bashing. 'I expect they told you I had a stroke. In that case, you were misinformed. I only had a very slight — what was hardly a stroke at all.'

Dorothy Hunter plunged her hands as deep as she could into the bowels of the dusty old uncomfortable chair; she would stick it out.

'In any case you flew — to make sure you'd see me die — or to ask me for money if I didn't. Basil too.'

'Oh God, Mother, don't you allow for the possibility of human affection?' The outraged daughter snatched back her hands from out of the depths of the chair: what her mother had said was the more cruel for being partly true. 'I can't answer for Basil. I never see him. Basil is capable of anything.' That was so unquestionably true it did away with her own spasm of shame by drowning it in a wave of loathing.

No, it didn't; she detested lies: most of all those half-lies she was sometimes driven to tell.

'You're so *unfair!*' A whinge developed through a moan into a downright blub.

It was only now that Mrs Hunter felt they had reached the point at which they might become one. At the same time she was chastened, as well as impressed, by the emotional outburst it was in her power to cause.

There was no need to call Dorothy to her: their impulses answered each other. Here was that still skinny, perpetually tormented little girl screwing up the sheet by the handfuls, laying her head beside yours on the pillow. You were soon crying together, though softly, deliciously.

64

'Anyway it did you good,' Mrs Hunter said when their self-indulgence could no longer be excused.

'What did?' Dorothy exchanged her lumped-up position, half on the bed, for a less embarrassing, more comfortable attitude; while the Princesse de Lascabanes started administering a series of flat pats to her coiffure in one of the distant looking-glasses: she wasn't consoled by her own reflection, nor by her mother's implication that she had benefited by a 'good cry'.

'Well, I mean — the air of Sydney,' Mrs Hunter selected out of the air. 'Isn't that why we came here? Your bronchitis. To escape from those severe winters at Gogong, after the burning hot summers.'

Knowing this was the official reason, Dorothy replied, 'Actually I can't remember much about the bronchitis. I expect I was too young.'

'Basil will remember,' Mrs Hunter said; it must have sounded complacent because she herself detected it. 'Basil remembers the least detail.'

'Basil is a genius.' Dorothy no longer resented it; in her wrung-out condition it would have been too exacting; now she only passively despised.

'I remember how quickly you revived in this balmy Sydney air. You never had bronchitis again.' In fact, it was herself who had bloomed like a different flower on the same plant; how exotic, how naked her body felt when the southerly began to blow at the end of a sticky summer's day, caressing her inside her dresses.

'The Sydney climate was always unreliable: changeable, treacherous,' the princess insisted feelingly. 'That's why the people are like they are.'

'Oh, but they are so kind, hospitable — *out*-giving.' Mrs Hunter came at it as though she were reading from a brochure of moral touristry.

Then perhaps because it was not clear who had won, Mother asked, 'In the winter — in Paris — do you wear woollen vests, Dorothy?'

'No,' the princess replied. 'Because indoors there are the — the *salamandres*. And when I go out I wear my fur coat. Fur boots too,' she added for good measure; her argument would have satisfied any reasonable Frenchwoman.

'But wool is best, Dorothy. And steak. My advice to any girl living on her own is to order steak—when she is invited out—by men.'

'*Bien saignant!*' Dorothy de Lascabanes laughed a rackety laugh. 'But I'm no longer invited out, Mother, by men. Or not very often.'

Mrs Hunter appeared not to believe it, anyway of herself: she closed her mouth so abruptly; then she opened it and said, 'There's this man—what's his name? Athol Something. I don't like him. We met at some dinner party. Athol Shreve? After we came to live in this house. I definitely don't like him. He's in business, or something awful—politics.'

Dorothy wondered whether she could stick it out.

'You haven't told me about your flight. Did they feed you properly, darling?' Mrs Hunter flickered her eyelids in the shallows of social intercourse.

Madame de Lascabanes was only too glad to accept the invitation. 'Yes. I saw to that: I travelled Air France. The food is frightfully civilized: none of your Qantas plastic.'

'Oh, but darling—Qantas—the best in the world!'

The mother heard her daughter give what she interpreted as a French sniff: the French were so certain of their values, and here was Dorothy, always knotted to the point of strangulation, aspiring to be what she was not, because of that parvenu prince.

Mrs Hunter saw him: the groove in the lower lip, above the cleft chin, beneath the pink-shaded restaurant lights. She had ordered *tournedos Lulu Watier*. After the first shock of mutual disapproval, she felt that she and Hubert were enjoying each other. Alfred said, 'Out with us, the food is plainer. We don't feel the need to titillate our palates by dolling it up with a lot of seasoning and fancy sauces.' He might have worsened the situation if she hadn't kicked him under the table.

They had gone over for the wedding because the old princess insisted she could not travel out to *ce pays si lointain et inconnu*. It was the first occasion the mountain hadn't come to Elizabeth Hunter: she couldn't very well believe it; nor that she would overlook the fact that her little Dorothy was being received into the Roman Catholic Church. But you did: at the nuptial mass there was your plain little girl in the dress by Lanvin *tissé exprès à la main à Lyon*, and none of it could disguise the fact that you were prostituting your daughter to a prince, however desirably suave and hung with decorations. For one instant, out of the chanting and the incense, Elizabeth Hunter experienced a kind of spiritual goose-flesh. (Ridiculous when you came to think you had never felt in any way religious, except occasionally at puberty, on clear mornings, down along the river bank. No, there had been other, later, more secret occasions.) Then she was carried on by the sea of words ebbing and flowing round her child's head. Her *child*! The eyes of several elderly Frenchmen were directed at the mother of the bride, from out of their aura of distinction and smell of mothballs. And the eyes of that priest standing on the altar steps. She had never met a priest's eyes, let alone felt them penetrate her: cold eyes can burn the deepest. She was glad of Alfred's shoulder: her rock, if not always, at least when necessary.

'Considering how uncomplicated Alfred was, it is surprising he never seemed surprised at anything that happened,' Mrs Hunter said. 'The Bullivants, Dorothy – will you be seeing the Bullivants?'

'Why should I?'

'But Cherry was your great friend. And the Bullivants took you to Paris that – that time – Daddy decided to send you. He had such faith in Charles and Violet – a reliable wing to protect you in foreign parts.'

'Are you blaming the Bullivants?'

'I'm not blaming anybody.'

'I'm relieved. It's only I who was to blame.'

Mrs Hunter thought she detected a masochistic tone of voice; she wondered whether she might take advantage of it.

'Well, I expect you'll see Cherry. She's married to a nice man. So I'm told—I haven't seen him: a stockbroker or something. They live up the North Shore. That can't be helped. Cherry's happy.'

An ambulance was screeching down Anzac Parade, or was it a fire engine? Madame de Lascabanes had not yet learnt to distinguish between the different Sydney emergencies.

'Dorothy, dear, I've been trying to understand why you shouldn't settle down in this house. Comfort each other. An excellent cook. Of course I had to take her in hand—pass on what I know—Mrs Lippmann. Have you met my housekeeper?' Dorothy was palpitating.

'In your old room. Practically as you left it. One has to respect what other people are—essentially—even when they try to destroy themselves. But I offer you your room—your latchkey—financial security—if only you will realize that badly heated Paris apartment is—so—so pernicious.'

Dorothy de Lascabanes had flown to her mother's bedside to pronounce an ultimatum, a brutal one if necessary, and here she was, her head literally so heavy she had to support it with her hands. 'I don't *know*, Mummy!' she muttered from behind her wrists.

'Think it over, darling. Nothing can be decided in—*you* know I would never let you *want*—and for *that* reason.'

They had lapsed. Both of them. The princess might have been sunk in a lake of mercury, but Mrs Hunter was probably born of that substance.

'Tell me, Dorothy—because you haven't told me—about your flight from Paris. Was the weather?'

In Madame de Lascabanes's experience most old people were deeply involved with the weather: an involvement which expressed itself superficially in a lament for rheumatics and colds, whereas on another level the hostile natural elements were charged with supernatural terrors, even if these were rationally laughed away or curtained off behind an apparently thick skin.

So it was no surprise when Mrs Hunter inquired almost fearfully, 'Was it *rough*?'

'No. That is, it wasn't most of the way. Except for one patch over the Bay of Bengal. Yes. Then it was.'

Again Madame de Lascabanes found herself guarding with one hand her pearls, with the other her coiffure. She need not be ashamed, of course, because Mother could not see. In any case the old thing was lost in what appeared a state of exhilarated anticipation rather than fear.

'It became so bumpy, so terribly rough, I was frightened more than I have ever been. I got beyond the stage of thinking how late the storm would make us in Sydney. I went on to visions of crashing in the sea. When a man sitting beside me gave me a sort of courage.'

'How?' Mrs Hunter had closed her eyes again; her question was followed by one of those waking snores; after which her mouth remained open as though expecting to receive some life-restoring draught.

'Simply by what he told me,' the princess replied, her private smile breaking up her face into something related to beauty.

'What?' Mrs Hunter snored back inexorably.

Madame de Lascabanes had been congratulating herself that none of the polyglot passengers surrounding her wished to tell their life stories. The sounds of flight made by the laborious machine gave cover, she liked to think, to her own more obsessive thoughts. On the whole, when travelling, she preferred anonymous company, till on this occasion the storm they entered whipped her nerves to screeching point.

Once or twice before now she had glanced, no more than formally, hardly out of interest, at the elderly man beside her on the aisle: neither French, nor English, she guessed; White Russian? the profile was not sufficiently irregular or blurred; too self-contained, probably materialistic. When, to kill time, her neighbour started ruffling the leaves of his passport, again she glanced – not exactly inquisitive – perhaps also to kill time. He was a Dutchman, she saw on the page.

This was to some extent a consolation: at least to her Australian soul steeped in the ethos of the white, the clean; though her French self grew bored and snooty. It was only after the storm took hold of them in earnest, and fear united the disparate halves of her entity, that she truly began to appreciate the Dutchman's presence.

Physically square set, his body was hard, she knew from lurching against his shoulder. The hands too, were square, hard-looking, and although no longer youthful, suggested a supple strength. At the same time she sensed an uncommon spirit, one probably prepared to overstep the physical limits most others submit to. He had something austere, monastic about him, nothing of the conventionally regimented ecclesiastic such as her mother-in-law used to collect; rather, you saw in the Dutchman some soul-ravaged, freethinking pastor.

While she was letting her thoughts wander, persuaded that his elderliness permitted her the freedom of her fantasies, the passengers were suddenly thrown as high as their safety-belts allowed.

'*Ah, comme j'ai peur!*' The Princesse de Lascabanes moaned and smiled, still half to herself.

'You are not frightened?' the Dutchman asked in round, correct English.

'Well, not really – or just a little,' Dorothy de Lascabanes replied, to be on the side of virtue; and after she had recovered a fundamentally Anglo-Saxon tone, 'I'm only afraid we shall be late'; she coughed because her eyes were smarting.

'It is probably a typhoon,' the Dutchman composed for his new acquaintance.

'Surely not!' she answered as coldly as she could. 'It couldn't possibly reach us up here – or could it? I know nothing of the habits of typhoons.'

'My experience is only of the sea.'

She did not know why hearing this should have given her so much pleasure, but she breathed more deeply, and observed his hand with fresh interest.

In the beginning he had inclined his head towards her shoulder, till discovering the angle and distance from which their voices might reach each other. Not once, even after establishing rapport, did the Dutchman turn to look at his neighbour. They were so private, at the same time so formal, Dorothy was reminded of the confessional, use of which was one of the more positive privileges she had acquired on marrying Hubert de Lascabanes. For a moment she was tempted to pour out she didn't know what—no, *everything*, to this convenient 'priest', till persuaded by his manner that he might not have learnt any of the comforting formulas.

She was only partly wrong, though.

'Some years ago I was at sea—master of a freighter,' the Dutchman was telling in his matter-of-fact, stubbornly enunciating voice, 'when a typhoon struck us, almost fatally. For several hours we were thrown and battered—till suddenly calm fell—the calmest calm I have ever experienced at sea. God had willed us to enter the eye—you know about it? the still centre of the storm—where we lay at rest—surrounded by hundreds of seabirds, also resting on the water.'

The airy rubble over which the plane was bumping became so inconsiderable Madame de Lascabanes was made ashamed; she was saddened, also, to think it might never be given to her to enter the eye of the storm as described by the Dutch sea captain, though she was not unconscious of the folded wings, the forms of sea-birds afloat around them.

'Sure, we had to take another battering—as the eye was moved away—and the farther wall of the storm rammed us—but less severe. You could tell the violence was exhausting itself.'

After that he closed his eyes. There was much she could have asked him, and perhaps would dare when he opened them. In the meantime, she sat half dreaming half thinking, her own eyes fixed on a full but tranquil vein in the back of one of this man's hands.

Actually, when he woke from his doze, he struggled out of his seat to visit the lavatory. Their paltry storm had passed, it appeared, though they were advised to keep their seat-belts fastened for the landing at Bangkok.

So she did not speak again to the Dutchman, except in mumbles.

They grunted, nodded and smiled at each other, amused, it must have seemed, by some shared secret, as they shuffled out of the plane at the airport.

It was here that she joined the Australian flight. She lost her Dutchman, probably for ever.

'Is that all?' Mrs Hunter opened her eyes.

'Oh, yes. I know I had nothing special to tell. Nobody would be impressed who hadn't heard from this ordinary, yet in some way, extraordinary man. He struck me as being'—she was struggling through the wicked jungle of language—'himself the soul of calm and wisdom.'

Just then Dorothy Hunter was startled out of her memories by some of the former mineral glitter in her mother's almost extinct stare.

'Dorothy, didn't I ever tell you of my experience in a cyclone?'

Mother was daring you not to have known. She was standing at the head of the stairs, one arm outstretched, pointing, in a dress of blinding white such as had suited her best: cold and perfect in its way. And now a mere daughter, in spite of trial by marriage, the exorcism of a number of doubts, and arrival at perhaps a few mature conclusions, was frightened to the edge of panic by whatever revelation this vision of earthly authority might be threatening her with.

'No,' she protested. 'You didn't tell—that is, I think I remember hearing—yes, about a storm.'

Somehow she must be spared: Mother must grant her this one concession.

'If I didn't write to you at the time, I must have been too annoyed with you—flying off like that—in a rage.' Mrs Hunter sounded reasonable, calm, just. 'It was when the Warmings asked us to stay on their island. They had to leave in a hurry. One of the children was sick, I think. Then you rushed away. You missed a lot of excitement—and made a fool of yourself.'

Mrs Hunter laughed gently; it sounded almost as though she

still had those small but exquisite teeth. 'What was the name of the professor man?'

Dorothy Hunter was frozen beyond answering. She shouldn't have been; it had happened fifteen years ago.

'Anyway, it was while I was on the island that this cyclone struck. Oh, I shall tell you—when I can find the strength. I can see the birds, just as your Russian said.'

If physical strength was letting her down, her capacity for cruelty would never fail her: to drag in Edvard Pehl. At her most loving, Mother had never been able to resist the cruel thrust. To have loved her in the prime of her beauty, as many had, was like loving, or 'admiring' rather, a jewelled scabbard in which a sword was hidden: which would clatter out under the influence of some peculiar frenzy, to slash off your ears, the fingers, the tongues, or worse, impale the hearts, of those who worshipped. And yet we continued to offer ourselves, if reluctantly. As they still do, it appears: to this ancient scabbard, from which the jewels have loosened and scattered, the blind sockets filled instead with verdigris, itself a vengeful semi-jewellery, the sword still sharp in spite of age and use.

She must try to define her love for her mother: it had remained something beyond her understanding.

And the cyclone: why was it given to Elizabeth Hunter to experience the eye of the storm? That too! Or are regenerative states of mind granted to the very old to ease the passage from their earthly, sensual natures into final peace and forgiveness? Of course Mother could have imagined her state of grace amongst the resting birds, just as she had imagined Mrs Hewlett's escaped lovebird and the mad or distraught gardener. Though remembering some frightfulness the prince had forced on her mind more painfully than on her body, Dorothy de Lascabanes suspected the lovebird's murder was not an invention.

Then the knocking, and in Sister Badgery's voice, 'Mrs Hunter? Here's a lovely surprise for you, dear. Dr Gidley is paying us a visit.'

73

Brave or foolish, the nurse pushed the door open without waiting for encouragement, and for once her judgment seemed correct.

Her patient spoke up in the voice of a little girl who has learnt a lesson, though it could have been an unimportant one. 'It is very kind of him,' Mrs Hunter said.

'We couldn't very well not look in—not as we were passing—could we?' The doctor was a large young man with a fatty laugh.

'Not very well—not after promising Sister de Santis on the telephone.'

The doctor ignored it, while the duty nurse pursed up her mouth, her cheeks near to bursting for the wickedness of her precocious charge.

Then she remembered, 'This is the—the daughter—Dr Gidley'; though her voice had a dash of acid, her eyes were radiating sunshine from behind the gold-rimmed spectacles.

'Ahhh!' The doctor recoiled, but put out his hand, sighing or hissing.

The Princess got the impression she was a rare disease he had not encountered before, and which he would have liked to look up furtively in a book; while avoiding his hand, she replied, 'How do you do, Dr Gidley?' Though recently grown up, the doctor would remain, for her at least, or at any rate for the moment, an enormous baby to whose somewhat featureless face had been added a pair of fashionable mutton-chops.

Apparently unconscious of a snub, he advanced on the bed, where he plumped his doctor's bag (humbler than himself) beside him on the carpet. 'How are we, Mrs Hunter? No strain on the Big Day?' Without waiting to hear, he took up his patient's wrist, which surprisingly she abandoned to him.

(Surely such enormous fingers would detect only a thundering pulse?)

'She's remarkable—truly remarkable,' the nurse nattered sideways and superfluously to the daughter who was a princess.

The doctor frowned, and the nurse, recalled to duty, stood to attention like a frail private.

74

'Normal enough,' Dr Gidley finally complained out loud.

And so did Mrs Hunter. 'Normal is the last thing I am—I hoped you might have gathered by now—Doctor—Dr *Gidley*.' The corners of her mouth were struggling to perfect a half-remembered technique of malice. 'Otherwise, what am I paying for? A—a dia-*gnosis* of my ordinariness?'

Dr Gidley flopped into the nearest chair, fingers dangling in clusters between wide-open legs. 'Okay! Dictate your diagnosis, Mrs Hunter, and I'll learn it.' Mirth bumped the banana-bunches against swelling thighs.

Sister Badgery hummed with suppressed pleasure.

The strength of these two acolytes lay in their belief in the rightness of what they were doing and the wrong-thinking of others; which drew Dorothy towards her mother: at her most imperious, her most declamatory, Mother's manner had suggested that the moment her will snoozed she might collide with some passive object or suffer buffeting by a directed one. Mother and daughter were both sleepwalkers, only their approach from opposite ends of the room ensured that their meetings should become, more often than not, collisions.

Now, faced with the forces of practical optimism, they were wearing identical smiles, while the opposition continued shining with the light of their mission: to prevent a human body dying, even if it felt like doing so.

In the circumstances Mrs Hunter murmured, 'My daughter and I understand each other implicitly.'

If it were true, it ought to be kept a secret; so Dorothy muttered, and stirred in her chair, and almost put up a hand to avert an indelicacy.

While Mrs Hunter continued in her determination to hint at sweetness. 'Before you disturbed us, we were enjoying a delightful conversation. She was telling me about her voyage out.'

'Flight, Mother,' Dorothy corrected; then blushed. 'And it was not a very spectacular one.' Her expression menaced Sister Badgery and Dr Gidley with her journey's uneventfulness.

This should have consoled them, but the large young doctor looked uneasy: if he had obeyed convention he would have inquired at least about the weather, only the problem of the title prevented him addressing Mrs Hunter's daughter.

Instead he made sounds.

Mrs Hunter slightly moved her head from side to side on the pillow, apparently about to start on a singsong, though when it came, the voice was thin, high and sustained, like the fine-drawn utterance of a single violin. 'She was telling me about a charming Dutchman she met—and a hurricane which overtook them off Curaçao—quite a mystical experience.'

The doctor and the nurse laughed to express their interest or hide their disbelief. Everybody but Mrs Hunter was obviously feeling uncomfortable.

Sister Badgery tried to remind her patient of the physical realities. 'Your pillows are looking lumpy, Mrs Hunter. Wait till I shake them up.'

While the nurse satisfied herself with the pillows Mrs Hunter was as much tossed by her own thoughts. 'Yes. I remember the birds—the waves shaped like small pyramids—black swans nesting between them.'

Dr Gidley accepted the swans as his excuse for leaving. 'If there's nothing we can do for you, Mrs Hunter, we shan't interrupt your reunion with your daughter.'

'Oh, but there is something! There is! I want you to give me whatever will make me sleep.'

Doctor and nurse looked at each other; then Sister Badgery said in a voice of such exaggerated kindness she might have been going to gobble someone up, 'But you do sleep, dear. You know you do—beautifully.'

'I lie and—and ramble around in waking. Once years ago somebody prescribed something, and when I took this pill the effect was like slipping on the sides of a smooth funnel, then through the hole, into darkness.'

She was listening very intently.

'Darkness is what I want,' she insisted. 'I'm too distracted by the figures which come and go through the grey of the other.'

She must have heard the catch on the doctor's bag, for she began to look pacified. He was dashing away at a pad, a sheet of which he tore off and gave to Sister Badgery.

'There's no reason, at your age, why you shouldn't have what makes you happy.' Dr Gidley spoke as though this moral prescription, on top of the medical one, had originated with him.

And Mrs Hunter seemed to think it might have: she was smiling up at the doctor with an expression of girlish gratitude; she might have received at least a kiss the moment before, whereas she was having to content herself with some clumsy handpatting.

When they were alone the Princesse de Lascabanes remarked, 'I'm surprised at your having a doctor of Gidley's type. I expected somebody older and more experienced—Mr Wyburd as physician, if you see what I mean.'

Mrs Hunter laughed. 'I know Gidley isn't much good as a doctor, but I can tell by the feel of him he's the kind of man I might have enjoyed as a lover.' She turned slightly. 'I've shocked you, Dorothy dear.'

Dorothy said, no, she wasn't shocked; even so she was glad of the blur which separated them: she could look more closely at her mother.

'Don't think I made a practice of promiscuity. Oh, I was unfaithful once or twice—but only as a sort of experiment—and it did prove it wasn't worth it. For most women, I think, sexual pleasure is largely imagination. They imagine lovers while their husbands are having their way with them, but in their lovers' arms they regret what they remember of the husband's humdrum virtues.'

The princess sounded all expostulatory mirth. 'I think you're tired, Mother, and are talking utter imaginary nonsense!' *She* was tired, anyway.

Mrs Hunter would have liked to see Dorothy as more than the blur she appeared, to decide whether she had ever had a lover.

Probably her trouble was that Hubert had been too much the lover for his wife to have experienced a husband.

'So now I'm going to leave you for my club,' the Princesse de Lascabanes announced.

'When we were expecting you for luncheon!' Mrs Hunter's recent wisdom shrivelled into a rag of skin. 'My housekeeper— Mrs Lippmann—will give you a splendid luncheon—in the dining-room by yourself—or a snack on a tray, here with me.' Then she added, out of desperation it seemed, 'You haven't met her, have you? Well, I mean, socially. Sometimes she dances for me. Are you surprised, Dorothy, at a dancing cook?'

'By now, Mother, I am not surprised.'

Mrs Hunter could hear her daughter drawing on her gloves; in the end, stitched to the bed by steel threads, you can only persuade the past.

While they were kissing, and she was sure of escaping, Dorothy de Lascabanes decided to ask, 'That fur rug in my old room—so soft—what is it?'

'Platypus.'

'But they're protected!'

'Yes. They're protected. It was Grandfather Hunter who killed them. Alfred was gentle.' (Then she did at least recognize it as a quality in others.) 'Alfred gave me the rug as one of my wedding presents. He thought that because it was so rare we might have had it on our bed, but I asked him to let me put it away. I didn't care for it as fur. I didn't care for *it*. When he was ill—when he was dying— he remembered the platypus rug and got me to bring it out. I used to arrange it over his knees—after we had sat him up in his chair—that last, bitter winter at "Kudjeri". By then I don't believe we thought any more about the poor slaughtered little creatures, or if we did, they had become willing sacrifices.'

Her memory was so positive, only the silence could compete with it.

'Dorothy?' Mrs Hunter asked, to confirm that her daughter had left.

Dorothy de Lascabanes was in fact stumbling down the stairs: dreams she remembered in which she was trampling recently-hatched nestlings swam into the actual waters of the sacrificial platypus. So she trampled and lurched. In the hall she found herself pushing at what? the only opposition was a void: and guilt, tenderness, desire, lost opportunities. She must never forget *Mother is an evil heartless old woman.* If you did forget, Basil would remember, himself Mother's only equal at driving the knife home. *Boo-hoo, poor you! if anybody ever told you they loved you you wouldn't believe that either now would you?*

The thought that she still had to face her brother started her tearing at the hall door.

Two

As the princess broke out there was the crunch of a key from the other side: a young woman had begun to let herself in. Each staggered while trying to decide who had the better right to the door. Of course Madame de Lascabanes knew that hers could not be denied, and to think that anybody might dispute it had started anger gathering behind her long face. Then her indignation and her sense of protocol left her. The girl was too young, too radiant, to be dispossessed; she was smiling besides, out of bland lips, on which was pasted a delicately aggressive pink suggesting ointment rather than lipstick, while her Perspex ear-rings cunningly gyrated, and a pattern of great suns on her pretence of a dress dazzled the beholder with their cerise and purple, particularly just off centre from the breasts. It was too physical a moment for speeches of apology. The half-smile the older woman had been induced to wear reminded her she had forgotten to restore her mouth: her thoughts had shed so much blood, she hadn't had the heart to resort to further crimson.

So the women passed each other smiling and murmuring, each suspecting who the other was, while avoiding confirmation. The princess tested the marble steps with wary feet, propping even more warily around the drastic swirl of path which would lead eventually to the gate and the taxi she had not ordered: to escape from the house was enough. During it all the relieving nurse was able to enjoy the luxury of a last look from her possessed doorway. Madame de Lascabanes did not glance back: it would not have been correct. Remembering her forgotten luggage (have Arnold Wyburd fetch it) she did not even pause. Carefully watching her classic shoes, she narrowed her French nostrils at the strange body-scent of Australian gumleaves, and sighed; while the nurse stood, legs apart, thighs radiating light and strength below the dazzle of minimal skirt.

She might have slammed the door at last, if she hadn't been trained to control her antipathies in the presence of the sick.

Sister Manhood walked through the hall swinging her orange plastic handbag. She went out to the kitchen where Mrs Lippmann would be dishing up lunch. Although it was agreed in writing that Sister Badgery should be given lunch before going off, it was never more than silently accepted that Sister Manhood should arrive in time to eat her share. Only reasonable, as Flora Manhood saw it.

'*So!* We thought you was going to be late, Floradora!' The housekeeper's solecisms went oddly with her civilized monkey's face: they roused Jessie Badgery's scorn—a scorn for all foreigners; but Flora Manhood was by moments at least something of an anarchist.

Now she nibbled at the housekeeper's unresisting ear. 'Anyway, I saw Her—the Queen Maree Antoinette Mother of all the Russias the Princess Lascabum.'

The housekeeper shrieked, and scraped the pan harder than ever; she wagged her behind as though stroked by the long feathers of light which float out across the empty floor, out of darkness, the moment before the act begins.

'*Wenn Mutter in die Manage ritt,*' Mrs Lippmann sang, and helped it along with the iron spoon.

'What's all these jokes I'm not in on?' Sister Badgery called from the breakfast room, in which she was already seated, and where Mrs Lippmann served the nurses' lunch.

Surprisingly, Sister Badgery had an appetite, though in manoeuvring the food past her lips her fork implied disparagement, and she emphasized her disapproval with an occasional flick of her accurate veil. What she could not disguise was a stomach like a small melon under the starched uniform, or her opinion of her colleague, who had sat down in her street dress and was scoffing the scrambled eggs, slithery with too much butter, in their cornets of smoked ham.

There was cucumber too, in sour cream, under a pretty sprinkling of dill; and a chocolate *Torte* oozing on to a paper doily in a Meissen dish. 'Ooh! **Yummy** yummy!' Flora Manhood squealed, her eye on the *Torte*. 'You've given away the milshig-fleishig today, Lottie!'

'No *milchig-fleischig*,' Mrs Lippmann muttered, from round what could have been an obstructive cigar. 'Only when I am at my lowest. I don't know why I am not today. But I am not.' If she had been smoking that cigar, her nostrils would have blown two streams of the fiercest smoke.

Sister Manhood examined her thumb and what was a fleck of sour cream; then she slowly licked the cream off. 'Can't think why you stick around here cooking for us and old Mother Swizzlestick upstairs.'

'Poor Mrs Hunter! Such names!' Sister Badgery protested. 'Why "Swizzlestick", for heaven's sake?'

'Because she likes to believe there's still a duty male, somewhere, drinking champers to her out of a shoe.'

Lotte Lippmann cackled. 'That's why I stick around cooking for Mrs Swizzlestick! *Ich weiss auch was Liebe ist!*'

'But the career and all, Lottie—how can you be content as a cook?' Sister Manhood's attempt at seriousness and gentility was sabotaged by her mouth closing on a forkful of *Torte*.

Mrs Lippmann hawked up her reply. '*Ach, die Karriere!* My art was a tiny, satiric one—to find what in all things is ridiculous—and all things are ridiculous if you look.' She laughed flat, and you could see her broad, purple tongue; you could see Lotte Lippmann tugging at the brim of her top hat, settling a cane under an armpit. 'My art was destructive—and soon finished—prick! pouff! along with all that it had pricked—*alles so schrecklich komisch*! Do you understand, ladies?' The cook was staggering under the weight of her exposition.

Sister Badgery did not like it at all when the housekeeper carried on like this; Sister Manhood, on the other hand, sat with her elbows on the table, her face in her hands, and felt she was experiencing life.

'No, it was not altogether like this,' Mrs Lippmann seemed to remember. 'My career ended in the gas ofens—in the smoke from

Jews.' It could have been ashes choking the seams of her burnt-out face.

'Oh, stopput, Lot!' Flora Manhood wanted to cry; she could have cried for everything, but principally herself.

While Sister Badgery was wondering how she might slip away and release the cucumber seeds trapped under her denture.

'So now I cook. That too is an art—a creative one, I tell myself—though I should be doing it in some huddle of Jews—all together mortifying ourselves and remembering the smoke from the incinerators of Germany.'

Mrs Lippmann laughed gently; but Sister Manhood burst into a spate of noisy sobs.

'You've been overdoing it, Sister. I can tell,' Sister Badgery said. 'You don't get your proper quota of sleep.'

'It isn't that.' Sister Manhood tried to wipe her messy cheeks. 'Well, it is too, I suppose—when you are *involved* with somebody—and can't make up your mind how deep.'

Sister Badgery sucked her teeth in sympathy or disapproval, and by so doing, managed to work out several of the pointed cucumber seeds; after which success, and the rich meal, she meditated, 'We've all of us got our job;' and swallowed the seeds.

Mrs Lippmann offered, 'I make you a double strong coffee, Floradora.'

Just then they heard a tinkling in the upper air. They sat and listened, and could have gone on sitting and listening: it was such a frail tinkling, of a little handbell, both supplicating and peremptory. All three became ashamed.

Sister Manhood said, after taking a good look at her watch, 'I must go up to the old bag. Bet she's wet the bed, or worse.'

Sister Badgery frowned and winced, and whipped the veil off her neutral, almost non-existent hair.

'*Unser armer Schatz!*' Mrs Lippmann sighed, sweeping crumbs off the table with her hand.

'Shan't be a couple of ticks, love, unless it's something urgent,'

Sister Manhood called through Mrs Hunter's door, and her practised, nurse's voice would have convinced all but the most sceptical.

Mrs Hunter, who had decided that it was one of her more pitiful moments, accepted the convention meekly enough. 'Nothing urgent,' she quavered back. 'Only they've left me alone for hours, and I feel I'm due for some sort of human attention.'

Nobody on either side ever bothered to wonder how much anybody believed in the untruths to which you were driven by self-pity and old age. Then there were those other genuine occasions when two minutes can encompass aeons of slow rot: that was something you couldn't explain to human beings who measure time by the clock.

Actually Sister Manhood was quick at changing from dress into uniform, because Jessie would be chafing to change and catch the bus. Sister Badgery insisted on absolute privacy: she couldn't bear to show herself even from behind a bra; and no wonder. So Flora Manhood resisted the temptation to contemplate her own body. She made do with her face, sucking in her cheeks after she had adjusted the veil, after she had pasted her lips a deeper pink for whoever would see them, not old Betty Hunter that was for sure.

'Well, here we are then! Did you have an exciting morning, Mrs Hunter?' Sister Manhood asked in a brisk voice unlike the one she knew to be hers.

'My daughter isn't an exciting girl.'

'It must have been nice, though. Wasn't it? After all this time.'

The nurse had to repair the bed: that was her duty; she began to do it.

'I suppose it was nice,' Mrs Hunter said as she was tossed about from side to side. 'But you can never really tell with people – what they like. My children – when they were children – always claimed to like the opposite of what I knew they did.'

'Oh?'

Flora Manhood couldn't care. What she herself liked she sometimes wondered: rich, yummy food; sleep; cosmetics; making love; not making love.

She remembered and asked, 'Supposing we rub your back? Or don't you want to be bothered?'

'Yes, please,' Mrs Hunter answered blissfully.

She could take any amount of treatment from little Manhood, whether buffeting or caresses, even her out and out bad tempers: an animal presence is something the mind craves the farther the body shrivels into skin and bone.

Sister Manhood had hoped her patient might refuse the back-rubbing; she had given her the opportunity; but it hadn't worked.

Once, while receiving Sister Manhood's ministrations, Mrs Hunter had put up her hands and encountered her nurse's throat. She had decided to feel it, and for a moment her hands had contained this strong vessel of flesh and muscle, inside which, it seemed, the whole of life was palpitating. Sister Manhood had pretended to be embarrassed; but that didn't deceive.

Now when the nurse had fetched the flask of alcohol, and turned the old thing over on her side, like a half-open pocketknife, or deck chair upset by the wind, she too remembered the time Mrs Hunter had held her by the throat: such a frail rat-tat she was subjected to, but subjected. She smiled to herself; now there was no question who had the upper hand.

How powerless I am, Mrs Hunter thought, the saliva becoming bitter in her mouth, till she realized: not quite powerless while my mind is a match for the lot of them—on its better days.

She was comforted by this fact as much as by Sister Manhood's soothing hand.

As she rubbed, the nurse droned, 'Mrs Lippmann has something lovely for your dinner, Mrs Hunter. You'll go crazy; it's so scrumptious.'

'Don't tell me. That will spoil the surprise.' Then she asked, from behind closed eyelids, 'What colour is it?'

'Shan't tell!' Sister Manhood giggled; she didn't have the vaguest idea what Lottie had got for the old girl's dinner, but this was one of the games they played.

When, as she rubbed, she was overcome by a revulsion, almost a paralysis of her strong golden arm. Oh God, my life is slipping away! Where the fumes from the alcohol had cauterized her nostrils, and straying farther, exhilarated her thoughts, now they disgusted, though not so much as this loathsome back streaked with sickly brown-yellow, the frail, fluttering ribs, and however clean, the browner cleft becoming a funnel to the anus.

What am I living for? The nurse crimped her forehead. One rabbit-blow might finish the party. Then she would run away, never set eyes on this house again, never see Col, Snow, or anyone, run till she arrived at some long, empty beach, and still running, by now miraculously out of her clothes, fall into the shallow foam, the bubbles fizzing and filling wherever there was entry, soothing wherever she was physically bruised or mentally troubled.

But even as she ran, he (or some other) would be running after, waving his thing to bludgeon her into childbirth and endless domestic slavery. So there was no escaping: on the one hand it was snotty noses, nappies, and a man's weight to increase your body's exhaustion; on the other, it was rubbing backs (grind your knuckles into the unsuspecting tissue-paper skin) and wiping the shit off sick or senile bottoms. She wished she was a plant or something.

Mrs Hunter's tone was one of resignation, 'I often wonder why more old people aren't murdered by those who look after them. A lot are, but usually by the relatives: those cases of "mercy-killing".'

'What ideas you get!' Sister Manhood could have bitten her own tongue off; when it was her thoughts which had given her secret away.

'I'm trying to be objective.' Mrs Hunter had trouble with that.

As for Sister Manhood, she had never known what 'objective' meant: it was a word Col used.

'That should have freshened you up,' she said, pulling the nightie down over the withered rump.

Flora Manhood felt frightened: the way the old witch could plug into your thoughts; she was frustrated, too, by what Col called 'your intellectual deficiencies'. She had never hoped, never wanted to be, clever, only to live, to know contentment, if she could discover what that was.

As the nurse stood the alcohol on the dressing-table – you could hear the flask jostling all your precious things – Mrs Hunter said, 'I expect you've been with that young man again.'

'Young man? Which?'

Mrs Hunter could tell from the thick voice that her nurse's lips must be looking swollen. 'The one – that chemist down at Kingsford – who doesn't mind delivering personally when we ring up about a prescription.'

Sister Manhood was so furious she wouldn't reply. She turned the body over and jerked it up against the pillows preparatory to pinning it down. At the beginning of her training she had persistently reminded herself that patients must remain bodies. (Yet bodies became pathetic, or, worse, vindictive.)

Mrs Hunter said, 'I can remember hearing a theory – that after a woman has been with a man you can smell her – like a doe after she's been to the buck.'

Sister Manhood was more furious than before. 'Sounds to me a pretty dirty theory!' She fixed the upper, hemstitched sheet under Mrs Hunter's chin, but never tight enough: everything you had ever been taught would always come undone.

The old thing laughed. 'Reasonable – and natural. I never kept a goat, but know from looking at one or two that we might have understood each other.'

Sister Manhood bashed one of the hairbrushes so hard with the jar of alcohol the brush fell on the floor. 'I'm not interested in men,' she said. 'Not anyway in Col Pardoe. That's just about over. Nobody – Col or anybody else – is going to dictate to me. I've seen the light. As a matter of fact my cousin Snow Tunks has asked me to share her flat.'

'*Snow Tunks?*'

'Yes. My only surviving relative. That makes you close – when there's only the two of you left.'

'But what – what is *Snow?*'

'A bus conductress.'

Mrs Hunter's lips continued mouthing incredulously, as though what should have been a meringue had turned into a stale bun; in the circumstances she could only finally answer, 'Oh!'

And Sister Manhood had said enough; the cool she cultivated was letting her down.

Fortunately, at that point, the housekeeper pushed the door open with a tray. '*Mahlzeit!*' Mrs Lippmann called.

An ugly, ridiculous expression, but Mrs Hunter loved to hear it; she loved food; if she could have remembered what she had eaten she would have spent more time thinking about it as she lay and waited.

'What have you got?' she asked, and tried to forestall the housekeeper by snuffing.

'It is beautiful steamed whitings – with a sauce. *Ach*, such a *sauce!*'

'Not out of a bottle, I hope.'

'*Ach*, Mrs Hunter, what you say and do to me! But I suppose we must have our jokes.'

'Which colour?' whispered Mrs Hunter; out of the whole of life the colours were perhaps what she missed most.

'It is very delicate – this colour.' Head held at an angle, Mrs Lippmann contemplated the possibilities; then she said, 'Flesh – I think.'

'Too variable.' Mrs Hunter sighed.

It made Sister Manhood sick, anyway this afternoon, to listen to such a game. After stooping for the fallen hairbrush, she grabbed the jar of alcohol. Flesh was variable all right: from her own smooth golden kind, to that great red angry club, enslaving and enslaved; you wouldn't think they were of the same stuff.

'Sister Manhood,' Mrs Hunter called as she was escaping; and you could tell it was going to be some awful drag because the old girl had postponed the first taste of her 'luncheon', 'there's something I want you to do for me – later on – after I've had my rest – when I'm in my chair.' Mrs Hunter paused before transposing her voice into another key, which made it so sweetly supplicating that many of those who knew her might have been filled with dread:

'Something only you can do, Sister. I want you to make me up for my son's arrival.'

Sister Manhood didn't go so far as to say she wouldn't have any part in it; instead, every sound she made as she left the room had a calculated clumsy ugliness.

Mrs Hunter was not deceived: she knew how to flatter little Manhood; while here was the faithful Lippmann sulking slightly because her thunder had been stolen: she had been prevented finishing the catalogue of praise for her own art.

Now she merely said, 'There's *Sachertorte*.' Her lips, Mrs Hunter guessed, had tightened.

And this gave you your next lead. 'I was never much interested in pudding.' Because, from the first day, Lippmann had made it clear that her greatest longing was always to feel more deeply hurt.

Actually it was true about the pudding: Alfred hadn't cared for it; on the whole the men hadn't; the best part of the dinner was always at the end as you watched them fork up their angels on horseback or whatever, their lips fatty with satisfaction while telling about their achievements and their aspirations. Your shoulders were at their whitest then, the mirrors showed, and your cleavage, from one or two glances, at its most mysterious: at such moments you were superbly conscious of your own power.

'*So!*'

The housekeeper was helping guide a forkful of whiting drenched with sauce, whether flesh-tinted or not, to its destination. Such power as she had exercised over other people, Wolf's love for instance, or her hold on an audience, had always been of secondary importance to her own enslavement; and now, with all her gods brutalized or gone up in smoke, or almost all, where else would she offer her limbs for shackling?

So Mrs Lippmann moaned, 'Careful! Careful, Mrs Hunter! I have seen one enormous bone I have overlooked go into your mouth. Masticate with greatest caution, and put out the bone on the end of your tongue so that I may secure it, please.'

*

89

Mrs Hunter was snoozing awake. Though she wouldn't have admitted it to her housekeeper, her lunch whatever it was—chicken? had been incredibly delicious; but light: she could have managed as much again. And a sauce: she remembered that. *Sauce maltaise*, Mrs Lippmann had said; *flesh-coloured*. It was too delicate to suggest anything human; it tasted of the scent of oranges.

Mrs Hunter rumbled, then she burped, without detecting, however, the origins of her recent pleasure.

She was greedy, always had been, though they hadn't guessed when she was younger because she had been so careful of her figure. Instead they accused her of devouring people. Well, you couldn't help it if they practically stuck their heads in your jaws. Though actually you had no taste, or no sustained appetite, for human flesh. There was this other devouring desire for some relationship too rarefied to be probable.

What was the housekeeper's story? something about an Aryan lover. Weren't they planning to run away together—to England—when she was arrested? The boy's family agreed to see her safely delivered into Switzerland—alone—and Mrs Lippmann had accepted for her lover's good.

Another idealist, but a realistic one; in your own case, your idealism was too abstract, improbable, under cover of the dinner parties, the jewels, the lovers, some of them real, but more often only suspected; or else a few individuals, sensitive up to a point, had guessed at some mysterious, not religious or intellectual, some kind of spiritual aspiration, and labelled you a fraud when you couldn't confront them with, not spiritual, but material evidence.

Anyway, you had eaten a mouthful of *Torte* to please Mrs Lippmann, only it didn't: one mouthful made things worse. But that was what Mrs Lippmann liked. If you had full command of your senses, and your strength, and could order a spectacular *bombe* for a party, and take a sword and slash it just as it was ready to be brought in, Mrs Lippmann would descend into the deepest of her infernal heavens.

Never see a *bombe* again. Those ponderous dinners the Radfords

used to give: always something on fire, or with a music box
playing inside; always an important guest—in Gladys's estimation.
*Betty—it's short notice—tomorrow night—I have Athol Shreve—I need a
woman—I mean, an exceptional one—Sidney tips Mr Shreve as Prime
Minister two elections from now—so you see darling your meeting could
be a historic one.* Play Gladys for ringing you after trying probably
everyone else. *Do you think I'd fit into your party darling? not as you
know the least politically minded—I'd half promised the Pritchetts—
then a migraine hit me this afternoon—I've been feeling impossible—and
isn't Athol Shreve—one hardly likes to utter the word nowadays—isn't he
'common'?* Gladys tinkled. She was one of those short thick slabs of
women who project tiny voices and specialize in shapely ankles and
dancing feet. *He has a certain brutish charm Betty.* Never liked
Gladys Radford, but you remained friends over the years. One of
the advantages of being a woman: you can do just that. After a
clash, men sometimes don't speak to each other again, but real
women can endure the worst in one another; must be because
they're debarred from all that honest-to-God mateship, and the
Masons.

Athol Shreve: upstanding hair and coarse skin in the photographs;
probably had acne as a boy. You couldn't fall—not immediately—
for the Radfords' importunate invitation; you were too obviously a
pis aller.

Sidney Radford, after inheriting coal, had sat about in an office
looking important, while somebody else managed the coal. Gladys
had money of her own; was it from—from—biscuits? or those
cakes and puddings full of burnt fruit and sand, in tins. Anyway,
with their two fortunes, and the Italian statuary and mosaics, the
French tapestries—said to be Gobelins—and Aubusson carpets, the
Radfords could put on a show. All their parties were *soirées*: some
of them musical. Sidney Radford played the fiddle, a famous one,
which rapidly became infamous. They engaged Moiskovsky? the
Russian pianist—to play sonatas with Sidney—but Moisenstein got
up and walked out. Stuck to the cheque, and Sidney and Gladys
were too ashamed to ask for it back.

This Athol Shreve Gladys finally hysterical was still going on about.

Perhaps you were a snob: perhaps being born into poverty had made you it. And Father's education, and suicide. Father was frail, as in the end, dear decent Alfred; you recognized the same quality when it was too late to do more than clumsily attempt to mend the breakages.

Gladys Radford couldn't leave off: *such a dynamic — a self-made man* ... Athol Shreve had been one of those paper boys who rise to position and fame; paper boys are among the *clichés* of the success story. *Aren't there rather too many of them?* It was a bad connection and Gladys couldn't understand, kept hitting the receiver. *Too many what?* Gladys's annoyance was growing; it was fun listening to it.

Shreve the trade unionist had ratted on the movement, to become the inspiration of the Nationalists. He was ripe for the Radford dinners.

Gladys — I'm not enthusiastic darling. Only crackle for the moment. *Well, if you're not:* Gladys's tinkle was becoming a sunken bell. *Except it's the holidays — which is something you can't appreciate — Dorothy gone to the Bullivants — Basil to 'Kudjeri' — to Daddy. I'm stuck here with a team of Irish maids fighting out their religious differences every other night. So I'll come darling — unless.*

Gladys Radford thought it would be simply marvellous. She had almost lost her voice achieving what she wanted. She hung up before you could modify your acceptance.

Mrs Hunter coughed a series of dry, exploratory coughs. She hoped she would not develop anything, grow feverish, or not before Sir Basil's arrival. Her star guest. She would be glad when it was all over, when night and Mary de Santis were in possession of the house. Of course Basil wouldn't want to stay any more than Dorothy had wanted to. Old people aren't quite human for those who are still capable of escaping from the past by moving about in what they like to think is positive action: movement, the great illusory blessing. Certainly if you are motionless you are more an object than a person: you are a less significant part of the design you make with the lives of others, particularly your children; children in particular get around to thinking how they can improve on the design, which ends in their wanting to eliminate superfluous detail. You had seen it before. You had heard it in Dorothy and Basil's letters, most clearly in the recent ones: *have decided to come out and discuss what will be best for you;* which could be interpreted as '*us*'.

Yes, it will be good when the guests have gone. You can hear the darkness clotting in the rooms below, Lippmann bumping into furniture and sighing for the Jews; outside in the park, screams from rape and waterfowl. Only yourself and de Santis are real. Only de Santis realizes that the splinters of a mind make a whole piece. Sometimes at night your thoughts glitter; even de Santis can't see that, only yourself: not see, but know yourself to be a detail of the greater splintering.

When the guests have gone: at the Radfords' they always seemed to stick, at the beginning and the end, on that great mauve staircase. Gladys and Sidney couldn't, or more probably wouldn't, encourage a flow after all the money they had spent importing the marble from Portugal; and Gladys liked to show off her feet and ankles: that was why she had to have an upstairs drawing-room, so they said, for her feet and her ankles to be noticed at the head of the mauve staircase, before the guests could concentrate on her slab of a body with its thick neck.

There on the staircase everyone was stuck as usual the night that Athol Shreve. You hadn't looked, or barely glanced, when introduced on the landing outside the drawing-room. Confidentially, he'd never come across an upstairs lounge: *isn't it a bit eccentric?* She had decided to create an impression of casualness. *Why not?* she asked; *you're not conventional yourself, are you? from what one reads in the press.* While half disapproving as a democratic Australian dependent on his constituents' approval, the other half of him was flattered to be tinged with an impropriety she implied. Caught in the crush, herself in turn crushing the cinerarias, she looked in a glass and saw that she had drawn her mouth all wrong, its bow

93

noticeably asymmetrical. Usually meticulous, her hand must have slipped on this occasion. Or perhaps it would establish the casualness she wished for.

She was wearing white. It seemed to make him ashamed of something; he began telling her, *when I was a boy* ... And again at dinner, *when I was a boy* ... Gladys had sat them together, so there was no escaping Athol Shreve's boyhood, nor his appearance which at last she could let herself loose on. Nobody, not Athol Shreve himself—nor *herself*—would have interested her in that before the second course.

Even now she only took quick bites, at the cratered skin, the heavy hands, concentrated eyes, and hair so thick and stiff you knew how it felt without having to touch.

He talked about his law studies (tedious), less about politics; if he was confident of what Sidney Radford predicted for him, he showed no sign of wanting to parade that confidence. He was boring her on the whole, and probably she him, though thoroughly masculine men seldom seem to become bored provided a female audience will pay them token attention.

So she felt at liberty to withdraw from his anecdotes and ideas to the company of her own thoughts while leaving him her physical presence. As the courses were delivered, acceptably anonymous food, on the Radfords' gold dinner service. Why she had agreed to be thrust together with Athol Shreve was not yet clear to her; so far there was nothing about him she could admire, or even like, she thought.

... never employ or trust a man who hasn't a worker's hands.

His cynicism appealed to a cynicism in herself. She laughed, but saw him look surprised, perhaps even unconscious of anything cynical in his remark. He went on stubbornly cutting into a chicken's too muscular thigh. Betrayal of the side to which he belonged had not transformed his own worker's hands, she noticed.

What would he think of Alfred, whose rather sensitive hands were scarred by the manual labour to which he committed himself on principle?

She was pleased to remember: *my husband*—not the mystic title contained in a humdrum word, but an expression of respect and affection. Whether Alfred respected her she could not tell: he loved her.

Are you married Mr Shreve? It ended in something between desperation and a cough; she took a sip of wine to hide a watering of her eyes.

It was not quite as she had hoped: Athol Shreve was another of those dutifully, sentimentally uxorious men with invalid wives.

At the same time his thigh, she realized, had come to rest alongside hers, or more than rest: it was plastered to her. If he was conscious of it he didn't show her, but continued telling about a daughter (her name Doris) studying economics in London. He was exceptionally earnest when it came to the matter of education, which again created a cynical situation. Only his hands were genuine: in shape and texture, at least, and if you ignored the history of his political betrayal.

And what about her own betrayal of Alfred? But she hadn't betrayed him, or only once, and that was little more than an afternoon's indiscretion, of no lasting significance. It didn't destroy the possibility of an ideal relationship, above the respect and affection she had for Alfred, and Alfred's (hurt) devotion to her. If she could to some extent understand or visualize this probably super-human relationship. But she couldn't.

It was in any case nothing to do with Athol Shreve the turncoat politician and tame social bull. Drunk by now. That was why his thick thigh was burning into her cooler, unresponsive one. Herself close enough to drunk. Gladys and Sidney served too many wines to show they were able to afford them.

She sat forward over the dessert, locking her hands against her forehead in the hope that this might cure an ache. Naturally it didn't. The bubbles continued rising and pricking, from the glass as well as in the head. Opened her eyes and there was a plain woman smiling opposite. Someone to whom you had been introduced, but who didn't matter while you were in full possession of yourself.

Some plain women smile at you genuinely grateful when you are at your prettiest, but perhaps it is only for the success of a dress, or some—some aura. And that imagined—not real.

So you couldn't or only half smile back to thank the woman for her kind interest.

Athol Shreve was what is real. This gross male. A fake: the real is so often fake. You had never recognized your own lust; you hadn't often been troubled by it. But it exists—alongside those unrealizable aspirations.

And husbands.

He said it was surprising they hadn't met before. Not at all surprising, you were tempted to reply, only you could no longer have aimed it at the heart of the matter.

There was a worm in the Radfords' de Lucca peach.

All Elizabeth Hunter's worst nightmares occurred at noon. She gritted her gums, crisped her jewelled fingers against being sucked farther down into the fug of afternoon sleep; its flannel tunnel daunted her; and to be dragged back eventually by someone who is paid to do it: that is why nurses, particularly little Manhood, remain so cool.

That man: the politician. Her lips tried, but failed to work the name free of her mind.

After dinner there was conversation and a pretence of music: two tall young men vamping at pianos; it was fashionable just then to engage them. You would have liked to slip away, but couldn't. Even accepted a curaçoa. Gladys so civil; and Sidney wanted to show you some Japanese prints he had bought: he had always bought something.

Where was Athol Shreve? she wondered. She couldn't escape him, she realized now. He was the reason she had told Lennox he needn't return with the car after the party. He was the awfulness, the reality, she had decided unconsciously to risk; if she had miscalculated the explosive force of her lust, she had felt its first tremor that evening when misdrawing her mouth in lipstick. She went at one point into the cloakroom to whimper over Alfred. The other awfulness is: you can sincerely love those you betray. She gashed again at that not so casually planned mouth.

Then everyone was leaving. There was something about a couple who lived somewhat in the same direction: as it happened, the plain quiet woman from opposite at dinner, and a husband, her male replica. Athol Shreve knew you would expect the offer of a lift, which you didn't, and did. Furs made you shiver: tonight they were too much a forfeit.

En route the gears kept tangling grinding before the eventual grudging release. The married couple on the back seat accepted gratefully to be dropped. He was wearing a white scarf, with a fringe and black monogram, she clutching to thin breasts a narrow moiré party handbag, as they stood on the pavement outside their house, stooping to call goodbye. They were smiling for what no one could explain: not yourself, certainly; and they were too nice to want to.

Athol Shreve had more trouble with the gears. It was an ordinary car for such an opportunist, but perhaps the ordinary is a better disguise for ruthlessness. Or the car could have been an innocent oversight, or convenience. They were bumping around against and off each other inside it. A pothole bounced them: she hit her skull on the roof.

'Seems like I'm trying to kill us!' (All your worst nightmares speak with actual mouths, but the mouths of megaphones.) 'Mightn't look too good, eh?' his thick, megaphone laugh, 'driving Elizabeth Hunter home, both drunk, after the shivoo.'

A sort of jollity in his voice made you wonder if it isn't a dormant instinct for evil rather than their thinking minds which drives men to dishonesty. A woman's knowledge of herself sees to it that she is aware of her guilt.

In Moreton Drive pulling up, 'This is the terminus, isn't it?'

Even so, he had no intention of turning round; was getting out: too big for the doorway of that smallish car.

A light was blazing illuminating your own solid yet unreliable house.

'There is this step — where the path turns: two people have broken legs.' Inwardly burning, her voice sounded cold.

Didn't listen to the joke he was making she was fumbling in her bag the gold mesh a wedding present from Alfred's mother in it the key to this house in which she was living.

Mrs Hunter groaned the cramps in her legs if night she would have allowed de Santis to give her one of Gidley's pills. After luncheon sleeping pills are immoral. Open her eyes at least. She couldn't. On the dark screen her lids provided the picture show continued flickering.

'I expect I should pour you a drink after your so nobly bringing me home.' A silly bitchy pretty woman after a party.

He recognized it. 'I think we had enough to know each other.'

They were driven together in a collision which sounded like that between two objects in solid bone or hard rubber so little surprising it might have happened before.

'Not along there. The maids are sleeping. If you're not careful you'll wake them.' She distinctly added, 'They might telephone the police thinking somebody had broken in and was assaulting or trying to murder me.' She was so sure of her innocence in the minds of everybody who didn't know her; nobody, not even Athol Shreve, knew her; only she knew herself.

'The police — you could deny anything the maids told them, couldn't you?'

Instead of answering she smiled at him, because she had no idea what she would tell until it was necessary.

Suspicion of treachery seemed to have made him determined to devour its source: her throat her breasts.

'If you don't mind — my dress. That might be inescapable evidence.'

He watched her prepare. They were watching each other. He had a vein in his forehead which swelled as he bent to ease, then to drag the cloth, down from his thighs.

Disgust for his body, his exploratory hands, the rasp of hair against her skin, did not diminish her own lust. Her enraged beast could have wanted to die of his: when there was some condition she knew she had aspired to above the placid waters of marriage the eruptions of adultery finally hatred of her own aspirant.

His thundering into her ear, 'God, Betty, we screw pretty good together, don't we?' Then squelching back out of their mutual revulsion.

You would have liked to separate, more than from your lover, from your own body.

Halfway into his clothes he began muttering, finally loudly whispering, 'What's wrong? There's nothing wrong, is there?'

Only everything; but how tell?

She could have lain resting for ever, not thinking; but roused herself. 'Is your wife politically minded?' That speeded his buttoning.

'Not very. Not now. She's too sick to take an interest. What made you ask?'

As well as husbands, wives had begun to haunt her: a strained, chalky menopause, but featureless.

Again fully armoured, he came and sat on the edge of the bed, seeming inclined to return to picking at a meal he thought he had finished.

When he put his hand she reminded, 'My husband might arrive unexpectedly from Gogong.'

Athol Shreve could behave very nervously for such a large, designated man. 'Thought the Gogong train reached Sydney in the morning.'

'It does. There's also a slower, daylight one Alfred sometimes takes because he enjoys looking at the country.'

She spent seconds on a total death wish.

'Better see me out, hadn't you? Make it look more like a social visit—if anybody—one of the maids.' For this final pretence she dressed herself in what she had been wearing, even made up her mouth; there was nothing she could have done about her eyes.

At the front door he was all for fumbling kissing sentimental respects. 'Night night, girlie. Thanks for the party. Next time we'll know each other's form better.'

She shut it out at last, not that the latch sounded convincing.

In the morning (it might have been today) Nora announced with a dignity which was a good copy of the original, 'Mr Hunter has come, madam. He hopes you won't get a shock—Master Basil fell out of a tree and fractured an arm.'

'Oh my God, when did they arrive?'

'Just now. By the night train.'

Alfred's anguished face; Basil, more gloomy than suffering, was wearing a sling.

'Oh, darlings!' She was too shattered to cry; and Alfred might have joined her if she had let herself go.

Basil was only ashamed of his parents. 'It's not broken; it's bent, or cracked.'

Alfred was so upset trying to trace Dr Moyes, to arrange an appointment, to confirm the bone had received proper treatment from the local man, he could pay no attention to anything else till later.

Then he remembered, 'Poor old Betty, it must have been a shock.'

She could only look at her husband: his vulnerable temples, kind mouth, eyes so much milder than her own.

It was Basil who suspected something, nothing specific, he couldn't have. It was just that he suspected his mother generally and on principle.

She used to say, 'Why are you so full of secrets, darling? What have we got to hide from each other? You can be so charming to other people—with Mrs Wyburd.'

Would he remember that? He had a phenomenal memory. As a boy he could recite whole scenes from Shakespeare. Sometimes they would read together from the plays, she taking the women's parts.

Now they were playing this scene at the top of the stairs.

'Anyway, a sling suits you—makes you look gorgeous: a hero back from the wars.'

'I stink! Haven't been out of my clothes since it happened. I stink of squashed ants.' His nostrils expressed a disgust which was aimed at her as well.

'Doesn't matter. Wait till after the doctor. Then we'll see how you can be washed.'

She could tell he was already preparing to resist her advice, let alone help.

The following day Dorothy returned from the Bullivants. If Basil was suspicious, Dorothy's absorbed little face was specially designed for locking up accusations. If she let them out, her emotions might get the better of words; though sometimes she saved them up for a better occasion. Now she was passing judgment on you for something she couldn't possibly guess, except that her stare sank deeper, her silence had intensified.

And she found a clue under the bedside table. 'What's this?'

'What on earth? A cuff link!'

'Whose is it?'

'It's one which belonged to my—my father—your Grandfather Salkeld.'

Dorothy, looking at it with a kind of horror, didn't at least ask to see its twin. 'Isn't it ugly!'

You couldn't deny that. She gave it to you, and you would have to think where to put it, before you could throw it away somewhere—in the park grass—and forget about the whole incident, if Dorothy didn't re-discover the link.

Only Alfred was trusting: he treated you as though you, not Basil, were the victim of an accident. 'I'll stay a few days, Elizabeth—keep you company—help you get your spirits back.'

The second day he suggested a walk together in the park. As they strolled between the formal beds he held her arm along his own, her hand clasped in his, in that position which most clearly demonstrates prerogative. His weathered face and grey eyes encouraged her convalescence from some melancholy nameless illness. In fact it was an illness they had shared, his expression implied, at the time Basil 'broke' his arm. Husband and wife were drawn very close inside the circle of her creamy sunshade.

'Is there anything special you'd like to eat?' she sighed and asked, since he had persuaded her to accept their convalescence.

He squeezed her languid hand. 'Anything simple that we can enjoy together.'

Should she drop everything, sell the house, put the children at boarding school, and leave with Alfred for 'Kudjeri'?

She didn't. She could not have worn indefinitely the veils of tenderness with which he wanted to invest her. Nor was she, except for that one necessary instance, the rutting sow Athol Shreve had coupled with. She would have given anything to open a box containing the sum total of expectancy, but as this did not happen (except in a single comforting dream, in which she discovered in a little marquetry casket a splinter of rock crystal lying naked and unexplained on the lead lining) she must expect her answers outside boxes, in the colder contingencies preparing for her.

While Alfred looked at her with much the same expression as the plain woman on the opposite side of the Radfords' dinner table: grateful for something they imagined you to be.

If you could have said: I am neither compleat wife, sow, nor crystal, and must take many other shapes before I finally set, or before I am, more probably, shattered. But you couldn't; they would not have seen you as the eternal aspirant. Solitariness and despair did not go with what they understood as a beautiful face and a life of outward brilliance and material success.

Over the years the letters: *My dearest Elizabeth, I realize our attempts at marriage are not bringing us any closer to success. From your last visit to 'Kudjeri' and mine to Moreton Drive I feel you find our pretences too great a strain, and that I should offer to let you divorce me. I have no further ambitions in the field of marriage, but although you don't care to admit it, you might like to look around you while there is still time to form a more satisfactory relationship. If I haven't suggested this before, it was on account of the children. Now that they have started thinking for themselves, they may feel less resentful, and even forgive erratic behaviour in their parents* ... oh the bitterness of your own inadequacies which people who give to charities interpret as selfishness yes you were selfish by some standards but did not bribe your conscience with good works or by acting as a domestic doormat certainly selfish beside Alfred's exceptional selflessness saints reap admiration when probably it is easier for them a saint is what Dorothy wanted and not getting could only blame the least of saints *it is easier for you Mother for anyone beautiful forceful to be admired praised worshipped that is what you are greedy for more and more worshippers* it was not true not when you understood your own faults better even than your children did yes praise perhaps but for some inward perfection you hadn't been able to achieve *My dear dear Alfred, how dreadfully guilty you make me feel. I am the one who should be making humble offers if there is any talk of 'freedom'. It is you who must call the tune and I shall accept whatever you choose. Personally I don't believe there is a state of freedom greater than the one we know and 'enjoy' — at least, not in life ...* but how you longed for it.

A silveriness about the room brighter than the mists of vision: a faint afternoon breeze deliciously flirting with your steamy hair, but chilling, alarming to boiled skin. This is the cool side of the house: the western rooms will be in flames. Nothing should alarm: at least you won't die; that has been proved over the years. And Basil coming, probably at dusk (you might look better by artificial light) to act out the scene an actor expects. A travesty, of course, but you can't condemn artifice without dismissing the whole of art.

An unnatural wraith of steam rising to the left in the humid evening is what is making you cough. You alone, not Alfred, probably responsible for Dorothy's bronchitis, for Basil's super-selfishness disguised as genius. Better a cow cocky or bank teller than an artist. Yes, now you've said it: what good is an artist to those who want to love him? We are never the one they think;

we are not one, but many. Father was expecting his daughter to read Browning to him as usual, when there she was dawdling beside the river of drowned dolls, plaiting grass, listening for the sound of hooves on the bridge, the evening he put the gun in his mouth. 'Blood exhaustion', Mrs Lippmann calls it. But there are still, even now, the little delights.

Out of the wraith a voice asking, 'Mrs Hunter? Did you have a nice rest? Are you ready for your sponge?' It is Sister Manhood with the Spode basin they are allowed to use for menial purposes.

'I had such horrid dreams.'

'I thought you didn't sleep.'

'Oh, you can dream, can't you? without sleeping?'

'I don't know.' The nurse had embarked, if not conscientiously, then at least professionally, on one of the duties for which she was paid: to sponge a geriatric case.

Mrs Hunter smiled. She would wait. She knew she could play Flora Manhood without her suspecting she was on the hook. In the meantime, the sponging made you feel better.

The nurse might have been peeling a fruit: she was so detached. In theory powerful. When it was the soft, tepid sponge which exercised the power, seeping into crevices, smoothing the wrinkles out of thoughts. Objects, including the human ones, are often more powerful than people.

'Anyway,' said Sister Manhood, 'it's a lovely evening, Mrs Hunter.'

'Is it?'

The life of Sydney was streaming past and around, you could sense as well as hear, pouring out of factories and offices: by this hour men in bars, a confraternity of Athol Shreves, had begun inflating their self-importance with beer; ambulances were hurtling towards disasters in crumpled steel and glass confetti; in semi-private houses, mothers would have started sponging little boys, their still empty purses, while nubile girls looked in glasses to pop their spots cream their skins dreaming of long-hoped-for but unlikely lads.

The children: thank God they didn't know it, they were the all-powerful — not that silly princess, nor, judging by his letters, the famous bankrupt actor, but Dorothy and Basil, more devastating in their silences than Elizabeth and Alfred Hunter with all their authority, money, experience of life, and practical, but finally useless, advice. Parents are wraiths beside their children, who are drained in turn by the business of living; sometimes their candour and perception are returned, but almost too late, when they have become thinking objects.

If Alfred hadn't died too soon it might have been different: you were learning to speak to each other in what seemed a revealed language, discovering unexpected meanings.

'Did I hurt you?' Sister Manhood asked.

'It was Alfred I was dreaming about. Did you know my husband died of cancer?'

'Oh, how dreadful!' It wasn't convincing: a nurse performing her professional duties shouldn't be called upon too suddenly to turn into a human being.

'And I nursed him. You didn't know that,' Mrs Hunter said, and laughed.

'No, I didn't.' Nor did she believe it: that was what made you laugh in advance.

'How did you manage — without the experience — if the illness was a prolonged one?'

'Oh, it was long — not in years, or months even. I managed. By will. Which I don't think you believe in, Sister. By instinct too, I suppose. Why do people start writing poems — or making love? You ought to know that — some of it at least.'

Sister Manhood had done with the sponge. This was the sort of thing which drove you up the wall: at times when you had got past pitying to liking, or farther, to almost having a love affair, the two of you and a sponge, the old bitch would start hacking, to remind you that you really hated her.

'Sister Manhood, you're making my nightie grate the length of my skin.'

Let it grate. 'P'raps it's a cheap nightie.'
'You're not angry with me, are you?'
...
'Sister?'
...
'About what I said? After all – isn't it our instinct to love – or try
to? Surely you must understand *that*? By instinct!'
'I don't know.' There was nothing you really understood, or so
they told you regularly – Col Pardoe and old Mrs Betty bloody
Hunter; you were either a body for fucking, or a log for the
axemen (or -women) to hack at.
'Where are you going, Sister Manhood?'
'To throw out the dirty water.' If you could have thrown the
baby with it.
'You won't forget your promise, will you?'
...
'Sister?'
...
'The promise!'
Like hell you wouldn't. Not for a moment. You were never ever
allowed to forget what you were there for.

Sister Manhood flung the water into the bath; sometimes it was
the lavatory, but because she needed greater scope, tonight it had
to be the bath. In that great bloody carpeted bathroom as big as
somebody's whole flat. The smooth mahogany seat on which Her
rich bloody arse hadn't rested since God knew when. The sealed
jars of bath salts, the bowl of brown dusty potpourri, were what
best explained the unused bathroom in terms of Elizabeth Hunter.
One day, Flora Manhood sourly decided, she was going to take
off her clothes and make use of that fucking bath, take her time on
the polished mahogany ledge, before slipping down the white,
sloping sides into untroubled waters.

Tonight the west was on fire outside the window: the bathroom
was Flora Manhood's furnace. From which she stumbled panting,
gasping, into the cooler, what Jessie Badgery called, Nurses'

Retiring Room (I ask you: as if you could ever *retire* with Her around the corner) to dab the wych-hazel.

Col's favourite perfume: said it was neither nursey nor tarty one of the sweet natural smells *just what I'd expect of you Flo.* Oh yeah? *I may be natural but nobody could call me sweet.* Not when you could never tell for sure the sincere from the sarky in other people; they never let you know, or else you were stupid. *Your trouble Flo you've got wrong ideas about yourself for that matter nobody knows what he really is.* Not according to Her: *only oneself can know what one is really like Sister.* So it was always this: hacking into you from either side.

Along the edges of the park the pines deepening in the silvery light grass whitening the lake silver which from close up was a mud colour smelling of mud invisible dead fish and the droppings from long-legged ugly birds. Coot, Col said they were.

Always Col! Or Mrs Betty Hunter. What if the old girl wouldn't let you go if you said you wanted to chuck up the job? E. Hunter was more powerful than any man you could remember. Or Snow. Must be from living so long that Mrs Hunter got the stranglehold. She'd sucked the living daylights out of all the people she'd killed: that husband for instance; or half-killed: Princess Dorothy you could see at a first glance had almost been swallowed; the real proof would be the son arriving tonight, whether he had survived the mother to become the great actor, or whether he would start acting her tame zombie.

Be fair though, Flora: wasn't the old girl always saying *this man Sister you're going with I can tell by your touch I can tell by his voice when he brings — no need — the medicines we've telephoned for — they've got the boy with the bicycle haven't they to deliver — that this is the man you're intended for.* As if it was any of her business. *Oh reely Mrs Hunter?* (snicker snicker). Made you feel such a silly drip. But the point was, she couldn't want to hang on to you for her own ends. Then there was nothing that you could truthfully accuse her of, except her scratchy bitchy ways; but she was old and oh God tired and sick.

So there was no one to protect or save you from Col Pardoe.
Only Snow.

All along the parkside the dead dwindling grass. It would be dark by the time the actor came. Snow was an albino though she called it a natural ash blonde. She'd develop skin cancers later on, specially working in a burning bus, and at the depot, sitting on a bench in the sun smoking with the blokes waiting for the handover. Snow smelled like white-coloured women do: more like a man. She smelled of the coins she had been handling, and sweaty leather, and too many smokes. But you had Coff's Harbour in common: my cousin—my only living relative.

While Mrs Hunter insisted *this man Sister you went with your last day off—to Noamurra—or wherever it was—tell me about it—I mean him!* As if you would have known how. *And what is this delicious cosmetic of which you are smelling? Ah* (snuffle) *that is wych-hazel I've often wondered.* Wonder what she smelled under the wych-hazel: perhaps those goats she went on about.

They had gone that day to Noamurra, it was true.

'Why Noamurra, Col? Such a godforsaken sort of a place!'

'That's what appeals. The bulldozer won't nose it out, or not yet. And that's what I want today.'

He was driving the old Mercedes SSK (whatever it means). He had traded in the Valiant, and done up this old car; he was clever at that sort of thing. Col would have been clever at anything he put his mind to, but said what he wanted was peace of mind. As if you didn't, all of you; but what was it? and how to get it?

'Noamurra! Who'd want to live *there*? Amongst all those old neglected orchards.'

'You could listen to yourself living at least—in between hearing the oranges drop.'

'Not very progressive. I'm for progress.'

'You could stand for mayor, Flo.'

In other circumstances she might have got angry but the warmth, the sound of the road, had drugged her. And the scrub: each swathe identical. She giggled slightly and it bumped her against the back of the seat. Col was smoking the pipe with the aluminium stem, which made the spit sizzle at the bottom of the bowl. Along the sandstone ridges the sun glazed and dazed: through the open window sunwind was flung harsh as sandpaper against the skin.

Farther back, while the suburbs were still streaming, she had tried to benefit from travelling by Mercedes, but you couldn't ever: this one was so old-fashioned nobody would have recognized it, not amongst the glossy up to date models. Now that there wasn't that much traffic, one or two dislocated fruit and vegetable trucks, here and there a family bus, what you looked like hardly mattered.

Was this being happy? If, as she suspected, it was, nobody, not Col, not even the Old Bitch of Moreton Drive, would have dragged the confession out from between her lips, parted like an idiot's, she realized, as she moistened their nakedness with her tongue.

'This Mrs Hunter, because she's old, comes out with the biggest nonsense. And thinks she can get away with it.'

'Such as?'

'Oh, I couldn't tell you!'

'If you can't tell, why did you begin?'

'I was making conversation.'

'That isn't conversation; it's frustration.'

'Oh, well.'

She settled down. She liked being with Col at times, and this was one of them. She would have liked to take a look at him, but might have given herself away. More than anything it's what you see; but that would not have done for poor Mrs Hunter, who had to invent theories about smells, and grow spooky over voices. Did the old thing remember with any clearness what she had seen when she had her sight? Men's hands, for instance; their hard throats: men show you their thoughts in their throats, or anyway Col does. She had to have just one look.

'What are you looking at?'

'Thought I saw a signpost. But there wasn't. God, scrub like this never stops once it begins.'

Or it only stops for Noamurra.

They were gliding at last into that different deeper green, paddocks with sprung hummocks, orchards with tangled, scaly trees, past a waterhole with scum on it: that was the deepest, deadliest green. Where there were houses they were faded or unpainted weatherboard, all old. Only the service station was new, the ads, and the drive-in pictures. The people too, seemed old, their weather-cured elephant skins, wedding rings eating into the leather. On a veranda almost screened by privet an old couple sat drinking tea out of white cups, and munching at something, probably scones. A daughter in a long straight cotton frock, and her simple brother, sat looking only at the road; they were younger than the old people of course, but elderly.

The privet which recurred round most of the cottages began to overwhelm, to suffocate. If you turned your head a tropical moisture was tumbling, bouncing around your field of vision: which was always of the same deadly green, sometimes splotches of oranges, or pallid privet blossom.

Col wanted to walk. So they walked the back roads. There was a child, a little girl squatting on the edge of an orchard, beside the road, fiddling with something in a glass jar.

'What is it?' She bent to ask the child, who wouldn't answer at first, but hid her face, as appetizing as dark plums.

'What are you playing with?' you tried again, more than anything to hold your own.

'A lizard.'

It was a lizard all right in the jar, and the lizard had already lost its tail.

'You won't be cruel to it, will you?' Silly the things you say to kids. 'If I was you I'd let it go.'

All eyes and glistening lips, the child gave the lizard a black look. 'He's my pet,' she said.

'All the same, I'd let him go.'

Or would you? It was difficult to tell what you would have done, squatting by the roadside in muddied dress and tattered pants.

Col said, when they had meandered on, 'She'll tear the head off as soon as we've turned the corner. To see what happens. You would have done the same, Flo.'

'How do you know?' She could feel her anger burning all the way up her neck.

'I don't *know*,' he admitted; 'but would guess.' The air was too drowsy to allow prolonged speculation.

'My own children wouldn't,' she said. 'I'd see to that. Whatever I may be, I'd bring them up different.'

He swung her hand, and laughed.

'Why not?' Indignation was blurring her words. 'I'd try to better myself in my children.'

They had cut across one of the green paddocks filled with spongy hummocks. The paddock might have been quilted on a large scale, the soft irregular quilting giving way beneath them as they tramped.

'I'm sorry', she said, 'if I seem bad-tempered. I know I'm quarrelsome. There's such a lot to quarrel about.'

'It's better to marry a girl with a bad temper. If you pick one that's sweet and she turns out cranky it's a big disappointment.'

'I was never sweet. And marriage was nowhere near my mind. I meant, it's a pity if you can't go on a one-day outing without doing your block.'

They ploughed ahead through the soft paddock, through probably many years, perhaps a human lifetime, of fallow.

'If I was domesticated I suppose I'd have cut us some sandwiches.'

'I haven't a single illusion, Flo'; making bite gestures down her arm as though it was a cob of corn.

'Stopputt!' It was too silly.

Or it wasn't; as they pulled up facing each other the silence was serious around them. A network of midges hung in a glow of sunlight; on the one hand scraggy, slanting gums, on the other the fuzz of orange trees, sooty branches and wax-clogged twigs struggling to escape from their own crowd. She realized from the stillness that she was caught again, if she had ever really broken free. Col, who had at first stood back, was coming at her, like a sleepwalker returning by instinct to the room he had left earlier in the same dream; the exhausted, but intent trees were collaborating with him.

She wasn't. 'What do you think I am?' she protested; when she knew too well; when they were already fitting together. 'Col?' If her voice resounded blatantly it was because her mouth was still under compulsion.

He didn't reply. He went on dashing his lips backwards and forwards in the readymade groove of her mouth: where she couldn't prevent them belonging.

She was part of the plan his fingers had worked out scientifically, and which, finally, was *their* plan. He only tore one button from where it was rooted in his pants.

In more conventional surroundings of sand and sea, their bodies never startled, but here against this hectic green their skins seemed a blinding, naked white. Immorally exposed at first, she was at last forced to ignore it.

But muttered incidentally, 'What if somebody comes?'

'Mmm?'

'That child with the lizard—we might influence her whole life.'

Not conceived along with their plan, the little girl was discarded. 'A cruel kid—anyway,' Flora Manhood remembered between gasps.

She began to moan for something else as he drove her deeper into the yielding mattress of pricking grass.

He sat up high above her. She was in love with the way his chest divided, till looking along her nose she became elsewhere riveted. She might have devoured her lover-tyrant if it hadn't been for having to face Elizabeth Hunter's grinning gums, her blind yet knowing stare.

As soon as he allowed, she extricated her softened body, on principle, from the torpor of half-thoughts and flesh in which she could have continued lying.

'You're all crisscrossed, Flora, about the bum—it's the twigs—and stained with green.'

'What have you done to me?' she moaned, trying to look over her shoulder at her quilted buttocks.

'Isn't it right?' he asked. 'Isn't that what we came here for?' Col too, grinning up at her.

'Someone may see us,' she began again.

When they were only half dressed they were drawn back against each other; but now it was as if he was the child they had made together, her big child buffeting her breasts, and she couldn't love him enough.

'I don't know what comes over us,' she said when they were decent.

'That's what we do know, and you won't admit it,' he answered quietly.

Along the road, near where they had parked the car, they found a house with a sign which read DRESSED POULTRY SNACKS BOILING WATER AS REQUIRED. The woman, in one of those long timeless cotton frocks, said she could fry them some eggs, if that was what they fancied. She brought them a dish of small, whole, eggshaped tomatoes. There was tea, from a brown enamel pot, in thick white cups.

While they were eating, the long woman hung around. She would have liked to talk. After covering the weather, she tried out a current murder case. But your mouths were too full to contribute.

'Arr, dear,' the woman sighed. 'It's lovely to drive around on yer own — when you're young,' she added.

Dribbles of egg were congealing with fat on the empty plates.

'No family yet?'

Col nearly swallowed the last egg tomato.

Because his mouth was full, and anyway, this was a woman's situation, you had to make the best of it. 'No family. This is only a friendly outing.'

The woman's eyes had begun searching for the ring immediately after dropping her brick; she was blushing up her scrawny neck and along her leathery jaw. 'I would of thought,' she said, 'but when it comes to some things, not everybody knows their own mind.'

Already slouching away from her mistake, she muttered above the sound of her sandshoes, 'Kiddies make all the difference.'

Col said too cheerfully when they were again in their car, 'A lovely day at Noamurra! Know what it means?'

She didn't of course.

He said looking at her, '"Man and wife".'

'I don't believe you.'

She did, though: Col knew everything; herself an ignorant girl off a North Coast banana farm, who took up nursing to catch a husband and then didn't want one.

They drove. At one point he put a hand between her thighs as though trying to show he owned her. If she didn't throw it off it was because she was again lulled by the road.

'There's the concert Thursday,' he reminded.

She turned away, speaking out of the window, at the scrub, the rocks. 'I don't know what you want me at concerts for.'

'Because I like to have you with me.'

'But I don't know how to listen to music. All that *Mahler*! All I can do is think of other things at music.'

He didn't seem to feel it mattered. 'That's fine. Go on thinking, Flo, and some of the music'll rub off on your thoughts.'

But he made her feel empty: the paperbacks, the records, knowing what Noamurra means. What had she got to offer Col, except her body, and her unborn children? Oh God those would come popping out of her like peas if she didn't keep her wits about her.

She might have felt content, so full of sun, and fried eggs, and Col; she might have snoozed if it hadn't been for the little children climbing on her lap kneading her breasts dabbling their lashes in her throat crimping her skin into the smiles she wouldn't allow herself to show how much she longed to take their golden cheeks between her teeth to test for love.

'Had a good nap?' he asked.

'I wasn't sleeping, if you think I was,' she answered, just like Mrs Hunter.

'You've been flopping like a half-filled sack most of the way to Hornsby.' And he squeezed her knee to annoy her.

Flora Manhood could have used the whole evening, elbows on the sill, hands folded against her cheek. She might have slipped the moment before from the attitude of prayer to one of dreaming, above the empty, faded park, above the traffic noises, facing the cut-out of convents on the skyline. Whatever else, she wouldn't like to be a nun. Better than anything she would have liked to be nothing, or a dream through which she let down her hair into the evening like in that opera Col told the long hair her lover tied to a tree and she was caught. But what lover? Someone unknown walking out of the park at dusk, perfect to almost not existing. But wouldn't she be caught? Yes, always!

The little tingle tinkle was coming from the bell the old thing kept beside her bed. Disgusted by the inevitable trap into which her own thoughts had led her, the nurse was now positively anxious to collaborate with her case. She adjusted her veil as austerely as Matron would have wished, and stepped out along the passage towards the still fretfully tinkling summons.

Almost twirling on the balls of her feet as she entered, Sister Manhood announced, 'We've been neglecting you, haven't we, Mrs Hunter? Now we must make up for it.'

So good-humoured: you wondered where the catch was; prepared for something else, Mrs Hunter could not match her nurse's volte-face. 'I don't suppose we can expect you permanently on the mat, but we don't pay you to ignore us — Sister.'

Sister Manhood ignored what was, after all, only a pinprick from Her. 'I'm at your service, Mrs Hunter. Anything you care to command.' She moistened her fresh lipstick with her tongue; she knew she must be looking pretty, though the old thing wouldn't see that.

'I want you to sit me in my chair.'

'Do you think you're up to it today?'

'I must be. I must be sitting in my chair — for — for his arrival.'

The nurse wheeled the chair, a functional contraption in chrome and leather, through that finicky rosewood and silver jungle.

'First my gown,' Mrs Hunter reminded; only she could remember the moves in their correct order.

The nurse fetched the gown, of crumpled, tarnished rose brocade. At some time or other moths must have got into the sleeves, edged with what Flora Manhood believed were real sables. The garment's tattiness could not lessen her respect for its intimations of original splendour.

'Don't be careless with my arms, please,' Mrs Hunter warned. 'Trained nurses have little idea how the human anatomy works.'

When the gown was arranged, the chair at the bedside, the nurse gathered up the bundle of creaking bones and acerbated flesh, and manoeuvred it into a seated position.

'So healthy,' Mrs Hunter murmured, inhaling the draught from her nurse's movements, under it the scented warmth of youth. 'And strong.'

'There, love. Are you comfy?' Suddenly Flora Manhood was filled with pity: not for Mrs Hunter specifically, but she had to spend it on somebody; and there below the nightie, between the panels of rose brocade and edgings of real, moth-eaten sables, were those legs like sticks of grey spaghetti.

The nurse knelt to put slippers on the chilly, transparent feet.

Mrs Hunter sounded almost tearful. 'Your hands feel kind, Sister. I hope you haven't forgotten your promise to make me up.'

Sister Manhood was ashamed: she would have given anything to be gentle, serene, loving by nature. It didn't come easy, and perhaps she would never learn.

'No, I haven't forgotten.' In standing up she curbed any further tendency to emotion.

'I hope it doesn't bore you.'

'No, it doesn't. It doesn't bore me.' In fact it was the only part of the performance she genuinely enjoyed; they both knew it.

Mrs Hunter grunted; she was happy at last.

Sister Manhood fetched the vanity case, of later period than Mrs

Hunter herself. In blue glacé leather with silver fittings, it was as much out of keeping as a chorus girl would have looked under the great silver sun which radiated from the head of Mrs Hunter's rosewood bedstead.

Mrs Hunter was happy; she snuffed up the smell of cosmetics which escaped when the case was opened.

Sister Manhood went to work, you could not have said 'voluptuously', because of a certain air of reverence; while her subject submitted her cheeks with pride. As Sister Manhood worked the foundation cream into the droughty wrinkles, even Sister de Santis might have respected such obvious dedication. Not the technique, though: some of it *was* voluptuous.

Elizabeth Hunter was at the first stage transformed into a glimmering ghost of the past. She could feel her cheeks rounding out. Those white dresses she used to wear: people stopped talking whenever she started coming downstairs.

'Turn the light on, Sister.'

'But there's still daylight enough, Mrs Hunter. Truly. I can see perfectly.'

'Go on—switch it on, please. I like to feel the light round me. It's so much warmer.'

Sister Manhood turned her annoyance into a mild sigh: smearing foundation cream on the switch. 'I was only thinking of the expense —using electric light so early.' At least the right sentiments.

'I have always been extravagant,' Mrs Hunter said, and smiled.

I bet you were—when it was yourself, Sister Manhood didn't say.

Something was hurting Mrs Hunter, it seemed. 'Alfred—my husband, considered that nobody learns to switch off lights or turn off taps till they have to pay the bills. That's true in most cases. Nobody ever thought of Alfred,' she said.

Sister Manhood was rootling around in the vanity case amongst the jars and cartridges. She had begun to hum, almost to sing, what was intended as 'I could have danced all night'.

'Where is my husband?' Mrs Hunter asked; the anxiety gathering on her face was undoing much of her acolyte's work.

The nurse was frightened for a moment; she didn't know how to handle it; then she said, 'I expect something has delayed him. He'll come, though.'

'Yes, he'll come.'

With the back of her hand Flora Manhood brushed the perspiration from where her moustache would have been. 'Which tones do we fancy this evening?' she asked in her brightest, classiest voice.

' "Dusk Rose" for the cheeks, "Deep Carnation" for the lips,' Mrs Hunter answered with conviction.

'Mmmh? I'd have thought "Crimson Caprice" for the lips. Not if you don't fancy it, of course.'

' "Deep Carnation".'

Mrs Hunter's cheeks took dusky wing. She closed her eyes: the perfumes rising out of the blue glacé leather might have been drugging her.

Comparatively languid dashing away at the cheeks, Sister Manhood was nursing the subtler resources of her art, or vocation, for the lips.

Her own lips invoked, ' "Deep Carnation",' and let it die in a breathy hush.

'You've forgotten the teeth, Sister. The *teeth*! You can't possibly work on my mouth before you've stuck the teeth in. Don't you realize?'

Sister Manhood was corrected. She fetched the expensively created, natural-yellow teeth: never without a shiver. It was Mrs Hunter who began to hoist; but *you* had to shove, until you were both involved in what must have looked like part suicide, part murder.

When she had sucked and glugged, the old thing would loll back exhausted. 'Hateful things, teeth!'

It couldn't concern a young woman preoccupied by her devotions; nor was the object of these rites more than a moment humanly distressed: breath held, eyes closed, she reached out towards the necessary level of abstraction.

After shooting the lipstick out of its gilt cartridge and making one or two conventionally mystic passes at nothing, the white-robed priestess began weaving deep carnation into the naked, crinkled lips. Anything she knew of art, all that she had learnt of sensuality, Sister Manhood drove into this mouth which was not her own. If she had never before attained to selflessness she succeeded now, forcing an illusion to assume a purple reality.

Not all selfless, however: her act became a longing; she could have cried out through her own brooding, swollen lips; she would have accepted humbly, if only for that moment, any delicious indignity he might have demanded of her.

'Mmmhhh!' Mrs Hunter dragged her mouth sideways with an unexpected suddenness and strength which almost ruined the work of art, and certainly curtailed any advances Sister Manhood might have been making in the direction of ecstasy. 'I'm not a thing, am I?' Or if you were, you didn't like other people's behaviour to confirm it.

'Oh, you're going to—you already are—looking *gorgeous*!' Sister Manhood sounded so throaty she must have meant it.

'Am I?' Mrs Hunter whispered softly.

'"I could have danced all night",' Sister Manhood distinctly sang; then she murmured, 'Are we going for eyeshadow?'

Mrs Hunter revived. 'Just a dash.' She smiled up like a little girl thrilled by her own daring.

'Blue?'

'Blue,' she agreed. 'No!' she luckily remembered. '"Delphinium-silver."'

Flora Manhood knew what to do: she traced on Elizabeth Hunter's eyelids the dreamiest of moonlit snail-tracks. Elizabeth Hunter, all but transmuted, lolled in a delphinium-silver bliss.

Till it occurred to her, 'You know Alfred never approved of make-up?'

'Didn't he?'

'Not even when it had become acceptable.'

Their weaknesses brought nurse and patient close. At times their unhappiness was transferable; at others, it was their joys.

Sister Manhood stood back after whisking a hair off the lips she had recently created. 'Are you thinking of a wig, love?'

'The lilac.' Mrs Hunter was definite on that.

'How will you wear it?'

'Flowing free.'

'For a big occasion?' The priestess had been prepared to give her all on a feast day.

'Yes. Flowing. I have decided to appear utterly natural.'

'I won't try to persuade you against. But I did think of bouffing it up a bit.'

The other members of the order, Sisters de Santis and Badgery, and the lay sisters, Lippmann and Cush, were aware it was Sister Manhood who renewed whatever was required for the ritual of anointment; what they didn't know was that Mrs Hunter had paid for Flora's course in the upkeep of wigs. The secret was one the two of them enjoyed, though Sister Manhood was inclined to disguise her doubly esoteric knowledge under a crust of irony, and to swing her hips and crook her fingers as guardian of the wigs.

When she had fetched the lilac one, she drew it on reverently enough, over the fretful wisps of unnaturally natural hair and meek patches of scalp. The lilac climax appealed to a religious sense Flora Manhood thought she had discarded outside the weatherboard church down the road from the banana farm: she had wanted a miracle and it wasn't granted; unless, possibly, whenever she assisted at Elizabeth Hunter's resurrection.

Now she backed between the furniture, feeling her way with her heels, with outstretched hands trembling between the pressures of emotion and air, till she reached the best distance from which to contemplate what in one sense was nothing more than a barbaric idol, frightening in its garishness of purple-crimson, lilac floss, and fluorescent white, in its robe of battered, rather than beaten, rose-gold, the claws, gloved in a jewelled armour, stiffly held about the level of the navel, waiting apparently for some further motive which might bring them to rest on the brocaded lap.

In spite of her desire to worship, the younger woman might have been struck with horror if the faintly silvered lids hadn't flickered open on the milkier, blank blue of Elizabeth Hunter's stare. Then, for an instant, one of the rare coruscations occurred, in which the original sapphire buried under the opalescence invited you to shed your spite, sloth, indifference, resentments, along with an old woman's cruelty, greed, selfishness. Momentarily at least this fright of an idol became the goddess hidden inside: of life, which you longed for, but hadn't yet dared embrace; of beauty such as you imagined, but had so far failed to grasp (with which Col grappled, you bitterly suspected, somewhere in the interminably agitated depths of music); and finally, of death, which hadn't concerned you, except as something to be tidied away, till now you were faced with the vision of it.

It was the spectre of death which brought them both toppling down. Mrs Hunter suddenly twitched as though someone had walked over her grave. Sister Manhood herself was stroked into gooseflesh.

'Am I looking—well?' The purple lips quivered with the necessity for confirmation.

Even if the nurse could have found a satisfactory answer, she was too distracted to offer it, what with Lottie Lippmann's far from obligatory crackle of excitement in the hall; men's voices; a thudding on the stairs; again men's voices, mounting, louder.

Elizabeth Hunter's armoured fingers descended to her lap, ascended to where her breasts had been; then the hands fell like the Fabergé they were. 'He's come, has he? He's come!'

Sister Manhood couldn't answer. Each of them was threatened by an imminence; but Elizabeth Hunter was the more afraid: her enamelled face was cracked with terror.

'Do you think he'll remember me?'

You couldn't console this poor old doll; you didn't know how to, any more than you could ever help yourself.

And then the door was opening: it was Mr Wyburd, his business suit, his correctly-mannered face, both ravaged by a day in which too much had happened. The solicitor might disjoint his fingers in trying to fit himself out with the right attitude and expression, as well as find words of an accuracy more painstaking than those he normally used. The old man looked properly grilled.

After muttering his way past the superfluous nurse, raising his voice, though he must have known it annoyed his client (*deaf is something I am not Arnold whatever else*) he managed to utter, 'Mrs Hunter—he's here! Sir Basil—heugh heugh!'

The laugh sounded awful: it creaked so; it obviously wasn't what he had intended. But nervousness, the nurse could see, more than nervousness—fright, had aged the solicitor. He had had almost more than he could take, as he stood twisting the signet ring with the blue stone, practically peeing, you felt, in those baggy trousers.

But what was inevitable, for everybody, happened: Sir Basil Hunter entered.

His mother's anguish was audible. What of his? Because the nurse did not know him, except from the legend of his career as told in pictures by the magazines, she could not guess. And now, faced with him in the flesh, she was further dazzled by the aura of charm and brilliantine the great actor was wearing.

On catching sight of the figure in the wheelchair, Sir Basil hesitated the tick of a second, as though he had found an under-study waiting on the spot where his leading lady should have been; then (your performance is what matters; curse the management only after the curtain calls) he continued across the carpet with that distinctive limp, probably a mannerism before it had set in slight gout, but which never weakened the power of his attack. One shoulder slouched a shade in advance of the other, he was presented in fact, though not objectionably, sideways to the audience of two, a hand outstretched beyond the custom-made cuff visible by a couple of inches at the end of his perfectionist sleeve.

He spoke, and the nurse thrilled to the riches in the voice. 'Darling —what a homecoming!'

As for the former goddess become a trembly woman, she, too, recovered her technique, her rings reaching up to clutch at her lover, his shoulder if she could get there, as soon as he arrived at her side. 'How I've waited, dearest! I believe the fat lambs mean more to you than I.'

Again Sir Basil hesitated, but drove himself at the understudy. When Elizabeth Hunter rallied. 'Why—Basil? Basil! Whatever happened in Bangkok?'

Sir Basil drew out of his breast pocket an enormous, enormously monogrammed, immensely expensive handkerchief to mop up what he hadn't reckoned with: not from an understudy.

'People, Mother. And then, I had a kind of—not exactly a turn—but needed a few hours rest. That's the only reason, darling.'

SHE was looking at him. 'You were never—I shan't say deceitful, Basil—but often disappointing.'

He parried it with Olympic expertise. 'Isn't disappointment something we've got to expect the moment we put our mouths to the nipple?'

Then they were clawing at each other; their 'darlings' ricocheted off the rosewood while they played their scene.

'I was not,' Elizabeth Hunter panted between kisses, 'what you would call a natural mother. I couldn't feed you—in spite of all that raw steak—as I must have told you—it seems. But that, you see—darling—hasn't deprived you of—of nourishment.'

As he knelt beside her, exposing his still considerable profile, while she buried her rings in his hair in an effort to reintegrate the fragments of a relationship, probably neither of them was more than formally conscious of an audience: which is how it becomes on those evenings when all the elements of a performance, on either side of the footlights, are perfectly fused.

Three

HE SHOULD have remembered his right knee was having one of its bad spells. In his response to the theatre of reunion, while disguising the shock of finding the Lilac Fairy standing in as his rehearsed-for mother, he had thrown himself at her feet, and was now paying the penalty for giving too much too soon. But he owed it to her — to them.

'Bless you,' he said, 'Mother.' He kissed the claw which had finally disentangled itself from his hair, and distinctly felt the sympathy streaming out towards him, the rapport he was establishing with the whole auditorium. (The nurse was quite a dish as far as he could tell, still only from out of the corner of an eye.)

He got up wincing for his age, his gout (left the pills in the bathroom cupboard in Eaton Place; not that they ever did much good). But the audience hadn't noticed; at least the nurse hadn't: she was too much like rapturous youth at its first play. He wasn't so sure the old Wyburd was on his side.

As you moved towards left centre Mother said, 'Is anything the matter with you, Basil? Why are you limping? Isn't your health in order? You never write to me — except when you're down the financial drain — so I don't know anything.'

It was not in the script; he tried to shrug it off. 'Oh — a nothing — a twinge.' The bedazzled nurse accepted it; the solicitor was one of those patches of silence which occur even on your best nights.

As for Mother, she said, 'All ailments are hereditary, I think — like moral flaws. I am arthritic, Basil. I had a great-uncle who went blind at the end. I am blind — physically, anyway.'

This time he more than shrugged; he raised his left shoulder. He could no longer look at her: greasy crimson overflowing the real mouth; the lilac silk sprouting from a withered cob. He felt he was to blame: the parents, those arch-amateurs of life, can't be held responsible for themselves, let alone their children.

'How is my granddaughter?'

'Hardly ever see Imogen. She does turn up now and again with offers to do me good. Doing good is her stock-in-trade.'

At least there was no mention of the wives, the mistresses, or any other moral blackmailers. He was conscious the pace was slowing up. Mustn't let himself get dejected after coming all that way, at such expense, on what he was determined to see as a positive mission; he would make it so.

'How's poor old Dorothy?' He pitched it to sound warm, mellow, affectionate, as indeed he had begun to feel towards a sister he hadn't seen in years.

'Dorothy is still poor old Dorothy,' their mother gravely answered. 'Full of the wrongs done her. She resents an experience I had on an island years ago. I expect she'll be here to dinner.'

The solicitor had to inform them the princess telephoned his office to say she had a headache. He didn't tell them he wasn't surprised. His loyalty, of an irrational kind, or else of such long-standing he was saturated with it, did not prevent him being caught in any of the cross currents.

'There! I knew!' The old lady was ablaze. 'And you, Basil?'

'I had booked a room at the Onslow. Didn't want to ...'

'... give anybody any trouble. My cook will be so disappointed. She was an actress, you know—in Berlin—and other parts.'

Not an actress! Nor daughter, nor wife, nor mother. He had reached that alarming stage in any actor's career where he loses the desire to perform. Suddenly. He would have liked to flop down, feel the tape closing round his neck, the clean, soft, white bib settling below his chin, then a detached hand feeding him slowly but firmly with spoonfuls of sweetened bread and milk. In such circumstances the mistakes would not yet have been made, and might even be avoided.

As things were, he could only answer, 'Very well, Mother, I'll stay to dinner. Actually it would give me great pleasure to meet your cook—and see some more of you, of course.' This too, was 'acting', but a diffident performance of a small part.

'Run, Sister Manhood, please—tell Mrs Lippmann Sir Basil will be here for dinner. She must—ex—ex*ceed* herself.' In her anxiety that minds shouldn't be changed, and that she scrape together words formal enough to compose her order, Mrs Hunter's tongue continued protruding from her mouth after the order had been given.

If he had felt less tired it might have shocked Sir Basil: that 'slight stroke' Wyburd had written about; though hadn't your first reaction been to hope for a second one? So many problems solved by a stroke; so much unpleasantness avoided.

Now as the nurse was hurrying to obey, he took it there was no danger. His conscience could enjoy the crisp swish of a departing skirt. If her nurse's smile was in a convention, it was a pretty version of it, and he thought he could detect that slight friction of silken thighs against each other, scissorwise.

He sighed brightly at his mother. 'A pretty nurse.'

'Oh, nurses! No end of them. And I'm the one who has to nurse the nurses. Take him, Arnold, and show him where everything is. The cloakroom lavatory doesn't flush when you want it to.'

'It does, Mrs Hunter, I assure you. We had it put right.'

'It didn't some years ago.'

Sir Basil Hunter persuaded himself to kiss his mother just below where the lilac wig joined the forehead. What looked dry, tasted clammy. He closed his mouth on his revulsion; whatever the conscious motive for his visit, he realized that unconsciously he had been hoping for some sign that life is a permanence.

She, on the other hand, seemed unaware of anything but her own exhaustion.

'I'll come up later,' he made his words linger; 'sit with you a while.'

She did not answer, nor probably care.

So, then, here he was, going downstairs with the Wy-burd, who was trying to talk theatre as though he thought that was the only stuff you were made of: well, there were one or two other components. The Wyburd wife and daughters, it appeared, had seen a performance of *Macbeth*.

Whatever else, all, even your enemies, even the flaming Agate, were agreed that you excelled as Macbeth. Though you yourself had endured agonizing doubts before the final flash of intuition. Perhaps you were after all the man of inspired mistakes.

The solicitor was demonstrating how the lavatory flushed perfectly. 'You see? She forgets.' He sounded mildly, officially kind.

'And remembers a hell of a lot that had better be forgotten.'

'I expect so.' There Arnold Wyburd would not wholly commit himself; of one thing he could not be sure.

As they strolled down the path which meandered back and forth along the terraces of the darkening garden, the solicitor all of a sudden gushed sweat to think he too might one day remember publicly what he had decided to forget. Would senility cause him to betray himself? when he wouldn't have wounded anyone intentionally: least of all, Lal.

Feeling he ought, Basil decided to ask after the solicitor's wife. The old man seemed pleased. It was becoming too easy to please: just as acting can become too easy, and you have to start again, imposing physical penance, and more painful still, by dragging up from the wells of the unconscious the sludge in which truth is found.

The solicitor remembered, 'My wife often tells how you made up your mind as a boy that you wanted to play Lear. And you did, didn't you?'

'Yes. I had a shot at it. I'm one of the many premature Lears.'

If you could remain long enough in this garden of ungoverned fronds, twisting paths, and statues disguising their real attitudes and intentions behind broken extremities and mossy smiles; if you could return upstairs and winkle experience out of the blind eyes and half-gelled responses of the Lilac Oracle, you might eventually present the Lear who had so far evaded almost everybody. But you had come here for a different purpose: short, sharp, and material.

Wyburd was making strangulated noises as though he had not enough of some foreign tongue to translate a simple wish into plain but consoling words. 'You actors of—of intellectual integrity, must find it immensely rewarding—to *immerse* yourselves in the great classic roles,' he at least attempted; poor old bugger, if he only knew!

Then the men were interrupted by a gate squeaking on rusty hinges; the figure of a woman was approaching under the fluorescent lighting and a cautious moon.

'Good evening, gentlemen.' Anachronistic, but not unpleasing.

'Ah!' The solicitor was prepared to do the honours. 'Sister de Santis—Sir Basil Hunter. Sister is your mother's night nurse.'

The woman bowed her head beneath a large, dark, dowdy hat. She was one of those who make the worst of themselves: the stately bust was clothed, before anything else, in an impersonal gaberdine which disregarded the lengths of fashion; the large, luminous eyes in the rather livery face looked almost phosphorescent in the street lighting; nothing about the night nurse provoked the actor's charm.

The solicitor and the nurse had launched into a duet on weather themes.

'A lovely evening, Sister, after the heat of the day.'

'Yes, Mr Wyburd—rain, though—a storm: I caught sight of lightning from the bus stop.'

The banality of the interweaving voices exorcised any mystery the night might have had, though the actor realized that he himself had contributed to this exorcism. He knew too much, alas. As he stood gloomily watching, a greenish sheet twitched for a moment against the cyclorama, making him listen for a rumble of zinc thunder from the wings.

The thunder missed its cue, and the nurse left them, climbing the terraces towards bedpans and thermometers.

'All these nurses and other characters must be eating up a fortune.' Sir Basil made it sound like a practical approach, when he knew himself to be the least practical of men.

'I don't think the cost need worry your mother, even if she lives to a hundred.'

'Hmmm!'

'And ought to be allowed—at her age—to choose what she most enjoys.'

'But does she enjoy? She seems to me full of grumbles.'

'That is part of her enjoyment.'

'Anyway we must talk, old Wyburd. I have a plan: a practical one.'

The solicitor took out his car keys as though to protect himself from any possibility of conspiracy by night; jingling his keys in retreat he went only so far as to admit, 'Yes, indeed. There will be plenty to discuss—for your sister and ourselves.'

He who had taken off from London Airport in the fever of a conspiratorial plan might have sweated it out of his system as the solicitor drove away. When he had thought himself ready for piercing the heart of the matter with a ruthless blade, he might, he feared, fall back on brandishing the theatrical counterfeit of a weapon. A lot would depend on Dorothy: had she been taught, tempered by, her mistakes? Most people aren't: an accumulation of failures either drives them inward or leads them to compassion for others; neither condition fits them to be partners in crime.

Weaving back along the serpentine path which climbed towards the house, he found himself snatching the ribbons of leaves from native shrubs and inhaling their scent to the depths of his lungs: to restore his own toughness perhaps? at the same time bashing senselessly at the heavy panicles of overhanging blossom, like a boy expressing helplessness confused by spite.

Something had happened to blunt his intention by filling him with his present malaise. If he hadn't committed a blunder of the kind which those who are jealous of you—wives, for instance, and certain actors, and crypto-friends—chalk up as a major crime, his age and a veneer of dignity made of this too recent incident a pretty squalid minor mistake.

Yes, Bangkok: thunder in the ears; a stickiness inside your unsuitable clothes; the bright, unquenchable inefficiency of the gentle

Thai airport officials; the equally unquenchable English hostess holding her chin high to boost her frustrated efficiency as the scrambled voice announced a four-hour delay, for repairs of such an esoteric nature no layman would have asked for further explanation.

He wouldn't, anyway, although it had been written, *there is nobody like Hunter for doing his homework*. Given a part which interested him, yes, he would ferret out the last refinement of lust in a Bosola, say, or just to show them, wrap up a homosexual bread-carter in all the oblique motivation required by the Royal Court. What concerned him now was how to keep himself company in the four-hour wilderness; none of the faces of his fellow passengers would have helped populate a ten-minute interval. The Scotch had been doctored. He sat on his stool, sideways to the bar, not entirely unaware of his own predicament as reflected in the peach-tinted mirrors: that of a vessel waiting to be filled. Had he always been empty, and not realized? God knows, actors can be! But not yourself: not with the press cuttings, the knighthood, memories of occasions when words and emotions fermented inside you, seethed upwards through the throat in a delirium to which you might have succumbed if you had been without the skill to direct it through the darkness at the many-faced monster. Hardly heard the applause sometimes; if there wasn't any, then you heard; that, and ruder sounds, were mostly on the road; a few occasions in the West End, for bad plays and mediocre support (politeness can also be daunting).

Everyone has had their failures: John, Edith, poor old Donald. (Donald would have had a damn sight more if he had allowed himself to think about them; or perhaps he used to. Anyway, dead now, and you mustn't muck about with the dead: least of all, dead actors. A wonder nobody had thought about that for a dressing-room superstition.)

You only couldn't prevent mirrors mucking about with empty disintegrating faces. At least before crumbling they acquire a kind of patina; and emptiness is not emptiness when it serves a purpose.

Many of the greatest have been empty. How else could they have filled with those necessary flashes of inspiration, the surge of words, emotion, if they had been a bunch of intellectuals stuffed with theories and 'taste'? Or Shiela (*not Sheila*) Sturges, the cerebral actress to bury other contenders. *What's eating you now Shiely?* Those intense, protruding, all but goitrous eyes. *I'm having a terrible time Basil with my self.* Always knotting herself tighter. Some critic had committed the crime of telling Shiela she was the 'second Meggie Albanesi'. Unlike Meggie, Shiela hadn't died, except mentally, daily, in her efforts to work things out, and in trying to coax inside her head a dead woman she hadn't seen, couldn't even imagine, only cerebrate on the theme of. *For God's sake you're late Shiela. What's got into you this morning? Here we are half an hour in rehearsal!* That was after you had separated, physically at least— for a long time Shiela continued to expect her professional perks— after Imogen was born. *I'm late Basil because I had to get off the bus—and rub earth into my hands. I felt it might help me understand this woman— this peasant;* how she mashed what she considered the more virtuous words. Poor Shiela: still having fits of cerebration when the grog allowed her; so you gathered from Imogen on her duty visits.

This is Imogen (pause) *my daughter.* What else could you tell actors about an actor's daughter who was a hospital almoner or something? They would have laughed, *oh really? how original, darling. I mean—so warm—helping people.* In any case, as old pros, the whole bang lot of them would be able to fill in the gaps in the story: *Shiela Sturges and Basil Hunter—he divorced her before the title; she never enjoyed her ladyhood, only the booze and L. C. Bottomley— hee hee!*

L. C. Bottomley, a reliable character actor and boring man (he played cricket) was always ready to give you a hand with your traps between station and digs, run out and buy you the evening paper, paid a bill or two on occasions and let you forget about it. A thin Bottomley; and Imogen a big, thick-ankled girl throwing back God knows where. *Daddy darling I want you to know that in any kind of fix—regardless of everything—and my living with Mother—you*

can rely on me. She must have inherited that from the Bottomleys.
It was a sad script if you were forced to study it:

THE ACTORS. Imogen — such a lovely name.

SHIELA (*dead serious as usual*). I hoped it might help her grow up
steadfast.

BASIL HUNTER *picks up his Number 9 and works steadfastly on his
face.*

There are the born actors: no amount of Cremine will wholly
remove their make-up; and there are the Bottomleys: clerks,
salesmen, and schoolmasters gone in the wrong direction. There are
also the Hunters in a special class of their own. Most of him derived
from Betty Salkeld, an *ingénue* stationed behind the willows at the
bend in the river to see who was clopping over the bridge, and
Elizabeth Hunter, a *grande dame* descending the stairs. Mother was
always on the stairs, in an inexhaustible wardrobe, white for
preference, and the smile which charmed innocent men, grateful
spinsters, seldom other wives, or servants, or children. That for
sure was where he got his — gift; let other people use the more
pretentious word. He had almost nothing of Alfred in him. For
God's sake, he would forget about Dad for years on end, then
regret it; but what was there to remember? The rams for which he
was famous within a circle of limited radius. They 'erected' a
monument to Alfred ('Bill') Hunter of 'Kudjeri' in the main street
at Gogong. The traffic parts at the point where this insignificant man
is permanently stood, in wrinkled bronze trousers, and waistcoat
carefully buttoned on a barrel chest, unexpected in anyone so short
and mild. The Council had invited Athol Shreve the politician to
unveil Alfred Hunter's statue; Mother hadn't been present, but sent
a cutting from a grey-paged country newspaper.

For a time you sent your own cuttings to prove the brilliance the
family hadn't been willing to believe in: 'Basil Hunter, a young
actor to watch, makes Guildenstern a real presence.' (Not getting
Rosencrantz had left you feeling sore till somebody spotted Guildenstern.) 'Basil Hunter's Orlando is a dazzling display of virile
sensitivity, enough to bewitch Arden girls far less perceptive than

132

Shiela Sturges's Rosalind.' (According to that old queen Hotchkiss; and poor Shiela had been awful, cerebrating into a boy playing a girl who becomes a boy: she got horribly tangled converting him back into a girl who was Shakespeare's boy.)

Then you left off sending the cuttings: you no longer had to prove you were an actor; there is only, finally, the need to convince that you can leave off acting.

He looked round the almost deserted bar, and out the doorway, at travellers lumped on plastic in a gritty expanse of chrome and concrete. Given better lighting, would any of these detached souls have recognized in him a human being as well as an actor? Hardly likely; who amongst them would have heard of Sir Basil Hunter? And who amongst those who 'knew', could possibly know? unless they were actors themselves: the eternal bloody actors.

This was where Basil Hunter, contorting on his perch between the mirror and the view through the doorway, tipped the chrome and plastic stool, and almost landed on his arse: for catching sight of what might be — what *was* a whole troupe of actors lugging vanity cases and overnight bags, dolls and paper parasols, trailing coats and stoles, and their own assorted tempers, one or two sustaining that roll of kettledrum brightness they had brought with them courageously from rep, years ago, into the jungle of the West End.

Averting his physical downfall at the bar, the lost actor couldn't wait to identify himself with the troupe, but skedaddled out, suede and rubber thumping tile and concrete, one trouser-leg still rucked at calf-level, his jacket showing too much shirt-cuff; a tie-end, flying, nicked his right eyeball.

Careering towards them, mouthing, he sprayed them at last with his relief. 'Madge! Waddayerknow, Dudley? For God's sake — not *Babs!*' Kisses for the girls; a shoulder clinch for good old Dudley Howard, a nice bloke, if just about the stodgiest actor.

'But darling, how in-*cred*-ible!' Madge Puckeridge was the brightest of all kettledrummers. 'And in Bang-*kok!*'

' 'Ere, not in front of ladies!' Born to the halls, Babs Rainbow

133

couldn't forget it even at the Royal Shakespeare: that's why they signed her up.

There was also a straggle of young things, he noticed, in too much costume and not enough make-up. Some of them he knew by sight, one or two by name, so he ducked his head. 'Hi, Gemma — Hamish!' Under his bonhomie he was shy of the young. Never let them see it, though. Some of them put on a moony, worshipful look for a famous experienced actor and knight. Others halted unwillingly, hand on sword, still too obviously in codpiece, and convinced they could run rings round this old ham it was their misfortune to bump into.

Here they were on their way from Japan, he remembered now. 'But why Bangkok?'

Madge explained. 'A British Council return gesture for a ballet or something they sent us.' Several of them groaned.

'Only a two-night stand.'

'Fabulous temples, if you can beat the heat to them.'

'Then Delhi.'

'And you Bas?' It was Babs, whose Nurse and Mistress Quickly were rather special. 'Where are you taking your one-man band?'

'To Australia.' He made the face they would expect, though not all of them did.

'I'd *adore* to go to Australia. Must be simply ravenous for theatre.' Herself a hungry thing: a mini-kirtled draft mare, about the thighs at least; the kind of face which is Plasticine to emotions.

'This isn't theatre.' Sir Basil Hunter could tell he was about to lose an audience, some of whom were already bored. 'It's a deathbed. My old mother.' He wagged his head from side to side to make it lighter, gayer, more acceptable for those it didn't concern.

'Better let's all have a drink, Basil old boy.' It looked as though Dudley had found the only possible way out of a difficult situation, not to say dead end.

Madge was sputtering and fizzing. 'Poor darling, how utterly tiresome for you! Alcohol is definitely called for.' Although a loyal and generally reliable actress, she was giving a bad performance, and knew it; but how could you make death convincing off the stage?

Suddenly he was disappointed; he hadn't found the hoped-for reality in these reinforcements of himself: these other actors. Time stretched almost as elastic as in the peach-tinted bar with its pretty little Thai barman and gusts of ice. He was more than disappointed: he was horrified.

'Yes. Alcohol. Why don't I come with you while they fix this bloody machine? I can keep in touch from the hotel.'

However little they had to give in the present circumstances, or perhaps ever, they were of his life, and that was in itself heartening: the 'pros' as opposed to the 'public'. Some of them had come in so far back they had probably forgotten you had slept together. (Madge Puckeridge one night in Manchester after particularly stinking notes from that cunt Arundel Hallett; that was before Madge's apparently endless marriage with Dudley, after Shiela had taken her child and gone; Shiela would have liked to make a barnstorm out of her departure, but her style wasn't broad enough.)

They were all bundling into a bus. 'We're staying at the Miramar —some of us,' Dudley said. 'The rest are on another flight, arriving later.'

Lights were spinning: the drinks Sir Basil had downed on his own must be catching up with him.

Babs Rainbow cackled. 'Remember Phyl Spink, Bas?'

'What about her?'

'She died. They found her in the bath with a gin bottle floating beside her.' Babs must have smoked a fortune in cigarettes: her lungs rattled worse than this complimentary bus. 'What a lovely way to die!'

'I won't, I *will* — NOT!' Madge was protesting. 'I'm a Christian Scientist in everything but the label.'

Some of the silent young were barely suffering the bus ride: those lithe boys still in their swords and hose, who seem to burn themselves out in the performance; nothing to give afterwards, unless perhaps to their equivalent girls.

He experienced another surge of anxiety: if he could no longer make contact with the Madge Puckeridges, the Dudley Howards, the Babs Rainbows, and certainly not with the silent young, where exactly did he stand?

'Are you terribly fond of her?' It was the mini-kirtled draft-mare, he recognized, as the street-lights played on the thighs beside him.

'Fond of who?'

'Your mother.'

'Oh, Lord—I don't know! I haven't seen her in more than half a lifetime.'

She had not been prepared for that degree of unconventionality in an old man and knight; perhaps it was surprise which made her near thigh increase its pressure.

Then they were signing the register, receiving their keys and mail, finding rooms, and one another. He lost interest: other people's hotel arrangements have an importance it is impossible to believe in; while they, from their side, had cast him off temporarily.

He looked in a mirror and tried to remember his mother, but couldn't distinctly: his own reflection got in the way. Funny he couldn't remember ever having known what it feels like to be a father; or not funny, considering.

It was better in Madge and Dudley's room after the bottles had arrived, and the ice, and Babs returned on getting rid of her foundations. There was a handful of the younger ones, on the whole only those who make a practice of 'sitting at the feet of'.

The draft-mare, whose name was Janie Carson, announced that she would contribute her duty-free to the party, 'to drink to the time I barged into Sir Basil Hunter'. (Possibly Janie embarrassed some of her contemporaries, to whom she might have explained herself more fully: *all right there's art we all know that but who's going to look after Janie if she doesn't look after herself and the ways of getting on are the same old ways it's only art that changes*.)

The refrigeration in a second-class tropical hotel was turning over groggily: you would see everybody's thoughts before the night was half over.

Two or three new faces put in an appearance at the door; the second flight had arrived, flogged, from Tokyo. They faded on seeing someone they knew only in the press or by repute.

One of them thought to call, 'Diana's sure she's pregnant. She thinks she took the seasick pills instead.'

A male guffawed.

That old bawd Babs Rainbow was grinning above her ginny-boo. 'Diana must leave it to Auntie Babs'; while Madge and Dudley, childless as far as you could remember, smiled rather thin, trying to show they were with it.

It was here that Janie rolled over and started fingering the clock on his sock. 'Possibly you don't know—I was at school with Imogen —your daughter.'

He swallowed half a tumblerful.

'Imogen and I were *chums*,' she added.

Not unlikely: two coarse-boned girls, equal in age; only Imogen hadn't Janie's plastic face: her missionary zeal would not have allowed it.

'Imogen sometimes asked me home. Shiela was ghastly, and Imogen always wonderful to her.'

He drank the rest of the whiskey in his glass. 'She isn't my daughter, you know. No blood offspring, I mean.' Why was he telling this young thing with the swinging hair and partially revealed twat? Honesty? Or masochism?

'I hadn't realized.' Some prude ancestor forced her to lower her eyes; a closer influence made her suck on her glass.

'Oh, no—definitely no!' he was emphasizing. 'Shiela admitted— out of spite. She made use of Len Bottomley, the most bloody uninteresting actor in the profession—butlers, friends, courtiers, all that—because she was jealous of me. She took Len as her stud, and Imogen—my "daughter"—is the result.'

Janie Carson looked as though she hadn't wanted to hear about it: confessions, when not launched as amusing details of gossip, can become embarrassing.

One of the burnt-up young men, Garth by name, was smouldering at him with what looked like contempt.

Janie said, 'What an awful time you've had, Basil, what with all that, and now your mother.' She delivered her line in a level tone of voice, except at the point where she swooped on his Christian name.

But he wasn't interested in the reactions, the preoccupations of Janie Carson or any of the present company. Although it boiled up in him at times, he was not interested in the past, or the messes he had made in certain corners of a successful career. What obsessed him was the future and its threats.

Again he was speaking to this girl, not because she offered him more than a token sympathy, but because her slight interest might help him give shape to some of his more shadowy thoughts. 'When I spoke of my mother's "deathbed" I was exaggerating – I think. I don't believe she'll die till she wants to. And I suspect she doesn't want to. What makes any strong-willed old person decide to die is something I've never worked out.' He looked round at the other faces, none of which, with the possible exception of Janie's, was giving attention to what he had to say. 'I haven't had much experience of the old and senile; in fact I've always gone out of my way to avoid that sort of thing.'

Good old solemn Dudley was dutifully automatically sleepily pouring you another drink. It was a relief to sink your mouth afresh; and no one had accused you of ignoble intentions.

'I must admit that when I've had a study I've longed for the star girl to drop dead.' Janie shook her hair and giggled at her glass.

'Not death again!' The word had broken through to Madge at the other end of the room; she was holding her chin too high to stretch the wrinkles in her throat.

Garth, the dark thin young hawk, had raised his beak; his eyes were contemplating no one else but Sir Basil Hunter the famous ham. 'Did you ever hear – sir,' he coughed for a word he used unwillingly; words probably made him feel awkward unless they were handed to him in lines: then he knew how to kindle them, 'I think I read it – that fear of sex underlies an obsession with death?' It was uttered with a seriousness so intense it fell wide and heavily.

'No. I hadn't heard it.' Sir Basil smiled the smile which had vanquished many.

Garth the hawk flushed darker, but wasn't vanquished. Gathering his shinbones inside sinewy arms, he sat and glowered.

Babs Rainbow blew one of her ripest raspberries. 'Tell us what's on in life for a change. Haven't you a nice play, Bas? Something old-fashioned and plummy?'

'I have a play.'

This was more in everybody's line, even the morose amongst them.

'Tell us!'

'The play!'

'Not old-fashioned. And if there's a plum, it's mine.' He hunched himself in mock apology. 'Aren't I an actor?'

Garth looked down his eyelashes and curled a lip.

Sir Basil Hunter drew in his nostrils. 'A sour plum, to shrivel the mouth.' You could feel their imagination catching.

Janie Carson had rolled over and was lying propped on her elbows. 'And who's written this frightening play?'

'It's not written—or not entirely. The greater part will be improvised.' To expose his daring was making him drunk.

'Darling,' Madge Puckeridge warned, 'you'll end up naked, and in the round.'

'Got to take the plunge, haven't we?'

Dudley, Madge, Babs, all old old; yourself, the high-diver, probably older than any of them, but from the tower on which you had climbed even the armoured young looked defenceless.

'It's only an idea—as yet.' There might still be time to throw the beastly thing off.

'But who's writing it? Who? This play—or idea.' Janie was rocking on her elbows, insisting.

'Mitty Jacka.'

'Never 'eard of 'er.'

Their ignorance might have deflated him if what they hadn't heard of could have been in any way important.

139

Then Madge remembered something. 'The woman who lives somewhere out—Beulah Hill?'

'That's where she lives.'

'Oh, but she's old! She's older than us.' Madge couldn't take it seriously. 'Writes poetry and things.'

'Mitty isn't old; she's ageless.' He believed it, and it frightened him.

'Has she got hold of you, Bas?'

'He's having a thing with a mummy.'

'The death wish more like it.'

'But at least tell us,' Janie Carson was insisting with her elbows, 'what's the *idea* behind this half-written non-play?'

'My life, more or less. Acted out with a company of actors. According to how we—the actors and audience—choose, it could go this way or that—as life can—and does.'

There! He was sweating. His glass was empty. This time Dudley didn't fill it.

Babs screwed up her face till the mouth disappeared and the glaring eyes and the dimple in the chin were her predominant features; then she said, 'No part for me, Bas, in any old non-play—swingin' me tits all over the auditorium—fartin' in the aisles. No thanks! No harm in a little embroidery here and there, but at my age I like a few lines to hang on to.'

There were visions in the faces of the others: Dudley Howard shorn of his reliability; Madge Puckeridge divorced from the affectations she depended on to disguise her thinness; Janie and Garth had slithered together, and could have been mounting on a wave, but of their own inspiration. So that he was again alone. All foresaw his downfall, he could tell, not by their smiles, but from the shadows under the cheekbones, their parted lips, as they watched the naked knight's exposure: the pendulous, vulnerable testicles.

Madge recovered first. 'It could be a perfectly marvellous idea. I only wonder—Mitty Jacka.'

Dudley, who grew earnest in drink, got you into a corner to warn you against a poison which could end in professional suicide.

Babs and Madge were not exactly quarrelling. Garth leaned over and began bathing Janie's cheeks with a spate of whispered kisses; his lips looked enormous, but no longer hostile; her hair, fallen to either side of her face, might have been dipped in water.

Suddenly you remembered. 'That flaming plane!'

Dudley took up the phone because it was his room and his responsibility as the equivalent of host. After the clicks, the polite voices, the re-connections and the explanations, he burped, and reported, 'They give it another three hours.'

It didn't surprise you by now; anything else would have seemed unlikely.

Everybody yawning mumbling mouthing the ice in empty tumblers.

You said you were imposing and would impose less in a public lounge if there was.

The key in which nobody said goodbye you would meet again if you didn't it didn't matter.

Known faces begging for forgiveness for past sins or to be loved in the indeterminate future.

He saw Janie Carson determined to pick up what must be the duty-free bottle. He could visualize her face as that of an old woman: a guarantee in the young—of? of?

Hands falling apart; the succulent kisses.

Long putty-coloured corridors smelling of soy sauce above refrigeration. Janie disappeared behind a door with Garth.

He went on through the cool but stale corridors looking for a hidden lift well. Found its cage just as the air started beating at him.

It was Janie the swinging bottle swashbuckling legs underwater hair. She took him by the hand, and it seemed natural: they had dropped their ages.

' ... why you should get a stiff neck in an armchair in a lounge.' Instead she was unlocking 365.

'Hospitality plus,' he foolishly and wearily contributed, but she gave no signs of having noticed its lack of sparkle.

Walking amongst the furniture (nineteen twenties pink

modernistic) she had begun taking off the little she was wearing. She was shaking and folding her shift. She lay on the bed having gooseflesh.

All the while the refrigerator was clonking over continuing continuously.

'Bed's pretty narrow, but ought to adapt.'

Reminded of what he was expected to do, he started taking off his own clothes but out of time with the airconditioner.

'Which parts are you playing?' he brought out from inside his shirt.

'Oh,' she sighed. 'Hero — Lady Montague — Gwendolyn. Gwendolyn's rather fun.'

'A compendium of females!' He wrenched himself pompous idiotic out of the tearing shirt.

The trousers clinging fashionably were more difficult. What if he toppled over?

'You know why I'm here? I've got to raise the money for this damn play. Even if she doesn't die she may come good with a few thousand.'

'I'd like to be in your peculiar play.'

'We'll im — provise it!' Tearing off the last of the trousers.

Why not? Mitty Jacka the master mind must have planned a few incidental harpies to tear into his nakedness.

Janie Carson almost didn't glance; she switched off the light soon after. It was thoughtful of her. His nervous shanks might tremble less in the dark, the slacker skeins of flesh not swing. Balls too.

When he reached her he lay along her let her at least feel his weight while dabbling his lips in her mouth. It would have swallowed him if he had stopped.

She gulped once. 'What I'd really like, terribly,' she spat him out, 'will you have me one day for your Cordelia?'

'Why?'

'I've never understood exactly what Cordelia's about. That's what makes her exciting.'

'I'll have you for Cordelia — if you — when we're both ready.'

He had to think of something to do—some *business*—between now and his apotheosis.

'That makes all of this madly incestuous, doesn't it?' Wriggling giggling under him didn't convert his limpness into enthusiasm only increased his shame.

'A dead loss tonight,' he apologized, before leaning off her into the dark somewhere in the right direction to do what he hadn't done for years.

'Sordid old brute! Vomited almost over me—anyway all over the carpet.'

'Serves you bloody right for tampering with old men.'

'But you won't understand, Garth. I've got to experience *everything*.'

'I guess you've experienced some of it, then.'

Janie a silk flame beside male body hair and white briefs: this one snapshot before you were acting the corpse you felt.

'Looks like the old bugger's passed out.'

'Let's move my things. That'll make the room more sort of his— as well as the vomit.'

The room did become yours as far as sleep could persuade a vast black chamber in which naked tumblers were playing a scene from birth to death it was the only scene in the play Mitty explaining for that reason fairly elastic somebody pulls your frightened prick to remind you the tumblers have formed a womb out of their stacked bodies through which you were expected to crawl under the encrustations of swallows'-nests out between the mare's legs whether Mitty approved of her Primordial Baby's interpretation you couldn't tell nor look to see whether Mother

The air had stopped flowing past him as he woke rigid on the narrow bed searching for some

The Flight!

'Flight 764 departed already one hour,' the sweet sleepy telephone voice informed.

'Then I must find—do you hear? a seat on another. As little delay as possible.'

Escape from this room, from Sir Basil Hunter his vomit. Thank God for your clothes: nothing like costume for security.

As he reached the upper terrace, his mother's house rose above him, black against the green-flickering sky, and almost as enormous as the houses of childhood: the dark had evolved a kind of beauty out of the pepper-pot turrets, dormers and bull's-eyes, fretwork canopies and balconies. At his return by half light, the same house had appeared a joke; now he had to take it seriously.

Respectfully he wiped his feet on the mat outside the door he had left ajar. From inside, sounds of cutlery and glass transformed his hopes into confidence, till he suddenly remembered he had to face another actress. It made him creep through the living-rooms, withdrawing his feet as though from a stickiness wherever a lamp had formed its pool of light. The portraits on the walls were passing judgment, his own disgusted little-boy's face the most relentless.

Someone had arranged decanters and glasses on a marquetry table in what had been known officially as the 'study'. He was glad of a couple of hairs of the dog before making his entrance for the scene with the housekeeper. He experienced as usual a faint excitement mixed with misgiving at the thought of playing opposite a woman whose work he didn't know, who had been chosen for him perhaps ill-advisedly, or even out of malice.

Then the housekeeper herself was standing in the doorway. 'Your dinner is served, sir, if you wish and it is not too early.' The opulent house filled with superfluities overemphasized the austerity of this stone figure.

'Nothing would give me greater pleasure than to eat.' He began moving with a grace which came easily when he was in his best form; he smiled, and the lights in his head were refracted in a glass hung above the fireplace. 'Basil Hunter,' he added unnecessarily, he hoped kindly, to put her at her ease.

But she must have been overdazzled: her lips, her chin, were in trouble to reply, 'Lotte Lippmann.'

Then she turned and began to lead him with as much seriousness as her black dress, her white crochet collar and scraped hair, had learnt to command; but her neatish bottom waggled, he noticed, because she couldn't help it.

Arrived in the dining-room, she indicated his chair with a languidly formal gesture, her eyes potentially communicative, though for the moment preoccupied with some irony of her own.

They had to get it over, so he said, 'My mother mentioned that you're an actress.'

As he sat down she was pushing at his chair from behind. '*Achhh!* Mere *Tingeltangel—Tingeltangel*, Sir Basil.' Her sigh expiring behind her as she left the room seemed to echo the sentiments of old honky-tonk pianos.

So he was invaded by her, or rather, by their common melancholy: of darkened theatres, or clubs where the stained tablecloths would be bundled up in the light of morning. The middle-class pomp of Moreton Drive gave no protection.

By the time she returned with a tureen, its lid rising to a climax in a miniature viridian cabbage, he had manufactured a whole arsenal of bread pellets, appropriately grey, to defend himself against a repetition of the hours they had both undoubtedly experienced.

'This *Tingeltangel* was my only talent.' Lotte Lippmann released the steam from the contents of the bulging tureen.

He would neither interject, nor hurry her towards the big speech for which, he sensed, she was holding herself in reserve.

She ladled out for him one of the German soups afloat with meticulously moulded *Knödeln*, the whole smelling a bit obscene of must or puffballs. '*Na*—you like it?' She was asking for praise out of her dark scar of a mouth.

The Englishman he had become, replied, 'Mmm—excellent—*yes!*'

They were laughing together in conspiracy, though she lowered her eyelids and withdrew soon after, out of discretion.

Outside, the thunder had begun. He could hear branches whipping the air. What might have been rain was still only the sound of attached leaves streaming in a wind.

He had come home to a foreign country. On the other hand Enid had once said, after one of the daily rows marriage privileged them to indulge in, *when we misunderstand each other Basil I must remember you are a foreigner we may speak the same language but we interpret it very differently.* Lady Enid Sawbridge, his second wife and the Earl of Burlingham's intellectual daughter, amounted to five volumes of verse besides a monograph on Aphra Behn, three novels, and the Travels in Asia Minor, in Outer Mongolia, and in Micronesia; with such a scholarly mind it was surprising the grasp she had of the facts of life.

He couldn't think why he had married Enid, unless to consume more of the unlimited flattery she appeared to offer, and for the doors she opened to allow him to indulge his lust for sociability. As a wife she was one long squabble. After the first week, in which they continued to share the triumphs of knowingness, they realized that beyond their few points of agreement, each knew something better and different. All through the quarrels Enid would smile: she had the grin of a borzoi bitch about to snap. The most amicable thing about their marriage was their parting. They agreed not to divorce for the moment, and the moment became permanent because it seemed as though no other arrangement would suit them better. Lady Enid Hunter was still about town: sometimes she made an appearance in his dressing-room, and they would rub cheeks and exchange endearments, perhaps go on to supper and have a good laugh at somebody's expense; it took the sting out of what they knew about each other. Possibly Enid liked to think of these occasional meetings as one of her many contributions to civilized living; in his own case they were the outcome of a fatal weakness, his inability to say no.

Certainly he had said it often enough to Shiela, but that was in the theatre: he couldn't tolerate a bad, perhaps even worse, an intellectual actress, holding her stomach to simulate an emotion her head had 'understood'. And yet in the beginning she seemed fired by intuitions, or was it the glow of youth, in the drab digs, the grimy Midland theatres? He had been in love with her—or the lines with which they wooed each other nightly. In any case, it was cosier for two to make the assault on the West End; whatever their ideals, that was their ambition.

Outside the house in Moreton Drive the storm effects had become more controlled: the zinc thunder was rolled only intermittently; the wind must have died; he had forgotten rain could fall as straight or as solidly.

He would have liked to continue listening to the rain, neither remembering the past, nor plotting the uncooperative future, simply being; but the housekeeper returned carrying a silver dish, molten it appeared, from her haste, and the sizzle of butter, and a considerable display of starched white cloth with which she was grasping the silver edges.

'*Du lieber!*' On the dish with which she smacked the sideboard lay a pair of flawless *Schnitzel*, the slices of lemon shaved to transparency, the anchovy fillets lovingly curled.

'Don't you find it tedious?' he asked, to disguise the greed which had risen in him.

'I enjoy myself to feed other people.' The hands which withdrew in a flurry of scorched napkin were trembling.

'But as a performer, I mean.'

'Oh, Sir Basil Hunter, I was never more than a kind of compelled firework. Night after night I was let off, and fizzed—*bang*—and went out. Till at the end I hardly fizzed. My firework was a sodden one.'

Inside its crust of golden crumbs her veal was succulent and tender. Instead of encouraging the housekeeper to reconstruct a life with which he would have to sympathize, he would have preferred his own company and thoughts. He was too much the victim of his own doldrums to be expected to enter anybody else's.

He could see from the corner of an eye that she was stationed by the sideboard, the hands below the white cuffs locked in an arrow pointing at the floor. The fact that she was standing guard made him conscious of the movements of his jaws and the silence he broke by masticating and swallowing. He was aware that one of his shoulders was raised, as if to ward her off across the intervening distance. She reminded him of some actresses, uncertain in their art, yearning towards an audience they feel they have not yet converted.

He half turned to compliment her. 'Whatever else, you're a first-class cook.'

'Oh, yes?' She laughed. 'That is important too—isn't it?'

The air was passive around the sideboard; he could not tell whether he had offended her.

'Cooks! Actresses! No one is all-important, unless the great artists: Mozart, Goethe, Bernhardt—Sir Basil Hunter!' Her rather Jewish compliment had him wincing; or did she intend it as a side swipe? 'If I could choose—if I could begin again—I would ask to create one *whole* human being.'

'Literally?' he asked, while knowing they were more or less agreed.

'Yes,' she said. 'Or two. Myself. And one other—out of my body.'

Though he had finished all but the rind of lemon and a thin ribbon of gristle, she did not attempt to clear away his plate or the quenched serving-dish.

'*Na, ja!*' she sighed from her formal attitude against the sideboard; 'though the life of theatre is necessary for us—for you and me, Sir Basil Hunter. This drunkenness! This is why—when my family is murdered—the man who is my *Lieb' und Leib* is lost—I still look to *Tingeltangel*—why, when I run out through the drenching lights, I can bear their worst laughter, their whiskey breath, afterwards the kisses, the praise and promises, the dirty gestures of both men and women. Even though these are only skulls, and false bosoms, and male vanity around the tables, I have to air my song—the little dance-step they expect—*ein zwei drei*.' She demonstrated round the Hunters' (four-leaved) mahogany table. 'I have no voice. Except that of drunkenness. Which is what they have been longing for. It is their need—and mine. They laugh. They wish to touch my hat, my stick, my coat-tails of almond velvet. They aspire—to what? to be translated out of themselves? to be destroyed? Certainly, Sir Basil Hunter, there is nothing of this that you will not have experienced.'

He was too humiliated to reply.

'At a different height, it goes without saying.' Her laughter made it sound more shameful, though unintentionally, he hoped. 'They tell me you've played Hamlet, Lear: all the great *German* roles.' As she went out with the empty dishes the housekeeper laughed quite recklessly. 'So you must understand, Sir Basil!'

He sat holding his head, staring at the place where his plate had been. *To create one other being out of my own body.* He had failed in that. Though Imogen his 'daughter' had shown herself willing to stand in. But with Shiela in the beginning, before the performance had set, he might have created a whole rather than a part. When all the parts were hanging from their pegs and out of sight, this whole might have reminded him that he was not wholly actor: he was also a whole human being.

On the other hand, the 'drunkenness'. Again this crazy Jewess was right. It is the next part which promises to bring the sum right. At the end another fly at *Lear*'s stony, perhaps unscalable mountain. He feared the prospect almost as much as Mitty Jacka's non-play. Worst of all he dreaded the sound of projecting a tattered voice into a half empty theatre. In Glasgow during that last tour someone had thrown a banana skin.

The housekeeper was returning to offer a crystal goblet; a perfume suggested peaches and champagne, together with a sickliness of almond? anyhow, inappropriate.

She planked her offering in front of him. She was too excited; emotion could have destroyed the servant's respect for a guest.

Though he had no taste for sweets, he began stirring the contents of the glass, poking at the bobbing gobbets of peach. 'Where did you learn this other art of seduction?' he asked in a voice which belonged to a different scene.

'Not from my old mother!' She laughed cruelly. 'I have learnt from a lover — no, we shall call him "protector" — a chef in Zürich. Berlin — Zürich — Haifa — Sydney: these have been my stations to date.'

Her recollections made her furiously active in the present. The Lippmann had shed any pretence of passivity. If her feet didn't go *ein zwei drei* the almond-green velvet of her coat-tails flew. Her hands looked younger for the shadows and her agitation.

'I don't *blame!*' she protested. 'Not this fat Swiss always smelling of the kitchen. Not any of the others. My one lover. My poor incinerated parents.'

She dragged up a chair and thumped down at the opposite end of the ponderous mahogany table. 'My parents, you see, are these liberated Jews who worship scientifically. Medicine, you might say, is their religion, their rabbi a physician, when not a psychiatrist. I, their daughter, must become a dietitian. I must study the Bircher Benner *und so weiter*. Right? But I cannot deny the drunkenness — which is also, by another light, my Jewishness. I run away to the *Tingeltangel* — certainly *ein Rausch* in its most unorthodox form — but *drunk!*' She threw back her head till she was all throat, her laughter at its most convulsive.

'And love!' Her face had returned. 'I love this one German — this *goy!* It is not desecration, as you perhaps, as certainly my dead parents, believe. There is no desecration where there is love.' The housekeeper's face at the opposite end of the table had grown old and terrible.

'What became of your German?' he hardly dared ask.

'I left him.'

'But others left together.'

'We were not as others. I left him because I loved him.' She got up, trying but failing at first to unlock her arthritic hands. 'Or because — as your lady mother insists — I am the original masochist.'

'No one ever knew better than Mother how to rub salt into other people's wounds.'

'But I love her!' the housekeeper gasped.

'How can you love what is evil, brutal, destructive?' If he were to survive, he must persuade himself to continue believing some of this.

'Yes. She is all you say,' her housekeeper agreed; 'but understands more of the truth than most others.' As her hands fell away from the table she added, 'And if I cannot worship, I have to love somebody.'

Then she removed the goblet of sweetstuff, which, it appeared to both of them, had been an unnecessary prop.

She brought him coffee in the study. She was again as self-effaced as she should have been in the role of servant: eyelids lowered; hands dutiful; bearing modest without trace of servility. When she had left him he scalded his tongue drinking her coffee, bitter-tasting, and strong enough to blow a safe let alone a human skull. But he forced himself to drink a second cup, because he must see his mother before leaving the house which, he had to remember, was only legally hers.

The storm had moved away, he realized. These were his footsteps thundering on the soft stairs; no other sound, not even the racket of traffic, to profane a perfect silence.

In the sanctuary the acolytes had created round the object of their apparent devotions, Sister de Santis sat writing with an old-fashioned, once elegant, gold-encircled fountain pen; on her knees a document, of no doubt esoteric significance, clamped to a board by a common bulldog clip. Seeming to take for granted that the intruder was of her persuasion, she looked up smiling as soon as he entered, then returned to her occupation. As in the garden earlier, the radiance of the woman's eyes and the opulence of her breasts surprised him. He could not entirely accept her in the way she appeared to accept him. Of course nothing of this would ever become acceptable. What he might have longed for, against his rational judgment, he stifled under repugnance in this house become shrine, in which there was even a hint of incense, if only from cypresses rubbed up the wrong way by the storm withdrawing from the garden.

By now the image on the bed was stripped of vestments and jewels, the festive paint removed from its face. What remained might have been a corpse if a fluttered breathing had not animated the shroud; and eyelids, otherwise like speckled seashells cast up on a beach by a storm, persisted in tremulous activity; and the light spun a nimbus out of the threads of dead-coloured hair. The total effect did not suggest a woman, less than any, his own mother: as the guardian of the relic may have wished him to believe. The shaded light, the scent of ruffled cypresses, the hypnotic motions of the fluttered sheet and tremulous eyelids, all invited him to share with the elect their myth of sanctity; when he had come here for his own and different purpose: his survival depended on the death a materialistic old woman had delayed too long.

He was relieved the attendant nun did not expect him to participate in any of their rites; at the moment she was having trouble with her antiquated fountain pen. Only in his first move towards departure it was suggested, 'Aren't you going to kiss your old mother goodnight?' Completely impersonal, impossible to identify, the voice was basically a woman's. (Could conscience be a woman, perhaps?)

At this point the night nurse raised her head, and he broke away, leaving her, he saw in one of the many mirrors, the token of a haggard smile, which she received with what he might have mistaken for an expression of pity or even selfless love.

He ran downstairs, feeling his pockets for he couldn't remember what, rang for a taxi, did remember his coat, the luggage he had brought with him from the airport, and the name of the hotel where they were keeping a room for him. The housekeeper did not appear again, and he was the happier for her avoidance. It also allowed him to fill his cigarette case from the full box he had found in the study before dinner.

Then the taxi was honking outside.

Sister de Santis did not approve of what she was doing: she got up, and cracked the curtains enough to watch Sir Basil Hunter leave. The moon had revived in the wake of the storm, but rode the sky groggily. From the house the garden below appeared a muzz of frond and shadow threaded with the serpentine path. Down the path the figure of a man was tentatively advancing, unequally weighted by a suitcase in one hand, an overnight bag and briefcase in the other. Sir Basil was made look older than when she had first met him at the gate; exhaustion could very well have shrunk him physically, without damage of course to his reputation. No, she didn't admire this elder brother of the great actor less; in fact, he benefited by her pity: he reminded her a little of her father, whom she had respected more than any other man, even in his frailty.

Down in the street the illuminated taxi was waiting for its passenger, its lights too brash beside the insinuating glimmer from the moon. Approaching the taxi's beacon, Sir Basil could have been dazzled by it. At a turn in the path, where an abrupt flight of steps spoiled its serpentine flow, he put his foot in a pool of darkness, and began to topple. The bags completed his unbalance. He fell right over into a border of heliotrope and thyme under one of the smirking broken-fingered statues.

Sister de Santis shoved the window as far open as it would go. She leaned out—to do what, she couldn't for the moment conceive, though in her mind she was already bent over the body examining it for injuries. Wasn't it part of her job? But her efficiency might have suffered from the scents of the garden. The heavy air was making her breathe too deeply; she could feel the sill cutting into her as she leaned out over the remembered face, from which she had banished any sign of disillusion or dissipation.

The taxi door sprang open on the driver's bronchial ribaldry, 'No need to watch yer step, mate. That's about the finest arse over tip I ever seen.'

Together the taxi-driver and Sir Basil were gathering up Sir Basil and his bags.

'Once you know you're a goner, it's better to let yerself go. And no bones broke. But I reckon you worked that out for yerself, eh? from experience.'

She could not decode Sir Basil's reply from its outburst of joviality overlaid by pique.

The taxi-driver carried the bags out through the gate, his passenger limping behind him.

'What is it, Sister?'

'Oh, I've woken you, have I? It was so breathless—I opened the window to let some air in.'

Through the window, you could hear the taxi driving away, alongside the silence of the park.

'Basil left, then. I knew he would.'

'He saw you were asleep.'

'He didn't want to say goodbye. Neither of us felt like it.'

'He didn't want to disturb you.' Sister de Santis hoped it was true; she liked to think the best of people, and night duty allowed her to: faces asleep surrender their vices to innocence.

'You know I never sleep,' Mrs Hunter insisted. 'Where is Manhood?'

'Sister went off as usual, soon after I arrived.'

They had met that evening in the dressing-room. Sister Manhood was in her slip. Under the colourless make-up she used, she was looking hectic.

'Have you met him?' she asked her relief.

'Mr Wyburd introduced us as I was coming in the gate.'

Sister Manhood was twirling: it emphasized her look of nakedness. 'I think he's gorgeous. Older men are so much more—distinguished.'

'I haven't met them all. And it's too early to say of this one.' Sister de Santis knew that she was not being strictly sincere, but Flora Manhood induced a show of principles.

'Oh, aren't you stuffy, Sister! So *literal*,' she added gingerly, because it was a word she had learnt from Col Pardoe.

Putting on her street dress she decided to provoke stuffy old Mary. 'I wouldn't mind sleeping with Basil Hunter.'

Sister de Santis knew she was blushing, but managed to laugh coolly enough. 'I expect he has the lot to choose from.' She took off the hat she knew Flora Manhood despised.

'Oh, it's easy for you! Have you ever had—have you ever *wanted* a man?'

'Surely that is my affair?' It should have sounded more casual, but Sister de Santis had pricked herself with a safety pin on sitting down at the dressing-table to unfold her fresh veil.

Fortunately for her self-control, she remembered, 'That friend of yours—the chemist—rang and left a message, Mrs Lippmann says. He expects you down at his place. He has some chops to grill.'

'Like hell I'll grill chops! I'm nobody's wife, before or after the ceremony.' Flora Manhood might have thrown a tantrum, with pouter breast and throat swollen to a goitre; but she thought better of it.

She nudged Sister de Santis in the small of the back with the orange plastic bag. 'Sorry, darls, for my indecent curiosity. I'll leave you to the pure pleasures of night duty with Mother Hunter.'

Because Sister de Santis was in no way given to frivolity, this duty would have been less a pleasure than a devotion. In her earnestness she was ready to forgive Flora Manhood her flippancy. She had tried before to explain away her colleague's frequent scurrilous attacks on Mrs Hunter by seeing in them youth's dread of the sacrosanct. She herself often feared the sudden slash or cumbrous intrusion of Mrs Hunter's thoughts. But tonight, it seemed, the old woman's weapons had been blunted in parrying the daytime intruders.

Paradox and heresy mingled with the night scents and sickroom smells after Mary de Santis had watched Sir Basil leave. She was forced to invent insignificant jobs, to prove to herself she had not lapsed from the faith which necessity and her origins made the only possible one.

'Már-o!' in her mother's despairing reed of a voice; 'Mar-*i*-a?' in her father's basso; till both parents were agreed she could only become an Australian 'Mary'.

If the child herself ever hesitated, she was never torn. Coming together at the centre of the suburban house, they would kiss and laugh, sometimes the parents above her head, more often all three conjoined. She realized while still small that her father and mother were in love with each other; and it remained so when the three of them were desolated.

She wasn't born in that brown Marrickville house, but might have been. Anything which had happened before hardly concerned her, even when they talked about it, and looked at snapshots, or broke into tears. Though when she herself was unhappy, or half asleep, or ill, the submerged wreckage of a past life sometimes floated out of the depths, and in her perceptive misery she recognized this as the important part, not the happy, thoughtless, unequivocal Australian present. She might have remained the unacceptable stranger, even to herself, if she had not adopted an attitude from which to make the most of unreason.

Before anything, the parents: Mamma a thin black stroke in any landscape; those narrow shoulders; hands too incompetent for manual labour except the dusting of icons (probably the 'real' in what was left of Mamma's life flowered only in front of the icons). Papa's hilarious scepticism transforming the Holy Roman Church into a vast elephant-house, *all hands shovelling*; then turning sour as his body shrank, his vision receded, *don't accuse me Mary as I see it the needle is my faith the only logical conclusion.*

They kept the records, buckled and specked, in a cardboard box. *Dr Enrico de Santis, 32, Italian subject ... Anastasia Maria Mavromati, 24, Greek ... both of Smyrna, Greece ... married April 26th, 1923, at Smyrna.* (It was never referred to as 'Izmir'.) In all the snapshots, the studio portraits, Enrico had remained the glossy charmer, after the paper had turned yellow, the inscriptions and humorous comments yellower to green. But Anastasia Maria had been born, like most Greeks, with a foreknowledge of everything that will happen: in her face the faith or fatality of old blackened icons.

Mamma would attempt to make what she was careful to refer to as her 'version of the Greek dishes', wearing an apron stained with tomato, her smile bitter for the oil she had spilt; because Mamma had only been taught to read poetry, receive calls, and discuss life on marble terraces beside the Gulf. *Most excellent are the soudzoukákia of Anastasia de Santis*—Papa would pretend to gobble, to emphasize this excellence, *though Greek food is fodder beside the subtleties of Bologna, Torino, not forgetting little Parma.* It was one of the jokes Mamma accepted, because they loved each other, even in Marrickville.

After deciding for nursing, Mary de Santis had once invited her fellow probationers Eileen Dooley and Verlie Rumble to a meal. Her gesture had been spontaneous enough, but misgiving set in as she watched her friends walking from the tram towards the junction of Warnock and Cathcart Streets, that brownest, most blistered corner in the whole suburb, on it the MIXED BUSINESS (Enrico de Santis) with residence above and behind.

Her martyrdom made public, Mamma appeared more desperate than ever. The black dress probably looked like mourning to the two summery visitors. Wearing over it a freshly stained apron, she brought them her 'version' of the Greek *soudzoukákia*.

'These, I believe, are also called "Smyrna sausages",' she explained to Eileen and Verlie, who giggled.

'Whatever they're called, they look tasty,' Eileen said to encourage Mamma.

It was a hot day. They were sitting beneath the trellis, its attempt at grapes mildewed by the humidity. Papa came out from the shop with a wicker-covered demijohn. Eileen and Verlie barely allowed themselves wine, and giggled as it touched their lips.

Eileen was pushing the food around the plate with her fork. 'Gee, they're rich, aren't they?' She had meant 'foreign'.

The girls had begun looking with a changed expression at their friend Mary de Santis, who grew reckless: she raised her glass and drained it in a purple, choking gulp. She could feel the wine returning to her cheeks, and what was almost insolence replacing her normal docility.

'This is the food it is natural for us to eat.' It was strange hearing herself talk like a bad translation, but in keeping with her foreignness, as she looked at Eileen and Verlie, the one dumpy, freckled, red, the other simply a pale girl.

By the time Mamma brought out the snapshots Mary de Santis had recovered her docility, and her agony was complete. Mamma sat holding the snaps, her hands like graceful paper fans gone sooty in the grate. The photographs caused so much pain, you often wondered why she had to produce them. Today in particular, under the eyes of these gawping girls, they were excruciating.

'These are at Smyrna,' Mamma explained, herself laid bare.

'Aren't they funny!' Eileen said. 'The houses! Do people live like that?'

'No. They don't exist. The houses were destroyed by the Turks. This is one of the cathedral. This is where the Turks crucified the archbishop—on the doors of his own church. Afterwards they put out his eyes.'

The two girls were gasping and perspiring for the monstrous event they were being forced to experience.

'All these are happier pictures,' Mamma suggested, though her sigh would not have allowed you to believe; 'all at Athens. After the Catastrophe we fled to Metropolitan Greece, and were some years as refugees. This is where Máro has been born. See? Máro as a small baby.'

They wouldn't have believed it! Mary de Santis: this papoose thing; and *black*.

Mary de Santis realized she had reached the apogee of her foreignness; that she accepted it as part of her Greek fatality she only understood in later life. Where earlier in the sequence of events wine had replaced her docility with insolence, she was now gently drunk with pride.

'Oh, what are these, Mrs de Santis?' Passing through the house to the street the two girls could not resist what might be another source of danger.

'These are icons, Christian—*Orthodox* icons.'

The girls breathed and mumbled. They said they were Catholic.

'My husband was a Catholic—until he thought better of it.' Mamma gently smiled.

The girls looked pained; one of them asked, 'What is he now?'

'He is nothing,' Anastasia de Santis admitted, out of her tragic depths. 'Oh yes, my husband is a courageous man.'

Brave? Perverse? Self-destructive? It was difficult to decide; or whether he was something of each: Enrico de Santis, the fashionable gynaecologist turned refugee and shopkeeper. 'What is the use, Anastasia? By the time they have chewed me up in examinations, and convinced themselves I am not disruptive to their system, what shall I have left to give? I shall take this shop, and make a decent living. We have each other—as capital, haven't we? And a shop will be entertaining for the child: all that pretty *prosciutto* and *mortadella*. Think of the geography she will learn from the labels on the tins! The linguistic advantages!' Papa was at his most ironical; while Mamma invoked her Panayia and the saints.

In retrospect, Mary de Santis realized her parents' love for each other had been their religion. Because she had grown up excluded from this, without their being conscious of it, she had evolved tentatively, painfully, a faith of her own.

On the surface it was her vocation as a nurse. During his worst mental torments Dr Enrico de Santis would ask to see her certificate. He seemed to find comfort in knowing that she was continuing in a tradition. In the final stages he would beg her for the needle, said she had the 'kind touch'. She had obeyed his wishes to the extent of breaking her vows. While Mamma prayed to the Panayia, Saints Anastasia, Barbara, Cosmas and Damian—the lot. Mamma's lips and temples grew transparent with prayer, as Papa's whole being revealed its increasing dereliction.

After several years of trial and attempted expurgation, all three had been involved in the great mystery. Mary de Santis, the only survivor, emerged as the votary of life: there were the many others she must save for it; or ease out as she had eased the failed man her father, and her equally failed saint of a mother.

In spite of her certificate and thirty-three years of experience, Sister de Santis still considered herself a novice; humility would not have allowed her to claim status in any hierarchy of healing, whether physical or spiritual.

But she was sometimes taken by the hand and shown.

She also enjoyed worldliness. At her first meeting with Mrs Hunter those fifteen years ago, her future employer had set out to clarify a situation. 'Although you are my nurse, Miss de Santis—God knows why I need a nurse for this—upset—"breakdown" my bitchier friends choose to call it—I don't want you to emphasize the fact. No ghastly uniform. I'd like people to accept you as my companion. I shall think of you as my friend.' Then, for the first time, you experienced Mrs Hunter's smile: a golden net she spread over the innocent or unwary; and because in those days you were both, you had been caught.

During the first weeks with this unorthodox case, the steps you took across the geometric rugs, on jarrah floors of a sullen red, were hardly more than automatic. The silence hypnotized no less than the strangely broken voice which commanded while inviting.

Mrs Hunter decided, 'I want you to make this your home. Go into the kitchen and see what you can find to eat if you feel hungry in the night. Take yourself off to bed if I'm boring you; I know I do run on at times—from being so much alone.'

Elizabeth Hunter spoke with such a studied earnestness she made all but the most cynical, or the most callous, believe. Mary de Santis was neither. She wanted a belief, which perhaps this ageing, though still beautiful woman could give her: secondhand experience must be more enlightening than that which may never come your way; and Mrs Hunter was composed of the many relationships she had enjoyed, with the many friends she was still seeing in spite of her myth of loneliness.

Certainly her husband was dead, her children gone—the daughter so recently and mysteriously after only a brief visit—but the maid was always running to answer the doorbell, to let in callers, or receive boxes of flowers, or single luxuries such as caviare or perfume, still wrapped, it sometimes seemed, in the sender's straining thoughtfulness.

On one occasion Mrs Hunter remarked, 'If only one could feel more grateful for what one doesn't want; and the poor things, I'm pretty sure they can't afford it.'

In the intervals when she found herself undeniably alone, the silence became a suppressed twangling, which broke free on one occasion not long after her nurse-companion's arrival. 'I'd like to show you something, Sister – I'm going to call you Mary; I'm old enough to take liberties – this little music-box belonged to the Prince Regent, or so the friend who gave it told me.' Elizabeth Hunter opened the lid of the pretty gilt and velvet toy, and at once the silence of the drawing room was vibrating with its gilt tune.

They stood holding the music-box between them.

'Play it if you ever feel like it,' Mrs Hunter invited. 'It does one good to give way to moods – even the superficial ones.' Then she looked very keenly at her companion to see how her suggestion had been read.

Sister de Santis did open the music-box sitting alone one afternoon in the drawing-room, stiff and guilty without the protection of the uniform she was not allowed to wear. She saw again the grime in her mother's fine, incompetent hands, and her father's wasted arm quivering for the drug she could not deny him in his last days. Mary de Santis was relieved when the music tottered note by note to a full stop.

But she almost ceased to be a stranger in this echoing house. She found herself running helter skelter across the slithering rugs, the waxed jarrah, to fetch something they had forgotten, thermos or handkerchief; while Mrs Hunter waited in the car. She kept a chauffeur, but liked to drive herself along the coast or into the country: drives which, the nurse suspected, bored the driver.

It was in the evening that Elizabeth Hunter came into her own. Resting on an Empire daybed while still officially ill, she expected her companion, not to make conversation, but to listen to the thoughts she was forced to project.

'When I was a child, Mary, living in a broken-down farmhouse, in patched dresses – a gawky, desperately vain little girl,' Mrs Hunter's eyes glittered and flickered as she flirted with the fringe of her stole, 'I used to long for possessions: dolls principally at that age; then jewels such as I had never seen – only a few ugly ones on the wives of wealthier neighbours; later, and last of all, I longed to possess people who would obey me – and love me of course. Can you understand all this?'

The nurse hesitated. 'I suppose I can, in a way – in a way. But you see, I've never had any desire for possessions. I couldn't imagine how I might come by them – or attract people, let alone have them obey me. We were a very close family. Outside that, I've only wanted to serve others – through my profession – which is all I know how to do. Oh, and to love, of course,' she laughed constrainedly; 'but that is so vast it is difficult to imagine – how – how to achieve it.'

Mrs Hunter suddenly looked angry and suspicious. 'What do you understand by love?'

'Well, perhaps – sometimes I've thought it's like this: love is a kind of supernatural state to which I must give myself entirely, and be used up, particularly my imperfections – till I am nothing.'

Mrs Hunter seemed agitated: she had got up and was trailing her long fleecy stole. 'Whatever they tell you, I loved my husband. My children wouldn't allow me to love them.' The stole had dragged so far behind, it was lost to her by catching on what must have been an invisible splinter.

'Oh, I know I am not selfless enough!' When she turned she was burning with a blue, inward rage; but quickly quenched it, and drew up a stool at this girl's feet. 'There is this other love, I know. Haven't I been shown? And I still can't reach it. But I shall! I shall!' She laid her head on her nurse's hands.

Mary de Santis was turned to a stick, though an exalted one, on feeling someone else's tears gush and trickle into her hands.

Next morning Mrs Hunter said, 'I'd like to give you something, Mary;' and produced a seal with a phoenix carved into the agate. 'You might wear it on a bracelet'; whether her nurse had one, she might not have considered.

Mary de Santis was embarrassingly touched. 'I couldn't,' she said. 'Or I might borrow it for a little.' Clumsily conveyed, it must have sounded ungracious.

Mrs Hunter only laughed. 'If that is how you are.'

As soon as the patient was considered 'semi-invalid' little dinners were arranged for long-established friends, who did not particularly interest the hostess, her nurse observed: they had eaten into her life like wire into a tree; they were also necessary for a discipline of kindness she had to practise.

At one of these dinners the Wyburds were introduced. The nurse had already met the solicitor professionally the day he engaged her for his client. There was no marked difference in his social behaviour, except that most of the evening he kept his eyelids lowered, probably tired out by a heavy day at the office. His wife, a thin plain, beaky woman, with dark-red hair and freckles, had something comically appealing about her. She must have been younger than a rough skin and wrinkles allowed her to appear. She was certainly younger than her solicitor-husband, but their hostess made her look old and dowdy, not that she minded, judging by her slightly ironical expression.

There was a second couple, probably friends of lesser standing: they appeared too grateful, as though they had borrowed money, or been able to do a rich and beautiful woman some unexpected favour. Sister de Santis did not catch the name of this unremarkable couple (another wife on the plain side) if indeed Mrs Hunter had introduced her friends to her companion.

The hostess was dressed very simply for a simple, perhaps obligatory occasion, but was able to shine the more for that.

She happened to remember, 'When we went over, Alfred and I, for poor Dorothy's wedding, we were actually invited—though only briefly, thank the Lord—to the family seat, Lunegarde. Exquisite wormeaten furniture. Gobelins by the acre. But the plumbing! The family used to rub themselves down with eau de Cologne, or if anybody ventured on a bath, Dorothy told me, it was brought from the village by the fire brigade.' The company was so enchanted they would have accepted almost any extravagance she dared them not to believe. 'And worse—far worse!' Mrs Hunter could not resist her own powers. 'You wouldn't believe, Constance,' though the grateful guest was obviously prepared to, 'the *cabinet de toilette*—to which nobody had to be shown: it announced itself so blatantly—the door, darling, opened outwards, so that if you valued your privacy, you had to sit holding a cord attached to the knob.'

The thin couple was most appreciative, the Wyburds less so. Mary de Santis wished Mrs Hunter had not told the funny story; it was almost as though her employer were determined to destroy somebody's good opinion.

Mrs Hunter turned to Mrs Wyburd. 'I've probably bored you, Lal. You must have heard it a hundred times.' Simultaneously she laid her hand on the back of her friend's, for the solicitor's wife was seated beside her owing to the shortage of men.

Mrs Wyburd neither denied nor reassured: she preserved her air of comical irony. The name 'Lal' still hung above the table; it had clanged too loud, as though Mrs Hunter did not give herself many opportunities for using it.

In the drawing-room over coffee the hostess remarked, again too aggressively, 'You're forgetting your duties as host, Arnold. Aren't you going to offer us a liqueur?'

He did so with a punctiliousness only slightly rattled by his omission.

Lal said she'd have one of those green things. 'Don't they call it a "starboard light"? I'm told it's a whore's drink.' Like other plain, dowdy women she would try springing a surprise.

'And what do you fancy, Mrs Hunter?' Mr Wyburd asked.

'Thank you, Arnold. I'm still my doctor's victim.' She looked at her nurse, half appealing for confirmation, or perhaps not in connection with the matter at all.

Later, when the gathering was threatening to break up, she aimed her voice very pointedly at the colourless couple, 'You can't have missed reading that Athol Shreve has almost finished his sentence.'

The husband and wife appeared wretchedly uncomfortable, as though they felt themselves responsible for something. The husband remarked that, to his mind, Athol Shreve was the greatest disappointment, ever, in Australian political life.

'I wasn't surprised.' Mrs Hunter scorned those who were. 'I

mistrusted him from the beginning. You remember the night we met at the Radfords' dinner, and he gave us all the lift? Oh, I shan't say I wasn't intrigued, too. He had something crude and real about him. Well, that was his reality—that of a thief.' She gave two or three short laughs, which for some reason increased the distress of the two friends for whom she was performing.

Not long after, the gathering did break up, and the couple were again gratefully smiling for the attentions of this rich and important woman. Sister de Santis realized they were not friends, only slight acquaintances. The Wyburds who were more inured to Mrs Hunter's friendship, might have felt sorry for, or contemptuous of them.

When nurse and patient were at last alone, drinking delicious, thirst-quenching, private draughts of cold water, Elizabeth Hunter confessed, 'Those Stevensons—I often wonder why I don't drop them, except that there are certain things—past events—which have to be faced in perpetuity. I suppose that is the reason for the Stevensons: now and then they lend themselves to one's self-mortification. And the poor creatures do enjoy a good dinner.'

The two women were passing through the hall. Elizabeth Hunter had linked herself with, and was leaning on, the one who for that moment was wholly her nurse.

'Why,' Sister de Santis noticed, 'you haven't read your letter'; it had come by the morning delivery, but still lay unopened on the salver. 'And isn't the stamp unusual. Is it Norwegian?' She could have been trying to encourage a patient who threatened to despond.

'Yes. The letter is from a Norwegian,' Mrs Hunter admitted, 'who was in this country recently—an ecologist—by repute an intelligent man—but weak, it turned out, and something of a boor.' She had begun tearing up the still unopened envelope.

'Shouldn't you at least read his letter?' asked Sister de Santis, who seldom received one.

Mrs Hunter said no, she wouldn't, and gave the pieces to her nurse to dispose of.

'One day, Mary, I shall tell you about it. Dorothy and I were invited by some friends to stay on their island, and this Norwegian, Professor Pehl, was our fellow guest. I'm too tired for it tonight.' Suddenly Mrs Hunter looked so old and haggard Mary de Santis decided she would always resist hearing the story; she herself was weak, sensual enough, to crave intermittently for the luxury and refreshment of physical beauty.

Normally Elizabeth Hunter appeared astoundingly young and beautiful for one who, from what she told, must be around seventy. Her face would certainly crinkle under the influence of impatience or anger, but only, you felt, to become the map of experience in general, of passion in particular. Untouched by any of this, her body had remained almost perfect: long, cool, of that white which is found in tuberoses, with their same blush pink at the extremities. If it had not been for professional detachment, the nurse might have found herself drugged by a pervasive sensuousness as she helped her patient out of the bath and wrapped her in towels, during her 'illness'. As it was, physical languor was absorbed into a ritual; physical beauty became an abstraction, in its way far more desirable to anyone hungry for a work of art or of the spirit, and who had not in fact come across one, apart from the dark icons inherited from her mother.

Elizabeth Hunter responded even to the abstract admiration she inspired, most noticeably at the dressing-table: her eyes opened to their fullest; her hair lent itself to tenderest weaving; the line of her cheek was rejuvenated. She liked her nurse to hand her things, particularly on nights when dinner parties were held; because now that she was practically 'well' she arranged a number of more formal functions, 'to give notice that I'm neither mewed up in a loony bin nor staggering down the ramp towards the everlasting bonfire. One's enemies, one's friends for that matter, don't really believe unless one shows them regularly.'

Preparing for such an occasion, her blue stare suddenly expanded to embrace a reflection in the glass deeper than her own. 'I must lend you something to wear, Mary.'

The nurse would have felt herself flush if she had not been able to see it. Her party dress looked frumpish, and though recently ironed, already crumpled; whereas the older woman shone: her form seemed to create an immaculacy out of whatever clothed it.

Now she rushed at a drawer in a burst of inspiration, tore it open, rummaged, and pulled out a broad ribbon or sash in turquoise silk, which she looped round the waist of the badly-cut muslin dress, and tied in a bow at the back as surely as impulsively.

Mary de Santis was too ashamed to move or speak. She was afraid to look at herself in the glass.

'Wait!' Mrs Hunter commanded.

She was fastening the strands of a pearl bracelet round a wrist too passive for resistance. Then, her hands trembling for the climax of her creative act, she tried out a pearl-and-turquoise star, first on a shoulder, before fastening it for preference on the muslin breast.

'I like it better there—in the centre.' She was standing back to judge her work. 'Less self-conscious. You are too pure, Mary, to follow fashion.'

Mary de Santis was only too self-conscious: so much so, she still had not dared look at herself.

Finally she did.

'See? I haven't altered you.' Mrs Hunter laughed. 'Only heightened a mystery which was there already, and which is too valuable not to respect.'

The younger woman was trembling for this self she had sensed at times, without ever believing anyone else would recognize.

In a last burst of confession as they heard the doorbell ring, Mrs Hunter said, 'How I wish I could have had you as a daughter. Or sister. Better a sister; then we could have told each other our secrets—and you would have helped me.' She even laid her cheek for a moment against her nurse's, and the latter felt the other's jewels freezing her skin, rustling and quivering against her dress.

Mary de Santis had never felt so desperately the need to worship.

That night she must have appeared a mysterious blur, or at her most positive, a dark presence at the fashionable dinner party. At least the women were amused by what they considered one of

Betty Hunter's experiments in the *outré*, just as her 'illness' had been an eccentric character's exhibition of caprice: they could take neither seriously. The men were at a greater loss: the knowing cats as well as the ingratiating dogs amongst them. Although the companion, or whatever, answered their questions pleasantly and accurately, she would not be rubbed up against, and it puzzled their male skins as well as their male vanity. They suspected her of holding in reserve some unidentifiable vice.

During the evening a gloom seemed to possess Mrs Hunter: she developed a staccato manner for the maids, and her irritation extended itself to her guests; perhaps she had undertaken more than she should have, or drunk too much. Anyway when the guests had gone, you felt it was a riddance. Or not to be simplified to that extent.

She approached, and her eyes were terrible: at the point where concentration becomes fragmentation. 'You know as well as I do, Mary, it would be self-indulgence on my part to continue making use of you now that I am well. I must ask you to go when you've found a suitable case.'

'Oh—yes? Mrs *Hunter*.' It was pitched somewhere between agreement and query: you too, were exhausted, or dizzy from the wines; or a dunce of a little girl in a turquoise sash.

What could have been interpreted as bland acceptance of her proposition might have increased Mrs Hunter's irritation: her mouth had taken on an ugly shape to express a bitterness. 'I wouldn't want to expose anyone of your worth and dedication—indefinitely —to a flawed character like mine.' It was as though, for some obscure reason of the moment, she had decided that love, whether given or received, was more dangerous than contempt; or else she saw the good in herself as an immodesty it was her duty to conceal.

As she climbed the stairs, her shoulder blades and a diamond clasp made her look more solitary. But this seemed her chosen intention.

Left standing below, Sister de Santis untied the turquoise sash with which Mrs Hunter had bound her. What she could not reject were the implications, human as well as super-human, which she had accepted while they were dressing for the party. Even her agnostic father had failed to commit her to unbelief.

Sister Manhood was given to speculating aloud to her colleagues, 'One day—any day now—one of us will go in there and find the old thing lying dead. I wonder which of us it will be? Bet I'm the one who'll cop it!'

It was an event Sister de Santis no longer contemplated. If Flora Manhood insisted on its possibility it could not be through fear of becoming emotionally involved with death. Flora's emotions were centred on Flora, and she simply didn't want the trouble of ringing Doctor and tidying up the body. Nor would Sister de Santis herself have been emotionally involved by this stage with Mrs Hunter's death: she was more concerned with the spirit she tended nightly, and which, in spite of a deceptive flickering, might have come to an arrangement with death. Sister de Santis would not have discussed this, of course, with any of the others, not even Mrs Lippmann. In spite of a broadminded attitude to life and contact with death on a grand scale, the housekeeper dreaded IT as an end; she could not see beyond the handful of ashes.

Mrs Hunter herself said, early the morning after her children had flown in, 'Now that my body allows me a certain amount of free-dom, I can roam about more—not my mind—I know my mind is a shambles; you're at liberty to tell me, Sister—but myself—all that I have been and seen, though not always done. I am free to gallop as far and as fast as I like along the banks of the river—nobody to call me back for meals or baths—or take the sword out of my hand because they consider it dangerous. Not understanding I may need it to cut my way through the last layer. Or that wind flows thicker and blacker than water. And hair. You didn't know one of the wigs is black, did you—Mary? Nor did Lilian. She only experienced murder—because that was what she believed—that her end was in death by her Russian lover. Poor Lilian—my other Nutley! She

169

hadn't begun to learn that love is not a matter of lovers – even the least murderous one. So she had to die.'

The old woman under the eclipsed silver sun, which radiated by day in the head of her great rosewood bed, sounded so far distant the night nurse took her pulse. Sister de Santis did not believe she would find the pulse had weakened, but this was what she had been taught to do.

'You see?' Mrs Hunter smiled, or forced her lips as close as she could to a display of affectionate sarcasm.

'Go to sleep,' the nurse advised.

'I may – if I'm favoured.' The nurse brought a pill. 'No! No! Not while there's work to do.' She clacked with her sticky tongue against her palate. 'Pills are all very well if you want to dispose of yourself, but I have an idea I'm not mine – to do what I want with.'

The nurse filled a glass with water and held it to her patient's lips.

Mrs Hunter's nostrils stiffened. 'You're not poisoning me, are you? I'm the one must decide – not Basil – Dorothy – Lal Wyburd – any of you. No, not even I.'

The nurse said, 'I thought you were thirsty. I brought you a glass of water.'

'Then I'll risk the water. It's my conscience I'm worried about: the pan mightn't hold it.' But when she had drunk, she seemed reassured. 'Did you have a kind night, Nurse?'

'Yes, thank you. About an hour ago I went down to the kitchen and fried myself some sausages.'

Mrs Hunter was laughing in her nose as if about to share a funny secret. 'Nurses were always whacking into sausages in the small hours.' When she became more serious. 'Quite right too. Feed the spirit. And kitchens are fascinating at night: full of things you don't notice by day. Sometimes a chair you haven't been seeing for years. Or a bowl of fat with fur growing out of its skin. I can believe such things interest you, Sister – because you are religious.'

Whether religious or not (that was something she would not have breathed about, not even to Mrs Hunter asleep) Sister de

Santis admitted to a belief in common objects. If you depend on something to any extent, you might as well learn to respect it; so she never kicked the furniture or threw the crockery about.

Clocks had begun to ping and reverberate in the depths of the house. In another suburb the hour was counted out, though so remotely, it had not much connection with time.

'Don't you think you might rest?' asked the nurse.

'I could have rested if I hadn't heard the doorbell ringing.'

'That was hours ago. It shouldn't disturb you now.'

'Who was it?'

'Sister Manhood's friend — the chemist. He wanted to know where she was, and I couldn't help him.'

'Ask the bus conductress!'

'I didn't think of that. But surely he must know about the cousin?'

Mrs Hunter had floated far enough not to feel concerned about anyone else, or so it appeared to the nurse.

Sister de Santis fetched the skirt she had brought for mending. As her rather naked-looking hands stitched at the torn hem, she thought how her legs, even in the finer flesh-coloured stockings she wore to the city or to afternoon tea with one or two nursing acquaintances, had never drawn much attention to themselves. When she was younger she used to wonder what she would do if a pervert started stroking her legs, as she read they did, in cinemas. But it had never happened, perhaps partly because she had lost her taste for films; she was too tired, anyway, by the time she came off duty. Only occasionally in buses an old man's watery stare would wash around her ankles and mount higher, though not high, for her skirts had never been of the shortest. Colonel Askew, another old man, and the patient who had left her an annuity, had sometimes gripped her knee, and she had not bothered to remove his cold blue claw; the colonel could not always remember his motive in raising food to his mouth, or why he had gone to the lavatory.

Comfortably and profitably occupied with her mending Sister de Santis should have felt protected. She was not, though: some disturbance kept heaving at the placid surface of her consciousness. She tried going over details of the voyage recommended for Colonel Askew's health, and one of the happier episodes in her own eventless life: how they had sat 'in mufti' (it was the colonel's joke) at a table for two in the dining saloon of the liner which was taking them, and eaten fish rolled in sawdust, and thin grey slices of roast beef; before lunch and dinner, the colonel always drank the one prescribed Scotch (he prescribed a white lady for his nurse, 'because', he remembered, 'women enjoy the sweet things') while informed eyes at the smoke room tables diagnosed a geriatric folly ('can't you see the old boy kneading her like dough; that hard, narrow berth must make a perfect kneading board').

Her recollections, in the end, were little more protection than her mending. She thought about the meaning of 'smug', what exactly it conveyed: in her mind's eye she saw the suet crust of a steak-and-kidney pudding, like the texture of an unpowdered nose. Colonel Askew used to enjoy his steak-and-kidney, but had been warned off salt by that stage, and was afraid they might put some in. He died at Brown's Hotel of a final, anticipated thrombosis. Before returning home, she had taken a brief holiday in Suffolk: the frosted roads, the hedgerows with their beads of scarlet bryony on withered umbilical cords, her own solitariness (when hadn't it been? though never a colder, harder one) shocked any smugness out of her. Her footsteps followed her hollowly. Safe behind the textbook flatness of her training she should always have been able to resist calculating death's dimensions. Just as the study of anatomy should ensure against preoccupation with the physical.

Sister de Santis threw aside her mended skirt. Before going downstairs she looked at her patient without seeing. All the way down, through the felted air of the staircase, the nurse's starched uniform might have been trying to remind her of possible missions. She couldn't very well cook herself another plate of sausages. There was her interest in objects, as Mrs Hunter had sensed. In a wire safe she found the basin of fat Mrs Hunter knew about: the green fur sprouting from the skin. There was a knot in the kitchen table polished by her own hand as she sat at night eating sausages and left-over scraps of potato.

Again she saw the whorl of hair close-clipped against the nape of a neck. 'She went off duty as usual. I'm sorry I don't know where she is,' she had repeated out of sympathy for the young man standing at the door. Mr Pardoe (Sister de Santis had been taught to use Christian names only after agreement and a ceremony) was not unlike another object in wood, turning bluntly away, smelling of nicotine agitated by hot spittle.

'If she isn't in her room I don't know what to suggest.' She could have hung on all night in the lighted porch offering non-suggestions to this knotty object of a young man; how would that whorl of hair *feel* if you touched it?

Mr Pardoe was moving off, when he turned, his teeth flashing ferociously. 'Did the actor come?' He laughed in no particular direction.

'Sir Basil Hunter? Oh yes, he arrived this evening. His mother was so excited; we all were,' she heard herself. 'He had his dinner here, and went afterwards to a hotel.'

'I bet Flora got a thrill out of meeting the great actor.'

'Oh, she *barely* met him.' To comfort the knotty object she added, 'And actors are like anybody else – in essentials, I should say.'

'Yes. In essentials,' he agreed; whether comforted or not, he decided finally to leave.

Watching him go down the badly lit path, she called after him, 'Don't forget those three steps just before you reach the bottom. They're dangerous in the dark.' In spite of her sympathy for him, and her faith in the honesty of ordinary objects, she knew it was herself she was trying to help: she was like a woman deep in the country trying to hold a stranger whose departure would leave her alone. Which she was at last. She was left picking the needles from a rosemary bush beside the porch. The perfume increased her isolation.

A sense of anger began floating around her, and kept recurring hours after he had left. She tried to direct it at Sister Manhood, because if Flora had not been diverted from the hoped-for meeting, the young man would never have arrived, a knotty problem, on Mrs Hunter's marble doorstep. Sister de Santis had gone in. The slammed door emphasized the silence of the house. She almost never slammed doors: that was more in Flora's style.

And here she was, hours after the chemist had left, standing in the study, Manhood's equal in faithlessness. The house had never been less a shrine; and you less its guardian. She walked about recklessly, nudged once or twice by a leather arm against which she bumped. Her anger was partly increased by the harsh glare from woodwork and gilding in a room she seldom entered, partly from having to admit that Flora Manhood and her knotty—oh yes, her undoubtedly honest chemist, were nowhere near the reason for her agitation.

In one of the many mirrors with which the house was overloaded, 'the big white lily' planted by Mrs Hunter the morning before, had begun swaying: all ready to be picked. As he bent her backwards with the smoothest, the most practised motion, her mind rooted through, her mouth lapped at, every detail in the catalogue: she drank through the pores of his just faintly bristling skin; dragged at the creases in tight clothes; inhaled the scents of brilliantine and stale tobacco; her fingers tangled with the grey-black (unfatherly) hair, laying open the bald patch she couldn't remember, but which must have been there because here she was discovering it.

Mary de Santis was flung into one of the huge leather chairs. It sighed, and sucked at, before settling around her. Whether she imagined it or not, it still felt warm. It smelled of. *You mustn't touch the basil Máro Papa has planted.* She did, though; she crushed it between her hands, and the scent of basil invaded, finally emanated from her body. She was anaesthetized by her own scent of basil.

Not entirely. Mary de Santis opened her eyes. Where two separate plants had been rubbing together so sweetly in bursts of glossy foliage and pointed spearheads of near seed, here was her knotty solitary self, trapped in the leather chair, in a distorting mirror. Not even Mrs Hunter's 'big lily'. Her anger broke around her. She began unbuttoning her uniform, tearing at the straitjacket beneath to free her smoothest offerings. Which he, or anyone, would have rejected, and rightly. Though dimpled under pressure, and arum white, their snouts pointed upward to accuse the parent sow.

Around her on the carpet the wasted basil seed was scattered. If Mamma were preparing to accuse, Papa would not. Nor Mrs Hunter, *along with acting Basil has made a profession out of disappointing.*

When St Mary de Santis was the disappointment. She heard her shoes chuffing as she escaped from the glaring room she had chosen for her self-exposure. All the way up the stairs the iron hedge, planted to protect her from space and the hall below, was catching at her skirt with iron thorns. In spite of buttoning her habit, she might arrive in the sanctuary stripped. In whatever state, she burst in. To fall on her knees at the foot of the bed. If not to recover what had passed for sanctity. She found herself pressing the palms of her hands together, in an arrowhead, as she begged (she had not been taught to pray) for grace.

Four

HER DELIRIOUSLY patterned dress, her gyrating Perspex earrings and orange bag didn't count for much in the dark. Not that it was *real* dark. Night was still in its brown stage: the sound of feet was not yet divorced from plodding bodies; you could still read the makes of cars, whereas in another quarter of an hour, all would be swallowed up in a great rubbery volume of traffic. If the lit windows of houses offered a human belief in permanence, the oil refineries ablaze down Botany way suggested other worlds, other more demoniac values.

Earthbound through her strong legs, her rather too thick, female body, Flora Manhood would have liked to destroy something tonight. She breathed deeply of the chemical air and hoped she was contracting lung cancer. What, she wondered, would happen if she picked up a stone and shattered the glass protecting one of these families seated at their monotonous meal? Rough hands; a bumpy ride in a police van; then Col would bail you out, explaining that he, more than anyone else, had the right to do so. Col's un-questionable 'right': other people, amongst them many women, would no doubt see it as 'fidelity'.

Flora Manhood did stoop, to pick up, not a stone, but an empty bottle which had begun swirling round her ankles. She half-aimed it at a window, and it fell short; it plopped amongst the oleanders. She walked on muttering, smarting for a feebleness which overcame her at decisive moments. There were moments when she won-dered what actual control she had over her own will, in spite of her latchkey, her training as a nurse, and her contempt for those who thought they would take advantage of her.

Probably she felt contempt for everyone she knew, except perhaps Mrs Hunter: why not Mrs Hunter, when half the time she hated the old thing, she had not yet been able to decide. She admired, possibly, heights to which she herself could not aspire. Flora Manhood remembered how she and Col had once watched a rather boring documentary of some mountaineering expedition on which the climbers never quite made the highest peak; the last shots in the film, with a commentary you had stopped listening to long before, were of this half-veiled peak, sombre at first in the distance, then for a moment, as the sun struck, breaking through to blind.

Of course it was silly really to connect this half-dead bed-wetting still spiteful old woman with a mountain, even though Mrs Hunter did at times break through the mists of senility and give you a glimpse of something else. You only hoped that one day she wouldn't frighten you with such a glimpse as you feared she might.

Down at the intersection the night closed in more grimly in spite of the noise, the traffic, the lights. At least from that level the refineries could no longer be seen, but the exhaust fumes thickened. It was frightening, all this lung cancer. She began breathing very lightly, tried in fact not to breathe at all, so as not to inhale the fumes. Along the pavement, in the shadow between lamps, a man was trying to pick her up, of what description she couldn't, didn't want to know. As she hurried along, the man followed on her darker side, mumbling half-intelligible words. A foreigner of some kind, which made it worse: foreigners were darker, and usually sober. To sleep with some hairy foreigner (*Yes I did it Col with my eyes open I am my own mistress aren't I knowing all the dangers—the risk of venereal disease which is actually what I have caught—syphilis has been diagnosed*).

By the next crossing at least she had shaken off the man. She was in the hell of a lather, though. Keep on along the same old everlasting stretch. Turn left, second right, and she would be 'home': Vidlers' back room with use of kitchen and cons. Fry herself a couple of eggs. Women are lucky: they can live on eggs if need be. And cheese. And chocolate. Then a long hot bath if the system wasn't playing up. She enjoyed her sleep: couldn't get enough of it;

and dreams. Sometimes she tried to choose her dreams. She would try to dream about Sir Basil Hunter.

At 26 Gladys Street decency prevailed: the dwarf shrubs pruned to shapes in their green concrete surrounds; the composition path, which Mrs Vidler scrubbed and mopped all the way from gate to doorstep; the letter-box poised at the top of a stiffened chain (Mr Vidler, a handyman at all times, had his artistic side). Sister Manhood rooted around in her bag for the key. What if she had lost it? It wouldn't matter all that much: Mr Vidler would let her in, into her own room, with its airless cleanliness, and lounge you converted into a bed. Mr Vidler would say, *no trouble at all, Flo—just as if you was our own daughter.* Mr Vidler was 'Vid', Mrs Vidler 'Viddie': they were such mates.

Because kindliness can suffocate, Sister Manhood went away, back along the composition path, past the letter-box standing on its stiffened chain. She wasn't going to Col's, though. She would muck around for a bit. None of Col's old chops and grease under your fingernails. *If you wash the grill Flo soon as it cools off you won't notice you're doing it—not like if the fat sets.* Oh, yeah? This was the kind of decisive moment which always slipped away from her: it left her elbow-deep in grey water washing up Col's greasy old grill, while Col played Mahler at her, or read out from some intellectual magazine opinions which confirmed his own. Then when you had hung out the damp, stinking towels, and you were what Col liked to call 'mooded' by the music, he would make 'love', he referred to it; and though you too, recognized it as such, you couldn't very well have admitted. Love as she tried, but failed to imagine, couldn't be so easy and cheap, or smelling of mutton fat and sweat.

Col once read her thoughts and said, *what if I've planted a baby in you Flo that'll give us something for real.* She downright panicked; she tried to remember how regular she had been with the pill; she couldn't.

Tonight she panicked, not for that reason, but for trying to come to the end of this street of deadly dolls'-houses, all painted up in emulation of one another, and behind their faces, either suffocating kindliness, or variations on her own theme of chaos. So her feet slapped the pavement. She almost broke her neck to reach the Parade: where a couple of blocks down she could read PHARMACY in crimson. She half expected to smell the chops he must have charred by now, for reading What's-his-name — Oonermooner, or some equally unreadable nut.

Flora Manhood crossed the Parade. She would go to Snow's; it was surprising she hadn't thought of it before. There was every reason why she should come to this decision: *my cousin Mrs Hunter my only relative left has asked me to share her flat I only have to make up my mind Snow Tunks a bus conductress.* Snow could be the answer: as good as a man without the disadvantages.

Flora Manhood went spanking through the night towards 'Miami Flats' where her cousin Snow hung out. There was nothing to recommend the street, except its convenience: close to the bus, the delicatessen — and the chemist. 'Miami's' barley-sugar columns were peeling; one of them had cracked; something, probably a runaway truck, had cannoned off a corner of the building and played hell with the roughcast. Just at the entrance a fluorescent light sat spitting at the top of its pole, so that all the potplants in the hanging gardens of 'Miami' were flickering sickeningly.

But Flora Manhood was almost puking with relief: she might have been walking through the steady white glare, like in the old days, along the road which ran between the banana farms. Snow, an older girl, told how *Ken Mathews asked me to go steady but you're the one Florrie I'll always love.* It tickled Flora. Not that she hadn't been, and still was in a way, fond. It was sort of comforting, close and easy, being cousins. But funny. Ken Mathews must have been simple or something to want Snow as a steady date. Even went into Coff's Harbour and bought her a diamond baguette ring. While other boys were laughing: she was growing muscles instead of tits. Had white hair as far back as you were able to remember. Certainly Snow was strong: Uncle's best hand about the place; no man, Uncle said, would ever regret his investment.

Helped Auntie Ol too, with the goats; the boys at the Saturday dance said you could smell the buck on Snow. (What would Mrs Hunter make of that?) Then Snowy decided to leave. In spite of the baguette ring she said Ken Mathews was unnatural. She was going to the city to find a job. She did. She became a bus conductress.

Though it was planned you should do nursing, so as to better yourself in life and perhaps get a doctor or other professional man for a husband, it couldn't be for some years yet. Snow went first seeing she was that much older. The night before she left you clung together and snivelled a bit; you had never been closer. Because she was tense, Snow pressed her hard body in between your thighs, her flat tits against the beginnings of your cushiony ones, while the moonlight was rustling between the rows of bananas, and the bandicoots went *frrt-frrt*. You had a cry, because the future was too enormous to grasp, and the bandicoots would still be making their farting noise in the country around Coff's Harbour long after Snow, or yourself even, had left.

There was no lift at 'Miami' and the several flights of steps had a look of brawn. On one landing the smell of gas was so intense it added to Flora Manhood's expectations: though she had never liked the idea of mouth to mouth resuscitation, being cousins could make it emotional, not to say heroic.

The flat was a small one and Snow appeared soon after you rang the bell, after she had squeezed aside a pleated curtain and tried to see through the frosted glass.

'Bugger *me*! Thought you must be dead, Florrie.' Snow stood holding open the stained pitch pine door.

Flora Manhood felt irritated. 'If I was dead you would have been notified. Haven't I named you as my next of kin?'

Snow laughed, and something—it was the fumes of gin—shot out of her. 'That's correct. Arr dear, it's lovely to see yer, love.'

All the while Snow Tunks was narrowing her eyes and smiling at her cousin Flora Manhood; it irritated Flora worse, when she had wanted to feel warm. But here were the white lashes, the blast of gin, and Snow's stomach sticking out, which she had eased by unzipping a hip since she came off duty from the depot.

Still, you had to come up with an explanation. 'It's a long time, Snow, I know. But I'm tired out with this case—this old tartar of a woman. I often think about you, though.' All considered, it was a necessary lie.

They were passing under the pink-beaded lampshade, with the same fly shit on it, and along the narrow, pitch pine and parchment hall.

'Arr dear,' Snow said, 'I reckon we oughter incinerate the old folks. What can they get out of it? You and me can't complain, Florrie—all of ours passing on.'

Flora Manhood hadn't come about death; she decided to hurry things and put the question. 'I've been wondering about the proposition—that suggestion you made—Snow—that I move in and share the flat. Does it still stand?'

Snow sort of burped.

Flora Manhood said, 'A person can't make up her mind without giving a matter thought.'

They had reached the back, the kitchen, and its other half, the dinette, its benches upholstered in a floral cretonne which might have looked brighter before the grease got worked in.

'You never ever gave me to understand you were so much as thinking of it,' said Snow. 'And now there's my friend Alix. Alix was sold on the idea from the start. She'll be home any moment.' Snow looked at her wrist. 'She's a sales-lady—at Parker's in the lonjeray.' Again Snow looked at her wrist, freckled either side of the watch strap.

She poured a drink for her cousin, who didn't go much on gin, but explored its shifting, blue glaze with extended, pink lip.

Flora knew by now she couldn't have stood her cousin's white-lashed lids, her protruding stomach, or her unzipped hip. Snow was sitting, knees apart, like a man sits, the cigarette hanging from the skin of her mouth. She had let herself go all right; you couldn't remember any such crude deportment in the old days at home, or even more recently, after she got with the public transport. On top of everything else, you felt that Snow was probably jealous, not as a man, which is bad enough, but something left over from being born a woman.

As they continued sitting on the cretonned bench, Flora said, 'I wouldn't want to butt in, Snow, on anybody'; testing the blue gin with her lip.

'Well, I realize that,' said Snow, looking up and down your wrists, your arms, your thighs—made you pull your skirt down—into the past perhaps, amongst the bananas, along the white road at home.

'This Alix,' Flora asked, 'is she a close—an old friend.'

'Well, she's close. I can't say she's *old*.'

'I mean, you've known each other a long time.'

'A coupler weeks.'

'No, you can't call that old.' Flora was determined not to show she was griped.

While Snow grumbled, 'You've gotter begin somewhere, haven't yer?'

They sat listening to the fridge. Snow was probably lit, from waiting for Alix who was late. Said Alix was first in as a rule, and put the tea on: that was what they were used to.

Flora Manhood wondered whether she would be able to submit to Snow if Alix didn't last a second fortnight. At least you came off duty too late to be expected to get the tea.

Just then they heard a key feeling its way inside a lock.

Snow laughed; her pleasure brought her out in strawberry blotches. 'That's her now,' she said.

Alix was a clotted-creamy woman, with the necklaces of Venus, and black hair built up high, which made her look taller than she was.

'Alix is late, Butch,' she explained unnecessarily. 'But I know you'll forgive her, won't you, love?'

Alix was less interested in Snow's forgiveness than in someone she hadn't been asked to meet; her eyelids, heavy with a load of shadow, or alcohol, were lowered specially for the stranger.

Snow had decided on manliness. 'We're not gunner chew the rag all night over why you was late and nothing in the pot, because here's my cousin Florrie Manhood dropped in as a surprise like.'

'Oh, rurlly? You didn't tell me you had a cousin. Or did you, Butch?' Alix put on what she understood as a smile, and approached the gin by little steps. 'Is she in business?' she asked, squinting at the bottle.

'Florrie's a fully trained nursing sister.'

'*Rurlly?* Perhaps she'll give us some free advice.'

Although she had already drunk, Alix was still thirsty; when she recovered her breath she asked, 'Which hospital do you favour, Sister *Manhood?*' looking down her own cleavage.

Flora explained, while feeling too sober and too cool, that she was nursing privately at present.

'That would be more in my line—Florrie, did Butch say? Only exclusive homes of course. I believe the loot is *incredible* if you know how to pick your cases.'

Alix was staring with such concentrated intensity, not at the prospects of private nursing, but into what she must have decided was the innermost Flora Manhood, that Flora looked to Snow to take her part; but her cousin had moved down the kitchen end of the kitchen, and was slinging the pots around. And chops—yes, chops.

A silence had fallen, outside the fridge and other kitchen noises, when Alix addressed Snow. 'Isn't she pretty, Snowy? Your little coz. Sweet.'

But Snow either didn't hear, or wasn't going to, and Alix, after she had tiptoed back towards the bottle, went and started rubbing up against her friend.

'You're not cranky with me, Butch, just because I wasn't on the dot? *Darl?*'

Though Alix was rubbing up and down against Snow's backview like a grater on a lump of cheese, Snow continued peeling a potato, holding it well away from her.

183

Finally she asked, 'Who wasut, I'd liketer know?'

'Not what you think.' Alix sighed into her glass. 'It was a gentleman.'

'Those bloody two-ball screwballs!'

'A buyer,' Alix extenuated, smoothing the black sateen over rather plump hips. 'You've got to stay the right side of the buyers.'

'Which side?' Snow hollered out of the corner of her mouth.

Alix said darl how could she, and soon afterwards Snow put down that long-distance potato; she turned and started kneading Alix, who submitted to the bumpy going.

Suddenly Snow remembered. ''Ere, we're forgettun the guest!' she shouted.

She poured her cousin a snifter, which Flora at once recognized as a snorter.

'She's pretty — your cousin,' Alix repeated, and sighed. 'Chawming.' She gargled a few notes. 'I think she's probably sensitive.'

Flora drank the gin because she had nothing else to do, except explore her own thoughts. These were occupied, she soon realized, almost exclusively by Col Pardoe: she saw him emptying the spittle out of the bowl of his stinking pipe; she saw that particular mole above the line of his pubic hair. By the time she could smell the chops Snow must have thrown on the grill, she had conjured Col into this kitchenful of drunken women. Seeing what would disgust him most, she began twisting in and out Snow and Alix. The woman shrieked; they loved it; they just on shot their hips out in imitation of a rumba from one of those old movies they drag up on the box; and as they pranced and wagged their bums they began to make a play for Snow's cousin Florrie Manhood. While Col's image, the mouth which in her weaker moments she liked to think of as 'strong', writhed for the obscenities he was being made to witness.

She'd teach Col.

Alix thought she had got hold of a breast, but what she caught was a handful of air; she almost fell over.

'Oh, *rurlly!*' Flora Manhood sang, 'Don't say it's chops — my favourite *cutt* – of murr-*heat*!' Then she went and sat down because the other two were so shickered it was no longer fun, toppling and giggling as they were from stored alcohol.

Only when the chops began to burn, and she smelt it, Snow brought them to the dinette. She had forgotten about potatoes, it seemed. The one she had peeled was turning brown on the draining surface beside the sink.

Snow said, 'I always think it makes a chop tastier to eat it with the fingers – like in the outdoors.'

Alix agreed through her opening mouthful. She was less a lady with a chop. Some of the fat had drizzled down her saleswoman's sateen. Her blue eyelids, hanging heavy like some old parrot's, confessed their wrinkles.

The company sat mumbling its chops, Snow and Alix as part of a necessary exercise after gin, Flora because she was young and hungry.

When she had licked her fingers, and no pud seemed forthcoming, she asked, 'What about the washing up?' as though it was her most natural function: the people who take you for granted are the ones who put you against things.

Alix sniggered close to the bone she was tidying, while Snow pronounced through a shower of shredded mutton, 'Never terday what yer can termorrer! Don't yer remember that, Florrie, from Banana Land?'

Alix added, 'It's easier after the fat's hardened.'

Flora snorted; she was so glad for what she was hearing, though melancholy in the end that these women should know better than Col. She noticed Snow's nails, bitten to the quick, and Alix's long, overhanging pearlshell ones; Col pared his nails to his broad blunt fingertips. (Though she would never have admitted, Flora Manhood was fascinated watching Col's blunt fingers perform unexceptional acts.)

Snow was yawning now, which made her look like a money-box, while Alix was inclined to hide her yawns in crumpled smiles. Flora herself suddenly felt a dead weight descending on her, from

Snow's snorter no doubt, followed by the hot meat. Her homelessness struck her afresh, since she couldn't face Vidlers' convertible lounge, any more than Col's possessive single. What she visualized, she dismissed almost at once, because it wasn't warm of her: she saw Mrs Hunter's great bed after the undertakers had been; she saw herself waking in its acres as the sun struck through the curtains, and Lottie Lippmann standing with breakfast on a tray.

Instead it was Snow Tunks saying, 'Early bed for working girls.'

And old Alix grimacing and asking, 'Is your cousin with us for the night?'

Since you had turned down the offer of a permanent lodging, perhaps Snow hadn't contemplated that, but jerked or burped at the suggestion. 'Nobody ever knew what Flora intends.'

Flora played for cautious. 'I could doss down here,' she said, 'if it was convenient;' patting the grease-stained cretonne.

The two friends looked at each other. 'We wouldn't expect *that*!' Snow was sentimentally reproachful.

Then they entwined themselves around the third party, and bumped their way as far as a black gulf which shot into light and became a bedroom.

Snow said, 'You can't always find the time of a mornun not even to pull the bedclothes up,' as she ruffled up the pillows and smoothed a sheet.

Alix giggled. 'Most nursing sisters can't see an unmade bed and resist making it,' she regurgitated before falling over on the one that offered.

Flora mumbled she had always found it resistible.

They were all three getting out of their clothes: Snow, that white gollywog; Alix riding a bicycle out of her black sateen; Flora, on account of what she had observed, kept her bra and panties on. Snow must have got through life without taking a look at the glass, but Alix would have liked to hide bits of herself, only she hadn't enough arms. Then they were pulling you down to be the ham in their sandwich. The two women flapping around, one white and the other black, reminded Flora of hens half paralysed by ticks.

After Snow had yanked the string which brought darkness down on them, the women became more frantic, and would have been united in a single aim if the drink hadn't sided with Flora Manhood: the drowsy dark blurred the ambitions of the two friends as well as affecting their sense of direction.

Half strangled chewed nuzzled Flora recovered enough of her wits to know she did not belong to this community of seething flesh. She managed to defect and stumble by the light of the spitting fluorescence in the street, as far as the window and what she remembered as an armchair. She flopped, but first had to jettison a well-heeled shoe buried in the nest of anonymous garments in which she finally settled to enjoy her independence. By comparison it was delicious and unlimited.

Snow's voice rose once out of the straining and muffled mumping on the bed. 'Watch out, Someone! Florrie? Alix! Those flamun nails of yours! Watcher take me for—a joint?'

'You know you always tole me, darl, I'm the most professional carver.'

'Carla Who?'

The flickering fluorescence was developing other pictures on the inside of Flora Manhood's eyelids.

'Eh? What about Carla? It wasn't that bloody buyer, then. It was Carla Abrams! Alix? Wasut?'

It will probably be a professional man a surgeon is more temperamental when you give away this private jazz dust down your ideals and go back to P.A. as theatre sister best for surgeons only counting the swabs puts the wind up you at times can't concentrate on the surgeon for concentrating on the count Sir Sir Archibald Humphrey no Valentine never knew a Valentine except the ones Col sends a black Daimler Jags are too common for Lady Valentine Parr *Parbury* not sit close riding to Admiralty House by air to seminars at Kuala Lumpur Delhi San Francisco all university men medical diplomats Prince Philip has his eye on *Lady Valentine Whatever in skinthin sheath of black leather yes the perfume is Shared Secret my husband adores it yes we are exhausted what with the seminars swab* counting the many responsibilities of diction deportment French archaeology there really isn't time except in the soundproof Daimler to discuss personal problems and for Sir Valentine to only very very occasionally put his hand under the rug.

Flora Manhood had to shift her dead arm. Her throat had dried. From 'Miami Flats' you could just see the fiery furnace blazing down Botany way. Those women on the bed must have reached a compromise the right side of sleep. They were all sighs as they were sucked under. Flora too.

Flora? Yes, Sir Basil. Not Sir Archibald Humphrey Valentine Whatever it's Basil Hunter you're after how could you have ever forgot remember quick the details you hardly had time for the peppersalt eyebrows meeting over what colour the biggest watch crocodile strap flattening hairs a vein suit you can tell the very best crumpled a bit up the back from sitting in a plane tie woven for winter everyone looks wrong who arrives out of the air *don't you remember your lines Flora* you can't neither lines nor anything important only the superfluous *superficial that's what I am* a swab count never chilled worse than the expression in Basil Hunter's eyes *do you think I'll learn the part Basil* so bad an actress in bra and panties too Mother Hunter would have booed you off the stage if she wasn't a lady as for Sir her son *if I teach you the technique Flora the rest is in you* coming at you bigger than the ad on a hoarding then bending down to part to look inside you for something no no you can't they're there all right all the children and none of them his pouring out and around he must recognize you are not the actress but acted on by all these children unlabelled uncounted warm and overpowering any reason you may find to offer.

Flora Manhood awoke to greylight and a street full of skittled milk bottles. She had been dreaming of what she wouldn't bother herself to remember though a bitterness made her suspect Col Pardoe was behind it.

Col or not, she must end by every means the goose chase with Snow and Alix: it was her worst madness to date. Snow was lying on her back, her gollywog mouth desperate for air, her stomach, with an old scar, rising and falling, but sluggishly. Alix, her curdled throat exposed, her flesh unsorted, would probably have settled for murder as the next best thing to love.

Having covered her bra and panties Flora Manhood slipped away very easily; she didn't even bother about her hair though she carried a comb in her bag. Outside 'Miami Flats' the street was looking extra livid: the fluorescence had not yet been switched off to accommodate the light of morning. She walked briskly, but suspiciously, as though expecting to skid on something: one of the empty milk bottles left to roll in the gritty shallows. Crossing the Parade she avoided glancing to the right because of the PHARMACY sign, and soon afterwards arrived at 26 Gladys Street, where Mrs Vidler was scrubbing the step.

She looked up: a large brown-skinned woman with suds to halfway up her arms. 'Vid and I might worry about you, love, if we thought there was any cause for it.'

'For all you know, I could have been prostituting myself with a G.I. at the Cross.' Flora Manhood was that exasperated she added for good measure, 'A Negro.'

Viddie laughed for the joke. 'Mr Pardoe called and left a message.'

'What message?' She could hardly bear it.

'Vid put it in yer room.'

Flora went in, and there was the envelope, exactly in the centre of the Vidlers' cleanly table.

She wouldn't open it at once, but did sooner than she intended, because what was the use?

Dear Flo,
    You can only misunderstand me. I honestly love you.
                                                    COL

Flora Manhood sat a while on the edge of the convertible lounge, her trembling fingers shielding her eyes from the gun which was neverendingly, inescapably, pointed at her.

Five

As she was rushed back from the depths of sleep in which she was being rolled and ground, and laid once more amongst the soft crests of comparatively placid sheets, Mrs Hunter became aware that something—some kind of transformation—had taken place at the foot of the bed. In the blur which the shaded light and mirrors made of her rudimentary vision, somebody was dwarfed.

'Sister de Santis—' she realized, 'what has happened? You're not kneeling, are you?'

The nurse gasped; you could see her veiled head shaken like a great white—not lily—Canterbury bell. 'I was looking for a pin I dropped.'

'Take care. I can remember a child—I believe it was one of the Nutleys—she knelt on a needle. It disappeared into her knee, and was lost in the flesh for weeks. One day they noticed a black speck on the skin, and drew out the needle with a magnet.'

The nurse said, 'This was a safety pin, Mrs Hunter'; and began getting up off her knees.

You couldn't believe in the safety pin. She hadn't been praying for you, surely? For that thing your soul; or an easy death. Extraordinary the number of people who insist that death must be painless and easy when it ought to be the highest, the most difficult peak of all: that is its whole point.

'Now that you're awake I might as well rub your back.' The nurse was laying a false trail.

'Don't invent unnecessary jobs.'

Because she had been caught out, the answer sounded stifled. 'I was only thinking of your comfort.'

'You can take out my teeth at least. You forgot my teeth. I don't wonder. So many visitors appearing—I might need them at any

190

moment. On the other hand, I don't want to lose them in my sleep.'

When she had carried off the teeth the nurse returned to repair the bed. Such a token raft, it didn't seem worth the trouble. But you could tell she was glad of the job. Sister de Santis must have been praying, not for you, but for herself, while she was kneeling at the foot of the bed.

The veil, as it swept back and forth, was so sharp it almost cut your skin open, while reminding, '*Campanula* is the botanical name.'

'For what?'

' "Canterbury bell" of course.'

'Oh, yes? They're pretty, aren't they?'

'They never appealed to me much. I was drawn to the more spectacular flowers.' She laughed. 'My enemies – and some of my friends – have called me an egoist – so other friends and enemies tell me.'

The nurse was trying to think of something kind but truthful to offer as consolation when she needn't have bothered.

'Lal Wyburd was the one for botanical names. They seemed to give her the feeling of superiority she needed. "Aren't you partial to an *Astilbe*? So feathery – delicate – but comical. Its common name, I believe, is goatsbeard." ' Mrs Hunter's laughter was wickeder for the rictus from which it issued. ' "The great tragedy of my life is that I haven't succeeded in growing *Mimulus* at Double Bay." Poor lucky Lal never to have had a tragedy!'

'You'll wake yourself up if you talk too much.'

'Don't worry. Sleep is what will wake me up.'

The nurse was adjusting the shade as though afraid the lamp might illuminate. Then she began to tiptoe out of the room. Silly girl: anybody on tiptoe lacks a sense of unbalance.

But the teeth you were glad without already drowning as you sink down horrid when sand gets under the false gums horrid teeth oh it is tiring yawnful the comforting true gums suck and gulp their way along the bottom of the sea nobody to want anything not love not money or illumination tell me the answer what it means tell me that you love me all that silly tiptoeing around you wait for answers to flow in quietly illuminating from the inside not if it is too rough sleep too can quench the light *the fire can't you make it up Betty my feet are can't you bring in another log bring me my dispatch case Betty we'll burn the letters together the love-letters they're too personal don't you think yes Alfred if that is what you wish burn all letters I agree* you don't the bottom of the sea is littered with old unburnt sodden letters the letter you have always kept of all letters it was so cruel untrue Dr Treweek's never liked him well he didn't like you you can't expect only Christians love their detractors an exercise in masochism *nobody can ever call me a masochist no you are right there Mrs Hunter Bill wouldn't have married you if you hadn't known how to use the whiphandle on his devotion.*

Oh the dreams with which the bottom of the sea is littered not always sodden like the old letters they will stand up in coral columns in whole cupolas and archways and long sculptural perspectives to confront entice you in where the daylight is solid and the expression in his eyes at that time perhaps the first clue I ever had to what is transcendent.

She was standing in the bow window at the end of the drawing-room at Moreton Drive, in that kind of light which can make a dream more convincing than life. Only she was awake. She was standing by the revolving bookcase, looking out over the park as she opened the letter they had brought her. (Miss Thormber had been admiring your hands while doing your nails. It was not a luxury bringing a manicurist to the house, more a charity: something had to be done about Miss Thormber, a hopeless manicurist – but an expert in flattery; therein could have lain the luxury.)

Elizabeth Hunter opened the letter, probably a tiresome one, and began to read, holding the indifferent paper at a casual distance:

Dear Mrs Hunter,

I am writing this letter against the wishes of one of those concerned, and realizing that what I have to say may be unforgivably distasteful to a second person ...

She flipped over the page to see that it was from Dr Treweek of Gogong, an unattractive elderly man with dandruff on his coat collar, and a habit of breaking wind regardless of who was present. What Dr Treweek had to say would undoubtedly be distasteful; at least she was on her guard against it.

... Briefly, I have to inform you that Bill is suffering from cancer of the liver, and is unlikely to last many months. This was established on a recent visit to a specialist in Sydney, of which you are unaware, as your husband's chief concern in life is not to cause others distress. I have strongly advised him to let me arrange for his admission to a hospital in the city, but his present intention is to see his illness out at 'Kudjeri'. Even with a nurse in attendance, and at present he refuses to have one, this will create difficulties, as perhaps you can imagine. The housekeeper is in a state of nerves, and may easily pack her traps rather than accept responsibility for an incurable invalid.

There you have the situation. Whether you are conscious of your husband's selflessness, any more than his stubbornness, I cannot tell, but *as you are his wife* it is up to you to make several important decisions. (Sorry if you can't forgive me for throwing such an unexpected bomb!)

Yrs truly
ROBERT TREWEEK

As it burst around her, distorting the view of the park, tingling in pins and needles down her limbs, and with particular violence in the freshly manicured hands with which she held the offensive letter (how had he dared underline the 'wife'!) she couldn't easily, perhaps never, forgive Robert Treweek. In the first surge of her rage and horror she almost went so far as to hold him responsible for Alfred's condition. At the mercy of a country physician! The physician no doubt would draw attention to the patient's neglect of himself (through selflessness, desire not to cause distress, etc.) to disguise his own ignorance and negligence.

So at first she could not weep, for anger, and because the charming

193

filigree of her life had been hammered without warning into an ugly, patternless entanglement.

Till she did begin to cry. She could only remember Alfred's hurt, never the joyful, expressions of his face. Not their affection for each other, only her ill-natured dismissal of some of his more tender advances. Lying on her unshared bed, the freedom of which she had so often told herself she enjoyed, she tried to recover her normal capacity for making up her mind. Unable to do so, she was glad of Dr Treweek's image, to match her rage against the explosion of his bomb.

Then, as the afternoon advanced, she exorcised her grief simply by letting it pour out. It seemed as though nothing would remain of herself, who had failed to recognize this gentle man her husband.

As light as unlikely probably as painful as a shark's egg the old not body rather the flimsy soul is whirled around sometimes spat out anus-upward (souls have an anus they are never allowed to forget it) never separated from the brown the sometimes tinted spawn of snapshots the withered navel string still stuck to what it aspires to yes at last to be if the past the dream life will allow.

Suddenly Mrs Hunter was leaving for 'Kudjeri'. Herself packed the crocodile dressing-case (tearing one of her nails on a hasp) as well as a larger bag, for what kind of visit she did not stop to think, only that she had to go. Nor could she give the maids any indication how long she would be away from home; she would ask Mr Wyburd to pay them weekly if she continued absent. She did not send for Lennox — it was late — but rang for a taxi to drive her to the station.

Throughout the train journey she sat pressed into her corner of the empty compartment. She felt cramped with cold, while unable to make the effort to raise a half-lowered window. The upholstery smelt of tunnels and night. She saw she had forgotten her gloves, and that the hands Miss Thormber had admired that morning were wearing a superfluity of rings.

It was again morning, though still only the dead of it, when she arrived at Gogong, at the Imperial Hotel. While she tried to rouse someone, she became increasingly aware of her own superfluousness. On the other hand, Hagerty the publican, as soon as he had recovered from his first annoyance, was impressed by the arrival of Mrs Hunter, of all people. He offered to run her out, there and then, to 'Kudjeri'. She said she would take a room at the hotel, and hire a car in the morning: she didn't want to upset her husband's housekeeper by fetching her down in her nightdress.

The remainder of those white hours trickled like sand under her eyelids as she lay between the rough sheets and tried to accept the small part she played in existence. A cock, a dog, and the moon were the major characters, it seemed. Till a cockatoo, evidently left uncovered, united its screeches with the crowing and barking. A man was cursing as he first muffled, then silenced, the cockatoo. Slippers slopped across the yard. There was the sound of somebody making water against stone.

She may have slept an instant. And did not really wake till the hire-car was approaching 'Kudjeri', her husband's property, never hers, though for some years her automaton had run his house and given orders for the rearing of his children. If she belonged at all in the district, it was from living as a little girl at Salkelds' rundown place. So she did belong: as inevitably as the brown river flowing beneath willows, as her own blood running through her veins. So she had to respond at last to these hidden jewels of hills. The same sun, re-discovering fire in dew and rock, was drawing tears and bedazzled acceptance from frozen eyes.

Too soon the car was crunching on the drive, bruising the laurels, swirling round the oval rose-bed in front of the house. Alfred had come out and was standing at the foot of the veranda steps, as though by appointment. At least he did not *appear* surprised, only so much thinner, smaller, than she remembered. She had to stoop, she found, to embrace her husband. This, and the hire-car man's abrupt departure, gave their relationship a special significance: they must have looked like lovers locked in one of the conventional attitudes of passion; whereas she knew by her own diffidence, and the response of her frail 'lover', each of them only wanted to comfort the other's spirit. Whether they would be given time or grace, remained to be seen.

Alfred said, 'It's the best month of the year at "Kudjeri";' as though this were her first visit.

'Oh, there'll be all the months, if you let me stay.'

As a man he was trying to pick up the larger of the two bags, and found he no longer could. Instead of going into the house, leaving the luggage to the groom, as would have happened normally, they began struggling, panting, for possession of the handle, converting a minor into a major issue; they needed to. By the time she had got control they were saved: Alfred must have decided he would not degrade himself morally by carrying the smaller dressing-case; she would lug the larger bag up the steps if it tore her side open.

Opening still on special feast days for Sister de Santis to put her hand in and touch the remains even that most unregenerate non-nun Sister Flora Pudenda is reconciled to a relic only it is not mine it is Alfred's whose liver is recommended worship remember any stench is sanctity the odour of each time a panful I lie again if I'm lucky in the arms of my DEAR LORD whose strength increases as he weakens I the guilty I will never be eaten away never purged because sin won't come out in the bedpan like what the walls call shit I like Kleenex best Sister it's softer and some nuns are heavy handed send for St Mary de Kleenex funny how the sinless overlook the stains understand the insufferable sins which can't escape or perhaps no one is sinless otherwise how would the night nurse get through her nights.

In spite of his autumnal complexion and the altered, more refined structure of his face, the first days were like a convalescence rather than an illness. Or perhaps that was how she wanted to see it. Alfred himself never referred to his condition in her presence.

Twice a week the doctor came out from Gogong. He was never

without a sleepless, often a glazed look. He drove himself to such an extent she sometimes wondered whether it was without assistance.

Once as she approached the pantry where he was sterilizing a syringe, she heard voices. Eldred the groom must have come in, and was addressing the doctor with an unashamed callousness, 'If you don't mind my saying so, Doc, you look like the ghost that wasn't laid.'

Dr Treweek was squirting the syringe at the ceiling as she reached the doorway. 'Not laid, but near enough,' he admitted. 'I feel just about fucked, Eldred.'

The groom looked shocked to see the mistress, and made his getaway.

She could not conceal from the doctor what was a mixture of dislike, apprehension, and petulance. 'Is the pain increasing, then?'

'Yes.' He sawed at a capsule till its neck broke. 'I'm going to show you how to give the needle. He'll probably want it more regularly now. If he seems real bad, you can ring me and I'll come out, but I'm nearly run off my feet as it is.' His contempt for her was obvious.

'I'm sure I can manage on my own,' she replied as coldly as she could; 'if you'll show me.' She was looking down her nose from under her lowered eyelids, but the effect was wasted because Dr Treweek had turned his back.

When he had filled the syringe, she followed him into the bedroom, where Alfred was lying waiting. He had a mysterious greedy expression which excluded her from the rite the doctor was about to perform. Even so, she was determined to help: she pulled down the pyjama pants over the wasted buttock, and only trembled on catching sight of the slender testicles, the blue head of the shrivelled penis.

'There we are,' said Dr Treweek.

'What—not now?' He thrust the hypodermic at her, when she hadn't bargained for it this side of some very vague interval of time.

As he explained the technique she stood holding the evil weapon she was expected to drive into her husband's flesh. Resistance to the whole idea almost made her vomit.

'Fire away!' the doctor commanded. 'If you're honest, I expect you've done worse in your time.' He laughed through what must have been phlegm.

Because of the truth in his remark she couldn't feel injured. But plunged the needle.

The doctor said, 'You'll make an expert, Mrs Hunter.'

While she withdrew the needle under cover of the wad of cotton wool, Alfred was lying, eyes closed, throat working, mouth relaxed in advance of relief: he might have experienced the perfect orgasm.

Then the doctor changed his tactics, his voice, bent down over his patient, and touched the sweat-stained pyjama shoulder. 'You'll be feeling better now, old feller.' It sounded as though he was speaking through a megaphone.

Again Mrs Hunter was excluded; till Alfred gasped in an unrecognizable voice, 'Thank you—Elizabeth.'

She asked the doctor, 'May I give you some lunch before the drive back?'

He accepted, and she served him herself, with a dish of spiced beef and salad, afterwards leaving him to it. Several rooms away she heard him belch, and as she was seeing him off, withstood the metallic blast of the pickled onions he had devoured too hastily.

'Don't hesitate to ring me,' he reminded while settling himself in his car. 'I'd do anything for old Bill.'

As the doctor predicted, she became adept at giving the injection, but all this was only later, after the 'convalescence' period of Alfred Hunter's fatal illness.

In the beginning they enjoyed this sere honeymoon of the hopeful spirit. They were full of consideration for each other, and hungrily discussed everyday matters in minutest detail.

'Send for Stanilands, Betty, in the morning. I'd like to ask him whether he thinks we could use Kilgallen. Still immature, I know, but a fine ram in the making. I'd be interested to see his progeny— if that will be possible.' At this first hint that it might not be, he began wriggling his neck inside the collar which had grown too large for him, and twitching at one corner of his mouth.

She brought him a pear she had specially picked; taking it from its muslin bag, she stood holding this enormous, perfect, golden fruit humbly in her two hands. 'Do you feel tempted? Let me peel it for you at least, so that you can enjoy the perfume.'

He agreed to that, and because he loved her, allowed her to feed him slivers which he tried to swallow, while the juice ran down amongst the stubble on his chin.

She coaxed Eldred to shave her patient. Alfred liked him; he had mentioned naming the groom's family in his will. She too, was revived by the man's presence, one of physical strength and health, none the worse for sometimes bringing with it smells of the stable, or of milk from the house cows in his charge.

Do you like ... ? was one of the games she and Alfred played. It was shameful how little they knew about each other, at least those childish tastes to which they confessed; if their honesty did not cut deeper, it was because the knife could not have prolonged their relationship: better to cherish surfaces in the time left to them.

Now that it was late autumn the evenings were what they most looked forward to. 'Ask Eldred to bring in another log before he goes down to the cottage.' After the groom had built up the fire and taken his leave, they would look through books together.

'What a funny old thing you are! To have been collecting this hoard of books over the years and kept so quiet about it!'

'You've never been interested in books.'

It was true; it had suited her purposes to adopt the opinion that to read is to live at second hand.

Now she could only murmur, 'I've read myself to sleep night after night. I'd say Goethe is my most effective pill.' She made a wry face to match her trumped-up explanation; farther than that she didn't go; nor did his kindness let him force her into an admission of frivolous tastes.

In fact, from the anxious way he immediately shifted his position, he seemed to fear she might have sensed a criticism he had not intended to offer. 'You had your life to live. It's different in the country – when you're on your own.' It was the bitterest reproach he had made: in one instant she experienced interminable nights aching with frost and silence.

She was looking through a book of French engravings and lithographs. Added to Alfred's remark, the artist's insistence on death, his marsh flowers, and detached, blandly staring eyeballs made her material self seem even more trivial and ephemeral. She quickly turned the pages to escape her unwilling fascination by reaching the end of the book; when she became spellbound by the artist's image of what he called a skiapod: not her own actual face, but the spiritual semblance which will sometimes float out of the looking-glass of the unconscious. Unlike most of the other monsters in the book, this half-fish half-woman appeared neither allied to, nor threatened by, death: too elusive in weaving through deep waters, her expression a practically effaced mystery; or was it one of dishonesty, of cunning?

'What are you looking at?' Alfred asked.

'Glimpses of the morbid mind of Odilon Redon.' She made this attempt at complacency as she snapped the book together.

He loved her to read to him. They were halfway through *The Charterhouse of Parma*, which he admired, he said, 'almost more than anything else'. Her own pleasure in it was sometimes lost in its longueurs, but she improved on those by listening to the sound of her own voice: when she made the effort, she read well.

That night Alfred began staring at her in what appeared like suddenly feverish, hitherto unrealized, admiration. 'Isn't she splendid?' he interrupted. 'What a dazzler of a woman—the Sanseverina!'

'A bit female at times.' If her voice sounded dry, it was from the length of time she had spent reading aloud.

'Womanly women don't much care for one another, I suppose.'

She herself certainly had never counted overmuch on her women friends. 'There's something else—a kind of freemasonry which brings them together, and they feel they must obey some of the rules.'

He laughed: they were united in a moment of such understanding she went and knelt beside his chair and started desperately kissing his hands. It was as close as they came to physical desire during those last weeks. But the hands remained cold and yellow.

Shortly after, he said, 'If you don't mind, Bet—you'll have to give me a shot tonight.'

As his strength left him, Eldred would carry him down to his chair in the library. Still later in his decline, she would call the groom to lift him out of or into his bed, till the day she discovered she could manage this bundle of dwindling flesh herself.

At once their relationship changed. Where she had loved, now she pitied. It was not pity in the ordinary sense, but an emotional need to merge herself with this child who might have sprung in the beginning from her body, by performing for him all the more sordid menial acts: tenderly wiping, whether faeces, or the liquid foods he mostly vomited back. Sometimes in the dependency of this new relationship she thought of her actual children: she had never felt pity for those, walled up in themselves, armed for emergencies with formidable moral weapons. But perhaps she had been wrong: they may have needed her pity; she might have earned their love.

On a day of steely, straight rain, she was forced to approach a subject Alfred was determined to avoid. 'Surely now you should allow me to write and tell the children?'

'I don't want to disrupt their lives.'

'If, when you go, they haven't been told, they may resent it terribly.' Of course she could not truthfully answer for their children, only for herself, the remorse boiling up in her.

Whatever Alfred's wishes, she took it upon herself to write.

Dorothy, in the grip of her unhappy marriage, replied in a translation from the French:

My dearest Father,
    You can imagine my feelings on receiving this truly shocking news. It grieves me deeply to be unable to do anything to ease your suffering. Here I am, living, though neither fruitfully nor

happily, at the other end of the earth, yet with certain obligations towards those who have become by marriage my family. Hubert I rarely see; we play Cox and Box between Lunegarde and Passy. But I shall not allow myself to hate my husband, nor shall anyone have cause to blame me for not trying, if our marriage appears to fail. The dreadful old princess my mother-in-law is eternally waiting to pounce, but I refuse to offer myself as her mouse.

So you will understand, my darling father, it is impossible for me to obey my instincts and come to you. This is how our lives have been arranged, and however brutally, in your case, or foolishly in mine, there is little we can do about it, beyond praying to God for deliverance from our sufferings.

You are always in my prayers and thoughts; in ever-increasing appreciation and affection—

DOROTHY

Basil was more genuinely Basil:

My dear old Dad,

You are the last man I'd like to think a victim of this most horrible injustice: as I remember you, the kindest and most generous of human beings. I am the more depressed for being unable at the moment to concentrate all my thoughts on you: we are in the throes of rehearsal (opening at the New a week from now in *Macbeth*). Since receiving Mother's letter, this is literally the first opportunity to sort out my feelings and attempt to reply. Even now it is only a few moments snatched in an empty auditorium. While a troupe of actors continues to agonize on stage, here I sit unshaven, unwashed, with a weight on my stomach after swallowing a wretched, fatty sandwich too fast; but I wanted to send you my very deepest sympathy however inadequately expressed.

We scarcely ever spoke to each other, did we? And yet, on looking back, I can sense that some kind of empathy existed between us. Oh, if we had our lives over again, I believe I'd choose to live! Not to renounce life for the grubby business of creating an appearance of it.

I'd like to sit a few minutes longer, Dad, and try to share your feelings at this moment of awfulness, but they are calling for me, so there is nothing for it but to leave you most regretfully.

Blessings!

BASIL

P.S. Nobody can realize the strain experienced by an actor who has taken on Macbeth.

Alfred Hunter was pleased to receive these letters from his children. 'They express themselves well, don't they?' His thread of a voice was not asking her to confirm what he wished to believe: that his clever children were the ultimate in rewards.

After reading the letters to him, his wife was still too confused to interpret them for herself. More collected, she might have used sarcasm on their considered insincerities; in the circumstances she preferred to accept their coldness, or, at best, their artificial warmth, as the formality imposed by distance and prolonged separation. As for being *her* children, she remembered them as sensations in her womb, then as almost edible, comfortingly soft parcels of fat, till later they were turned into leggy, hostile, scarcely human, beings, already preparing themselves for flight.

But she said to Alfred, 'I'm glad we told them. We did the right thing.' She ended as virtuous as the Princesse de Lascabanes probably felt.

Then she began to realize that the brief, exquisite phase when she had been able to speak to her husband in words which conveyed their meanings was practically past; from now on, they must communicate through their skins and with their eyes. It was a climax of trustfulness; but of course they had nothing left to lose.

Dr Treweek drove out from Gogong almost every day. Technically grateful, she could not altogether overcome her irritation for his uncouth habits, nor disguise her satisfaction at having routed his scepticism. Once she only just restrained herself from recommending a cure for dandruff.

'We can expect it any day now,' he said.

She felt so exhausted it hardly moved her to realize the doctor was referring to death, not even when she reminded herself it was her husband's.

'Call me if you want me.' Dr Treweek himself was glittering with weariness, and, she was pretty sure by now, the stimulus of drugs.

She replied with deadly calculation, 'You can't expect me to want to share my husband's death. Strong as your friendship was, I think I have precedence.'

One glance at the scurfy back, and mentally she was wringing her hands. 'Don't think I'm not — *truly* — grateful, Doctor,' she was forced to add.

He was shrugging his way into the muddy car. 'Please yourself. Some people are afraid.'

She was not afraid, either in contemplating what must happen, or when it did. They accused her of being cold. She was not: she was involved in a mystery so immense and so rarely experienced, she functioned, it could have been truthfully said, by reverence, in particular for this only in a sense, feebly fluttering soul, her initiator.

On the night, she was roused from her half-sleep, not by sounds of death in the next room, but by her instinct to participate in a miraculous transformation. She snatched her gown, and hurried in.

Here was this dear husband of her flesh still lying waiting for her, it appeared, to come to his bed. Only now, the fading eyes implied, it was she who must take the initiative. So she laid her hand as gently as she could against the chamber of his yellow cheek.

Immediately Alfred Hunter's mouth, the lips with their rime of dried salt, was stretched to its utmost, to utter, '*Whyyy?*' before the last of his fire froze.

What remained of the night she spent mostly stumbling through a labyrinth of rooms, trailing the gown she had bundled into so hastily she looked lopsided from unequal sleeves. Motion saved her.

Often in the past she had wondered how she might behave as a widow, and enjoyed in her imagination comfortable and respected status. For the time being she was neither widow, nor wife, not even a woman. She could not yet bear to think of 'Alfred'. For a moment or two she dipped her toes in hell, and made herself remember the bodies of men she had dragged to her bed, to wrestle with: her 'lovers'.

Towards morning she caught sight of a reflection in a glass and was faced with her *Doppelgänger*: aged, dishevelled, ravaged, eyes strained by staring inward, in the direction of a horizon which still had to be revealed.

'My God, what a fright you can look!' she said aloud.

Somebody—a nurse? was holding her by the wrist: they never stop taking your pulse or or

'What is it, Mrs Hunter? Were you dreaming?'

Then you realized, less by the voice than through the fingertips on your skin, that it was Mary de Santis, and not in her professional capacity: she was trying to make amends for something.

'Not dreaming—living,' Mrs Hunter gasped out. 'Alfred has just died. I shall have to ring Dr Treweek. That is what I don't look forward to. It's one thing to know, another to tell.'

'Lie still, and all these bad dreams will pass,' Sister de Santis advised.

To a certain degree it was practical advice. The palmetto leaf in your side was agitating at cyclone strength; but those at sea level, including St Mary de Santis, could never understand that this was only a physical aspect of the storm: you alone had experienced transcendence by virtue of that visit to the Warmings' island. There was Dorothy's Dutchman, too. The Dutchman may have recognized the sanctity and peace reflected in the eye of the storm, but to dry Dorothy, who ran away from Brumby and storms of her own imagining, the Dutchman's vision would have appeared like the fascinating though constricted view from the wrong end of the telescope. Dorothy had wasted her Dutchman.

'Or do you think we'll be wasting time ringing the doctor? He'll never forgive. Treweek is afraid of tenderness.'

'I know nothing about Dr Treweek,' the nurse replied. 'If we ring anybody, Dr Gidley is the one.'

'Gidley?'

'Isn't he the doctor you like? The one you chose?'

'Fat, soft Gidley!' Mrs Hunter was grinning. 'If you could look, there'd be yellow wax in his ears. Treweek is a man: hateful, ugly, dirty—all those foodspots—and the dandruff. But tormented. I think Treweek has suffered. That is why he understands. What he doesn't understand is that he's a man's man: that's why he won't forgive me my failings as a woman.'

'Don't get worked up, Mrs Hunter. It's morning.'

'I know it's morning. Haven't I been measuring out the night?'

'Let me bring you the roses. As soon as it was light, I went down and cut them. There's such a flush.'

'Oh—the roses—yes.'

On leaving her patient asleep Sister de Santis had forced herself to descend once more into the dark body of the house where she had betrayed her vocation earlier that night. She passed the study: lights still burning filled the room with glaring reminders. She went to switch off the lights, but changed her mind, and fetched a cloth to mop up a pool the housekeeper had overlooked in clearing away the decanters and his glass. Wiping the slops, Sister de Santis thought she might have exorcised her lust, if not her shame. Probably, she would not be allowed to forget that; certainly not if Mrs Hunter, at her most cunning, cornered the reason for a moment of panic at the foot of the bed. Now on guard against those other snares, the scents of cigarette smoke, whiskey, and leather, Sister de Santis moved imperviously around and through them.

She went back into the kitchen. This was Mrs Cush's day, and the night nurse sometimes started it for her. Mrs Cush the cleaner suffered from varicose veins, a smoker's cough, heart murmurs, an epileptic husband, and logorrhea. (*You're the real pal Sister Mary*

*don't know what we'd do without yer Mrs Hunter Lottie any of us would
yer believe it Sister Dad went off again Tuesday evenun threw isself
on the stove took Donald Mavis all three of us all our time to pull im
back Sister e fell down at last such a eavy man bit through the cork would
you believe it e bit Donald's finger I been under sedation ever since poor
Dad the bruises ooh Sister don't bear lookun at Mavis took me to a picture
ter cheer me up it wasn't the one Sister with the nice scenery and the lovely
music it was about a mob of sailors trapped in a submarine we come out
Mavis bought me a brandy and dry in the Ladies Lounge at the Lancaster
we went ome Sister Mary after that because it was time ter get the tea.)*

If Sister de Santis genuinely wished to compensate the cleaner for
some of the injustices suffered by her, she was not unaware that her
acts of charity could also be sly attempts to lighten her own darkness
through a discipline of drudgery. This morning after taking off
her uniform, she got down and began scrubbing out the kitchen.
She worked in wide sweeps at first, tossing ahead of her the veils
of suds she gathered back into the bucket. The electric light was
pursuing a policy of flattery: wherever she had knelt the lino
blazed; her arms, her shoulders, looked and felt strong and white;
if her bra was torn (by whatever accident) her full breasts were less
constrained. She continued scrubbing, ruffling the night silence
without threatening their relationship. As an emanation of night she
could flow like water and back into her secret self. Whether there
was anything narcissistic or sensual in her behaviour, she was saved
from toppling over by the precedent of her failed father and the
threads which bound her to the human object of her dedication.

By the time Mary de Santis, still plodding on all fours, backed into
the scullery, her shoulders had begun to ache, her knees were
numbed, the glory had gone out of penance. She saw herself as the
eternal novice, muddling around this narrow cell, thrown back off
its walls whenever she blundered in the wrong direction; yet her
attempts, like any of her other bursts of desperate clumsiness, would
be registered as experience in the eyes of innocents. Only Mrs
Hunter was aware; Papa had seen, perhaps: reflected in a white-to-
ivory skin his own failures and permissiveness. Mamma of course

had her relationship with the saints, which prevented her identifying the sins of those she loved.

The penitent bumped her head on a strut supporting one of the scullery shelves. The heavy breasts quaked and settled. Grey water, no longer sudsy, had seeped into the knees of her stockings. She lumbered up, staggered by the change of attitude, and found herself staring dizzily into a bowl of oil in which a light was shining. The light floated and rocked, not by grace of the electric bulb: she saw through the bars on the window that day had come.

When she had dressed herself again in uniform and veil, and generally restored professional neatness, the nurse took another look at her patient. A breeze was very slightly lifting the curtain of grey light. The old woman lay breathing and murmuring through one of the calmer passages of sleep. Once the lips fluttered apart; the words dragged themselves unstuck, and forced their way between the gums, 'Still only thorns. Locked buds. This long frost.' By a gigantic, creaking manoeuvre she pushed away a strand of shabby hair. 'Speak to each other beautifully in silence.' Till wrapping the spiral of a sigh, 'My darling silence', around a cherished privacy.

The nurse recognized the silence which comes when night has almost exhausted itself; light still barely disentangled from the skeins of mist strung across the park; at the foot of the tiered hill on which the house aspired, a cloud of roses floating in its own right, none of the frost-locked buds from Elizabeth Hunter's dream, but great actual clusters at the climax of their beauty.

After she had rummaged for the shears and the ravelled basket under the pantry sink, Mary de Santis let herself into the garden. A dew was falling, settling on her skin; vertical leaves were running moisture; trumpets of the evening before had furled into crinkled phalluses; grass was wearing a bloom it loses on becoming lawn. Encouraged by the rites of innocent sensuality in which she was invited to take part, she tore off a leaf, sucked it, finally bit it to reach the juicy acerbity inside. Not a single cat appeared to dispute her possession of its spiritual enclave as she rubbed, shamefully joyous, past shaggy bark, through flurries of trickling fronds. If her conscience attempted to restrain her, it was forcibly appeased by the tribute of roses she saw herself offering Elizabeth Hunter.

As soon as arrived, she began to snatch like a hungry goat. Dew sprinkling around her in showers. Thorns gashing. Her heels tottered obliquely when not planted in a compost of leaves and sodden earth. Nothing could be done about the worms, lashing themselves into a frenzy of pink exposure: she was too obsessed by her vice of roses. When she stooped to cut into the stems, more than the perfume, the pointed buds themselves could have been shooting up her greedy nostrils, while blown heads, colliding with her flanks, crumbled away, to lie on the neutral earth in clots of cream, splashes of crimson, gentle heart-shaped rose rose.

Breathing deeply, still automatically snipping by spasms at the air, she regained the grass verge, her basket of spoils heavy on her arm. Poured in steadily increasing draughts through the surrounding trees, the light translated the heap of passive roseflesh back into dew, light, pure colour. It might have saddened her to think her own dichotomy of earthbound flesh and aspiring spirit could never be resolved so logically if footsteps along the pavement had not begun breaking into her trance of roses.

A man of dark, furrowed face and inquiring eyes was asking the way to Enright Street. Though looking at her closely, he did not appear to be soliciting. She knew the street, and directed him with a care which the early hour and its exquisite details seemed to demand, the man listening intently, his eyes concentrated half on her directions, half, though in an abstracted way, on her rose-embowered figure.

When she had finished he smiled and thanked. They were both smiling for different and the same reasons. From his humble, creaking boots and still apologetic glance, he was not only a stranger to the street, but to the country, she suspected. She was reminded of her own alien birth and childhood; whether the man guessed it or not, he gave the impression that he recognized an ally.

Nodding at her veil he suddenly asked, 'Somebody sick?'

'Not really. There's an old lady living here, who has to be taken care of.'

'How old?'

'We don't know exactly. I don't think it matters once you've reached a certain age. You're no longer altogether a person: more like an electric bulb going on and off, and perhaps, if you're lucky, you may throw a light on something that hasn't been noticed before—by you or anybody. At least that's the way I see it.' Truthfully she had never looked at it from that aspect; it was the early morning leading her on, and her audience of one simple foreigner.

The stranger seemed seriously trying to visualize the image she had offered. Then he smiled full at her, and she looked down to hide her pleasure, and noticed that her white shoes were caked with soil.

The nurse was at once recalled to duty. 'I must go in now,' she said, awkwardly, almost harshly. 'My case may be needing me.'

The man's sculptured boots were creaking into motion. 'Yes. I also go.' By the expression of his eyes he had already left her; when he turned, as though at the last moment he must force her to admit to something. '*Tí ximaíroma kánomay!*'

The words went shivering and chiming through her veins. If their meaning was lost on her by now, they echoed through her head in her mother's voice. All the way up the path, the stairs, a melancholy murmuring recurred: of words, and bells, and women's voices rejoicing or lamenting, she could no longer have told which.

The sweetness and distraction of only partial union with the past began to mingle with anxiety that her patient might be preparing a crisis. Sister de Santis only gave herself time to stuff the roses by thorny handfuls in an old washstand jug left over in the mahogany bathroom, before she hurried in. At the same moment, the relic in her charge was tossed up out of whatever infernal depths, and stranded on the shores of consciousness.

Taking the fairly normal pulse, the nurse had become irrationally and unprofessionally afraid. 'What is it, Mrs Hunter? Were you dreaming?' she began the constant reprise.

'Not dreaming—living. Alfred,' Mrs Hunter gasped, 'has died.'

For all her sympathy, Sister de Santis could only follow the trail of the stranger's words, pursuing her *ximaíroma*.

'Ring Dr Treweek ... ' Mrs Hunter was panting.

' ... Gidley is the one ... ' Sister de Santis heard herself bleat; then in desperation, 'Let me bring you the roses. As soon as it was light I went down and cut them. There's such a flush.'

'Oh—the roses—yes.'

The nurse ran to fetch the chipped, washstand jug. The resplendent roses scattered their dew their light their perfumed reflections over the sheet into the straining nostrils the opalescent eyes staring out through this paper mask.

'Look!' Mary de Santis forgot.

Elizabeth Hunter answered, 'Yes. I can see, Mary—our roses.'

And at once Mary de Santis heard in her mother's voice the words she had not understood when the peasant-migrant spoke them, 'What a sunrise we are making!'

It was: the roses sparkled drowsed brooded leaped flaunting their earthbound flesh in an honourably failed attempt to convey the ultimate.

'Yes—our roses,' Elizabeth Hunter repeated.

Which Mary de Santis interpreted as: we, the arrogant perfectionists, or pseudo-saints, shall be saved up out of our shortcomings for further trial.

Six

WELCOMING THE princess, the president of the club had pointed out that the room was a cheery one. Madame de Lascabanes supposed it was; but the flowered chintz (green and beige) and the reproduction of a landscape with daringly stylized eucalypts, aggravated the disease of foreignness from which she suffered. There was a white telephone which intimidated her fearfully; what if it went off before she was prepared to cope with it? She felt better when her things, collected from Moreton Drive after a long delay by that decent soul Arnold Wyburd, were delivered below. Just to unpack her toothpaste calmed her nerves; and in the meantime she had begged a headache powder from a maid. Yes, she was feeling better.

Unless reminded of her escape from where she wanted but feared to be: that housekeeper hovering with something raw and German; and the mummified head of Santa Chiara Hubert insisted on visiting *elle a quand même une influence extraordinaire* which the jealous Franciscan refuted *vous savez c'est une tête quelconque que les soeurs se sont procurées pour en tirer profit.* Alone in the lift on her way down to dinner, Dorothy de Lascabanes whimpered a little thinking of poor Mummy.

Discretion reigned in the dining-room, where six or seven powdered ladies lowered their eyelids over the roast chicken or stewed apple they were pretending not to masticate, while an ancient maid in stiff white led the honorary member to a table of her own, from which she was expected to impose. It had the effect of exposing Dorothy Hunter, alone with her cutlery and the tight arrangement of Queen Elizabeth rosebuds. She spread her hands on the cutlery as though she were going to strike a chord, and sat staring at the vacant air.

'Poor Madge, she is so tahd,' one of the ladies remarked now that the climate was restored.

'Yes, she's tahd,' her companion agreed. 'It's the humidity. And Madge is over generous of her energy and time.' Perhaps to quash any such impulse in herself, the second lady added a minimum of stuffing to her forkful of breast, with the merest smear of bread sauce.

It must have brought on recklessness in a third, in no way connected lady, who swallowed her mouthful of stewed apple and started coughing. She coughed and coughed. Intent on ignoring this indisposition, Dorothy Hunter was fascinated to see what could have been a bubble of syrup appear for an instant at each of the lady's nostrils; and as instantly, each of the bubbles was sucked back.

Oh dear, if only Mummy were here 'at the club' to order for you! And what if you blew bubbles with your syrup, or dropped a dollop of bread sauce on the elderly maid's spotless cuff?

Or if you screamed.

When the maid approached with the menu Dorothy barely glanced at what she could not have read; she remembered leaving her glasses in her room. 'Do you know what I'd like better than anything—I mean, if it isn't any trouble—if you have one—I'd like a nice, thick, mutton chop. And make it rather pink.'

'Oh yes, milady—of course—I'll see.' The maid looked terrified; somewhere she must have heard about a curtsey, but hadn't the courage for more than a bob.

The members raised their heads like so many disturbed cows.

The Princesse de Lascabanes had not succeeded in vindicating herself: between the inspiration and the command, or perhaps even farther back, after changing airlines at Bangkok, *le mutton chop* had shed its exotic implications. Dorothy Hunter was left to get by heart the mumbled syllables of her gaffe. It didn't help to catch sight of herself in memory holding the chop over the embers on a sharpened stick, and to hear the even less articulate, but naturally sincere, voice of littlegirlhood, *no Daddy it isn't burnt only charred that's when it's scrummiest.*

Though most of the members had left the room, a couple had lingered purposely to watch the maid serve the chop to Princess Thingumabob: one of those Hunters from Gogong if you please.

By now the princess had completely lost even the pretence of an appetite. In any case the meat, when brought, was too red, too fat: *en effet écœurant ce chop australien*; it would have warmed her late mother-in-law's heart to know it.

When she had eaten a mouthful of tepid cress and drunk a glass of water, Dorothy pushed away the mutilated chop. 'Thank you, nothing else.' She smiled at the maid, while appealing to the woman with her eyes not to tell on her.

Coffee in the drawing-room could only have been a greater ordeal than dinner in the dining-room. There was the question of where to sit: not so far off that it might appear offensive, yet beyond hailing distance of any of the other inhabited islands. In the end she ran up the two flights to her bed, where her exhaustion promptly left her for the night. She passed this between dipping into *La Chartreuse de Parme*, which she knew too well, and remembering the motives for her return. In consequence, any of the homelier images were a comfort to the mind: for instance, her tube of French, soon alas to be expended, toothpaste, or a rather boring family solicitor. She shepherded in procession anything that might be considered safe, but was forced repeatedly to sit in judgment on herself.

Let's face it: I've come back to coax a respectable sum of money out of an aged woman who happens also to be my mother, whom I do sincerely love at times, but have also hated (God, yes!) so perhaps it will be more pardonable, if coaxing fails, to bully the money out of her, most pardonable because she herself has been the greatest bully, and hateful remember hateful the visit to the island the jade sea grey jade is subtler than green if Mother hadn't thought of it first *there's something so comically banal about these Pacific islands don't you think Professor I mean the sea is just as jade as advertised the grey days a positive relief of subtler less expected jade* Mother lighting candles to illuminate her conversation to profess herself on the over appealed-to professor whose name is EDVARD spelt with a V unlike Mother you would not pronounce it in his hearing any more than abuse a sacrament the white flakes of his skin the sun has shredded.

The half-sleepless princess drew her thighs up closer in her bed until she was all thighs and buttocks a knot of flesh or pile of bones under which the pea revolved.

Edvard with a V is telling of forests whether the rain forest of Brumby Island or spruces larches rowans of Norway has no importance. Ashes too. The wild horses racing at dusk along the beach sting your cheeks with flying sand horsehair whips. *Not afraid Professor* only that my ribs may batter their way through your side in this electric moment of locked hands clamped bodies.

Trust Mother to cook the fish the professor caught and lay it on a bed of wild fennel with all this chichi of native flowers round the edge of the dish the electric moment has galloped into the dark tossing its mane only hope Mother's fish will taste of sand.

The princess, grinding around on her colossal ball-bearing of a pea, continued munching on her waking sleep. If neither coaxing nor bullying what if you should kill an old woman or mother what can money mean to the aged except as a reminder of triumphs no longer desirable or possible? It wouldn't be killing, a shock, not murder. Definitely not. You can scarcely step on a cockroach for all your pus which spurts out.

Basil could: my genius of a brother of a famous actor why why has he come Mr Wyburd don't tell but I know don't I Basil and Dorothy = brother and sister = hunters lurking in the fuggy depths of Elizabeth Salkeld's cave. When you could have stayed curled indefinitely in Mummy she pitched you out unarmed not Basil an actor is born with clubs instead of inhibitions your inhibitions can only have been inherited from Alfred a deformed statue at the point where the road forks the other side of Gogong his inscription at least speaks for him also the wrinkles in his waistcoat and trousers around around well the fork poor bill hunter DAD.

Yourself a father Mr Wyburd tell me won't you about my father this newspaper cutting you so kindly sent to remind.

The princess stirred. She regretted the solicitor bored her so intensely when she had much to ask but fathers forgive we are told this one of practically the same height thickness fastidious habits as yourself untying the pink ribbon which holds your character your deeds together Arnold W as methodical as Edvard with the V will only profess when he has considered all the facts then when they are quite naked the solicitor is prepared to admit only a good man could have married Alfred's wife.

Oh Father Father she wanted to cry for what he had suffered she was only consoled by the touch of milky legal silk his long old transparent testicles dangling trailing over her thighs.

The Princesse de Lascabanes was so shocked to see Mr Wyburd his shanks his blue veins his everything embossed on the darkness she sat up in bed and switched the light on: to be faced with her reflected self instead of a dream solicitor. Her breasts, leaner and longer than she would have cared to admit, looked askew inside the reflected nightie; her thin, naked lips were parted; she was scarcely less disgusted by reality than by the dream which had been foisted on her.

After this perfectly ghastly night in the cheery bedroom Dorothy swallowed an aspirin and considered whether she ought to confess. But to whom? in Sydney. Some anonymous Irish peasant would scarcely appreciate her spiritual bruises, and might even despise her for her educated voice. She had never thought anonymity in the confessional more than a dubious, theoretical comfort for special occasions. But wasn't this a special occasion? Yes, but she personally, on all occasions, preferred acquaintanceship with the hand which strokes the soul. Moist-eyed, she lay regretting her beloved Abbé Passebosc, then grew haggard remembering her mother. Mummy would somehow worm out that shameful dream. Dorothy lashed the sheet around her. Never! Better to suppurate.

After she had rung for coffee, and innocently drunk a draught of unmistakable essence, what she had been dreading the day before began to happen: the white telephone exploded.

'Good morning, madame. I haven't learnt your habits, so you must forgive me if I'm disturbing you.'

On identifying the solicitor's punctiliousness, the princess was in fact disturbed; she avoided her own reflection in the glass opposite. What to say? Their bodies had already communicated with greater expressiveness than words could offer.

' ... the meeting I want to arrange—yourself and your brother—to discuss Mrs Hunter's situation. What are your plans, madame?'

Her plans? Ever since leaving Mother for Europe, she had hoped somebody, some *man*, would materialize to make them for her. If an elderly, not to say fatherly, solicitor could not, who then would?

To disguise her own ineptitude she heard herself suggest in a high bright voice suspiciously like the Queen of England's, 'I do wish you'd call me "Dorothy"—won't you? Mr Wyburd?'

He sounded understandably gratified, but did not make a reciprocal offer, because after all, he was quite a bit older—desirably so; instead he said, 'Thank you, Dorothy. I'll be glad to. As a matter of fact I've always—my wife and I, that is, have been in the habit of referring to you by your Christian name, for old times' sake.'

None of this meant he wasn't still expecting to hear her plans; he fell silent waiting for them.

'Well,' she began desperately, 'I had better pay my mother a short, early visit—before she has tired.' The shortness of the visit would ensure that you could not initiate your real, your infernal plan, on this occasion. 'Any time later in the morning—I know nobody, and have nothing else to do—I shall be at your disposal.'

The solicitor was too discreet to react in any way emotionally to her admission; but she had impressed herself by the pathos of her nothingness.

Mr Wyburd suggested eleven-thirty at his office provided Basil also.

'Yes, yes, provided Basil—naturally,' Dorothy earnestly agreed.

But was it 'natural' that she should confer with her brother at any time about their mother's affairs? Basil's character was such that he must accept without hesitation the most ruthless details of her design. And had the solicitor perhaps smelt the crypto-plan? Bad enough; but worse if he had some more convincing, *legal* solution to share with his client's long-suffering children. He could be the wily Wyburd in fact.

Madame de Lascabanes felt desolated as she put down the phone, not so much because the good solicitor might turn out to be yet another dishonest man, but because, when a victim of injustice, she preferred herself as the sacrificial lamb rather than the justified crusader in burnished, many-faceted armour; brilliance at its best is a quality of heartless jewels, at its worst, of supple, ultimately self-destructive intrigue. So she forgot the solicitor for seeing herself in an ignominious light.

She forgot the whole issue when the white telephone went off again, far too soon. 'Is it the princess—the Princesse de Lascabanes?' Not a bad attempt at it.

'Yes. It is.' There was no escaping the caller, except through a downright lie; alone in the chintzy bedroom, there was no escaping yourself.

'This is Cherry—Cherry Cheeseman—Bullivant that was.'

'Why—*Cherry*!' In the train of your false enthusiasm a dark pause filled with breathings: Cherry Bullivant Cheeseman sounded bronchial, or corseted, or perhaps she had taken the plunge too quickly.

The princess threw in something appropriately banal. 'How clever of you to have tracked me down.'

'Oh, but everybody knows—Dorothy. It's in the papers.'

Dorothy de Lascabanes frowned. 'I haven't read one—not since I left *Le Monde* behind in Paris.'

It was Cherry who filled the current awkward pause. 'You can buy it, Dorothy—at least I think so—all the foreign papers—from a stall outside the G.P.O. You remember the G.P.O., darling?'

Helpful Cherry could not have seen herself as the unwelcome revenant she was; ghosts are never so insubstantial that they don't breed others, and strings of ghostly incidents, and odd, chilling, ghostly phrases. Cherry Bullivant had been present on too many first occasions: the First Meeting (accidental) in the Crillon lounge; first to see the ring after the improbable engagement; she should have played First Bridesmaid if Mrs Bullivant hadn't been overcome by Methodist misgivings. A sweetly pretty girl, dark and glossy to match her name, Cherry was also practical: *shouldn't you ask for a settlement or something?* it had occurred to her to ask. Born plain and shy, Dorothy Hunter, too, was of a practical, if more disillusioned nature: *don't you see Cherry I'm the one who's expected to bring the settlement?* If she had been less wealthy, though as luscious as Cherry Bullivant, she suspected even then that this desirable man would not have been enticed. No, she was born without illusions, about life anyway, and other people; instead she had been given determination which enemies saw as stubbornness, and Hubert failed to understand as love. Just as he could not believe in fastidiousness. It was her delicacy in sexual matters rather than his perversities which had ripped the ribbons off their marriage. *Oh Cherry why did you make this telephone call?* Dorothy Hunter, whose self-confidence began trickling away on her arrival as a bride at Lunegarde, glanced down as though expecting to catch sight of a last pool on the club carpet.

'The point is,' Mrs Cheeseman's wheezy voice returned to insist from away down the tunnel of the telephone, 'when are we going to see you, Dorothy dear? From all he has heard, Douglas would adore to meet you. I thought perhaps a little dinner — here at Warrawee.'

Mrs Cheeseman *sounded* comfortably middle-aged, and Dorothy de Lascabanes, still *au fond* a jittery girl, was grateful for it. 'I'd love it, Cherry — just ourselves — so that we can talk;' when to talk was the last thing she wanted, unless to be confronted with a whole battery of listening faces.

'Oh, we'll keep it *small*!' Cherry Cheeseman lowered her voice to make her promise. 'What about Thursday?'

All the way to Mother's that morning Dorothy de Lascabanes was half conscious of a malaise from which she should not have been suffering: the steam of yesterday had lifted, leaving behind it a glossy morning; the taxi was diving, describing curves with such daring she could easily have claimed for herself expertise in living; she should have felt as free as she was ever likely to be on earth, returning to the country she knew through her instincts, but to which at the same time she was under no further obligation. Oh yes, she was free enough. Only the sickness persisted. Supposing. She had intended to have that check-up. Perhaps she should ask the advice of one of Mother's army of nurses – while appearing not to, of course: you could look too foolish if the trouble wasn't physical, as it more than probably wasn't.

So she tried, physically, to shrug the sickness off, as the face of a television star on a hoarding, skin stretched, teeth bared in a ravenous imitation of youth, towered for the instant before dismissal.

'*Mais qu'est-ce qui vous prend? Vous êtes fou?*' the passenger in the taxi screamed as she was shot against the roof.

Who was *fou* was immaterial: the driver, or the elderly pedestrian, his pace abnormally leisured, too uncertain in crossing, the face too white, the bags under the eyes too blue.

'Is he ill? Drunk more likely!' shouted the princess: the bump (what if her skull had been fractured?) together with the fright she had got, made her feel extra virtuous.

'Some flaming metho artist!' The driver himself had had a fright, his passenger screaming down his neck: bloody hysterical foreign woman.

Of them all, the drunken, sick, or possibly only aged man continued gently, unsteadily, on his undisturbed progress.

'How can they?' How dirty, smelly, frightening, so many old people are: the Princesse de Lascabanes felt more virtuous than ever.

While the driver remained appropriately incensed. 'The Council sweeps the rubbish off the streets, and leaves the half of it behind! Eh?'

Dorothy Hunter's sick sick not sickness only a malaise returned: herself potentially a murderess.

At Moreton Drive peace was pouring in a bland golden flood

out of the park opposite. There were birds in Mother's garden. Somebody had put out seed for them in a little terracotta dish suspended from the branch of a tree. Sparrows and finches were fluttering, flirting; a rain of seed scattered from the swaying dish. From the lawn at the foot of the tree, a flight of blue pigeons took off clattering, and away.

Oh dear, this is what I must keep in mind, at all times: the light, the movement of birds. Climbing the path, the princess knew she was giving herself a piece of hopeless advice: as if you can possess the moment of perfection; as if conception and death don't take place simultaneously.

It wasn't the housekeeper, it was that boiled nurse who answered the doorbell. 'Isn't this a priceless morning, mad-*dahm*? Priceless,' she repeated, evidently proud of her adjective. 'Let's hope it's the end of the humidity. Your mother would be so relieved. The old backs do play up when there's any humidity around.' Sister Badgery oozed professional sympathy, not only for her patient, but for a caller she suspected of being, behind the voice and the fal-lals, a neurotic inexperienced girl.

Dorothy coughed drily; she didn't think this was the nurse she would pump for information on the symptoms and whereabouts of cancer in women of a certain age. 'I see you've been feeding the birds.' A feeble comment, and the more annoying in that Sister Badgery was so obviously stupid.

'That is Sister de Santis. She puts out seed for them before she goes off duty. It's quite a little ceremony. Sister de Santis is so good.' Though Sister Badgery's gold-rimmed spectacles radiated approval, you couldn't help feeling that any admiration she had for her colleague was strictly theoretical; just as 'goodness' was probably a theory, one that you were supposed to get sentimental about.

So Sister Badgery beamed, and stood aside for her patient's daughter to enter.

'Is my mother *well*?' Nervousness gave the question an exaggerated emphasis; it sounded ominous, Dorothy thought.

'Never better. Mrs Hunter is unexpendable.' Sister Badgery laughed so gaily leading the way upstairs; if her calves looked strained, her step was springy.

All of this helped increase a gloom gathering in the princess. 'Such a ridiculously large house for one old woman to be bedridden in!' She sighed. 'I know from experience how unpractical. So much work for everyone involved.'

'It isn't work when your heart's in it,' Sister Badgery reminded rather breathily from over her shoulder. 'And I think I'm safe in saying we're all devoted to Mrs Hunter.'

'That isn't the point. The housekeeper alone must be run off her feet.'

'Mrs Lippmann's such a grateful soul—after all she's been through —she wouldn't begrudge her services. No, she wouldn't begrudge.' Sister Badgery never ran out of breath though she seemed permanently on the point of doing so. 'And then she has the help of Mrs Cush—that's the cleaning lady—two mornings a week. Though sometimes she doesn't come. Today—if she comes—is Mrs Cush's day. But Mrs Lippmann has gone to the dentist.'

One less to face, Dorothy Hunter was relieved to think; besides, her French self, overlooking the housekeeper's Jewishness, disliked her automatically as a German.

'Poor Mrs Cush! Her husband is an epileptic.'

Perhaps after all you could ask Sister Badgery, though prudently, about the cancer symptoms and the check-up.

But *epilepsy*!

Sister Badgery said, 'I think today Mrs Cush more than likely won't be coming—considering she isn't here already, and the hire-car sent to Redfern to fetch her.'

'*Qu'est-ce que ce* ... ? The *hire*-car?'

'Yes. Mrs Hunter believes—in the goodness of her heart—the least she can do is send a car for poor Mrs Cush—what with the varicose veins and the epileptic husband.'

But is my mother mad? Madame de Lascabanes fortunately prevented herself exclaiming in her most disapproving voice:

outside the bedroom door too. Instead she remarked weakly, 'Epilepsy must be frightening—quite frightening,' and touched her pearls.

Then Sister Badgery opened the door, and she was allowed into the sanctuary, where the shrunken head was still lying on the pillow as she and Hubert had seen it at Assisi. (That night he had been unusually kind, simply holding you in his arms, stroking, in no·way sensually, but with that same reverence you were conscious of sharing earlier at the shrine.)

Mrs Hunter opened her eyes. 'Leave us, Badgery,' she commanded; 'I want to talk—confidentially—to my daughter, the Princesse de Las—ca—banes?'

The nurse looked pained, but did as told.

Dorothy felt weak at the knees. For a moment she feared she might be forced down on them, but succeeded in staggering as far as the bedside chair.

'Mummy!' she began mouthing in a genuine attempt at affection. 'I should have brought you something.'

'What?'

'A present.'

'Don't be silly! It's too late. I'm too old. Though that doesn't mean I'm going to die.'

'Did you have a good night?'

'Oh—dreaming.'

'What about?'

'My husband.'

'Won't you share him with me as my father?'

Mrs Hunter ignored it.

'I hope at least they were pleasant dreams,' her daughter persisted.

'Yes, and no.' She began wheezing like a bellows. 'Oh, Alfred—oh, his face! His teeth—or throat—suddenly clicked. That's how I knew he was dead.'

Boiling tears were pouring down the dry canyons of Dorothy de Lascabanes's face.

'I'll tell you something,' Mrs Hunter's voice warned the listener not to expect an abstract confession. 'For many years I couldn't love, only respect him. Then I—well, I never loved enough. In all our life together, I didn't touch his penis. To touch would have shown, wouldn't it?' Hands moved on the sheet as though to gather a rare flower; lips twitched back, exposed naked gums. 'Or would it have seemed—whorish?'

The Princesse de Lascabanes was horrified; she couldn't answer: her best intentions were destroyed at every move.

But she tried again, making conversation with what after all was only a dotty old woman. 'As a matter of fact, I too had a bad night.'

'I knew you would.'

'Why?'

'You were always such a fretful thing. And in a club bed. Those women in the dining-room must have frightened you stiff.' Dorothy was about to protest, when her mother asked, 'How did you pass the night if you couldn't sleep?'

'Oh, I read—and thought.'

'What did you think about?'

'I don't know. Business matters. People I've known.' Dorothy progressed with caution.

'Money and lovers,' Mrs Hunter corrected dreamily; then she laughed. 'Or non-starters.'

The pearls the princess was wearing could have been billiard balls: they cannoned so deafeningly off one another.

'Tell me what you read last night.' Mother could never leave well alone.

'The *Chartreuse*,' Dorothy replied *tout court*.

'It was your father's favourite book—*The Charterhouse of Parma*.'

'Oh? But he wasn't a reader. How do you know?'

'I found out a lot of things when I got to know him. He'd been reading books. This one in particular: there were crumbs between the pages, coffee stains. He admitted he loved it. We read it together the weeks before he died. He loved that woman.'

'Who—Clélia?' she hoped.

'No. The other—the duchess. He admired her brilliance.'

224

'I find her dishonest in some respects.'

Dorothy looked for signs of exhaustion in her mother, but this morning the mummified head seemed filled with steel wheels.

'Everyone is more or less dishonest. They may not murder, or forge cheques—dishonest with themselves, I mean. This—San-severina was no more dishonest than any other beautiful woman, or —or jewel. An emerald isn't less beautiful, is it? for the flaw in it?'

It was Dorothy who was exhausted; she mumbled, 'I can't think.' In fact, her thoughts, her aspirations—which were also her dishonesties—were rattling round inside her like the loose seeds in a maraca.

At least the state into which she had been plunged gave her the opportunity to hate her mother more honestly.

'How do you find Arnold? Do you think he's deteriorating?'

Why Arnold? Yes, Dorothy hated her mother.

'Not in the least deteriorated,' the princess answered primly. 'Now Mr Wyburd is a man who is completely honest, I'd risk saying.'

Mrs Hunter laughed. 'Upright.'

And Dorothy hated her mother for reviving in her the milky white caress she had experienced in her half-dream the night before.

It was a relief that Sister Badgery should appear with a tray.

'Better late than forgotten completely! Here's our egg, Mrs Hunter—our lovely, *coddled* egg—topped with cream and a pinch of herbs—and all prepared by me because poor Mrs Lippmann broke her bridge and had to rush off to the dentist.' Sister Badgery gave the princess such a look she wondered whether this odious nurse wasn't more than her accidental ally.

Mrs Hunter said, 'You know how I hate egg.' She clamped her jaws to show she would resist.

'You like brandy, don't you, dear? There's brandy in the coffee for those who eat the eggs that are good for them.'

As the jaws were unclamped the aged child's lips began filling with desperation; they looked blistered. 'But I *need* the brandy.'

'You need the good eggs that nourish.' Sister Badgery arranged the bib.

'I need fire — when the fire's almost out.'

'Whatever for? It's summer, dear.'

'To inspire me.'

'If you eat up your egg, that will be inspiration. Think of the phosphorus.'

'All nurses are the same,' Betty Salkeld gulped through a splather of forced egg. 'Kate Nutley's wouldn't allow her the toffee on the caramel custard if she didn't pick the fish's head.'

'Phosphorus again!' Sister Badgery, who always knew when she was right, celebrated her own wisdom by driving in another spoonful. 'You never told me what became of this Kate Nutley.'

Revolving the egg mess on her tongue, Mrs Hunter spluttered, 'I — don't — know. Well, of course, I really do. They must have driven her — nutty.' At least the nurse and her charge had a giggle.

The Princesse de Lascabanes was by now so revolted she got up. Her elastic was eating into her; influenced by other behaviour she dragged it down by ugly handfuls.

'Coffee, mad-*dahm*, if I fetch a second cup?' the much-occupied nurse managed to call over her shoulder.

'Thank you, no — Sister.'

'Dorothy's going to the lavatory,' Mrs Hunter whispered, and watched the right direction.

It was such an unexplained exit it might have suggested just that: which was what the princess hoped. She had even considered pulling the chain at a certain stage, but decided against wasting time on realistic detail as you couldn't wholly depend on the nurse's continued dedication to the egg ceremony. So the princess went racing down to where her serious business lay. As she hurried, steadying herself on a rail which was burning her hand, she already heard in her mind's ear, a tray pursuing her down the stairs with empty or rejected crockery jumping and stamping on it. However important it was for her to investigate, it would be equally important for Sister Badgery to observe.

So the Princesse de Lascabanes's pearls bounced, and Dorothy Hunter's eyes were set in an anxious glaze, as they reached the hall Of course it was ridiculous in a house where you, not the German-Jewish housekeeper, not the boiled nurse, not even your senile mother, were mistress; and what you now heard in actual fact, was something crashing in the room above, subsiding in waves of porcelain fragments, and finally, instead of slaps, ripples of united giggles. Sister Badgery would almost certainly never be your ally.

Since the whole house was against her, in spite of the claims to which she was entitled from having spent her childhood in it, Dorothy de Lascabanes stalked more warily than before. Somewhere she brushed against a very old raincoat. A parasol she upset in passing, fell between her legs and might have brought her down, but she saved herself, and it, carrying the parasol along to use in her support.

The kitchen, the pantry, all the offices, were at least spotless: trust the German creature. The *belle-mère* herself could not have looked so keenly into cupboards; yet there was not a scrap of incriminating evidence, until, in the scullery, a bowl with a growth of green-to-bluish fur. The princess slammed the door on an obscenity; before it struck her that probably everybody has their basin of fur.

For the moment directionless as she revolved on the shining linoleum, Dorothy Hunter tried to persuade herself: remember the light through leaves, the movements of birds, a sweaty but honest pony plodding homeward under casuarinas, Stendhal the laser beam; while she continued hearing the *trit-trit* of a hollow maraca.

'*O mon Dieu, miséricorde!*' Instead, you are losing touch with all the positive signs and your own better intentions; you are led in the direction of the garbage bin, to tip the lid with the ivory ferrule of Mother's dilapidated parasol.

Then the Princesse de Lascabanes began to rootle, in the practical, but joyless tradition of domestic bloodhounds, stirring up an inevitable stench: of coffee grounds, cabbage stalks, a whole alphabet of grey potato peelings, and the damp rot which sets in

227

when newspapers fulfil their other function. To rootle was the real reason for her descent to the kitchen, the princess herself almost had to admit. To create a stink. Which she now managed. She brought it out, skewered to the ferrule of the lace and ivory parasol: as much as *two whole kilos* of good *filet de bœuf* on the point of putrefying.

'*Quelle salope! Que les gens deviennent de plus en plus malhonnêtes!*' Dorothy de Lascabanes could hardly breathe for having justified herself: in exposing the immoral unbalance of her mother's crazy economy. If Mother hadn't spent a lifetime hacking into the defenceless, yourself included, you might have been moved by a different horror on discovering that her parasites, the artistic housekeeper, pampered cleaner, and frivolous or over indulgent nurses, were sucking her dry without her knowing. As things were, the princess stood a moment by the bin to taste the flavour of an ironic outrage which was also her own triumph, while the wrist of the hand holding the parasol twitched to her thoughtfulness, and as it twitched, the beef fillet revolved limply, a silent klaxon attached to the ferrule.

If she allowed the meat at last to subside, it was because it had such a horrid smell, and because, if you came to think, the solicitor was probably more than anyone to blame; though you couldn't expect a man, however watchful and devoted, to conceive of the self-interest, the want of conscience, the cunning of such a gaggle of women. No, you would have to absolve poor Arnold Wyburd who, you had been made to realize, was such a dear, not to say a comfort.

The princess firmly scraped off the lump of putrid meat on the edge of the bin; the lid clattered back into place, too loudly perhaps: Dorothy was afraid Sister Badgery might suspect an intruder; when she still had to carry out an even more daring detail of her plan.

So she went barging out, again too loudly, clumsily, and up by what used to be referred to as 'the servants' stairs', an expression probably discarded along with the luxury of professional servants.

The bare, though scrubbed boards, sounded alarmingly frail as she climbed; the air was as dense as felt in this claustrophobic, matchwood and plaster tunnel. She regretted her foolishness now, but had to continue as she had begun.

And arrived on the landing, at the passage leading to the cells of the released prisoners. The doors she tried opened on rooms which must have been unoccupied for years, except by their wire stretchers, deal chests, and the corpses of moths; till in the last, the most imposing cell, intended for some more important, semi-responsible inmate, she found signs of life; for the housekeeper's spirit lingered in it, together with the scent of her facepowder (understandably cheap) and a few visible possessions such as ground-down, yellow-bristled hairbrushes, a hare's-foot stained brown, the framed snapshot of a woman and a young man enlaced against an empty bandstand, in front of an expanse of white sea.

For a moment the Princesse de Lascabanes suspected herself of having committed an indecency, and her expression in the dressing-table glass looked pained—then worse: it was that of a flogged and panting horse, nostrils pinched, veins in relief on the saturated skin. Till the past excused her: she had always been fascinated by the maids' bedrooms, by their mysterious otherness, above all by a suspicion of what was talked about as Love. Dorothy had lowered her fringe over Nora's birthday book, and was honoured to write her name in it.

Now there was time for little more than to fling open the ricketty wardrobe, to discover the balding silk hat, the tails with their accretions of mildew, greasepaint—oh God, whatever else. And leaning in one corner, the imitation malacca cane: its tinny, dented knob.

Forgetting why she had come there, unless to add to the housekeeper's moral reprehensibility, Dorothy Hunter slammed the wardrobe shut, then the room (she hoped) and ran, the whole passage shaking and creaking; till she reached the world of carpets and her shoes began to glide again, decently and prudently, towards her mother's door. Emotions which a moment before had exploded in her in a burst of anarchic madness were stilled by the silence of old, sumptuous, superfluous furniture: impeccable intentions can always warp, given the wrong climate at the right moment. Recovered from her sentimental aberration in the housekeeper's room, Dorothy de Lascabanes was persuaded she had a more lucid understanding of her mission.

The fact that the awful nurse was hurrying downstairs (you could hear the bits of broken crockery slithering and chattering on her tray) to find out what you were up to, confirmed a sense of rightness strengthened. And the telephone, dubious on the least suspicious occasions, had begun to ring. And ring.

Downstairs, Sister Badgery had put down her tray to pick up the receiver. 'Who? ... Oh, yes! ... Yes, *yes*, YES ... Isn't it? ... Oh, she will ... Yes ... I'll tell ... Yes ... '

Maddening! The figure on the landing flung itself at the extension, to lift what might have been a butterfly, in bakelite; then it was fluttering against her ear: not one butterfly, but two, and having a love affair it seemed.

'I know she'll be disappointed, but has taught herself to bear disappointment: she's such a strong character. And of course others will be disappointed too. I, for one, was looking forward to getting to know you. I have to confess I'm *avid* for *people*—though there are some in particular—you can always tell in advance—who are somehow on the same wave ... '

Thus flirting her wings, the white butterfly made them appear excessively fragile and sensitive. As her insect body writhed and squirmed, the male butterfly was vibrating round her, warmer in tone (copper to red) veined in black, with heavy black knobs or horns.

' ... My own disappointment is enormous—needless to repeat— and it's only because this business meeting is so utterly important, that I'm postponing the visit I'd planned this morning. Tell her she's an old darling, and that I love her, won't you? As for what you say—it's flattery of course—flattering to know one can mean something in advance to strangers—but nobody was ever any the worse for, only strengthened by, encouragement.'

Dorothy thought she could see a spotted foulard butterfly bow fluttering, but with masculine conviction, as the adam's apple bobbed in time.

As for the white butterfly, if he wasn't careful her frail wings might remain stuck together in their ecstasy. 'Oh oh Sir Basil I do yes I do agree Sir Bas ...'

'I'd like to send her something when I can think send all you nurses but what? stockings? perfume? chocolates? we must talk it over every opportunity now that I'm here now that I've re-established a relationship making fresh ones too ...'

'Oh oh Sir Basurl ... ' The white butterfly's antennae were bridling, buckling.

' ... some little trifle to show I do appreciate the attentions you're paying my mother ... '

At some moments the white wings quivered greenish at their more transparent tips. 'There's one thing I'd like to ask you, Sir Basil—a personal favour ... '

'What?' The male butterfly could have had enough of love dalliance.

' ... a young girl—I can't tell you how she admires—we all do from reading about you in the papers and magazines—I would like to ask you for your autograph. The girl would kill me if she knew ...'

The male was stroked back, if only for a flutter or two. ' ... delighted to write in her book if you send it.'

'Oh, a signature would be sufficient—to make it more of a surprise—to stick in, Sir Basil—in the book.'

'Send her a photograph when I get back. What's your friend's name?'

The white butterfly must have swooned; then she returned, though fainter, through their abstract firmament. '"Lurline" is the young girl's name.'

' "Lurl ... " ' the male was repeating gravely, to let it be under-stood, between audible munches and sups at an invisible breakfast, that he was engraving the word on his heart, if not writing it in his diary. 'To do the job thoroughly, what's the girl's second name?'

The female might have sunk, battered and exhausted by the rigours of courtship, but rose again on the wings of inspiration. '"Lurline *Skinner*,"' she barely managed to bring it fluttering out.

'"Lurline Skinner." Grand!'

Dorothy Hunter heard herself rumble. Her brother she believed to be not only dishonest, but also, she regretted, humourless.

The white butterfly could have flopped around a whole lot more, but the male was for drawing away in a last burst of coppery condescension.

'I shan't forget—Sister … ?'

'Badgery.'

' … neither the photograph, nor our agreeable conversation … '

' … urmssurbasurl … '

' … already old friends … '

The Princesse de Lascabanes was glad she had married, however unsuccessfully, away from Anglo-Saxondom.

'Now I must get myself ready for this chore at the solicitor fellow's. To meet a sister I haven't seen in half a lifetime. Don't much enjoy the prospect either.'

'Poor Dorothy!'

'How is she?'

'She hasn't complained about her health.'

'I'm surprised she hasn't added that to the list. But the poor girl had a raw deal—not that she didn't get what she wanted.'

'Ideal marriage is as rare as snow at Galle, Mr Badgery used to say.' His widow suggested she would have liked to tell the story of hers if Sir Basil had allowed.

' … only the deal could have been less raw for someone less rigid and less humourless.'

The princess was so deeply cut she cut herself off. Chin sunk, eyes bulging unnaturally, pearls heaved so spasmodically, she might have been suffering from heartburn. If only it were! Better unchaste than humourless, better dead than a dead weight.

On opening her mother's door she bumped against it, and Mrs

Hunter's head started up from the pillow, a relic miraculously raised from the timelessness of a morning nap.

'What is it? Why—oh, Dorothy! I thought I saw a statue walking at me—out of the Botanical Gardens. It's worth a visit. Ask Arnold. Will you be seeing Arnold, dear?'

'That is what has been arranged.'

Her daughter seated beside the bed, Mrs Hunter might still have suspected a statue: the practically sightless eyes were swivelling at an apparition in marble, if it wasn't plaster.

'You'll treat him kindly, won't you, dear?'

'There's no reason why I shouldn't.' Madame de Lascabanes spoke as though she inhabited a world sans butterflies.

'Because Arnold is kind—blinkered, but kind. The blinkers were torn off him probably only once, and I believe his whole life has been an effort to forget it.'

Dorothy thought the word 'kind' sat uneasily on Mother's lips, but she bent to kiss them, and was at once possessed, dared to question authority, cajoled, then rejected by an imperious but tired old woman.

'And Basil—has he arrived? Tell him, if you see him, I didn't expect his visit. I don't expect anything of anyone—except myself— and one's self, Dorothy, lets one down worse than the others.'

Neither of them dared ask, either through words or fingers: who then, is there?

Basil Hunter wiped the crumbs off. He had eaten three croissants (passable imitations) and drunk two cups of coffee (surprisingly, excellent: must be the Swiss management). He had received one telephone call, and made another, each in its way achieving something; he liked to think he was living positively even when he wasn't working. But he couldn't dismiss a suspicion of self-disgust, in spite of his still presentable features and body, a satisfied stomach, a sense of duty done: in agreeing to a meeting with the worthy Wyburd that same morning; in sending love-messages to his aged mother; and in promising a photograph to the nurse's protégée, if it wasn't the nurse herself. (More than likely he would forget the photograph, but to promise one pleased the nurse, and the minor gestures are often the most gratifying to those who make them.) Even the prospect of meeting a sister he hardly knew was only half a drag: to overcome her dislike would add significance to his conquest.

He should have felt brisker in the circumstances. No doubt the change of climate had been too sudden. He was suffocating in this hotel room, stuffed with everything that is comfortable and hideous in walnut veneer and glaring chintz, and sprawled on the Axminster roses, a great slippery monster of a Prussian blue eiderdown dismissed from the bed during the night. But it was the refrigerator, however homely and practical as a thought, which offended worst of all: ticking over ticking over, when it wasn't simply standing mute.

He was forced out into the garden, where the few hungry, city shrubs, and a plaster bird-bath painted to imitate brick, but suggesting slabs of uncooked beef, failed to provide the morale booster he was looking for. Nor did distance lessen the effect of the refrigerator's racketty movement; and worse, a clunk clunk in overtone recalled the airconditioners of Bangkok. Oh God, his head, his mouth, were still frowsty with Bangkok! Against this background of mere mechanical threats and physical reminders, the Jewish housekeeper's irony continued pricking: her celebration of failure, her own in particular, but anybody else's as well, 'They tell me you've played Hamlet—Lear—all the great "*German*" roles, so you must understand, Sir Basil!' *ein zwei drei*. (EXIT) Laughter from the gallery.

He glanced up. A sonsy maid and a chronically unemployed valet were talking on a balcony. They were looking at him from out of their frame of cast-iron lace. Well, he couldn't pretend it didn't go with his profession to be looked at, though he was hardly prepared for it at the moment, with his growth of stubble, and dressing-gown crumpled by the journey. Still, his head, his shoulders, could take it; when the maid and the valet burst out again; and he hadn't been playing for laughs.

He withdrew into his hideous but comparatively charitable room, away from what might take its place amongst the rankling moments, like that banana skin in Glasgow, brown-blotched and clammy-wet. How they laughed that night, till the decent among them shushed, and he forced himself back into the character he was playing. Dangerous attempting Richard Two at forty, but isn't an actor proved by danger? and the original notices (he still had them) were too seductive to resist. If they couldn't respect the accolade, there were the notices – if you could have shown them to the bastards: *Of all our younger actors, Basil Hunter* ... Produce the notices, however tattered and discoloured, and the laughter of all trumpery chambermaids and Irish-thug-valets would be stilled.

Sir Basil Hunter, who always felt better after shaving, less frayed, splenetic, awful, began to lather himself. (Remember too, Basil old boy, that when you see people laughing together at a distance they are more often than not acting a scene in which you don't appear.)

Like make-up, the white lather usually seemed to protect him from both past and future – if only temporarily. But this morning these red rims, dragged into view by fingers preparing a path for the razor, destroyed the authority, the chances of renewal, of an ageing, blighted fool. Have another go at Lear at least. During that other jinxed run he had seen himself in every other part but the one he had accepted to play: the Fool if you had been younger, smaller, a shade more fly, and considerably more selfless; Edgar, whom some find a bore – again if you had been younger, nimbler – and lower in the hierarchy; Gloucester, simple and rather stupid, can't fail to win sympathy: those empty eye sockets a gift to any actor. While Lear, that other loon, or human landslide, must work for pity which, unlike tearful sympathy, can survive on tragic heights, and is harder to rouse because purer, perhaps only begotten by purity of the inner man. Is it why almost everyone can fail as Lear – not completely of course: *Hunter's monolithic, weather- and emotion-haunted king* ... Produce those notices, too, for anybody troubled by superficial doubts, anyone short on 'purity' (doesn't it cut both ways?) remind them of the 'monolithic' triumph some critics and co-operative playgoers had more than witnessed: which they too had *lived*.

In spite of the inverted corners of his mouth and a bitter taste, Sir Basil found reason for perking up at his still only half-shaven reflexion; snow could not have brought out the ruddiness of the skin, its morning glow, more brilliantly than the drift of lather. Then he began to laugh, and finished snorting for what he didn't care to admit: that you were as remote in character from Lear and any of his attendant 'forces for good' as only the eternal bastard could be; if nobody else knew, God and yourself did. Who but Edmund, at a hint from the Guiding Spirit, would have taken plane for Sydney and Mummy's bedside? The real, utter bastard: so much so, he nicked the lobe of an ear, the worst possible place, usually bleeds for ever, leads from fury to wretchedness and depression, unless the styptic, which had more than likely been left behind, along with the anyway useless pills against gout.

Murderously, while pitifully bleeding, Sir Basil rootled his overnight bag into worse chaos, to find an invisible styptic pencil among the lozenges, the Jermyn Street handkerchiefs, the useless and expensive tackle in leather and silver which acquaintances (the recent ones) force on you for journeys; rootling always more hopelessly amongst the crumpled notepaper, unanswered letters, and one small book.

There was this scruffy paperback of plays he had snatched off a stand at the airport, to protect himself with something familiar: *Lear* in fact, and in spite of bitter associations; a shield against Mitty Jacka's last, still unanswered, for that matter, unread letter.

Here they were: in one hand a once more dogeared, smudged, pencilled *Lear*; in the other the latest directive in that awesomely elegant, convent-formed calligraphy from which he recoiled, hackles up; he couldn't say he feared, when its absence from his letter-box made him resentful.

Her letters might have been love-letters, but they weren't. There had never been a hint of love in their relationship: in his own case, perhaps the need to exorcise a dread of staleness with the dread of danger; in hers, he had not yet succeeded in deciding what.

He wouldn't open the Jacka letter: he was already late, he realized, for the appointment with Arnold—yes, time you called the old bugger by his first name; and it wasn't as though the letter hadn't lain already several days ignored and crumpled in your bag.

Basil might have kept to his intention of snubbing the Guiding Spirit if he hadn't taken another look at the glass, where he saw that the blood had started to clot, while glittering like a single jewel hooked into his left lobe. Distracted by this rather pleasing conceit, he found himself fumbling the letter out of its envelope, the parchment sheet still basically stiff and formal in spite of its martyrdom during the journey. Again he might have decided to postpone reading, if he hadn't already begun sifting.

... those who are younger often allow themselves to be gulled by the old: by purblindness, which doesn't necessarily prevent them seeing very clearly; or by some distressing tic they exaggerate because they have found it pays; or by a general pathos of old age. The aged are usually tougher and more calculating than the young, provided they keep enough of their wits about them. How could they have lived so long if there weren't steel buried inside them? ...

... beware of the saintly in particular: the tactics they employ are often the most subtly elastic. I believe aged saints are made through the waning of desire more than by the ripening of inherent sanctity; nor does diminished desire mean they cannot draw on a knowledge of the world they have been forced to renounce ...

... dear creature, you can't be unaware that my spirit goes with you on your flight. That you must succeed in your mission and return to collaborate in this work of ours, which will add another dimension to the art of theatre, is something I take for granted ...

Hooey, of course! Still trembling, he sheathed the letter. As a young fool he had dabbled furtively in the arcane; as an old one, the possibility of controlling events normally considered uncontrollable often kept him awake at night. One of her more ribald associates had referred to the Jacka as the Witch of Beulah Hill. He had met her on a wet night, on the deserted upper deck of a bus: it could have been to compensate him for a walk-through performance in a sick contemporary play with which he had unwisely become involved. ('They' said he didn't understand it, when—balls to them—he understood it so well he hesitated to convey its putrescence.)

The woman on the bus was dressed in black: woolly leotards under transparent waterproof cape; over her head, and tied beneath the chin, a scarf in colours which might have looked flaunted on someone less oblivious. The rain had brushed with as much of her hair as you could see, and freshened the long parchment-coloured face, the thin, naked lips, on which the last words spoken still seemed vibrating.

As the empty bus staggered and panted with suppressed speed, the woman's body, her long legs and pointed shoes protruding at an angle from the seat, appeared to derive a weary and in no way voluptuous pleasure from its motion. Facing straight ahead, the half-lowered radiant eyelids and live mouth began to suggest that you might have something to say to each other, only it was up to you to confirm.

On a thumb of the hands laid together in her lap he noticed a ring, the twin of one he had sent his mother some years ago; he had often regretted parting with it, though the gesture had produced material results. As for the woman, she was aware of his interest in the ring, and could recognize a crucial moment.

'Is it Ethiopian?' He was pointing at the Orthodox cross in the nest of plaited gold. 'I knew another, exactly like it—as far as I can remember.'

'I can't say. I haven't asked'; and after a pause, 'I took it from someone who didn't appreciate what they had. It's the only thing I ever stole—except flowers from over fences.' The bus lulled her back into silence and a half-smile, though she appeared to take it for granted that it wasn't the end of their conversation.

He was certainly fascinated, if also mystified by the woman across the aisle: ageless rather than old; not a whore as he had suspected at first; probably more willing to receive a stranger into her thoughts than into her still supple body.

Presently she said, 'If I could choose, I'd lead my entire waking life at night. Well, I *can* choose, I suppose, and I do more or less.' She turned towards him. 'Don't you feel more aware at night? Of course you must—Sir Basil Hunter!'

Recognition was common enough for him not to feel embarrassed in normal circumstances; but in this instance, a grey stare acted like blow lamps (cold ones) on any hidden flaws. 'A lot depends on the performance,' he mumbled while looking at his hands, at a place scarred by a forbidden jackknife; he must have been seven, or thereabout, at—at 'Kudjeri'.

'Day or night a lot depends on the performance,' she agreed. 'There are nights when I sit for hours—locked.' She smiled at him with understanding. 'This is where I change buses.'

Though nowhere near his destination, he got up and followed her down; they both seemed to find it natural, or at any rate she did not behave as though frightened; some women would have wanted to throw him off, star actor notwithstanding. It was simply that there was nothing sexual in their encounter; yet she was leading him, and he could feel himself more subtly possessed than he had ever possessed either Shiela Sturges or the Lady Enid, his official wives.

Her long feet reached for the damp pavement. He was standing beside her. They did not speak again till after she had chosen their bus.

When they were re-settled, she told him, 'This house where I live—which I inherited—is too big, too demanding.'

Was she after all making a proposition?

She didn't seem to be. 'Still, it's where I've got to live, and I don't normally complain—only that my dependents make it impossible for me to lead my life wholly at night.'

'You have a large family?'

'Not family in the usual sense: various *old* people, women mostly, dotted all over London—who won't die—and at home, animals.'

He thought he wouldn't inquire into the animals; he didn't care for them, except as an English theory he had adopted, and as engravings.

Instead he rounded on her with what might have sounded like reprehensible enthusiasm. 'Now that I come to think of it, I haven't any dependents—one of a kind, a pathetic *failed* actress to whom I pay what is necessary—no need to the other—nor to my well-balanced, committed daughter. I have no one. I ran away from my family, my country, to become an actor.'

She was waiting.

'I've done what I set out to do,' he insisted, he felt, modestly.

She didn't disagree. 'You were knighted by the Queen,' she reminded with appropriate gravity.

When it wasn't his achievement he wanted to recall, but his childhood, from which Macbeth, Hamlet, Lear, together with other paler apparitions, had sprung, out of the least likely drought-stricken gullies, brown, brooding pools, and austere forms of wind-tattered trees. Only the bus was not the ideal place in which to begin his invocation; and for once the sound of his famous voice would have made him wince.

'I've seen some of your performances,' she was telling, 'though I don't make a habit of going to the theatre. I remember your Lear—and I've been to the present thing.'

This drew him. 'Will you admit it isn't as bad as they said?'

'No, not bad—in fact good, in its stunted way.'

He could feel himself inwardly bridling; perhaps vanity was the source of his greatest sensual pleasure.

'But might have been better if you had dared *give* yourself.'

'How do you mean "give"?' He could hear the anger in his voice; and he looked at her afresh, wondering whether this old bag was leading up to what would materialize as an unmade bed.

'Nothing physical,' she formed the word with almost prudish

240

care. 'I don't doubt you've given yourself physically, night after night, in the parts you've acted—to the wives you mention—mistresses probably (I know nothing about your private life because I don't read newspapers). And I don't mean creatively either, because that's unconscious where it isn't disciplined physical labour. Nor do I mean what used to be called "spiritual" before we shed our *illusions*. Perhaps I should say you haven't yet given yourself "essentially".'

His mind felt numb, his skin clammy. Was she preparing to introduce him, not to the unmade bed with its coffee stains and importunate ageing flesh, but to a far more daunting prospect: the other side of that grey screen, or backcloth, he had seen in his boyhood as standing between himself and nothing; and which he resurrected even now in times of flux and fallibility. So he armed himself with scepticism against anything else she might have to say.

'Why I don't go to the theatre more often,' she continued, 'is because it exhausts and irritates me to watch a set of cast-iron figures trying to drag their weight around in a disintegrated world. Since our conglomerate existence became less conglomerate, less controllable, more fluid, how can we express, or become part of it, unless we flow too, by giving—or losing—ourselves "essentially"?'

Cock, he resisted answering; I have been able to control my own life ever since I learnt the technique of living, which is also the technique of acting; my gift, which is myself, is something no critic, no ratbag witch, no banana skins, only senility or death, can destroy. But what she had said stimulated him to the extent that he would have been tempted to flow with the darkness and the rain, and beyond them, if she was prepared to show him how.

Instead, the bus jolted and stopped. 'This is where I get out,' she said, looking younger for the moment and unexpectedly shy. 'My name is Mitty Jacka.' It could have accounted for the shyness.

She got up lugging a string bag filled with awkward, lumpy parcels, which had been lying on the seat beside her. Again he tagged along; at some point on their nightride they had come to an agreement.

The rain had stopped, or rather, he could feel only an occasional flurry of moisture, fine enough to have been shaken in his face by plant tendrils, or out of human hair. The glistening pavement they were mounting rose sharply enough for Mitty Jacka to sound breathless, though she looked more youthful for her breathlessness whenever the lamplight showed her up. He too was breathless, from the strangeness of what he was letting happen.

'My house will put me to shame,' she said, and you knew that she was being no more than formally truthful. 'Other people find it dirty.'

'Other people? I imagined you leading the life of a recluse, apart from those dependents "dotted about".'

'Oh, no. They pour in. Droves of them. At all hours of the day. That's why I prefer the night. Night is for the elect.'

Though she gave no direct sign of including him amongst the chosen, he was moved by vanity for the second time since their meeting. He brushed against her, partly by losing his balance, if also a little by intention. She didn't appear to notice, unless awareness was the reason for a sharp clout he received from the loaded shopping bag.

Soon after, they arrived at a gate in a flint wall at which a cat was on the lookout, back arched at first in anticipation of danger, then subsiding into a serpentine blue glimmer.

The cat's purring and the drip of moisture from branches lifted in a gentle breeze made the sound of his voice an inept and impertinent intrusion on their dark surroundings. 'What's its name?' he asked, stroking air instead of fur.

'Oh, I don't know—Cat! It was called something in the beginning, but I forget. We're always together, so a name isn't necessary, is it?'

After identifying him on the bus, she hadn't addressed him by name, and he felt pretty sure he would never venture to call her by hers.

All around them were wet, needling branches, patches and trailers of faintly moonlit ivy; he caught sight of an irruption of fungus on the scaly torso of a tree. Here and there he had to stoop, not always successfully, to avoid being hit in the face. She too, was tall, but there the difference began: she had been initiated into the ways of darkness, while he might remain the blundering intruder.

As soon as her key grated in the lock, there were sounds from inside the house: of scuffling, and snuffling, and a pop pop popping. Then, by light, a brace of pugs had begun to seethe around them, laying their faces flat against a stranger's ankles, squeaking joy for those they were re-discovering.

Mitty Jacka was no demonstrative dog lover; she allowed devotion to flow around her, which it did: her pugs were ecstatic. After his experience with the cat Cat, he suppressed an impulse to ask their names. Instead, he was learning to adapt himself to the flow, if not to the smell of rubber hot water bottles and peanuts, evidently the distinctive smell of pug.

He sat with a glass she had brought him, filled with something sweet, unacceptable, finally insidious, while she went about her animal business. Around him smouldered an upholstery of garnet plush, against panelling which looked like ebony, but couldn't have been. At least it was an ebony pedestal on which a figurine stood holding its curve under an ivory parasol. He found he had begun smiling into his sweet and fiery drink, while the voice of Mitty Jacka in the distance flung a few ritual 'darlings' to her animals.

He realized she was with him again on seeing her drop a piece of paper about the size of a visiting card into an urn on the shadowy outskirts of the room.

'What was that?' The drink inside him made him feel less brazen than spontaneous.

'Oh — an idea I might decide to use.' She sounded unwilling, even a bit sour.

Then she was gone, followed by her anxious retinue. He continued sitting. Perhaps the smell of raw liver she left behind deterred him from investigating her 'idea'. Instead he waited: for what? His future as an actor of some importance no longer seemed relevant.

When she returned, not to settle — her behaviour suggested she might never do that, anyway during the hours of darkness—she freshened up his drink, more of which he had meant to refuse. As she moved about the room a cigarette she had lit for herself trailed its streamers of smoke, or described more elaborate arabesques as she stopped to look at and sometimes re-arrange objects she might have been seeing for the first time. She smoked so furiously that he was more drugged by her cigarette than drunk by whatever was in his glass.

From adding up a couple of her remarks he decided to risk her displeasure again. 'I gather you write.' Carefully composed, the words shot out of his mouth like a handful of independent marbles.

She drew harder on her cigarette. 'I hammer away.' The smoke she blew looked peculiarly solid. 'Sometimes it takes a recognizable shape—or one which *I* can recognize, though more often than not it isn't what it was intended to be. Yes, I write verses,' she added, by way of obeying a social convention. 'And all my life I've been putting together I don't know what you would call it—a work—which will convey everything there is to express—if I can extract and compress it—or if in the end I don't find it has melted down of its own accord into the word I started with.'

Surrounded by the smoke with which she had been filling the room, he began telling, 'When I was a boy—I forget how old, but quite young—I had an illness—no, I must have broken my arm: I can remember the sling, and the clammy feeling of my skin from the arm strapped against my unwashed body—in bed. They had fixed me up for the night—tried to make me comfortable. My father lit one of the night-lights left over from when we were smaller. And stood a screen across one corner of the bedhead—to keep the draught off, I imagine. During the night this screen began to terrify me. The fall—the broken arm—must have left me a bit delirious. As the night-light flickered I kept trying to turn—the strapped arm made it agony—to watch the screen. It was of a pale grey, or some nondescript colour, with the skeletons of trees stencilled on it. Or that was how the light made it appear. As the night dragged on and I became more desperate, I longed to look behind the screen, but was too afraid of what I might find. I was running with sweat. I suppose I fell asleep in the end.'

Nor did the wine, or whatever the Jacka woman had poured, help him decide whether he had been speaking or dreaming. She had come and was sitting beside him on the couch, in a heap of drowsy pugs. She could have been smiling as she watched him, while stroking the rise and fall of a pug's exposed teats.

'This screen—how it's continued cropping up. So solid and real— as real as childhood.' He laughed uneasily for his discovery. 'I've built speeches round it, rehearsing parts which have worried me. It's always protected me from the draught.' He sniggered, sipping the drink which had let loose his confession. 'This screen thing—it materializes again when you feel you're beginning to slip—in musty provincial theatres—a piece of disintegrating silk stretched on a ricketty, tottering frame. You're less than ever inclined to look behind it. And you're pretty sure that if it blows over, you're lost.'

His lips were almost paralysed. He was no longer aware of her as a face but as a smile beneath water. What else he told he could not have unravelled for sleep in a white dress streaming light from the top of the stairs. Did she touch his forehead?

Towards morning he needed to relieve himself, stumbled through the curtains of smoke and plush, and against a low, object-laden table, but reached the garden, where cold and a sprinkling of rain revived him. A sweet scent, cold too, rejoiced him as he did his business. This piercing scent of night flowers was threaded through the smell of damp rot which finally predominated.

Returning to the house, he looked up, and caught sight of Mitty Jacka seated by a naked light, in an upper room, either 'hammering away', or, more likely, 'locked': for the moment she was perfectly still, her expression desperate by that searching light.

He felt so sober burrowing back into the darkness where he had slept, it occurred to him to investigate the urn in which she had dropped her slip of paper. He made light, put in his hand, and skimmed the surface of an urnful of similar slips for what was probably the most recent: there were traces of raw liver on it, as well as a bloody fingerprint or two.

Sceptical this morning, not to say cynical, he opened the folded paper to read:

> ... an actor tends to ignore the part which fits him best *his life*
> Lear the old unplayable is in the end a safer bet than the unplayed I ...

His breath sharpened as the words blurred. He didn't have with him the glasses he used, not to read (he seldom did) but to study a part. So he held the paper at arm's length. After the first attempt to focus on words too perfectly formed in a severe, anachronistic hand, he saw he might as well give up. Depressing the way his sight had deteriorated: after shock for instance, or abusive letters, selfish performances by the vindictive young, and especially after alcohol. Considering how the Jacka had dosed him the night before, it was no wonder half the message was lost. He was glad to re-fold her squalid paper, and toss it back into the urn, where it couldn't remind him of physical decay.

Then he proceeded to arrange himself again on what had become an uncomfortable unsprung sofa. He drew himself into an appropriate form, only it wasn't: he realized he had taken on the shape of a prawn, and that it was too TIGHT. When sleep seeped back shallowly around he was lashing and kicking, more transparent than the words in which he was netted.

His hostess brought him a cup of coffee at a most untheatrical hour. After she had dragged the curtains back, a grey light touched their reunion with fatality. Even so, Mitty Jacka, all gooseflesh and shivers now that day had succeeded her elective night, would have liked to float on the surface.

She said too hastily, 'Poor you – you must have been uncomfortable! The sofa's a disaster. It belonged to a great-aunt.'

She stood chafing thin and elderly arms; while he sat muttering approval of the sofa into his coffee. The cup, a once sumptuous Empire, had a brown chip as large as a thumbnail.

'We'll keep in touch,' she predicted, looking out uneasily through the amorphousness of a wet garden, 'because I know we're meant to write a play together.'

She had him at her mercy: she could attack him at the theatre where he was playing; whereas he had neither her number, nor address – nor did he want them.

'Plays cost money,' he replied, showing her his smile, which she ignored.

'It can always be raised from somewhere. What about this old rich invalid mother?'

What had he told her in the night? He wasn't aware he had mentioned Elizabeth Hunter.

'She's pretty tight,' he mumbled, staring at his white knuckles. 'Oh, she's generous enough, I must admit – in little handouts – from time to time.'

'Wouldn't a personal appearance make a difference?'

'Not worth it. Too many others waiting to jump in the moment you leave the West End.'

'Money is worth it. Money is power, isn't it?'

'Oh, but it's hers!' As though he believed.

'Only if her life justifies her keeping it.'

'Aren't the lives of beautiful women works of art? They deserve the fortunes men pay for them. And Elizabeth Hunter is a great – an incredibly beautiful woman.' Now he honestly believed in what he saw: himself as a youth deriving from this radiance.

'She had a stroke.' Mitty Jacka sounded her coldest. 'Mightn't she die?'

More than this voice, he had begun to detest himself. 'Not on your life! Or anyway, not in a hundred years. Nothing will persuade Elizabeth Hunter to die.'

He must get up; he must move; or succumb to slow poisoning. He felt as though not a skerrick of live flesh had been left clinging to his thought-infested skull.

Mitty Jacka might have tried persuading him some more if her blue cat had not forestalled her. It strolled in out of the garden

247

flicking the tip of its tail, carrying in its jaws a folded thrush: a corpse judging by the lolling head, resigned eyelids, and a necklace of blood against otherwise decent feathers. The cat flattened itself and growled, to warn off possible intervention, then glided under the sofa.

The mistress had bared her teeth. 'Ohhh!' she cried, whether distressed or elated by the enactment of her argument, it was difficult to tell. 'There's nothing one can do. Isn't it natural,' she insisted, 'that some should die for others to live?'

Holding forth in its rasping, high-pitched growl from under the sofa, the cat made it clear who should live, while its mistress remained only an aspiring murderess.

Seeing that the moment could provide him with a reason for his exit, the actor advanced firmly, professionally, on his hostess, and took her hands in his. 'Thank you', he said, 'for your hospitality — the ideas you've shared — and this memorable house.' Make it sound final. 'I shan't forget any of it.'

There was a faint trembling, it seemed, in the cold unresponsive hands, till he realized it came from his own warmer, fleshier ones.

'Next time,' she said as they were walking through the rooms towards the front door, 'I'll tell you how I visualize this play.' Their shoulders collided in conspiracy: his well-cut, actor's sleeve, and her shabby, black silk, rustling kimono, with stains become part of its embroideries.

Mitty Jacka was still apparently speaking. 'A man develops only one of his several potential lives. There's no reason why he shouldn't live them all — or at least act them out, if he can liberate himself. This is what I'd like for you: this nightly liberation instead of the cast-iron figures dragging themselves from one prescribed attitude to another.'

By now he had dragged his cast-iron, proven self as far as the front door, from which he could see, through foliage and boughs, the gate set in the flint-studded wall. The gate was still a long way off.

He replied cagily enough, 'A lot would depend on who else was available at the time; not forgetting a theatre. That's after we've raised the cash by whatever immoral means!'

'In this case almost everything would depend on yourself; and aren't you a great actor, Sir Basil Hunter?'

This time he saw to it that she didn't raise a flicker out of his vanity. 'I'm a man who's been bitten more than once, and who intends to go carefully.' In spite of long experience, he could not tell how his audience had reacted to this touch of false humility.

'If it's a matter of life and death, wouldn't you choose life?'

At the moment he might have chosen death rather than go through another performance for Mitty Jacka. So he ignored her question.

Then, when retreating down the path, he remembered the convention in which he must behave, and looked back, not so much to raise, as re-tilt his Homburg with the right show of insouciance. She was standing on the step, an archaic figure in the black gown she had gathered around her with her arms, her face an expressionless white, except for a grey shadow of what could have been anxiety.

'Don't forget to write to that old woman—your mother,' she called after him in practical tones. 'You'd be surprised how many people are longing to be asked to collaborate. It gives them the illusion of living.'

The gate jingled, clicked; he was free, thank God.

His footsteps resounding down the hill, the sky awash with early morning colours above the telly grids and wet slates, restored his faith in himself as future. If he did fly home on a brief visit, it would be from his own choice, not a mentor's, his object not to bully an old woman into handing over a fortune even if it killed her, but to renew himself through bursts of light, whiffs of burning, the sound of trees stampeded by a wind when they weren't standing as still as silence. And mud: in spite of the pavement and his shoes, he could feel it almost, oozing upward, increasing, between the splayed toes of his bare feet.

Fortified by sensual realities such as these, it was easy to dismiss as hallucination the incident at wherever it was. Certainly the woman made no attempt to get in touch. A week or two, and it began to surprise him; once or twice he caught himself resenting Mitty Jacka's neglect.

Then the notices went up. Though there had been rumours, the management (a second-rate, recent lot) hadn't so much as hinted that their miserable play was likely to close abruptly; and himself carrying the thing for weeks, in support of a young Geordie graduated overnight from bricklayer to leading man.

Well, that was the way nowadays. He belched at the sheet of paper pinned to the board.

'We're off, I see,' he mentioned to Peggy Digby, her perky tits and jumper in a hurry down the corridor.

'Yes. Didn't you know? Wadda*relief*! Now I guess I'll make the panto.'

He continued staring, not so much at the announcement on the board, as the brand-new drawing pins, and the image of that woman on the bus.

On the night of the fourth last performance he poured himself a tot purely to moisten his vocal chords. The walls of his dressing-room at the Delphic were painted poison green above a chocolate dado: both green and brown had blisters in them. He poured himself a second tot: the first had been thoughtlessly done, and weak.

But his voice stayed hoarse all that evening. Nothing he threw in —and God knows he performed—nothing helped them out of the doldrums in which they were stuck. Except in the second act, when the Geordie bricklayer bared his torso, a girl's voice nearly squealed the darkness down. The audience (mostly paper) laughed.

Taking off his make-up after the performance, which normally revived his spirits as much as putting it on in the beginning, he was nauseated by the smell of Cremine to the extent of trembling. And his disgusting old rag of a towel. Surely he wasn't becoming a professional trembler—or Parkinsonian?

He longed for somebody to come. He listened for the sound of a formal dress; he might have put up with his second ex-wife, the Lady Enid; even a worshipful, crushed macintosh wouldn't have come amiss. But nobody appeared, and in the absence of visitors, he poured himself a tot. Walker handed him the Homburg.

He went out. In the green-and-chocolate corridor, Peggy Digby gave him a big, skilful kiss. 'Promise to come up to Glasgow to see the panto. You'll find I'm the Number One Dandini.'

It was parky outside under an etiolated lamp-lit drizzle. He had no appetite for the meal he would eat in the corner of some stale Soho joint: no point in cutting a dash when he was on his own. He could have rung any number of bells, where groovy young pros or business swingers would have dragged him in raucously, and scooped out the *foie gras* and got him drunk, but he couldn't think of one who might satisfy his hunger—for what? For substance perhaps, for permanence. Friendship, as he saw it, was more and more like an ingenious farce with too much plot and too many characters all acting frenetically, in spite of which it closed after the routine run. (Marriage too; though that was a different sort of play.)

This was where Sir Basil felt the damp in his right foot, looked at his sole as soon as he reached a quiet lamp-post, and noticed that he needed mending. All right, simple enough: he wasn't on the rocks, only shortly out of a job. He had his experience, his title, his technique, his voice, and, it had been demonstrated, women were attracted to him.

What was the—Mitty Jacka! Of Golden Hill? Of Beulah!

He took the bus to Beulah Hill looking for signs of a disturbing presence: on the seats of an empty upper deck; at a flint-studded gatepost apparently much favoured by dogs; then along the path, slippery with snails, till he was again standing on her doorstep about that same hour of night.

'I've come', he said, 'to hear about the play you spoke of. Remember?' Perhaps it was his position on the lower step which made it sound suppliant.

The two pugs were poppopping at his ankles, while around hers curved an arc of luminous fur.

'Yes,' she said. 'I've been giving it thought. I'm glad you've decided.'

He could feel his mask grinning up at her, the teeth grown jagged in its mock flesh: that of the Second Conspirator. Or was it the First Suicide?

Anyway, here he was as a result, in this other sunlight, dazed by it as he lolled in the cavorting taxi, prickling with grit, streaming with sweat in spite of his recent bath and shave. He was feeling fine: not the shadow of a conscience for keeping them waiting, old Arnold the Wyburd and the bloody princess, probably three-quarters of an hour. It was hardly his fault, was it? if the *Herald* and the A.B.C. chose to ring, one after the other, just as he was making a dash for it.

So he was determined to relax and enjoy this whizzing vision of a city which had grown out of his childhood recollections: of a Pitt Street peopled only by acquaintances, all of them converging on the Civil Service Stores. Though he had played no active part in his city's transformation, though he had rejected it in fact, he accepted some of the credit for it. He had to share his recovered self-respect with this self-important metropolis. However late in the piece, he offered his love to its plate glass and neo-brutal towers; at the heart of it, his old mother. He would forget his horror of the lilac wig, the deliquescent smile: these dismissed, he could love the whole idea of mothers, as of Sydney. (Recall the horrors later if you are short on ruthlessness. Remember to send the better suit for pressing, for your interview with the telly girl of the mellow-'cello voice.)

Mr Wyburd glanced at the clock. Unpunctuality was one of the vices which roused him to anger, an ugly and intemperate emotion, though perhaps not as deplorable as unwillingness to forgive the offender; and the Hunter children had both failed to keep an appointment made for eleven. One of them could have been involved in an accident, but not both, surely? unless they had shared a taxi, and there was not love enough between them for that. A regular churchgoer (he had kept it up as an example to his own children, then found it had become a habit), the solicitor would have liked to conjure a material banner embroidered with the concept CHARITY to hold between himself and his clock, to prevent the anger rising again, peculiarly physical and bitter-tasting, out of his stomach into his mouth. Or in any event, he must dissociate his irritation from the face of a clock for which he had a longstanding and sentimental attachment.

It was a carriage clock, and had been sent him by Mrs Hunter as a memento and token of esteem after her husband's death. The clock had belonged to the late Mr Hunter. Arnold Wyburd could remember exactly where it used to stand on the library mantelpiece at 'Kudjeri'. He remembered, not from that first brief stay when he had arrived unsuitably dressed, timid as a boy, bringing for signature the agreement to their purchase of the block in Moreton Drive, but from later visits, by which time he had proved himself worthy of his clients' trust, and could unbend sufficiently to take pleasure in their hospitality. His respect and affection for Mr Hunter grew, until (it had been something of an ice-breaking) he could be included among those who addressed him as 'Bill'.

Under the carriage clock, in the library at 'Kudjeri', Bill Hunter and Arnold Wyburd would sit talking: each had a respect for functional objects such as clocks, telescopes, razors, barometers, as well as for acts of God; often they were content simply to stare into the fire. Arnold Wyburd wondered how many of those present at Bill Hunter's funeral had noticed him crying, and how many still remembered. He was half ashamed of it himself. He hadn't thought about it for years, till this morning Bill's pestiferous children gave him the opportunity. Had Bill loved his children? You didn't believe he could have, then felt guilty at thinking such a thought.

Standing beside the devotedly accurate carriage clock on the bookcase in Arnold Wyburd's office was a framed studio portrait inscribed in Bill's angular hand (it reminded the solicitor of arrowheads) *To Arnold Wyburd—in affectionate friendship—Bill*. Several years before her husband's death, this, too, had been sent by Mrs Hunter, almost as if she wished to suggest the inscribed photograph were one of her own little inspirations (though wives usually do up the parcels). She had enclosed a note in her familiar, awful scrawl (she must have started writing large as an affectation, then found it came naturally) ... *an exceptionally good likeness I consider and as you more than anyone else Arnold love and appreciate Alfred you must be the first to have one* ... She hadn't inscribed the photograph herself, but you could see her standing over him with advice. It embarrassed you still to remember the wording of her note. What, Arnold Wyburd sometimes wondered, did Mrs Hunter understand as 'love'? For that matter, he wasn't too clear what he understood by it himself: probably, from personal experience, many years of honourable conjugal affection interspersed with decently conducted sexual intercourse.

The solicitor coughed. On top of everything else that morning, he couldn't help resenting Mrs Hunter's intrusion on his memories of Bill.

To restore mental order, he moved one or two objects on his desk. There was no question of settling down to work. Avoiding the eyes of the photograph he might have glanced again at the infuriating clock if Miss Haygarth hadn't appeared with the cup of pale, milky tea (*normally* she brought it earlier) and the two biscuits he seldom touched. Miss Haygarth went away.

No need to look at the clock: his mind was keeping pace with it. Rage, he had told himself, is generated by those of unreasonable temperament, and leads to the courts. As for irritation, simpler, though more often than not, perverse, it could bring on stomach ulcers, when his health, apart from appendicitis at the age of thirty-seven, had remained exceptional all these years, thanks to regular habits, plain food, and a prudent wife. Yet now, all seemed threatened, if not by rage or irritation, by an uncharacteristic restlessness. He had spent a most disturbed night; and at breakfast Lal had joined him in one or two cynical remarks (unlike either of them).

'Poor Dorothy—I'd be curious to see her again—to find out whether a plain girl can make a glamorous princess.' Then she laughed, and her teeth looked—no, not really. 'I expect she can,

because underneath I'm a bit of a snob.' The honesty of her admission together with too large a mouthful of corn fritter made her
cheeks bulge: his reliable Lal.

'Yesterday she said she'd love to see you.'

'That's what they say.'

'Oh, Dorothy will come—unless there's too much of her mother
in her.'

They had such a laugh together he promptly suffered from a fit of
disloyalty to the Hunter family. He stabbed the sausage on his plate.
Lal bought beef because they were more economical, and less
greasy, but even so, when he pricked the skin a jet of liquid fat shot
out on to his waistcoat. He covered the stain with his napkin in case
she should notice and feel she must do something about it before he
left for the office. For his additional discomfiture, the napkin, he
realized, was one of a good Irish set the Hunters had given, on no
formal occasion, simply as a spontaneous gesture between Easter
and Christmas. (Because it was Mrs Hunter who must have thought
of the napkins, it made him feel almost as guilty as when she had
referred to his 'love' for Bill.)

Now Miss Haygarth was returning, not to remove the cup and
saucer and the two rejected biscuits, but to announce with unusual
enthusiasm (she was a rather phlegmatic, though efficient girl, from
Bexley North), 'It's the princess—Miss—Miss Dorothy Hunter.'

At almost the same moment the Princesse de Lascabanes came
pushing in. What the solicitor suspected of being worldly abandon,
perhaps inspired by her inexcusable unpunctuality, seemed to have
replaced the reserve, the diffidence of the day before. If her manner
was still harsh, recklessness had tempered it. She approached, hatless,
taking off her gloves, smiling a smile, some of which had come off
on her teeth. It surprised the solicitor that a princess should not be
wearing a hat, and considering the gloves; though lots of ladies, even
the older ones, went hatless nowadays. (He wondered whether Mrs
Hunter, if she had the strength to rise from her bed, would have
broken into his office hatless, and started dictating to him from the
leather chair.)

'I'm not horribly late, am I? I expect I am,' Madame de Lascabanes opened in a voice loud enough to cause a sensation in the outer office.

The solicitor formed the word No, but it sat soundless on his pale lips as he unnecessarily rearranged a chair.

Dorothy observed, 'My brother is late at least;' and could have been drawing attention to one among many other flaws.

She could not have been better pleased: things were turning out as she had planned, when she imagined she had botched it all by her expedition, however rewarding, to the kitchen and the housekeeper's bedroom.

'I'm so glad.' Her sigh was perhaps too little-girlish.

For a moment her diffidence returned as she reflected that the solicitor might plunge her abruptly into business matters. What she had wanted by forestalling Basil was to talk, not to a solicitor, but to an elderly man, one old enough to be her father. It had been her intention originally to ask about the father she scarcely knew, but she had changed her mind at some point since waking from her dream of the night before.

'Are you comfortable at the club?' Mr Wyburd kindly inquired.

'The beds are comfortable.' She blushed, and added, 'Yes, I am comfortable — thank you.'

She thought she would begin, after all, by discussing her one and only father. 'I believe you and he were very close friends;' she was launched well into it before she realized: too intense, but there was nothing she could do about that; she was only grateful for the unusual impetus. 'So you must have understood him, Mr Wyburd — as we never did. My brother was certainly too selfish, too much concentrated on his own ambitions; I, too shy — and yes, too stupid'; on a different occasion she would have been ashamed to make any such admission, but now she was offering a wise and consoling confidant what she hoped he might recognize as virtues; whether he did, there wasn't time to calculate before she fired her last and most necessary shot, 'as for my mother, she never allowed herself to understand anybody in case it might interrupt what she liked to see as her own continuous triumph. Mother specialized in slaves, of whom Father was the most valuable. She must have tortured him cruelly.' Dorothy Hunter looked at the solicitor and begged – no, not this morning; this morning, for some reason, she was the Princesse de Lascabanes, brave enough to command this man to become her ally.

But in his position of trust Arnold Wyburd was above alliances; and even if he hadn't been, he imagined prudence would not have allowed him to desire one; so he wet his lips, and answered, 'I can't remember your father ever referring to Mrs Hunter in the conversations I had with him, except formally, in legal matters, and – oh, you know the kind of jokes men make about their wives!'

The princess was rather put out. 'No, I don't, exactly,' she had to admit; then she blurted, 'But what on earth did you talk about all those years?'

'Well, business. Wasn't I his solicitor?'

It infuriated Madame de Lascabanes. 'But a relationship isn't only business! There must have been other, personal topics.'

The solicitor had a brainwave; he smiled mildly. 'We shared an interest in clocks.' Not avoidance when it was a fact. 'You see the clock on the mantelpiece? That was one of Bill's. Your mother very thoughtfully presented me with it after his death. And there's your father's photograph beside it.'

Dorothy got up, handbag, gloves and all. 'Oh, yes! *Dad!*' when she hadn't meant things to go this way.

She hadn't wanted to be moved by her dead, though actual father, only morally roused on his behalf; whereas here were lines of kindness round eyes as mild as the solicitor's own, and a mouth too sensitive to be associated with rams – or Elizabeth Hunter. She must concentrate on the absurd collar of an in-between period and the laughably conventional photographic pose. But the inscription, in a hand as stiff and awkward as some of her worst moments, was convincing enough to make her regret this confrontation more deeply.

She turned and said, 'I'm afraid nobody—*none of us*—loved him as he deserved.' While expressing her own inadequacy, it should at the same time have paid the solicitor out.

He didn't reply.

When they were once more seated, she noticed his hands clasped in front of him on the desk: they were older than she would have liked. But he probably hated her. Everybody hated her.

Madame de Lascabanes opened her handbag, looked inside it, and closed it again.

She held up her head, and smiled a bright forgiveness. 'Tell me—didn't you have a little girl called Heather? I seem to remember measles. Or was it *chicken* pox?'

Miss Haygarth came in and whispered in her farthest from Bexley North, 'Sir Basil Hunter.'

Dorothy was seated with her back to the door. Would her pearls, her coiffure, help her after all endure the presence of her un-speakable brother? Before anything else, she did not think she could bear his laughter: for herself, as she remembered it, the rattle of a metallic shutter clashing with her most private thoughts; for others —the grown-ups—dreamy rippling chuckles delighting by what passed for uninhibited boyishness.

Now only silence in this steel and concrete cell, in which the paraphernalia of another age, in sagging leather and buckled paste-board, collaborated with austerity to make it appear more sinister. She looked to the solicitor to protect her from the calculated brutality of the blow which must be preparing for her; Basil's malice was capable of the greatest accuracy.

Arnold Wyburd had stood up, himself a party to the silence: lips twitching, but silently; eyelids flickering rather foolishly she thought, showing their blue veins and unnaturally white wrinkles. It was as though the silence had isolated and exaggerated this decent man, no longer solicitor, pseudo-father, least of all the mysterious lover whose dream flesh and silky testicles had caressed her thighs in the club bedroom, but a mediocre actor continuing to mime his part during a break in the sound track. He looked particularly unconvincing as he pretended to accept from across the flickering silence of the Keemis and Wyburd office apologies for late arrival which would in any case have sounded insincere.

She sat frozen by Mr Wyburd's impotence: deep frozen when unseen hands grasped her shoulders from behind in a display of familiarity, moulding, positively mauling; then she was nuzzled between her right ear lobe and the pearls.

At the same time sound flowed back to assist the performance in a series of broken, not quite vibrato, amplified whispers. 'Good—old —Dor-o-thy!' Basil breathed down her neck; and she realized that she was faced with, perhaps not star-, but co-stardom, in this flawed film, in which she had hoped to play only a modest part, like the solicitor, and slip away without being blamed for her innate gaucherie as an actress or the vicious tendencies of the character she was supposed to represent.

Instead, Basil her brother kept coasting round the somewhat sticky Keemis and Wyburd leather chair till their situation of reunited brother and sister was complete.

As she looked at him she came to her own rescue. 'Don't you think we ought to get on with things? It's late enough as it is, and Mr Wyburd may have a luncheon engagement.'

No doubt Basil was struck by her amateurishness; he burst out laughing, and it wasn't the metallic shutter of their youth, nor yet the dreamy chuckles which had charmed innocent adults, but a peal of vibrant organ notes: specially for her, she horrified herself by suspecting.

'For God's sake, Dotty—' nobody had ever called her that, 'allow me the pleasure of your eyes for a second or two.'

It was perfectly ghastly. The few press photographs to come her way in the years between had shown several different men all of them either dimmed or distorted; till here she was faced with the lustrous truth: Hubert de Lascabanes himself had not appealed more disturbingly on the occasion of their first meeting in the Crillon lounge.

As for her brother (it *was* her brother), he remarked, 'You've improved quite a bit, darling!' pursing up his lips, either in irony, or sharing with her an interesting secret.

So she was helped recover her balance by being unable to interpret his attitude and words with any certainty.

This was where Mr Wyburd came into his own, professionally, reliably: he opened the meeting as it were. 'You will realize this is hardly what you would call orthodox procedure: for your mother's solicitor and attorney to reveal any of the details of her private affairs. But considering Mrs Hunter's advanced age and the state of her mind—not so far deteriorated that she isn't determined to continue dictating general policy as well as giving decisions on many little personal matters—I am taking it upon myself to make you, her mature children,' here he grew excessively grave, 'acquainted with the line of management I have been pursuing, and so convince you—I hope—that your mother's confidence in me has not been misplaced.'

Only fretfully impressed by the solicitor's periods, the princess was left brooding over the reasons for his failing her earlier on when she had needed his moral support. Instead she should have been studying the boring memos he had provided for them: a sheaf for each. The furrows in Basil's forehead advertised the intensity of his concentration; several times over he ejaculated, 'Quite, quite!' the clipping of which showed he agreed with the substance, while not wishing to interrupt the flow, of the Wyburd monologue.

Once, after riffling ahead through the typed evidence of the solicitor's integrity, impatience almost shouldered aside his studied discretion. 'Oh, I can see—it's all here! You've done a superb job, old Wyburd.'

The solicitor was not to be flattered or diverted.

Dorothy wondered whether he had learnt his speech in advance. The fact that two men were taking tedious matters in hand had made her momentarily languid. Still looking appropriately serious, still *listening*, she opened her handbag and tilted the little mirror: she was curious to discover what Basil had found in her to inspire his peculiar remark about improvement; it might have explained an affection he had never shown her in the past. What she saw in the mirror pleased her no better than it usually did: she had a flair for general effect, but her details let her down—except perhaps the eyes; perhaps Basil admired her eyes; the possibility made them swim.

She glanced up and he was actually looking at her over the typed sheets, through the solicitor's reiterated jargon. Basil was looking, not at her eyes, which at their most appealing she liked to think liquid and gentle as a deer's, but into her mind: he was sifting her thoughts, perhaps to confirm the reason for their meeting voluntarily in this office. He looked rather frightening; just as she knew that she could look frightening in her moments of indignation, frustration, or rage.

However far he may have wormed his way into her mind, he suddenly winked at her, then openly smiled; and she smiled back, or parted her lips enough to ratify an alliance.

Basil Hunter half snorted, but gathered the other half into his handkerchief, as he recognized *Horse Frightened by a Thunderstorm*. A handsome horse: a Regan of a horse. Did it mean that he was to be cast as a drag Goneril? (Shades of Mitty Jacka and the 'unplayed I'!)

At least he and Dorothy both understood the purpose of their presence in Sydney. Now that it was made clear, he could unwind a little; he yawned; and when the solicitor finally came to the surface with a flash of pride in his old eyes, Sir Basil contributed a non-committal 'Possibly'. In the pause which followed, he held his head on one side, and the sunlight glittered on a wing of steely hair, folded casually enough if it hadn't been for the marks of the comb which had sculptured it between his temple and his occiput. 'Nobody can deny you've protected a client's interests and administered her fortune with admirable devotion. So—if I suggest we've been considering the situation, until now, more or less in the abstract—Arnold—it in no way reflects on your irreproachable behaviour.' His smile glistened, also by grace of sunlight from high above street and traffic. 'But in fairness to everybody—including my—*our* mother,' the princess acknowledged his civility with an awkward little jerk of her head, 'I think we should review the position from another angle.'

The solicitor lowered his eyelids, it could have been to protect his rather watery eyes from the glare.

'What we have to decide is whether a person who has reached our mother's age derives happiness and comfort from her *half*-life, in proportion to the elaborate and — and shockingly expensive *machinery* needed to maintain it.'

Arnold Wyburd reminded, 'You know from last night, Basil, when we only touched on the subject, that I believe Mrs Hunter enjoys her life even now.' He wished he could have expressed himself more passionately, but cutting an emotional dash had never been his style.

Basil Hunter screwed up his face so tightly only its rudiments were visible. 'Surely she could continue to enjoy her life — if she does enjoy it — within a less pretentious framework?' Then he allowed his face to fly open, and stared from the solicitor to his sister with a candour which should have won any but the most uncooperative audience. 'The needs of old people, by the time they're almost gaga, must be so simple: not much more than a comfortable bed, a kindly hand, and plenty of bread-and-butter custard, I should have thought.'

'Though Mrs Hunter's mind wanders at times, it always appears to be searching after subtleties.' Arnold Wyburd was feeling his way. 'I'd say she is still the most complex woman I know.' He couldn't confess the rest: she terrifies me as much as ever.

The Princesse de Lascabanes stirred; she coughed as though trying out her voice, which had been lying, as it were, deep down with her sunken thoughts, and might not at first be flexible enough. 'Personally,' she began, and found she was up to it, 'I think you are both shilly-shallying — avoiding issues — playing about with words and theories. You in particular, Basil.' The accusation was cold enough to remind her brother that, although she had been bowled over on his first appearance, by the cleft in his lower lip, by the steely hair, the glowing complexion, and for a moment thought she saw the husband she had failed to devour, she was not on any account prepared to be carried away to the point of incest.

Apparently disbelieving, Basil laughed and played with a pencil. 'Tell us some more, darling,' he coaxed.

Dorothy ignored it. 'I mean to say—I've already gone as far as making practical investigations of my own. One fact, for instance, of which you can't possibly be aware, Basil, though Mr Wyburd must, I imagine,' she looked with regret at her dream lover of the night before, 'is that Mother has given orders for a hire-car to be sent regularly to fetch the cleaning woman from Redfern. That, one might argue, is a caprice, and anybody old should be allowed a caprice here and there, to show them their will is still theirs to use. But I discovered something else about which she can't have known, and if she had, would most certainly not have approved.' The princess narrowed her eyes to fire her shot. 'I went down this morning into the kitchen ... '

'You didn't, Dotty!' Basil sniggered.

She closed her eyes for an instant to shut out the brother she had known, in spite of his deceitful overtures, to be as malicious and hateful as ever. 'I went down and found in the dustbin at least two kilos of good *filet de boeuf* deliberately thrown away and already putrefying.'

Sir Basil roused himself to renew his entente with his French sister. 'Nobody can have known about that except the housekeeper. Who, I wonder,' he looked at the solicitor, and looked away, 'engaged a crackpot Central European cabaret dancer, or whatever she is, as our mother's cook? That was madness on a grand scale.'

'But she loves Mrs Hunter.'

'Loves, does she? Then love in the kitchen ends, apparently, in the dustbin.' He was pleased with that; and Dorothy was visibly impressed.

'It's the waste. Wastage', the additional syllable made her feel she was giving birth to a word, 'has always been immoral, but in an age like ours, it's unpardonable.' Almost as soon as she had said it, she wondered which of the immoralities she pardoned: at least you have no control over your dreams.

Basil was preparing to lead the charge farther afield. 'Whatever their professional skill, nurses are renowned for being unpractical creatures, unless, as private nurses, they find themselves in a position to fleece their wealthier patients. Then some of them become most realistic. Tell me, dear old Wyburd, where, for instance, does our mother's army of nurses *eat*?'

'Naturally they're entitled to a meal if they're in her house at the time when the meal is usually eaten.' He could see Dorothy Hunter's eyes still trained on that chucked-out fillet. 'If the night nurse eats a meal at an unconventional hour, it's because she must feel hungry in the middle of the night.' He was appealing to his prosecutors.

Sir Basil nodded: that woman in the awful hat.

'What I'm not altogether prepared to accept,' the solicitor admitted, typing with nervous fingers on his desk top, 'is that Sister Manhood should arrive in time to share Sister Badgery's lunch before Badgery goes off. Manhood made the arrangement to suit herself—economically most desirable from her point of view—and difficult to put a stop to, now that the precedent has been established.'

'Is Manhood the pretty one?' Sir Basil Hunter asked.

The solicitor drew in his mouth; he looked frightened; he nodded.

Madame de Lascabanes hated her brother, even her pseudo-lover, not to mention that healthy nurse in skimpy shift patterned with palpitating colours, who had stood in the doorway yesterday watching her go down the path.

'If the girl isn't entitled to a midday meal, you, in your position of authority, should have told her so,' the princess considered.

'She's Mrs Hunter's favourite.' The solicitor began to protest, then slightly hesitated. 'She makes your mother up.' He hesitated more noticeably. 'I understand Sister Manhood took a course in—wig—management, for which Mrs Hunter paid.'

Sir Basil clapped his hands above his head: a burst of percussion in their hitherto stately string music could not have startled his fellow artists more. 'Good for Mum! As an actor I can hardly disapprove of her tendencies to theatre. Can I?' It was one thing to arrive after many years and find a daubed mummy standing in for your real mother; but now Sir Basil was bored, and his vision of the Lilac Fairy tittuped deliciously amongst the law books and steel filing cabinets, her cupid's bow strung for mirth. 'Nor should I mind a pretty girl like Manhood slipping the bedpan under me.' He took one of the two biscuits lying in the solicitor's saucer, and shamelessly gobbled it up.

Dorothy was revolted; she unclenched her jaws with an effort to mutter, 'So much still to settle. I should have thought you might control yourself.'

'Mmm. You are right, dear Dorothy.' Basil reached for the second biscuit. 'Only there's a frivolous bum hiding in my soul of reason.' He munched, swallowed ostentatiously, and might have been preparing to burp; but folded his hands instead. 'Now I am— ready—to resume—our discussion, which is important enough, God knows.' And looked at her for the approval she couldn't very well withhold; and smiled.

Why did he have to play the fool, and in so doing, make a fool of her? He seemed unaware that his coarseness might cause others to suffer. She couldn't bear an elderly fool.

Arnold Wyburd, who might have enjoyed a clash between his critics if he hadn't been distressed by what he sensed as the same motive behind their different approaches, shifted and mentioned, 'What I think we must bear in mind is Mrs Hunter's need to spend her last years in the house she knows, surrounded by dependents to whom she is attached.'

'In the house she knew, Arnold, but no longer sees, not even the room in which she lies.'

'What do you mean, Mr Wyburd, by dependents? Has our mother no obligation to her children? Elderly children, too!' Dorothy de Lascabanes wrenched it out, and laughed, but mirthlessly.

Basil stuck out his lower lip till it looked bulbous—tumerous. She would have seen him ageing before her eyes if she had looked at him, but she did not want to.

Then, she heard, he had lightened his tone of voice, and was using a staccato delivery by which he no doubt hoped to hustle their opponent. 'What I am unable to believe is that this apparently evolved city can't provide some kind of asylum for the aged. Oh, I don't mean the poor house—but a simple life in agreeable surroundings which a woman like our mother might accept.'

'There's the Thorogood Village,' Mr Wyburd admitted. 'A great many people of both sexes retire to it and enjoy one another's company in a more bracing climate than ours. I think Mrs Hunter would not accept it,' he added simply.

'What about the nuns?' the Princesse de Lascabanes asked with appropriate reverence and a wistful smile. 'I've known several old unregenerate ladies end their days very happily in convents.' Mother, who hadn't the rudiments of a religious faith, could not be expected to appreciate the spiritual balm the Church had to offer; it would be too tiresome if she refused to see the practical advantages of an organization to which she need only be superficially obliged.

Arnold Wyburd said, 'I think Mrs Hunter would die rather than have her way of life dictated to her.'

'To talk sense into her wouldn't be dictating.' Sir Basil's recent flight out of fog, to the indulgent air surrounding him ever since arrival, appeared to have made him drowsy: he stretched, and one of his shirt buttons flew off, which his sister and the solicitor pretended not to notice.

Dorothy de Lascabanes could hardly help being conscious of something so revolting as a glimpse of bodyhair through the gap, as well as ribs arching under a transparent fabric. At the same time it inspired in her parallels of languor. It is I who am revolting, she was forced unwillingly to decide.

While Basil had started kicking at her from round the corner of the desk; Basil was shouting, 'You, Dorothy—you're the one who must talk to Mother.'

'Why should *I*?' So precipitately jolted from her thoughts, she found herself shouting back.

'Because you're the woman, aren't you?'

She was perspiring with injustice. 'I like that! Why shouldn't Mr Wyburd — he's the solicitor — and Mother's — well, intimate — talk?' She struggled, gulping uglily, to get it out.

As for Arnold Wyburd, he realized he had lost his faith in words, when his life of usefulness had depended on them: they could be used as fences, smoke-screens, knives and stones; they could take the shape of comforting hot water bottles; but if ever you thought they were about to help you open a door into the truth, you found, instead of a lighted room, a dark void you hadn't the courage to enter.

Perhaps he had come closest to illumination in some of those talks with Bill Hunter in front of the fire in the library at 'Kudjeri' after Mrs Hunter had gone to bed (you suspected her of being bored by the preoccupations her husband had in common with yourself). There was, in particular, the night Bill told about the earthquake he had been through as a young man travelling in Baluchistan, and which you were soon experiencing together, while the house shuddered and crumbled around you, smoke rising not only from the immediate hearth but from the shambles of rubble with its clusters of dark bodies lying limp or struggling calling sinewy arms stretched begging for mercy sometimes out of the cracks in the earth. After Bill had come to the end of his 'story', you both remained precariously suspended, it seemed, while dark fingers still raked and clawed at your ankles from the smoking chasm. Words, as Bill had already realized, were pitiful threads to dangle above those whom actions had failed, and God was swallowing up. Even after you had been returned to the leather chairs in the library at 'Kudjeri', you continued sitting in silence, daunted, but in some sense toughened, by what you had shared.

Basil had left his chair, and was insisting, as he stamped about the office, 'Yes, I agree, Dorothy, the old Wyburd's the one who must persuade Mother. However well-meaning our proposal, Arnold's honesty has been proved. She won't have any doubts about him.'

If this building were to fall, we might, all three of us, be purified in the mass destruction, Arnold Wyburd hoped. He did truly long for Bill Hunter's earthquake, to save him the humiliation of an alliance with the Hunter children; or would the earth refuse to swallow him? His prayer lasted only an instant, because of course there were Lal, Marjorie and Heather, the girls' husbands (whether you liked the fellows or not) and children: the *grand*children; Jenny already dancing around with undesirable young men.

While Basil, holding on to the window frame as he stared down into the gulf, had begun declaiming what sounded like a speech, 'My God, how it would crash, all this concrete and glass, and we—the insects—ground together with other insects. Well, there are worse ways. Worse to be picked out for your colour, or your spots, or unorthodox behaviour, and impaled by a pin—alone!'

'Oh, *darling*—' Dorothy was surprised her insincerity could sound so warm, 'why be morbid on such a heavenly morning?' She was laughing incontinently; she was mauve gooseflesh along the visible half of her arms.

'You're right. Why should insect life panic while it has the sun to flatter it?' But as he turned away from the window he mightn't have convinced himself: the arch-enemy could have confused his instinct for survival.

The solicitor remembered a duty still to be performed, and opened a drawer in his desk. 'Mrs Hunter particularly wanted you to have these.' He came round, and handed each an envelope inscribed with full name, not forgetting the title.

The Hunter children were enchanted, feverish it looked, to discover the Christmas tree still existed. Dorothy hissed with surprise as she scrabbled at her envelope, but recovered her 'breeding', and with it the approved functions of her long thin manicured fingers. Basil, on the other hand, tore an ugly handful out of the end, just missing the contents; the heavy breathing reminded the solicitor unpleasantly of what he would always have preferred not to hear: himself approaching an orgasm.

Dorothy was genuinely dazzled by the cheque signed for

Elizabeth Hunter by her attorney Arnold Wyburd. 'Isn't that kind? So *kind!*' she kept repeating, as though kindness were a virtue she had forgotten about; she must really start practising at it herself: there was no reason why she shouldn't; except that the thought without the attempt was enough to make her feel virtuous.

'Yes, very. Very generous,' Basil was mumbling over his cheque. 'The old girl was always generous—if nothing else.' His voice had acquired a huskiness he was probably going to make the most of. 'If one's wives had been half as generous.'

'Oh, Mother was noted for being the soul of generosity: selfish, but generous in countless material ways.'

'Must ring her up. Send some flowers. Look in later in the afternoon.' While exploring the range of his huskiness, Sir Basil was folding his cheque and putting it away.

The Princesse de Lascabanes would have loved to see how much it was worth. Not that she could complain. But out of curiosity. Had Basil come off better from being the boy?

The solicitor was relieved to find the cheques had cut short an argument which promised to prolong itself over weeks: the Hunter children were encouraged to leave.

As they passed through the outer office the princess walked ahead, smiling for Miss Haygarth, the typists, a spotty boy with sausage roll halfway to his mouth, and a junior partner emerging from a frosted booth. It was a vague, general sort of smile, but she couldn't have directed it: she felt too languid.

After her came Sir Basil Hunter, the shining actor, holding old Wyburd where his biceps would have been. ' … at the moment several irons in the West End fire—one especially exciting—but I can't go into that. How long I stay will depend on how quickly we clear up the matter we have been discussing—and on my mother's health. Don't want to exhaust the old lady, do we, Dorothy?'

She did not consider it necessary to answer, nor to speak again. As the lift closed, she raised her head, parting her lips to breathe some kind of wordless message at the considerate solicitor. How really grateful she was that they had Mr Wyburd: he was so necessary; strange though, how the most necessary characters can be dismissed so easily.

When they were alone in the lift Basil made a vulgar noise with his tongue, and dug her in the ribs with a stiffened index finger. 'It's my turn to be generous. What do you say to a spot of lunch? I'll shout you, Dot.'

'Thank you,' she said, recovering her primness, 'I have an appointment with a hairdresser.'

'Where?'

He couldn't possibly be interested.

'Oh, some-where: I have it written down in my book;' and with her arm, she pressed her handbag deeper into her side.

She had lied, and he knew it, but neither of them could be bothered; in any case, there was nothing wrong with the social forms of dishonesty.

Outside in the street it was one of the days when all human beings are handsome: young, casually mooching men in lightweight light-toned suits; perfectly articulated girls, born to their brilliant shreds of dresses as to their own skins.

'It's encouraging, Dorothy,' Basil was saying, 'to know we're in agreement over Mother.' As they lingered on the pavement he was looking at her almost passionately; but of course it was only part of the Basil Hunter performance, to which, surprisingly, she found herself warming (you had to admit he had looks of a deliquescent, actorish kind, if none of the distinction of Hubert de Lascabanes her husband). So that when he moved in on her, and she found herself fitted to Basil Hunter, she was less surprised, or when he kissed her on the mouth: it was probably as close as she had ever come to spontaneous surrender.

'We shall meet soon, I hope.' He spoke in what she recognized again as those nostalgic, husky tones of which he was the thrilling master, while looking at the hands he was holding – the rings more likely; but noticing for the first time whatever had attracted his attention.

The Princesse de Lascabanes toiled on alone up what had been till recently a bland hill in a rural landscape. She felt emotionally squeezed out. She went and sat on a bench, amongst the statues and the salvia, in the Botanic Gardens, at her back a wall of succulent evergreen spattered with gold. There she crossed her ankles, and might have enjoyed contemplating her classic Pinet shoes if it hadn't been for a young couple stretched on the grass, in a bay scalloped from the evergreens. The young people were conducting themselves disgracefully, with the result that they impinged on the thoughts of the princess, till she too was writhing, upright and alone on her bench, in almost perfect time with their united, prostrate bodies.

It was ghastly.

For some reason she conjured up the image of the nurse: that Sister Manhood. To distract herself while the pseudo-Manhood was undulating with her lover in the scalloped bay, she took the cheque out of her bag, to re-examine, and confirm the sum. In spite of which, she had never felt so purposeless.

Turned at a sharper angle to exclude the lovers, she leaned forward, plaiting her long fingers together: there is something I must find out about, which is neither marriage, nor position, nor the procedures of formal religion, nor possessions, nor love in *that* sense. If I could only ask Mother; but Mother was always a greedy, sensual woman, and is now dotty with age.

She looked round to see whether the lovers had heard her thoughts. But they hadn't. 'Ohhh!' she moaned in spite of herself.

The Princesse de Lascabanes ground her knife-edged buttocks into the park bench, till she was positive she had struck a splinter; and whom, in all this foreign city, would she ask to dig a splinter out of her behind?

Thinking to board a ferry and agreeably waste the rest of the day, Sir Basil meandered down towards the Quay after parting from his sister. First he bought a pound of cooked prawns. Then he decided against the ferry: in his boyhood the other side of the harbour had meant the other side of the world; and today, what with his return, and the warmth, he was womb-happy. So he plodded back up the hill, plunging a hand intermittently into the paper bag, gorging himself on prawns: he was illustrious and foreign enough to make a pig of himself in public. Even so, many of those he passed, appeared to glare at him; their own suburban laws would not have allowed them to guzzle in the streets, and here was this stranger dragging them down to a level they might have been yearning for. He was not influenced by their unspoken strictures, but went on climbing, shelling prawns, stuffing them into his mouth and spitting out any fragments of shell, some of which lodged in the transparent shirt, in particular on the shelf his stomach was beginning to provide. From time to time he brushed off the prawnshell, but only half-heartedly.

On this day of vacillations, which are also details of the overall design, Sir Basil Hunter found himself walking through a side gate to the Botanic Gardens. He sat down on a bench, amongst the statues and the salvia, against a wall of evergreens, the other side of which the Princesse de Lascabanes had begun worrying about her splinter.

Sir Basil had no worries, or not for the moment; he was enjoying vegetable status in the city to which he no longer belonged. So he dragged down his tie. And stuffed in some more of the prawns. Around him the fortified soil, the pampered plants, the whiffs of manure, the moist-warm air of Sydney, all were encouraging the vegetable existence: to loll, and expand, fleshwise only, and rot, and be carted away, and shovelled back into the accommodating earth. He closed his eyes. He loved the theory of it. The palm leaves were applauding.

He might have snoozed a little.

Because the tree was writhing around him none of the flattering palmate hands but the human denuded ones in bone stringing him up not against the halcyon cyclorama the Department of Tourism advertises but on branches of the pure anguish this is why He is unplayable by actors anyway at those moments when the veins are filled with lightning the Fool flickering in counterpoint like conscience conscience dies first so that you can feel more thoroughly destitute nothing else matters but this pure destitution not all the stalking the blood Goneril and Dorothy not jellied eyes not even the misunderstood Cordelia nothing is truly solved unless at the last button why Mother is closest but how close to the undoing Mitty the Jacka would cut it off before its time in one of those bursts of negative fulfilment.

Basil—Hunter? woke back. The salvias were stifling him. He (or He?) had undone the button. Not surprising: it had eaten into his throat.

He began to decide against visiting his old mum that evening. No, he would write a rather *charming* Letter of Thanks which all the nurses—and the neurotic Jewish housekeeper—would read and variously interpret. They would read it to Elizabeth Hunter, who cannot see except by flashes of lightning. (Has Mother inherited a lost art?)

Basil Hunter leant forward on the park bench, trying to interpret the blades of grass. There had been a time when he saw clearly, right down to the root of the matter, before his perception had retired behind a legerdemain of technique and the dishonesties of living.

Seven

MISS HAYGARTH announced, 'It's the second week the house-keeper hasn't collected her money.'

Though the nurses had called, in accordance with Mrs Hunter's original decree, and received their weekly due, it was Miss Haygarth who had attended to them. Mr Wyburd would have been un-willing to admit, but he had avoided contact with Moreton Drive since becoming an unwilling accessory to the Hunter children's 'plan'. If Basil and Dorothy had visited their mother since the meeting at his office, he presumed they had not raised the subject of her future; if they had, they would have been proud to mention it; he was only relieved they had not reproached him for not acting as their emissary.

Now he told his secretary, 'I shall go out there, I expect. Yes, I must;' and took from Miss Haygarth the two envelopes intended for Mrs Lippmann.

When the housekeeper opened the door to him, she appeared overcome by a diffidence as palpable as his. In fact, Mr Wyburd's recent guilty involvement made him feel so awkward he came to the point with unusual directness. 'You've forgotten these, haven't you?'

'Money keeps, Mr Wyburd.' As she accepted the envelopes she stuck out her lower lip. 'And I was so depressed all these days.' She drew down the corners of her mouth, determined as always to exaggerate her ugliness by her most grotesque mannerisms.

'What can have been depressing you?'

'Oh,' she was searching for a focus point apparently in his right shoulder, 'it is the cloakroom lavatory. It will not—spill?'

' "Flush" is the word. But we had it put right. And in any case, you only have to ring for the plumber. He's been coming here for years, and knows its habits.'

Relieved to fix his mind on the temperamental lavatory, the solicitor made for the cloakroom.

'I have rung Mr Jackson. He came. And now it spills correctly.' She was following in the slippers Mrs Hunter allowed her to wear on account of the pains in her feet. 'Yes, it *flushes*, Mr Wyburd.'

In the dark closet he had to switch on the light. Together he and the housekeeper stood looking into the lavatory bowl. After he had pulled the chain once, and the bowl was flushed perfectly, they continued looking into it a while, as though expecting oracular guidance.

'Well, Jackson has done his job. And you have no reason for being depressed.' He began to laugh too heartily, and at once felt foolish. 'Did you pay?' he asked, 'Or tell him to send his bill?'

'There is no bill.' Mrs Lippmann's eyes were lowered to concentrate on the settling water. 'Mr Jackson has said he will not think of payment over such a simple matter. He is a so honest man,' she added.

The solicitor made his clicking sound: they couldn't stay for ever round the bowl waiting on an oracle who had withdrawn her patronage.

'Mr Wyburd—' now perhaps Mrs Lippmann's real preoccupations were beginning to unfold, 'it is not only the affair of the lavatory which has made me so—*so furchtbar furchtbar deprimiert*. It is this plan to remove Mrs Hunter to a home, or convent, or somewhere—*ich weiss nicht genau*.'

'A *home*? At any rate, it's no plan of mine!' He was escaping into the hall with the housekeeper in pursuit.

'It is dreadful only by contemplating,' she continued in a high voice which must draw attention from upstairs to the scene she was making here below.

There was no avoiding it; and he might calm her. 'Where did this rumour originate?' he asked when he was facing her.

'I don't know. I think it was Mrs Badgery—and Mrs Cush—that were talking of it.'

'But this is a monstrous babble—whoever's to blame! Has Mrs Hunter herself been told?'

'I cannot be sure. But Mrs Hunter has her ways of knowing.'

'If she doesn't know about this, I hope none of it will go any farther.' The solicitor spoke with the vehemence of a once upright man.

'Yes, Mr Wyburd,' Mrs Lippmann said, and went away.

In her absence he was threatened by the not quite silent house. The light was retreating from rooms in which furniture had begun to swell and brood. At intervals ill-regulated clocks were sounding the hour. Bill Hunter, with his passion for clocks, had distributed them throughout his wife's house at Moreton Drive as well as his own 'Kudjeri'. For Arnold Wyburd, the clash or tinkle of the sounding clocks was the worst accusation yet: of his part betrayal of a trust.

All the way up the stairs his feet seemed to pad dishonestly; the sickness in his stomach made it the predominant part of him; his knee was grazed by the formally tangled iron hedge which stood between himself and the hall below, but he was scarcely conscious of what in ordinary circumstances would have struck him as physical pain.

Arrived at the landing, he wondered which of the acolytes he would have to face: better Manhood than de Santis, he decided; though it still left Mrs Hunter who, asleep or awake, would remain the irremoveable cause of his distress.

Sister Manhood came out from what he had heard referred to as the 'Nurses' Retiring Room'. She might have been waiting for him. She had already changed from her uniform, which should have made her less formidable: the dresses young women were wearing gave them so little protection, or that was how he would have liked to see it at the moment. But Sister Manhood was clothed in addition with a threatening air; she was standing with her legs apart, and the legs looked aggressively youthful: she had something of the swashbuckler about her, or the principal boy from a pantomime, who, he reminded himself, is only a girl in disguise.

'Good evening, Sister Manhood!' His intended cheeriness sounded wretched to his own ears.

Sister Manhood cleared her throat. ' ... Mr Wyburd' was as much as he caught; the fact that she had swallowed the rest of her greeting added something ominous to it.

He must keep in mind that the girl was surly by temperament, and clearly sulking now. 'Getting ready to go off duty?' He couldn't shed the cheeriness.

'If Sister de Santis remembers she's taking over. She promised to be early tonight.' Sister Manhood glanced at her wrist. 'Because of something important I'm planning on doing.'

'How is your patient?' Mr Wyburd was forced to ask.

'Not bad,' the nurse answered casually. 'In fact, pretty good— considering.'

She looked at the solicitor, and her mouth was full of accusations; or the sulks, he hoped.

'She's sleeping now.' Was the girl throwing him a rope?

'Then I shan't go in.'

'Oh yes, do! That's what she loves—the coming and going. That's why she says she never sleeps. Mrs Hunter would like to be always awake—ready for a brawl.' Sister Manhood laughed brutally.

So he would have been forced to go in at once if the nurse hadn't felt the need, he now realized, to play him a little longer.

'Mr Wyburd,' he heard as soon as he had passed her, 'may I have a word with you?'

It was impossible to refuse her, and already she was drawing him into the room behind, a place he had always avoided as a repository of the concentrated past: that row of built-in cupboards with Mrs Hunter's dresses still hanging in them. (*One day I shall surprise you Arnold I may get up and go for a drive and what should I wear if I didn't keep a few dresses to choose from? Nowadays I'm told one can look fashionable in almost anything that's been put away.*) One of the cupboards was standing ajar, and a smell, half antiquity, half musk, but faint and stale, rubbed off on him from the shadows inside; in his present state of anguish, the shadows in the wardrobe suggested figures rather than limp, empty dresses.

Even if he had felt the desire to let his memory fossick amongst the contents of the cupboards, he would not have been so imprudent: the Manhood girl was staring at him moodily.

'I just wanted to make sure', she said in a significantly lowered voice, 'that Mrs Lippmann didn't give you a wrong impression. Most of these foreigners are so hysterical at times—particularly the Jewish ones. Don't think I have anything against Mrs Lippmann —she's a heart of gold—but that doesn't prevent her getting wrong ideas. I did *not*, Mr Wyburd, throw anything down the cloakroom toilet.'

The solicitor heard himself laughing quite crazily. 'I assure you Mrs Lippmann made no such accusation.' He even patted the girl's arm.

But Sister Manhood wasn't reassured. 'There's another matter I might as well mention, now that we've got down to talking.'

Mr Wyburd's wretchedness returned as sweat.

Her eyes had grown distant, glassy, moist. 'It's the job,' she said. 'For some time now I've been thinking of turning it in.'

Recurrent reprieve was becoming too much for the solicitor. 'Then you haven't thought it over enough,' he gabbled. 'What should we do without you, Sister Manhood? Aren't you—I understand—Mrs Hunter's favourite? You can't possibly let her down.' Hearty overtones were turning the situation into something incongruously schoolboyish: better that, however.

'The truth is,' she said, halfway between the giggles and a blubber, 'I no longer know what I really want. I don't seem to have control over myself.'

Was she about to twitch back the curtain from some other equally distasteful problem of her own? He wanted that no more than this.

'I should have thought a position like yours would have given you a sense of security: good money; at least one excellent meal a day,' *to which you aren't entitled*, he prevented himself adding; 'and your patient's appreciation and affection.'

'Nobody's appreciation and affection helps, Mr Wyburd, when

it comes to making decisions for yourself.' Then Sister Manhood's voice inflated, and he was reminded of a windsock filling and tearing at its mooring, only the wind was a noisy one, at a deserted country airstrip on which they stood facing each other. 'Anyhow, if I stay, what good will it do Mrs Hunter when you dump her at the Thorogood Village?'

The solicitor began backing into the passage. 'No decision has been made. That is, nobody has the intention, I'm sure, of forcing Mrs Hunter to do anything against her will.' Desperation was fuddling him. 'Is this another of Mrs Lippmann's delusions?' In asking, he felt he was wildly grabbing.

Sister Manhood said, through swollen lips and what sounded like a blocked nose, 'It was Sister de Santis who told me. That's why I have to believe it.' Then, growing panicky, 'I don't want to get Sister into trouble. You won't go for her, Mr Wyburd?'

'Nobody will be "got into trouble". We must only—all of us— keep our heads.' How could he console others, himself a ricketty thing even before the termites had gone to work?

Sometimes Arnold Wyburd wondered whether his being surrounded in his family life by too many women had nourished a streak of weakness in him. As he escaped from Sister Manhood he was pursued by some of the sounds he most disliked hearing: the sniffs, the sighs, tissues ripped from the box, the blown (female) nose. Much as he loved and depended on his regiment of women he often regretted their sogginess. He feared rather than despised their weakness: now especially it seemed to equate—let's face it—with masculine duplicity.

So he not exactly scuttled down the passage towards Elizabeth Hunter's door, where he was brought up sharply against woman's strength. This, perhaps, was what he feared, not the flattering demands of feminine weakness.

And yet, when he stealthily opened the door, the concrete reason for his almost physical fear was reduced by the enormous bed to the form and the feverish innocence of a sleeping child. Not even a child, her breathing or dreams were stirring her like a hank of old grey chiffon; the cheeks, sucked in on time, were puffed out as regularly against the breathing; a strand of hair blew less frantically than a moth. Yes, that was how he saw her finally; because it would have been to his advantage to stoop quickly, crush the soft creature between his hands, and be saved or damned for ever: each a remote possibility, for the soft moth's steeliness precluded her destruction.

'Arnold,' Mrs Hunter said, 'I've been trying to cal – cul – ate,' the breath of a sigh tormented her, 'how many weeks you've neglected me.'

'It's only last week, Mrs Hunter – or anyway, the week before – ten days I should say,' her whippersnapper was actually trying to tot it up. 'Not neglect, surely?'

'Not in employment. It's hellish long in a love affair. Or a good marriage – which can be the same thing.'

They both decided against developing the theme.

Her eyelids had opened, but continued batting. 'What I think I wanted you for was to show you the letter I had from Basil – our son.'

'What did he write to you about?' The solicitor thought that when the time came to leave the house he would never have felt so glad. (Lal and himself eating a simple meal together: that would be the ultimate in gladness; and to tell her what he had been through.)

'Basil wrote to thank me for the cheque,' Mrs Hunter said. 'All the nurses have read it – Mrs Lippmann too – Mrs Cush – all agree it's a sweet letter, which of course it is. Basil is a great actor, and knows how to choose words for their – marrow; he's learnt the business thoroughly.'

The lids stopped batting. Her stare would have been trained directly on her visitor if sightlessness and the position of the lamp had not made the eye sockets look hollow.

'I would like you to read it.' Her intense seriousness turned it into a command, while a certain invalid tone appealed for sympathy for herself rather than his approval of the letter. 'See whether you don't also agree it's sweet.'

'Of course I'll read it if you show—if you'll tell me, Mrs Hunter, where it is.'

'It's here on the bedside table so that it can be easily found.' Waved vaguely in that direction, her hand collided with his, which at that moment could not have looked more ephemeral: under the transparent skin, bones awaiting distribution for the final game of jacks.

He had no difficulty in unfolding the letter: it must have been read so many times.

'Aloud please,' Mrs Hunter ordered.

'My dearest Mother,
    On opening The Envelope in Mr Wyburd's office I was moved before anything else by your kindness in devising such a stunning surprise. No, it was not surprising; you have always been the soul of generosity. Now, if I am the richer for your gift, I am also humbler for your thoughtfulness ... '

Mrs Hunter cleared her throat; possibly she also laughed. Because he had to continue reading to the end, the solicitor was unable to distinguish laughter with certainty.

' ... Soon I shall come in person to thank you. In the meantime, I send my grateful love, and leave you in the hands of those whose affectionate dedication, unexpected charms and rare skills are all that I could wish for you in your life of trials.'

'You didn't read it very well, Arnold,' Mrs Hunter complained. 'You sounded like some old man—trembly and addled.'

If he had been more than temporarily relieved by the evasions of the letter, he might have rejected some of her scorn. But he did feel old, and would not grow any younger trying to guess how the fatal blow might fall.

So he joined in the hypocrisy. 'It's—yes, it's a wonderful letter.'

' "Sweet" is what the others call it,' Mrs Hunter corrected. 'And I am inclined to think that is what it is.' From movements of her tongue on her lips she might still have been testing the letter's flavour.

'At any rate, I expect he's been to see you since—probably more than once,' the solicitor ventured.

'No. And I didn't expect it. I expect nothing with absolute certainty,' Mrs Hunter said, 'but death.'

It started shocked sensibility battling in Arnold Wyburd against immense physical relief.

Somewhere in a lull of his own, he tried to offer consolation. 'I seem to remember he did mention not wanting to tire you out with talk.'

Then it must have been Dorothy who had dropped the rumours at Moreton Drive; a sly, vindictive woman, she couldn't have resisted flashing her knife prematurely. 'Well, the princess—daughters don't forget their duty so easily. I don't doubt you've had visits from Dorothy.'

'She came—oh, several times. And each time I was asleep.' Mrs Hunter was so definite about that, he had to dismiss his theory.

'I don't know whether I'm sorry,' she continued. 'Dorothy gives the impression she would like to start discussing money. And that's boring. Think about it if you must, but don't talk about it. Almost any vice is more interesting than money.'

They languished after that, and the solicitor might have become the victim of his thoughts if the night nurse had not saved him, anyway from their lower depths. Sister de Santis was so much a presence he was not used to thinking of her as a person. Since she had begun trading in dangerous rumours, he looked at her tonight for further evidence of womanhood, but found only what pleased his old-fashioned, shy tastes.

After she had greeted him by bowing her veiled head, Sister de Santis became too intent on her patient's welfare to bother with any visitor. 'Have you spent a happy day, Mrs Hunter?' she asked as she took up the token of a wrist.

'How innocent you are, Mary! Oh, yes—I suppose I have,' Mrs Hunter was forced to admit. 'Happy, or un-happy: by this stage there's not much to choose between them.' She turned to the solicitor and asked, 'Is there any reason why I shouldn't feel happy, Arnold?'

'Not that *I* know—unless you know of one yourself.' He had staved her off, he hoped, and would not expose himself to further danger. 'I'll go now, Mrs Hunter, if you'll excuse me.'

She had lost interest.

Sister de Santis seemed to be trying to apologize for her patient's lapse. The immaculate lips were smiling at him, though the lamp was so placed, he could not judge the expression of her eyes. Probably she was on his side, but even if he had dared ask for confirmation, he suspected her discretion of being as great as his.

So he went down through the house, its silence alive with clocks, suggestions of subterfuge, the blatant echoes of downright lies, together with hints of the exasperating, unknowable truth.

The house in which he lived (judicious Georgian borrowings by a once fashionable, now forgotten architect) was making a last stand against a Central European pincer movement in yellow brick. He let himself in, and at once Lal, in an apron, was coming towards him across the hall. 'I've done us some haddock,' she said, 'with a couple of poached eggs.'

As they sat down to enjoy their simple nursery food, it relieved him to find life still as he hoped it might be the other side of the hectic shimmer of apprehension: they were free to masticate the requisite number of times in silence, or mumble about grand-children's ailments, and discuss the price of things.

Over the bottled pears (Lal was for making a religion out of the country virtues) he thought to mention, 'I paid Her a visit this evening.' In masticating, he didn't pretend to emulate Gladstone, but managed a ritual twelve to fifteen chews.

'How was it?' He only faintly heard above his absorption.

Lal's face was inclined over the brown and leathery, but healthful pears. Their friends must always have seen his wife as plain, he imagined; he too, at times: some species of modest, monochrome bird, her low, and uniformly agreeable call unexpectedly punctuated by an ironic note or two. Now he surprised himself thinking Lal looked downright ugly; he was repelled in particular by that single pockmark on one cheek beside the nose, which he must have noticed every day of their life together. Disloyalty to this loyal wife made Arnold Wyburd swallow a mouthful of unmasticated pear.

And Lal was repeating in a louder, slightly reproachful voice, 'How was the *visit*?'

Suddenly he was leaning forward. 'It was *awful*!' he ejaculated with such force that some of his mouthful of pear shot on to the surface of the mahogany table; some of the juice must have spurted as far as his wife's bare arm: from the way she jerked it back against her side she might have been spattered with acid.

But the account of his discoveries at Moreton Drive had to come pouring out on Lal. Wasn't she the only recipient for what might otherwise have eaten him away? With age, the half hour of mutual confession had practically replaced their sexual life, after which, in normal times, they fell deliciously asleep.

'On top of the children's criminal intentions, to find a houseful of half-informed, speculating nurses! The housekeeper too. Even the cleaning woman, I gather, is in the know.' If he had been able to restrain himself till later, it might have sounded less reprehensible after the light was turned out. 'How far it has gone, I couldn't tell, but suspect.' *Is there any reason why I shouldn't feel happy Arnold?* he was stabbed by a voice which memory made appeal and accuse more pointedly. 'Or how the leak occurred.' It was torn out of him in what, for Arnold Wyburd, was almost a tortured shout.

Lal had finished her pears; she laid her spoon and fork together, her behaviour the more seemly for his display of dry passion.

She looked at him and said, 'It was I who told, Arnold.'

'*You!*' Who was this woman he hadn't got to know in a lifetime of intimate exchange? Because of his faith in her, a greater criminal perhaps than Basil and Dorothy Hunter themselves.

'After what you told me, I had to tell someone. I rang Sister de Santis. That is all,' Lal was saying. 'I was so upset,' she continued

284

with more difficulty, 'not that I ever greatly cared for Mrs Hunter, I may as well admit; she was always too selfish, greedy, in spite of being over endowed—with everything. And cruel,' she gasped. 'But I suppose I also looked up to her as somebody beautiful, brilliant—occasionally inspired.'

He couldn't help approving of the way his wife was choosing her words to express his own feelings; but her treachery came back at him; the dishonesty which had lurked behind her homely virtues increased her physical ugliness.

'I knew you respected Sister de Santis,' she was continuing when almost run down. 'And I was so shocked that they could even contemplate discarding this pitiful old creature, I suppose I didn't stop to think I had been told in confidence.'

'Stop to think? After all these years—not to be—*ethically conditioned*!'

She looked as though she expected him to dash his napkin in her face.

He had never seen Lal crying convulsively before; not even after Heather's premature baby died. Her present anguish was streaming from a source far less rational than death because more unexpected. She was at her plainest. And Arnold Wyburd knew that he would not have wished her otherwise. Nor did he attempt to hide his own few spurts of tears: in that way, Lal and he completed each other.

He only removed himself while she was blowing her nose without thought for her table napkin. He went, as coldly as the undertaking demanded, to the upstairs telephone; not that there was much point in telephoning pretentious people at that hour. Indeed, at the Onslow, Sir Basil Hunter was not receiving calls; and the Princesse de Lascabanes had left the club for dinner with friends. So he was frustrated; or saved up.

That night the Wyburds went to bed earlier than usual. There were no confidences after lights-out. Instead, they were clutching at a flawed reality they had been allowed to discover in each other, perhaps even taking upon themselves the healing of a wounded conscience.

It was an occasion when it did not occur to Arnold Wyburd to regret the snoring sound he made as he approached an orgasm.

It was the night of the Douglas Cheesemans' dinner for Princesse de Lascabanes: one of the club maids had read an announcement in the *Telegraph*. As the evening approached Dorothy increasingly regretted her too hasty acceptance. She had always practised social deferment at the risk of suffering for it: from being 'hard to get', she was gradually forgotten. Now, she thought, she would have given anything to be dropped by one who was never more than a casual girlhood acquaintance. If Cherry Bullivant had been proposed as bridesmaid it was because Dorothy Hunter had not been encouraged to form close attachments; she had never had what is called a Best Friend. In any case, if it had been expected of her to go in search, she might not have known how to find. So, whatever her legend and her weapons, she dreaded her entrée into Cherry Cheeseman's world.

After receiving her mother's cheque Dorothy had considered splurging some of it on an important dress: an armature to intimidate any possible adversary, and to warn off what could be worse, an importunate admirer. But on sending for a statement almost immediately after paying the money into the bank, she thought she could not bring herself to reduce such a lovely round sum; she would make do with her trusty Patou black enlivened with a jewel or two. Moving back and forth as far as the club bedroom allowed, she felt temporarily safe, acceptable to herself, which after all, she had decided, is more important than being acceptable to others; and as she moved, she slightly and indolently rocked, grasping her shoulders, the bank statement pinned to her breast by her crossed arms; she derived considerable consolation from the chafing of this toughly material paper.

On the night, then, it was the Patou black, of such an urbane simplicity it had often ended by scaring the scornful into a bewildered reassessment of their own canons of taste. And the diamonds; everyone must bow to those: their fire too unequivocally real, their setting a collusion between class and aesthetics. These were some of the jewels the colonial girl had been clever enough to prise out of her husband's family by knowing too much. If they had been more than a paltry fraction of the realizable de Lascabanes assets, and if she had not detested all forms of thuggery, Dorothy Hunter might have seen herself as a kind of female Ned Kelly.

She was standing at the dressing-table mirror massaging the lobes of her ears before loading them with moody de Lascabanes pearls encrusted with minor de Lascabanes diamonds. The ear-rings made her suffer regularly, but it was all in the game of self-justification. As she pulled on the long skins of gloves, she noticed the mauve tones in the crooks of her thin arms, in her salt cellars, and at her temples; she was not displeased with her angular looks – for that moment, anyway.

The princess licked her lips, and rang down for a hire-car; then, on second thoughts, remembering the round sum in her account, she changed her mind, and asked them for a taxi instead.

The night through which she was being driven seemed on a curve, as a bow is strung, herself the arrow shooting out of it, into the heart of the North Shore, which was where – who were they? the Douglas Cheesemans, lived. The princess could not recollect ever having crossed the bridge, and would have preferred not to be doing so now. She saw herself lying propped up in bed with an *oeuf à la coque* on a tray, and bread and butter as thin as only nuns know how. Instead, she was allowing herself to be driven, because by now it could not be avoided. (Unless she told a really super lie, one which even bread-and-butter nuns might not condone.)

So the expressway curved, flaunting rival but spurious jewels, past the windows of some unidentifiable club, above pavements darker for the tongues and maps made by the pissing of slanted sailors. The taxi drove her at that other curve, the great bridge, and here the north-easter tore in through the crack above the glass threatening the composition of her hair. Her first impulse was to close the window, to shut out the marauding wind, when the sense of her ultimate powerlessness returned, and she sank back inside the taxi, inside her Paris dress, her stole (not less modest for being sable), inside her own ruffled skin, shivering like a bitch temporarily parted from her owner (whoever that might be) on a railway platform.

She only vaguely and too suddenly realized the arcs of speed, the explosive missiles of light, had diminished, and that the taxi had pulled up on an ellipse of raked gravel: where Dorothy Hunter would have chosen to remain, encapsulated.

Mr and Mrs Douglas Cheeseman lived in an impeccably maintained, shamelessly illuminated, fairly recent Colonial mansion, surrounded by European trees and Japanese shrubs at a stage in their development which suggested they must have increased their rate of growth in an effort to keep up with their owners. The perfectly tended garden was not more personal for the attentions it received, except in parts of its thickets where nature had intervened, leaving an impression of assault and battery. Some of the deciduous trees had begun to colour in keeping with the season, but their leaves looked as though jaded by peroxide rather than thrilled by autumn. There was a smell of something: blood and bone, Dorothy seemed to remember it was called.

No time for more, except to invoke her de Lascabanes self: a man had pushed past the white blur of hovering servant, and was opening the taxi door.

'Doug Cheeseman—Cherry's husband.' Haste and alcohol had stunted whatever he may have prepared by way of an introductory speech. 'We were beginning to worry about you.'

The princess unsheathed her voice as though it had been a sword. 'Don't tell me I'm late! Your wife said eight-thirty, didn't she?'

'I expect she did.' Mr Cheeseman laughed; he was one of the stringier males, of a freckled, reddish persuasion.

'Eight-thirty, I'm positive.'

'Yes, yes,' he mumbled out of his good nature. 'Cherry sometimes makes a mistake.'

Since she had settled the matter in her own favour the princess narrowed her eyes and gnashed a smile at Mr Douglas Cheeseman as a reward for his being reasonable. He appeared dazed, but delighted.

Dorothy was surprised to find it so easy. She would often surprise herself, and could not think why there were those other moments when her skill left her; if only she could have remained in permanent control of her de Lascabanes technique she might have rivalled Basil as an actor, or a hoax.

'So charming—quite *charming!*' The princess was taking notice of what were only too obviously Antiques as her host brought her through the chequered hall. 'I do congratulate you.' She reined in her kindness just this side of sincerity, because to have admired such ghastliness wholeheartedly, would scarcely have been honest, would it?

Again Mr Cheeseman's sounds and glances expressed delight. 'It's one of Cherry's hobbies. She took a course in home decoration.' He had those paler eyelids, intensified by rimless glasses; the back of his neck was as wrinkled as those of other Australian males of the same age and complexion: saurian, but defenceless.

Douglas Cheeseman's neck made Dorothy feel she must keep a tight hold on herself: she might easily topple over, not into compassion—self-pity. She must rely on her sword of a voice, and remember that the face can be transformed into a visor by narrowing the eyes. (She had practised that one in the glass to defend herself against her late *belle-mère* the old Princesse Etienne.)

In the Cheeseman *salon*—or whatever their own word for it—there was a galaxy of personages, a shimmer of pastels, a simmering of frustrated, but rearoused expectations. Square men in black alternated with others more demonstrative and decorative in ruffles and plum to midnight velvets. The women must have emptied their jewel cases, while one or two exposed invisible tiaras last worn for royalty.

The Princesse de Lascabanes narrowed her eyes at it all, and the smiles of some, she could see, commended her for her humble spirit, adding pity for myopia, together with forgiveness for the sin of unpunctuality. That she was in fact terribly late Dorothy had to admit to herself, for several of the company were swaying on their heels, the level of alcohol in the Georgian tumblers clamped against their waists, tilting, and in one case, spilling down a pale blue front.

The pale blue lady, crimson to purple in the cheeks, was her hostess, Dorothy de Lascabanes saw: pretty, glossy Cherry Bullivant swollen into a festive turkey.

Mrs Cheeseman's nerves rose in her for an instant, but were sucked back at once into the sea of brandy in which they had been conveniently submerged. As she plunged forward, her garnish of jewellery and tulle bobbing and frothing round her thickly powdered neck and shoulders, her lips preceded her, to express a warmth her hand certainly impressed, even through a glove, deep into the comparatively chilly fingers of her former friend, a *princess*: Mrs Cheeseman could hardly believe in her own luck.

'Dorothy!' she moaned and glugged for everyone to hear.

The princess was so close to it she could only give in. While Cherry Bullivant Cheeseman wheezed and expostulated against her cheek, about time and life and other comforting complaints, Dorothy Hunter de Lascabanes nuzzled and whinnied her way back to fillyhood, till both were again standing corrected in the Crillon lounge, two young girls bedazzled by a real prince one of them was daring enough to imagine she had fallen in love with.

Her major gaffe reminded Dorothy of the minor trials she had to face in the present, so she withdrew from Cherry's rather too adhesive embrace with one last, isolated, high-strung giggle. Madame de Lascabanes was so embarrassed at herself, she blushed; though from the glances exchanged by some of the older ladies present, they were impressed to discover signs that Dorothy Hunter hadn't lost her Australian 'warmth'. If an ambush was to be expected, the princess scented it in another quarter: several girls, stunning in their pant-suits and their youth, were smiling sceptical smiles, as though they understood too well, or misunderstood more dangerously.

To allow them to share in her triumph and pay homage, Mrs

Cheeseman led her guests on a somewhat uncertain course towards the objective. They tottered, or stomped, or tittuped, or swayed past: the blue and the pink, the pink and the blue, the double-barrels and the knights, Rotarians who squeezed your glove till they had practically emptied it, those op deceivers whose naked faces and mermaid hair disguised ambivalence as innocence, the lissom younger men, who might have been longing to take you to their ruffles.

'And this is Zillah. She's an actress.'

'How is Sir *Basil*?' the actress whispered in professional tones out of an expert mouth; a hairless kangaroo-rat of a woman, she vibrated in basso from deep down amongst the Iceland poppies stencilled on her velvet shift.

Mrs Cheeseman explained that Zillah Puttuck was dedicated to serious drama, and had played all the major Chekov roles—in North Sydney.

The hostess was entranced to reveal her own artistic connections. 'And Brian Learmonth.' She gave her wheezy giggle. 'If you're not careful, Brian will write you up for his paper.'

The princess saw she had been written up already.

When suddenly Mrs Cheeseman reverted to more important matters, and spun round, a topheavy top. 'Is there time for her, Doug, to knock back a teensy one? Or will that bloody woman walk out if we keep dinner waiting any longer?'

To which her husband replied, 'Don't work yourself up, Treasure. If a crash comes, it comes. To start expecting one, gives a person blood pressure.'

The princess was persuaded to accept a drink they did not want to give her, and which she did not want. As nothing would have moistened her by now, she slid her glass behind the lavishly inscribed photograph of somebody in tights called 'Bobby'.

At dinner she was sat between her host, and, she was alarmed to discover, an Australian Writer she hadn't heard of. It was perhaps his increasing awareness of this which made him slash at the wings of his Dickens hairdo, while glancing in the mirror opposite at the woman who continued to exist in spite of her incredible deficiency.

'Don't you read?' he inquired, when he could no longer leave her unmasked.

'Not adventurously,' she admitted. 'I'm reading *La Chartreuse de Parme* for I think probably the seventh time.'

'The who?' The Australian Writer could not have sounded more disgusted.

'*The Charterhouse of Parma*.' Repetition made her throat swell as though forced to confess a secret love to someone who might defile its purity simply by knowing about it.

'Oh — *Stendhal!*' He gave her a rather literary smile; and slashed at his Dickens wings; and turned to his other neighbour to explain — again a waste of intellect — how he was adapting the Gothic novel to local conditions.

At least Mrs Puttuck was appreciative of the Australian Writer: she leant across the table to inform the ignorant princess which awards and grants he had received in the name of brilliance; though if the actress continued to lean across from time to time it was usually in honour of herself: to tell what Larry had said of her Arkadina, or Sibyl's praise of her Madame Ranevsky. Once she observed in her most vibrant basso, 'Coral would be mad to attempt Lubov Andreyevna. She's petite — and like all Chekov's major women, essentially feminine.'

In the course of it all, and the changes of dishes, Dorothy poked at something on her plate, and found that by coincidence Cherry had chosen roast turkey as the *pièce de résistance* of her dinner.

Noticing what could have been a repugnance, Mr Cheeseman remarked, 'Bit dry, isn't it? Turkey's always a bit of a sell.' He would have liked to do something for their guest of honour, and had an idea, which he popped on her plate from his own. 'Liven it up with the parson's nose!' Better than that he couldn't think of; a tip for the stock market might have offended such a pernickety princess.

He was so pleased with what was obviously his sacrifice, she had to eat the fatty morsel; but behind her smiles of 'gratitude' lurked the sense of guilt which little acts of unpremeditated kindness on the part of others roused in her.

Again, after dinner, while the ladies were rinsing their teeth under the taps, and reconstructing their faces, and telling their fellow masons what their husbands did to them, or didn't, the old and crumbly wife of a detergent knight detached herself from the others, approached the strangers, and revived the theme of kindness.

'I do think it's good—so kind of you, to honour us this evening,' she began to quaver.

That the old lady, herself obviously innocent and kind, could yet be so wrong, threw Dorothy momentarily into a panic of despair. 'Oh, but I am *not* kind!' she blurted in a loud voice through painful laughter.

The old lady, faced with such unaccountably odd behaviour, could only smile tremulously, crumble some more, and murmur, 'I know, dear, you have a modest nature. Anybody can see you are kind. And it must be a great joy to your mother—to have you here: such a kind daughter.'

Which Cherry Cheeseman overheard. 'Why, yes, darling, your mother—is she well? How shabby of me—forgetting to ask.'

The others had by now scented something peculiar: their faces were turned towards the princess while awaiting the revelation they craved.

For this agonizing instant you might have seemed odd, if you hadn't been too much yourself your little-girl's voile damp with evening crumpled tortured by hot hands resisting Your Own Good *Dorothy dear you're running the risk of a relapse if you don't come in out of the damp there's salmon loaf you know how you love and caramel custard* they stick in your throat like kindness in your ears the truth as Mother playing the piano she likes to when she remembers playing and talking at the same time *if I'm to tell the truth Dorothy you're going out of your way to develop a warped character* tinkle ping.

For this split instant of anguish Dorothy saw that the knights' ladies, the pant-suits and the op mermaids, all here gathered watching in the Cheesemans' ideal-home bedroom, were probably agreed.

Then the Princesse de Lascabanes succeeded in taking over. 'Yes, Cherry, Mother is well—old though. You can't say anybody old is altogether well. To some extent, I suppose, if their minds are active. And Mother's mind is certainly that. She takes an extraordinary interest in what goes on around her.'

This was where Cherry Cheeseman cut in. 'Activity, you see? That is what old people thrive on. That is why we got Mummy into the Thorogood Village.'

From the way she looked at you, Cherry must have had an inkling; more, you might be sharing a secret.

'And she enjoys it?' Dorothy asked.

'She adored it from the beginning: the company of others her age, the discussions—the flower gardens, my dear! There are certain beds planted with perfumed flowers specially chosen for those whose eyesight is failing.' Cherry Bullivant aimed an extra significant look at her friend Dorothy Hunter.

'I'm so glad, Cherry, your mother is happy at the Thorogood Village.'

The ladies only vicariously involved were standing almost at attention as they waited.

'Mummy died a few weeks after being admitted, but Matron assured me she appreciated what Douglas and I had done for her.'

Dorothy's heart was bounding in her side.

Then a gust of apprehension seemed to blow amongst the silent ladies; and Mrs Cheeseman's voice suggested, 'Don't you think it's time to go down to the boys?'

So they did.

Downstairs the men might not have had enough of talking bawdy and money, except for Brian Learmonth and the Australian Writer, who had ganged up in a corner, and who looked a case of two people too much alike, who had exhausted their stock of malice, and were bored with each other. When Mrs Cheeseman led in her retinue of women, all with the bland eyelids of those who have recently exchanged confidences and flushed the lavatory, the Australian Writer announced to his companion, 'This is where I help myself to a stiff one.'

After dinner was more intimate than before, if also more tedious. The novelty of a French princess, who was only an Australian underneath, had already worn thin. The detergent knight at one stage was unable to contain a fart. While Christian names of absent acquaintances were being flicked back and forth as light and hollow as pingpong balls, Dorothy was allowed to withdraw inside her thoughts, as though she had really been speaking a foreign language and everybody was exhausted by their own smiles and efforts to communicate.

Only the wife of the detergent knight would not leave well alone, but came and sat beside her new friend. 'I'm going to ask you a favour,' old Lady Atkinson begged; 'if one day you will visit me, my dear, and I'll make you some of my pumpkin scones.'

The princess thanked the kindly old thing, and immediately asked Mr Learmonth to find her a glass of water.

'Nothing wrong, I hope?' Lady Atkinson anxiously asked.

No, there was nothing wrong, Dorothy assured; actually, it was the murder she had been contemplating, and was pretty certain to commit since her visit to the house of one who had brought it off successfully.

Ever since dinner Cherry had been, not avoiding her, merely too busy pouring coffee and urging her guests to get drunker on liqueurs. At times you caught glimpses of a hectic eye, a back less powdered than before, as Mrs Cheeseman circulated with noticeable heaviness.

When suddenly she appeared to force herself to approach the Princesse de Lascabanes, and bending over her, offer a personal message, however indistinctly delivered. 'Drink this, Dorothy; it will do you good,' as she stood a brandy balloon, more than half filled, on the table beside her guest.

Because Mrs Cheeseman moved away at once, Madame de Lascabanes hadn't time to refuse: not all the brandy in the world would have melted the sobriety in which she had been frozen by Cherry's earlier admission, not to say her recognition of a capacity for treachery equal to her own.

While Lady Atkinson continued smiling: at the balloon; for the generous hand which had poured such a quantity of brandy for a friend; for her own good luck at meeting and being accepted by such a distinguished lady as this princess. The old woman was beginning to weave around their relationship a cocoon of the same golden threads from which, as she told it, her marriage had been spun, and by which she was joined to her beloved grandchildren. Lady Atkinson was most anxious for the princess to visualize these children in their perfection, and had already dashed off a water-colour or two when Dorothy felt she must escape from the old woman's delicately tinted world in which she was a harsh impostor.

At first she tried making excuses for herself. 'I've been neglecting my mother. Tomorrow I must spend more time — the whole day with her. We never succeed in dealing with all we have to talk about.'

Lady Atkinson was charmed. 'She'll love that, dear, I'm sure. It's hard for anyone old and helpless to kill time.'

Finally her own hypocrisy spurred the princess into going in search of Mrs Cheeseman to say goodbye. At least nobody inter-fered, or offered to help: either she had gone about it too discreetly; or was she unlikeable? she wondered at the mirrors she passed. Certainly her mouth had grown thinner from preoccupation, her cheekbones chalkier and more exposed. So she moistened her lips and reminded herself that her friend had arranged this dinner out of affection for her. She hoped her eyes, her best feature, would not let her down while expressing in return the grateful affection she ought to feel.

She found Mrs Cheeseman lying on the bathroom tiles, crumbs of plaster in her hair.

'What on earth happened?' Knowing perfectly well did not prevent an increase in Dorothy's desperation.

'Nothing happened. I fell down.' For somebody so huge and

purple who had suffered a recent fall, Cherry did not sound unduly plaintive. 'I fell, Dorothy. And the curtains came—with me.'

When her friend had heaved her as far as the bed, again Mrs Cheeseman wheezed, 'Thank you, darling. You're a real—ppal,' each word flickering inside a fume of brandy.

Dorothy thought she was entitled to feel virtuous. 'Would you like me to send your husband?'

'Oh, husband! Husbands aren't any use—they know too much.' Cherry's head was rolling uncontrollably in the rucks of ice-blue satin. 'And you, Dorothy—I let Ethel Atkinson bore you—ad naus ... ' She coughed the rest of it away.

'But Lady Atkinson was sweet! She was telling me about her grandchildren.'

'Nasty little bastards! Last week they pulled the legs off a clutch of live chickens, and poked out their eyes with sticks. But that isn't what Grannie sees.'

Through her own nausea, Dorothy was clinging to a hope that Mother—but Elizabeth Hunter always saw: she saw the worst in everyone.

Then Cherry Cheeseman, who had closed her eyes, opened them wide at something she appeared to have discovered. 'Why do you hate your mother, Dorothy?'

'How can you be so cruel, Cherry?'

Fortunately she was saved from further interrogation: her friend passed out.

As Madame de Lascabanes fled, snores pursued her from out of the ice-blue satin. If there was no running away from herself, she must at least escape from the Cheeseman house, with its implications, and downright accusations. But more was prepared for her, it seemed.

On an antique sofa, in an alcove halfway down the stairs, the Australian Writer had arranged himself, or perhaps more accurately, had been arranged, in an attitude more decorative, though no less drunken, than Cherry Cheeseman's on the bathroom floor. He could have been put there on the sofa expressly for the discomfiture and humiliation of the Princesse de Lascabanes, on whom his eyes began to focus purposefully. As she slipped past the unavoidable alcove, his mouth was working to expel the words it was loaded with.

'Only turn me on, princess,' was what she heard; 'I love everybody.'

Naturally she paid no attention, but was horrified to see him fling himself from his sofa at what he judged the level of her knees, as though she were a footballer whose evading tactics he had set out to queer by a flying tackle.

The princess was almost crying her relief to find herself slightly ahead of the thud the Australian Writer made with the banisters. She ran on, clutching, not the ball, but her intention of getting away as quickly as possible from the Cheesemans and their guests, her furs streaming, the tails of sables galloping behind her on the stairs.

She ran out into the night, through the more emphatic, at the same time liquid black poured around her by trees, till she reached the suburban street, slower now, and holding her temples. Above her were stars she might not have noticed since—oh, too long—since 'Kudjeri'. If only the lid could be lifted from her head to let out the bursting rockets of thoughts alternating with evil smog, she might see more clearly; but clear vision, she suspected, is something you shed with childhood and do not regain unless death is a miracle of light; which she doubted.

Although she was walking, her mind continued running.

Since Sister Manhood thought up her idea she had become pretty obsessed with it. Actually she couldn't claim to have thought of it in the sense of reasoning it out; she would probably never learn to reason as people did in books, or famous doctors, or even a comparatively ordinary man like Col Pardoe; her idea, it seemed, had been lying quietly somewhere inside her till the time came for it to spring into her head. She liked to believe it was what they call an 'inspiration'.

The day Flora Manhood felt her embryonic inspiration ready to convert itself into a positive event, she had woken early, but drifted a while longer, enjoying the ripeness of her intention. She lay glowing and expansive on what was normally the Vidlers' un-yielding convertible lounge, but which this morning responded to her form with an almost sensual recognition of their possibilities, so that she had to smile and rub one cheek against a shoulder, and enjoy lazily scratching a flank; the smell of her hair and her flesh was so delicious she thrilled with an unusual sense of her own power. But wasn't she, anyway, about to take her fate in hand? In the circumstances, she only faintly frowned at the stench of fowl manure intruding through the open window in opposition to her own drowsily voluptuous scents.

No more than four hens, in any case, and not all that much shit: Vid was too clean (cleanliness was Vid and Viddie's life). And so decent, not any of the neighbours would have dreamt of lodging a complaint with the Health Inspector they thought of other reasons for their asthma; or how they might scrounge a handful of manure for the aluminium plant. If anybody was to complain, Flora Manhood knew, it could be herself in one of her nursier moments: didn't you have to prove your status from time to time, to other people? But with Vid and Viddie so decent, never ever had she complained. She was fond besides, she thought perhaps she loved, certainly she depended on them more than any other person (her parents dead; Snow Tunks in the dyke racket; and there was no one else, thank you).

Flora Manhood opened her eyes so suddenly and wide there was a distinct scratching sound. Although she could have lain in bed most of the morning as she mostly did, she got out of it quicker than usual. She would take her time, though, on such a day: do her nails, run the bath later on, make herself extra nice before afternoon duty at Moreton Drive. One pyjama leg had hitched up around a thigh, which she sat a moment stroking in the way someone exceptional, chosen for the important part he must play, would most likely — caress (none of that take-you-for-granted stuff). Her skin was smooth, hairless, suntinged, except for the two white cups, and lower down, less than a triangle, a line. She had thought how she might give up pyjamas (cut down on laundry apart from anything else) but Viddie walked in one morning, so shocked to see what was only another woman's breasts, you hadn't taken to sleeping starkers.

The girl stood, rather abruptly. What makes people grow up decent? she wondered while washing the sleep out of her eyes. It could be from not wanting anything enough. Like Vid and Viddie, and Mr Wyburd, and de Santis, and Lottie Lippmann, even binding Badgery, though Badgery put on dog and liked to be thought better than she was. Not the Princess Lascabanes, from what others had to tell. Or Sir Basil Hunter.

Flora Manhood soaped her armpits. After she had rinsed them, she got out the pale lipstick and clothed her mouth: her lips looked healed, and neat, and meek. Yes, you could thank the pale lipstick for meekness.

And Mrs Hunter: nothing meek about old Betty; she wouldn't be selected for the Decent Team. Trample you when she felt like it. Even at her oldest, most pitiful, feeblest. Because Elizabeth Hunter, judging by the studio portraits, and the oil painting, had been a beautiful, a passionate woman. And that, together with money, was power, wasn't it? Power couldn't resist trampling. Not even while mumbling a prayer through bluish gums. Was it prayers Elizabeth Hunter mumbled on? or dreams of her own beauty— and men? All together, they had given her the power which can't help trampling. Doesn't God? On whole nations, as well as decent inoffensive individuals like Vid and Viddie; they must have it coming to them as sure as any Vietnamese.

Flora Manhood—'Flo' as she had been to Mum and Dad, and someone else more recent, but as dead, 'Florrie' to Snow Tunks; made you fetch up only to remember—looked in the glass and wondered if she had gone too far. She was not irreligious, she didn't think. Right down from the banana days and the miracle that wasn't—vouchsafed? she had more than respected, she needed God.

So virtue plumped out her lips as she went into the kitchen she had the use of (together with cons) her bare feet this moment enjoying the cleanliness, the reliability, of Viddie's lino. Indeed, she stamped once or twice, to drum her pleasure into her soles, before taking the Magic Wand and making the gas explode around the burner.

Presently Viddie came in from cleaning: front path, doorstep, and hall were the first details on her schedule. 'Early for you, isn't it?'

Flora said, 'It's an important day.'

Seated at the shining laminex table, she was still no more than warming her lip on the steam from the cup. For once her appetite for food had left her, though if she had wanted, there were eggs with dates on them, gifts from Vid, from his four hens.

'Is it to do with Mrs Hunter?' Mrs Vidler asked. 'About what you told me? It's a scandal!' Whenever she was outraged, something of Yorkshire rose up Viddie's throat, until, as it overflowed, it was joined by a sound like as if the adenoids hadn't been taken from her. 'Her own flesh and blood!' she gasped.

'Yes,' said Sister Manhood, sipping her cooler tea, 'it's a shame.' She must try to feel it more deeply; she did: only Elizabeth Hunter her sleeves embroidered in gold thread and pearls in that studio portrait on the desk turning her flower her *face* in all the radiance of its arrogant beauty holding it up coldly to the light or camera made you concentrate on an old munching skull if you were to raise sympathy — and there you were back at a geriatric case no more than a job.

'I'm thinking of giving it away,' she said.

'Giving away what, dear?'

'Nursing Mrs Hunter.'

'But if they send her to the Thorogood Village, won't the job terminate — automatic?'

'She may be dead by the time they finish talking about it. They'll talk all right. Sir Basil and the princess see themselves as highly civilized.' She laughed through her nose, but didn't convince herself.

Nor Viddie Vidler. 'Must be that, I'd say. They've had all the time and the money. And Sir Basil — he's a great actor. Anyway, they made him a Sir.'

'He's a gorgeous man. Going a bit in places. But lush. How civilized I wouldn't like to bet. Personally, I don't think any man is all that civilized.'

Viddie sucked her teeth; she was picking non-existent fluff out of a broomhead. 'What thoughts you have, Flora! You ought to settle down, dear – marry – have some kiddies.' It was a great sadness in Viddie that she had none of her own.

'I could do with a kid,' Flora went so far as admitting. 'Yes, I'd love a little child.' She gulped so greedily at her tea she choked; the tears came into her eyes.

Again the Yorkshire rose up Viddie's throat to unite with that sound of adenoids. 'You wouldn't have one without the other – would you, dear?' she gasped.

Flora rinsed her cup and saucer. She flung the leaves from the pot, she realized too late, into the bin reserved for scraps suitable for hens; but Viddie didn't notice that.

'Expect I'll be late in tonight,' Sister Manhood told her landlady.

'Enjoying yourself, are you, dear?'

'I'm going on the streets.'

Viddie laughed, but grudgingly, at one of Flora's off jokes. 'And what shall I tell Him, if he comes, or phones?'

'Tell who?'

'Why, Mr Pardoe.'

'I'm not his property, am I?' She was so enraged.

'Nobody is anybody's property, dear.'

'Not if I can help it, I won't be!'

'I was only asking,' Viddie complained.

So the irritations began collecting as early as early like real fluff you can't pick out of a broomhead what ought to be a solid permanent core the too tidy too-decent-by-half Vidlers spilt the varnish doing your nails on their old convertible moquette oh dear oh God the green the best straining at your just about every direction how would you look if you ever got preggo the genuine bloaterbella to stare at climbing on buses now it's only greed it's

Lottie's lunches too much of what should have been today the dreamiest Stroodle if she hadn't burnt it only slightly bloody Badgery crooking her finger *my husband* as per usual *a public school man of Brighton College Sussex England never accustomed his ear to the Australian twang.*

When the nurses had finished their lunch, or 'luncheon' as Badgery called it, to copy Mother Hunter and put on extra dog, Lottie said, 'I apologize for the *Strudel,* if it has burnt itself frightfully.'

'Mmm. Didn't notice.' Sister Manhood scraped hard so as not to lose the merest flake.

'It was delicious.' Sister Badgery might have invented the word; she smiled the kind of smile which rewards, but which knows better at the same time.

'It is burnt,' said Mrs Lippmann with a simplicity which emphasized the tragedy. 'I have planned this *Strudel* during several days, but on the morning did not reckon with the plumber.'

'You've had the plumber?'

'The cloakroom lavatory has been blocked—by somebody throwing superfluous matter down the hole.'

Sister Badgery lowered her eyes. Mrs Lippmann's clouded expression was directed, only incidentally perhaps, at Sister Manhood.

'Don't look at *me,* Lottie! And anyway, if the plumber unblocked it.'

'Oh, it is nothing. The plumber unblocked it.' It was nothing and everything.

Sister Badgery hoped to put an end to the post-mortem, for herself at least. 'After nursing several cases in the country—all of them prominent graziers—I would never dare throw anything foreign down a toilet. Septic tanks taught me my lesson.' That was final; so Sister Badgery got up.

'It is not the lavatory only. It is Mrs Hunter.' The housekeeper looked visionary today.

'As if the old girl will know about it, Lottie—not if you don't tell her—or care if she did.'

'She will care about what *they* do to her,' Mrs Lippmann said, 'her children.'

'Do you think she has any idea?' Sister Badgery was taking off her veil and folding it; her hair had thinned at the parting, and was of a neutral or sludge colour.

'Who knows?' Mrs Lippmann had to suffer everything herself, or so it sounded.

Much as she disliked men, Sister Manhood began to think women got on her tits as badly, anyway this afternoon. Irritations must be in her stars. She went up and found the old biddy had done it in the bed. (Bet it had happened before Badgery handed over: her so pleased with herself at lunch.)

And Lottie Lippmann and the loo.

As Sister Manhood stripped her patient's bed, gathering together in one exasperated crumple of sheet anything 'foreign' (trust Badgery) the tears were as good as shooting. Perspiring too. And no spare deodorant, more than likely, in the Nurses' Room.

When Betty Hunter said, 'I haven't done anything, Sister – have I? I must have been dreaming. My nurse was so unkind to me. She told me I must eat the cold mutton or spend the rest of the day in my room. Or was it Kate Nutley's nurse? I don't – believe – we could afford one.'

'P'raps it wasn't you that did it.' What bliss to be a geriatric nut.

It was a long afternoon. Sister Manhood fetched a mag to have a read in an easy chair by Mrs Hunter's window. She should have felt relieved her patient had withdrawn, it seemed, into sleep. But she wasn't relieved, the magazine too full of old women displaying the fluffy toys they had made, and crochet bedspreads, and tea cosies, themselves with scone faces and enormous overstuffed cosies for bodies. Sister Manhood could feel the wrinkles prickling as they opened in her own cheeks. She went at one stage and patted her face with wych-hazel. This evening it didn't soothe; it fed a burning which had taken possession of her skin.

Then the gate squealed, and Mr Wyburd was coming up the path. Slowly. Another geriatric: if his head was still his to use, it wouldn't be for long; you could hear the arteries hardening in him in pauses between chosen words. Just your luck old Wyburd turning up the' night you wanted off early; worse luck still, de Santis (Mary the Saint of Saints!) letting you down.

She came in at last in that same navy hat. 'I see Mr Wyburd's car is at the gate.'

Flora Manhood was perked up, quickly and efficaciously. 'He's in with Betty—having his turn,' she snickered.

'I expect in the end he'll be the one who'll have to tell her what they propose doing to her.'

'Oh hell—yes!' Flora Manhood felt breathless now that she was actually faced with the prospect for her evening. 'Yes, he might. I can't think why I—why we've got to worry—not personally—about what happens in a patient's life—outside her *sick* life, I mean.'

Sister de Santis said, 'But the princess and Sir Basil—it worries me when I find human beings more disappointing than I expected.'

'I never start by expecting too much,' Sister Manhood maintained; though she often did, of course, she knew.

Seated on the stool, her own reflection in front of her in the dressing-table mirror, she became aware that Mary de Santis was looking at her from under the awful navy hat.

Flora tried to protect herself. 'And I never had tickets on Princess Dorothy—or Sir Basil Hunter.'

De Santis didn't answer, but continued, probably, looking. What was she trying to winkle out?

Sister Manhood turned and said, 'Why don't you get yourself another hat, Sister? It's gay colours today. And I don't think navy suits you. Makes you look livery.'

Sister de Santis had begun to remove the offending hat. 'I grow attached to things.'

'Not clothes, for God's sake! They're not for permanent, are they? It would turn women into statues, sort of—clothed statues.'

That made Mary de Santis smile, and Flora Manhood realized her colleague did in fact have something of a statue about her: a statue with live eyes. Funny how old de Santis could make you feel inferior and you didn't mind.

Then she saw that Sister de Santis was not smiling for anything that had been said, but for thoughts she had been turning over. 'I know it's really none of my business as a nurse—it's the doctor who could say something—but as an old friend who is fond of Mrs Hunter—that is why I feel I'm entitled to speak to Sir Basil. Not here where it's all so cluttered—too many associations to get in the way—I might go to his hotel, and appeal to him to consider the distress he's in danger of causing his mother.'

Flora Manhood was surprised to see Mary de Santis had begun to blush. She had never thought of her as being exactly beautiful, and now only for a moment, because of something shocking about it all.

'You'd be wasting your time,' Sister Manhood mumbled, and got up. 'Or that's what I think.' She wished it had been a hospital, when she could have produced a chart, handed over with efficient, completely impersonal cool, and swept off without further yakker.

She did sweep off, even so.

She couldn't skip quick enough bang the door she didn't care down the dark treacherous path a shrub hitting her across the eyes could have been a wire switch made her whinge she couldn't see what some people saw in trees (it was Col Pardoe who was so sold on trees on nature: its *spontaneous recurrence*).

Nobody could say she wasn't spontaneous; it was spontaneity which had ended by making her regret the situation she was in. It was too much spontaneity which persuaded her for a time that she needed Colin Pardoe. *I am not whole Col except when I feel you inside me then we are truly one person*, she had been fool enough to even put it in writing; the spoken word fades out, but writing lasts for ever if a person is mean enough to want to prove something.

After passing Wyburd's car she began to act more—more *prudently*. It was not her word, but one she had heard the solicitor use: *I don't think it would be prudent Sister Manhood to allow Mrs Hunter to go for a drive she would see nothing almost certainly overtire herself and perhaps catch a chill*. To live, to love prudently. That meant to think so much about it you didn't get anywhere at all. It wouldn't pay today. If it mightn't be desirable in the long run.

As she walked (more prudently) along Moreton Drive towards the bus, she wondered what and how Sister de Santis, who suggested she was capable of thinking things out, would say and do to Sir Basil Hunter. One thing for sure: he wouldn't take her seriously wearing that hat. But perhaps St Mary would buy herself a new one, a real whirligig, on the solemn occasion of her intercession for Basil's mother.

Flora Manhood was slightly sorry she had brought up the subject of hats. With or without, what would de Santis know to do with any man, let alone Basil Hunter? You could only imagine her sitting alone in her room, mending, or, to turn it into a holiday, leafing through the *National Geographic*.

Then Sister Manhood felt wholly sorry for the colleague she did respect. Sincerely. *I am sincere aren't I?* She often thought you can never know truthfully what you are, when you are the one and only who ought to be in a position to know.

On the bus she caught there were several men looking at her. She looked away from the dirty men. She tried to adopt a comfortable position, to pull her skirt down, but it wouldn't come, or only so far: her green. The bus wasn't all that full because it happened to be a between period. (She could reason things out for herself when these ran along practical lines.) There was a pretty bitch of a conductress: no dyke. (You would have died if it had been Snow.) The conductress looked down her nose at you. Well, you couldn't deny it was you the greasy old men coming off shifts and out of pubs, scabby, horny men, were looking at, wasn't it?

The betweentime bus rumbled along.

She had worked this out at least: she would catch him before his dinner, perhaps changing into dinner gear for some gala occasion when the presence of a great visiting actor might be sought. She would send up her name: Flora Manhood. Miss? No, *Sister* Manhood. Give him a clue, for Christ's sake.

After she had left the bus, and found her connection, and arrived, she hung around the bright thoroughfare a while before going down the hill to the hotel at which he was staying. Take her time. She could hear the voice through the receptionist's receiver asking for them to send her up, like a meal on a tray. Upstairs Sir Basil would have dropped to which nurse, the 'pretty one', the one his eye had roved over, the night of his arrival. If she was to be completely frank, it scared the shits out of her now that it was approaching.

So she hung around a bit, looking at the cheap engagement rings in the windows; in the souvenir shops, the opals and the kangaroo claws. (Wear a kangaroo coat—white—for her first press interview —her hair a short bleached Mia Farrow.)

But what she never ever wanted was marriage. Col had taught her that, if not about MAHL-er. She turned her back on everything that made her want to puke, and her skirt, what there was of it, swished in the plate glass. She didn't seem able not to swish tonight however prissy she walked. Along the pavement the men were looking at her: the disguised G.I.s on leave from that war; the Hungarian Jews without, and even with, their wives; the spotty, fish-eyed kinks. A pair of poufs had a good giggle, as though recognizing their own act. She looked in a window and caught her green swishing, her body barely camouflaged by the pattern of deeper greener leaves. Shoot said the eyes of the G.I.s on leave from war the kinks picked their noses and rolled it at least the Jewish gentlemen were dry and professional in their glances a queeny giggle sprayed her up one side of her neck.

She turned her head, looking into the shop windows. What Mrs Hunter said about goats that had been with the buck could apply also perhaps to women who were on their way there: other people scented it. As she stretched her neck, her green seemed to fit closer to her hips. You couldn't say she hadn't been what they call 'chaste' for some time now, though that didn't mean she hadn't let her mind roam around a bit, or hoped that some completely satisfying dream might descend on her during sleep. All the while making her calculations, by the calendar too, with pencil and paper, on Vidlers' wiped-down laminex.

Till you were ready according to figures.

That was why the men were looking at her. Because she was ready. And unprotected. All men, she suspected, not only Col Pardoe, hated the pill as being unnatural. It was natural for men, even if they didn't know it, to want to pump a woman up, then in watching, feel their self-importance expand.

So all the men were watching her as she turned down the darker street on her planned visit to Sir Basil Hunter. If she slipped in a bit of advice on how to treat his old mother, that was to save de Santis the trouble. It was in no way related to her plan, the hands of which had begun to articulate, the feet to kick: she felt dizzy, if not crazy, with all that was forming in her head.

The receptionist, a dark shiny girl who looked as though she didn't do anything about her armpits, made a tight mouth, and said, 'I fancy Sir Basil will be changing for dinner;' which was exactly as Flora Manhood had hoped.

The receptionist frowned before smiling at the bakelite cup she was addressing. 'A Sister Manhood to see you, Sir Basil.' There were the usual formal gulps and clicks from the phone; then the receptionist stuck the phone back on its stand, and without looking, condescended, 'Up the short flight, and follow the passage to the left. It's number Five;' her voice as impersonal as bakelite: whose business was it if a casual, if *Sir* Basil Hunter (Guest of Honour on the A.B.C.) received a prostitute in his room?

The dark shiny receptionist had already begun pressing her damp handkerchief against her catarrhal nose before Sister Manhood started mounting the short flight, to follow the passage to the left.

The visitor had hardly given Sir Basil time to come out from under the shower; but he came, in a dressing-gown she recognized as 'luxurious', tousling his hair with a rough towel. 'What can I do for you?' The voice was natural, weary rather than elderly, at any rate not as old as Arnold Wyburd's.

He must have dropped to himself, because immediately he settled for a sharper expression, both mouth and eyes, and stopped drying his hair.

She felt a spurt of fear, which might have shot deeper into her if it hadn't been for Mary de Santis coming up with guidance. 'It's your mother,' Flora Manhood said, 'I thought I'd like to have a word with you about—Sir Basil.'

'Oh, come!' He laughed; and she reckoned the eye-teeth were probably hitching posts for the false. 'I was hoping you were paying me a sociable visit.'

Legs apart, back turned, rubbing stuff into his hair in front of the dressing-table glass, Sir Basil Hunter gave the impression it was the most natural thing in life to be receiving sociable visits from girls, in hotel bedrooms, in his dressing-gown. As for herself, she felt for ever rooted in her origins: in spite of your training at P.A., the diploma, the gear you had dolled yourself up in, a pretty intensive sexual life (till recently at least) and a lengthy spell nursing a rich bitch who had many cranky but often pointed answers to the questions, your basic knowledge was that of the girl reared amongst the banana palms up country from Coffs Harbour.

All of this made her mumble past the trembling cigarette she had lit for a purpose. 'Mrs Hunter has been my case for over a year. Why can't you believe I have her interests at heart?'

He stooped a bit, so that his reflection could stare back at her. Without turning, he gave her a look of what she suspected was—commiseration? Seeing that he knew the hypocrite she was, she dragged on the jittery cigarette she had only lit to help herself. (Never got more than a screen, you couldn't say it was pleasure, out of smoking.)

While still taken up with the hair he was dashing back into shape, the lights in it intensified by repeated blows from the brushes against the crisp waves and unctuous tonic, Sir Basil sighed. 'Yes—Mother —poor darling!'

After that he laid the brushes down; it was as though his visitor and he had settled a matter between them: they had done their duty by Elizabeth Hunter.

Sir Basil brought a bottle of Scotch. He brought ice from the fridge, which was ticking over the other side of the room; while she removed from her tongue a shred of tobacco she wasn't sure existed, but it was what they do.

(How to raise her glass without giving herself away? There was the two-handed method she had practised while a trainee on her first dates with residents: young pukey milk-skinned doctors, themselves nervous enough not to notice the trembles in somebody else; but Sir Basil Hamlet Hunter?)

'If you don't mind, I prefer a lighter one.' Not quite, but almost, Badgery lining up a tea planter as the sun went down on the equator.

He added soda. She felt the draught prickling upward, and lowered her eyes. She sank her pale lipstick in the glass as she noticed the hairs on the backs of the actor's fingers.

'Right?'

'Thank you.'

Even if the half of her tried on and off to kid the other half into believing her standards were basically moral, and that she was genuinely concerned for Mrs Hunter's welfare, the more positive half had declared its intentions by choosing the sofa; just as he declared his by sitting down deliberately beside her. The sofa was neither very large nor very new; the springs protested, but the occupants were brought unavoidably closer as from the sides of a shallow funnel. More unexpected was the sudden change of climate, from temperate to tropical, as the steam from his freshly showered body burst out of the dressing-gown. For a moment or two she had trouble getting her breath.

Sir Basil seemed unconscious of the effect he had produced without evidently trying for it; he was too intent on the touches with which he would build up a performance into something recognizably his.

'Thank you for coming here tonight,' he said, focusing a lustrous eye on his opposite lead. 'You couldn't have known you'd be saving me from myself.'

'Oh?' The most she could summon out of her stupor was this pathetic moo, like a cow sunk, but passively, in a bog.

'One of my black days.'

'I don't want to latch on—not, I mean, if you have anything else in view.' A pellet of gum flattened on a back tooth couldn't have given worse trouble than the words her jaws were trying to get rid of. 'The girl at the desk said you were dressing for dinner.'

'Dinner with myself—unless the girl at the desk knew more than I.' All the time he was looking at, or into her, his right hand was picking over the upholstery somewhere at the back of her head.

She must make the effort to overcome this stranglehold of huskiness on her monotonous, her charmless voice. 'Don't imagine I came here expecting dinner.' She hawked up the words, it sounded, out of her hoarse throat.

Instead of answering he smiled at her with an indulgence to dismiss diffidence for good and all.

He was certainly going out of his way to make it easy for her. She was by now almost sealed up with Sir Basil in his envelope of steam. She should not have had to think out a further move, only adopt a grateful expression.

What then prevented her taking immediate advantage of his consideration? It wasn't Mrs Hunter, though in the absence of an admissible reason, it would bloody well have to be: not the old incontinent carcase whose mind maundered after the dolls she had played with and tortured as a child, till suddenly and cruelly, she was back inside her right mind, the dolls turned into human playthings. You would have to concentrate, not on this real woman, but the pale ghost of a saint Lottie Lippmann and de Santis persuaded themselves to believe in.

Instead, what Flora Manhood had begun to see was not the ghost-saint, it was Sir Basil Hunter's knee—and calf—slowly released by the slippery folds of the dressing-gown. 'I mean, I did honestly come here to ask whether you were considering your mother's feelings in putting her in the Thorogood Village.' She seemed to have achieved at last a low, soft, perhaps even appealing voice, while making circular passes with the palm of a hand over her own uppermost knee, unwisely, it soon appeared, because it emphasized the naked-ness, not to say the closeness, of his.

The eyes of each were concentrated on the other's knee; when the telephone went off, knocking their attention, as well as their bodies, sideways.

Sir Basil handled the situation. 'I'm not taking any calls tonight. I'm too exhausted.' To prove it he closed his eyes, and smiled rather bitterly for the switchboard before dumping the receiver in its cradle.

He was back in brisker form. 'Nothing has been decided. It was an idea, only. And more than likely won't get any farther, if everyone who pleads for my mother is so pretty and so tender-hearted.' He squeezed her knee, very warmly, through the hose.

Touched by a famous hand, Flora Manhood jumped up; she was on fire, and liking it. What was more, she hadn't altogether ratted on old Mrs Hunter. So she was now free, not to enjoy the situation she had so carefully prepared, but to go through with it for the sake of the fruit it must bear.

'If it was only an idea,' she panted, 'we've got that straight at least. But your other ideas may be as crook,' she threw off in the brassier voice she used as one of her weapons of defence.

Sir Basil would have liked to follow suit by standing up as quickly from the musical sofa, but could have felt a twinge in his back. His moody smile became a bare grin as he got to his feet, but he came on in the only possible direction: he too, had his plan to carry out.

And grabbed.

Probably on account of the twinge throwing him slightly off balance, he caught hold of a handful of flesh she wasn't proud of (it was superfluous) above her right hip; and Basil Hunter looked angry that his technique should let him down, converting a smooth pass into what must look an act of vulgar clumsiness.

Even so, they were thrown together on the edge of the room, and rebounded so abruptly off the pounding fridge they almost over-turned a Queen Anne walnut veneer table with piecrust edging, the lot.

'I should have thought,' Sir Basil got it out while eating his way along her shoulder, 'we understood each other, Sister Man—Clara, is it?'

'Flora.'

'Oh, yes—Flora! Perfect! *Flora!*'

They were seeing eye to eye, both literally and figuratively: they understood each other's inquisitive lust as it tempered and tried them out. How much else she understood of this ageing man, desirable, if only in bursts, she could not try to think. That he had no inkling of her real intention, she was a hundred per cent sure. Which gave her the advantage.

So she collapsed somewhat in his arms and made no secret of her breathlessness. '*Whoo!* Aren't you making the pace a bit hot?'

It gave him an opportunity to pass the buck. 'I'm hardly responsible—am I? Flora?'

Having kicked free of her shoes, she walked across the carpet on practical, flat feet, and pulled herself out of her dress: the green.

Sir Basil remarked, 'Now that clothes have become so rudimenary, we can't offer to help, can we?'

It did seem to become increasingly practical, and solemn. Till there she was.

'A genuine Botticelli!' He glanced over his shoulder, half expecting some unseen spectator might have overheard his corny remark.

'My what?' she giggled as he stood out of his dressing-gown.

The breasts of this elderly man—her lover—were developing relentlessly inside the fur bra.

'Please,' she screwed up her eyes, 'must we have the lights—Basil?' Mention of the sacred name seemed to add just that extra touch of obscenity.

As he switched off the lights, she had a blinding vision of that old sightless woman his mother: Mrs Hunter would surely smell out the whole circus, and to make it worse, keep her dignity.

You lay and felt Sir Basil limbering up: he might not be the artist you would have expected. Nobody is what you expect; and all great artists, you had read, suffer from nerves.

'You don't know what you're denying me,' he said in a sort of peeved voice, 'insisting on darkness.'

She grunted. She couldn't very well tell him *her* idea might breed more fruitfully in the dark, though Sir Basil had already shown his approval of ideas, anyway his own.

He was going on again a bit about his 'Botterchelly Flora'.

She would have liked to ask Col about this 'Botterchelly'. She was so *uneducated*.

'What is it, darling? Did I hurt you? Aren't you comfy?' He spoke with a tenderness which should have delighted any blessed Daddy's girl.

But she couldn't play up to it. Instead, she choked what must have begun as a whimper, or turned it into a sigh.

Which appeared to satisfy her lover.

He was all over and around her: exploring. She felt she had stopped being a woman, to become a mountain range. She saw herself spread out, under a Technicolor sky, on a picture postcard: *Greetings from the Sleeping Sister*.

He seemed to be trying, unsuccessfully, to drink her eyes. Then he climbed down. He kissed the soles of her feet. It tickled.

'What's the matter? Don't you like it?' He too, laughed, though he didn't sound amused.

Again, he was burning inside her ear. 'Do you think you'll be able to love me, Flora?'

'What are we doing I'd like to know?'

'Yes,' he sighed, while undeceived.

Because she might have sounded cranky, and because she owed him something in return, she must make the effort to deceive: perhaps deception was what an actor expects of life.

So she put her arms around him; she must think about this child he was going to give her: the child who would be the embodiment of unselfish love. 'Yes,' she muttered. 'I'll love you all right. I've only got to get used to — the idea.' And she crushed him with all her health and strength, as someone else had crushed, and mauled, and possessed her into a state of resentment.

Sir Basil seemed to like it. He grew young and excited. Even if he slit her open, she must love it for the sake of this golden child he was going to plant inside her.

So they were giving a great performance.

Whereas at the beginning his supremacy had been assured by ambition, now it was she who had become the guiding force. It was this desire to create something tangible, her only means of self-justification: as she must make others understand. *I'm not oh God oh Col I'm not the fucking whore you think*, she moaned the shapeless words into her lover's mouth. *Col?*

'Mmmm?' The getter of her child this pseudo-husband drove the word back into her she had wanted *oh Col Col ohh* she wanted her own her flesh her child *ohhhhh*.

Sir Basil keeled over, finally, and slithered off her left flank. He lay beside her trying to show he wasn't exhausted.

'Have you,' he panted, 'everything you—need, Flora?' He sounded anxious.

'Yes.'

She felt becalmed rather than calm, let alone fulfilled. There was nothing she needed beyond the certainty—she might even settle for the faint hope—of conceiving. She couldn't visualize her child except as a burst of distant gold. Would Col bash her up? She would have to tell him to his face because the letters she wrote made her want to puke, and on the phone she was at her dumbest.

Sir Basil Hunter was snoring. Although she would not have imagined she could fall asleep beside a man she didn't know, and without his clothes, she must have snoozed to find herself walking it could only be with Col Pardoe amongst the green hummocks of Noamurra printed up large on a hoarding A NOAMURRA WELCOME TO MAN AND WIFE Col if it was it was his arm seemed pleased to confirm what he already knew.

Basil woke. The surrounding darkness must have reached its lowest depths of black. He drooled for the glass of Alka-Seltzer he would presently brew, not on account of a hangover, but because it was a drink which soothed and restored him in the middle of the night; he slept more innocently, he liked to believe, after gulping this pristine draught. He scrabbled after, and found his watch, only to remember his eyesight was no longer up to reading the time on its luminous face. So he groped farther, till bumping the lamp he realized he ought not to switch it on: there was this girl, the nurse he had gone to bed with. He could hear her beside him, breathing in her sleep.

He hankered after light more than before, to stare at the flesh which had given him such a surprising amount of unexpected pleasure; but he might not be dispassionate enough, and the nurse could return to her body and start bossing or abusing him.

So he lay flickering his eyelids and thinking; there was no alternative in the trap in which he found himself. Oh Lord, if only he could kick her out and spread a bit; but in an effort to rearrange himself he found he had been brought closer, plastered to her ribs, almost part of the movement of her heart. He tried listening for signs of waking; but there weren't any: if anything she was sinking deeper drawing him under with her a voice calling in his mind's ear from a long way off BASIL his own slippery name nobody he could recognize not even the sex behind the voice only that it was persistent clearly articulated though faint. He shut it out at last by forcing himself full awake.

His thoughts began steeplechasing, spurt after spurt, a string of competitive images. He looked his best in sombre, fur-trimmed robes: that photograph of Alvaro, the one from the Third Act. Nobody could deny you made a fine figure (in fact, there is always some bastard aiming a banana skin, but dammit). Fly back as soon as it is practically possible, and revive *Malatesta* perhaps, or *The Master of Santiago*. On the whole they preferred your Alvaro: an austere, destructive, while self-destroying soul—a noble inquisitor. Yes, revive *The Master*, with its shorter, cheaper cast; woman's part not big enough for her to think she can rob the kitty or throw a tantrum. Impress anybody with some of those lines—and your voice: *God neither wishes nor seeks anything. He is eternal calm. It is in wishing nothing that you will come to mirror God.*

317

Oh God, if only he could have switched the light on: he was driven to speak the remembered lines, address Alvaro in the mirror; but the damn girl; and on this narrow bed he couldn't tear himself free of the adhesive skin. He was stuck with her.

So he sank back. What he had never been able to understand was how he had moved them in certain scenes night after night while wanting and getting everything, the whole jackpot, for himself, and not believing in 'God'. Every night the faces stirred, the breathing rose out of the darkness. Only the author was unmoved, a cantankerous, hostile Frenchman arriving unannounced to catch you out. When the critics had more than hinted that his play was corn. Some of the lines *were*; everything depended on the voice which spoke them. But the Frenchman couldn't forgive himself his own corn, so he wanted to hold you responsible.

It was becoming the nurse's play. Rolling violently, she was trying to throw off her dream, get her lines out. 'Donthigkbecolsidoancallyoudarligidoanfeeloralway—sfelt.' Well, you would have expected her to love somebody, probably the whole pack: this Botticelli, not so much vulgarized as pop slanted.

He was unable to resist stroking the surface of her dream. The hot skin responded to his fingers without her waking. He felt a bit guilty for doing her so easily, and considering what she had given in return: she had made him see and hear himself again, moving with authority under the weight of his winter-toned, fur-trimmed robes. Perhaps this Alvaro was a little more in love, sensually, with his Mariana than the text demanded. Not an easy part to cast, herself always too much the sheath to his sword, particularly in that last duet:

MARIANA.   O rose of gold! Face of a lion! Face of honey! At your feet! My forehead on the earth before Him whom I feel!

ALVARO.   No, rise up higher! Rise up more swiftly! Drink and let me drink of you! Rise yet more!

MARIANA.   I am drinking and being drunk of, and I know that all is well.

Sister Thing—Flora Manhood—was stirring. He, too. Without her knowing, she was filling him with more than pleasure, poor girl: positive joy. He had to impress it on her whether he woke her or not. She gave no formal sign of waking, but this time they were more gently and completely lovers.

What if he did fall for some pretty, healthy, but ordinary girl like this? Would her love for him survive his bitches of friends? Would he be turned by her perpetual clangers into a pillar of sullenness? Come to think of it he had never been 'adored' by any but unattractive girls who came to the performance night after night, and hung about the stage door blushing through chlorosis or acne; or by some elderly, often deformed woman usually without means, whose permanent, near stall was her one shameless extravagance, in which she sat devouring with her eyes, her open dentures, perving on a codpiece. Esmé Gilchrist (E. Gilchrist she signed herself) invited him to tea at Islington, and he went because at that age he was still so incredibly innocent, and—she must have guessed—shockable. She received him in a lace whatyoume—teagowns in those days—and hoped to excite him with her truss. As a bonus, shit on the sheet. He got away so quickly the knocker could hardly have stopped knocking by the time he reached the bus stop.

What he had always longed for, he now knew, was to be loved by some such normal, lovely, insensitive but trusting hunk of a girl as this Flora Nightingale beside him: he had done her twice and felt progressively younger. Then why Alvaro? at one level a rewarding part for an elderly—let's say 'mature', actor of voice and presence; at another, the mouthpiece of asceticism preaching its withering gospel from the foothills of tragedy. As he climbed higher into a rarefied atmosphere, he breathed more deeply to satisfy his youthful lungs. It occurred to him: only an old man should aspire to, and would be capable of enduring, the fissions of Lear, but an old man with the strength of youth. So he paused, on a ledge as it were, to huddle closer to this warm girl who had received him unprotesting for the second time.

He began to feel lonely at last, on his narrow ledge, and thought

319

he would wake his companion: have to sooner or later; probably shamming anyway. 'Darling,' he addressed in turn, an ear, her mouth, each of her nipples, his arms as deep in her flesh as wire in the bark of a tree after a long relationship, 'I have a feeling we're starting something that's—most important—for both of us.' If he had resisted writing a play for himself to act in, it was because it might have sounded something like this.

'Mmmm?' She was too sleepy; or not so sleepy that the resident crowbar of her will could not prise her apart from her lover. She turned her back, her moody rump. Was she corrupt? Nurses— when you come to think of it. And when he had wanted to worship at the altars of health, purity, innocence; to lay his head on a pair of breasts which sympathized with the hunger of his thoughts.

Anger doused the rosy flame he had gone to so much trouble coaxing. He had nothing, or comparatively little, against this poor cow, who had simply flopped from running backwards and forwards at the beck and call of Elizabeth Hunter throughout the afternoon, then flogging half the night. No, he must look farther for somebody to blame, farther even than Mitty Jacka expecting him to find the money for the spectacular suicide she was devising for him. Look right back to the original grudge. *I was never a natural mother—I couldn't feed. But that—you see, darling—hasn't deprived you of—of nourishment.* She had told him, by God, without his asking. And doled out a cheque for five thousand—dollars, not pounds. Again only a wretched nibble.

He dragged the sheet up, tight, sawing at his throat, then settled down to hugging his resentment. Forgetful of his love, he must have rocked his anger to sleep.

In the cold awfulness of this fur-trimmed robe feelings unshutter only for brilliant glimpses watching the old painted skin give its last gasps through every frightened pore as well as the purple cupid's bow no need to use the dagger in your sleeve words are fatal if pointed enough *money is life while there is life left otherwise it is time to die die then* she can't protest against the truth only use her automatic bellows on the not even half-life she is giving up for life for say

320

The Master if Alvaro's own attitudes are sterile that is only to make a play to forego the wrack the storm and put buggered to the Jacka's version of suicide by the *unplayed I.*

Flora Manhood lumped herself together in the bed. Already there were flashes of tawny light through the rattling blinds. The light blew cold on her nakedness raising goosepimples as she watched.

Basil Hunter looked frightening in his sleep. His expression twitched, and on and off, it was twisted into tight knots of wrinkles. She too felt frightened at last.

She put out a hand, before bending over him to say, 'You must have been having a shocking dream.'

'Yes. I was murdering — or being murdered — I can't remember — or who.'

Though it sounded sleepy enough, he was watching her keenly to see whether his explanation had satisfied her. But she was not interested in his dream: she looked preoccupied by some unhappiness, or murder, of her own. It had given her something more than her rather commonplace, healthy prettiness: she was beautiful, her hair an equal of the tawny light; only her expression remained remote and sad.

Flora Manhood did in fact feel unbearably sad. Here was this strange, not bad, but boring man, unconscious of the part he was playing, or the child she could conceive by him, regardless of whether he, or the child, wished it. She herself would not have wished to be born; sometimes she wondered whether her parents had wished it; or whether it was something that had happened because it was too long a drive to the pictures, so they stayed at home. Of course they would never have admitted to it if you had been brave enough to ask them; they were honest, religious-minded people.

She was the dishonest one, the deceiver. Her own child, whom she could not help seeing with the features of Colin Pardoe, would grow up as the visible proof of her deception, and she would have to disguise her remorse as love for her boy. Whichever way she looked she could see no end to her dishonesty: a vista of mirrors inside a mirror.

At least the actor would go away, and need not know. It was the rightful father who would remain and know. Passing them in the street or sitting opposite in the bus, he would look for his own features in what should have been his child. Oh, but she would take her boy away to another city, and there perhaps she would be able to love him enough to prevent him suspecting her deceit and ending up hating her.

While Basil Hunter, the more he looked at her brooding over her secret thoughts, wanted to make amends for what must have seemed a capricious seduction: on the contrary, he had been feeling tired and dispirited, not to say disgusted with himself for his intentions towards that old woman who was also his mother. Actually there should not have been any question of making amends to Flora Manhood; he was by now sure—or as sure as you can ever be—that it was not merely a matter of sexual desire: he could love this girl for the beauty of her simplicity, and her still unformed character would respond gratefully and happily.

'What is it?' She didn't really want an answer, but felt that, for politeness's sake, she was bound to ask.

'I'd like you to kiss me.'

His request was so simple she laughed, and bent over him; she more than kissed him: she raised his shoulders with her strong arms, and began dashing her lips against his forehead, his hair, as though trying to give expression to some deep-seated, natural passion.

So that, from being at first only her patient, he became her baby. He could have been wanting that. He did in fact nuzzle at those breasts overflowing with kindness and—and 'nourishment', unlike the reluctant official tit recoiling from his importunity.

As he sucked, and made all the sounds of gratified fulfilment, she felt herself to be doubly a deceiver: for she was holding the past in her arms, under the staggy orange trees, amongst the hummocks, in the green haze of Noamurra. When the haze cleared, and here was this ugly substitute.

But she went through her part in the play, of wife and mother, without showing her distress, let alone disgust.

Basil was saying, 'Don't you feel this is real, Flora?' He did honestly want to believe it.

She smiled, and began putting on her clothes.

'When shall we see each other?' he asked. 'It's going to be a right old lark phoning you in that house! Don't you appreciate the irony?'

She pounced on finding her mislaid shoes.

'Wait a minute,' he said. 'I'll get into something and come out to the gate with you.'

'Won't there be somebody at the desk?'

'Only a man at this hour. And a man is less likely to chalk it up against me.'

For the moment she couldn't think which sex she despised more; neither man nor woman would silence the objections which kept raising their heads in her mind.

So she preferred to kiss him formally, and go. She had a thumping appetite too: she could eat a plate of bacon, and a couple of Vid's numbered eggs fried till the whites were crisp round the edges.

While Basil got back, looking forward to another stretch. Till now his thoughts had been mostly of love; but he might even marry the girl. Himself as husband. In the days when marriage had implied Shiela's drunken slanging or Enid's spiked epigrams, he couldn't take it; matured since, he was again tempted by this peculiarly exacting role; above all, the idea of a woman keeping the bed permanently warm, was beginning to exercise its appeal. And a nurse: look after you; go out and work if necessary. It wouldn't be. There was the money, your own and rightful. Little Flora could only respond with gratitude.

Half asleep he tried out the variations on a name: Sister Manhood; Lady Hunter; Sir Basil's wife; all of them strong, and the total woman a conspicuously attractive addition to the cast of his play.

He continued drowsily smiling, till a hair bent in one of his nostrils, making him sneeze.

*

323

Flora Manhood looked in at the breakfast room where Badgery had begun her lunch, Lottie Lippmann in attendance.

'You're late, darling.' The housekeeper was not accusing. 'We began to wonder.' If anything, there was awe in her voice, as though she believed in the sanctity of youth and beauty; she would have liked to start at once stuffing this pretty young thing with food, because it was the only way in which she could express her belief.

'I'm not staying. I'm not hungry.'

'You're not *ill*, are you?' Badgery asked rather too loud through a mouthful of chicken liver and rice.

'I'm late. I got up late.'

'Not *ill*!' Mrs Lippmann's scorn rang out. '*Sie sieht so reizend aus! Strahlend!*' she chanted.

'What is that, may I ask, when translated for ordinary persons to understand?' Sister Badgery might have looked provoked if the foreign language had not allowed her to feel complacent as she sat spooning more of the sauce over her food. (She never understood how people could 'make a practice of foreign food', but she tried to do justice to it.)

Herself reduced to Sister Badgery's earthly level, Mrs Lippmann answered in dulled tones, 'It means, if you'd like to know, Floradora is looking good.'

'Ah, dear!' Sister Badgery sighed; she gave a peck or two, for propriety's sake, then settled down to gobbling her mash.

Sister Manhood didn't *feel* good. Going upstairs, going on duty, she could not have described her feelings. On arriving home she had eaten four of the Vidler eggs and as many rashers of bacon. She had slept too long and too heavy, and jumped up, and got into her clothes too quick. If she looked good to other people, it was, to put it crudely, on account of the friction: there's nothing like the friction of one human skin against another, she had often noticed, for bringing the complexion to life.

At least Mrs Hunter wouldn't notice your complexion. But what would she know? What would she smell? Remembering their talk about the goats, Sister Manhood was possessed by dread, her whole body numbed with it, on the soft, relentless stairs. With her own Basil involved, Mrs Hunter's sense of smell would surely be all the more acute.

Much as Sister Manhood would have liked to change quickly, to avoid Jessie Badgery in the Nurses' Room, she had no wish to go bursting in on her patient, to act the spirit of light when she was feeling the complete leaden bod. So she camped around a bit, making mouths at herself in the glass, and peering into the crammed cupboards. It cheered her to some extent to think that Lottie must soon come with the tray, after which Mrs Hunter would indulge in her guessing game of what there was to eat.

'Ooh, pardon *me!*' Sister Badgery put her hand to her mouth, as they did, no doubt, on tea plantations and P. & O. liners, before observing to her colleague, 'She's spent really—whatever she may tell you—a cheery morning. Pulse normal—bowels open at ten-thirty—everything the relieving nurse could desire. Oh, and Dr Gidley called. Doctor couldn't have been better pleased. He's such fun, isn't he? I do think Doctor's a jolly man.' Then Sister Badgery shook her wattles, her comb, and raised her disdainful beak, as though suddenly remembering she was superior, in the hierarchy of the yard, to this shapely but scatterbrained pullet. 'Appetite excellent.' She shuttered a yellow eye. 'Mrs Lippmann says Mrs Hunter ate an *enormous* luncheon, and asked for more—which of course she wasn't allowed,' Sister Badgery added.

'She's *had* her lunch?'

'She's had her lunch. Because you were late. We couldn't keep her waiting, could we?' Sister Badgery was so cheerful to be going off duty.

Then Sister Manhood knew that nothing stood between herself and her patient: she had the whole afternoon before her, and some of the evening, with Mrs Hunter.

She went in.

More often than not a wind would be blowing through the house in Moreton Drive, but this was only a wafting breeze fidgeting the muslin curtains, the rather grubby folds of which could become convulsed at other times, with violent shudders, or swell into great majestic sails. This agreeable afternoon breeze would in the long run dull the furniture by laying a film of moisture on its rosewood and mahogany. On the dressing-table, too far off to benefit the patient, was one of the vases of roses Sister de Santis made a point of standing beside the bed, and Sister Badgery of moving to a distance. Sister Manhood could never make up her mind which side she was on in the Wars of the Roses. Because nobody had ever brought her flowers, she failed to see a reason for them, unless plastic: plastic lasts. The current roses had wilted, and she hated both the feel and smell of dead roses. Later on she must remember to throw them out: something to do in the desert of the afternoon.

Mrs Hunter was looking gentle. The breeze from the ocean might have laid its film of moisture on her forehead already: the skin glittered where light caught it. Once or twice she stuck out her under lip blowing at a non-existent lock of hair; her actual hair, thin, dank, indeterminate stuff, lay along her cheeks and on the pillow.

Matching her patient's gentleness, or obeying her own wariness, the nurse made a silent approach and felt for the pulse: there was much else she must investigate, but warily.

Mrs Hunter said, 'The butterflies—there used to be those big red ones—*brick* red, as I remember—making love above the lantana. I often wondered why they chose horrid stuff like lantana. Its smell. He hated it. It used to make him sneeze. So that was an excuse: I had it rooted out.'

It was one of the many moments in life when Flora Manhood could not think what to answer; and the remark, which started by seeming to accuse, had fluttered off in some other direction; or perhaps it was still hovering, not for you to see or understand, but for those who control their own and other people's lives.

So the nurse asked, 'Did you have your lunch, love?' to make certain this too was not something Lottie and Badgery had dreamed up: like what you were supposed to have done to the cloakroom loo.

'Yes, and it was lovely – if I could remember what it was. Breakfast was better. Kedgeree. I can remember better the things that happened long ago. Except that this foreign woman I've engaged isn't in the kedgeree tradition. But he was so kind – talked so sympathetically. I'm the one who should have had more understanding. But of course, the breakfast – he always loved kedgeree. He likes an early breakfast.'

In her disbelief Sister Manhood ran the tip of her tongue along the line of her lipstick, but said, 'That was fine, wasn't it? To both have enjoyed yourselves so much.'

This slack man panting on top of you in his fur bra then dashing off to early breakfast with his old mother when you read that actors lie in bed till afternoon exhausted by acting in the play and love and suppers. Basil hadn't had the supper, though. He hadn't exactly acted in a play; though it is always hungry work. Perhaps it was pure hunger drove him out to early breakfast. Or else, the love he imagined he felt for you, had done a boomerang and come back as thoughtfulness for Mum.

Either way, Sister Manhood's sense of her own deceit returned.

While Mrs Hunter had brightened: she had begun to kindle, to shine, as she did when following up an inspiration; her shoulders twitched on and off. 'I've thought of something –' she was spitting slightly, 'something I want to give you, Sister – to wear.'

'I've got all I need, love.' It was a lie anybody must see through; but you couldn't be in any way indebted to old Mrs Betty Hunter: the next moment she would turn the thumbscrews.

'What you *need*! Praise, love, beauty – anyone can do *without* them.' Mrs Hunter snorted. 'They aren't necessary. You can live on potatoes and a cup of milk – like an Irish peasant – in a bog!'

Flora Manhood was convinced that, without the least encouragement, Elizabeth Hunter had started tightening the thumbscrews.

When she had licked her lips, Mrs Hunter ordered, 'Fetch me the box, Sister.'

Sister Manhood brought the jewel case from where it was kept, and the old piebald fingers began actively running over its contents till they found what they could more or less identify.

'These,' Mrs Hunter said, and showed. 'Alfred took to giving me sapphires: one year he gave me the blue, the following year the pink. He had a passion for star sapphires. I never liked them,' she confessed; 'too much like lollies. But lovely trans—cend—*ental*? lollies;' she gave a hiccup, and the jewels rattled in spite of their velvet nest. 'Well—aren't they?'

Because she didn't know what 'transcendental' meant (she couldn't remember Col ever using the word) Flora Manhood brooded. Or sulked.

Mrs Hunter must have decided to ignore her nurse's mood and develop her theme. 'You will have to tell me', she was forced to admit, 'which is which. Which is the pink, Sister?'

'Why the pink?'

'It's feminine, isn't it?'

'I don't know.'

'Yes, I think so. Blue is more intellectual—*spiritual*,' she hiccuped again, 'compared with lush lollypink.'

Flora Manhood had begun to feel unhappy, both for herself and her patient, then, incidentally, for others. 'That's the pink,' she said, stroking it where it lay in the palm of Mrs Hunter's hand.

'Take it.'

'If I don't want it?'

'But you must. You must wear it for your engagement.'

'I'm not engaged.'

'You will be. There's hardly anyone doesn't go through it.'

'I might be an old maid.' Sister Manhood cackled.

So did Mrs Hunter.

Then the latter composed her lips before delivering the gipsy's warning which rings a bell in most women, and which surely this silly nurse would hear. 'It's your fate. And he loves you,' Mrs Hunter said.

Flora Manhood pouffed. 'I don't know so much about that.

They make use of you. In any case, I could never ever marry a man so much older than myself.'

'A boy!'

To his monument of a mother, no doubt.

But an old man: he had let out a short fart, his buttocks quivering and hesitating, before he came; she had felt the elderly lips tasting her eyelids, bunting at her breasts. Then he had run hungry to his mother, and they had hatched this Hunter plot over the early kedgeree.

'Even if there was any question of my getting engaged, oughtn't the man to give me the ring?' Because she was afraid of falling into one of a number of traps, she made herself sound as ungracious as she could.

'He might be embarrassed—if I gave him the ring and told him to give it,' Mrs Hunter replied. 'He'll see it as a practical arrangement if you explain why you're wearing it. Women *are* more practical. Some men know—though they mostly won't admit.'

Since you had allowed the old thing to transfer the pink lolly to your hand, you were growing greedy for it: from certain angles the buried star would come alive.

'It's all very well for me to take the ring.' Flora Manhood sounded harsher still. 'There'd be nothing to show I hadn't snitched it, if—supposing—you died all of a sudden, say.' It was she who wished to die: she was so ashamed; but had been pushed to it. 'You did say we're practical,' she blurted, 'didn't you?'

'You are perfectly right. Telephone to—What's-his-name—my solicitor, Sister. Ask him to look in—to write it down that the ring has become your property.'

It sounded awful: she had never owned any property until this ring, her right to which existed only in the old girl's attic of a mind.

So she went out mumbling, neither agreeing nor refusing; though she had gone so far as to put the ring in her pocket.

The afternoon was the desert she had feared, in which she invented little unnecessary jobs for herself and disciplines to impose on her patient.

Twice Mrs Hunter remembered to ask, 'Did you get through to

Arnold—to come about the sapphire—to put it on paper?' On the first occasion Sister Manhood was able to avoid answering: she was engaged in seating her patient on the commode; at the second inquiry, she snapped back, 'I wonder if half his clients realize what a busy man Mr Wyburd is?' That would not have entered into it if she hadn't been afraid of how the solicitor might look at her, for winkling a jewel out of Elizabeth Hunter. But she would have to keep the ring; she knew by now: from its continued presence in her pocket, from its smooth motions against her thigh, from its burning itself into her flesh.

Then it was time at last for de Santis to arrive; soon you would escape to your own room, to fondle your jewel. Which would never fulfil its purpose, because you wouldn't accept a proposal, not even another proposition, from Basil Hunter, however hard his mother worked to prostitute you to her son.

This evening de Santis appeared unusually thoughtful. And was wearing (good grief) an orange hat.

'I decided to take your advice,' she explained, 'and buy myself something gay. How do you like it?'

It was more than awful; there was something sort of sacrilegious about Mary de Santis in this orange hat, not worse if she had bent down, switched her skirt over her back, and shown she was wearing a naked bum underneath.

'Or don't you?' Sister de Santis was waiting.

'It'll take a bit of getting used to. It isn't part of your—your image, Sister.' Flora Manhood was sweating with her own daring.

But she was able to start giving the details of their patient's condition during the afternoon. 'I'd say she's a bit constipated, whatever ideas Badgery may have. Badgery sees things as it suits her. The old girl could do, perhaps, with an enema. If you like, Sister, I'll stay back and give you a hand with the enema.'

Sister de Santis smiled; she was so thoughtful: was it of her own reflection in that hat? 'Is she?' she said. 'We'll see. I might phone Dr Gidley and ask what he thinks. In any case, there's no need for you to stay. I can manage the enema. Poor old thing, she's only a husk.' All the while Sister de Santis continued smiling, for her own thoughts, or the orange hat.

Sister Manhood was beginning to lose patience, when her colleague said, 'I'm going to let you into a secret, dear.' Never in history had Sister de Santis called you 'dear'.

Sister Manhood was dumbfounded: coming from someone as remote and respected as de Santis, the gesture shocked rather than touched her; St Mary should never set foot on earth.

'I've made up my mind,' Sister de Santis said, that smile still afloat on her face, but graver than before, 'I've decided to go to Sir Basil's hotel, tomorrow, to ask him what they really intend to do about their mother.'

You could have pushed Sister Manhood over. 'But do you think you ought to?' she could scarcely ask. 'I mean – meddling in family affairs. Is it any of our business?'

Sister de Santis said, as though she had been reading it, 'It's up to us not to remain what they call the silent majority;' and at least took off the orange hat.

Sister Manhood was horrified. 'But what could you do? And him! If a man's dishonest enough to dump his mother, he's immoral, probably, in other ways we don't yet know of.'

Sister de Santis only smiled, and began taking off her dress. Overfulness in the bust showed her to be what you always thought – but never liked to admit – out of proportion.

Disappointment raged in Flora Manhood. 'I think you're bonkers!' Not that she desired, having experienced, Sir Basil Hunter; not even though his mother had sealed a long-term contract with a star sapphire ring.

But Mary de Santis!

'I'd be very careful, Sister,' Sister Manhood advised.

'I have no intention of being anything else.' Sister de Santis had clothed herself in her uniform; there remained the veil: nobody adjusted a veil more religiously.

But Flora Manhood was unnerved. What if you could not trust this stately figure any more than you could trust yourself?

What if St Mary was a whore behind your back? Everyone knew about that colonel she had taken overseas in a liner, and got an annuity out of when he died. The colonel might not have been as old and gaga as she made out, and his nurse more subtle. Flora Manhood did not want to think such thoughts, just as she wanted no more of Basil—oh dear no; it was the threatened fall from grace of somebody revered which shocked her.

Presently, on seeing there was nothing she could do, either by persuasion, or helping with an enema, Sister Manhood left. At one point, she slithered on the steep, coiling path, and nearly fell. When there was nobody left to respect, neither Sister de Santis, nor Mrs Hunter (poor Lottie couldn't help it if she was foreign and out of the running), certainly not Sir Basil Hunter the Great Actor, she must concentrate on this child who had, perhaps, been planted in her and whom she would love with all the love and strength she could raise. But who was there for her boy to love and respect?

She went skittering away, in her bargain shoes, into darkness.

Nurse is sitting you down upon your sit-upon.

'Do you think it will happen, Mary?'

'What will, Mrs Hunter?'

'Well—I must remember.' Seat's too cold in the beginning the old commode to think or do.

It has these very delicate arms curving down like swans' necks. Feathers are rough, not the heads, not the beaks even; swans' beaks, in life, look knobbed—pustular.

'You see these carved heads, Sister? They were polished by Alfred's hands. He used this same commode during his—his *fatal* illness, at "Kudjeri". Eldred used to sit him on it. I did myself—sometimes—at the end.'

'Really? Fancy!'

She'll go soon, leaving you to fate. They do. Yes, they have always gone.

'Hold on tight to the arms, Mrs Hunter. Do you think you'll be all right on your own?'

'Perfectly. It's such a reliable piece of furniture. Isn't it useful?'

'Useful, and elegant too. Here's the bell beside you. You can ring if you want me.'

'Yes.'

She is going. And why not? Constipation is caused by nurses hanging around bossing, treating you like a bundle of dirty linen.

All afternoon evening wanting to drowse back to some difficult situation you were not allowed a nurse's heel indenting the brain (ugh! not brains Nurse) carrying the sound of brittle roses the two later voices hammering together and apart in other rooms on words and names Elizabeth I must only ever be called without foreshortening ELIZABETH that is my isn't it my given name whatever else parents parents are given too whether you like it the one her bones crumbling the other a rifle in his mouth children are dolls the parents leave for nurses to hoist I'm not a doll Nurse lolling on the cold commode however drowsy cold does not cut the will to discover which direction you must take the island was it the storm of course you had *desired* the man Dorothy ran away from but only desired as a last reflection in the little tin looking-glass a nocturne was hammering out that last of nights nothing else after the trees had bent double some snapped the house carried off like any human relationship then walking down towards the piled water the swans from dipping their beaks rose hard precise yet loving admittedly only for the bread you had and sodden unhallowed by the eye of the storm the swans accept the bread no longer hissing like children why had you called them Basil Dorothy ugly names hatched out of pride by Elizabeth Hunter a swan herself but black.

Ooh don't kick mahogany only hurts the heels. Sister? No. What can they do for a jack-in-a-box once the spring's gone? Not worth it. Throw it out. Boxes and islands. I must not think myself on to the island. I am not *hallowed*—therefore—I must *eschew*? all such thoughts—for the time being.

Love is closer anyway and warmer than adoration of some vast and unknowable cloud. Think instead of the silly human Manhood.

Womanly: that's it. Elizabeth Hunter was never womanly enough, her flaws too perfectly disguised under appearances: enormous, gaping, at times agonizing flaws. Even so, perhaps you are reserved, through these same flaws, for other ends. Whatever and when, it is more comforting to drowse over this Flora silly Man you gave the pink sapphire to belove her to her chemist.

After failing so many—worst oh far worst my darling Alfred born without the machinery for getting his own back—you could not expect fulfilment as a woman only as an all giver.

Little children come tumbling out like sheeps' pellets but unexpectedly hard into the cold commodious world.

When love is what my Alfred has longed for what the chemist prescribes it is what the nurse and I withhold.

Perhaps it will drop pink at last the lolly sapphire like any common brown penny.

'Sister? If you don't leave the bell, how can you expect me to ring? Sister de Santis! Lungs aren't leather, either. Urrr! I might die on this damn commode and nobody know.'

Mary de Santis sometimes wondered how she had chosen to live where she did; except she had to live somewhere. She was always promising herself she would move, but something in her, of the passive mollusc, or solitary female, had so far prevented it. And after all, she was only here in her 'conveniently situated flatette' to spend a few daylight hours, most of those asleep. And the rent was low: not low enough, perhaps, considering the view of visceral plumbing exposed against the wall of ox-blood brick opposite. She could stand a plant, however, on the window sill; and if the stove was obsolete and smelly she was not interested in food, or not when on her own: plenty of bread and butter, with strong tea, and just the occasional cigarette, had become her normal diet. Above the narrow divan where she slept, she had nailed Mamma's icons, which caused a film to form, she noticed, almost always on the eyes of the casual caller; to her own eyes the icons were by now little more than atavistic windows, so choked with age, grime, and conflicting sentiments, they failed to open. In any case, she had decided not to make a cult of the past, though she had hung Papa's diploma next to her own certificate on one of the walls of the superfluous triangular hall, and still had his medical books arranged with her own on the adjustable shelves she had wisely bought as far back as graduation. She loved her books. She owned some of the classics: George Eliot, Conrad, *The Cloister and the Hearth*, *The Moonstone*. If ever she felt particularly serious, or lonely, she might read a poem or two; she could read Dante, haltingly, in Enrico's voice. Then, at the window, there was this exceptionally beautiful, velvety, deep crimson cyclamen she had nursed by regular attention and affection over several seasons: she liked to feel something growing, living, in the room where she lived if only during the less significant intervals. For she had her work: that was her life, and she was happy in it.

This at least was the comfortable theory well-meaning people had thrust on her. Reserved by nature, and not given to argument, she accepted it, while sensing that the visible ramifications of her work were no more than a convenient *trompe l'œil* to distract attention from that shadowy labyrinth strewn with signs through which she approached 'happiness'.

Rational beings are pacified by evidence of efficiency: a scoured bedpan veiled in starched white, the geometry of linen, a temperature chart; or uplifted, rational though they claim to be, by a mystique inherent in the pretty confetti of capsules, and less demonstrative, more insidious, ampoules, locked for safety in the steel cabinet behind the bathroom door. All of which has only indirect bearing on your significant life, revealed nightly in the presence of this precious wafer of flesh from which earthly beauty has withdrawn, but whose spirit will rise from the bed and stand at the open window, rustling with the light of its own reflections, till finally disintegrating into the white strands strung between the araucarias and oaks of the emergent park, yourself kneeling in spirit to kiss the pearl-embroidered hem, its cold weave the heavier for dew or tears.

335

Frequently Sister de Santis grew ashamed of her opulent obsessions; just as, in a physical context, she was embarrassed by her own bust when men sitting opposite stared at her cleavage, or when Sister Manhood's disapproval was stretched as remorselessly as a tapemeasure.

This morning after returning from duty Mary de Santis was unable to rest: neither her mind nor her body allowed her. She was this heavy slab, turned, and again, turned, on the narrow, rigidly sprung divan; but a slab holed by insinuating thoughts. As she tossed, her breasts bumped around, in search of independence it seemed, while never parted from her. And the orange hat so obviously condemned by Flora Manhood: she went cold thinking of her hat; she tried to wring it out of her inner vision by squeezing her eyes tighter shut. Sometimes by daylight, and particularly on this important morning, she could not believe that Mrs Hunter would survive till night, or herself experience again the peace which darkness offers.

At a point when the small box enclosing her seemed about to fly apart, from the orange light, the sounds of traffic, the fumes of petrol collected in it, she was forced up. If only to wash some stockings and hang them on a line at her viewless window. To sit a while over the morning paper without deciphering the print. Before she began bathing herself, putting up her hair, examining the angles of her appearance, all according to some more than ordinarily complex ritual, performed it could have been, for the first time.

When she was ready, she had no doubts about putting on her usual navy hat, and a matching, old, but presentable coat (which Flora M. dismissed for being as dowdy as the hat). Though not wearing a uniform, she looked as though she were, Sister de Santis realized, not disapprovingly: she felt safer in her unofficial uniform.

It was neither too early for actors, nor yet too late to have lost one of such charm and fame, she had calculated; and the receptionist's words, so carefully enunciated at the telephone, her smile so beautifully evoked, together with the single dimple she must keep for favourites, made it at once clear that Sir Basil was in his room.

'He'll be down presently,' the girl announced through the last glimmer of her waning smile.

Gratefully enough the nurse accepted the receptionist's bounty. She sat down to wait opposite the desk, crossing her ankles as though seated beside Colonel Askew on the liner's deck or in the lounge at Brown's Hotel. It also occurred to her, but fleetingly, embarrassingly, that Mamma had claimed descent from three Emperors of Byzantium. Mary de Santis averted her thoughts, settled the crown of her navy hat, coughed to clear her voice of a suspected huskiness which might obscure the meaning of what she had to say.

And Sir Basil Hunter came running down the last short flight of stairs, presenting a figure she would not have expected, perhaps because his clothes were more casual than she—well, she had not attempted to *foresee*; but they were in fact casual: silk paisley-patterned scarf, its crimson reflected upward on to his already ruddy, shaven skin; suede jacket, the cuffs of which were turned back over shirt cuffs of a halcyon blue. But it was not, after all, the details of his dress which surprised her, so much as a breathless jollity, his soles squelching across the foyer carpet in what would have seemed a parody of loose-limbed boyishness if the actor had not ended by persuading you that it was the real thing.

Sir Basil made Sister de Santis feel artificial: she must have looked like one of those great soft ponderous dolls in felt or kid sometimes referred to nowadays as sculpture; and as though that were not perverse enough, she heard herself giggling like some trainee nurse telling about an evening spent at a night club with a reprobate surgeon.

While Sir Basil tried to raise her to a less ignominious level, by squeezing her elbow, sinking his chin in the paisley foulard, and directing his stare full at her face, his eyes as charismatic as Mrs Hunter's were in the beginning. 'This is a most agreeable surprise,' he admitted in the greatest confidence.

'Oh, I didn't want to *disturb*!' Sister de Santis protested in painfully lumbering contralto. 'I only looked in,' she blundered on, 'to say how much I—how we *all*—appreciate Mrs Hunter.' There she fizzled out, the dismally inept bungler of a mission.

Sir Basil was leading her somewhere, into the garden it began to appear from the yellow light which was filtered on their faces through the leaves of autumn plane trees.

'Mother—yes—isn't she an extraordinary—beautiful—exceptional person?' His boyishness let him down at last, and he began to look the grave man she had anticipated; still not wholly grave, however. 'I'm glad you've come,' he continued confiding, 'even if you've stolen a march on me, in a sense.' He laughed, for her personally, making it clear she was not to take his remark as an accusation. 'Because I've been meaning to see more of those who— who've been devoting themselves to Mother's care—to—to get to know you more intimately.'

At his most hesitant he was also at his gravest. It was what she had hoped for, and now that she had found it, must resist. It was Papa: an elderly, distinguished, but weak man, asking for love and understanding as well as the drug he depended on. Mary de Santis was so shaken she lowered her eyes.

Sir Basil came almost too promptly to the rescue. 'What, I wonder, can I offer you to drink?'

'Oh, it's early, isn't it?' She laughed. 'I didn't come here expecting hospitality,' she added, and blushed.

But Sir Basil was waiting for her to name her fancy, and as her confusion mounted she was unable to think; then remembered the White Ladies Colonel Askew had prescribed before lunch (the name prevented her asking for one now) and before dinner, knew she had enjoyed a sherry (sweet). She might have settled for the sherry if she had not gathered, long after the colonel's death, that there was something shameful in confessing to a taste for sweet sherry.

Sir Basil Hunter was growing impatient, shooting his cuffs. 'My lunchtime poison,' he said, 'is a dry martini.'

'Very well.' She laughed and blushed again. 'A dry martini would be perfect.'

'How dry?' He raised his eyebrows and cocked his head, as though to show he recognized a knowledgeable guest.

'Oh, *dry*!' If she had been true to herself she would have in some way resisted the cloak of incongruous worldliness he was laying on her shoulders; but she rather liked it.

Then he had gone inside to give the order, and she was left amongst the white furniture, the plaster storks, and a bird bath painted in mock brick. A sadness began to filter through to her, perhaps caused by the jaundiced light, together with the blotched leaves, and seed-clusters in moulting plush, of the expatriate planes. She was alone in the hotel garden. She sat down on one of the mass-produced iron chairs. There was a dusting of smuts on the iron-lace table. As she waited for her host, bag still wedged between arm and side, she was tempted to forget the reason for her being there, and slip away through the smell of fallen, half-rotted leaves, rescuing her susceptibility from a disturbing presence. But she owed it to Mrs Hunter to stay.

Very resolutely Sir Basil returned. He had decided to adopt a dogged look, for the part of a tarnished ex-brigadier in a play which didn't appeal to him. It couldn't be helped: for the moment, there was nothing else offering.

'Incredibly lackadaisical service,' he nattered, 'at the Onslow.'

And this Sister de What's-it raised her incredible eyebrows: they were broad and glossy, almost furry, reminding him of moth down; only he had never seen, as far as he could remember, a black moth.

'Though nowadays, isn't it the same everywhere?' he continued tediously, while resigning himself to the cast-iron acorns already eating his buttocks. 'London and Paris are, if anything, worse.' He looked to her for the confirmation she would not be able to give.

He knew it was wrong of him, but she did so intensely bore him: in her fright of a hat; when he had half expected the little Manhood to return for the other half. Surely this deadly Hera had not taken it upon herself to warn him off, or worse still, stand in for the nymph she was protecting?

339

But it was his mother's nurse reacting in earnest monotone to his (pretty lamentable, he had to admit) cosmopolitan ostentation. 'I remember the year I travelled over with Colonel Askew, the poor colonel never stopped complaining—often with reason—in hotels and restaurants. It was not long after the War. Everything was down at heel, I suppose. Certainly the people were depressed. And the colonel was old, and sick—a cardiac case. But for me it was enough to have arrived in a great city of which I knew nothing. After the colonel died I took a short holiday in the country. I roamed around on my own, along those wet, narrow lanes. The trees were bare by then—everything very austere—but somehow strengthening.'

Oh God, 'anaesthetizing' was the more likely word; as he resisted the isolation to which she would have liked to introduce him, under a colourless sky. He tried to remember how it felt just to have arrived in a great, unknown city, but couldn't; or did, and wanted to reject this momentary vision of himself in a cold, empty, darkened theatre, looking for an identity to replace the one he had lost.

Sir Basil Hunter shifted on his iron chair from one uncomfortable position to another. He must listen to the woman, if not with interest, professionally. There had been that immensely turgid, endlessly melodious Ethelyne Perry who had played opposite him in a piece he let them talk him into, at the Duke of York's; it must have been about the year Sister de Santis arrived in London with her colonel. (She hadn't mentioned visits to the theatre.) In the second act there was a scene with Ethelyne on a bench; wasn't there just: ten good minutes every performance of the fortnight's run he had concentrated on Ethelyne while she lowed her way through her monologue (she was married to the management) himself so tensed with interest it was a wonder his body hadn't broken up, scattering his irrelevant thoughts around her feet.

Almost as melodious, quite as stately and monotonous as Ethelyne Perry, the de Santis woman was forcing him to give the same kind of performance now. 'What did you do when you returned to London after your holiday in the country?'

She looked at him with an expression of surprise. 'I came back here.' Her throat knotted, she appeared startled, as though it might not have occurred to her that life offers alternatives.

They were saved by a waiter in grubby mess jacket presenting a tray with their two martinis.

'Gin fumigates,' Sir Basil informed his guest somewhat sternly; 'it blows away any night thoughts. That's why there's nothing like a dry martini before lunch.'

She was not sure how she ought to react to his remark: the self she acknowledged could not have shared her beliefs with him, but she seemed to have been parted from that real self on entering the hotel garden.

Because the glass was filled too full, she gulped quickly at her drink's teetering, colourless surface. 'Isn't it a bit strong?'

'So it ought to be. That's what you ordered. Dry. Personally I feel vermouth is only an excuse for gin.' His knowingness appalled him.

She had only mildly complained; her drink was too agreeable: perfumed and cold; the scorched leaves of the plane trees had begun to clap; lemon and alternately, greenish screens, were being slid one behind the other; a sudden more emphatic burst of light suggested that louvres had clattered open to admit it.

'I expect you're right,' she murmured; the unbelievable circumstances justified her giving the matter serious thought.

In an upper window of what was probably a residential overlooking the hotel garden, a woman had appeared. All of her shouted for Basil's attention: the plastic curlers in the whitened hair; the cleavage in her plump form above the pink chenille; and the feather duster, more a toy, as variegated as the curlers studding her formally informal head. The fat woman began camping with her duster round the window sash. She hummed a few broodily self-conscious bars, winked once or twice at this man in the situation he was preparing for himself in the garden, and let it be understood she was on for a joke, the dirtier the better.

Basil Hunter might have responded surreptitiously if it had not been for the flash in which he saw that the pink woman took it for granted he belonged to her level of vulgarity.

As he did; at any rate for the moment, in the presence of this other, subdued creature unconscious of the pantomime going on above her head. So much so, the nurse smiled at him just then with such innocent gratitude and pleasure he bundled his commonness out of sight. (Anyway there are some parts, important ones, you can't hope to play without a touch of common.)

'I have an idea,' he said. 'I'll buy us another drink, then drive you out to Watson's Bay. There's a place where we can lunch—not brilliant, but not impossible—and the weather's with us.'

She said she had not intended; she ought to rest before her night duty. She had never felt so undecided, powerless.

He had gone to order the second round and she knew this was as she really wanted. She must not forget the reason for her coming was to plead for Mrs Hunter. She would speak soon, not the moment he reappeared, but after a decent pause, before they left. The light predicted that she would sit beside the sea, eating—it didn't matter what: light, and by glimpses, when she dared, a face.

What, she wondered, would Papa have thought of Basil Hunter? She almost had not known another man, excepting doctors, whom she externalized as colleagues, and patients: the human beings to whom she had dedicated herself. But never men. Unless during the last years of his life, when Enrico de Santis had crumbled, and she, no longer his daughter or his nurse, had been united with him in a dangerously rarefied climate where love and suffering mingle.

Distracted by her thoughts, Sister de Santis decided it might be wiser not to look at Sir Basil, just returned from ordering the drinks. She found herself staring instead, from under the brim of her hat, at his ankle. And that was worse. She had never before considered a man's ankle, or only as bones and ligaments. Now she was fascinated, if also disturbed, by what should have been no more than another ankle. But this one displayed, besides the silken elegance you might expect in a man of wealth and taste, a cruel menace.

Sir Basil sat waggling his ankle. Could he have been conscious of the effect he was creating? No, she thought, it isn't possible; nobody, except probably Mrs Hunter, knows the effect they have on others; it is fortunate, or sad.

'An actor in a play—does he allow himself to be carried away by his emotions?' she asked in a desperate burst of what might have been inspiration, or again it might not.

At least it was not what he had expected; it dragged him back from his distant thoughts. 'Of course he's got to *feel* the situation. But he mustn't drown in it. That's where his technique saves him—leaves him free to speak and breathe—to convey.' Just how much was he conveying to this nurse, he wondered, and how much did she know already?

'Much the same as in nursing: there's the question of how far to become involved.' She tried deliberately to make it sound matter of fact; then immediately hoped she had not succeeded.

Sir Basil did not allow her to see; he remained moodily distant: an assured, handsome man.

In the circumstances it was a relief to be holding the second drink; in fact she was so relieved she was reduced to clumsiness: some of the fumigatory gin slopped over the edge of the glass, and she drank too deep to hide her confusion.

'What do you know about theatre?' He seemed to be looking at her intently; till she realized he wasn't at all, and perhaps hadn't been from the beginning.

'Practically nothing,' she had to admit, in spite of a desire to please. 'What I mean to say is—I don't go very often.' One half of her lumbered with a heavy sincerity she knew to be her own, the other was feeling its way into a groove faintly remembered, in which she hoped to glide with the same aluminium brightness as some of the women at those dinner parties Elizabeth Hunter had given during her convalescence, in the first months of their relationship. 'I adore the theatre,' she heard herself mouth. 'But it isn't always possible. Sometimes to a matinée. I like to see something *light*. To make me laugh. There's so much unhappiness in the world;' which is what they say, she recalled.

343

He was looking through her, and at once she wanted to confess: oh no, this isn't what I think; the words are borrowed. But because you never can, and he would not have believed anyway, she could only close her eyes and drink up the bitter dregs from her glass. A tenderness she might have conveyed petered out in a shiver as she stood the glass on the gritty surface of the metal table.

He too, had finished. She would not have dared chew the lemon peel left behind in the gin shallows, but Sir Basil Hunter could and did. More, he could afford to spit out the last shreds of pith on the surrounding gravel.

His eyes watered, and he attempted a comic face to disguise a nausea of words and sensations he could feel rising in him. 'I'm glad you're not of the theatre,' he was saying. 'It's seldom one talks to anybody who isn't. It's seldom one *talks*,' he added with what, for that instant, he recognized as sincerity deserted by technique; his voice had an uncontrolled, an unregretted wobble.

His confession made her feel duller, more ignorant, farther removed. When she tried expressing sympathy, it sounded to her like a low moan.

What he was going to say, he was not sure, but had to say it. 'All my life I have wanted—needed to be of the theatre—even before I became an actor—when I was a mere boy here in Australia, taken to an occasional panto or musical comedy. I only began to breathe, to live, the first time I got inside a part—only a few lines, mind you—in a play. And outside the theatre, there was always the gossip, the bitchery, the question of billing—lights! Your name in lights—after the physical drudgery—this was the *summum bonum*: an electric crown. The perks are far less gratifying—the accolade, for instance—because it's like falling off a log after the blood and sweat of acting. Suck up to a few *personages*, give a charity performance or two, alter your tempo, your thinking a little—and you're home! From now on, you are the one who is sucked up to. Till you reach—let's call it "the age of disgust"—when you can feel something taking place in your metabolism, and a change comes over the expression of other people's faces, and you want to reject the whole business of—of acting: all its illusions and your own presumption—not to say *spuriousness*.'

Mary de Santis would have liked to think he was not serious, but he was, she saw. She could not bear to witness this second death of the only man she had ever loved. This time she was unable to offer even a needle. She sat looking at Sir Basil Hunter's silken ankle.

'To reject,' he said, 'before you are rejected.'

He was horrified by what he had spewed up. Though only a lymphatic nurse was to any extent aware, he might have been speaking in a dressing-room full of pros: the smell of greasepaint, the authentic gusts of superstition were overpoweringly present. For a moment he wondered whether he ought to suspect the vacuous though probably innocent eyes of his actual audience.

'Well,' he said, slapping her on the knee with what he hoped would be interpreted as *joie de vivre*, not brutality, 'aren't I supposed to be taking you out to lunch?'

Sister de Santis gasped, scrambling up, dropping, then quickly retrieving her navy handbag so as not to give him the trouble of forestalling her. 'Oh yes, that will be fun!' she seemed to remember the ladies at the dinner parties, as she and Sir Basil scarified the coarse gravel, cannoning off each other once, under the shabby plane trees. 'Aren't those plaster birds *ghastly*!' she heard her dinner party voice, followed by a nurse's giggle: that of a young girl just down from Kempsey or Coonamble.

'Execrable!' Basil Hunter hid his half-heartedness in pronunciation.

Glancing up, he caught sight of the chenille woman leaning on her sill. The light splintered on her multi-coloured helmet. She was looking as though she had proved a point.

Perhaps from having already exposed themselves, and unwisely, Mary de Santis and Basil Hunter were for the most part silent on their drive along the foreshore in the rented car. The nurse would have expected something more streamlined, more spectacular, to further the legend of a star actor. Then instinctively dismissing her pretentious thought, she remarked on the 'glorious day'; and felt miserable for the glazed post-card she was substituting for subtler glories experienced by a different light.

Any subtlety on this journey was soaked up by the glare of sun off brick, as on their arrival, what should have remained primitive forms, timber surfaces untouched except by the crackle of age and a patina of weather, were overlaid with painted slogans and scuffed posters. At least the sea was unspoilt, but only as an expanse, or in its pretty lapping round the stilts of a bleached jetty; along the skirting of sand and detritus which passed for a beach an earlier tide had hemmed scallops of oil scum.

Basil Hunter asked his guest to grab a table while he organized a bottle of wine from the pub round the corner. So she sat and waited at one of the tables on the pavement in front of the little restaurant. Perhaps I am the one to blame for anything dull or disappointing in the landscape, she tried to persuade herself; a muzziness from unaccustomed drink could be clouding her vision, and was certainly blurring her thought; though she could not be held responsible for the actual litter on the beach, only in the background of her mind her half-silted intention of pleading for Mrs Hunter. She roused herself. She would speak of course; it was just that the auspicious moment had not yet occurred.

Basil returned with a green bottle. It was wearing a chill, and looked a very special wine, at least beside her memory of the wicker-covered demijohns Papa used to buy from a compatriot, and which left those purple stains on the cloth under the trellis in Marrickville.

'I took a chance and picked a dry one, seeing how we started dry.' He was not convinced his voice disguised the canker of gloom eating at false heartiness: wine bought over the counter from the Bottle Department of a pub could only turn out to be cat piss; and deeper still, there lurked the continued mystery of why he had invited the nurse.

But Sister de Santis, it seemed, was finding everything agreeable. After the waiter had uncorked the bottle, and she had put her lips to the doubtful wine, she looked at him and composed them in a smile. 'Delicious, isn't it?'

346

The word alone made him wince; he did not know how he would match her genteel composure.

'Why don't you take off your hat?' he surprised himself saying; and again detecting a brutal tone in what was more a command than a suggestion, decided to play it lighter. 'Here we are in the much publicized outdoors—no formalities—no cares.' His chair grated on the concrete. 'And I'll be able to see you better, shan't I?'

Taken unawares, Sister de Santis glanced round quickly: certainly everyone else lunching at the little alfresco tables was hatless; but her unconformity and his cheek could not have been the sole causes of her expression of guilt and embarrassment. She was probably one of those subservient souls always afraid they have not spread the gratitude thick enough.

Whatever it was, the nurse recovered her moral balance, took off her forbidding hat, meekly it would have appeared if she had not immediately shaken her head and disclosed the curve of her throat: it was too unconscious a gesture, and too noble he realized, for meekness. Once more he was disturbed by the confused motives in their being seated where they were on the edge of this rubbishy beach.

'That's better. You're right,' she said with gentle command of her voice. 'One feels free.' She smiled with a candour which threatened to bring to light shortcomings he hoped he had well and truly sunk in the depths of his being.

As for Mary de Santis, she had recovered faith in her own purpose, not through the company of this amiable, if also occasionally unnerving man, but from joy in a life which still stretched ahead of her, for which the sun assaulting a barricade of cloud, the steam-boat tooting towards the jetty, and a launchload of children dangling their hands in the transparent wavelets as they moved parallel with the shore, appeared as affirmations.

While Basil remembered with surprise his easily satisfied sensuality of how many nights ago, his 'love' for his Primavera, even a fantasy of marriage with a young and healthy nurse. Such illusions

347

as he had about her colleague were scarcely of the same kind: he would have recoiled from touching this statue of a goddess.

The waiter brought the food they had ordered: a rather nasty looking mess of scallops for Sister de Santis and grilled lobster for Sir Basil Hunter.

Sir Basil sighed. 'Looks as though I'm the greedy one.'

But Sister de Santis seemed satisfied.

One of two women seated at a table nearby nudged the other.

The nurse glanced down at her front; or perhaps it was the fork she was using; then she blushed on realizing she was lunching with a famous actor.

'Tell me,' she said, raising her voice to the level of the occasion, 'which is your favourite part, Sir Basil?'

'Oh Lord, my favourite *part*?'

She knew she had pronounced it as 'port' in her effort to make conversation with Sir Basil Hunter. The blue-haired ladies at the nearby table chafed their rings and laughed. Everyone was laughing. A party of six or seven businessmen had moved from the pub on the corner and were descending on the table waiting for them. The men were laughing. Their skins oozed. Glassy-eyed, teeth bared, the executives were looking around for something on which to whet their wit or their appetites.

Sir Basil Hunter groaned, and struggled with his lobster. What to tell the woman? He had been a riot as Horner, though you might not believe it today.

'Surely there's some part—or play—which gives you special pleasure in looking back?' Sister de Santis was gently determined.

A curse on all nurses!

In her abstraction, wondering how she might rouse her patient's interest, the nurse looked full in the teeth of one of the cheery businessmen, and he closed his mouth as though he had swallowed a bad oyster.

'There's Lear, I suppose,' Sir Basil offered, God knows why: he had not got there with Lear.

'Oh yes—*Lear*!' She made it warm and bright: Lear might have been a cousin she hadn't met for years, but for whom she would always have a soft spot. 'I've never seen it, though.' Too high for a contralto, and aggressive, but she had to compete against the laughter, the general noise.

Still standing round the table reserved for them, the businessmen were having difficulty sorting themselves out. They were all drunk, it seemed.

The blue-haired women had got into some kind of menopausal huddle. 'You sit tight, I tell you, dear. It'll pass in a year or two. He'll come round. He's probably going through the same thing. Men do you know.' The eyes of the menopausal ladies were focused on their own plight.

'You must have read it, though—haven't you? *Lear?*' Sir Basil shouted.

'Yes,' she shouted back; then corrected herself. 'No. I didn't succeed in finishing. There was a lot I couldn't understand.'

She was honest enough, poor thing. He was the dishonest one. And a bloody superficial Lear.

When a brief crunch began, followed by a positive crash. In seating himself, one of the businessmen had gone through the ricketty chair. Every one of his party roared. Still embraced by a bentwood skeleton, the victim sat heaving on the concrete, a vast purple bladder palpitating with mirth and tears.

Sister de Santis heard herself explode while half-glancing at the blue-haired ladies to ask their permission. It was too late. Her example had put them against laughter: their flaked lips were working restrainedly against their teeth as they stared out over the solemn sea from above the bones of the fish they had devoured. One of the ladies was massaging a pearl ear-ring.

Sister de Santis was appalled by the unlikelihood of her own behaviour. But laughed. It was the wine. It was not all that funny. But was. She vaguely wondered whether she should feel sorry for the purple man flopping around and scratching his wreckage against the concrete. Somebody would pick him up. So she continued laughing. Till plunging her mouth in her glass, she drank a great, choking draught. The wine had not lost its cool, but tasted more insipid than before. She went on laughing, for nothing funny, merely settling whimpering down. Exhausted.

She was shaken by what she had in her without having realized. 'I'm so sorry. But it *was* very funny,' she protested guiltily to her host, when perhaps it had never been that.

'Yes, I expect it was funny,' Sir Basil answered; he had spilt some barbecue sauce on his thigh.

Distressed by the way things had gone she finished her wine. 'Tell me, won't you? about the play,' she sighed, 'about *King Lear*.'

As if their small frail table would have allowed either of them to rise to it: his hollow lobster was battering the plate; the remains of her scallops encouraged his worst memory of a Channel crossing.

Welladay, Sir Basil broke bread; he drank the lees of the wine (unfortunately he had a head for it, at any rate today, whereas the nurse, drunk or sober, could be absolved for her innocence). 'Lear—' he had got it out from amongst the shreds of lobster with which his teeth were stuck, 'nobody has ever entirely succeeded as Lear, because I don't think he can be played by an actor—only by a gnarled, authentic man, as much a storm-tossed tree as flesh.' He looked to see whether he had dared too much, but encountered fleshy scallops of eyelids. 'So he can probably never be played.' Sir Basil hit the lobster shell with his fork. 'Blake could have, perhaps. Or Swift.' That didn't mean you wouldn't have another go at it yourself.

He tried to decide how much the nurse had gathered, and saw her swaying, very slightly, above her shambles.

'I see,' she said, solemnly, thickly.

At no stage had she looked more opaque: a giant scallop, and raw.

He felt suddenly maddened: not by this heavy woman, not even at her worst, putting on a social voice for the occasion, or giggling and shrieking when the business bum landed smack on the concrete; no, what infuriated him was his own worst, or what she had seen of it. Mercifully not all. She would have to be profoundly innocent, if not downright mad, to suspect him of hoping to commit so much as a discreet murder.

But his uneasiness increased as she continued brooding opposite. Perhaps she was preparing to accuse him.

In fact, Sister de Santis was accusing herself of her own fall from grace which had begun with the arrival of Mrs Hunter's son. She would scarcely have believed she had given way to lust, if she had not found as proof, those tears in her clothes, scratches in her flesh; there were times when her breasts, becoming snouted, were still pointed at her, when all desire for this man was dead. She would have liked to substitute pity, which is one aspect of pure love. But between Basil and her soul's eye, hovered the face of her pitiful father. Whom she had desired to love in some way never made clear to her during his lifetime, only recently in the line of Basil Hunter's jaw, the veins in his temples, the bones of a silken ankle. Her whole vocation of selflessness was threatened if she offered this man her pity, grown as it was on decomposed lust. Now too, in the context of slovenliness and apathy presented by the half-deserted restaurant, she knew she would never find the strength or opportunity to bear witness to her true faith and plead for the one who was also, incidentally, Elizabeth Hunter.

Sir Basil turned, partly to avoid the nurse's eyes, partly to pick with a finger nail at the worst of the lobster shreds nagging at him from between his teeth. He too was oppressed by the squalor to which their surroundings had been reduced: disordered tables, crumpled napkins, lipstuck glasses, the skeletons and shells of fish. Only the party of executives, silenced by business still in hand, continued guzzling food and drink. The sweat gathering in enormous balls round Basil's eyes was almost ready to fall; if it did he was afraid Sister de Santis might notice it bounce.

So he wrenched himself round, and still avoiding the patch of silence in his audience, began to declaim, 'There, you see—this is where we must concentrate our attention—on all this which was given to us to take pride in, to cherish;' at the same time indicating with what had become his jewelled glove, embracing with the sweep of his heavy, fur-trimmed sleeve, a vision of sky and sea, towers and domes, conjured up for his wimpled queen.

But he no longer had the power (he had known his delivery temporarily affected before this, by physical exhaustion, indigestion, mental strain, or quite simply, if he over-moistened his vocal cords). Now he was sucking on his words, audibly, though he would have liked to think it was one of the businessmen at work on a lobster claw behind him. The sun had gone in besides, behind a drift of dirty cloud. And once your vision is withdrawn from you, there remain the lapping shallows, the littered sand, one competing with the other for the sludge to which the human spirit can sense itself rendered: an aimless bobbing of corks which have served their purpose, and scum, and condoms, and rotting fruit, and rusted tins, and excrement.

'Yes, isn't it glorious?' murmured Sister de Santis from memory.

But she was too conscious of the wicker-sheathed demijohn floating at a drunken, slanted level a little way out. To recognize those purple stains round the mouth pained her more than anything else.

When Sir Basil Hunter began dragging on the tablecloth, practically shouting, 'What's that? That filthy object—the black thing!' hysterically for a man.

Then she caught sight of it: something black drenched swollen and obscene rolling slightly in imitation of life somewhat like the full waterskins Colonel Askew pointed out the Arabs were holding as the liner sailed through the Canal.

The thing was slowly washed or rolled on to the sand almost directly in front of where they were sitting. It was the corpse of a dog, a not-too-well pickled Labrador. A sick stench was rising out of the natural smells of salt and weed.

Sir Basil appeared to take it personally. 'Isn't this the ultimate in filth? This barbarism! But only what can be expected,' he screeched, like an old parrot she thought, its tongue stuck out, hard and blue; like—oh no, his mother caught in what could be a seizure, at the point of aiming her deadliest insult, or curse.

Unlike Sir Basil, Sister de Santis was not immediately shocked by the drowned dog; she was more passive of course, and less articulate; while most of her life she had been personally, though objectively, involved with the physical aspects of death. Till now a nameless anguish began seeping, and she put her handkerchief to her mouth, to stanch it. She could do nothing about the smell: this continued penetrating, and would probably haunt her nostrils, cling to her clothes for ever; or the gelatinous sockets where the dog's eyes had been: they were staring at her so intently they gave the mask a live expression.

Sir Basil got up as though meaning to go in search of the waiter and ask for the bill, but the waiter was already approaching, carrying a saucer with the bill on it. Sir Basil passed him, walking on as straight a line as his somnambulant condition allowed, and disappeared at the back of the restaurant.

Only then Sister de Santis noticed the wire eating into the dog's neck.

After putting down the saucer, the waiter grinned, and said, 'Never know what next! Last month they fished out a woman. I been looking for the case in the papers, but nothing come up yet. It adds interest when you've taken part in it like.'

Sister de Santis had been sitting staring a lifetime at the strangled dog when a man dressed in eroded jersey and washed-out pants rolled above the knees, seized the tail, and dragged the corpse farther down the beach.

'Good on yer, Joey!' the waiter called. 'Takin' on the undertakin', eh?' He followed for some distance, flicking the air with a stained napkin.

While two little boys ran squealing, ploughing the sand, pitching pebbles at the carcase. One of them caught up and gave it a kick with his bare toes. But fell back afterwards.

The businessmen were all applauding, though what, they might not have been able to tell: they were too full, their faces running over with sweat and melted butter. One of them seemed to imagine the sea air had tarnished his ex-service badge: he had raised a sleeve to his buttonhole, and was rubbing the brass with exaggerated, yet completely detached, solicitude.

Basil returned. A tautening of the skin had dismissed the blur from the edges of his face; his hair was grooved, steely, again perfect; his clothes had resumed the careless worldliness of an important man who grants interviews to journalists.

He clapped his hands together, looking at her whimsically, when it might have been his intention to convey forcefulness. 'We must go!' he announced. 'Oh yes, the bill—the bill!'

He plumped down (none of the restaurant chairs seemed too stable) and dragged the wallet out of his pocket. Distantly she noticed it as a beautiful crocodile, monogrammed affair, and no dearth of money.

Basil doled the notes out, then hesitated, mumbling and fumbling.

'What is it?' she asked, leaning forward from her side.

'The tip. I can never work out the percentage.'

'Just like Colonel Askew,' she consoled; 'he could never work it out either.'

Basil offered a handful of coins from which his nurse, kindly and gently, extracted the necessary.

'It's so much easier with dollars,' Sister de Santis reminded.

'Yes. One has to admit it's easier with dollars.' Perhaps this was what he had needed all along: to be nursed by some such competent but impersonal creature.

Both were rehabilitated, or so it seemed on the drive back.

Till Sister de Santis, remembering, looked at her practical, man's wristwatch, and began to murmur, 'How late it is! For me at least.' Unexpectedly for someone so placid, she was twitching. 'I ought to be resting. My patient.'

It was the performance again, he realized; she had his sympathy.

He tried to console her from his own experience of life. 'Well, yes—I know. We cling to our principles—arrive two hours before curtain-up—go into a trance—get the smell of the greasepaint in our nostrils. Then, sometimes, you may have been held up rather

354

delightfully. You run in at the last moment, make a few passes at your cheeks, go on stage and – take wing as never before.'

He could not see whether she understood: she was too self-absorbed probably; and he driving: nothing mechanical ever came naturally to him.

They got into a traffic jam between 'Santa Monica' on one side and 'Key West' on the other. The nurse began to sway, to rock, to grunt. The hold-up allowed him to look at her.

It must have triggered her off. 'I can't help it!' she burst out. 'It *was* very funny, wasn't it?'

'What?' The stink had risen again; the wire was cutting into the throat: which probably only he had seen.

'The man falling through his chair!' She was rocking beside him in the stationary car. 'I thought it was a scream!' It went on echoing in her memory *screama screama*: it was Lily Lake chambermaid at Brown's Hotel to whom she had sent post-cards till several years after the replies had stopped coming; there were so few people to write to.

Basil Hunter was relieved when the traffic started moving and he was no longer forced to look at or listen to Sister de Santis. It was his own fault: he must have got her more than a little drunk.

By the time they reached the block in which she lived her face had recovered its characteristically refined expression, though her lips looked twisted, her eyelids crimped: she could have been suffering physically.

'I do hope I never – in any way – let your mother down.' She had to force it.

'How would you expect to?'

'Oh, I don't know – *by being late*,' she suddenly thought up.

Already she had hunched herself, and was halfway out of the small car. He would have liked to put out his hand, to touch her; but would not risk causing further damage.

As for Sister de Santis, she made the extra effort to drag herself out through the car door, and had practically reached her full and normally impressive height, when she stumbled, and fell forward on her knees. For a moment she stayed kneeling on the pavement, her shuddering back turned towards him.

By the time he had raced round and almost reached her, she was again on her feet. 'Don't!' she gasped. 'There's no point. It's nothing.'

One knee had burst through its stocking. She was trembling, horrorstruck by more than her fall, when he was to blame, for the second time he was made to see: he could not have felt guiltier if he had come to his senses and found that, not even of his own will, but by malicious inspiration, under some cloud of unreason, he had defiled this pale nun.

The details of their parting were not clear to him, only that she reeled away into a dark hall with its accumulated gas and cooking smells, and up a narrow stair, to bathe her face, compose herself, perhaps pray for a remission of unorthodox sins, before presenting herself as usual at her evening devotions in Moreton Drive. Blood which had risen to the surface of the unusually white flesh was left smeared across his mind's eye.

His mechanical self drove off by jerks in the tinny car. Because he never felt at home in one, he knew he would be sitting upright, his shoulders narrowed. *Pray you, undo this button. Thank you, sir.* Why? Only that on his last performance as the old king he had never felt so personally bereft, so bankrupt; technique could not protect him from it. This last gasp; and the poverty of a single bone-clean button. In this you may have conveyed the truth, if in nothing else.

Eight

THOUGH HE went to bed conscious of having degraded an innocent creature, then condemned her to share in his own disgustful mortification, he woke without any feeling of guilt. In fact less than guilty: under cover of sleep, that scene at the water's edge, searing though it was at the time, could have been sharpening his intentions, steeling his will.

He would have liked to telephone somebody, almost anyone would have done, to hear his own voice, and try out a thrust or two; but it was still too early. Instead he drew up the blinds on a green dawn, or what could be seen of it above the roofs, amongst the telly aerials and branches of defoliated plane trees. Time and light at work on the forms of man-made ugliness both chilled and exhilarated, as they had, he remembered, on the first of his visits to Mitty Jacka.

In a fit of frustration he sat down at the pretence of a desk and began doodling words on the hotel writing-paper. The Jacka might have approved: to watch the long pale worm-thing's first attempts at uncoiling itself in non-play:

Scene: A Room. Table, chairs, a gas fire. The presence of ACTORS *should make other furniture unnecessary.*

ACTOR'S 1ST WIFE. Can't you see, darling? What she must convey in picking up this cup is the abject humility her husband's behaviour has driven her to, but which at the same time may be a sort of *pseudo*-humility—something she may eventually throw off. I mean, the gesture should not convey despair pure and simple, because there's the possibility of re-birth.
ACTOR (*undoing his collar button*). Oh, come off it, darling! It's

357

two o'clock. If we don't get our sleep we'll look like a couple of silkworms at rehearsal.

1ST WIFE. I've got to work this out. Always, Basil, always, if somebody not yourself is making a serious effort to break through, you have to kill it with flippancy. (*Pours herself half a cup of whiskey.*)

ACTOR. You'd break through all right, Shiela, if you'd realize it's a paper hoop, not a stone wall.

(1ST WIFE *sniffs, sulks, gulps from the cup she is holding.*)

1ST WIFE. I've always understood nothing is worth anything if it hasn't been a struggle.

ACTOR. Constipation in the theatre doesn't pay, believe me. In some London basement perhaps, with half a dozen hand-woven devotees in front; not when you take it on the road.

(1ST WIFE *sits holding the cup as though she hopes to abstract some first principle from it.*)

ACTOR. And don't you know you're drinking whiskey out of that bloody cup? A cup!

1ST WIFE. Yes. A cup. Why not? A cup is so much more *real* than a glass.

ACTOR (*grabbing the bottle*). By that token, not as real as a bottle! (*He swallows a good slug, then lets out a burp ending in blatant laughter.*)

1ST WIFE. For God's sake! You'll wake the child!

ACTOR. Yes, poor innocent! Find out about it the *real* way!

1ST WIFE (*guzzling whiskey*). You should feel less responsible. She's hardly yours, is she?

ACTOR. As you never stop reminding me.

(1ST WIFE *takes the bottle and pours herself another generous one.*)

1ST WIFE (*warming the cup drunkenly against her cheek*). I'll love her! How I'll love her!

ACTOR. Not if it's like your acting. No one ever loved by head alone.

1ST WIFE (*shickered snicker*). Oh, fuck off! I'll love my child—

when I've learnt how you do it. That's something nobody—
not you, not Len Bottomley—can teach me. I've got to work
it out for myself.

ACTOR. I've often wondered, Shiela, what Len has that I
haven't.

1ST WIFE. He tells me I'm good. What he means by 'good' is
that I'm a 'subtle actress', in case you misunderstood me.

ACTOR. What I don't understand is why you don't go off and
live with Len? Why not marry him? I'd divorce you.

1ST WIFE. He may be a dear decent ordinary man—and I must
say I'm deeply appreciative of ordinariness—but I couldn't
live with, let alone marry—a bad actor.

(*She drifts* OFF *with cup.*)

ACTOR (*tilting his chair*). Principles could have been her downfall—more than the booze.

SCENE FADES *into a* LIMBO *of half light in which the* ACTOR *is
still visible and gradually the* FIGURE OF A WOMAN. *She is
wearing a black kimono embroidered in silver and raw liver.*

WOMAN (*approaching, putting a hand in his hair*). That's a start.
But you're still only telling the truth about other people.

ACTOR. Give me a chance, won't you? I'm only beginning.

WOMAN. It ought to be easier after you've done the murder. It
ought to flow.

ACTOR. I'll bring on the Second Wife. There's no one like
Enid for telling others the truth about themselves. Enid can
make turnips bleed.

WOMAN. It's you who have to do the murder.

ACTOR. Give a bloke a chance. I'll ring my sister later on. It's
too early for a princess.

WOMAN. You're the star.

ACTOR. I don't think I can face it, Mitty.

WOMAN. Nothing to it. No blood—or not that anyone will
see. Only half a dozen words—spoken kindly. Oh, come, Sir
Basil Hunter!

ACTOR. First I've got to learn my lines. Got to rehearse them.

WOMAN. Enid will rehearse them with you.

ACTOR. Yes. Enid. (*He is handed a magnificent robe which he slips on as a disguise.*) And as you say, there's nothing to it. Half a dozen words ... (*His lungs expand.*) ... when I've got away with speeches lasting half a lifetime, and even for a fortnight the Lady Enid Bullshit herself.

SCENE: *A boudoir crammed with too many rare and incongruous bibelots. A desk at which* SECOND WIFE *sits writing. She is dressed in a rich stiff kaftan. Her head is that of a well-bred Borzoi.*

2ND WIFE (*without turning*). Basil?

ACTOR. I hoped you mightn't recognize me.

2ND WIFE. Huh? (*writing away*). What is it, darling? You haven't come to interrupt me, have you?

ACTOR. What are you writing, Enid?

2ND WIFE. My memoirs of course.

ACTOR. Still?

2ND WIFE (*dashing away*). Always! Isn't life one long incredible memoir? All the journeys, all the friends—the husbands!

ACTOR. I want you to hear me my lines for this play in which I'm supposed to do a murder before committing suicide.

2ND WIFE (*writing*). What—again? (*crosses out something with vicious pen.*) In each case no doubt you'll survive—as on the other occasions.

ACTOR. More likely not. This is the part I've never played.

2ND WIFE (*glancing through what she has written, correcting*). When I married an actor I thought it would mean going to bed with a different man every night. I found he always plays the same part—Himself. (*She looks up, gnashing her bitch's smile.*) Rather a boring part, too.

ACTOR. That's how you become a star. (*His nerves remind him.*) Give them too much—which is what I'm proposing to do— and they may tear you to bits. Because it isn't what they expect of you.

2ND WIFE (*yawning*). It's time I went on a journey, Basil. I think I'll fly to the Sahara—get me a Tuareg. Besides being veiled, a Tuareg doesn't talk. His ego is essentially physical. (*She stretches, and the garment she is wearing is released. She is left with her long plume of a Borzoi tail, lean human breasts and thighs.*)

SCENE FADES *into the* LIMBO *of semi-dark in which* FIGURE OF A WOMAN *in black silk kimono is visible.*

WOMAN (*to* ACTOR). Better, but it's you who must take your clothes off. (*Withdrawing*) It will probably come more easily after—after you've done the murder.

ACTOR (*mechanically*). Yes.

While he had been sitting at the desk scribbling, the light of morning had established itself so unequivocally in the hotel bedroom he saw that this must be the day when they would go out to Moreton Drive; it was in Dorothy's interest as much as his own to face Mother with the arrangements they were making for her future. As a result of his decision his face looked younger, he thought, his nails closely pared, the skin round his fingertips more clearly defined than usual.

He would ring Dorothy after he had drunk his coffee, as soon as he had shaved. Not that he had much respect for the princess his sister, but there were certain convenances he found it difficult not to observe. If affection were among them, it was because this morning at least he had to stress a collaboration she ought, but did not have to concede.

'Who?' Before being told, she was sharpening her tone in defence.

'Basil. Your brother.'

'Oh.' She sighed; she cleared her throat; she was giving an amateurish performance as a woman woken earlier than her rule allows. 'Oh, *Basil!*' She sighed, and coughed. 'Of course your voice is unmistakable. It's only the suddenness. Haven't collected my wits yet.'

' ... know it's early, Dorothy. But this, I think, will be the day, darling.'

'Which day?' A tone of suspicion, not to say hostility, was darkening her delivery.

'The day we tell Mother what we've decided for her.'

'Have we? Well, I know we've talked about it. But nothing's been positively arranged, has it?'

'As good as. In my mind, anyway.'

'You may kill her.' Dorothy spoke with such conviction she could only have intended to make him fully responsible.

'Most old people are tough,' he heard himself repeating a lesson. 'In case this one isn't, I'm asking you to come along with me. As a woman, you'll know how to soften the blow.' Ha-ha!

Dorothy was trying to impress him with the thought she was giving their grave situation. She sighed again, and even moaned once or twice, while in between (he recognized the technique) she was drinking her coffee.

'Is it good?' he asked.

'How do you mean—is it *good*?'

'The coffee.'

During the pause it might have been her stomach rumbling; then she said, 'As a matter of fact it's the most ghastly awful stuff—not that I expected anything better.'

They enjoyed a sympathetic laugh together.

He said, 'I know what neglect of the little important unimportant things does to your sensitivity, darling.'

She could have been lashing about in the bed. 'Are you flattering me?' she asked.

'Naturally. Haven't you found flattery pays?' Though it was too obvious she hadn't: Dorothy would not have known how to flatter, least of all the opposite sex.

She ignored his question. 'What time do you want me?' She made it as coldly practical as the circumstances seemed to demand; so much so, he was taken aback.

'Well, this morning, I suppose—since we're agreed.' If she

needed the moment pinned down more accurately, he was not capable of it—for the moment. 'Should we coax the Wyburd along? As a sort of witness?'

'An unwilling and disapproving one. No. Embarrassing and unnecessary. What time?' she persisted, it sounded irritably; and as though either of them could keep an appointment.

'Well,' he hesitated, 'towards the end of the morning—at Moreton Drive.'

'Say eleven.'

'If you're there.'

'I'll be there. Then we'll get the morning nurse. She's the silliest— and under your spell, Basil, I should say.'

'Sister Badgery?' He bridled.

'Whatever her name, the skinny hen. It might be unwise for us to encounter the young one. She despises us for class reasons, while probably having hopes of Mummy; and you, Basil, could easily make a fool of yourself with anyone so pretty, and doubtless ambitious.'

He said, 'It's far less complicated, at any time of day or night, than you would like to think. Leave it to me.'

Dorothy laughed. 'That's my intention. It's what you want, isn't it?'

He was not sure. No, he didn't; he had wanted Dorothy to take the dagger.

Madame de Lascabanes had dressed for what looked, from behind the closed window of the club bedroom, a brisk day: the harbour waters slightly shirred, newspaper rising and flapping in gutters, the paintwork on recent buildings and a moored liner as glossy as the makers advertised. The princess was wearing one of those timeless suits designed to silence criticism of an austere figure by emphasis of its bones and angles. Daring, anyway in this department, had remained a paying investment. And this morning her thin mouth looked right: no need to invoke her eyes in defence of a face where experience had routed ugliness, at least temporarily. Yes, she was pleased with her lack of compromise, in honour of which she had renounced jewellery even of a semi-precious variety. Why should she feel naked when realism was to be not only her weapon but her shield?

Walking down the corridor she heard the bones click once or twice from somewhere about her, and was reminded of early morning gallops on her first horse (as opposed to barrel-bellied pony) storming across the river flat in one long burst of thunder, till finally controlling her mount only by riding him, humped and groaning, at the steep of a hill. In the club corridor Dorothy Hunter's breath came faster; her nostrils thinned; she surprised a chambermaid by smiling, then by positively whinnying at her. Realizing at once that she had gone foolishly far, the princess fell silent and sober. In the taxi she sat looking with less demonstrative pleasure at her crossed ankles.

Some little apprehension, though only of a momentary nature, rose in her at Moreton Drive. Where a sharp wind had prevailed amongst the wharves and along the expressway, here more of a breeze, or circular languor, inspired the mops and switches of the native trees. Overcome by what should have been happy surprise, the princess almost tipped the driver twenty cents, before scotching that foolishness too: she made it ten.

Was it morning that caused the squeal made by the hinges on the gate to sound so penetrating, yet private, and somehow melancholy? She could remember listening as a child for the sound of the gate, wondering whether this time it was announcing the arrival she had always half expected: of the person in whom beauty was united with kindliness? Would she be listening still if she had continued living in Elizabeth Hunter's house?

Strange that Mother should have thought to preserve, stranger still to plant, native trees in her garden: herself an exotic even down to her hypocrisies. *I shan't feel happy till I've tasted everything there is to taste and I don't intend to refuse what is unpleasant—that is experience of another kind.* There must have been some Australian streak still existent under the posturing, the opinions and habits borrowed from another tradition. *But how can you possibly love them Mother? Scarcely trees—monotonous ugly scarecrows—ugh!* When they broke your heart at times, just from thinking of them, and in another hemisphere. *I can't reason about it Dorothy only swear that it's a true passion whether you believe me or not tell me if you can why confident responsive women are attracted to withdrawn shadowy men? or gentle girls to hairy brutes? Oh Mother—must we descend to that level?* At any level Elizabeth Hunter could make you feel you had inherited some of her moral pretences, and added to them, if you were honest, a dash of priggishness all your own.

Now the princess went warily as she climbed the path which wound amongst the contentious trees. Wary of the light too. Round the suspended terracotta dish, which the night nurse kept filled with seed, birds were hanging in fluttering clusters. Instead of the normal clash and shattering of light, here it glowed and throbbed like the drone of doves.

She opened her bag and looked distractedly inside, without knowing, she realized, what she expected to find. She shut the bag. She wet her lips. She must forget about the light, the trees. She rang the bell, and heard her authority resound through a house, the size and misuse of which, made it redundant, if not downright immoral. (It occurred only very briefly to the Princesse de Lascabanes that she would have been horrified in other circumstances by the attitude she was forced to adopt.)

As on a previous occasion, the bell was answered by the nurse on duty.

'Oh, dear!' Sister Badgery was sent flying several paces back. 'I got a shock!' she clattered.

'Why—whatever shocked you?' the princess heard a bleached voice inquire.

'I expected someone else, I expect.' Sister Badgery laughed and gawked, unlike the widow of a tea planter.

'Who is expected?'

'I don't know I'm sure.' Behind her spectacles the nurse was trying to look mysterious. 'Not you anyway—Princess Dor—

mad-*dahm!*' She was bubbling up again. 'Maybe Jehovah's Witness!' she shrieked.

Neither of them could decide whether to take it as a joke or a revelation. The nurse at least was in a position to turn and lead the caller upstairs.

Dorothy thought it prudent to avoid inquiring after her mother's health; instead she asked with deliberate coldness, 'Has the house-keeper broken a bridge on this occasion too?'

'Oh, ne-o!' Sister Badgery twittered, and shook her veil. 'She's a bit under the weather. That's all. Her feet—and everything.' She half turned while continuing to sidle up the stairs. 'Between our-selves, mad-dam, many of these Continental Jewesses are more than a little neurotic.' The nurse herself had a tic in one cheek as she turned back to give full attention to the climb, with a less crablike, more of a perching-Leghorn motion. 'In any case, it's no hardship for me to answer the bell. I love people.'

'I'm told that's why some women choose to work at news stalls on railway stations,' the princess remarked. 'But surely, with a tempera-ment like yours, you must feel lonely in this big old unused house?'

Looking down into the gulf of the hall which she had known intimately, Dorothy herself half-admitted to loneliness.

But Sister Badgery was protesting out of a flurry of veil, 'Oh, ne-o, ne-o! Mrs Hunter is such a happy—such an *original* soul! She makes a person see things in a different light from day to day. We all worship Mrs Hunter—your mother.'

Dorothy was more than ever determined not to inquire after Mother's health. 'I'm expecting my brother at almost any moment.' She made it a cheerful warning.

'Oh, Sir Basil!' Sister Badgery gasped. 'Then there will be two of you,' she added rather pointlessly; even more so, 'I had three brothers. I could rely on each one of them for moral support.'

The two women had reached the landing, where they were glad to draw breath a moment.

'Though it amuses you to answer the bell, I'm sorry you've had this exhausting climb,' the princess thought to apologize.

'Oh ne-o, it's really nothing. I love the exercise,' Sister Badgery insisted; in between panting and smiling, she seemed to be drying the buckle of her teeth with her under lip while developing a line of thought. 'Actually, for some people it's a climb. Poor Mrs Lippmann has her feet. Actually, what upsets Mrs Lippmann more than anything is to think she may become so incapacitated she won't be able to dance again for Mrs Hunter.'

'Have you seen it?' the princess was tempted to ask about what she had vaguely heard.

'Only Mrs Hunter has seen.' Sister Badgery bowed her head and led the way along the passage, lightly tossing over her shoulder, perhaps to frustrate the visitor some more, 'In her day Mrs Lippmann was a great artiste we are told – by Mrs Lippmann.' Standing with one hand on the knob, head inclined against a panel of the door, the nurse might have ended by sounding vindictive if it were not for looking as though physical exertion and some demanding pre-occupation had blanched the malice out of her.

Other questions were rising to the surface of Dorothy's mind, but there was no time to ask them: the nurse had opened the door of Mother's room, and you would have to go inside. What made the moment more portentous, Sister Badgery was clinging to the knob, holding back, while an intensified flickering of eyelids and the directionless drift of a pallid smile implied that she personally would have no part in anything reprehensible anyone else might be plotting. The princess hesitated, to give protocol a chance. But the nurse failed to announce her; she closed the door, shutting out her own blameless figure and a last simper of apologies.

'Is that you, Dorothy? I can't see.'

'Yes, Mother.' The Princesse de Lascabanes felt her nylons turn to lisle.

The figure on the bed – her mother – continued treading the waters of recent sleep, till rising above the wave she was to some extent clothed by the myth of her former beauty.

Alone, Dorothy was already quailing for the kind of sentimental weaknesses a raking of the past might uncover. At the Judgment, too, you stand alone: not only Basil, all other sinners will contrive to be late. Your only hope in the present lies in indignation for whatever disgusts most: from faecal whiffs, breath filtered through mucus, the sickly scent of baby powder. Thus fortified, you may hope to face the prosecution and conduct your own defence.

Madame de Lascabanes stripped off her gloves, dumped her bag: it tumbled off the bedside table, and lay; she seized the freckled claws, and asked, 'Do they look after you, darling?'

'What do you mean?'

'Rub your back regularly. Change you often enough. Keep you fresh.'

'Why? Do I smell?'

'Of course not! I was only inquiring generally.'

'They spend far too much time messing me about. But that's what they're paid to do, isn't it? Poor wretches!'

'I shouldn't have thought of them as "poor wretches". They're paid very well. The award's ridiculously high.'

'What do you know about awards?'

'Only what I've found out.'

Overcoming her repugnance for the signs of human decay, the princess stooped to kiss the papery cheek, and was again victimized by the past. *Oh Mummy can't we stay together? can't you come into my bed?* To sleep blissfully secure. *In this dress? do be sensible Dorothy you must know Mummy's expected at dinner.* The fingers as pink-tipped the dress as slippery scentful white as—what was it? *Tuberoses darling somebody thought they were paying me a compliment.*

Cling, for God's sake, to the present. 'Only what I've found out,' Dorothy de Lascabanes repeated, and what that was could have been as distasteful to her as the body's corruption.

Even so, screwed up for ruthlessness, she felt inside her a movement too physical to be ignored, as though conscience had become the baby sterility had prevented her having. Her lips seemed to grow thick and blubbery as she withdrew them from her mother's cheek. She had to go quickly and stand looking out of the open window.

'Basil will be here presently,' she flung back over her shoulder as hard as she could.

'I expect he will have found out a whole lot more.'

'I doubt it. Basil has his gift; beyond that, I suspect him of being a wobbly, helpless male.'

'Basil was the affectionate one.'

'His manners were always flamboyant. And it's an advantage to be a man, Mother.' Dorothy's mirth was so dry, she herself was reminded of a lizard, possibly a deadly one; again she felt guilty, no longer on this old woman's account, but for the people she could see strolling through the park below, innocent of what might be in store for them, at any thicket, even in the open grass.

'What was that man's name, dear?'

'Which man, Mother?' As if your instinct for danger had not forewarned.

'You know—the Norwegian—when somebody invited us to an island.'

Dorothy did not think she could bring herself to force it out from between her teeth; but Mother seemed to have lost interest since she had got her own back. If she had. Out of a haze of sentiment and tuberoses, she had conjured for you this solid land mass, or island of hate: its stinging sand, twisted tree-roots, and the brumbies snapping at one another with yellow teeth, lashing out with broken hooves as they stampeded along their invaded beach.

Dorothy de Lascabanes did not have to remind herself she had never hated anyone so bitterly as she had hated their mother on their brief visit to Brumby Island. She should remember Elizabeth Hunter's treachery on that occasion could only make the most brutally reasonable plan her children might now conceive for her seem morally defensible.

Jack and Helen Warming were going on ahead to the island, to open up the house and get in some serious fishing before the arrival of their guests. The Hunters would fly up later from Sydney to Oxenbould, and there transfer to the helicopter Jack was chartering

369

to take them across to Brumby. From the beginning Dorothy wondered why they were invited. The Warmings had never been more than superficial acquaintances living in another state. Though Helen and Dorothy had gone to the same school, Helen had been a junior when Dorothy was at the point of leaving. Then there was Mother, a most incongruous element: on finding this out for herself she would develop the fidgets, and start rearranging other people's furniture and lives.

'I know what's on your mind, Dorothy. Don't worry; I shall fit in. Though the island's uninhabited except for a few forestry workers, the Warmings don't pig it, so I'm told. In any case, I've never had a craving for luxury, and know how to pull my weight under primitive conditions.' Her Edwardian man's slang made it the more irritating.

The thought that the Warmings might be doing them a kindness started to fester in Dorothy. *There she is Jack ditched by the Frenchman back on old Betty's hands shouldn't we do something about them only a couple of weeks won't ruin the holidays.* Becoming an obsession it nagged and throbbed, bringing on a migraine at times. *Wouldn't you think Jack the unfortunate Dorothy has probably reached the menopause it must be ghastly for her mewed up with that hideously successful ex-beauty of a mother.* Till she looked to reason to rescue her from her thoughts: surely the Warmings would not have invited Mother if they had been taking pity on you? Dorothy knew that one of her worst faults was to suspect ulterior motives in others; and kindness always roused her suspicions.

Now, at the end of the journey, arrival practically upon them, everything smooth-running, so far no one specific to accuse, she felt afraid. It must be the helicopter. She was no good at this sort of thing: beneath them the straits burnished to silver by the heat; ahead of them the solid island trembling just perceptibly with the motion of their flight. If she could have heard a door closing behind her, and hidden herself, not only from strangers, but from kind friends. She had been wrong to come. Yes, to be perfectly truthful, it was the menopause, which Helen Warming would see, if she had not already guessed – or more likely, Mother told.

Seated beside her mother, Dorothy Hunter (still 'de Lascabanes', it might help to remember) pressed her hands together in her lap: held in the vertical position they would have suggested one of the Gothic attitudes of prayer; laid in her lap, they revealed too plainly the white pressure of nervous frustration, and by some law of architectural stress, helped to narrow her shoulders. By contrast the young pilot was relaxed, brown, naked it would seem, under his khaki shirt and shorts. Not that she was in any way impressed by this young man, only envious of his detachment.

As Mother would not have understood. Who was at the moment trying to burn her way into your thoughts using those blow-torches of eyes. You were not deceived, nor by the counterfeit smiles, the quirked corners of which were hung with webs of faint silvery wrinkles.

Dorothy looked away. She might have drawn comfort from the wrinkles if she had not imagined she could hear laughter trailing cool and indulgent through the noise and the suddenly torrid air. The pilot was bringing them down, she realized, on a strip of grey sand. Whether their landing would mean her mental release remained to be seen.

The women bowed their heads simultaneously as the helicopter touched down; its rotor, slashing at the light, collaborated with it in a whirligig of blue and green which scattered normally reliable values. In consequence Dorothy started throbbing again. On one side was the strait, flat and listless through a fringe of mean-looking mangroves; on the other, beyond pickets of eucalypts, rose the dark mass of a more esoteric rain forest which obscured, presumably, the ocean.

After climbing out of the machine, Dorothy's legs felt as brittle and spindly as Mother's looked.

But Mrs Hunter was not admitting to any of the physical shrink-age which can occur in lesser beings in exotic surroundings. 'I must thank you for delivering us as sound as when we left the main-land.' She advanced on the pilot while keeping him at a distance with an outstretched arm and white-gloved hand.

The young man saw with surprise he was meant to accept this cleanly hand. 'No trouble at all,' he whinged rather than spoke, as though punched in the thorax, and gave her a lopsided smile.

Dorothy noticed that the wrench her mother's whole arm sustained from the pilot's mechanical handshake did not make her flinch, and that the legs, far from being brittle and spindly, justified exposure.

Dorothy looked in vain for the car which must surely come to meet them.

While Mother had decided to make the best of a hitch in the arrangements. 'Is there much wild life on the island?' she asked the pilot in a clear, rather jolly voice.

'Lousy with it.'

'Then I shall spend my time studying the wild life of Brumby Island.'

Dorothy winced for the tone, even if the pilot did not understand. Mother could start a flirtation at a street crossing, waiting for the lights to change.

After thinking things over, the pilot informed them, or more precisely, Elizabeth Hunter, 'The wife likes to watch birds— whenever the kids give her a break.' He added, 'She's got a bird book.'

'Have you a bird book with you, Mother?' The pilot's presence made it sound more sardonic.

'Don't be *silly*! I don't propose to go into it scientifically, only for my own pleasure.'

Of course you were silly, not to say boring: wasn't it what Hubert had given you to understand, by exquisitely tactful innuendo, long before margarine had started offering its rival charms?

'And I haven't yet decided whether it's birds I'm interested in.' Mother was still at it though the pilot had obviously dropped out. 'For all you know, Dorothy, I may take up trees—or sea creatures.'

Dorothy looked down, and caught sight of a land crab, claws raised in anguish as it moved sideways over the sand by bursts of protective choreography.

She enjoyed a reprieve from her own anguish when an ancient car dashed towards the airstrip from out of the tallowwoods and sassafras, bucking, almost pig-rooting, at every ridge it had to cross. Jack Warming had driven across the island to fetch them as Helen had promised in her letter. He was a large man, with large, extrovert manner allied unconvincingly to that faded, quasi-mystical expression of those who spend their lives searching the shimmer of distance for the sheep or cattle dissolved in it.

Mrs Hunter responded enormously to Jack Warming's arrival. 'Now I can feel we're really off to the races!' She offered her cheek, bravely patted the Chevrolet's overheated bonnet, and advanced on two little children dressed in the tatters of the rich, who had come with their father.

Jack bellowed in appreciation of Elizabeth Hunter, 'We've been wondering whether you realize what you're in for. We lead a pretty simple life on the island. Helen thinks you're tough, though.'

Dorothy suspected the Warmings were among the many Mother had taken in. Jack was innocent enough to attempt drawing 'old Dorothy, here' into the circle of his own pleasure: with good-natured clumsiness he took her by an elbow, squeezed it, but let go at once. The quasi-mystical expression was averted, though light still lingered on the tips of teeth exposed in an uncertain smile.

As for Elizabeth Hunter, she was engaged in seducing the children. 'The stones are turquoises. It's a tremendously *old* chain. It belonged to my mother before me — one of the few pretty things she possessed: we were poor, you see. I'll allow you to wear it, Sara,' she promised the girl child, 'tonight.'

The children were entranced by the kind of stranger Elizabeth Hunter excelled at being. Then they looked at the one who was the princess, and looked away.

Dorothy was not hurt: if children disliked, or perhaps feared her, it was because they recognized one who understood them too well. Mother's strength lay partly in not knowing what other people were like.

With revived bellows, Jack had begun recalling 'the MacGregors' party', apparently the last occasion Mother and the Warmings had been together.

As Mrs Hunter left off courting the children she lowered her eyelids, raised her chin, and smiled faintly at the others. 'It was a riot, wasn't it?' she said in the softest voice.

Dorothy was surprised, even shocked: she failed to equate the MacGregors' party with anything she knew of her mother's life; she had a stampeded vision of Elizabeth Hunter in a paper cap, then, too brutally sudden, Mother's naked, white body as seen through a sheet of water or curtain of tropic light.

Mrs Hunter opened her eyes very wide and said with studied emphasis, 'You won't believe, Dorothy—I cooked bacon and eggs for about twenty people at three in the morning.'

It was a relief to be getting into the car. Dorothy made sure she had the seat beside the driver: in this way she would be separated from the children. She was appalled to think there were five other Warming offspring, fortunately 'farmed out for the holidays' their mother had written, 'at points between Rockhampton and the Monaro'.

Nonchalantly the Chevrolet leaped away from the airstrip, tore through a belt of thinnish scrub, and started its climb through the rain forest.

Compared with the other islands strung out along the Queensland coast Brumby was considerable. Grabbed by a Warming grandfather early on, most of it had been resumed for its timber. The present Warming owned no more than a few acres on the ocean side and a house to which he brought his family as a respite from the inland summers. The island was uninhabited, except by a permanently stationed gang of foresters, and the Warmings on their infrequent visits.

Now it hushed the strangers it was initiating. At some stages of the journey the trees were so densely massed, the columns so moss-upholstered or lichen-encrusted, the vines suspended from them so intricately rigged, the light barely slithered down, and then a dark, watery green, though in rare gaps where the sassafras had been thinned out, and once where a giant blackbutt had crashed, the intruders might have been reminded of actual light if this had not flittered, again like moss, but dry, crumbled, white to golden.

The Chev skirted a clearing in which stood three or four tents coloured by permanence, as well as a Nissen hut, a couple of hatless men outside it, their leather visors of faces expressionless below white, vulnerable foreheads.

Jack bellowed. The children waved and shouted. The men waved back. Out of the corner of an eye Dorothy caught sight of Elizabeth Hunter languidly wooing the foresters with the flicker of a white arm.

The Princesse de Lascabanes failed to animate the stick she was changed into. More than anything, she feared that the secret joy she had experienced while carried onward and upward through the forest, might overflow through her eyes, and give her away. So she screwed it up as tight as she could, together with the equally terrifying sobs which were rising in her. Ten minutes later, as they sprang into the open and down a grass-stitched slope, she might have prayed, if her prayers had been more successful in the past, that their car should continue charging into the immensity of light and water, as far as the ocean would support its wheels. Better blinded by green glass, ear drums burst by a black roar, infinity pouring into the choked funnel of your throat, than the paroxysms and alternating apathy of a lopsided existence.

Instead they were pulling up alongside what must be the Warmings' house, a ramshackle ricketty structure in the easygoing Queensland style: where breezes are encouraged to blow through lattice nailed to unequal stilts, behind which any old thing you want to forget about may be stashed away, and children hide, to share their more sinister imaginings. Standing on a shelf between the forest and a strip of powdered coral, the house had been stained a practical brown with trimmings of glossier, though blistered green, the whole so placidly domesticated it was a wonder it had resisted the throbbing, the threats, the apocalyptic splendours of an ocean perpetually unrolling out of an indeterminate east.

The visitors were still meekly disengaging themselves from the car, when the stairway reaching to what looked more a continuous balcony than the veranda of the stilted house, was shaken by a woman's descent. She came thumping barefoot down in a cheap faded cotton frock which did not detract from the chatelaine's authority. Dorothy would not have recognized Helen Warming: she had let herself go; her hands had been coarsened by menial grind, her body made slommacky by childbearing. Then, for an instant, the little girl looked out of the fulfilled woman, and quailed, if smilingly, beneath the prefect's stare, before the woman resumed control, and flung on towards her objective.

'Dear Mrs Hunter! How brave of you to take the risk! It's only a primitive humpy—as I warned you.'

It was not the pretentious gush it might have sounded, even Dorothy was forced to recognize. Helen almost swept Mother away, after which the two women embraced with a tenderness approved by husband and children.

The girl child told, 'That chain she's got—with the tur-*kwoys*—she says I can wear tonight.'

But personal honours were irrelevant beside the family triumph in having come by a living breathing object of worship and source of oracular wisdom. With a twinge Dorothy de Lascabanes realized she had been invited, not because the Warmings had wanted to be kind, but because they adored her mother.

A galling discovery was further inflamed after the devotees had bundled their idol up the creaking stairway, and sat her in the room prepared for her visit. 'Do you think you'll be comfortable, Mrs Hunter? The shutters are a bit stiff. Look, these are biscuits in case you're hungry in the night. And books. Have we remembered matches? Don't touch the biscuits, John. We've only got the old kero lamps. John! Please! I still think oil lamps give the only truly benign light. Cleaning them's a drag, but once you get into your stride it's like saying the Lord's Prayer. Jack, darling, why don't you lay Mrs Hunter's bag on the stool? Sara, *nobody* likes being *mauled*. Oh dear, poor Mrs Hunter!' Helen stooped to give an extra hug.

The fractured light in the shuttered room gave back to Mother's hair the aureole it must have worn in youth, of what again appeared as palest, purest gold. Her eyes, at their deepest bluest, expressed the resignation of one receiving her due.

Till she said with some severity, 'There's something I can't allow if I'm to spend a fortnight as your guest. All this "Mrs Hunter"! My name is "Elizabeth". Nothing less. I detest diminutives.'

The Warmings were variously enraptured.

Somebody had stuck a bunch of flowers in a pottery vase, and stood it on the chest. The Name insisted on knowing who had gathered her nosegay.

'I did,' said Sara.

'We did,' John corrected.

'How thoughtful of you; and how clever to know nothing would please me better than natives.'

'They're all there are,' John confessed.

Elizabeth Hunter ignored him. 'In whatever other ways we fall short, we have our native flowers: there's nothing subtler — nobler;' and getting up, she advanced on the erect bunch to rearrange it.

Unable to endure any more, Dorothy had stepped outside on to the veranda. From where she was standing she might have been on board a ship, one which would never weigh anchor. Heat had bleached the colour from the sea, and reduced the coastline to a dead green, except at a point to the south where it rose into a curious cliff layered in reds and yellows. The cliff glared back at her ferociously.

'What is it, Dorothy? Is anything wrong?'

'No. Nothing to speak of. Well, I do have a wretched head.' She turned a wince into a smile. 'I'll take something I've got with me.'

Helen would no doubt have been prepared to dredge up a generous ration of the sympathy which seemed to be her stock in trade, but Dorothy feared to run the risk of accepting it, with a white sun staring at her, and those angry cliffs.

Behind the shutters of her narrow cabin of a room, after the tablet had begun to take effect, she was to some extent soothed. She lay wondering at the helicopter pilot with the bird-watching wife, and Helen Warming's husband in that rank-smelling stockman's shirt he had worn to meet them; she wondered at the law which decrees that almost everybody shall desire some other human being. She could not have desired the lean, gauche young pilot, or for that matter, any man she had known or could imagine, least of all Hubert de Lascabanes, who had been her husband, and still was in the eyes of God.

Mother could be heard at a distance charming her hosts with an impersonation of the character generally accepted as Elizabeth Hunter, involved for her present purpose in some mock-dramatic situation. Through the cracks in the floorboards the threads of children's voices were interwoven in conspiracy. All always conspire. None so secretively as waves. But you were laid to sleep in them at last.

And woke, not refreshed, but the despair wrung out, the children clattering chattering along the veranda outside. The room had darkened by now; it smelt of stuffiness, damp sheets, and what was probably dry rot.

She ought to face the children.

When she had touched herself up, she went outside, and smiled at them, and said, 'I believe you have something to tell me.'

They looked embarrassed, not to say frightened, and she realized she must have put it badly; mutual understanding did exist at another level, if the children would admit to it.

She tried to improve her position. 'I heard you underneath the house. Playing?' She looked at them, not too significantly she hoped.

The boy was the first to respond, looking away, his voice rapt for the scene he saw or was dreaming. 'There was somebody murdered here in the beginning. They were wrecked on the island. The blacks killed the men and made the woman their slave.'

Though it was hardly night, Sara was already wearing the promised gold-and-turquoise chain. 'They undressed this woman,' she said, 'till she was quite naked.'

378

'It's supposed to have happened down there.' John pointed with a wishbone gesture at the striated cliffs; his arm must have been double-jointed.

Sara said, 'But we think it was here,' stamping with bare foot on the veranda boards.

'Why?' asked Dorothy Hunter, not intending to question their belief: she hoped they would allow her to share their myth.

'Because – underneath the house – there's the smell of dead bodies, sort of,' John explained.

Sara added, 'There's the oyster shells the blacks left.'

The children began to giggle, but not on account of the murders: she suspected they were laughing at the person who was a princess, and it made her unhappy again; she wanted to be one of them.

While everything was in the balance, she looked out along the coast where the light had dwindled, and saw a man approaching. He had beached a dinghy, evidently. He was wearing no more than a pair of faded scarlet trunks.

'Do you see that man?' she asked the children. 'Who is he?'

'That's Professor Pehl.'

'He's staying with us.'

'He's – Norwegian.'

'They invited him, but I don't think they like him much.'

'They felt they had to ask him.'

Dorothy looked in the direction of the unwanted Norwegian. From that distance it was difficult to estimate his age; but he had not yet gone to seed. The streaky hair had been bleached lighter by the sun, and arrested in the chaos wind and salt water create. Not adapted to the climate, his skin looked shabby: except that it was almost of the same complexion as his faded trunks, it reminded her of dried cod hanging from the ceiling *chez l'épicier*.

'At least he must be interesting,' she ventured, 'a professor – and a Norwegian.' She could not remember ever having met a Norwegian; perhaps as a Frenchwoman she was proud of it.

The children were hardly encouraging.

'He's all right.'

'He doesn't come out of his shell all that much.'
'He writes in an old notebook.'
'And picks his nose.'
'And lets breezers, as if he didn't know there was anybody else in the room.'

The children burst, Sara more violently than John, to show her appreciation of a coarse masculine joke. Though they wandered off soon after, the princess person tried to persuade herself she was already more acceptable to them than the professor could ever become.

In the kitchen Mother was peeling potatoes. As one of the characters it amused Elizabeth Hunter to project for sympathetic strangers, she was wearing an apron. There was a scent of gin.

' "Pehl" – did you say?' There had been giggling in the kitchen too.

'Yes. Don't think I'm running him down, will you? He's not bad, only serious. And I'm really all in favour of serious men.' Helen realized the (ex-) Princess Hubert de Lascabanes had intruded on their cosy conversation. 'Oh, Dorothy, do help yourself to drink.' After doing her duty, she altered course automatically. 'I only wish, Elizabeth, you hadn't insisted on peeling potatoes. Potatoes are half the ruin of my hands.'

'I'm wholly a ruin without potatoes.'

Elizabeth and Helen sighed: they had been interrupted.

The Princesse de Lascabanes helped herself to a generous squirt of soda. She folded her arms like a thin man.

While peeling a grave potato, Elizabeth was assuring Helen, 'Scandinavians are clean. I can't bear those French lavatories – *footprints!*' Helen and Elizabeth became convulsed. 'Helen – you won't believe – I knew a woman who dropped her passport down the – *hole* – between the footprints!' The friends cried with laughter. 'At *Montpellier!*' Elizabeth invited Helen to shriek.

In spite of a decision to suspend hate, Dorothy hated Mother.

'What is Professor Pehl's subject?' the Princesse de Lascabanes cut in coldly.

In self-defence, Helen remembered almost too quickly. 'Why, he's a—a marine ecologist, Dorothy.'

'Interesting.' Elizabeth sighed.

Then there was the sound of a potato being peeled, and Helen hauling pots around the stove, and men's voices, and water sluiced.

'By the way, there aren't any baths, not even a shower, because we depend on rain water,' Helen explained. 'When we become self-conscious about our dirt, we water ourselves with a jug. That's what Edvard's doing now.'

Mother said, 'I came prepared to rough it, darling. It's Dorothy who grows uppity if all the cons aren't mod—living in France, too.'

'Really, Mother!'

Dorothy's irritation was not given a chance to develop: Jack came in, somewhat improved by an old tussore suit and a crimson cummerbund.

Elizabeth remarked, 'I do like my men with a dash of colour.' She had tired of peeling potatoes.

Jack laughed. 'You should see old Edvard's back. It's almost the colour of this cummerbund.'

'Did you say "Ed-*vard*"?' Elizabeth asked.

'Yes. With a "v".'

'Turns it into something different—quite attractive.' Mother had raised her head, pursed her lips, as though tasting the Norwegian's name.

It was a characteristic attitude, one probably intended to bear out the legend of a neck and throat. To hide her contempt, Dorothy took up the knife, and began peeling the three or four potatoes Mother was obviously not prepared to finish.

Jack lowered his voice. 'With or without the "v", he's one colossal bore. Wished on to us by somebody we thought our friend. If you don't take care, Elizabeth, you'll have him explaining benthic aggregations.'

'You can rely on me to avoid anything of that description,' Mother solemnly promised; merely by opening her mouth she made others laugh.

The moon was rising, full and red, a legacy from the flamingo sunset. Jack Warming had come round, seated himself on a corner of the table, and put an arm round his wife's waist. Perhaps not altogether unconscious of the picture, Elizabeth Hunter's still imperceptibly shrivelled lily offered its effulgence. Brumby Island appeared a world of harmony with which Dorothy de Lascabanes had been made to clash, and now, it seemed, Edvard Pehl; though she would not dare envisage him as an ally. In the circumstances she was humbly grateful for being allowed to peel potatoes.

Helen had started fussing, wondering where her children could be, and Elizabeth said, 'Sara looks delicious in my chain. I hope she doesn't lose it. Not that it's of great value. Precious only because it's practically the first thing I can remember.'

'Lose it? God forbid!' Perhaps it had been Mother's intention that Helen should suffer. 'I'll go and round them up at once.'

'Do let me go, Mrs Warming.' The Princesse de Lascabanes had finished off her potato less meticulously than she would have wished; but she was again in danger of feeling desperate.

'You wouldn't know where.'

'No. I'll look around – I'd like to – and find them.'

Without waiting for considered permission, Dorothy escaped. By moonlight the house almost convinced that it had put to sea. Under the heavy red moon the distance undulated gently as her feet spanked along the deck. Silence had fallen in the galley. No other sound but the whirring of a bird somewhere between sea and land.

When a door opened and Edvard Pehl stepped out on to the veranda. In one hand he was carrying a towel, in the other, the pair of bathing trunks. Nor did darkness help clothe him; if anything, a phosphorescence emphasized his nakedness. She was conscious of the parting of his rather fleshy, though firm breasts; then her glance, decently averted, was drawn for a flickering instant – no, worse: she was hypnotized. *Mon Dieu, des seiches!* When in all her married life she had not allowed herself to notice.

That she did not collide compulsively with a monolith of flesh was due to the professor's self-possession. He slightly swerved, not ungracefully considering the stolid first impression, rather as though playing a bull, and continued firmly along the veranda, or deck, or slatted nightmare. Though large enough to run the risk of wobbling, his buttocks looked hard as marble. She was compelled to watch them, and saw the moonlight glinting in a polished saucer as he disappeared inside the cabin next to her own.

Under her retreat the veranda swung groaned she might have been prising the slats wider open without giving thought to direction hadn't she been directionless ever since coming to this island heels now trapped in mattresses of coarse hair or grass now bogged in wet sand. Logically, on arrival at the water's edge, she should have taken the smooth path distance offered. Instead she turned, and walked or wallowed back, and was received into the room which was hers for want of another.

The walls might have been felt-lined: they were breathing at her. She bolted the shutters. Nothing could be done about the door: its lock was not provided with a key.

So Helen was able to break in and attempt to coax this troubled child. 'Dorothy, darling, aren't you coming for some dinner?'

'No—*thank you*—Mrs Warming.' She had not meant her voice to explode.

'What, I wonder, can we do for you?'

It made Dorothy laugh cry. 'Nothing, really—*chère Hélène. Je vous en prie*—Helen.' All the more humiliating in that you were the prefect and Helen Warming the junior girl.

It was a relief to remember, 'What about the children? Did they turn up?'

'Yes. And Elizabeth's chain is safe.'

Very slightly, Dorothy twitched; while the Princesse de Lascabanes guiltily allowed herself to be comforted by kind arms.

Prescribing sleep, Helen went away. Not sleep but spasms. Sewn into the silver to reddish sheet the worse than red the angry ejaculating moon shoots to kill *ah non Hubert je suis déjà morte d'avoir tant souffert* Edvard may understand that basic aggravations breed at the greatest depth it is hope dead or alive which floats on the surface to be identified and gently netted.

Dorothy woke, still not rested, but surprisingly calm. Some intention, she was not sure what, had tautened her body while insulating her nerves. The light, when she opened the shutters, was of a silver so cool she did not quail at thought of the approaching blaze, or its white aftermath which would smoulder through the middle of the day. Cherishing her delicately balanced contentment, she tiptoed along the veranda as soon as she was dressed, to brew herself coffee (*sans doute immonde*) or at worst, a pot of Indian tea.

In the kitchen somebody else, alas, was already disturbing the pots.

'I was thinking to boil myself some coffee,' Professor Pehl explained in a thick and gloomy voice. 'The Warmings have no liking for coffee.'

Dressed, she observed, in shorts and shirt, he had already started the operation.

'I am lost without my coffee,' she heard, not herself, but Mother preparing to deal with a man. (Well, why not? there was nobody to listen in.) 'And I like it French,' she added rather too stridently as she took possession of the pot.

'Not French,' Professor Pehl objected. 'French is muddy. I favour the American style of coffee—since I am at San Diego.'

'Are you, now?' Dorothy tried to visualize the distance between Mother's room and the kitchen; but she couldn't; which distracted her. 'San Diego—is it interesting?' she asked, for safety's sake, in a softer voice.

'Interesting? That is where I am recently attached—for better or worse.' The professor spoke through a crust of bread he had torn off and started chewing.

'When you say "attached", do you mean "engaged"?' The princess enunciated very clearly in addressing this Scandinavian; while remaining distracted, vague.

'I do not by any means mean "engaged". I mean I am attached for my research to the University of California at San Diego.'

Imbécile que je suis! The percolator squealed, she dragged it so rudely across the stove.

'I am formerly engaged to a young lady at Bergen. For a short time I entertained the idea of marriage, but decided it was early days: it would have interfered with my research projects.'

'Your work must be fascinating.' In the circumstances, the princess plumped for an insincerity she might have condemned in someone else.

When the coffee was ready, and herself prepared to pour, an inspiration whirled her round. 'I know what I'm going to do. I shall make you an omelette.' Even Hubert had complimented her on her omelettes. (*Si tu es Française, chérie, c'est par ton talent pour faire les omelettes.*) They sometimes stuck, however.

'I take only coffee to my breakfast.'

'But a man should start the day with something more substantial,' she heard the Australian countrywoman in her.

Professor Pehl made no further comment: Mother may have known, after all.

Dorothy was elated to rediscover her lapsed art. The perfectly folded omelette shuddered as it settled on the plate, not so much from resignation as voluptuousness.

'How is it?' She would claim from his stolid lips the praise which was her due; though if she had achieved perfection, surely he would not have munched so?

'It is good. It is only—for my taste—too much slime.'

'*Baveuse!* That is how we like it.' Her tone had sharpened. 'And the French invented the omelette.' Or had they? She was no longer certain.

'Ah, the French!' He laughed and forked in another yellow mouthful.

When he had swallowed, his looks returned; and she remembered what she liked to believe she had succeeded in hiding: *bien baveuse ma chere petite—Australienne—peur-euse.* No, it was slime. How could she have been so depraved as to collaborate in depravity? She wiped away all trace of it, but could not rid herself of her disgust: it had festered and left a scar, visible only in a certain introspective light.

As he munched, Professor Pehl moodily stared at the maker of omelettes.

For her part, she wondered whether his eyes, trained to observe underwater life, would notice her skin leaping. She saw her hand as it would have lain, like a narrow, snoozing, white fish, in the pale hair, its thicket still sticky from salt and the shortage of rain-water; she avoided the phosphorescent pubics, recurring anyway only in one of the briefest flickers.

She went to her room to remove physical temptation and spare herself renewed mental shame, but knew she was listening for movements: ostensibly Mother's. But Mother's 'insomnia' allowed her the luxury of rising late, so there was not much likelihood that she would accuse you of chasing after a professor.

He returned to his room, on no more than a short visit. The Princesse de Lascabanes dismissed her reflection from the dressing-table glass: it might have ended by unnerving her. She heard what sounded like final departure. Recklessly casual, she opened her own flimsy door.

'Are you working while you are here on Brumby Island?' Would the increased volume of her voice impinge on Mother's insomnia?

'I am invited here for a holiday, but yes, you could say I am working. I always work.'

One after another, the planks were buckling under the weight of his descent. She followed him down with the same intention of disembarking. Arrived on shore, the professor was starting out on what he had obviously planned as a solitary trek along the beach in the direction of the striated cliffs she had noticed the evening before.

'Shall I disturb you,' she asked, 'if I walk some of the way?'

He murmured no she would not disturb; 'I can shut myself off if necessary.'

The princess gladly accepted the arrangement they had reached. Though normally she did not wear a hat, she began putting on the big straw pancake she had brought to Brumby as protection from the tropic sun. She was feeling better—indeed, restored. Her shoes were unpractical, though: she must remain a plodder beside this sturdy, self-sufficient figure tamping the beach with his rawhide sandals. Even so, she managed to keep level physically; it was morally and intellectually that she tagged along some way behind, but would have consented in the circumstances to become a sumpter mule to this—yes, boorish male.

She risked the boorishness to ask, 'Will you tell me what ecology is about?'

He gasped at first; then he shrugged. 'To put it simply, you might say this is the study of the structure and function of nature.'

'And which part of such a vast and, to me, frightening subject is your special interest?'

Professor Pehl seemed to be compressing reserves of steam inside his fired cheeks. 'If I am known as a marine ecologist it is for my work on burrowing crustaceans of the neritic region.'

A fine drawn sigh from the Princesse de Lascabanes might have signified appreciation.

They continued marching, or plodding, while the professor stared ahead, from under bleached brows, out of pale eyes.

'Then, since you are interested, I have gone on to, and am presently investigating, benthic aggregations: that is, briefly, the types of level bottom substrata and the parallel groupings of invertebrates supported by them at similar depths in different geographical regions. These invertebrates make a chain of ecologically similar aggregations that replace one another according to latitude and temperature.'

Dorothy said, 'I understand.'

Professor Pehl turned on her his actually fervid eyes. 'I shall explain in greater detail when we are less heated,' he informed her.

Dorothy agreed to listen in the cool of the evening. At the same time she was amazed at herself: at her instinctive insincerity. Or not altogether insincere: almost any mission is better than none; and she could perhaps in some way serve, she would not dare hope to comfort, this boring and complacent man contingency had given her.

Professor Pehl had brought with him a clutch of plastic bags, and would stoop to examine shells, weeds, all kinds of anonymous sea rubbish, and sometimes pop a specimen into plastic; at one point he pounced on and bagged a distraught crab.

It was the crab which made Dorothy exclaim, 'Can't I at least carry the bags for you?'

Nothing would have struck the professor as more consistent with the nature of things, judging by the promptness with which he surrendered the specimen bags.

Gratitude for being allowed to make this small but positive contribution launched the princess into a dangerous recitative. 'Sometimes I feel I must take up a definite subject—I won't go so far as to say scientific—but something to make a study of—now that I'm at a loose end. I may as well tell you—after years of a a failing marriage—my husband left me. That is why I am here. I mean,' she quickly explained, 'why I came home—or perhaps I should say *back*, to Australia—to visit my mother.'

The professor was picking at a sea urchin: it smelled putrid and was of no interest. 'I think, if I count, I was invited to assist at more divorces than were marriages.'

The princess primly recovered herself. 'I'm sorry if I bore you. And in this case there is no divorce: my church does not recognize it. No ceremony could alter the fact that my husband is living with a woman not his wife. An American,' she made the extra effort to disclose.

'Ho! So you accuse your husband?'

'I don't *accuse*', here she blushed, 'anybody.'

'I am happy to hear it. Each party is almost always partially to blame.' Inside his overheated body, he remained only coldly, distantly, scientifically involved.

'Oh, yes.' She sighed. 'I expect you are right. We were both to blame.' She laughed bitterly, while not entirely believing what she had just admitted.

She was again enclosed by an emptiness. She dreaded being racked by the physical pain, though its less precise attendant, the fragmentation of mind and future, could inflict worse tortures. Through her own hovering mist, she stared at the coloured cliffs fluctuating in the haze of distance. Till the unreality of the cliffs became transformed into what she was sometimes forced to believe the only reality in life: that of the past, and more specifically, her own not particularly happy childhood. She was looking at the ornament in Nora's bedroom: the glass dome filled with layers of coloured sand, a Souvenir from the Isle of Wight, where as a girl its owner had vowed herself to slavery. Dorothy loved the parlourmaid; indeed she had loved most maids, for the mystery surrounding their private belongings, such as this striped dome, and crochet collars dipped in tea, and lockets preserving likenesses, or twists of greenish hair. Now as she toiled along the beach there rose around her scents she had forgotten, of innocence and trustfulness, out of an open deal drawer.

The Princesse de Lascabanes swept aside the curtain of perspiration distorting those already overpoignant cliffs. The heat was increasing. Professor Pehl had started dragging off his shirt, and as he did so, she was conscious of the aggressive stench, sweet but acrid, of fair-complexioned men. It was nauseating, or so she tried to persuade herself before dismissing her discovery.

The professor made no concessions to the woman who had tacked herself on, but continued striding. His hairless, noticeably developed calves, could have been trying to outdistance her. He did at times, and then at others, he was forced to stoop, to examine a potential specimen. So she caught up, and was again drugged by that penetrating male stench.

Under its influence she was moved to exclaim, 'Oh, your back — how horribly painful it looks, Professor!' Days of exposure to the sun had turned the more prominent parts into a scurf of skin, or salt codflesh.

He straightened up. 'The worst is over,' he said, but continued fiercely working his shoulderblades together.

'I expect it's too late to have any great effect,' she hesitated, 'but if you would like—I'll rub you with sunburn lotion—tonight.' Automatically she listened for Mother's comment.

'Thank you.' It was neither acceptance nor refusal.

She was exasperated: a Frenchman would have let her know the extent of her success or failure; but with this Norwegian she could not be sure.

Of course it did not matter to her, and to show it she asked, 'Do you suppose the cliffs over there are a mirage?' But either he did not understand, or he considered her remark too fanciful.

For a moment they were overtaken by the forest pressing through the carob scrub which had so far fringed the beach: great eucalypts, themselves shedding skin, and darker sassafras, were massing to obscure the tantalizing coloured cliffs of childhood. She noticed grass of the same green as moss, sombre, yet glowing, clotting in hummocks at the roots of some native cypresses. What began by giving her pleasure, ended as a virulent glare.

And the Norwegian decided to take up the subject she had offered in the first place. 'These cliffs beyond are where a ship was wrecked. The crew and officers were murdered.'

Yes she said she knew about the murder.

'And the master's wife taken by the blacks for their slave?' He was looking at her more with his teeth, it seemed, than with his eyes.

Yes she knew about that too.

The throbbing had begun again. For some unreasonable reason directionless fears were shooting through her. However seductive the moss at the roots of the deformed cypresses, she must not give in, nor to the increasing ejaculations of her head.

So she disentangled herself from the plastic bags. 'This is where I shall leave you.' As she tore free, one of the bags fell on the sand between them. 'My mother will be wondering where I am. I can't leave her indefinitely—not at her age,' she snickered.

The professor was more intent on retrieving the fallen specimen bag, but thought to gasp, 'Is Mrs Hunter an invalid, then?'

'No. Only elderly.'

Dorothy de Lascabanes and Edvard Pehl stood looking at each other from either end of this telescopic situation. Because hers was the wrong end, she could feel him staring into the pores of her skin, through them, and beyond.

After she had turned and moved away she looked back once, ostensibly to re-focus on those mesmeric cliffs. In the foreground the Norwegian's tattered shoulders were already exerting themselves on their solitary ecological trek.

The Princesse de Lascabanes was glad of her shoes after all: she found the return journey strewn with oyster shells.

Dorothy had noticed in the kitchen an antiquated telephone, its varnished box fastened to the wall, a receiver attached to a hook on one side. Its ancient air suggested that it might provide an even frailer lifeline than its more compact, outwardly more efficient, contemporary counterpart. There was a connection with the foresters' camp, one gathered; but calls to the outside world were made through the mainland town of Oxenbould.

When Dorothy reached the house, Helen Warming was standing at this antique telephone, her comfortable shoulders tensed inside the cotton frock, while Mother sat at the kitchen table making the formally sympathetic noises a sense of one's own superfluousness induces.

Helen was speaking with Sydney it seemed, the subject their eldest boy, 'Oh yes, I'm sure ... You've done everything that can be done. I know practically nothing of Sydney doctors, but accept your choice ... No, it's far better that he should go into hospital ... Yes – every care ... Yes yes ... We must wait for the results of the tests ... Thank you, Dugald – and Barbara. I'm truly grateful.'

Helen hung up. When she turned, her face was blotched, her eyes were streaming. She probably did not see the friends instinct forced her to address. 'Hugh collapsed. He's been taken to hospital.

They shan't be able to diagnose before they have the results of the tests,' she explained while walking out of the kitchen. 'I must find Jack.'

In the sense of inadequacy they had in common, and the increasing paroxysms of her own migraine, Dorothy was at first grateful for her mother's presence. For a shameful instant she almost fell on her knees: she could have buried her head in Mummy's lap; but managed to direct her anguish outward.

'Oh,' she cried, 'is there nothing I can do to help?' To demonstrate, not to Helen specifically, but to *everybody*, the love they suspected she was incapable of giving.

Mother said, 'Nothing, Dorothy. There's nothing you can do, dear – except try to control yourself.' She was becoming absorbed in contemplation of her own lustrous fingernails.

'If you aren't *intolerable*! And as usual, right! There's nothing I can do for anyone. I should have gone all the way – as the professor wanted me to on this expedition.'

'You'll only make it worse, dear, if you work yourself up emotionally. I advise you to go and lie down.'

'That is something I have no intention of doing. Who knows – Helen may find she needs me after all.'

Her rage might have erupted ceilingwards if Jack Warming had not come in. Like Helen, he no longer saw these guests. He began tinkering with the phone, talking with the mainland, organizing. There was a promise of the helicopter, at Brumby airstrip, at two; this should allow them to join the afternoon flight from Oxenbould to the south.

Temporarily relieved, their host was able to concentrate on his guests' future. 'Though we shan't be here, it needn't prevent you enjoying the rest of your holiday. There's food enough to see you through a couple of days. Ask the forestry people to help when you have to renew supplies; they'll ferry anything across from the mainland.' He showed them how to re-fill the two laborious kerosene refrigerators. 'You'll find wine in the bunker, there, behind the house. I rely on you, Elizabeth, and Dorothy, both of you, to be kind to the professor whatever your private opinions.' Jack even laughed.

In the circumstances it was a plan nobody could reject, and towards the time the helicopter was expected, Edvard Pehl, who had returned from his expedition, prepared to run the Warmings and their two silenced children down to the strip.

Elizabeth Hunter stood on the veranda waving a scarf. She called out they could rely on her — and Dorothy. It was a flamingo scarf, the colour also of sunsets, which made the gesture more nostalgic, if not fateful.

Because there was nothing else to do, the princess rested during the heat of the afternoon. In her room the other end of the veranda Elizabeth Hunter was no doubt resting too. If one could care. And Edvard Pehl?

Dorothy turned a cheek to the rather coarse gritty pillow its scuffed-up skin salt-smelling sea-rinsed that is where She had it over most others insomnia rinses out the wrinkles the tide of years erodes but only imperceptibly in her case not in a hundred.

A hundred eyelashes are distinctly becoming Dorothy Hunter. Never oh Lord anything but. She must have slept for she had dreamt of something if she could remember. She got up as the light was waning. The pillow had scored her face and left it looking like a washboard. After she had sponged it with soft though tepid rainwater from the jug, and put on a dress nobody could have seen before, she started on a walk, this time in a northerly direction, along the beach at first, then pushing inland through scrub, towards the darker rain forest. Till the trees began to frighten her. It was the light. She saw a man, nobody recognizable, in fact most improbable. Though there were the men up at the forester's camp. There was, she became convinced, a stench of man in the undergrowth.

After making her discovery she scrambled down, back to the beach, to return to the house. The sun was setting: this bronze tyrant lowered into the flamingo litter and encircling host of haze-blue trees. The splendours which were being enacted kindled tongues of expectancy in her, for the dissertation he – Edvard, had promised for the evening. Though she also swallowed a giggle or two: what if his benthic aggregations should put her to sleep?

Then in the dusk she caught sight of an actual man, head down, crunching towards her, and from the thickset body, and the intense seriousness of his mission, knew it could only be Professor Pehl.

'Ah, you are there!' The lightening of tone, she felt, was intended to convey pleasure. 'I have come to bring you,' he announced while marching to a halt.

'That is kind – thoughtful of you.' She was genuinely touched by this, after all, amiable Norwegian.

Walking beside her he proceeded to explain, 'Yes, your mother has sent me. She has seen you walk along the beach, and now fears for your whereabouts.'

'She needn't have worried,' the Princesse de Lascabanes replied. 'I've managed to survive till now without help. However old and wise parents may grow, reasonableness is a virtue few of them seem to develop.'

She shut up at once, as though finding her own contribution to reason had curdled; but the professor showed no sign of having detected a prig.

'I have caught some fish,' he was pleased to confess, 'which Mrs Hunter will cook for us.'

(Wonder what Mother will make of the fish, beyond the big tra-la?)

They walked on, blissfully alone, through the forests of Norway. He was telling her about the birches and aspens; rowan berries were clustered overhead; cold air blew funnelling down from the glacier higher up, making her twitch closer the folds of a long heather-tinted cape.

When the actual beach over which they were squelching, began thundering behind, then around them, sand hissing, spirting, flying in great veils – whinnying, it seemed, finally.

'It is these horses!' the professor called in a loud but unsteady voice. 'Oh, the brumbies of Brumby!' she shouted back between gusts of nervous laughter.

On reaching them the horses propped for an instant; a couple of them reared; others wheeled and spun into spiralling shadows; there was the sound of hooves striking on hide, bone, stone; a flash of sparks, and of teeth tearing at the dusk.

Edvard Pehl and Dorothy de Lascabanes stood supporting each other. She could feel his thick body breathing against her negligible breasts and palpitating ribs, while outside their physical envelops their minds flapped around in bewilderment and fright.

Then the brumbies had passed, lunging and stampeding farther down the beach, kicking up their heels, some of them audibly breaking wind.

'Were you afraid?' his trembling voice laughingly inquired.

'Nohh!' If she had been honest she would have answered: I was glad of you; I was glad even of your trembling; but would have been equally glad of someone else, provided that person was a man.

They walked on. He continued in possession of a hand he had grabbed hold of at a moment of crisis, until he realized; and dropped it.

They walked, and Professor Pehl started pointing. 'There, you see, is a light.' It sounded as though he was spitting with excitement brought on no doubt by relief after fear. 'Mrs Hunter has lit a lamp.'

'I dare say. I'm surprised they haven't electricity. Lousy with money as they are.' In her case, relief had dredged up the slang of her youth. 'Haven't you noticed how the very rich so often stint themselves of the obvious?'

The professor did not appear to be listening, or not to her. 'Is she a musician—Mrs Hunter?'

'No.'

'I swear I have heard the Warmings' piano.'

'Oh—well—when I say "not a musician", I can remember her playing the piano—yes—when we were children. As a matter of fact, she was pretty awful at it.'

'I was sure I have heard a piano.'

Now that she was warned, and reminded, Dorothy too, could hear. Somebody was very deliberately 'playing the piano'. It came through the dark, sad and monotonous and maddening. It was Mother hammering away at that same old nocturne—whose was it? (*I got it from Miss Hands. Every Thursday they drove me into Gogong. I was to learn the piano, along with other accomplishments.*) Still hammering, she managed to intensify the ambivalence of a tropical evening. Her tenacity was remarkable: it explained not only her worldly success, but also perhaps her only slightly faltering beauty.

Elizabeth Hunter had opened up what was officially the living-room. Under Helen, they had congregated almost exclusively in the kitchen, in an atmosphere of fry and good-fellowship. Elizabeth's accession promised subtler nuances. She had stood a pair of candles on the old cottage piano, and further tricked it out with a piece of music, the banality of which, together with a certain hypnotic sweetness, partly accounted for its being a performer's first choice when shaking the dust off a long neglected talent.

She might have appeared to greater advantage if the piano had been a concert grand set in a waste of uncluttered carpet. As it was, however high she raised her head, exposing her famous throat, her lily neck, the size of the instrument and the rather warped, salt-cured keys, made it look more as though she were hunching her shoulders over some harmonium. There was her back though, white amongst the shadows, and light in her hair, and she had obviously dressed herself for an occasion, in a long white robe of raw silk, of unbroken fall if it had not been for a corded girdle, and faint flutings which gave her slenderness an architecture.

The dress was one Dorothy could not remember. She decided not to notice it again. Nor listen to the wretched hammered nocturne.

She said in her harshest voice, 'Shall I fetch you a drink, professor? After being almost trampled to death I feel we need something strong to revive us.'

'Trampled? *How?*' Elizabeth Hunter did not turn because she was having a fight with the treble.

Music seemed to excite Professor Pehl. 'It is great chance, Mrs Hunter, that you have this gift, and can entertain us.'

She bowed her head, and broke off playing only then. 'But how,' she asked, turning to face them, 'were you nearly trampled?' A vague concern troubled her candle-lit surface.

'It was these wild horses which galloped past us down the beach.' Professor Pehl got it over as briefly as possible. 'But tell me, Mrs Hunter, you who perform the piano, what persuades you to waste your time on this mediocre composer Field?' He aimed his perceptiveness like a dart which the target must gladly suffer.

'I play him because he is easy,' she admitted with exquisitely serious candour, before allowing the smile to come, 'and leisurely enough to show off one's wrists.'

Dorothy went to get the drinks. When she returned, Mother was explaining the insignificance of her gift, while Edvard Pehl had developed an itch to discuss Brahms.

'At least we have music in common,' Mrs Hunter said. 'I shan't have to make a fool of myself trying to take an interest in – science.'

The professor laughed so vibrantly he made the candle flames shudder on their wicks.

Mrs Hunter modestly ignored her success. 'Amuse him, Dorothy, while I go and cook the fish.' In passing, she draped herself for a moment on this difficult child. 'The brumbies! How fortunate I sent you to fetch her, Professor.' Could some of Mother's concern have been sincere? 'I was somehow told that danger was in store for Dorothy.' She kissed a bony cheek with what could have been tenderness.

Dorothy was silent; and Elizabeth Hunter, silent too, left for the kitchen. She was barefooted, her daughter realized with disgust.

What had brought on coldness in the Princesse de Lascabanes provoked a restlessness in Professor Pehl. As he roamed around the room guzzling his drink (many Norwegians, she had read, were incurable alcoholics) he asked while mopping the sweat from his forehead, 'Has the temperature perhaps fallen? I think I hear a wind has arisen.'

397

'Not that I've noticed.' She could not make it cold enough.

The professor announced he was going to put on a coat, and came back wearing a linen jacket, all creases, as though dragged straight out of a suitcase, or more likely, a rucksack. But the coat was Edvard Pehl's contribution to dressiness, and the colour, ultramarine, emphasized the blue as well as the clear whites of his eyes. (Bitterly, Dorothy visualized a figure equipped for a path winding round a fjord: the rucksack needless to say, hobnailed boots, woven tie, and a meerschaum.)

'This is better!' As he settled his shoulders in the creased jacket he seemed to be angling for a compliment, which he did not get from the princess: she had been made too ashamed by her novelettish fantasy.

When the cook called from the kitchen, 'Ed-*vard*? I shall call you "Edvard", shan't I? These magnificent fish haven't been scaled, and I think — don't you? it's a man's job to scale the fish.'

So Madame de Lascabanes found herself alone. Only she had failed to dress in celebration of the fish caught by Edvard Pehl. Or was it the contingency which had brought all three of them together in this unlikely house beside the sea? Or simply, Elizabeth Hunter's voracious beauty and vanity?

Whatever else, Mother had transformed 'Ed-*vard*'s magnificent catch' into a work of art: she had grilled it, and laid it on a bed of wild fennel, and strewn round the border of a fairly common, chipped dish a confetti of native flowers.

On the wings of her second whiskey, the Princesse de Lascabanes was taken with a sombre glee. 'Do you realize that for every fish cooked, a still life is sacrificed?' When she fell foul of her darker humours. 'Or has it been said by someone else?'

Neither Edvard nor Elizabeth could give attention enough to affirm or contradict.

As though a martyr to the appetites of others, Mother was no more than picking at her fish; whereas Edvard frankly stuffed his mouth, then fossicked for bones with his fingers, lips grown shiny with gluttony and oil.

He cried, 'The head is always best!' and seized the largest.

Though she lowered her eyelids, Elizabeth Hunter seemed prepared to accept whatever behaviour might demonstrate a man's rights.

If Dorothy too, only picked at her fish, it was for a different reason: she believed she could detect, between her teeth, traces of sand. Slightly appeased by this flaw in what should have been perfection, another thought kept recurring: that the cook might be practising her art, not for art's sake, but for immoral purposes.

Because why leave off her shoes? In Helen Warming's case, it was from force of habit and living in a hot climate. But Elizabeth Hunter had done it to impress, if not to seduce. She was sitting sideways at the table, sipping the wine she had brought up from the bunker, exposing her slender, miraculously unspoilt feet from beneath the white, raw-silk hem. Her feet had the tones of tuberoses.

(Why are others given the physical attributes which belong to your true, invisible, hence unappreciated self?)

The white of the throat was mottled with green to golden reflections as the wine she was holding floated in the glass. 'Isn't it a bit sweet?' she asked. 'That slight *Spritz* is interesting, however.'

Perhaps she had overdone it; she threw back her head and more than sighed, she whimpered, 'That poor child!'

'Which child are you referring to, Mrs Hunter?' The professor was gouging the last revolting fragment of jelly out of a fish's skull.

'Why, the Warmings's of course! That boy who's developed God knows what—polio? leukaemia even!'

'Oh—no!' Dorothy dug the points of her elbows into the table: she was weeping not only for the good Warmings's innocent child, but for her own intransigent, and worse still, Mother's possibly compassionate nature.

Professor Pehl remained more equable than either of them. 'It is very unfortunate, that is for sure. But medicine is making all the time remarkable advances.' He licked the juices from his knife, and having cleaned it, propped the blade against the edge of his plate.

He saw there was a pineapple to come. Mrs Hunter had torn out the flesh, and returned it to the shell, and replaced the crown of stylized leaves. Now when she lifted the lid, an insidiously sugared perfume mingled with the somewhat hostile smell of bruised fennel and the stench of charred, oil-tinctured fishskin.

For some reason Mrs Hunter and her daughter barely touched the pineapple, while watching Professor Pehl feasting on its jagged flesh.

Tonight the moon was glinting green above black water, the princess noticed, and could have lingered, brooding over this capricious image, together with the injustices to which a sensitive human being is inevitably subjected.

Till Dorothy, in redemptive mood, jumped up and as good as insisted, 'Why don't you let me do the washing up?'

Elizabeth Hunter made the appropriate murmurs by which acceptance is disguised as protest, while the professor, as replete male of some importance, could see no reason for dismissing the suggestion. So, when he had finished picking his teeth from behind a formal hand, he bowed, and followed Mrs Hunter, not without actually sidestepping the visible thoughts of this Princesse de Lascabanes who had already taken up her duties at the sink.

Mother's voice on the veranda floated like the flamingo scarf with which she had waved the Warmings to their son's sickbed. 'Obliging of the moon always to do the right thing in landscapes like these.'

By the time the princess had finished the washing up (which failed to purge her of her spleen as she had hoped) the piano was at work again, though with a masculine authority, if not male heaviness. Hardly musical herself, Dorothy could only guess at Brahms, by the clotted chords, and what she recognized as an unmistakeably Germanic-skittish *brio*, as she slung the dishes around, and wiped a fleck of offending detergent off her upper lip. As a Frenchwoman she was bound to condemn the Germanic; as an Australian daughter she was contemptuous of a mother who could lie by moonlight on a chaise longue (where else would Elizabeth Hunter have chosen?)

flicking her ankle at the music whenever she thought about it, making the tuberose tones come and go in her naked feet.

Her martyrdom folded, or stacked to drain, Dorothy went outside. The screen door clashed harshly with the mood Elizabeth Hunter would have wished to invoke. Her daughter hugged her fish-scales and a patch of sticky pineapple juice: they were honest humiliations at least. She went and sat on the higher ground outside the bunker where the Warmings stored their wine.

If he failed to scent you out by your fishy fumes, you would identify him by his characteristic reek and the sound of blunt toes exploring the formless surroundings. *Here I am—Edvard—your skiapod.* Not surprising he should hesitate; and still clogged besides, with Brahms. *My which is it you say?* Laughter—by courtesy of Mother (you can't dispense with her entirely.) *Fish shadows are more substantial than they seem—as you, an expert, must know.*

He did. Her own no more than shadowy innuendo of a body had been pinned down, flattened flatter surely, by his substantial weight.

Dorothy de Lascabanes had so appalled herself that she sat up holding her elbows, while the grass, starved and vindictive, continued tilting at her thighs through her dress. Brahms must have stuck somewhere in mid-actuality; voices had broken out instead, in the kitchen, only a short distance from where she was aching on a hummock.

In different circumstances, Dorothy felt, she would not have allowed herself to eavesdrop. Now she was too frustrated to resist. There was a barrel, moreover, visible amongst the stilts on which the house was raised.

It did occur to the Princesse de Lascabanes: what if I topple off the barrel? tear my leg on a rusty nail? *Quelle horreur*—tetanus at least! But hearing, and eventually seeing from eye level as she clung to the sill, reinforced her limbs with steel.

Without his shirt, Edvard Pehl was seated astride a kitchen chair, arms folded along its back, one cheek resting on a forearm, eyes closed in what the expression of his face suggested must be bliss.

The princess almost whinged in anguish: there, standing over him, bottle in hand, was Elizabeth Hunter, anointing this peeling, though still inflamed Viking with what appeared to be calamine lotion.

'Don't you find it soothing, Edvard?'

The professor answered, 'Yes,' or barely: it reached Dorothy as '*esss*', the pearly tips of his little-boy's teeth for a moment visible in his man's flaming face.

She was infuriated. But of course Mother was to blame.

Elizabeth Hunter must have had faith in her own healing powers: she was radiant with charisma. 'You poor dear!' she murmured, as she stroked the scruffy, burnt back. 'Somebody should have attended to you before. Before the worst.'

Edvard Pehl did not answer, but snuggled visibly against the chair.

And Elizabeth Hunter poured herself another pink handful, and clapped it, but ever so gently, between the suffering shoulderblades. 'There's nothing like calamine for driving out the fire.' Now it was she who closed her eyes, as she raised her face, willing the inflammation to subside.

The Princesse de Lascabanes was so incensed she could feel the barrel tottering under her, and did not care.

'You will tell me if I'm hurting you, Edvard?' Mother commanded, but her little boy only sighed, and smiled out of the cushions of his own dreaming flesh.

After that there was the clop clop of renewed handfuls of calamine lotion.

As Mother stroked and soothed, her white, classic form poised at an admirably cool, though unconvincing, parallel distance from the body to which she was ministering, you could tell from her face that she was preparing to outdo the night, with its background of sea and moon on the one hand, and on the other, scrub stirring, wings brushing, frogs croaking out of damp-leather throats (also, alas, the creaking of a barrel). Dorothy could tell that Mother was about to change the slide in her magic lantern, and trembled to discover what its successor might be.

Click! Here it was, as the face revealed, and the raised voice commented, not on a single image, but a whole series, while preserving a tone both velvety and dark.

'Do you know, Edvard, there's a dream I dream—on and off;' and her hand encouraged a deeper participation in this recurring velvet. 'Naturally the details vary, but always in my dream I am walking on the bed of the sea.'

She paused until her fellow sleeper stirred.

'I expect those clever people who *know*, would accuse me of all kinds of obscene desires. But there—I can't avoid telling the truth—and the truth was always beautiful,' the hand insisted.

Whether she had put her patient into such a dead sleep that her dream narrative would be wasted on him, it looked unimportant to Elizabeth Hunter, herself once again walking on the sea bed.

She had grown so luminous even Dorothy, perched on her barrel, was precariously spellbound.

'What I remember in particular from each of these dreams is the light I found below—sometimes flowing around me—like water—then, on other occasions, as though emanating from myself: I was playing a single beam on objects I thought might be of interest.'

Without opening his eyes or shifting position, Professor Pehl announced in his most direct voice, 'Many deep-sea animals are provided with luminescent organs, you know, to enable them to produce the light they need. Some fish use this light to attract their prey.' Still without opening his eyes, the lines around them deeply engraved by the seriousness of the subject, he asked, 'Were you, in the dreams, a fish, Mrs Hunter?'

Mother looked only fairly amused; nor could Dorothy blame her, but would not go so far as admitting they might have united in a 'good laugh' at the expense of this turgid male—or human turbot (the princess quietly sniggered at her own conceit).

When Elizabeth Hunter continued. 'How can I say? One is always rather fluid in a dream. Or if I took on a form, I don't believe I was ever more than a skiapod.'

Dorothy was breathless with resentment for what she herself

could no more than half-remember, had perhaps only half-discovered—on the banks of the Seine? in dreams? as part of that greatest of all obsessions, childhood? and how could Elizabeth Hunter have got possession of anything so secret? Only Mother was capable of slicing in half what amounted to a psyche, then expecting the rightful owner to share.

Professor Pehl also seemed surprised: his eyes had flickered open. 'A what did you say, Mrs Hunter?'

'Oh, a kind of shadowy fish, but with a woman's face. The face was not shadowy. Or some of it at least was painfully distinct. I saw it years ago in a drawing, and it stayed with me. You couldn't say the expression looked deceitful, or if it was, you had to forgive, because it was in search of something it would probably never find.'

The Princesse de Lascabanes heard her own dry gasps; possibilities were shooting, like minute, brilliant, electric fish, in and out of her sunken skull; she heard her ribs fluttering against the equally frail boards of a rickety house; but the professor closed his eyes again because Mrs Hunter had led the conversation outside his sphere of interest.

'There *were* fish of course—real ones. I was often surrounded by them. Enormous creatures. All the fish I saw were in fact much larger than myself. It should have been frightening. But I don't think I was ever frightened.'

The professor remained equally calm, as might have been expected on his own ground. 'A characteristic of some deep-sea fish is the enormous mouth. It makes it possible for them to swallow prey much larger than themselves. A very practical arrangement: meals are few and far between.' Because it was meant to be a joke, he laughed.

Though Dorothy doubted whether this turbot of a man, eyelids again closed, could possibly have seen the point of his own remark, she was rejoiced: her equilibrium had been restored.

Mother only smiled as she drew her hand back and forth, very slowly, three or four times, across the small of her patient's back; if you had not known more, she might have been wiping him off.

404

The professor suddenly opened his eyes, their expression so concentrated the tone of their blue was that of anger. 'Did you ever come across any interesting invertebrates at the level to which your dreams have taken you?'

'No. Definitely, no. I was never interested in invertebrates.'

Professor Pehl looked momentarily incredulous. 'They are the most greatest interest in my life,' he confessed. 'It is remarkable,' he added, 'that a woman of your intellect have been born with no inclination to science. I would be happy if you would grant me time to acquaint you at least with my special subject. That way is it only possible for you to get to know me.'

Elizabeth Hunter may have been temporarily daunted by the prospect of a walk hand in hand with Edvard Pehl amongst the invertebrates, for she altered course. 'Poor Dorothy,' she suddenly said, out of her conscience, 'where can she be? She's so good. I do hope she hasn't taken offence. She's going through a difficult time, you know.'

'So I've noticed.'

They both slightly laughed for the knowledge they shared.

Dorothy felt sick from the physical distaste this peeling Norwegian roused in her, as well as morally disgusted by a mother's perfidy. Though Professor Pehl was prudently buttoning up his shirt, you did not believe 'that a man *au fond* so stupid, however 'distinguished', could avoid providing Elizabeth Hunter with her next meal. If he had survived courtship by calamine lotion, and that floodlit tour of the sea bed, it was because she was saving him up: to blind him with the first glimpse of her still formidably sensual body.

The Princesse de Lascabanes could not spider down quickly enough from off her barrel; she did not care who might overhear its creaking; she already looked too abject, worse in her own eyes than in the eyes of others. Lust and disgust are one, she suspected, the same shooting pain in both mind and body. Love: she must learn love. Tearing off some leaves, she plastered them on her forehead; if she could only have parcelled her entire head in leaves, and dropped

405

it in the sea, together with all memories of husband 'lover' mother
SELF.

So she continued blundering around in despair, as well as through
the actual dark, till restrained by thought of the wild horses galloping along the beach. It would be wiser to return, she decided; I hate
to be hurt.

Once during the night the horses might have galloped past:
again her feet were taking root in sand, and the arms offering protection trussed their common fear tighter.

She did not wake from what could hardly be called sleep. Somebody—Mother, was it? yes, Mother had come to spy.

'Dorothy? I've been worried. I had to satisfy myself you're here.'

'*Satisfy* yourself?' It was a matter for laughter.

'Why not? Aren't I your mother?'

Dorothy's laughter grew more rackety.

Till Elizabeth Hunter gave warning. 'Ssh! You'll wake him.
Don't you know he's in the next room?'

'Yes, I know. *Officially* he is! Isn't he?' She did not know; she
knew she was babbling.

'My poor darling, if only I could help you! If you would have
confidence in me.'

Oh yes! But without confidence in yourself you could not have
confidence in others, least of all your mum—*Mother.*

For a moment it seemed as though Elizabeth Hunter would try to
insinuate her physical self into this void where trust should have
been: she began stroking; she was threatening to hug; while
Dorothy prepared to resist: she must not allow herself to be seduced
by anyone so expert in the art—by anyone, for that matter.

'Thank you—Mother. I am quite well—only tired. Thank you,
I'll see you in the morning.' If she could lie, so could you.

'At least you'll allow me, I hope, to kiss you goodnight.'

You submitted to it. She smelled still of calamine.

When her mother had gone Dorothy de Lascabanes lay and
composed a schedule which had so far only erupted in her head by
fragments. While through the wall a snore broke. A Norwegian

snore could bore a hole. Her beloved, hateful Hubert had never succeeded in piercing her head.

But the princess survived the night, and on this morning fore-stalled Professor Pehl in the kitchen. That it was more than a fore-stalling, even this stupid, self-centred man must see. Anyway he kept looking at her with the eyes of a hangover, when he, a Scan-dinavian too, had not been in the slightest drunk. He was looking at her because, without being told, he had noticed she was dressed for better things; and what better than departure?

'Professor Pehl,' she began, 'I have a favour to ask.'

A favour so evidently stern might have made a less phlegmatic man recoil.

'I have been in touch with the mainland,' she said. 'The helicopter will come for me at ten. I would like you to drive me to the airstrip as soon as you have finished your coffee.' She poured it for him; *pas d'omelette aujourd'hui.*

The professor could have experienced a shock. 'You are leaving us, then?'

Without answering, she began picking over the things at the sink; till recognizing in her dry precision the movements of some bird, possibly a guinea hen, she gave up.

The professor had scalded himself on the coffee. 'If we leave presently, as you wish, we will have the most of three hours to wait for this helicopter.'

'I don't expect you to keep me company in waiting. We might exasperate each other.'

He was so mystified, so anxious to please, he scalded himself a second time. 'I do not understand what we have done to you.' Coffee bubbled at his puzzled nostrils.

'Nothing.' She composed her lips in two strips which the hour and an absence of lipstick failed to make more communicative.

While they were driving down through the flickering trees and stationary ropes and trapezes of vines, he dared ask her, 'Have you informed Mrs Hunter?'

'No. And I must ask you not to tell her, Professor.'

'But she is your mother,' he groaned.

'What of it?' Then she shrieked, 'I am not her doll, am I? Or am I?'

They were driving through the clearing in which the forestry workers were camped. Several of them had come out of the Nissen hut and were washing mugs and plates in a trough. Peering through the leather visors of their faces they had more than ever the air of zombies.

Were they expecting to be waved at? The Princesse de Lascabanes waved, describing an arc wide enough for men of a lower order to interpret as heartiness. The men did not wave back.

When the nonchalant car reached the airstrip, and the princess was standing beside her suitcase, holding the superfluous straw hat, she thanked Professor Pehl, and added, 'My mother won't fail you: she'll keep you entertained, I'm sure.'

Then Madame de Lascabanes sat down on a log at the edge of the field and began to spend her several hours. The heat had already begun pricking at the silence. The ants were climbing up her stockings. She opened her mouth, but the bitter drought inside was increased the more she sucked and gulped. Again she could feel Mother, rustling around her in the dark room, offering the suspect sponge people call affection. She saw the men standing in the clearing, not waving, but watching.

Thank God for the helicopter, though it would have the pilot in it; blessed the anonymity which would clothe her at last in the great plane flying her back with speed and discretion to Europe.

'What was that man's name, dear?'

'Which man, Mother?'

'You know—the Norwegian—when somebody invited us to an island.'

Standing at her mother's window in Moreton Drive waiting for the brother who could not keep an appointment. Madame de Lascabanes was no longer sure she had reached the pitch of ruthlessness she had sensed that morning in her dressing-table glass. Certainly

408

the several looking-glasses in Mother's room, survivors from a hey-day of vanity, disclosed nothing that might suggest vacillation. (Ah, but you know yourself better than any glass. And how much does Mother know? Whatever the old thing remembered of Brumby Island, she had handed you a whole armoury of weapons; if you had the courage to choose and use the most vicious of them.)

'Pehl—Edvard *Pehl* was the name.'

Mrs Hunter kicked at the upper sheet. 'I'm surprised you remember—after all this time. But you're young, Dorothy—anyway, younger. And perhaps you were fond of the—*ecologist*?'

Dorothy swallowed: keep your rage from exploding till after Basil's arrival. 'I thought he was *your* interest, Mother.'

'I had to do my duty by him, stupid though he was.'

Dorothy longed to reply: Women of seventy can't afford to reject a man simply because of his stupidity; but in spite of keeping Brumby in mind, she was not brutal enough; nor was Mother, who might have dealt a counterthrust: For a plain woman of any age, though especially while in her Frightful Forties, a man's stupidity is a negligible fault.

Well, all that was over now: neither of you would ever be tempted again by a man. Or would they tempt Elizabeth Hunter's mummy?

'It was the island I loved, Dorothy. After you left I got to know it. After I had been deserted—and reduced to shreds—not that it mattered: I was prepared for my life to be taken from me. Instead the birds accepted to eat out of my hands. There was no sign of hatred or fear while we were—encircled. What saved me was noticing a bird impaled on a tree. It must have been blown against the sharp spike left by a branch which had snapped off. I think I was reminded that one can't escape suffering. Though it's only human to try to escape it. So I took refuge. Again, it was the dead bird reminding me the storm might not have passed. Afterwards I found out—the man told me—the bird was a noddy.'

So truth was beginning to seep through this vision of an island conjured up by a senile mind. 'Who told you, Mother? If, as you say, you were deserted?'

'It must have been the man driving the lorry.'

Madame de Lascabanes was so enraged by this piece of deceitful evasion she understood the urge to commit physical murder, when up till now the thought of gently prising a confused soul out of an exhausted body had been enough to cause an attack of moral misgivings. The voices she heard approaching from the other side of the door were, in the circumstances, godsent.

Whereas the nurse must have decided to forget the princess was lurking in her patient's bedroom and to shut the door smartly on admitting the latest and far more acceptable caller, Sir Basil Hunter looked as though he could not wait to shake off his tedious guide and take his sister by the hands. This, and the expression of moist-eyed, hesitant inquiry Basil was wearing, surprised, then charmed Dorothy. In every other respect his appearance advertised masculine self-command: freshly shaven cheeks giving off gusts of an aggressive, though not disagreeably pungent lotion; hair cleverly trimmed to within an inch of Romantic excess; clothes pressed or laundered to a degree that the man of the world demands, then ignores.

At the reunion after their independent return, Dorothy had been disturbed on finding Basil reminiscent of Hubert. Now she was not at all reminded. In spite of the dreadful intimacies forced on her by the man with whom she still considered herself spiritually united, she had never arrived at the real Hubert. Each meeting might have been the first, in which hope of reciprocal love was dissolved by her breathless adoration, and moral qualms anticipated physical repulsion. None of which could enter into her relationship with a brother whose moist eye in the assured façade was a peephole she would not hesitate to use; in fact, she had already peeped, and found that this was a Basil she knew better than the mirror knew him. She knew him, she thought, as she knew her actual self, as opposed to the one which others saw. She even found herself warming towards their mother for having made a less animal version of identical twins: mutually appreciative siblings.

(Oh no, Mother must, of course, be resisted at every instant. Remember the island, the calamine lotion, the skiapod equipped with a mouth large enough to swallow an ecologist.)

Basil did not greet their mother, perhaps because guilty of arriving late and in a rush, though Dorothy preferred to take it as a sign that he meant business.

Till he shook her by asking, 'Have you started anything, Dorothy?' when nobody knew for certain that Elizabeth Hunter was deaf.

'No. Why should I? Haven't I been waiting for you?' Her anger might have returned, but she could sense shudders appealing from the sibling conscience to her own.

Mother herself helped them out of their impasse. 'I never saw you act, Basil. When there was the opportunity — after that de Lascabanes wedding — when we went across and spent a few weeks in London — I couldn't bring myself to go to the theatre. You were in something at the time, too. You were clever enough always to be *in* something. But I just wasn't brave enough to find out for myself.'

'The only time you were not brave, I should say.' Sir Basil Hunter had recovered his jewelled scabbard, his sleeves sumptuous with fur. 'I expect you were busy, Mother darling, trying on hats, and patiently enduring all those fittings at the dressmakers'.' A particularly splendid movement brought him *from L.C. to bedside, C.*, laughter glistening on the points of his teeth.

Dorothy was reassured on finding the teeth pointed — if they were not false: that day at the solicitors, before Basil had her sympathy, she had decided some of them were false.

Elizabeth Hunter's gums were grinning in her son's direction. 'Yes, the hats and dresses! You're laughing at me. But hadn't I my own art to consider? Admittedly a minor one.' As she stirred, there was a faint rustling of stale perfumes; light clashed with light and was ground still finer, brighter; the air was swizzled. 'What really prevented me going to the theatre,' she sneezed as though memory had pricked her eroded nostrils, 'was the thought that I mightn't find perfection—which is what I have always looked for—wanted so desperately to find, in my children.'

Dorothy could no longer bear to look at Mother, but saw that Basil had been stung; which was all to the good.

When Mother played her next. 'Your father went.' A card they had not expected, it strengthened her hand by the love they had withheld from a man there seemed no point in knowing.

Basil was in the position of one who still cannot tell how deeply he has been wounded. 'If Father saw me act, he must have given you a full report. Strange he didn't come round after the performance —unless he found so little to approve of.' On top of the social omission, an unenlightened judgment ruffled his actor's vanity.

'He didn't go round, I expect, because he was shy. Nor did he report on the performance. I tried to pump him—because half of me was curious to know. Well, he didn't utter a word. Alfred, you see, was a man of great delicacy.'

Basil licked the salt off his lips on deciding Mother's game was less cunning than fortuitous.

'They were both gentle, sensitive men, my husband and my father, and each died of his disappointments.' Elizabeth Hunter's eyes were staring like two saucers of frozen milk. 'Do you think I could have prevented any of their suffering?'

Again playing for compassion, she might have won it if Dorothy had not remembered.

'How can one tell? I hardly knew my father, and my grandfather was always only a name. Or a myth of failure and suicide. Oh, and one other thing—funny it should come back to me—that cuff link of his. Do you remember, Mother? The one I found under your bed. Rather an ugly object in brown agate, I think it was, in a heavy gold setting. Mother?'

Dorothy looked at Basil. Though he could not have known about her find, as her accomplice he must sense its importance, and that she should go carefully—or no, not even carefully now.

Mother's head protested against the pillow. 'No, I don't remember, dear. Do I?'

'Have you got your father's cuff links? In your jewel case perhaps?'

A claw, without its armour this morning, fumbled at Basil's hand for pity: Basil was the affectionate one. 'No, I don't know, Dorothy—whether I have them. There was too much to keep.' Basil had accepted the claw. 'As a matter of fact, I seem to remember, I threw the cuff link—into the park grass. You saw what an ugly thing it was.'

Dorothy looked away, and Basil knew it would be he who must drive the knife home: Sir Basil Hunter the Great Actor.

Seated beside the bed, still with the claw clasped in his experienced hand, against his breast (actually damned uncomfortable, on a little, tipsy chair, your guts pushed up into your thorax, the jockstrap pinching your balls) he began to blandish this ancient queen. 'Such a welter of morbid thoughts, whatever they amount to! I can't keep pace with them. Don't you feel—Mother darling—living alone in this great house full of associations, not all of them happy—does tend to make you morbid?'

Like a child at the dentist's, Elizabeth Hunter had clamped her jaws.

'What you must miss more than anything, I should have thought, is the company of your contemporaries. Which you could enjoy in some efficiently-run institution—or home, dear, home—such as I understand there is on the outskirts of Sydney.'

He looked at his sister. Who saw the sweat lying blue in the field of bluer, incipient stubble.

So it was her responsibility as well. 'Yes, Mother. As Basil says. Sympathetic company in bright surroundings. There's one place I've been told. And a garden. At the Thorogood Village. There's a *scented* garden laid out specially for those whose sight isn't of the best. I was told that by Cherry Cheeseman. You remember the Bullivants, Mother? Well, her mother ... ' The Princesse de Lascabanes did not normally perspire.

'I know, Dorothy. Violet Bullivant died at the Thorogood Village.'

'That was sad,' Dorothy admitted. 'But everybody dies eventually. Let us at least be realistic.'

'And you, darling,' Sir Basil added, carrying the blotched claw to his lips, 'will not die before it is time.'

'Not before my time,' Elizabeth Hunter's unclamped jaws agreed.

To her children she had become an enormously enlarged pulse dictating to the lesser, audible valves opening and closing in their own bodies.

'Something I found out,' she panted, 'on that island — after you had all run away — nothing will kill me before I am intended to die.'

If you could describe your storm; but you could not. You can never convey in words the utmost in experience. Whatever is given you to live, you alone can live, and re-live, and re-live, till it is gasped out of you.

So she lay gasping, as though the tide had almost fully receded from this estuary of sheets, while they watched her, she could tell, with their unregenerate, gulls' eyes.

She had got up earlier that morning: it must have been a changed light, the latticework of bird sounds, then an enormous span of wings spreading creaking (or was it a car?) compelling her. She had taken to wearing a minimum of clothes on the island. Although she had scarcely been near the beach, sand which had collected in them set up a dry, cleanly friction with her skin as she was putting them on. Round her hair, unkempt by now, she tied the flamingo scarf, before deciding to discard it. Would that slab of a Norwegian, or worse still, would Dorothy have thought you were wearing the scarf for a purpose? As you might have been: which was all the more reason for undoing the knot.

She laughed for the conspiracy she was having with herself.

Then she was alone. Not even herself for company.

Never one for self-pity, or not more than a normal ration, she snivelled a bit on reaching the veranda. She recognized her own type of useless, beautiful woman, whose husband had got the number of children required by convention from the body he had bought at an inflated price because he was over-loving, and regretted the contract — secretly (he was an honourable man) and perhaps died grieving over his lack of wisdom. She was a woman who had encouraged her lovers' lust; indeed she had made it inevitable; not in the Norwegian's case (she only half-wanted the Norwegian: he was peeling). Above all, she was a mother whose children had rejected her.

Oh God! Rooted to the veranda, she opened her mouth, and the sun blared back across the glass-inflected Pacific Ocean.

She had come across the coffee dregs in the kitchen when Professor Pehl drove up, between the bunker and the house, stopped the car, and got out.

She could not have felt less amiably disposed, but her upbringing and the dregs made her inquire automatically, 'Is that you, Professor? Will you drink a cup of coffee if I make it?'

He stood to attention beside that wholly utilitarian machine. 'Thank you. I have already drunk.'

His sobriety struck her as grisly.

So she bared her teeth while calling lightly, 'Where is that silly Dorothy my daughter?'

She regretted it: he returned her stare so seriously she might have lost not only Professor Benthic Aggregations Pehl, poor Princess Menopause de Lascabanes, Alfred the Good, Basil my Beloved Only Son, Athol Shreve the—ugh! Arnold the Pure—but Everyone.

Professor Pehl dutifully replied, 'I am not permitted to reveal the whereabouts of your princess daughter.'

He disappeared after that; and Elizabeth Hunter bowed her head.

Instead of brewing coffee for herself alone, she drank a draught of tepid water. Under her nails she could feel an irritant from the dregs her secretive daughter had bequeathed her.

Of course you could not altogether blame poor old Dorothy, what with that devious Frenchman, and now her unfortunate condition. Only natural that she should bear grudges, whether imaginary or justified, especially against a mother whose love of life often outstripped discretion, in the eyes of those who were drab and prickly.

415

To confess her faults (to herself) and to accept blame when nobody was there to insist on it, produced in Elizabeth Hunter a rare sense of freedom. As she wandered up past the bunker, past the abandoned Chevrolet, into the bush, she even went so far as to admit: in some ways I am a hypocrite, but knowing does not help matters; to be utterly honest, spontaneously sincere, one should have been born with an innocence I was not given. Which Alfred had.

Yet Alfred, not she, had been hurt, deceived, tortured, and finally destroyed. While she had continued demanding and receiving more than most women would have dared envisage. Even her beauty had only just begun to dim; her body remained supple at the age of seventy. For the first time she was disturbed by the mystery of her strength, of her elect life, not that frequently unconvincing part of it which she had already lived, but that which stretched ahead of her as far as the horizon and not even her own shadow in view.

Walking more humbly, as much for her solitariness as for the powers and honours so unreasonably conferred on her, she let herself be led into the cool depths of the rain forest, striped by the occasional light which fell between the shafts of its trees, rubbing past vines which had survived their writhing to become abstractions. It occurred to her she had read of elderly women lured into the scrub by an instinct for self-destruction, and of an old man driven mad after days imprisoned in a blackberry bush. Obviously none of this was reserved for her: she was too rational. So she went on.

Soon after setting out she had unpinned her hair, that most recalcitrant, though habitually controlled part of her. Now it floated round her face, almost completely veiling it at times, at others opening for her mind to surface and identify a foreign substance, or translate her present movements into recollections of another person's sensuality.

In a clearing she came across flowers: a variety of ground orchid, each tongue returning into the tufts of fine-drawn green sprouting from the gristle of its own sickle-shaped ear. Overjoyed at her find she got down on her knees: to insinuate herself into secrets, to pick, to devour, or thrust up her nostrils, or carry back to die on her dressing-table. When she discovered the desire to possess had left her.

Ah, but temporarily, and flowers. Sitting back on her haunches, taking a detached look, she knew she was still annoyed at Dorothy's behaviour, and irritated by that Norwegian, not only for his presence on Brumby Island, but for existing at all. She picked a blade of pale grass, and sucked at it, and wondered what Edvard Pehl could be doing at the moment.

By allowing her inescapably frivolous and, alas, corrupt nature the freedom of its silence, the forest had begun to oppress her: she could not believe, finally, in grace, only luck.

This was where she heard the sound of an axe. And more faintly, voices. She got up, not without a warning twinge. She was longing to talk to somebody, nobody, somebody quite simple, stupid even. She needed to reassure herself that she could still fit into the pattern of someone else's life.

She was soon given the opportunity to prove it. After blundering some way through the undergrowth she arrived at the spot where two men had felled a blackbutt. Peace and light were flooding in where violence had recently exploded. One of the men was systematically lopping minor branches off the desecrated crown; the other was tending a saw, filing its teeth, feeling, almost stroking the blade, with trembling hand.

At once Elizabeth Hunter realized it was going to be practically impossible to make herself credible. The man with the axe left off lopping. His stomach heaved under its hairy entanglement. His rather prominent eyes would have withdrawn deeper than the sockets allowed. A chain dangling from the waist of his thinner, stringier mate struck a slight music out of the saw he was holding.

'I heard the tree crash,' she claimed; when she hadn't. 'I came to see. May I watch?'

The pursy man mumbled something and returned to lopping, but delicately now. The stringy fellow laid down his saw, then thought better, and took it up again.

She breathed rather than spoke. 'Isn't it a wonderful smell?' Indeed, the heavy air was impregnated with bleeding sap. 'More than a smell—a perfume.'

The men laughed, but softly. She suspected they might not look at her after that.

She sat on the trunk just above the fatal wound they had made. 'And taste!' She did actually taste a chip from the tree, and might have dropped this transmuted wafer as quickly as she could; but managed to put it down instead. It slithered off the trunk and fell to the ground.

For herself she was again brittle and pretentious, but the two men appeared to be enjoying the unexpected.

The big fat one went tiptoeing alongside the trunk chopping through branches turned to butter. His thin mate had begun smearing the saw with oil, an operation he might have taken slower if she had not been there.

Undoubtedly neither of them would look at her again. Perhaps it was her loose hair. Or was she old? Or mad, perhaps?

Whatever it was, they respected it: the men were as reverent as a cloister of nuns.

'I expect you live over at the forestry camp.' A pointless remark, but one which she hoped might put them at their ease.

Yairs, they lived at the camp; they were employed by the Department.

'I'm staying with the Warmings.' It was too obvious, but she told. 'They had to leave. One of their boys was taken sick.'

The men probably knew this: telephone lines in remote places are usually public property; but the hairy belly murmured, 'Go on, eh?' out of regard for convention.

They still would not look at her; to do so might have been irreverent.

In the end she could only ask, 'Now if I start back in *that* direction shall I come out somewhere near the house?'

Yairs, they began to explain, their reverential arms making signposts, their blackened hands trembling from recent exertions.

Some of the hairy creature's sweat flung off his jowl on to the back of one of her hands. He realized, and looked embarrassed.

When she left them, they were smiling, but at the ground.

The walk back was monotonous. She would have liked to put up her hair now, but there was no means of fastening it since she had thrown away the pins. She went on. Just before entering the carob scrub which fringed the beach, she licked the back of her hand, sucking up her own salt together with what she liked to think the axeman's sweat, and went sweltering or weeping through the glare off sand and ocean. As it happened, she was not a great distance from the spindly house. She walked slowly, less than ever capable of explaining the gifts which were showered on her.

The house felt empty, though somebody had made use of the kitchen. It could only have been Professor Pehl: a sliver of corned beef fat on a plate and a scattering of crumbs on the oilcloth had been left for a woman to dispose of. The sulks, or else her migraine, would have prevented Dorothy contemplating food.

Elizabeth Hunter tore off a lettuce leaf, and cut herself a wedge of mousetrap cheese. Eating her blameless cheese she envied the Warmings their complementary lives; she even envied them their child's illness. In a burst of sympathy rather than inquisitiveness, she marched along the veranda to their room. They had barely stopped living in it, leaving off as they had, in haste and anguish. Behind curtains dragged together at the last moment, there was still a smell of privacy: Helen's powder on the dressing-table, Jack's shirt rolled in a ball in a dark corner. Children's faces looked at the intruder out of framed snapshots. Neither of her own children had looked her full in the face, either from photographs or in life.

It was really too irritating, not to say maddening.

'Dorothy?' When she reached the door which she knew must open to her, Mrs Hunter rattled the knob.

Now she was feeling old; she would be looking haggard: just how old and haggard Dorothy alone would see.

To get it over quickly, she sprang the door, and practically lurched into this narrow glaring box. Dorothy's room was so empty it might never have been inhabited.

Elizabeth Hunter could not have hated Dorothy more than she did at that moment. More than Dorothy, she hated Edvard Pehl for having a part in her daughter's defection. She was glad she had not washed up his insolent plate.

Till suddenly faced with her own insolence, her childishness, she returned to the kitchen, and scraped and washed the plate. The sliver of sweating fat, and the iron roof crackling at her in the language of heat, reminded her of the foresters, their misguided gentleness, and a reverence to which she was not entitled.

Because she was alone, she lay down and snoozed, or simply lay, during the afternoon. (If he was there at the other end of the house, he gave no sign.)

She was roused by hands, it seemed. No, by thin fingers twitching at the corrugated roof. Only wind after all.

She got up and washed herself as well as you can from a jug and basin. She powdered her revived skin. She anointed herself. Why not? Her life had been a ceremony. She put on the dress she had worn the night before. Though in fact old, age had not tarnished its splendour, nor blunted its fluting: like certain classic sculptures, the dress was designed not only to ravish the human eye, but to seduce time into relaxing its harshest law. Tonight she plaited her hair, and wound, or moulded it, into a crown; then bowed her head before slipping over it the gold and turquoise chain she had allowed the child to wear.

She dared only a quick look in the glass.

The wind had dropped. There was a breathlessness before sunset; irrelevant feathers of cloud were strewn on a white sky, just as she, at another level, was an irrelevant figure hanging around the veranda, living-room, kitchen, for no purpose she could think of, and in what was after all a ridiculous get-up. Well, she could cook something for the professor when he came: that would be purpose of a kind. She would make something simple, an omelette, say; though Dorothy had never approved of her omelettes. (You

420

were not prepared to join your French daughter in the cult of slime.)

Waiting, she sat down at the piano and listened to her own affectation hammering part of its way through the Field nocturne she had played last night (it was the only one she could remember). She had been waiting then for a man to approach and recognize that she had control over more than this hackneyed, girlhood piece, over music itself, and the threads of a brilliant sunset, and experience in general. Whereas now the most she could expect was a dull Norwegian, to hammer at facts, as she was hammering at the warped keys, fetching the thrummed, disjointed phrases out of the salt-eroded, motheaten depths of the piano.

Thrumming. Drumming in the end. Until she was outdrummed.

She went outside, and there were the flying brumbies approaching down the beach, their veils of manes, and in the sky the cloud feathers more tenuous than before. The sun too, was curiously veiled and pallid above the single stretched black hair of the horizon. At least the brumbies were outrunners of life, and she was gratefully prepared to watch them stampede along the beach in the direction of the striped cliffs. But this evening the mob propped, wheeled, and broke off through the scrub, smashing and trampling as they charged at the hinterland.

Quite suddenly a bluish dark had possessed and contracted the landscape. She lit her gentle lamps. Out to sea a blue lightning tattered the sky, which gradually lost its paper flatness, becoming a dome of black, thunderous marble. The night below had begun to snuffle. From undulating at first, the wind slammed hard at the land. She saw trees recoiling, heels dug in as it were, like a crowd resisting physical prostration.

She ran down out of the house, possibly falling once, but thinking less of selfpreservation than of finding and shepherding her deadly companion. 'Edvard!' she called, then screamed into the wind, 'ED-VARD!' His stupidity was what worried her: all his science would not save his limbs from breaking.

Something flying could have been a board grazing her temple oh but sharp. For the moment a wound was less frightening than

421

exhilarating the wind roaring into her lungs inflating them like windsocks. The bluest lightning could not make her flinch.

Till cold and sober, she saw black walls on the move across what had been a flat surface of water. She was blown back no longer any question of where twirled pummelled the umbrella of her dress pulled inside out over her head then returned her breasts rib-cage battered objects blood running from her forehead she could feel taste thinned with water a salt rain.

In this solid rain herself a groping survived insect a staggering soaked spider fetching up at what must be the bunker behind the house where they keep their wine.

A child's broken celluloid doll lying in the sand at the entrance.

She looked back to see the groaning house break into sticks and flame a cardboard torch thrust high above the heap at once rain wiped it off.

Trains were rumbling, it sounded, over the wreckage, and continued rumbling, across the roof of the bunker.

It was dry inside her funnel. The walls, she could remember from daylight, were concrete buried in the dune which rose behind the house, but how resistant to acts of God she was not of a mind to calculate. She felt around her, through cobwebs and other accretions, and found the shelves of wine bottles. She began rolling the bottles off the uppermost shelf. Their thudding as they hit the tamped floor could not be heard above the thunder, roaring of the gale, groaning of the sea, lashing of wiry rain, until in a last desperate sweep she cleared the shelf entirely: out of the slithering torrent rose a shattering of glass. She clambered up, stiff with salt, sweat, and age, and stored herself thankfully on her shelf.

More awkward to dispose of than her jackknife body was the mind which kept lumbering around inside the walls of her bruised head, or streaking off independently by flashes. The lightning was soon as free to enter as her thoughts to sky-rocket, for the sturdy door of the bunker, till now wedged ajar in a drift of sand, was forced off its rusted hinges: she heard it somersaulted away.

There was a continual juggling of fireballs, either in the sky, or was it at the back of her eyesockets: *rub hard enough Kate to see the coloured spots it's bad for the eyes but I don't care*. All night long the rumble of goods trains passing through Gogong, and on into precious memory, where it was Alfred trying to protect her storm-threatened body with his. As though she were the vulnerable one.

About three, if she could have looked at her little shagreen travelling clock (a present from Alfred, one of several, when Basil was born) the hour when she normally woke, to drink a glass of water and read a chapter, Elizabeth Hunter let herself down from her shelf. She was standing in water up around her thighs, nuzzled by several stiff objects, bottles, and dead fish.

Outside the hole where the door should have been the night was still hurtling. She could hear the ocean rising to accuse her. Well, she would stand accused: for the suicide of that contrary man who refused to come in; or was it murder if you were the cause of his staying out?

It was not the dead fish Edvard guiding you back on to the shelf more likely Alfred or solicitous Arnold. Arnold was born with a highly developed Sense of Responsibility which did not make him immune from irresponsible lust at least that one attack. For which you as much as he. Or more. Perhaps it is you who are responsible for the worst in people. Like poor little Basil sucking first at one unresponsive teat then the other the breasts which will not fill in spite of the nauseating raw beef and celery sandwiches prescribed by Dr Whatever—to 'make milk to feed your baby'. Instead of milk, 'my baby' (surely the most tragic expression?) must have drawn off the pus from everything begrudged withheld to fester inside the breast he was cruelly offered.

This night (morning by the shagreen clock) it is the earth coming to a head: practically all of us will drown in the pus which has gathered in it.

Elizabeth Hunter was almost torn off her shelf by a supernal blast then put back by a huge thrust or settling of exhausted atoms.

She lay and submitted to someone to whom she had never been introduced. Somebody is always tinkering with something. It is the linesman testing for the highest pitch of awfulness the human spirit can endure. Not death. For yourself there is no question of dying.

She could not visualize it. She only positively believed in what she saw and was and what she was was too real too diverse composed of everyone she had known and loved and not always altogether loved it is better than nothing and given birth to and for God's sake.

It must have been the silence which woke her. No, not woke: she had been stunned into a state of semi-consciousness from which light as much as silence roused her.

She waded out of the bunker through a débris of sticks, straw, scaly corpses, a celluloid doll. Round her a calm was glistening. She climbed farther into it by way of the ridge of sand and the heap of rubbish where the house had stood. At some distance a wrecked piano, all hammers and wires, was half buried in wet sand.

Without much thought for her own wreckage, she moved slowly down what had been a beach, picking her way between torn-off branches, great beaded hassocks of amber weed, everywhere fish the sea had tossed out, together with a loaf of no longer bread, but a fluffier, disintegrating foam rubber. Just as she was no longer a body, least of all a woman: the myth of her womanhood had been exploded by the storm. She was instead a being, or more likely a flaw at the centre of this jewel of light: the jewel itself, blinding and tremulous at the same time, existed, flaw and all, only by grace; for the storm was still visibly spinning and boiling at a distance, in columns of cloud, its walls hung with vaporous balconies, continually shifted and distorted.

But she could not contemplate the storm for this dream of glistening peace through which she was moved. Interspersed between the marbled pyramids of waves, thousands of seabirds were at rest; or the birds would rise, and dive, or peacefully scrabble at the surface for food, some of them coasting almost as far as the tumultuous walls of cloud; and closer to shore there were the black swans—four, five, seven of them.

She was on her knees in the shallows offering handfuls of the sodden loaf the sea had left for her. When they had floated within reach, the wild swans outstretched their necks. Expressing nèither contempt nor fear, they snapped up the bread from her hands, recognizing her perhaps by what remained of her physical self, in particular the glazed stare, the salt-stiffened nostrils, or by the striving of a lean and tempered spirit to answer the explosions of stiff silk with which their wings were acknowledging an equal.

All else was dissolved by this lustrous moment made visible in the eye of the storm, and would have remained so, if she had been allowed to choose. She did not feel she could endure further trial by what is referred to as Nature, still less by that unnaturally swollen, not to say diseased conscience which had taken over during the night from her defector will. She would lie down rather, and accept to become part of the shambles she saw on looking behind her: no worse than any she had caused in life in her relationships with human beings. In fact, to be received into the sand along with other deliquescent flesh, strewn horsehair, knotted iron, the broken chassis of an upturned car, and last echoes of a hamstrung piano, is the most natural conclusion.

Logically, it should have happened. If some force not her absent will had not wrenched at her doll's head and faced it with the object skewered to the snapped branch of a tree. The gull, a homelier version of the white predators, had been reduced to a plaque in haphazard bones and sooty feathers. Its death would have remained unnoticed, if her mind's ear had not heard the cry still tearing free as the breast was pierced.

At least the death cry of the insignificant sooty gull gave her back her significance. It got her creaking to her feet. She began scuttling, clawing her way up the beach by handfuls of air, an old woman and foolish, who in spite of her age had not experienced enough of living.

So she reached her bunker. She re-arranged herself, amongst rust and cobwebs, on her narrow shelf, protecting her skull with frail arms, to await the tortures in store for her when the storm returned.

For the eye was no longer focused on her, she could tell; and as it withdrew its attention, it was taking with it the delusions of her feeble mind: the black swans feeding out of her hands and seabirds nestling among the dark-blue pyramids.

As the storm came roaring back down the funnel in which she had clenched herself, the salt streamed out of her blinded sockets.

Some time that morning day evening the thin ribbon of silence was stamped very faintly then more distinctly with voices. The thing on the shelf, becoming a body again, began painfully trying out joints to see whether they still worked.

An old woman appeared in the hole which had once been the doorway to a bunker in a sandhill, behind what was now the ruins of the Warming family's summer 'place'.

The woman said, 'Yes. I am alive—after all.' The breeze even lifted her hair, or one lock less sodden than the mass.

Elizabeth Hunter smiled at the still tentative sunlight; no, it must be evening: the light was waning. She was glad to find herself reunited with her womanly self, and to see that these were actual men. One of them she recognized as the stringy Second Forester whose modesty had started him anointing his saw when she intruded on their privacy. His present companion was not the man with hairy belly; she had never seen this one before. He looked important, above physical employment, from the way he stood with his hands on his hips.

Legs astride the ruins, the man of authority congratulated the survivor. 'You've had a lucky escape, Mrs Hunter. We've come to take you back to the camp and across to the mainland. The line's out of order, as you'll appreciate. So we can't call the copter. But some of the boys 'ull ferry you over in the boat.'

She smiled, and bowed her head without comment, the ropes of sodden hair hanging like plummets from around her face. One of her breasts, she realized, had escaped through the tatters her dress had become. She could see no way of covering it without drawing attention to herself.

As they trudged through the sand towards a truck standing on high ground she noticed the storm had blown the bark off several trees. There was that bird too, impaled on one of them, skewered by a snapped branch.

The stringy fellow wanted to contribute something to their meeting. 'Most of these trees are gunner die,' he confided; then, after wetting his lips, he pointed. 'See that bird? It's a noddy.' She saw her friend had left his teeth out.

Elizabeth Hunter, while listening, was more intent on following the movements her feet were making in the sand. The men seemed to be accepting the exposed breast as a normal state of affairs. Which it had to be, in the circumstances; only Dorothy would have condemned it and everybody.

The Forestry foreman, if that was his status, told how the cyclone had cut a swath halfway along the ocean side of the island, turning out to sea before arriving at the camp. This time the mainland was untouched.

'Oh really,' she said, 'a cyclone, was it?' formally.

She could hardly bother: nothing mattered beyond her experiencing the eye.

When they reached the truck they helped her into the cabin. They sat her between them. They behaved as though guarding a treasure, something of great antiquity and value uncovered by the storm. Whereas she was simply herself again.

In their erratic and roundabout drive, while the foreman was forcing the truck's nose through, and sometimes over, freshly piled barricades of scrub, the stringy, toothless fellow asked her, 'Feelin' okay, are yer?' She caught a possessive tone in his voice, induced no doubt by their first meeting how many aeons ago in the rain forest; he had that over his boss, who was now merely the driver of the truck.

But she felt no desire to be possessed, by anybody. Like the black swans, she never had been, except for procreative purposes.

Suddenly she blushed for her self-indulgence; she thinned herself out from between her companions, to lean forward, to impress on them the urgent need for action. 'I forgot. There's a man—a guest of Mr Warming's—Professor Pehl, who didn't return yesterday evening. He may have gone inland looking for shelter. He may have seen—he's a scientist—that a storm was preparing. We must start looking for him at once. No,' it was she who had taken command, 'better drive on first to the camp so that we can brief as many men as you've got, and organize search parties. Or he may be dead,' she thought to add; 'but we'll still have to find him.'

'What—that Norwegian bloke?' the foreman shouted unnecessarily loud. 'He walked over yesterday evenin', before the storm started up. Had 'is wotchermecallem—rucksack on 'im. Some of the boys were going across to Oxenbould. They took 'im along with 'em in the boat.'

'Oh?'

Bumped roofwards in the leaping truck, Elizabeth Hunter chafed the gooseflesh on her arms. She was only saved up, whereas that deadly man Edvard Pehl, had been saved. Did he join his accomplice the Princesse de Lascabanes on the mainland? She speculated no more than vaguely on the possibility of it, because she was still too weak from the great joy she had experienced while released from her body and all the contingencies in the eye of the storm.

All the years she had spent lying on this mattress of warm moist sand the gulls had not deserted her. She had never been quite sure of gulls: even the stupid sooty kind, the noddies, are probably waiting to plunge their beaks and empty your sockets.

'Mother? You're not asleep, are you?' Sea hunger, or continued use of the French language, had sharpened the voice. 'You might give some thought to our suggestion. We don't want to rush you into anything you'd dislike—but time can trickle away when decisions have to be made—and we'd like to see you settled before we leave—for Europe.'

Dorothy feared her approach had not been resolute enough: too vague and womanly. Basil pretty certainly thought so: he shook off Mother's claw as though getting rid of it.

'Yes. Dorothy and I shall have the practical side to attend to. This house—the furniture alone.' Movement helped him: his robes swirling and ballooning around him increased his confidence at every turn. 'I imagine they'll allow you to take some of the things you're fond of. We'll ask the matron. If necessary we'll *demand* that you have your own furniture in your room. We must go up there and see them; why not tomorrow, Dorothy?' he looked at his sister from out of the figure eight he was cutting in the middle of the carpet, 'to discuss the matter.'

Dorothy couldn't help feeling moved by her brother's famous voice.

'Though of course,' he had to remind her, 'we may find they haven't a vacancy for the moment.' He too was moved, by the warmth which collusion had brought to their relationship.

Mrs Hunter said, 'If there isn't a vacancy, somebody will conveniently die. They must be dying all the time.'

It shocked her daughter. 'Oh, darling! Now we're being morbid again.'

'I thought we'd decided to be realistic,' Mrs Hunter said and laughed.

At the same time, something liquid, sticky—oh dear, ancient eye-muck, began to force its way out, first a drop, then a positive driblet, from under one of the mottled lids. No *tears*! In Dorothy de Lascabanes a sense of revulsion was trying to get the better of her own anguish. Mother, one should remind oneself, was able to cry at will; she had quelled rebellious maids with tears, so that they stayed on worse enslaved than ever.

Mother's weakening, if it was, had a more personal effect on Basil. Professionally, he had to guard against his excessive sensibility. He remembered advancing on an audience, his dead Cordelia (that lump of a Bagnall girl) weighing down his arms, himself snuffling, then blubbering. The audience loved it, while he and the cast (trust your fellow artists) were too aware that his generous emotional response was destroying the concerted tone of a performance.

Now his sensibility must resist this artful old creature, only incidentally their mother, by calling short her attempt to invoke pity and drown their plan in mawkishness. 'Remember,' he said, 'that what we are doing will eventually be for the best, and for your happiness.' If his voice trembled, it was because it suddenly occurred to him how the old bag might hang on and see the two of them reduced to ashes.

Dorothy advised, 'Don't upset yourself, Mother;' *and start my poor Basil wavering*, she did not add.

Dorothy de Lascabanes had never before scented the opportunity of underpinning a weak man: the prospect, though alarming, was exhilarating: to react to the tremors, taste the tears, of someone ostensibly stronger than yourself.

While Mother was explaining, 'It's something to do with my ducts—an oversensitivity, Dr—Treweek, I think—told me.' She ungummed her gums to masticate a smile stored in the cavern behind.

Basil had forgotten the doctor: an uncouth G.P. who used to come out from Gogong to 'Kudjeri', dandruff on his shoulders, and a smell of sweat from the leather band inside the hat he left hanging in the hall. Dr Treweek had a manner guaranteed to discourage the patient from ever falling ill again. Mother must have hated him.

'I shouldn't have thought Dr Treweek sensitive to oversensitivity.'

'Perhaps you're right. It must have been Gidley. He likes his patients to think him kind. Perhaps he is.'

'Dr Treweek attended to my arm. Surely he's dead, isn't he?'

'Who's dead—who's alive—I no longer know.'

But Basil was haunted by the smell of sweat, and of dusty casuarinas in the home paddock, and the scent of beeswax, at 'Kudjeri'.

'It was Dr Whichever who discovered about my hay fever. Did you know I am only ever infected in one nostril?' Sure enough, one nostril was in full flood: Mrs Hunter tried to guggle it back.

Écœurant, mon Dieu! In the absence of a nurse Madame de Lascabanes tore out a Kleenex and wiped the snot from the old baby's nose. She could have more than wiped: she might have broken off what she remembered as a work of art as late as Brumby Island. Instead, she pinched the gristle together till it showed white, and thus prevented any tenderness giving her away by running out of her fingertips.

'*Whurr — err — urrh!*' Mrs Hunter went.

'Are you off your nut, Dorothy? Can't you see you're hurting her?' Basil's protest was halfhearted; his memories of 'Kudjeri' still possessed him: of pears in muslin of roses under tussore sunshades of children in gauze masks against the Spanish influenza there is no protection against poetry as perversely flavoured in the beginning as Isabellas damsons and Sevilles as much a secret vice as a first stream of sperm.

Dorothy stood looking at her brother. His sharp words had wounded her. She could have wept for the unhappinesses he might not allow her to share in.

But Mother had put on her social voice. 'I do think it's sweet of you both to pay me a visit — to tell me what you're arranging for me. I so appreciate your kindness.' She coughed, and tussled with the sheet. 'I'm ready to die when you want me to.'

Standing either side of the trussed figure on the great bed, the two avoided looking at each other.

'I've experienced enough. Brumby Island alone would have satisfied anyone less — voracious. Now I've only got to work out how you stop the machinery.'

Basil whispered, 'Tomorrow, Dorothy? I have a little rented car.'

'Tomorrow? Mmyeh-ss ... ' Desperately searching for the other engagement she must have, Madame de Lascabanes could not find a convincing one.

Her essentials only cobwebbed by the fine sheet, Elizabeth Hunter looked as good as naked. She was so perfectly lulled, Alfred might have been caressing her breasts, her navel, the Mount of Venus, till suddenly she became contorted, as though her children were jostling, elbowing, fighting each other to be first out of the womb.

Dorothy shuddered; but Basil was again entranced. ' "Kudjeri", Mother — who lives there now?'

431

'Don't ask me!' she moaned. 'Oh, some—some McDonald or Mackay, I believe. Arnold knows. Ask Arnold. A girl married an overseer, and her father bought a place for them. He bought "Kudjeri". I don't like to think how it must look nowadays. Scribble on the walls. Half-naked children sitting on their potties. The rugs threadbare. And a stench of pickled onions. Some people have a craving for them, because, I feel, they want to mortify themselves. I used to keep them to feed to that kind of person. I'd give them to Dr Treweek when he came out visiting my dear Edvard during his last illness.'

'Edvard?' The hackles of Dorothy's shame and suspicion had risen: that grotesque, menopausal version of herself staring at her out of the glass. 'But Edvard—we know too well—was the Norwegian we were stuck with on Brumby Island.' Her mouth stiffening, she could not elaborate.

'Yes,' Mother agreed, 'the one you were prepared to fall in love with—only you weren't in your right mind at the time—and he too self-centred.'

'*I* fall in *love*? with you preparing to carry on under my nose! That's why I made sure I shouldn't be a witness—why I sent for the helicopter—and booked on the first plane which would fly me back to sanity and Europe. Edvard Pehl, indeed!' *Que cette vieille garce crève sous mes yeux!*

Mrs Hunter lay grinning. 'Looking back, lust is always difficult to understand. And ugly. One's own is uglier than anybody else's. Edvard Pehl was in some respects, I suppose, a desirable man. But tedious. Frightened. He ran away that same afternoon. I thought he must have caught you up—and that was why you've never wanted to mention him.'

'*Oh, Maman!*' Dorothy de Lascabanes opened her bag: if she knew what might help, she could not find it; she shut the bag; she wept.

Basil probably hadn't noticed: he had half-closed his eyes, and his nostrils had a pinched look, as though detecting a stench of pickled onions in shuttered rooms. 'I'll ask the old Wyburd to approach whoever they are and come to some agreement. I must see "Kudjeri" while I'm here.' Return to the source of things, and in doing so, perhaps even save yourself from Mitty Jacka and the death play.

But it did not allow him to forget that a future of any kind hinged materially on Elizabeth Hunter. 'In the meantime, Mother darling, Dorothy and I shall investigate the Thorogood Village.'

His smile as he left the room looked irresponsible, Dorothy thought, like that of somebody falling asleep or setting out on an obsessive journey.

'Dorothy, are you still with me?'

You became, inevitably, Mother's dutiful girl awaiting dismissal.

'Kiss me, won't you? Before you go?' One of the organisms Elizabeth Hunter's skiapod depended on for nourishment, you let yourself be sucked in. 'Come back tonight—both of you,' the mouth withdrew enough to bubble. 'I'll get hold of an ambassador, or foreign professor. That's the sort of thing people seem to like. However perfectly foreigners use words, one can blame them for what one doesn't want to understand.'

Tear yourself away from this mouth, the underwater implications, from a simple dangerously illuminating beam, and from love, as Elizabeth Hunter understood it. (Could Mother have loved, ever? She loves offering herself for love, but that is a different matter.)

Madame de Lascabanes went: a woman of tensed calves and variable age, her handbag sealed to her ribs to avoid losing the keys and documents from which one cannot afford to become separated. Though anything really important, such as incriminating letters, can be more safely carried in a chamois bag pinned to the slip, in that sanctuary below the division of the breasts.

Walking quickly along the passage towards the landing, she intended to glance through a certain doorway at her own virginal sufferings, when she heard voices in the nurses' room, and caught sight of Sir Basil Hunter talking at that healthy, pretty nurse. Was it so late that the tea planter's widow had been replaced by the gaudy strumpet? To distract herself from her twinges, the princess looked at her watch, which confirmed that everything was, in a broad superficial sense, in order; the details are what grow disorderly as they take it upon themselves to sprout in conflicting directions.

'Basil?' she called in passing, in a high, light, deliberately disinterested voice. 'We shall be late if we don't make a move.' Late for what, she could not have told, but continued down the stairs with an obduracy to convince anyone but herself.

If Sir Basil had heard his sister's warning, he delayed answering it. Unable to resist just a peep into the room where the nurses changed, he struck lucky: the little Manhood, already in uniform, was checking something, it appeared, in an exercise book. It was also obvious she had taken it up very recently and too quickly: the pages had not yet settled down.

Sir Basil had meant to close the door after stepping inside the dressing-room. Whether he did, he was not aware; in any case, his only reason for doing so would have been to avoid pandering to Dorothy's inquisitiveness. But he soon forgot his sister.

He was too intent, while too uncertain, how to behave now that he had a foothold in this room, with its closed cupboards and a scent of wych-hazel; but no doubt Sister Whatnot—his Primavera! would come up with his cue.

Instead she continued squeezing and releasing the end of her ball pen, as she gave herself to whatever she was reading in her exemptive notebook.

It became a question of interrupting or looking a fool. 'I half expected you to follow up our meeting of the other evening.' His voice was no longer that of a successful actor playing a part he knew inside out: he detected in himself the quavers of an elderly amateur.

'Oh?' Though she condescended to raise her head, it was surrounded by the forbidding veil, and her eyes showed him she was taking in no more than the tip of one of his ear lobes, and that as a favour he had scarcely earned. 'I don't know why you would 'uv even *half* expected it,' she finally said. 'We didn't arrange anything,

434

did we?' While breaking her silence, her face remained opaque, seemingly sullen, the eyelids thick and half-lowered.

'It didn't occur to me to suggest a business deal.' Nor to snigger now. 'Not where mutual tenderness exists.' Oh Lord! He had always hated his matinée performances.

Again, 'Oh?' but this time Sister Manhood's swollen lips smiled enough, under the pale lipstick, to show the concession did not mean a thing.

Then she tossed her veil, swished what she was wearing of a skirt over her dimpled flanks. 'I must go in to my patient,' she announced with a busy officiousness.

'Anyway, you know where I am,' he pointed out, 'if you care to repeat what I personally found most enjoyable.' To make it sound less like a meal, he added, 'I even felt we cared a little for each other,' bullshit though it was.

Sister Manhood gave no clue to what she may have experienced at the Onslow Hotel.

He was going downstairs having made a fool of himself over a cocktease nurse on a one-night stand, at this crucial point in his life when he should have been concentrating instead on persuading his mother to die, so that he might survive. He went down, lashing out now and then with a foot at the cast-iron Hesperides and thorns put there to protect him from space. He remembered only at the bottom of the stairs that his sister and accomplice would be waiting for him with a knowing, and probably vindictive, smile.

At once he saw he had done poor old Dorothy an injustice. She must have guessed what he had been up to, but decided to half-veil her knowledge in a virtuous woman's understanding. She had gone out into the garden leaving the hall door ajar. She was standing in the sun waiting for him, her intolerant brand of elegance at odds with the blowsy light and tree fronds indolently stirring. But it did not prevent her offering a smile in which her own virtue waived virtue in the male, particularly one to whom she was related. It restored his virility. He took her by the elbow, and squeezed it.

'You're giving me a lift, aren't you?' To beg her tender favour she had turned her bony face towards his, almost as though expecting a kiss into the bargain.

Walking down the path together he slipped an arm under hers, and actually thought how pleasant to be connected with this Princesse de Lascabanes, all the more since she happened to be his confederate as well.

'How do you think we have done?' he asked.

'Mother is unpredictable.' She gave one or two curious, apparently genuine sobs, which she tried to turn into grunts, before continuing in her driest voice, 'I'm more than ever convinced old people should not be encouraged to live for ever.'

They were in agreement, but it made him feel alone again: with his failed Lear of some years past; and the prospect of leaping into darkness under the guidance of Mitty Jacka.

Till the fantasy he had woven for himself at the height of the unpleasant business in Mother's room returned to screen him from this other vision of a puppetry more sinister because it concerned him personally. 'When I said I have a strong desire to re-visit "Kudjeri", I don't believe, Dorothy, you took me seriously.' He must will her to share this obsession of his. 'I very definitely mean to go, if it can be arranged—not just as a sentimental pilgrimage—more as a—' the false ones amongst his teeth were offering stumbling blocks to the simple words he was trying to utter, 'I mean this journey might put me in touch with a reality I no long—— which *everybody*, right? tends to underrate and forget—and which no artist, of any kind, can afford to ignore.' His clumsy tongue had finally forced this foolish confession past the teeth.

He had come to a standstill with his sister at a turn in the path overhung by an old weeping bottlebrush. The light, together with the fronds through which it was spilling, had imposed a lattice between himself and Dorothy's face. Was she mocking him from within her purdah? Or had she simply closed down, like a woman for whom abstractions hold no interest? He could not tell, much as he wished to; she was perhaps as necessary for his regeneration as for the crime they had agreed to help each other commit.

436

'Why don't you come along, Dorothy?'

As though performing an act of love on a still doubting mistress, he inserted his suggestion gently but firmly in what he could only guess to be her imagination. At the same time, he reinforced the square of their clasped hands. They continued standing in the semi-shade of the bottlebrush, while he half swung the hand she was only half attempting to withdraw.

At first Dorothy made a series of rudimentary bird noises. She was surprised at herself: it was not her sort of thing; and because he was unaccustomed to them, her tentative chirps probably sounded as odd to him.

She became more herself when habit had her flash the knife of her face, just for an instant. 'Won't it be horribly uncomfortable?' She winced. 'I can't bear discomfort, Basil — sharing bathrooms and all that — not at my age.' To confess to your own age, as opposed to others implying it, is something of a luxury.

'It used not to be uncomfortable. Far from it.'

'Once upon a time!'

Visions of strangers' hair stuck to the bath, country cisterns characteristically refusing to flush, breakfast conversation while fat congeals around the ruins, little hands invading your dressing-table, to touch, try, upset, and leave codewords written by finger in spilt powder, roused in her a repugnance she must have inherited from Mother.

'It would give the old girl time to make up her mind — and soothe the nerves of her murderers.' He spoke the word with saving gusto.

Dorothy laughed to please him, but without mirth and shapelessly. 'What if she makes it up the wrong way?'

'She won't. I've appealed to a sense of duty which has always been there in the depths, and depths are easier to reach in senile minds.'

'Senile minds are infinitely stubborn, let me tell you.'

He did not see it that way because it would not have suited him to.

'Stubborn or not,' she prepared to console, 'our present concern is whether this ghastly village will have a vacancy in the possibly near future.'

They bounced down a flight of three steps, at that dangerous corner, still swinging hands. 'Bless you, darling!' At the bottom he raised her knuckle to his lips. 'And I salute your French in-laws for bringing you up so practical.'

If ever she should have hated Basil, it was now; but the warmth of his hand, the hint of his lips, had stanched the wound from which hatred flows: in her imagination she raced ahead tied by conscience to this brother she had never accepted as a blood relation and as they bumped in the rented car the dusty miles even united them physically freshly burnished not repulsively barbecued by the sun they recognize an avatar in every skeleton tree then their own totems of casuarina and willow the oval rosebed in front of a house from which the no longer vengeful siblings tumble down the veranda steps to greet the travellers and merge at last into one another.

Basil may have sensed some of the dangers of exaltation. 'Whatever we decide about "Kudjeri", tomorrow it's Matron, the clergy, and any other ghastliness the Thorogood Village has to offer.'

'The inmates!' Dorothy unaccountably shrieked as they reached the gate of their mother's garden. 'Those who aren't vegetable will be looking us over—from the moment we arrive. Old people with nothing more to do about their lives develop a nose for weaknesses, like dogs and children—as we ought to know.' It appalled her to think they might scent out ambitions she kept more or less veiled from her conscious mind; nor could she hope to hide behind her brother.

Nine

'WHAT'S THIS?' Sister Manhood owed it to her profession to disapprove of the unorthodox; but you couldn't knock Lottie, who apart from everything else was looking such a fright in her drag.

'Mrs Hunter asked me for to entertain her.'

'Never in the middle of the day. First her dinner, then her shut-eye.'

'Today she has no appetite for food. That is why I am to dance for her.'

A laugh was a laugh, but Sister Manhood was losing patience. 'Mrs Hunter doesn't always know best—not about everything.'

The housekeeper took off her top hat; she stood to attention as it were, balancing the scurfy cylinder on a level with her right breast. Less disciplined because expected to remain unseen, her hair also looked skimpier, from having been screwed up and stuffed inside the ancient hat; one dusty lock stuck out straight and stiff at an angle from an unexpectedly pretty little ear.

'I'm the one who will decide.' The nurse spoke as though she actually believed in her own infallibility, and marched down the passage.

Lotte Lippmann tagged along behind. If her pumps had not forced her to walk flatfooted, time and arthritis would have clinched the matter. In her worst moral doldrums, she thumped; and this afternoon the polka bow, flopping between throat and bosom, took on a more wilted look, grubbier for the flesh tints a performer's sweaty painted neck leaves on oyster sateen.

'Wait in the dressing-room, please,' Sister Manhood ordered; but was tickled into relenting a little. 'I'd say, darl, you've been to town on yourself!' She could not bottle up the laughter frothing inside her authority: she let it rip; and went so far as to give Lottie a quick cuddle while disguising it as condescension.

'*Bin zerschplittert!*'

'Eh?' As there was no means of deciding whether these harsh noises were tragic or merely funny-foreign, Flora Manhood went on laughing.

The lips out of which Lotte Lippmann had uttered her fierce cry were formally drawn in twin peaks almost as far as the nostrils, with a heavy crimson loop swooning in the direction of the chin. Where lips and cheeks had not burnt through, the skin was whiter than powder could make it: she had more than likely floured herself.

It was a good giggle. Till the nurse took fright.

Something in Lotte Lippmann's eyes pierced an unhappiness at Flora Manhood's core so that it squirmed. This baby, if she did have it inside her, was already a disaster; and how would she ever atone for all the child must suffer after she had given birth to it?

She said in her hardest voice, 'You've only yourself to blame, Lottie, for letting her push you around. Making a fool of you.'

'She is making no fool. This is what I am.'

'Those feet alone! How you'll ever dance!'

Swollen flesh and contorted bones had deformed the scarred, once sprightly, skintight pumps.

'Sit, anyway,' Sister Manhood advised more gently, 'while I give the old cow hell for turning down her lovely din din.'

Lotte Lippmann did as told. Resigned to waiting, she sat herself on the dressing-table stool in company with the looking-glass.

As the nurse went into her patient's room a voice was coming from under the bed, ' ... Dad threw another of 'em Thursday just after sundown a new moon too I forgot to wish what with Dad flounderin' around Mavis and Donald pretendin' they pretend upstairs since Donald's finger got bit instead of the cork it turned septic I told Mavis it was time to squeeze it she rousted on me 'er mother and Donald looked as if it was me not a sick man bit 'is bloody finger for 'im ... '

If Mrs Hunter had not been strung for listening, she might have looked dead. Sister Manhood, after her first shock, realized the old thing was living someone else's life.

'Yairs.' Mrs Cush crawled sighing from under the bed soaked with perspiration and O'Cedar. Her seams were grey where they weren't pricked out in black. She was a formerly spry, smallish woman; the smaller women surrendered themselves more willingly, it seemed, to enslavement by Betty Hunter.

'Well, I don't know,' and Sister Manhood no longer did; 'it was your *morning*, Mrs Cush, wasn't it? not your afternoon.'

'She asked me to extend.'

'Weren't my children here this morning?'

'Couldn't get on with me work—not with all the yakker that was goin' on in 'ere.' Mrs Cush leered, and sucked her teeth back into place.

'I asked her to stay,' Mrs Hunter confirmed, 'and tell me something to divert me.'

'And that is what I was just tellun.' Mrs Cush frowned at the snooty sister.

'Where is my cook?' Mrs Hunter asked. 'I was expecting her to dance for me.'

Her patient's whims, as well as the slaves who ministered to them, were getting Sister Manhood down; she made an effort, however. 'What about your luncheon, Mrs Hunter? I believe you refused your luncheon. You might try to take a mouthful, and everybody will be pleased.'

'Oh, but I did. Or didn't I? Yes, I did! They rammed it down my throat by handfuls. Chased me round the nursery while Nurse was out. There's nothing like older children when they have you at their mercy and want to get their own back. That's something Lilian Nutley escaped. She galloped away, and was murdered at the foot of those orange cliffs—down the street. They found her bones amongst the oyster shells. So they say. Personally I don't think she was murdered: she died of all she remembered.'

Mrs Cush was so distressed she flipped with her duster and sent a little silver tray spinning off the dressing-table. It clattered through Sister Manhood's nerves like wind bashing into a curtain of metal beads.

'If that's how you feel,' said the nurse, 'it's better for you to take a nap.'

'Oh, I have! Haven't I been sleeping all my life? That's why I asked Mrs Cush to tell me something real.'

'I'll give you something to help.' It was not like Sister Manhood to make offers.

'I may take you up on that, Mrs Pardoe. But not now. I want Sister Lippmann to dance for me.'

Sister Manhood went to fetch this old clown from the dressing-room where she was waiting to perform.

Lotte Lippmann had her nose in one of the cupboards.

'What are you up to? Fossicking through other people's things!' It was at least an opportunity for the nurse to revive her collapsed self-righteousness.

Lotte Lippmann said, 'This is the dress she has promised me after she dies. Only, as I see it, they will not believe. Or if I shall take my dress, they will say I have stolen it.'

'Have it put on paper, dear.' Sister Manhood snorted with some bitterness. 'That's what the solicitor's for. To see that debts are paid, and everybody legally tidied up.'

'But Mrs Hunter is in no way indebted.' As Lotte Lippmann stood fumbling the dress, it did seem that this rustling, materially insubstantial stuff, of foggy moonlight as well as gauze and sequins, absolved the owner from obligations other than that of continued being.

Inklings of transcendence had washed against Flora Manhood before, if only by brief moments: after some dream had driven her out from a house of threatened cardboard into a solid white night, to which her own white particle suddenly and miraculously belonged; or swimming with Col Pardoe against the tide of music, where inadmissible eddies would occur in which she was almost whirled to an understanding of mysteries such as love, beauty

442

fulfilment, death. Now, thanks to this crazy Jewess, she was again troubled: by the shimmer from a grotty dress in Elizabeth Hunter's wardrobe. When, like every good Australian, she must continue to believe only in the now which you can see and touch. But did she make sense? She had given away all that is most touchable along with Col Pardoe: the ribs which enclosed his thudding heart; in her own groin a trickle of semen she had made a show of wiping off and secretly let dry on her finger. Or their children: however hard they pummelled, and hollered for life, she had seen to it that she would never allow them their rightful features.

'Stop mauling that mouldy old dress!' Sister Manhood's sticky finger was rankling with her. 'We'd better go in, Lot. She's waiting for you—to *dance!*'

So they went in to Mrs Hunter's room.

' ... I always sweared by the bark meself but Mavis would never do it without she used a hairpin.' Mrs Cush was having trouble removing from the pierglass a reflection she was rubbing with a damp rag.

'Here is Mrs Lippmann,' Sister Manhood announced in her classiest voice. 'She's come to dance for you, Mrs Hunter.'

Elizabeth Hunter replied, 'So I see,' without opening her eyes.

Lotte Lippmann put on her napless hat. The cane protruding from her left armpit wobbled for the human being in her as she stared out of the chalky face at the figure on the bed, or farther, probably much farther. For that reason she could not resist, finally, whatever it was that took place: translation, or dislocation. A whip almost audibly cracked: the limbs twitched into jerky action; the face was split by a patent-leather smile, the more deathly for clenched jawbones and one or two gaps somewhere earwards. Lotte Lippmann was again breathing the spotlit dust as she went into her song-and-dance, *ein zwei drei*, the painful pumps thumping the carpet, a voice unfurling like a raucous favour from away back around the uvula.

Out of the gaps and the gold in her crimson slot of a mouth, accompanied by her possessed body, she sang,

443

> '*Wenn Mutter in die Manage ritt,*
> *Wie jauchzt' mein Herz auf Schritt und Tritt*
> *Hoppla, hoppla, tripp, trapp, trapp ...*'

And Mrs Cush, who must have taken part in it before, echoed, '*Oppler!*'

> '*Bis mir die Schuppen von den Augen fielen*
> *Ich sah den Dreck in allen Dielen*
> *Hoppla, hoppla, tripp, trapp, trapp!*
> *Es ist das alte, fade Lied*
> *Nichts macht mehr einen Unterschied*
> *Es ist 'ne Welt für leere Laffen,*
> *Ein Zirkus mit dressierten Affen*
> *Die Löwen und die Löwenkätzchen*
> *Die Dame ohne Unterleib,*
> *Die Hohe Schul' mit allen Mätzchen,*
> *Was ist es schon? Ein Zeitvertreib!*'

Poor Lottie! Flora Manhood was reminded of a golliwog moneybox on a nursery mantelpiece.

While Lotte Lippmann persisted with her perpetually unsuccessful trick of trying to disentangle her voice from its distinctive raucousness, she continued to point her toe, or hobble in pursuit of the authoritarian spot, tapping with the dented knob at the end of her cane on tables which were not there. Screeching. Choking once. Fighting with gloved fingers a hair stuck to her lips. Always smiling. The neck muscles screwed tighter by the *clack clack* of the patent-leather words.

Sister Manhood could get on with the job at least, take her patient's temperature, feel her pulse, plump the pillows; whereas the cleaner, who appeared to have finished her work, was stranded in the middle of a pantomime which frightened rather than amused. Even less sure how she ought to react when grabbed round the waist and dragged into a wheezy, undulating waltz,

444

Mrs Cush might have got the wind up if she had not bumped foreheads with Lottie, breaking up their partnership.

After re-settling the topper, Lotte Lippmann danced alone; and as she danced, she sang,

> *'Jede Nacht, seit ich geboren,*
> *Hat meine Seel' ihre Unschuld verloren.*
> *Verdammt sie nicht, versteht es nur,*
> *Sie war zu schwach in der Struktur*
> *So geht's einmal in der Natur.*
> *Am selben Platz wo sie verwelken,*
> *Da wachsen wieder andere Nelken.*
> *Sie gehen nie verloren,*
> *sind ewig neugeboren.'*

Mrs Hunter, who had not yet opened her eyes, did so as she rejected the thermometer with her tongue. 'No longer necessary, thank you, Sister. This morning they drove the temperature out of me for good and all.'

Even so, Elizabeth Hunter's smile, her eyes, suggested a slight fever as she lay looking inwards at an image possibly invoked by Lotte Lippmann's song-and-dance: was it herself? light slithering off the long legs, men's eyes not to be detached from the stockings; ignore it of course, but that is another convention which deceives no one.

Elizabeth Hunter's head was beating a different time to the music to the brisk pebbles of the kettle-drum and goo from the foggier saxophone: as you dance you pretend you are not practically naked you are what is accepted as virtuous but men call cold.

'Not cold.' Elizabeth Hunter's head lolled. 'Part of you will never be touched. That's all it is. Not even by Alfred.' She turned to her nurse. 'That's what nuns understand, isn't it, Sister?'

'I wouldn't know.' Sister Manhood was busy disinfecting the thermometer.

'No. You're the breeder. Sister de Santis would know. Where's Mary? I haven't seen her since we were girls.'

'She was here last night,' Sister Manhood corrected; 'and will come again this evening,' she offered as consolation.

'Oh, yes.' Mrs Hunter accepted it.

So they were all dancing: the nurses lined out even skinny Badgery that potato sack is Milly Cush all pelting the patrons with crimson rosebuds from little trays attached to the neck by halters of variegated ribbons.

> *'Die Rosen können nie vergehen,*
> *Die Liebe lässt sie neuerstehen ... '*

The singer withdrew to one side, apparently about to reveal the reason for their shenanigans. The stale-perfumed, over-throaty words faltered as the line broke and re-formed; and there at the apex stood Elizabeth Hunter.

Nursing at her breast an ammunition of roses (hers were white) she hesitated a moment to allow her patrons to recover from the dazzle, then took aim. Thanks to her height and her supple body she could throw farther than anyone. She threw the handfuls of white petals, torn off so extravagantly they might have been paper, or flesh, sometimes an eye fringed with stamens, and stems which made her hands run. She flung her offerings over the men's smarmed heads and those of their jealous tight-permed women, to lob amongst the pyramidal waves of deepest cobalt, the muslin balconies dissolving around them to be thrown up afresh and contorted by the storm of applause.

'Oh yes,' she smiled at her human satellites, 'I have only to learn to re-enter and I shall be accepted. Their beaks were crimson, with staring nostrils, but innocent of cruelty.'

She must have known that her attempts to convince others would remain hopeless and might even be interpreted as pretentious, not only by a sceptical audience, but her fellow artists, for she opened her eyes as wide as she could, to shock the lot of them by exposing those opalescent cataracts.

Her impromptu had electrifying consequences: a voice tore itself out by the roots and lashed the air with an excruciating scream. It was her housekeeper, Mrs Hunter realized.

'*Ich kann nicht mehr weiter. Ich fürchte mich. Immer. Immer. Dieser entsetzliche Gestank. Ich halt's nicht aus.*'

Mrs Hunter heard what sounded like a silk hat bowling across the carpet on its cardboard brim till abruptly halted by furniture. She felt Mrs Lippmann's cotton gloves grappling her; and—please not! convulsive lips fastening themselves on the backs of her hands.

'*Barmherzigkeit! Ich verlier' auch SIE! Verweile doch!*'

Because she was so repelled physically, not to say otherwise embarrassed, Mrs Hunter replied, 'Every serious German I ever came across fell back on quoting from Goethe in a crisis—if not the real thing, their own version of him. I don't understand this dependence—unless the absolute stinker in a great man makes him more human.'

It did not persuade Mrs Lippmann to release the hand she was slobbering on. 'I am no German. I am a black Jew from anywhere between Hamburg and Bessarabia—who have escaped the gas *Ofens* by my own imperishability—and since then a *Gunst* you have shown me—till that too, will be taken from me.' She began slobbering afresh, or trying to devour the relic she would not otherwise be allowed to possess for her own desperate purposes.

Mrs Cush, herself an expert on slobbering, gnashing, and possession, slunk off.

A wind had risen. The muslin curtain which Sister Manhood had flung back to dismiss the smells of exertion, soggy powder, musty clothes, and perhaps a whiff of putrefaction from the corpses she had laid out in the course of her short career, was billowing and fluctuating inside Mrs Hunter's room.

Shuttled between controlling a curtain and dragging the housekeeper off her patient, Flora Manhood's voice was trembling, 'Mrs Lippmann—come, please! I'll have to give you something if you can't get a hold of yourself.'

'I am again sedate, Flora.'

She did appear all of a sudden surprisingly calm. Above the craters

447

and runnels of the cheeks and advanced deliquescence of the lips, the eyes were afloat, if darker for their recent plunge.

'I do not see why I should fear what I have already always known.' She rubbed her cheek with her coat sleeve, then looked dispassionately at the evidence she found on the cuff.

The nurse accompanied the housekeeper along the passage as far as the door which separated the servants' quarters from the landing.

'You will leave Mrs Hunter unattended,' Mrs Lippmann asked, 'after her—experience?' Though her own life depended on the mortality of this old woman, exhaustion made her sound disinterested.

'She'll sleep now. This is her time for a nap, and she'd hold it against anyone who made her miss it. Specially today, when it may help her forget what they're going to do to her.' Sister Manhood listened to her own chatter while guiding a friend who had been proved almost less calculable than herself.

At the baize door she longed for the housekeeper to invite her in to the bare, but emotionally overcharged room, in which she slept. Flora Manhood would willingly have allowed Lottie to tuck her up in the narrow bed and afterwards take her temperature; from behind closed lids she would have listened for the verdict: you are several lines above normal Floradora as you would expect of somebody who imagines herself with child by this crumby old farting famous actor sleep and you will wake up to find you are under obligation to nobody but yourself least of all to a geriatric case approaching the expected conclusion.

As she could not be cured so simply, the situation continued billowing in Sister Manhood's mind like the live curtain in the room to which she must return. Till the front doorbell rang. And that same muslin of her uncontrollable mind was ripped to flapping shreds, then scattered in what had become snippets of tinkling zinc.

Mrs Lippmann was again the golliwog money-box in cast iron, its paint martyred by inhuman children. 'Is it these murderers coming already about their business?' The possibility was more than she could face. 'You will answer for me, Flora? You see I am not after

448

all in my own control.' The baize door, expiring on its hinges, masked a whimper.

Left alone on the landing, Sister Manhood could feel her hypothetical child become a fact: he jumped inside her long before his time. She went downstairs. Colin Pardoe would be standing in the porch with the parcel of drugs Badgery had forgotten to mention, and which Col himself had perversely decided to bring. He would begin staring immediately at the little window with which her womb had just been fitted, to make it easier for him to identify a foetus by its features. If she could snatch the deadly drugs Dr Gidley had prescribed for his patient in a moment of misguided compassion (he little knew it was the nurse who needed his help) Flora Manhood thought her shame and desperation would help her tear the wrapping, fumble out the plug of cotton wool, and in spite of Col's iron fingers, nails pared to the quick as she remembered, and brutal thwack of male arms bare as far up as the biceps, she would more than swallow, she would first chew the bitter-tasting capsules, only for the necessary instant, because she would feel the poison thrust its prongs through her entire system, and fall oh God briefly convulsed before the cold took over on the chequered tiles at Colin Pardoe's feet.

She wrenched so hopelessly at the door she sent the pains shooting down her side, and found old Wyburd standing, not inside the porch, but out from it in the sunlight. He was holding his hands edgeways to his face as though saying his prayers.

'What is it, Mr Wyburd?' she practically bellowed: his attitude was no more than slightly peculiar; she only felt so relieved it was not the person she had imagined, and yet, a man. 'Is anything wrong?' She laughed, and it would not disperse afterwards; it hung in the air, the same brassy tones as her spoken words.

'Nothing *wrong*,' he answered, removing his hands from his face. 'I've been smelling this.'

'O-ow-hh?' she ended up giggling through her nose, and it might come back through her mouth as the raspberry vinegar had, she was a kid, in Con's Caff, at Coff's Harbour.

'It's rosemary,' Mr Wyburd explained. 'My wife is an expert. She can identify any plant you care to show her. I couldn't compete – but do know rosemary when I see it.'

The solicitor too was laughing by now. It made him look rather silly: old men's dentures, the cleanest of them, have a look of slime, their mauve gums.

'Go on! Is that rosemary?' She peered into his open hands though he was not really offering them to her; she looked inside the cradle the old fingers and creased palms were making for the crushed silvery spikes smelling of furniture polish.

'Yes, of course. I can tell now. Isn't it a – nostalgic perfume?' The woman visitor at P.A. who brought, instead of the pink carnations, what she said was 'pinks' (actually they were wine colour) in a twist of crumpled brown paper: *it's the hot day making them smell nostalgic.*

The solicitor was saying, 'You can stuff fish with rosemary. You sew them up afterwards.' Then they were both giggling, himself and this Sister Manhood, together. 'I've never tried it. My wife and I prefer plain, wholesome food.'

Though she could take it as rich as it came, Sister Manhood was only too ready to agree. From giggling too much she would probably end up with a goitre. There was no medical reason; she might though, from the knotting and unknotting of a convulsive throat.

The solicitor was looking at her from under the brim of his Akubra: the way she saw it a hat is only one more thing to lose.

'Won't you come in, Mr Wyburd?' she remembered, and started coaxing.

When she had got him past the door, he asked, 'How is Mrs Hunter?' as though he might find her in some way different from what she had been at any time that century.

'You know they were here this morning?' She had lowered her voice, and was treating the latch with the greatest care.

'I don't know, Sister. Who? You must be more explicit.' He wanted to hold it off.

'The children.'

If it did not occur to Sister Manhood to see the princess and Sir Basil as anything but evil and elderly behind the label she had given them, they flickered through Arnold Wyburd's mind with the attributes he would have liked them to keep: grass-stained, scab-kneed, still a vision of potential good.

Irritated by the presence of this nurse, waiting like anybody else to accuse him, he mumbled, 'Isn't it natural to want to visit their mother?'

'It could be, but isn't – knowing what we do,' Sister Manhood persisted as they accompanied each other towards the stairs.

Annoyance made Arnold Wyburd bluster. 'I'm sure I don't know what you're hinting at. None of us knows for certain what Dorothy and Basil's intentions are. And in any case, they may change their minds.'

He was so furious with himself for letting Sister Manhood trap him into what amounted to an admission, and for referring to the Hunters as 'Dorothy and Basil' in her presence, he stubbed his toe on a stair, and might have fallen forward on his knees if the nurse had not grabbed him by an arm, as though he were one of the geriatrics she was experienced in nursing.

'Are you all right?' she asked with unnecessary concern.

'I only came here this afternoon,' he panted, 'because Sister Badgery rang me about a document Mrs Hunter wants drawn up.'

Ah, then he must have known all along! Badgery could never bottle up information of importance, and what more important than the Hunters' visit?

'About what time were the princess and Sir Basil here?' he lowered himself enough to inquire.

'I don't imagine it was too early. People like that don't get moving early.'

His voice brightened. 'You're quite right. When Sister Badgery rang, I had just reached my office. She knew nothing about a pro-jected visit from the young Hunters – which no doubt they decided to make on the spur of the moment.' He hoped he had shown this girl that there was no good reason for bullying him.

Actually she would not have dreamt of it. She was too busy wondering what the 'document' could be. Was it a fresh will, perhaps? It was almost certainly a will. If she herself was dishonest enough to sleep with the son behind his mother's back and conceive without his ever knowing, Badgery and Wyburd might be cooking up some plan to forestall the children by diddling the old girl out of her lolly. Naturally the solicitor would lie. Flora Manhood knew she would have perjured herself all the way, denying that she had seduced Sir Basil, anyway till she was certain of a positive result.

It was understandable that she and Wyburd, a couple of crims more or less, should nurse their silences for the rest of the climb.

Outside Mrs Hunter's door, Sister Manhood whispered, 'You must be very gentle with her, Mr Wyburd: she's had such a dreadful morning.' But you could not tell from glancing at him whether he suspected what was genuine anxiety.

When they went in, the room was practically filled with the ballooning curtain, though as soon as the solicitor closed the door the muslin was sucked back, flapping and battering, before subsiding in tremors, to cling like a transparent skin to the face on the pillow.

The nurse ran forward to deliver her neglected charge from this great caul. 'There, dear. You're all right. We're here.' Her sense of guilt quickened by thought of her own future trials, Flora Manhood comforted her baby.

Mrs Hunter emerged working her gums. 'You know I'm not all right,' she gasped, 'and your being here can't make me any better. I'm past that. Though nobody can do me harm either—or not in ways that matter.'

The solicitor thought her body had shrunk since he was last with her; on the other hand her spirit seemed to billow around them more forcefully.

So he attempted a jolly voice to boost his own flagging spirit. 'I've come, Mrs Hunter—you remember me, don't you? Arnold Wyburd,' then sotto voce, 'to discuss the document you have in mind.'

Sister Manhood began rearranging several unimportant objects in case the old bloke might show his hand. He wouldn't, though. And it didn't matter. Betty Hunter was right: she couldn't be harmed, any more than you could kill your baby, if you had conceived it; you might get rid of the embryo, but its spirit would haunt you for ever after.

'Oh yes,' Mrs Hunter was feeling her way, 'it's you,' she said. 'I sent for you—because—I must try to remember.'

Sister Manhood could have slipped out to the nurses' room, free at last to do her nails, consult the stars, or just sit mooning away the flattest stretch of the afternoon, if it wasn't for having to satisfy herself about the blessed 'document'.

'It couldn't be the rates and taxes, could it?' Mrs Hunter asked.

'You've never had to bother yourself, Mrs Hunter, about the rates and taxes.'

'Always,' she said. 'Only oneself bothers enough. But perhaps this was more personal. Oh, yes! Nurse, fetch me paper—for Arnold. Something formal, and white. Arnold was the whitest—and the smoothest.'

Poor old Arnold, what he came in for! Sister Manhood almost started giggling again. She would have if the solicitor had encouraged it, but when she looked he ignored her. Nor would he look at Betty Hunter. He was all for his own thoughts, it seemed. He had turned red, except where his jawbones showed up white. Arnold Wyburd, she saw, would look a very naked man when stripped.

As Sister Manhood returned from the nurses' room with the pad, Mrs Hunter was making her solicitor recite, ' ... Marjorie four, Heather three.'

'Surely there were more? For years the talk was all of babies. Some of them must have died, then?'

'Yes, some of them died; some miscarried. They don't count, I should have thought.'

Sister Manhood was pretty sure she was right: the 'document' would be a will, and Arnold Wyburd would influence it.

For a moment Mrs Hunter's attention was distracted by matters more important than life and death: her fingers were flittering over the topmost sheet of the writing-pad her nurse had fetched. She was feeling for concrete evidence.

'What's this?' The fingers almost gouged out the upper edge of the paper. 'This isn't it. Not important enough – Nurse. A common *pad*! Go down to the study – to Alfred's desk – the *embossed* paper from Sands.'

Old snob.

'I want it done properly,' Mrs Hunter insisted.

When Sister Manhood trailed back with a wad of the super parchment, old Betty was explaining, ' ... people think if it isn't in writing, it's stealing.'

Mrs Hunter's hearing was good enough for her to fall silent after that, and the solicitor of course was too discreet to show he knew she had been talking at all.

Flora Manhood would have liked to cry, not only for the un-necessary journey she had been forced to make, but also because these inhuman beings were letting her see the outsider they thought her.

'I was explaining', Mrs Hunter took up the thread again, 'that you are going to marry a man you don't value enough.'

'*Marry*? What man, I'd like to know?' Sister Manhood exploded.

Elizabeth Hunter went off into what might once have convinced as laughter. 'Come on, Arnold. Did you bring him a pen, Sister? And ink?'

Now it was the solicitor who was pleased to explain: he had his Parker, a present from the staff on his seventieth.

'But who can the fellow be? Who I don't intend to marry?' Sister Manhood raged.

'Write something, Arnold – in your beautiful hand, which I hope you haven't lost – put something like, "I hereby confirm that I give my pink sapphire to Florrie ... " Is it Florrie? " ... Manhood – to celebrate her engagement ... " Or do you think "betrothal" sounds less suburban? her – her ... ? But that is beside the point.

What it all amounts to is her—*marriage* with … ' Mrs Hunter started coughing, so her nurse was able to occupy herself offering a glass of barley water.

When the coughing fit had passed, Flora Manhood announced, 'I am not going to be conned into marrying any man—however important. Anyway, you don't know what was behind it. You're mad', she said, 'to get any such idea. I won't! And you can keep your ring!' She would bring it back from Vidlers' tomorrow, and better if Sir Basil was here: she would show the pair of them, mother and son, how little a pink sapphire impressed her.

'But we must mention the man's name, Mrs Hunter.' The solicitor paused, suitably grave above his presentation pen.

'How do I know?' Mrs Hunter grumbled. 'I can't remember names any more. But liked his voice. Once when he brought the prescript—the medcins!' She smiled the taste of words down. 'I liked the feel of his skin. I don't know why they brought him up to my room. Perhaps I asked for him. I have always liked men around me.'

Sister Manhood stood the glass so abruptly it chinked with the crystal jug. She removed herself so quickly these cold old devils probably didn't even notice; though you were the reason for the game they were playing, its only object to cause distress.

Well, she would take her child to anywhere—to buggery—or Adelaide—throw the ring out of the bus window, rear her poor bastard with the love she already felt for him, and hope he would not end up murdering her with a hammer for forcing life on him.

Mrs Hunter said, 'That should pacify her. Give it to me, Arnold.' He did, and she put what she remembered as her signature, slashed across the paper, after which he witnessed it in his deliberate hand.

'Now,' she said, 'another matter. Bring me the jewel case. Well,' she said, 'it's where it's always been—over on that what-not I've had to put up with because it was a present from Emily.'

He fetched the case. She sprang the catch, and her fingers went to it, verifying. 'Oh, that! Ugly! Now this—this is what—I've often thought of—of giving Lal Wyburd.' She collected herself immediately. 'Your wife, Arnold.'

Turquoises were clustered at intervals along the chain she was drawing out.

'Very simple, as you see. We were poor farmers. (My father died of mortgages.) This chain of my mother's I was wearing when the storm struck. Otherwise it would have gone the way of everything else.' The voice was reduced to such an introspective key, the solicitor might have lost track if it had not been suddenly raised to a pitch of blatancy which suggested Elizabeth Hunter had manned her battering ram. 'Do you think Lal will care for anything so unimportant? People expect you to hand out something showy when they've decided you're sitting on treasures. So she may be hurt—by the insignificance—of this little chain. When one doesn't set out—deliberately—to ruffle these sensitive souls. If she doesn't like it, at least she can wear it on family occasions.' The mouth rasped shut.

'Yes.' He was tired. 'She will like it.' His eyelids were the heaviest part of him.

He was no master of disguises: he could not have watched the condescension with which their benefactress would have received thanks for her gift to his wife; so he simply put the chain in his pocket.

She had sunk back, gummy-eyed and thoughtful, before remembering, 'Have you got the paper? To give that nurse?'

'Yes, I have it, I have it,' he nattered.

She was grinning at him from the pillows. One of her nonbreasts had worked free of the nightdress. As he put the jewel case back where it belonged, his discomfiture was laced with a spirt of horror. He stumbled on his way out of the room.

'Sister Manhood?' He knocked on the door shut between them.

She took so long to open, he had begun to wonder whether she would, but she did, and he told her, 'Here's Mrs Hunter's statement. Which you wanted,' he added, to hold her partly responsible.

'I didn't want it! Because I don't want her bloody ring!'

She took the paper, if only because this old man, the older for being Mrs Hunter's solicitor, had withdrawn so deep into his thoughts he might continue standing at the door.

'Mr Wyburd,' she said in a burst of exasperation with herself and desperation over almost everybody else, 'you are the one who must reason with them – a legal man and their father's friend.'

'Mrs Hunter is the one who will decide,' Mr Wyburd hoped.

He went away.

Faced with the remainder of the afternoon Sister Manhood engaged in the most elaborate succession of activities she could invent: she opened windows which were closed, and closed those which she found open; she fetched a duster and dusted ledges and corners Mrs Cush had conveniently left to occupy a nurse; she generally tidied the already tidy. In doing so, she was forced to ignore Mrs Hunter's official declaration, which she had shoved for the time being under the pin cushion on the nurses' dressing-table; why, she couldn't think, when she meant to tear it up.

Nor would she have known whether a tinkled summons by her patient's hand-bell was a godsend or an evil omen.

When she went in, Mrs Hunter ungummed her voice. 'I want to use the seat, Sister.'

'Are you sure you're strong enough, dear? Hadn't you better let me bring the pan?'

'I am strong enough,' Mrs Hunter said.

Though normally Sister Manhood hated the business of bundling the old mummy on to the ugly-looking commode, today after all that dusting and emotional hullabaloo, she made a soothing cere-mony of it. The commode itself, if you were in the right mood, had a kind of half-cocked dignity, with its knobs and scrolls, and the curved handrails ending as swans' heads. Flora was reminded of the picture of a real throne in the history book at school.

When she had enthroned her ravaged queen, the waiting-woman upheld procedure, 'Say if we're not comfy, love.'

Because everybody ought to know she had not felt comfortable in years, Mrs Hunter did not answer. She sat as though resigned to face a moment of self-imposed terror in a fun fair, clutching rails polished by the hands of other compulsive thrill-addicts rather than the flannel Mrs Cush loved to saturate with O'Cedar.

Flora Manhood, all bash and busyness till lately, felt curiously lulled. 'When I was a kid,' she could feel her lips opening, swelling with a lovely warmth and indolence, 'I seemed to spend half my life in the dunny. Half of that time only looking. Or dreaming. Or reading ads from the papers Mum had cut into squares. I dunno — they can't have been there that long, but all these papers had turned yellow. In the dunny up the yard. There was always fowls outside picking around amongst the mallows. They'd come and peck at your toes, like they thought your toenails were grains of white corn.' Never before had she talked to Mrs Hunter like this: it made her feel sort of drunk. 'Some of the hens used to roost on the seat at night. I could never ever decide if it was the hens that smelt of lime, or the lime of hen dirt.'

Flora stopped. She was ashamed.

Mrs Hunter cleared her throat, and it was going to be serious. 'What did you dream about — when you were at the — lavatory?'

'About getting rich, I reckon. Escaping to the city, away from the humdrum of the farm. Oh, and love!' She was careful not to make it 'marriage'.

Mrs Hunter was considering the gravest issue. 'Do you love me, Nurse?'

'What a thing to ask! Of course I love you. We all love you.' It was too bright and bouncy, too Big Sister; though it mightn't strike an old person.

'If you love me as you say, perhaps you would do me a favour,' Mrs Hunter persisted. 'Even if it went against what I suppose one would call your better judgment.'

Sister Manhood smelt a rat. 'I don't know about "better judgment". It all depends what you want me to do.'

The old girl's eyes were clenched so tight she was more than straining on the loo. 'The little capsules Doctor prescribed — to make me sleep—would you leave them by me, Sister? So that I could help myself?'

Sister Manhood felt herself perspiring: her upper lip must be wearing a moustache of sweat. 'Not likely!' she cried. 'What a thing to expect! It wouldn't be ethical.' She was genuinely shaken.

'Love is above ethics. And you love me. You said.'

'That's unfair, Mrs Hunter. How would I stand if anything happened?'

'If you love me.' Her eyes still screwed up.

Flora Manhood shepherded her breasts inside her arms, no longer a nurse, but a woman defending her threatened virtue. (Well, more or less: when technically no virgin, and ethically not altogether blameless, there's still a theory of good you like to hang on to.)

Mrs Hunter said, 'Let us forget about it. There are other ways.'

'But it's downright immoral—wanting to do away with yourself!' Oh, cock, cock; the way things were going, you might have to come at it too. 'And not so simple, believe me.' As though anybody would.

'Simple enough. My will shall withdraw, if I decide it's necessary.'

Sister Manhood blew her top. 'This may be the time your will doesn't work. See?'

A silence fell between them.

Flora fumbled for her handkerchief; the old thing would never realize what she did to people.

Presently the nurse asked, 'Have you finished, dear?' However others might study to break the rules, there were still formalities to be observed.

'Have I finished? I haven't begun!'

Flora remembered Mum used to whistle: that was for the other, though.

Then she heard the pink pink, of one or two pellets, or three, as from an afterthoughtful, or costive, goat.

'I believe I've finished, Sister.'

When she had wiped, and was preparing to hoist the bundle back

459

into bed, Sister Manhood asked, 'Would you like me to make you beautiful tonight? Wigs and all?'

Mrs Hunter smiled, and answered, 'No.' But enjoyed the bosomy waves into which her nurse was lowering her. 'No,' she repeated, and her voice rocked and settled. 'I'm looking forward to a cup of tea. Do you think my cook-housekeeper will have made me anchovy sandwiches? Not if they're not thin.'

Sister Manhood's thinned-out smile was the visible expression of her sigh. 'We'll see,' she said.

She had to admit the old cracked gramophone records they played together, over and over, sent her at times, but she would be glad this evening when night came, and with it her relief.

Then as the last quarter approached, and she dusted the crumbs off her embalmed patient's chin, and sorted out in her mind what to report to de Santis, Flora Manhood knew that for some reason she would have given anything to defer her colleague's arrival.

You could as easily hold off the night as defer de Santis. Soft and silent, she was standing in the dressing-room. In her navy hat. She was more than usually considerate: just when human was what you mightn't be able to take.

Sister said, 'You'll be glad of your rest, Sister. You're looking drawn. Nothing wrong, is there?' Taking off that hat, she held it raised for a moment, detached and purposeless, above her head. 'Nothing personal, I mean?'

Sister Manhood snort-laughed. 'Nothing that a boiled egg and a hot bath won't put right.' Jesus Christ!

Sister de Santis was airing her dark, rather matted hair by lifting it in places with a hatpin.

'She must be upset, isn't she?' she asked; 'so much happening too suddenly.'

The grotty old pin, which you had seen often enough before, had an onyx knob: tonight the streaks dividing it were whiter.

'Upset?' Sister Manhood would not have liked it known, let alone confirmed. 'She's constipated—anyway, a bit—last time on. I've dished out the calomel, Sister. You'll have that to brighten your night.'

De Santis was taking off her coat in such a way it became some kind of dark robe.

Flora's head was aching by now. 'It hasn't been an easy duty,' she admitted. 'I think Badgery sees to it that the worst of the morning will take effect only in the afternoon.'

Sister de Santis had begun the more intricate, personal moves in her disrobing. She was a bloody onion tonight. Not that anybody had to watch. Not if they could uproot themselves.

'They rang the Thorogood Village.' It sounded muffled from inside a dress. 'They're going out tomorrow.'

'Oh?'

'Yes, the princess rang them.'

Flora Manhood took a look at St Mary's great dollops of breasts as she stooped and hunched to get her slip off.

'It was the princess, was it? Not Sir Basil?' Sister Manhood needlessly asked.

Sister de Santis confirmed that it was the Princesse de Lascabanes, not Sir Basil Hunter: which might have been a consolation or, on the other hand, a disappointment each had half expected.

When Sister Manhood rounded. 'How do you know they rung, Sister?'

'Matron Aspden phoned me to ask what sort of woman Mrs Alfred Hunter is—whether she would adapt herself to life at the Village. Matron and I were same year at P.A. She's good. She's down to earth.' The flatness of their conversation might have been a comfort to both of them.

Sister de Santis was setting her veil in the orthodox folds. 'So tomorrow they will drive out—to interview Matron and Mr Thackray the chaplain—to decide—officially, that is.'

Sister Manhood stopped tweaking the corner of the document she had stuck, for want of a better place, under the pincushion. 'I'll go now,' she said.

She did, but shortly returned, to collect for safety's sake, Mrs Hunter's written promise.

Strange in one so professional, Sister de Santis would have liked to postpone appearing in her patient's room. Later, in the small hours, it might be easier to convert this old woman into an abstraction of age, or justification for your own existence, or see her in both physical and metaphoric terms, as the holy relic to which your faith bowed down in worship; but for the present, as mother of her children, Mrs Hunter remained distressingly human. Mary de Santis turned once or twice in the narrow cupboard-lined room, itself a narrow cupboard, or suddenly transparent repository in which those other relics were piled hugger-mugger: a silken ankle; a shrunken, needle-punctured arm; a woman's white, bloodied knee; the body of a strangled dog. The least brutal of these images flickered in Mary de Santis the most subtly and persistently. Grace would never abound in one who was frivolous, sensual, irresponsible enough to shiver still in contemplating the relic of Sir Basil Hunter's silken ankle.

Fortunately, it was given to her to escape her thoughts in remembering the calomel.

Sir Basil's mother was asleep at least in theory. As the nurse approached the bed the old woman's breathing grew more complicated: it sounded like a crumpling, then a tearing, of tissue paper. The level of the barley water slightly swayed.

Sister de Santis was moving around.

'What are you doing, Mary?'

'They left your jewel box open.'

The old woman lay managing her bones, grimacing.

'Did you have a good time?' Sister de Santis asked. 'Did Sister dress you up?'

'No. I've been giving some presents.'

'I hope they were appreciated.' Mary de Santis felt duller, heavier for her sententiousness; the darkened room shook as she tiptoed around: a hypocrite's movements should have been more skilful.

Mrs Hunter said, 'I've never given you anything. Or nothing of consequence. You seem to me complete, Mary.'

The nurse mumbled.

'What did you say?'

Oh, Lord! 'I said there's nothing I need.'

The old woman floated off again.

The nurse pulled up her usual chair. At first she sat forward, arms round knees, gasping, panting, till noticing in a mirror the white contortions of a throat, dark lips struggling to contain the hole which opened in them. What if she lost control and sounds blared out across the silence?

She sat back after that, to await the motions of a patient's bowels. She had her work, which was her faith. Whatever images might distract, seduce, even spiritually strengthen her in the course of this life, her formal faith would remain as plain as a bedpan. Nobody could destroy *her*.

Yes, she had her faith her work her work.

Ten

BASIL WAS driving very cautiously amongst the concrete mixers, the semi-trailers, the lopsided vegetable trucks, and parti-coloured Holden sedans. The long road out of the city repeated itself in hills and hollows, in rows of red identical villas, and blocks of equally conformist shops. The used-car racketeers added something of daring by mooring their fleets under canopies of garish pennants permanently fidgeted by a wind. Still, the predominant colour of the highway was that of cement dust.

Basil drove sitting too upright. Neither of them was yet resigned to the circumstances they alone had wanted: they had badgered Arnold Wyburd into organizing their visit to 'Kudjeri' against his wish.

'But they're very ordinary, quiet people;' the solicitor tried to fob his clients off.

It clashed with Dorothy's sense of what was due to her. 'Are we such hectic monsters that we shall disjoint the lives of ordinary quiet people? *And,*' she turned on the *vox humana* Australian style, 'isn't "Kudjeri" our old home?'

So it was engineered. It would be one way of killing time while the details of Mother's future were fully arranged. And yet, having satisfied her wishes, Dorothy narrowed herself as they drove north. Was it in imitation of her brother? Basil was so unnaturally erect he would surely break this side of Gogong. She preferred on the whole to be driven by somebody she did not know; knowing a driver made her nervous. The exception was the man she still referred to as her husband: with Hubert at the wheel, she accepted the wall which would spring up straight ahead of them.

Now ostensibly driving on a positive mission with her brother, they were in fact allowing the past to suck them back through this choked intestine recorded on maps as the Parramatta Road. Faces to either side of them were watching it happen: streaming, muscular men and their drier, scorched women aimed sideways glances at the couple swaying with assumed discretion in their unconvincingly modest car. Emotionally at least, things were what they used to be, the tall poppies bowing mock apologies to those who held them guilty of the worst.

At an intersection a truck had spilt half its load in slewing to avoid collision with a milk van: burst open or slackly contorted, the flour bags lying on the grey concrete had a disconcerting dead look. A tall young policeman was noting details of an accident which only lacked blood.

Dorothy began to snigger.

'What is there to laugh at?' As a driver Basil was incensed.

'Nothing,' Dorothy admitted, but the laughter bumped out of her. 'Actually, I was thinking of that woman – Matron Whatnot at the Thorogood Village – the day we went.'

'A stout lady, and worthy.' Superior to Dorothy, Basil did not laugh; he smiled.

'Worthy – yes – I grant you! I'm only too thankful!' Dorothy laughed with greater restraint, till a veil of flour draped across the road, and in her mind's eye an image of blancoed shoes severed from a pair of ankles, shocked her short; she was relieved when Basil had driven her past.

Basil, too, was uneasy for something. 'Seriously though, Dorothy, with plenty of warm-hearted attention – and Matron Aspden is obviously the personification of what they call "warmth",' Dorothy could not resist a giggle, 'there's no reason why Mother shouldn't be happy at the Thorogood Village.'

'In her day she was an intelligent woman, and is still, *au fond*, reasonable.'

'She thrives on flattery of course.'

'Don't we know! And she'll get that. Mother is one of those who generate in their slaves the flattery they're hungry for.'

Basil drove. The factories were gone; the shops, the houses were thinning out, offering glimpses of a still shamefaced landscape. He tried coughing away a suspicion that trees appear real only when artificially lit. At 'Kudjeri' perhaps he would re-discover the real thing—if there was enough of him left to fill so large a stage.

'What I thought most frightening,' he formed his words with foresight because the road had some treacherous bends in it, 'was the row of inmates sitting along the veranda as we pulled up—before Matron came out to jolly them. That was an audience I shouldn't care to play to. You could act your head off, and they wouldn't let you know how they were responding.'

'They were old. Old people are detached.'

'Made me feel an awful outsider.'

'Mother will be on the in-side.'

'There was one old girl—the one with the bone bracelets and a hank of pink chiffon round her shingle: a kind of musical comedy queen. Mother will hate her. She'll queer Elizabeth Hunter's opera.'

'Mother won't know. She'll be too wrapped up in her own past. The outer world doesn't exist beyond her bed.'

Yet the frieze might encroach, with a rattle of bone bracelets, a creaking of arthritic limbs, a clutching of sticky, remindful fingers, the kiss of chiffon.

Whatever might happen to Elizabeth Hunter, her children were determined to resist encroachment.

Basil said, 'The bed will be a problem. I hope they can fit it into the room.'

'They'll have to.'

'She'll give them hell if they don't.'

'Matron's a resourceful woman.'

'I can't see—short of taking a saw.' It was a scene in which you could laugh; so he did.

'Nothing so brutal.' Dorothy's voice rose, harsh and querulous, not to accuse her tasteless brother, but to defend herself. 'Anyhow,' the voice subsided, 'somebody's got to die first. There isn't a vacancy. The matron explained that.'

'Somebody's got to die,' he agreed.

He drove, and said, 'Arnold Wyburd's the one who's going to have it in for us for ever after.'

'Men like old Wyburd are so vain about their own integrity in serving a family and keeping its fortune together over the years, they lose sight of the fact that the actual members of the family are human beings with human desires. I think Arnold only realized that when we descended on him out of the air. It gave him a shock.'

Dorothy looked at her brother: she would have liked him to recognize her humanity. She was feeling more youthful since they had left the suburbs behind.

But Basil was intent on driving: it absolved him from appreciating his passenger. When Dorothy started acting it filled him with dislike: he recognized at such times the hard, greedy, scene-stealing pro she might have become. He glanced for re-assurance in the driver's mirror: men on the whole were more generous, both as artists, and as human beings. On the windward side his hair had been ruffled without appreciable damage to his looks. (Might give *Richard Two* another go.)

In the mountains the weatherboard and fibro townships were minding their own business. Chummier shops displaying pragmatic goods had nothing to hide. But doubts set in among the stragglers, towards the fringes, where houses built for permanence had reached the lurching stage, above the rich humus spread by their shrubberies to soften the logical collapse. The shrubberies themselves, planted by their owners as a sober duty, were touched with a cold apocalyptic fire. Here and there at the foot of a tree, old, broken, black umbrellas arranged singly or in clumps, were seen to stir at times, then to move, slowly, sideways, asymmetrically. Some of the old umbrella-forms were trundling through an undergrowth of rhododendrons and azaleas assisted by what appeared to be part of their own aluminium frames, which had become conveniently unstuck, and could be used as crutches.

Basil was stopping the car in front of a shop. On a blind wall a square of faded bluebag blue was advertising some illegible commodity. Without explaining why, Basil was getting out. Nor did

Dorothy ask for explanations: she was frantically searching for some face or object with which to identify herself. As Basil was closing the car door, a boy in jeans followed by a high-stepping spotted dog, came jaunting past. Dorothy tried smiling at the boy, but her smile must have looked directionless, or old; anyway the boy was plainly ignoring foreigners. When Basil had gone inside the shop, Dorothy was left with gooseflesh up her arms. The silence around her might have been solid if it had not been for the sound of the boy's departing thongs and the notes of a currawong floating on the mountain air. Something was eluding her; it will be different, she said, when we reach 'Kudjeri'.

Basil returned with the two pies. He was wearing the expression of a man who has laid hands on a symbol of his boyhood: it made him look somewhat ponderous.

'Oh, Basil — you're not going to *eat* them!' She spoke with the languor of an older girl.

'What else?' The light through a sycamore illuminated his sheepish words.

He handed her the second pie. 'Oh, *really*!' She couldn't refuse it, and at the same time it was too hot, too greasy: she didn't know what to do with the thing.

Basil was already stuffing his mouth. She doubted whether his boyhood could be recaptured so easily. As a trickle of pale gravy meandered down towards the cleft in his chin, she was reminded, rather, of a boyish, slightly sweaty commercial traveller in a train. Only the dustcoat was missing.

Dorothy sighed. 'Oh, dear!' She bit into her horrid pie.

Flooded with the flavour of hot soggy cardboard and floury gravy, her unwillingness and contempt turned to loathing; worse on discovering something loathsome in herself: she was filled with a guilty voluptuousness as though biting into her own flesh.

'By God, it's *good*!' Basil sprayed the windscreen with several fragments of gristle.

'*Naus*-e-ating!' She sucked back anything else that was trying to escape.

And turned her head to prevent Basil's noticing. The same boy, returning with his cold insolence and high-stepping, swivel-nosed dog, must have seen. But that did not matter. She could feel the tears hurtling hot down her cheek to join the mess round her mouth. (Her faith would never have allowed her to contemplate suicide, but she came close to committing it each time she betrayed the past.)

Basil had swallowed his last mouthful. He was wiping fingers on his breast-pocket foulard. One currawong floated longer and closer than the others. It seemed, as always, that the answer might have been found in the country town you were leaving; if you had not already left.

'Admit you enjoyed it, Dotty!' Basil sounded brisk and ruthless.

Searching through her normally organized handbag, Dorothy was all cunning. 'The wretched thing was warm, at least – food of a kind. But only in the wildest moment of sentimental excess could anyone admit to enjoying that pie.'

'I did.' It was what made him an artist, he decided, as opposed to what kept Dorothy, alas, Dorothy.

Although driving, he looked at her with what she might have interpreted as compassion. But she did not need it.

She had found her mirror. There was no getting away from her face, for today she had abstained from make-up, in celebration of nature. Now the cynicism she had been cultivating of late helped her bear up against the drought furrowing her skin. She quirked the corners of her mouth. A touch of sunburn lent her courage while emphasizing the desiccation, except where some grease had overflowed the naked lips. She began rubbing at the ghastliness: that grisly, gristly pie. After restoring her true self, she relaxed her throat. She was looking bright rather than anxious. She glanced at Basil, wondering to what extent he could distinguish between vanity and courage.

Basil was lowering his eyes, smiling as they plunged down through the glare, which was all that could be seen of the bleached plains. A sombreness lay in the depths of his stomach. He converted a belch

into flatulent silence. Soon he would be forced to do a pee. He
stopped. And did. Even Dorothy, a lone emu, casually flounced
into deeper scrub.

When they were reassembled, she asked, 'Doesn't it make you
feel guilty, darling?' while surveying a non-existent landscape,
smiling a bright, casual smile.

'For what? And why? For God's sake!' If Dorothy de fucking
Lascabanes wasn't the archetypal rat.

'For foisting ourselves on these poor Macrorys.'

'Would they have let themselves in for what they didn't
want?'

Basil and Dorothy Hunter were getting back into the car. The
scrub around them was of the poorest. Left-over blue metal at the
roadside petered out in stones, then rocks. There was a dry scuffle
of heat and lizards.

Dorothy advised practically, 'Whether they want us or not,
we'd better push on. It's worse arriving after dark.'

All women, wives even, are fundamentally big sisters: Dorothy
he saw and heard easing her elastic in front of a brother.

'Would they have accepted us,' he harked back, 'if they hadn't
wanted us?' She had got him upset.

'Mr Wyburd suggested they were rundown. Perhaps we could
offer them something—as rent, I mean.'

Basil grumbled, and drove.

Dorothy, for her part, was ready to dismiss the idea of making too
large a hole in Mother's cheque; though she had bought the little
dress she was wearing: burnt umber for longevity.

'It was only a thought,' she murmured.

She pointed her elbows at the windscreen, and the wind blew
down the short sleeves into her armpits liberating her from obligations. Basil must have felt included: he snuffle-laughed, and
rearranged a thigh.

Only in competing with distance, the gongs and drums made it
difficult to maintain a human balance. He had to remind himself
I am Sir Basil Hunter—the actor; while the Princesse de Lascabanes

kept looking in her handbag for something she was unable to find.

What he, what either of them expected of the Macrorys, it might have been indelicate to enquire. Or he might not have known. He was pretty sure Dorothy had no idea, though if asked, she would pretend to one.

Where physical hunger heightened by the crudest sentimental longing had prompted him to buy and guzzle the pie, now a deeper, more confused desire made him urge the car across the blinding plains towards this mythical house in which a real family was living. He anticipated flopping into bed, pulling up the sheet till it became a hood to intensify the darkness, curling as tight as his stubborn bones would allow, as he remembered possums, beans, a foetus in a bottle. Around him as he fell asleep he would hear the sighs, the muffled assertions of people living in the house from which he had run away in the beginning.

Intimations of frost reached them as they drove into Gogong. Sheets of fluctuating copper had replaced glass in shopfront and window. Barking dogs, thinner for the approaching cold, slavered and gulped at the silence. One little shit-coloured bitch, wearing a strap for collar, was threatened with drowning in waves of dust while chasing after this foreign car to head it off. All the watching faces looked curiously opaque, some of them blinded in addition by the spectacles they were wearing.

'Gogong, eh?' The metal had entered into Basil's voice.

'Yes, indeed! The same as all the other ghastly little towns.' She knew it was not. 'Let's get it over.'

She had hunched herself sideways in her seat as though to take advantage of her brother's protection, or if this were not forth-coming, to shoulder off any unpleasantness she might not be able to endure.

They were nearing the point on the outskirts of the town where the road forked, one branch stretching unequivocally north, the lesser straggling over the hills to 'Kudjeri'. In the cleft between the two roads a clump of dark conifers had survived the larger design

471

for a park; drought and neglect had done for the rest; though at its insignificant most, the park would never have become more than the background to a monument in bronze, which no doubt had been the original intention.

From the newspaper cutting Mother had sent years ago Basil knew what to expect. So he slowed down. Whether Dorothy, too, was in the know, he had never heard; the way she was turning her back to the thing she was probably unaware the monument to Alfred Hunter existed. But he had to look. And was fascinated by this ugly marriage between civic bombast and innocent human purpose and achievement; for if the head, the chest, the stance aspired to the heroic, the wrinkles in the bronze waistcoat and pants dragged the attempt back to earth and a hand which might have been propped on a bamboo occasional table instead of the horn of a merino ram.

Basil could have lingered, grinning and squinting up at 'Father' if Dorothy's fist had not started drumming on his thigh. 'Go on—do! I can't bear it!'

So that he accelerated, and they spurted forward, shot over the level crossing, and bumped their heads on the roof of the car.

He thought he would not mention the statue which his mind was busy resurrecting; when Dorothy murmured, 'He wasn't like that.'

'Can you honestly remember?'

'Oh—yes—no—not distinctly.'

It was his own recurring predicament.

To cheer them up, he shared a malicious fantasy, 'I wonder Mother didn't insist on their working her into that deathless group.'

'On a chaise longue!' Dorothy's laugh dropped like a stone.

After that they fell silent, driving through the hills this side of 'Kudjeri'. By the light of dusk, paddocks were thrown wider open; on the other hand, rock and scrub were double-locking themselves against intruders. The car ranted on, over grit, and potholes filled with a thin mud. A sky drained as shallow as a sheet of colourless waxed paper had resumed its cyclic promises: all of them mysteries which strangers drowning in their purple depths must fail to solve. Perhaps the car would at least stall: it stuttered and faltered enough at times to encourage hopes. Then in the darkness of a hollow, opening out ahead and below, the house you could remember only by flashes or in dreams, was pinpointed as a cluster of lights, flickering and failing through a great mushroom-clump of trees, before becoming fixed by the car's approach.

Dorothy said, 'This is what I dreaded – arriving at nightfall.'

Basil too, if he would have admitted.

Doubts failed to discourage the car: willows were swooning round a river bend; then the sweep of Portuguese laurels, battered by age, animals, and children. At last, the oval of a rosebed.

'I've never felt more frightened,' Dorothy chittered and giggled; 'not even on my wedding night.'

Basil knew his lips were trembling with the smile he would normally compose with confidence, to take a call, or to impress those he was meeting for the first time.

As they got out, people were coming down the steps towards them.

However it might strike their hosts, Dorothy ducked back, looking for some something – anything – roses, a rose! She trampled the edge of the unkempt bed, and came across one or two autumn buds, cold, tight, pointed, which would dry on their stems without opening. She had torn her wrist, but that was the least of the situation.

'Come on, Dot!' Basil was chivvying his awkward sister.

Then the Hunter children were holding hands, by whose choice they would not have known, prepared to face a music which was bursting on them, agonizingly clear, but discordant.

' ... you'll just have to get used to it. It won't be what you remember – will it, Rory? do you think? Children, don't make a nuisance of yourselves ... '

By degrees they might furnish the house with their memories. For the moment it looked bare: the Macrory establishment did not run to comfort, let alone luxury. In the hall Sir Basil caught his toe in a rent in what must have been an oriental rug before dust and decay had taken over. Beyond the rug, there was simply a sound of feet grating over grit, in corridors, on stairs, and in some cases, whole rooms.

Halfway up the stairs Mrs Macrory paused and gasped, 'It must seem odd to find strangers living in your house.'

Basil could at least turn the Voice on. 'Hardly ours. We left too young.'

Dorothy had for protection her authentic upper-class stridency, as well as the legend of nobility, both of which worked as a rule. 'We were sent back for part of the holidays,' she blared, 'almost always. To our father.' The mystic word troubled her more than when it cropped up in her prayers.

'Gosh, yes, those were holidays!' Basil had a brief glimpse of himself as juvenile lead, carrying a tennis racquet, in a farce.

He felt at once that the line had misfired: they were possibly expecting the tattered crimson of a grand manner, but he was too exhausted, too travel-sodden for histrionics; nor was it any advantage that one member of his audience had her back to him, and the other coming behind with the baggage was little more than a heavy breathing. If Mrs Macrory were to turn, he would win her over with that infallible moist stare; but she would not.

It was he who turned, to introduce some business into the scene in which they were stuck. 'Anyhow, I see no reason why I shouldn't carry my bag.' He might have matched heartiness with a wide gesture, but the stairs cramped his style: in the play he made for possession of the suitcase, his hand slithered ineffectually past an unresponsive, hairy arm.

Macrory made a devious lowing sound, and continued mounting. His wife would do the answering.

She looked over her shoulder laughing somewhat automatically. 'Physical exertion is Rory's speciality.' Finding she had embarrassed herself, she showed them her back as before, and brought them shortly to the landing.

Mrs Macrory — 'Anne' in her reply to Wyburd's letter — was a woman neither young nor old, her distraught hair prematurely grey, or dusty in keeping with the state of her house. If she had not been in the middle of a pregnancy, her cheeks might have looked less gaunt, her eyes less hollow and flannel-edged. By nature coldly explicit, the voice would have carried conviction if it hadn't sounded permanently surprised. Anne Macrory had the air of a social worker trapped in a life she had warned against.

As the party reached the landing, various children on whom the social worker had not been working, appeared in doorways in bitty costumes, while one or two were still stumbling up the stairs in the wake of the invasion. Some of the children were already tall and thin, with knobbly wrists and noticeable salt cellars, but the mother had not yet shown herself in the little stumbling tumblers, tripped by curiosity and their hems.

Anne Macrory showed the Hunters into what Dorothy remembered, at first scarcely, then with repugnance, as their parents' bed- and dressing-rooms.

'I hope you'll be comfortable.' Mrs Macrory looked around what was a room in her own house, and touched a towel hanging on the rail at the foot of an enormous Hunter bed.

The Princesse de Lascabanes murmured and blushed: she would have liked to help her hostess out of an embarrassment, but lacked the skill.

Macrory dumped the bags in the suite the visitors would occupy. (Basil gloomily supposed he must settle for the stretcher and the dressing-room.)

The younger children seemed drawn to their father. They clustered round him. The youngest began climbing up one of his legs, but was thrown off just before grabbing a handful of crutch.

Rory Macrory was a physical man. Black, wiry hair made him look younger than his gaunt and dusty wife. But he might not have been. He was crude, perhaps deliberately so: shirt open almost to the navel to advertise his opinion of a famous actor and a princess. Though his smile was impressively white, and he flashed it often enough, it did not express pleasure.

Dorothy found herself remembering Brumby Island: it was the smell of sweat.

'Think you can doss down here?' His body thrown into a spectacularly plastic stance, Macrory dared all takers.

'Why ever nn-n-ott?' Sir Basil caught himself stuttering.

The Princesse de Lascabanes returned out of an apathy. 'We are the ones who should apologize for complicating such busy lives.' The stalactites of charm dripped and glittered in this cavern of a room.

It was too much for the musclebound Macrory, who staggered out, smiling his joyless smile, strumming his exposed chest as though it were a hairy guitar.

Anne Macrory was the one who did the talking, in a voice she must have refurbished for the benefit of the princess: her words were formed so cleanly, however confused their sense of direction. 'Oh dear,' she started sighing when the guests came down, 'I meant to lay the table in the dining-room, but have fallen behind—as you see—with everything—tonight.' A used saucepan she was clutching escaped from her hands to bounce on the kitchen floor. 'Timing is essential, isn't it?' She opened the door of one of the ovens in a fuel range and let out a smell of burning fat. 'That is not what it seems,' she explained; 'mutton is more digestible if overdone.' Though a forthright opinion, it was haunted by a waning spirit; while almost simultaneously, a precarious mountain of unwashed pans slid crashing into the sink, and a middle girl appealed to her mother for help with a stringy hair-ribbon.

Sir Basil Hunter welcomed the idea of eating in the kitchen: it would save both time and trouble, and they would get to know one another quicker. The princess, who had noticed the marmalade smears on the table, was more niggardly with her enthusiasm. It cheered her only slightly to think she might give the oilcloth a wipe while their hostess was dealing with the burnt mutton. But the children would be watching, and children's eyes daunted Madame de Lascabanes.

476

Just before dinner, Basil nipped out for a pee, in a darkness full of animals. From the veranda edge he became part of the conspiracy: his water and the frost hissed together. A beast stopped cropping at the grass, but saw fit to start again.

Basil stood listening and shivering awhile. To be passively accepted by your natural surroundings is only temporarily gratifying. What he craved was confirmation of his own intrinsic worth as opposed to possibly spurious achievement. Which might not be forthcoming, however. The darkness continued to offer the kindly indifference of nature at its domesticated fringes, while the house behind would probably never share its secrets with one who had renounced life for theatre.

Upstairs, a child began to cry, then a man to comfort in broken resonances. It worked in spite of, perhaps because of, the absence of technique, in a scene in which Sir Basil did not take part.

He broke away after that, back into what was more simply a darkened set where in accordance with some rule of nightmare he had been denied the opportunity to rehearse. He barged on, without exactly panicking, his person the victim of knobs and corners and low-hung lintels, before catching sight of a crack beneath a door. He had to reach this splinter of light, and did, after grazing his heels on a downward flight of steps, and thumping the flags with an abruptness which numbed his kidneys, took away his breath, and let off fireworks inside his skull.

When Sir Basil made his entrance with a real limp instead of that mannerism which passed for one, he advanced a shoulder, exorcised the wrinkles from his brow, exposed his jaw, and waited for the recognition he was not accorded. Again he found it was not his scene.

Anne Macrory was launched on a speech regardless of the colander she was holding, and from which the cabbage water was dripping in runnels down her skirt. Dorothy (a bad actress) had borrowed an apron and was standing frozen by the kitchen table. On and off she touched the cutlery to imply she had laid the places. A child positioned at the sink was running her finger round the brown at the bottom of a basin of fat; a smaller child was seated on floor L.C. pulling the legs off a toy horse.

Dorothy Hunter suddenly realized somebody had mistimed an entrance. She frowned ferociously, not at a star actor, but at her tiresome brother.

Anne Macrory did not care: hugging the colander, she continued, '... that was after our first child. Until then, Rory wasn't accepted. Could you blame them? Only a stockman.'

'We were told the overseer.' Dorothy remained engrossed in the patterns she had made with cutlery: however exact, she might improve on them.

'Never an overseer.' Anne spoke with a candour she must have developed in facing the crises of life, at the same time exploring her skirt where it was sopped with cabbage water. 'Or only after they decided they'd better accept the whole situation. When he'd got me pregnant for the second time.'

Dorothy glanced at the children. Either they did not understand, or knew it all by heart.

Basil plumped down at the table, to wait for the meal in this play to which he didn't belong. Dorothy, it seemed, had wormed her way in with the management: considering her lack of talent, nothing else could explain their acceptance. Well, he would go on waiting, protecting his eyes from the crude lighting, and hope that his Swiss wristwatch and signet ring would not discredit him further by being so blatantly out of keeping.

Anne Macrory continued, her voice pitched clear and high, like a girl's. 'Then Daddy came good. He bought us "Kudjeri".' Anne and Rory had moved from 'Kirkcaldy': 'Kirkcaldy' was Anne's myth, her 'Kudjeri'. 'Of course I love "Kudjeri". But it isn't the same. You'll appreciate that, I'm sure.'

Dorothy said yes she did; though pudding spoons were more important since she had discovered them. 'You can't have been here so long,' she said, polishing one of the spoons on her apron. 'None of your children looks very old, though there seems quite a number of them.'

'I've been here a lifetime. You'd believe it if the children were yours.'

'I never asked to be a child,' said the girl who was cleaning out the brown dregs of dripping.

Her mother shushed her. 'Robert is sixteen. He's the eldest. He's away. Yes, it must be fifteen years since we took over "Kudjeri".'

Now it was Dorothy's lifetime which did not add up. 'But what happened here in between—between your coming and my father's death?'

'Surely you know better than I? Your mother put in managers, didn't she? Though she didn't like to come here, she tried to keep it, I think, for sentimental reasons. Didn't your father love the place?'

'I expect he did.' Dorothy blushed. 'I don't know. One was out of touch, living in Europe.' She looked to Basil, hoping he would either know, or else share her ignorance.

'Oh, yes—vaguely. Yes—I knew.' When he hadn't a clue.

What he did know for certain was that he would like to get the mutton over: food would fill a gap. He would probably never discover the point in time at which he had taken the wrong turn. It might have helped if he could have spoken some lines from one of the parts he had played, but his memory had become a blank.

Nor did Macrory improve matters by coming in with a whiskey bottle a quarter full. 'Would you care for a drop, perhaps?' He seemed to defer the moment of addressing the princess by name.

Dorothy took pride in refusing.

Macrory poured for Hunter and himself. 'My wife is a saint. She doesn't drink.'

'The best saints were the greatest drunks,' Mrs Macrory snapped, and tipped the colander of flopping cabbage into a brown-chipped tureen.

'How do you mean, Anne?'

But she wouldn't answer her husband. She went on scraping the colander with a big iron spoon so as not to waste any of the cabbage.

Macrory laughed. 'My wife is educated,' he complained; he was already half gone, on whiskey taken in advance to avoid wasting the stuff on guests.

'I'm educated, aren't I?' asked the girl who had been at the dripping; her fat cheeks aglow with it.

She came smoodging up at her father, and he answered, but gently, 'Yes, Mog;' and kissed her. 'Yes.'

He improved a little; and his wife put on a better face. 'Rory's tired by evening,' she explained. 'The work's exhausting.' She brushed against her husband in passing.

When other children had been called or sent for, and all were seated, the father began to decimate the mutton, the mother to dole out the pale cabbage as well as some grey-complexioned potatoes.

Speaking through a mouthful, casting up his eyes, corrugating his parti-coloured forehead, the host asked of the actor bloke, 'Tough, isn't it?' hopefully.

Sir Basil smiled. 'You must give me time to get my teeth round it.'

'It has the authentic flavour. Delicious.' Dorothy despised the words she had chosen, but did want to contribute something.

'You can only call it tough — to tell the truth.' Macrory looked at his wife; he wanted to hurt somebody, and in doing so, himself.

'But it's not bad, Dad.' One of his boys, who did not understand, was trying to help him.

'To you it isn't.' The father sighed; he was considerate of his children.

They were all eating the gristly meat, some of them genuinely loving it, others persuading themselves. The Hunters looked at each other with unforced tenderness.

'Will anyone have some more?' Anne was enunciating again so bright and clear she might have been fresh from 'Kirkcaldy'.

This would be the test. Some of the children accepted; the guests declined with sugared smiles.

Macrory could relax again.

Now it was Anne who carved the mutton. 'And what about Rory?'

Cocking his head, lowering his eyelids, his lashes so thick they looked as though they were gummed together, or fringed with flies, he agreed delicately to accept another help of mutton.

Anne brought it. Again she brushed against him; while arranging the plate, she leaned over his shoulder lower than she need have. The Macrorys tended still to communicate by touch; words were the dangerous weapons some malicious daemon from time to time put into their mouths.

During the pudding a child began wilting and moaning. 'I'm sick of spotted dog, Mum!'

'Eat it up! When I was a little girl at "Kirkcaldy" spotted dog was my favourite pudding. Certainly the spotted dog was lighter. I don't pretend to be a cook. But you can't say it isn't wholesome. We had a professional cook at "Kirkcaldy".'

'At "Kirkcaldy"! At "Kirkcaldy"!' The husband bowed his head. 'Everything was lighter, sweeter—better class. Only the fences were the same. Barbed wire never changes.'

Anne was not going to be caught. 'Isn't it a weakness everybody suffers from to some extent?' She looked from Dorothy to Basil, who smilingly agreed not to disagree.

Rory was addressing his knuckles, white except where one of them was scabbed. 'Any "Kirkcaldy" I knew was only ever from the wrong entrance.' He rinsed his mouth with what remained of the whiskey, and left them.

His wife murmured, 'Rory's tired.' She was at her gauntest, her saddest, the social worker whose job has got the better of her.

The Princesse de Lascabanes suggested that everyone was tired: her revenant certainly felt exhausted.

'Oh, but I must show you!' Anne revived. 'Rory had the idea of turning your father's study into a private sitting-room. So that you can escape from children—and think your own thoughts.' She had got up. 'I believe he's lit a fire. Come and see.'

The Hunters followed her warily. It was obvious that Anne wished to rehabilitate a delinquent husband. But what sort of ambush had the husband prepared? Or did he reason that your own thoughts in Father's room would be dynamite enough?

Basil had some difficulty in remembering their father's study, except as a scene of embarrassment and lockjaw. As in the rest of the house by this stage there was hardly any furniture: a burst, leather armchair; a day bed, probably burst too, if it had not been draped with a faded Indian counterpane, scorched in places by an over-heated iron; general collapse among the books on sparsely tenanted shelves.

'Don't you remember your father's chair?' Anne Macrory was daring them to let her kindness down.

'Why was the chair left here, if, as you say, Mother was so determined to do the right sentimental thing?' Dorothy's voice had begun hammering again.

'She let it stay because it was too old, I expect. She made us a present of a number of things. We were glad of them.' Anne tried draping the counterpane into more artistic folds. 'Books, too. Though we're not readers. There isn't time.'

Dorothy was particularly outraged by Mother's abandoning the books: apart from their sacredness as literature, books are the most personal possessions. Basil did not care: he had dragged the chair closer to the fireplace and two great smouldering knots of wood. He sat smiling down at the fire.

Dorothy pounced at the bookshelves. 'I'm sure none of these were my father's.'

Anne offered proof. 'Here's his signature in one.'

'*The Charterhouse of Parma!*' Dorothy turned on Basil. 'It was his favourite. She told me. She could leave his favourite! And mine!' She was chafing the book between her hands. 'No one can accuse us of heartlessness.'

Basil could not care. 'I never read it— *The Charterhouse of Thing*.' He was too drowsy: couldn't read a book in any case, unless a play, if it had the right part in it.

Dorothy was so engrossed in their father's book, in checking the text, shaking out the crumbs, fingering a tea stain (or was it faded blood?) Anne Macrory must have withdrawn. Dorothy herself must have sat down on the washed-out cotton counterpane. She

482

must have been, anyway half-reading, half-drifting, in their sitting-room.

While Basil must have half-dreamt he had grown old, as people do in life; you can't afford to grow old in the theatre. Perhaps if he sat long enough over the murmurous fire the most calamitous events might seem inevitable, even become acceptable: his wives; his non-child Imogen; the attempt to prolong what he and Dorothy understood as living by condemning their mother Elizabeth Hunter.

He opened his eyes wide. Her legs drawn up on the decrepit daybed, the open book dangling from her fingers, not as book but as artifice, Dorothy was staring at him, and not. What reminded him of their mother he could not think, or did not want to.

Still looking at him Dorothy said, 'That little, decent man struggling to escape from an unnatural bronze attitude. Which she imposed on him. The most grotesque idea Mother ever conceived! Say if we're not justified?' She was looking wholly at her brother, in the ruin of their father's room which had been made over to them.

He would have liked to close his eyes again, but as she would not allow it, he had to use the socially approved channel of evasion, 'Don't let's talk about it;' yawning, stretching his comfortable drowsiness to its full extent. 'We didn't come here, I feel, simply for that purpose.'

'For which other, I'd like to know? unless to wallow in discomfort.' She laughed. 'We must admit it's the rock bottom, darling.'

'We can slip away when we've had enough.'

'Yes, we can always slip away.' Sunk in an apathy of sagging leather and faced with the pleasures of martyrdom, she wondered if she would be able to.

Overhead, voices were wrenched and slamming rather than talking.

'Listen to them!' Basil said.

'Poor wretches!' Dorothy murmured dispassionately.

'Perhaps we should go to bed,' Basil suggested. 'That appears to be what the Macrorys have done.'

Unexpectedly, Dorothy awoke to a morning filled with explicit forms, after a night disordered by equivocal thoughts and suspicious, finally not unpleasant, dreams. She had woken once already, during the hours of darkness, to a sensation of being surrounded. She had switched the light on. Basil was snoring in the next room; beyond them silence was heaped on silence. She browsed here and there in *The Charterhouse of Parma*. She thought she might get to hate Macrory; although she had renounced men, at her age, she found his physical presence disturbing. She read, but could not become involved with this pale ghost of the novel she knew. Not that it was lost for ever: she could invoke its flesh and blood by reading it again in the original; thus her vanity was satisfied.

Sometimes at night Madame de Lascabanes allowed herself a touch of brilliance which should have been hers. Under the sheet she crossed her still estimable legs, an involuntary legacy from Elizabeth Hunter, and thought how she would enslave others, Anne Macrory for a start, and perhaps one or two of the children, simply by using her eyes. Her Sanseverina wandered after that into deeper velvet. One of several presences was entangling almost tripping before fitting her closer than a skirt. It could not be called adultery: Anne Macrory herself had confirmed it was the parents' bed. Love which has been imprisoned a lifetime in this tower which is also incidentally a body can only be the purest noblest occurring with a delicacy Stendhal cannot realize till Fabrizio breaks open his bronze and there is the knuckle with this one ugly scab oh Basil Bas Ber Bazzurl *tu es le seul à me comprendre.*

Dorothy Sanseverina woke. Again it was dark, Basil snoring in the next room. Supposing she had called out, as women do, she had read, in their ecstasy? She was relieved Basil continued sleeping. She could not have explained such an exquisitely elusive pleasure to her brother, or any of the others who came to mind:

that monument her father; the disgusting man with shirt open as far as his navel; less perhaps to Mrs Macrory; least of all to a vengeful Elizabeth Hunter, whose bed it was.

So Dorothy slept uneasily.

And got up too quickly: she had heard it was dangerous for people beyond a certain age to jump out of bed on waking; but had meant to rise early, to introduce some sort of order into the ghastly Macrory kitchen. Instead, here she was, listening to her anxious breathing as she bumped around in a grey light amongst the scant furniture.

Nor could she enjoy her own virtue to the utmost for finding Anne already in the kitchen, fire roaring in the flue, and beside the sink, additions to the unwashed plates. On the range stood a black pot, from which porridge had dribbled down to burn. In spite of the range it was cold in the kitchen at that hour. Through the rent in a fly-proof door, Anne was throwing chopbones to a pack of dogs in the yard beyond.

Anne said in her frostiest 'Kirkcaldy' voice, 'I hope you slept. I hope Rory and I didn't disturb you. We were not quarrelling. We were discussing whether to send some old ewes to market. My brothers say Rory hasn't a business head. That was my father's opinion also.' But suddenly Anne Macrory descended from her mythical-pastoral level, and exclaimed quite passionately, 'Come away! Whatever are you doing?'

'Preparing to wash up these pans and dishes.'

'But you mustn't! We wouldn't hear of it—Princess.'

'Truly, once I've drunk my coffee—and I can do that comfortably standing at the sink. How else shall I spend my time?'

'Oh dear, that's not for you!' moaned the social worker *dérangée*. 'And we don't have coffee.'

'Tea, then. I adore tea.'

Madame de Lascabanes stuck to her pans. She often surprised in herself a practically mystical attitude towards the ordering of chaos, even in its more squalid manifestations. In different circumstances, she might have made a devoted and uncrushable *femme de ménage.* Strange that it was her French self which abounded in humility, while the Australian in her aspired to a place among the 'happy few'.

'Has she come to live with us?' asked Mog, the fat girl who had scoffed the dripping the night before.

The mother was too distracted to attempt an answer. Before each of her children who had appeared in the kitchen, she set a plateful of burnt porridge. For the recalcitrant princess she managed to slide a cup of tea in amongst the litter at the sink.

The tea tasted bitter and stewed. It thrilled the Princesse de Lascabanes, as did her own consummate industry and the tongues of frosty air licking at her through the yard door.

'What about Sir Basil?' Mrs Macrory thought to ask, and became more distracted than before.

'No idea. You know, I hardly know my brother.' Indeed, Madame de Lascabanes was more intimate with the inside of this pan she was scouring.

It was too immoral for poor Mrs Macrory. 'We were a close family.' She sighed, and drifted to the screen door, and warmed her hands in her soiled sleeves, and returned uncomforted. 'Rory's gone to fork out the silage to the calves. He'll be back later on, and we'll see what plans he has for entertaining Sir Basil.'

The Princesse de Lascabanes narrowed her eyes, her lips, at the saucepan lid she had finished. She was holding it like a buckler between her self and the unspeakable Macrory; or herself and Basil, even; Hubert might not have existed; Father was at least dead; Fabrizio, a character she saw differently at successive readings, offered the greatest difficulties because substantially affected by the climate at waking.

Half opening in her, this dream of the night before was a wound more exquisite than any she had yet experienced.

By the time Sir Basil Hunter woke the frost must have thawed. The light reflected on the bare walls was suggestive of glossy, yellow-green apples. It had probably been a child's room before the visitor turned him out: in one corner stood a toy cart. Early in the night Basil had grown resigned to the stretcher: he was too tired to sulk at discomfort. On waking, he was still tired and stiff, as though he had been on a journey in his sleep far longer than their drive to 'Kudjeri'. Now he continued lying curled in the shape he had been longing to assume: that of a sleeping possum, or a bean before the germinal stage, or a foetus in a jar. He might snooze some more if nobody came to scold him. Each of the women in the house was a scold. If it were that thug Macrory he might have a knuckle duster with him. None of it greatly mattered to Basil in bed.

In fact nobody bothered about him. He shaved unevenly in cold water, and tried to decide which of his unsuitable clothes to wear for 'Kudjeri'. His mind was beginning to grope around amongst its surroundings regardless of what the Macrorys had reduced them to. The physical context should not matter; but it always did. He patted his face in the flawed, deal-framed mirror. He wasn't too bad, considering. Reassured, he roughed up the foulard at his throat, and wondered what Dorothy would be wearing.

When he went down he was surprised to find her in the kitchen, looking far less incongruous than he expected. She was arranging things in cupboards as though she had taken possession of the house.

Because of the march she had stolen on him, he asked with some severity, 'Where are the Macrorys?'

'She is starting the children on their lessons. He's out around the place, doing something occupational, but will be back shortly to entertain you.'

Only then she looked at him, to give him the opportunity to grimace.

He took it, and at once felt annoyed with himself for having fallen into the trap: he was no longer sure which side Dorothy was on. She had tied up her hair in a Roman scarf, as though she were again a child dressing up on a wet afternoon. The scarf made the face fend for itself, which it did by not communicating. Her arms, he noticed for the first time, were not only lean, but leathery and muscular. No doubt her hands, with their long nails which usually

487

exempted them from any form of drudgery except boredom, had already acquired a film of household grime, not to say kitchen sludge. No, he could not be certain which side Dorothy was on; when he needed her on his.

'What do you want for breakfast?' she asked.

'There you've got me. Whatever they have.'

'Men eat charred chops,' Dorothy reminded him with every sign of gravity.

She even produced from out of a fly-proof cupboard a dishful of drought-fed, mutilated chops, and held one up, not for him to laugh at, mercifully he realized at the last moment. 'Rory himself does practically all the outside work,' Dorothy told; and let the chop fall back on the pile.

'Well,' he said, 'I'll have a chop, if that's what you advise. Or two.'

The Princesse de Lascabanes actually knew what ought to be done. Not only was she grilling the chops, so the stench told him, she was melting a lump of dripping in an enormous blackened pan, to fry up a mound of grey cold potato laced with ribbons of pale cold cabbage.

The blue fumes, the spitting, then the revolver firing a blank at memory, brought the image jerking to life. 'You know—' he wanted somebody to share it, 'we might be on tour—in digs up north—doing for ourselves. Before anybody knew we existed.' Encouraged by the fug of sentiment, he moved in on her and squeezed a buttock.

The princess did not like it. 'Watch the grill!' she shouted. 'See if the chops are far enough gone.'

They looked infernal. 'They should be. They're writhing.'

In her irritation, she pushed him aside, to stoop, to peer, to frown: her recently contracted partnership with life made her as damn humourless as she had been when a girl. 'A tough chop is easier to swallow if frizzled,' she announced with bossy assurance.

Her opinion of him was probably as low as Shiela's or Enid's. Faced with his trio of contemptuous women, what he desired most, as ageing man and precarious actor, was respect rather than admiration.

Dorothy at least handed him a plateful of food, all the better for being primitive and mountainous: he tucked in, devouring with particular appetite the charred fat round the edges of the chops and those bits of the fried-up veg which had stuck to the pan. He had forgotten something, and Dorothy pushed the bottle at him to test his reaction to ritual. She stood watching obliquely, and only turned away, whether hissing or sighing it was difficult to tell, on seeing him consecrate amorphous matter, first with a turgid clot or two, followed by an ejaculation of authentic, plopping red; while the act transformed him into a boy, greedy for life as much as food, as he watched an old rain-soaked drover still sitting in this same kitchen chewing the greasy mass of tucker a boss's cook had doled out as charity.

Macrory appeared too suddenly, as though bursting in might deliver him from a predicament by intimidating a pair of impostors.

He ignored the woman and jerked his head at the actor bloke. 'I'm gunner muster this mob of ewes we're sending in.' He showed his teeth in the ambiguous smile. 'If you'd care to come,' the offer was a grudging one, 'we'll make tracks as soon as you've put away yer breakfast.'

Macrory drove his jeep at such a bat he might have been prepared to sacrifice himself if it would dispose of Sir Basil Hunter. On the back seat stood a bleached and matted kelpie, whinging old womanishly and draping a purple tongue over the driver's shoulder.

Like dark, grounded birds, the casuarinas shied and flapped as the onrushing steel shore into their dusty feathers; along a rise, skeleton trees upheld the tradition of martyrdom; at each neck-breaking jolt, the sky showered sparks of light; and a decapitated thistle-head grazed Sir Basil's cheek as they curved around the shoulder of a hill.

Leaping off the eroded ridge, the jeep bore down on a brown dam framed by a stand of withered tussock.

'There!' Basil pointed and shouted. 'That's where you can drop me.'

Shocked by the unorthodox demand, Macrory shouted back, 'Why?'

Sir Basil Hunter explained, 'Used to come here after yabbies. I'd like to poke around a bit.' What he did not dare confess was that he wanted to feel the mud between his toes.

Even so, Macrory's surprise turned to surliness: he could hardly reconcile himself to what amounted to a perversion. 'Dam's near as anything dry. Couldn't drown in it, anyway. I'll pick you up on the way back—if you're still here.'

Basil said he would be.

Macrory pelted off, but returned in a swirl to deliver a warning. 'May be gone an hour or so.'

Basil assured his host he could use every minute of that time at the dam.

Again Macrory drove off, tensed and disgruntled: perhaps he had been hoping to ferret a secret out of his guest, or to make some more of company he despised.

At the far end of the dam stood a single tree, of tremendous girth beside the comparative sapling rooted in Basil Hunter's memory. Mentally he could still put his arms round the tree, instinctively shinning up its shagginess, grasping it with bare knees, while a stench from the ants he crushed and the motions of his chafing limbs drowned the scent of gorse and the twittering of tits as they hovered above the fists of blossom with which the spiky bushes bristled. Overhead, the cries of a desperate magpie were sawing away, and once or twice a beak struck at the marauding skull almost close enough to bump the nest. Tits' eggs were peanuts to maggies'. He hoped he would find a nestful of reds: what he hadn't got was a maggie red.

Perhaps never would. The moment of falling his heart descended bounding ahead his vision a whirligig of fear. Then his lungs must have collapsed: they were spread on the ground as flat as perished balloons. That he was still alive he knew from the pain in his arm, the bone of which should have been protruding through the skin. But the arm looked normal: no sign of the sick throbbing going on inside the flesh. Though alive now, he would probably die of his arm.

The roan mare was coming at a canter. *For God's sake boy what have you done?* Father was shorter, more breathless than usual, the seat of his breeches too tight as he arrived on the ground out of the saddle. *What is it Basil?* His pores were open. *I think I broke my arm.* Those red, staring pores. *The deuce you did—we don't know—got to find out.* A man's a father's hands shouldn't tremble it was frightening: if you cry you may make him worse. *Have it put right. Get you up in front of me. Shove the good arm round my neck.* Too close his breath on you like the trembling and that scalding sweat your own as cold. *Now lie back son lean against me I'll support you.* Awful bumpy hard half on the mare's withers the pommel of the saddle and half lying on Dad's stomach the bone shrieking under your skin deliciously delirious his fire dripping into your cold sea of sweat. *Won't be long Basil boy.* It was Dad trying to love. It made you want to cry, to reach up with your crook arm. So you laughed.

Sir Basil Hunter limped towards the tree he had fallen out of. He would lie down under it a while: even his omissions are a luxury to the expatriate of a certain age and reputation. The ground was suitably unyielding. The scents returned: of ants competing with gorse blossom.

And Alfred Hunter offering downright love disguised as tentative, sweaty affection. When Mother was the one you were supposed to love: *you are my darling my love don't you love your mummy Basil?* Bribing with kisses, peppermint creams, and more substantially, half crowns. *I don't believe you love me at all perhaps you are your father's monopoly or is it yourself you love?* So the game of ping pong was played between Moreton Drive and 'Kudjeri', between Elizabeth and Alfred Hunter (Dad at a handicap).

You all played. Dorothy was playing it still.

Sir Basil Hunter opened his eyes. The other side of the branches of the great tree the empty sky was staring at him. Suddenly he would have liked to feel certain that he had actually loved somebody, that he had not been only acting it.

He sat up, looked over his shoulder, then began taking off his shoes: whether it was self-indulgence or not he would have to feel the mud between his toes.

Around him the silence was watching, which made him stealthier in his movements. No, it was his soft white feet: still elegant, he had liked to think, long and narrow, formed by generations walking in the furrow behind the plough and sticking their toes into stirrup irons. But become useless, except to stride imagined miles around a stage; incapable of trudging the actual miles to Dover. Perhaps this was why he had failed as Lear.

Along the edge of the dam the hoof-prints of sheep had set in a fussy clay sculpture. Painful, too: he was regretting the sentimentality which had driven him to paddle back towards little-boyhood. At least he was unable to see his face, but his feet looked foolish mincing over the fanged clay. Till the soft, softer than soft, the effortless squelch: flesh is never so kind, nor as voluptuous, as mud: certain phrases, lines, can become its equal when delivered by a practised tongue into darkness on a propitious night.

'In such a night,' he aimed at the Australian daylight, while throughout the ritual dark he had conjured up in his mind, the pale discs were raised to receive the seed he was raining on them;

> 'in such a night,
> Stood Dido with a willow in her hand
> Upon the wild sea-banks, and wav'd her love
> To come again to Carthage ...'

Legs apart, pants hitched their highest and tightest, he listened for his own voice (his worst vice) and some of it returned out of that extrovert blue. He listened again: as the circles widened around him on the muddy water, magpies' wings were clattering skywards; but the silence burning into his skin was the applause he valued. That his art should have come to terms with his surroundings gratified Sir Basil Hunter.

But what if the disapproving Macrory should reappear sooner than he had reckoned? Sir Basil began frowning; he started swirling

around, shouldering off his not reprehensible, but in the circumstances, embarrassing gift. He stumbled into a pothole: could have
come a gutser. Walking not so steady now on his Shakespeare
legs. When beneath the soles of his feet a tickling, a prickling of
life, restored his balance. Putrefying meat was the best bait for
yabbies, he remembered. He could remember the jar: to be kept
beyond smelling distance; that Easter Sunday he fetched up his
breakfast tying the string round a lump of green, stinking mutton.
Catching yabbies might not have given him so much pleasure
if it had not displeased HER: *I shan't darling you smell so don't claw
at me Basil smelly boys aren't kissable.*

The light now streaming over the eroded ridge was her same
glistening white, still blinding him. And another crueller, more
relevant trick the light was playing, as its meaner refractions
flickered on the face of the dam: this old freckled claw was twitching,
clenching and unclenching, or beckoning through the brown
water, perhaps appealing to him. *Poor Mum's acold.* Oh yes, he
pitied her, but had to think of himself (no need to include Dorothy, a
thriving hive of self-pity). And remember Mother's practical
ethics: *one can drown in compassion if one answers every call it's another
way of suicide.* All the best aphorisms have a habit of doing you dirt
sooner or later, and the illusory claw reflected in the water conveyed something of the same distress of the actual hand lying on the
hemstitched sheet.

This was where the Thing, no yabby playfully tickling memory,
rose up out of the mud under Sir Basil's right sole. Because his
innocent morning's pastime had made him spiritually vulnerable,
the submerged object wounded him more deeply than rusty
spike, broken bottle, or jagged tin. In his state of aggrieved anguish,
his arms began swimming against the air as he made for land,
jaws clenched, gristle straining in his throat. He was not yet able
to hobble, except mentally, because his legs were still swathed in
sheets of brown filthy ooze, in promises of septicæmia, anthrax—
perhaps death, simple and unassuming; none of the Jacobean
trappings when Y O U are the one concerned.

At least he reached the bank: the clay impressions of hooves, or teeth, bit into his flesh regardless of existing wounds as he hopped towards the not much more charitable grass, trickling lustrous scarlet behind him. He was bleeding all right.

What to do? Wash in stagnant water? Tie up infected flesh in a far from aseptic handkerchief? Sitting in the coarse grass Basil for a moment got his foot almost as far as his mouth, to give the wound a good suck, but realized he was not the contortionist to bring it off.

Nor a boy. Unless an elderly one. Abandoned by everybody. Stranded in his own egotism and ineptitude. Though he listened for it, the reliable roan was not coming at a canter.

When he had pulled himself together (it was nothing more than a cut, an ordinary cut) he went so far as tying the dirty handkerchief round his wounded foot; he made quite a neat parcel of it. *And at least there had been nobody to see, or hear;* hearing might have been the more humiliating: the way his thoughts at one stage were pumped to the surface.

About noon he heard the barking. A mob of sheep was advancing in his direction: though fairly compact, its individual members were bobbing like scuffled cocoons, at first in silence, then as a rustling, then a dry panting. They halted on seeing the figure at the dam. The leaders stamped. Here and there a cough muffled by flannel. The faded kelpie ran back and forth, rejoicing in any emergency which gave him the opportunity to work; while Macrory's jeep, by nudging the straggling rear with its bonnet, tightened the invisible string which kept his string-coloured flock intact.

The figure with bandaged foot seated on a clay hummock between the dam and these dedicated workers, was irrelevant to their whole delicate operation.

At last Macrory allowed himself to notice. 'How are we?' he deigned to shout.

Sir Basil Hunter, aware of his own superfluousness, could have been sulking: he did not answer. Carrying one shoe, he began hobbling towards the jeep, which did not intend to stop for him.

'Wotcherdoneteryerself?' Monotony had bleached Macrory's voice; dust had clogged it.

Sir Basil mumbled. 'Cut my foot.'

'Waddayerknow! Can't be much of a shoe yer've got. Pom made?'

'I'd taken them off. It happened in the dam.'

'Good Christ! What were you up to? *Paddling?*'

'Exactly. Paddling in the dam.'

As they continued the uninterrupted droving of their flock, Sir Basil found himself hating the jeep as an extension of its owner. Like the metal excrescence on which the injured actor was allowed to perch, Macrory's body looked inviolable. Basil's foot began throbbing, out of time with the loutish jeep. On and off, the grazier glanced down: where the thought of paddling had disgusted, even shocked him, the bandaged foot was no more than a harmlessly passive object from the way he squinted at it through his black, gummed-up lashes.

Suddenly he said, 'It'll be all right,' surprising himself, it appeared, more than anybody else.

Basil recognized the tone of voice in which the man addressed his children: for the moment you were accepted as Macrory's additional, if idiot, child.

But the fellow regretted his mistake: he tried to disguise it by shouting curses at the dog, who seemed to be laughing back at his master, in little whinges, from behind a splather of tongue.

Basil gloomed and throbbed. A gout of moody crimson was gathering on the crude bandage. Obviously he could not expect sympathy at 'Kudjeri', either from this boor, or the two shrews of women; the ghost of his father was insubstantial; and his mother's image would refuse, understandably, to respond to invocation.

Anne Macrory disguised her concern. 'Oh, Lord—we'll soon see to that.' She spoke too loudly, with a show of determination which suggested the incident might be her final test.

She began fetching and dropping things. 'Dorothy's down at the river with some of the children. She'll be back soon,' she added

495

hopefully, looking out through the ruptured screen, though the kitchen faced in the wrong direction.

Basil's hopes of his sister were less optimistic than Mrs Macrory's.

A year-old baby in a high chair started crying. The mother, who had been feeding her and bottling pears at the same time, returned to battering with a spoon on a plastic dish, from which a mess of predigested pap showered the immediate kitchen.

'Eat, love! Look, Mummy's eating. We're eating it together, aren't we? It's going to be so good for us.' The social worker had adopted what she understood as a dual purpose voice: sweet and stern at the same time.

In her distraction, she pushed the spoonful of pap into the blank of the child's cheek; the baby roared.

Sir Basil sat watching a fly drown in a half-filled bottle of brown pears.

'Where's Rory?' his wife asked as though she needed to know; but flipped on. 'Dorothy is so dependable.' She sighed.

Through what metamorphosis, Sir Basil wondered, had his sister possessed herself of this distraught woman's respect? He would have to learn the trick.

Presently Dorothy came. The two Macrory girls in tow were still loving up to her. Her dress and one elbow were stained green by grass. Her eyes were overflowing with languor, and what Basil recognized as river light: greenish to golden-brown.

Fat Mog was pointing. 'Ooh, look! Basil's cut his foot!'

The older girl, who had grasped something of protocol from associating generally with a princess, and from looking through the drawers and cupboard where their visitor kept her belongings, blushed to the height of her fleshless cheekbones.

Dorothy was still too dazed by light to assess the situation. She looked beautiful, he thought; almost not his sister.

Then the truth struck her. 'Oh, darling, what have you done to yourself? Ohhhh!'

While the Macrory women were flapping their wings ineptly, Dorothy Hunter swam across the kitchen, to arrive, to settle herself

496

at her brother's feet, and untie the dirty handkerchief. She dipped her head; for a moment he thought she was going to put her lips to the wound: they protruded so noticeably, and were besides so tremulous.

Basil basked.

'You're not feverish?' Dorothy cried. 'Or are you?' She began tenderly exploring, while giving icy orders, which Mrs Macrory and her girls were glad to obey.

Only the baby gravely stared from above the dish of unfinished pap, wondering whether to grind her brows together and scream.

Whereas most of the Macrorys accepted the princess as the same woman who had arrived at their house the night before, and whom they had got to know, if not intimately, anyway enough to have formed a relationship of trust and affection, Basil could not recognize his sister; and Dorothy, with her competence, more than that, her authority, and the obvious compassion with which she approached his wound, seemed to be avoiding recognition: not once since her bemused entrance had she offered him her eyes.

After she had bathed the foot, using a tin basin Mrs Macrory had first dropped, and Mog retrieved and filled, she disinfected the cut with a powder Janet fetched from upstairs together with lint and an assortment of grubby bandages.

When she had bound him, coldness took over again in his nurse. 'There you are!' She turned away, and confessed to Anne Macrory alone, 'I don't trust our own crude methods. I shall have to ring the doctor.'

But it was no longer the age when doctors could be summoned at will to 'Kudjeri'; and that evening a sulky Macrory drove the Hunters to Gogong in the jeep.

The bronze version of Alfred Hunter had its back towards them as they flew across the railway lines approaching the township through the dusk. Basil nudged Dorothy, but she was in no mood to encourage family jokes. He must remember that his sister was essentially a solemn bore.

On the return journey, a long wait at the doctor's made it easier for him to resist glancing at the sculpture of their father. They tore up into the hills, through an amorphousness of dark, in the smell of antiseptics which accompanied them. The sequence of events and the drugs he had been given made him feel light-headed. Dorothy's hair had escaped: once or twice it touched his cheek. Macrory cursed the road, the dark. From time to time Basil and Dorothy in the back seat were thrown at each other and stirred together. They recovered themselves. They might have been returning from a country dance, separating the pleasures from the disappointments. Not quite drunk.

When they walked into the kitchen a hardfaced Mrs Macrory looked at her husband and said, 'I thought you must have had an accident.'

Everybody was hungry by then.

Basil went to bed soon after what they were coming to recognize as the standard meal at 'Kudjeri'. The inflated importance of the day's events as they occurred, had begun subsiding: they would soon no doubt assume their actual, flat significance.

Dorothy escaped into the study with Father's *Charterhouse of Parma* which she had only slight intention of reading: holding the book would be her safeguard against anybody's intrusion on her thoughts. Again a fire was burning, but tonight it had been only recently lit: the room was cold and smelt of ash. After drawing up her legs beside her on the broken springs of the daybed, she lifted the Indian counterpane draped to disguise the cracks and deforming bulges in the leather. By stretching out she was able to peer into the space between the floorboards and sagging springs to confirm that there was nothing to fear. Settled back, she felt tolerably comfortable; if also, yes, deprived.

After a lifetime of luxurious isolation she had been left alone hardly at any point in this huggermugger day: her neck was sticky from children's hands; under her nails she could feel grease and grit from the pans she had scoured that morning; her dress and an elbow were still stained with grass juices. Any attempts at washing or grooming herself had been slapdash gestures made out of obedience to habit: unconsciously, she could have been cherishing her patina of grime. Now as she lay turning the pages of a book she was not reading, increasing warmth from the fire intensified the burning in her arms. Normally she would have deplored a sensation which conjured up images of zombie women, their shrivelled, leathery faces, beside the road or driven in lorries. But tonight her own rather dry skin was prickling with life.

Of course the whole situation was thoroughly perverse, whatever Basil had persuaded himself he might get out of it. You would have to extricate him, not crudely, but in a few days time, after gently paving the way towards escape. From the squalor of this ugly, crumbling house, with which neither had any rational connection. Certainly not with the people at present living in it. Not even Anne Macrory your friend: that was what Anne seemed aspiring to be. That was why you ran to scour pans, feed her regurgitating baby, help raise the mother from the level to which she had been only half-willingly reduced.

By the brute Rory.

Madame de Lascabanes made the extra effort to concentrate on her book. *She did not want Count Mosca to see her talking to Fabrizio.* Unfortunate that the English language should transform a great work of French literature into a mock-Italian novelette. Still, it was in this version that Father had found consolation; so Mother implied.

Dorothy rested her cheek against the padded scroll of the daybed on which she was lying. She closed her eyes and willed the spirit of Alfred Hunter, his charity, his innocence, his essential goodness, to possess her. Without the innocence, would he have been so effortlessly good? like Arnold Wyburd, that other virtuous man; and neither of them memorable. Dorothy Hunter opened her eyes: better perhaps insignificant and good, than insignificant and bad.

No, you were not bad, only dishonest in socially acceptable ways, and then only slightly, out of necessity; it was a dishonesty inherited from Mother.

When it was Alfred's charity Dorothy Hunter was determined to woo, she was most haunted by Elizabeth's greedy sensuality, and in Alfred's own room, where he had enjoyed chaste and manly discourse with his friend Arnold: of clocks, moreover. Dorothy glanced. There was no clock. She could not have been more helplessly exposed to Elizabeth Hunter's influence. There was no doubt Mother, whatever she said, had desired other men: Edvard Pehl for one; more successfully, for certain, the owner of that cuff link lying under the bed. On the whole, though, Mother's adulteries had probably been mental ones: to possess rather than to be possessed.

Why did Mother fill the room tonight? Had she perhaps died? Oh God, never! She was too cunning, cruel, to release you from your hatefulness by dying.

While listening for the telephone, that urgent ringing through a silent, country house, which suggests that the instrument is about to tear itself from the wall, Dorothy heard steps. She did not doubt it was Macrory: the sound was too heavy, too boorish, to announce anybody else. It was what she had been dreading. Would she be forced by terror to submit to her friend's husband? Or by curiosity? she had time to wonder.

Then Macrory was knocking; after which, he barged in.

Scorn for a man who knocked on doors was followed by a feeling of outrage that he had not waited for her invitation. She must have looked idiotic besides, stretched out rigid on the daybed, stiffly raising her head to stare at the intruder.

Macrory giggled, his eyes too brilliant, his lips moister, fuller than she could remember.

'Took you by surprise, did I?'

'Why should I be surprised?' Madame de Lascabanes mumbled back.

He did not answer, but crumped down in Alfred Hunter's leather chair.

Basil would save her if she needed saving. Though she did not want Sir Basil Hunter to see her so much as talking to Rory.

(She was contemptuous of herself for letting the name enter her head.)

'Isn't it late?' she suggested; and was vain enough to add, 'Won't your wife be wondering where you are?'

'I often prowl around the house at night, knock back a drink or two, and think things over, after she's gone to bed.'

She could see he had knocked back the drink or two. His less evident thoughts he would not, or more likely, could not share. In their absence she visualized them as trussed and writhing, a bundle of instinctive snakes, or no, hairy caterpillars. Her cynicism made her draw down the corners of her mouth, lower her eyelids, not so far that she could not contemplate one of her own limply dangled wrists: with or without jewellery wrists had been among her assets.

Like many plain women, she was vain. But wasn't Macrory vain of his thoughts? Would he have dangled them otherwise? He might even have been wanting to suggest that his mind could outshine his effortless, but otherwise repulsive, body. Rory Macrory was a man who had not been designed for clothes: they emphasized all they were meant to conceal. Madame de Lascabanes made herself concentrate harder than ever on her own wrist.

'You people have it all over us,' Rory suddenly blurted, and his pants shot higher up his calves.

'Which people?' the princess bitterly asked. 'And how do you mean "have it over you"?'

'Anne "Kirkcaldy" Robertson—Sir Basil Hunter—and you.' He would continue to punish her, she suspected, by refusing to address her by name, let alone title. 'You're all of you cold perfect, arrogant people.'

Poor stained Anne!

'You love your wife, surely, to have made all those children with her?'

There was no logic in it, and Rory did not reply.

'Whatever my own shortcomings,' Dorothy hurried on in case he should absolve her, though he showed no signs of preparing to, 'my brother is a most distinguished man—and great actor.'

Macrory said, 'I've never been inside of a bloody theatre.'

It did not matter that she had never seen Basil act; no one, not even Mother, should accuse her of disloyalty, or of being stingy with affection; affection is a pure pleasure, and costs nothing, unlike the tortuous proposition, love.

But Macrory had other thoughts. 'That book you're reading—I had a go at it once.' He was picking at the scab on his knuckle.

'Well?' Her faith in truth, as opposed to the orthodoxies, made her stiffen.

'Seemed to me a fuss about nothing.' Then, 'I couldn't understand it.'

This was where the Princesse de Lascabanes, surprised by a comparative humility, surrendered to him. 'It is a "fuss", admittedly;' she realized she was perspiring at the roots of her hair, 'but it is about something—whether we find out or not.' The conviction she could not convey was distended painfully inside her; the broken springs of the daybed were driven into her straining back. (At least you can always close your eyes, but whether you like it or not, you have got to listen to a man's breathing.)

Rory was as unmoved as the chair in which he was sitting. 'I only ever believed,' he said, 'in what I can see and touch. I expect that's why we get children. Did you have any kids, Dorothy?'

'I'm childless.' His use of her name made the admission sound more wretched.

'And Basil?'

'Also. No, he has, I believe, one child.' 'Imogen' had never been convincing; less, in the present circumstances.

While Macrory was stung by his own dilemma. 'You people can get away with it. You don't need kids. You have the time—the nerve—to con yourselves—and others—with words and ideas.'

There was no reason why his rejection should hurt: all her life she had lived with her own emptiness. *Macrory*: his arms alone filled her with revulsion.

'Time to spend a morning mooning round a dam! D'you know what? He was shouting something at the top of his voice. I couldn't see him, but heard it from a distance. It sounded like bloody poetry. Why d'you suppose he was spouting poetry at nobody?'

'How should I know?' She was floating on her own breathlessness. 'He was showing off, perhaps, to himself—listening to the sound of his voice.' She had not intended to make Basil look foolish; it was this clod Macrory who had brought her to it.

Macrory laughed, like a boy. 'I admire old Basil.'

Dorothy's lips were at their thinnest, she could tell. 'I thought you thoroughly despised us both.'

'Shouting at the flamun air! He can get away with it.'

'He ought to. Isn't it his profession?'

'And shoes! Those Pom shoes! He's sharp—Basil!'

Dorothy said it was time she went to bed. Her arms were thin. She felt as though she had been trampled on, actually, physically, and for no good reason.

Macrory, who was kicking the fire together, called after her without turning, 'Sleep good, Dorothy!' If an inarticulate, practically retarded mind, his body was highly articulated; every muscle in his back worked.

Elizabeth Hunter was having the last laugh, in this dark, seemingly deserted house. The sound of her dress filled the draughty staircase. On the way up, on a half-landing, Dorothy leaned her head against a cedar post. She would have liked to cry on a shoulder if Mother had been more than a presence. At least Basil had not seen her talking to that boor; he had not heard her betrayal, nor witnessed an adultery of which Macrory himself remained unaware.

Some way back from the house, across a yard, the meticulously planned stables now fulfilled only a memorial function. A clock face pale amongst the ivy had long ago ceased to express time. But dogs liked to frequent the yard for snoozing and shitting; and hens to stalk, and peck between the pavings; and through an archway with which the clock-tower was pierced stood a slightly less neglected, because more utilitarian, shed. Built of iron and slab, with a reinforcement of solidified cobweb, the whole ramshackle barrack had taken on the colour of dust except where the weather had left on the iron a look of dried blood.

Basil Hunter had paid several visits to the shed, and was on his way again this morning in the leisurely fashion he found himself adopting for 'Kudjeri', where his responsibilities remained spiritual rather than technical.

On reaching the closed door he paused to pick a splinter or two from the slab wall, then to expend his splinters by plunging them one after another into the dust-cemented cobweb funnels. It achieved nothing, but he found the pastime as absorbing and consoling as any of the many rituals of childhood.

When he had finished he glanced round to see whether anyone had noticed: he could have deceived an adult by turning it into a joke, but a child would have recognized the dead seriousness of such behaviour. There was nobody looking, fortunately.

The great door creaked and staggered wide open once the wooden arm which held it had been withdrawn from the iron hasp. Instead of the door a curtain of spangled light hung protecting the secrets of the cavern beyond. He pushed through, needlessly stooping, for the swallows' nests encrusting the lintel were several feet above his head. As on previous occasions, his heart was beating noisily for the pleasures of renewed acquaintance.

Stashed away in the shadows of the barn, all these implements and machines were by now more believable as sculpture, though here and there, traces of a practical function clung still to esoteric forms: soil to a ploughshare; grains of unsown maize in a row of wooden box-compartments; a faint pungency of fertilizer lingering where he had lifted a lid. From touching the scant remains of super-phosphate his ephemeral fingertips became as shrivelled as the ageless grains of corn.

He was lured farther: to bounce on a harvester's rusted though resilient seat, while walls of green fell before his progress down the river flat. He could feel the hand at his shoulderblades: to prevent young Basil falling off. Hating at the time this indignity of protective hands, you would have had them back long after shrugging them off for ever: strong but submissive, insensitive, while abrasively solicitous.

Mucking around always deeper in the shadow, Basil knew he was deliberately saving one corner till the last. Where most of the utilitarian machines had returned to being the bores they always were, nothing would dull his delight in what that far corner contained. He was trembling to such an extent he was glad to bend down and pick up a boot he could not remember noticing on other visits. A bloom of fungus on leather cast in iron wrinkles discouraged any normal foot from prising its way into the boot. Suddenly Basil was determined to wear it, and got it on. He was able to hobble around too, heel raised higher than the inturned toe. And was not handicapped more than he already knew: he could have been wearing this same unnatural boot on his walk to Dover.

So he stumbled at last on the corner in which Alfred Hunter's 3-litre Bentley stood waiting for him on flat tyres. The most reactionary of all these pieces of sculptured memory assembled in the shed, Alfred's car stole the show. With its straight-set hood and goggling lamps, its nickel corseting, and once cobby, now deflated tyres, it suggested some mild, deposed monarch. Or Alfred Hunter late of 'Kudjeri'.

Basil hobbled in the iron boot to fetch the nail from where he kept it, to continue digging grasshopper-corpses out of the radiator in which they had been incinerated. He picked, picked, the dribble soon running out of his mouth, then the grunts, or half-sobs, for murders and tortures perpetrated on earth, for others not yet conceived; only if you were lucky enough, a decent harmless death.

What you doing Basil boy?

Nothing Dd-dadd. After defeating that slight stammer, your voice had developed what seemed like unlimited power; but the limp came to replace the stutter.

Basil stopped picking at the corpses, to leave something for next time. He climbed inside the car. Airlessness, and the scents of luxury embalmed, made him gasp. But his touch received from the gears a vague promise of motion, and wiping the dust off upholstery and the more frivolous fitments, restored something of a former life, both elegant and sybaritic. He got half an erection running his hand over his surroundings. He lifted a walnut-veneer lid: did he imagine the smell of grazed flint still hovered around the lighter? No mistaking the trail of perfume from the little flask in fluted glass. She so deplored *vulgar overscented females driving in motorcars scenting themselves some more en route.* Had she ever used it? like what she called a *public woman.* People do what they most deplore. *Just a dash darling for fun.*

They were driving along that same old endless road into Gogong. They overflowed on him from either side so that he hardly existed: in any case only their little boy. *Isn't it a lovely light Alfred the hills look soft.* Because he was a man Daddy said it was the Good Season making everything soft-looking. He spoke in the voice he used for Mother when they were alone: sort of croaking, which also stroked. Mother sat not looking at the hills. After a bit she laughed. *Certain words I can't bring myself to use for doctors – at any rate not Dr Treweek the word* B-R-E-A-S-T *for instance.* Father laughed his smoky laugh. *Why not Betty it seems to me natural enough.* The smoky laughter like a bridge between them over your head. *Oh yes natural I'll admit.* She put out her hand towards him, but stopped on seeing you were sitting between. For driving he wore doeskin gloves, turned back at the wrists into cuffs. The gloves made his wrists look naked, except where his watchstrap was eating into one of them. Dad was hairless at the wrists. Mother suddenly remembered *look Basil darling the lambs aren't they sweet the newborn lambs* for their little boy. *Do you think he understands?* Father was a careful driver; he slowed down always over culverts. *Don't see how he possibly could – not when you spell it.* They laughed some more. For each other.

They drove on, and the wind started coming from another direction. She lost control of her gossamer. It flicked your eyeball.

It was still not crying, running. Sir Basil Hunter was forced to take out Enid's Christmas handkerchief, to mop the trickling.

'Basil?'

The voice was too real, more forbidding than the figure, its substance diffused into a dark blur by the curtain of light hanging in the doorway. Foolish of him to forget to close the door. At least she could not have noticed him jump: all those rusted machines cluttering the space between them were serving a purpose.

'What are you doing?' she asked like everybody else.

'Nothing.' Now he was angry. 'Playing with this bomb. Don't you remember Dad's car?'

'Do I? I suppose I do.'

He had found that girls remember less. Though the glare behind her did not allow him to see her face, he knew Dorothy was wearing the expression to match her voice: that of an older, responsible girl, the thinner for her earnest disapproval.

As she chose her way between the obstructive machinery, narrowing her shoulders narrower still, flattening her chest if possibly flatter with one long glimmering hand, he started scrambling out of the car. However deeply Dorothy and he were committed to each other as partners in a crime, she must not catch sight of the train of images and emotions which had barely stopped flashing past.

Just before she reached him, he managed to slam the car door shut, and stand with his back to the nickel bonnet.

'I wanted to talk to you,' she said. 'And this ought to give us more privacy than most places.' She looked around them, slightly shivering.

He knew he would not want to hear whatever it was she planned to discuss.

Dorothy had indeed planned, after observing Basil make for the shed on other occasions. Unnoticed by any Macrory children, she had kept watch this morning from behind the screen of the scullery window. Though a smell of milk on the turn had roused her fastidiousness, she decided to stick it out.

And now was reunited with her brother, who resented it; she could sense that. To butt in on his private games had usually made Basil hurtful.

For that reason, as she spoke, she was carefully tracing a seam in his coat with one of her long fingernails. 'I want to talk about this situation we've got ourselves into and have to get ourselves out of. I mean to say, we can't go on sponging indefinitely on strangers.' As she traced, or rather, dug out the intricate seam, she smiled for her own thoughtfulness.

Outside the theatre, Basil had been inclined to favour postponement; so he blew a raspberry. 'You can't call it *sponging*, can you? They'd be the first to notice. You can be sure Macrory would have let us know.'

'Macrory the archmasochist? He's probably writhing in silence. After all these weeks. How long do you suppose it is?'

They were not prepared to join in an accurate reckoning.

'We have our lives to live,' Dorothy looked at Basil for approval; 'however long it may be before the Thorogood Village can offer a vacancy.' He recognized in her eyes his own fear of developing the theme too explicitly.

'We might simply go away,' she said, 'farther than "Kudjeri", I mean—out of this country where we don't belong.'

'Never did.' As he confirmed her assertion, he saw she had been watching for him to lie.

Now she was positively disappointed. 'To you it may mean something—something you aren't prepared to admit.' She had raised her voice, to force its scorn past the knots in her throat. 'I've always hated—HATED it!' Though insulated with dust and cobwebs, the shed failed to muffle Dorothy's voice: it continuted ululating.

As though he had ratted on her.

'Yes, yes.' He began moving her towards the door. 'We'll talk about it. When we're calmer;' hobbling helplessly beside her.

'What is it?' she hissed. 'Is your foot troubling you? The wound? Oh, darling, I thought it had healed—*perfectly*.'

'It's not the foot.' They had both stopped, and were looking down through the shadow in which they were standing waist deep. 'It's the boot!' Though they were motionless he contrived an exaggerated stumble.

'*Boot?*' She was staring, brows pleated, eyeballs straining, with such distaste, not to say horror, at something so unexpected and still partly obscured by shadow, he might have been showing her his cock.

She started hurrying towards the door.

'I found it. I put it on.' Hobbling, stumbling after her, he was trying to exonerate himself. 'Don't know what got into me. I had to try it. An impulse, that's all. Don't you have impulses, Dot?'

'I don't know. I don't think I do.'

He had reached her side after cannoning off a scarifier.

'And now I've got to get rid of the thing.'

'Oh, Basil, aren't you absurd!' She sounded shattered.

He had plumped down on what had been, judging by its scars, a chopping block, and was pulling at the offending boot. 'All right, I'm the one who's the fool!' Panting pulling. 'Aren't I? So why worry?'

What if it wouldn't come off? There was no sign of its giving; a natural deformity could not have stuck closer.

'Dorothy—you may have to—fetch a—*knife*!' The words too, were a struggle.

'A knife? What shall I tell them?' His sister was to that extent humourless.

She had got down on her stockinged knees, on the dust and slivers of bark, and had started wrenching at the filthy boot. 'If we can't, between us—we're—not—much,' her teeth bit the rest of it off; her long fragile nails ran skittering tearing over the surface of the mildewed leather; as the Hunter children fought for their self-justification and freedom from awfulness.

The Princesse de Lascabanes fell sideways at last, holding the boot which together they had torn from Sir Basil Hunter's foot.

'How could you?' she gasped. 'You're such a shit, Basil!' She was crying, or at any rate laughing, as she thumped the dirt with the boot. 'God only knows what sort of actor you are. Oh, fuck—fuck everybody!' she moaned in a whimpered whisper: her Australian self was tormenting Dorothy de Lascabanes.

'Yes,' he agreed.

509

He got her to her feet.

By the time they burst through the curtain of light she had calmed down.

'We shall think of something,' he promised, and squeezed her elbow.

Dorothy knew it was she who should think. 'You didn't close the door. Hadn't you better go back and close it? On top of everything else, Macrory might object, Basil, to the door left open.'

'Yes,' he agreed. 'I'll go back and shut it.'

For the moment Dorothy knew better. He also realized he must find his other shoe, or limp across the yard in his sock, perhaps bump into their host, and stand accused.

So Sir Basil Hunter doubled back inside the shed, and the princess went on alone. It was preferable that way: those watching would be less likely to interpret conspiracy of any kind.

Anne Macrory remarked, 'I don't know, Dorothy, how we managed before you came.'

Dorothy bit off a thread.

Anne could not stop herself totting up the virtues. 'And Basil— he's such good company. Rory admires him.'

Dorothy would have re-threaded the needle if her hand had been trembling less. 'I think all actors are pretty useless, except as actors.' She had not met another. 'Basil, I know from experience, feels out of his element with laymen.' Her voice had suddenly tightened.

Anne was mystified by something. 'What is it, dear?'

'I pricked my finger,' Dorothy lied.

After the customary women's lunch they had come upstairs to what was still the sewing-room, and were renovating dresses for the girls. ('You're so imaginative, Dorothy, and clever. This year the poor things are going to look presentable.') In a corner of the room Dorothy Hunter used to hate for what she was submitted to, both blandishment and slaps, Mother's form had stood through the years, stuck with pins and several needles trailing multicoloured threads. There was the table in which Dorothy and Basil, during an armistice, had burnt their names with a poker. Over optimistically, Basil had pricked out an asymmetrical heart surrounding them.

The bare room where the women were working was kept just warm enough by a thin winter sunlight and a rather smelly kerosene stove. The horizon was so distinctly drawn, frost must have started gathering in the hollows. The night would be cold.

'Do you actually *enjoy* sewing?' Anne asked respectfully.

'Cutting is what I like,' Dorothy confessed.

She enjoyed hearing the crunch of the heavy, dressmaking scissors. And was an adept cutter. Though she had only recently been told. She was surprised to realize the number of ways in which she excelled since her friend pointed them out.

She frowned at the dress she was finishing off, and brought it closer than her sight required. If she could have remained enclosed by this circle of love and trust, she might have accepted herself by living up to their opinion of her. But her heart sickened on her thinking that her commitments made this impossible. As the surrounding hills shrank under the pressure of cold, and the warmth from the rusty governess-stove decreased, so the love her friends appeared to feel for her became more poignant and undeserved.

Anne Macrory and her girls were inured to cold, but Dorothy chattered and laughed while delivering a blow she had been contemplating. 'That old dummy in the corner—is it of any use?'

Anne looked up. 'Not really. We use it as a pincushion.'

'I wonder you think it worth keeping. It was Mother's form when we were children—indispensable in those days, in the dress-making department. But by now it's probably full of borer and dry rot—what you might call a hazard.'

'I hadn't thought. It's always been there.'

Mog said, 'We dress it up. Don't we, Jan?'

Janet blushed along her cold, milky cheekbones. She was waiting greedily for the frock the princess (her friend!) was sewing for her.

Dorothy inclined her head above the dress. 'You remember those figures stuck with pins? You made them out of wax, and threw them on the fire—and the person you wanted to die was supposed to.'

Anne said, 'No, I don't know. What sheer superstitious rubbish! Anyhow, I can't remember ever wanting anyone to die.'

'And did they die?' Janet asked.

'Apparently, if you wanted it enough.'

Mog was sticking a few additional pins into the dressmaker's dummy. 'Did you ever have a go with the wax?'

'No,' said Dorothy, looking through the window at a landscape she did not see. 'I know somebody who went as far as making the image. Then she hadn't the courage. I think she felt—in fact she told me that merely to conceive such an evil thought starts you withering up, and you go on—withering.'

Like flies in amber, the Macrorys hung transfixed in the light which for a moment had set solid in the quiet room; till Anne began to fidget, to glance at her watch, to twitch. 'How morbid we're being!' She laughed, and looked over her shoulder at the window.

'Here's Janet's dress at least.' Dorothy shook it out for them to see; she was relieved to be making what was to some extent a positive contribution. 'All it needs is a sash of sorts.'

'Yes,' said Anne. 'Blue for Janet.' Her own preoccupation made her vague; the vastness of the sky bewildered her.

'But I hate blue!' Janet blazed, crumpling the dress against her thin body. 'You know I decided on red, Mother.'

Anne was too tired, too absent, to give the matter thought. 'Blue is what suits you, darling. Red would look—well, eccentric.'

'How do you know what I am? How do you know I'm not eccentric?'

Janet looked to Dorothy, whom she loved, and who must understand and save her; when Dorothy knew that the most she could do for Janet would be to trim her dress with a red ribbon, and from a distance, carry on a correspondence till it died of natural causes.

The mother sighed. 'Red, then.'
Mog Macrory chanted from behind the dressmaker's dummy,

'Red red he went to bed
Silly blue she went too
But nobody wanted purpurl!'

At the last word, she stuck the scissors into the dummy, and a smell
of must came out. It was disappointing. Possibly she had hoped for
something better, like worms, or blood. She stabbed again, deeper —
but nothing.

The mother seemed reconciled to defeat over the colour of the
ribbon: she was free to give herself to other worries.

'How late it is!' she was amazed to find, standing at the window.
'Rory drives off, and never tells us where he could be found if
needed. Supposing there was an accident here at the house? Or for
that matter,' she had opened the window and was craning out, 'he
could overturn the jeep — kill himself. Well, we do know of somebody who broke his leg, and was found at last, lying out in the
paddocks, in the frost. But Rory considers nobody — least of all his
wife.'

The blaze of light and her obsessed relationship with her husband
gave Anne Macrory's grey face a resplendence. Dorothy tried not
to envy her friend her gratuitous embellishments.

Mog murmured, 'If I broke my leg I'd go to the Cottage Hospital
and Matron and the sisters would make a fuss of me. There was
a lady used to let me get into bed with her and cuddle, when I
had my tonsils out. A broken leg would take much longer than
tonsils.'

Janet would have liked to apologize to the Princess Lascaburn
for her embarrassing family. As she did not know how, she could
only wait for the princess to do or say something to loosen the
tangle in which everyone was caught.

But Dorothy continued sitting at the table, and it was Anne
who roused herself finally; she came and took their friend by the

hands. 'What you must think of us! And how you've put up with it all this time!' For a moment it looked as though Anne's hovering face was going to plunge into Dorothy's.

Dorothy raised her shoulder: being kissed made her feel awkward; she had almost always tried to avoid it. 'Is it so long?' She broke away from Anne. 'Of course, it must be. I'm ashamed.'

'Truly that isn't how I meant it!' Anne moaned for her own tactlessness.

Pinned to the sewing-room door was a local chemist's calendar, the leaves of which had been neglected after the first couple of months.

'But it's true!' Dorothy's insistence made her voice boom. 'The calendar will prove it.'

In her determination to resist what she most desired, her chair groaned, then screeched, before falling over sideways, giving a bentwood bounce or two.

While arms were grappling, laughter straining, Mog shouted, 'I've got her by the leg. Gee, she's *wiry*!'

Janet put her cool, virgin hands over her friend's eyes.

'No, Dorothy darling, you're ours! We need you!' Anne struggled gasping to make her point. 'Don't you understand?'

But Dorothy only understood that she must reach the calendar, on the leaves of which flies had printed their sepia riddles. She must tear away the leaves one by one till she unveiled the truth.

She did succeed in tearing MARCH before they carried her, as part of their female Laocoon, past the door and on to a landing, all still writhing and laughing. Somebody was sobbing: or it could have been interpreted as that. Winter fire followed them a certain distance from the sewing-room window down the creaking stairs before being doused in the darker regions, with a noise of hissing, or anguished breathlessness.

Mog kept repeating, 'She's *wiry*! That's how I'd like to be—a wrestler—or acrobat.'

When they reached the stone flags below, it was impossible to ignore the sound of a car driving into and pulling up short in the yard. The women composed their mouths, and began fiddling with their hair.

'That's Rory,' Anne murmured religiously.

Mog continued to caper, showing her muscles. 'Or *boxer*!' Dorothy decided the child was subnormal: another reason for throwing off the influence of 'Kudjeri'.

'Don't listen to Mog,' Janet appealed to her friend the princess.

Perhaps the telephone would break out; you never stopped listening for it to ring so frantically that it would tear itself off the wall.

Instead Anne Macrory, who had run outside, had met her husband and was bringing him in. Dorothy saw that Anne must have laid the wafer on his tongue: they both looked so meek, as though returning from communion. And Rory was working the last particles out of his teeth.

'Dorothy has been helping as usual.' Anne made it sound a pious afterthought.

Macrory went so far as to smile at their guest, but immediately after, coughed and swallowed.

The Princesse de Lascabanes announced that she would go and tidy up. She lowered her eyes. She might have committed a sacrilege: she felt pricked by pine needles; at the same time willow branches could have been paddled in her. And Basil her brother was not present to share her shame.

Mog Macrory bellowed, '*Haw-haw-haw!*' as she ran her short-cropped head at the thighs of the princess.

In their preoccupation with each other the parents did not attempt to restrain or make apologies for their child; and Janet only winced for all that she sensed without entirely understanding.

After the episode in the shed Basil took care to keep to himself. The warm sun, conflicting with overtones of cold, heightened his sense of expectation. The climate was that of diminishing freedom, as on the day before returning to school, or in the half hour to curtain up. Even so, his will had never been less inhibited by design or demands of any kind; his lack of connection with anything happening in the lives of others had a delicious, if also sickening, immorality about it.

Around noon, after the sound of women's voices had drained away from the kitchen quarters, he nipped in, tore out a handful of bread and broke off a lump of cheese, driven not so much by hunger as by habit. Swallowing the saltless bread, the insipid cheese, he fetched his book and hurried out before anyone could deprive him of the solitude which was his present need.

He found quiet intensified in what used to be the orchard, amongst espaliers turned from fillets into actual trees, in grass bleached by sun and frost, amongst the skeleton suckers of raspberry canes and naked gooseberry scrub. Here he lay to study, if not to understand, the Part. It was foolish of him to bring it to 'Kudjeri' to remind him of past failures; though better to fail in a part than as a whole: Lear rather than the Jacka's threat.

So he rubbed his nose in it. *Is there any cause in nature that makes these hard hearts?* Some of the lines were flung back at him like stones; others melted on his snoozing skin, *I have one part in my heart that's sorry yet for thee*; or battered on his sleep, *thou art the thing itself; unaccommodated man is no more but such a poor, bare, forked animal.* Stick to the text reality is a mad king not an aged queen whose crown won't come off for pulling whose not quite fresh eyes live by lucid flashes as hard as marble.

Not even at the moment of waking could he remember his dream. Fish. The fishmonger? Or cemetery. Certainly the ground was hard enough in what had been the walled orchard. He would have welcomed the scent and sound of plums; instead, whips and thorns had been used against his whole length. The sun was on its way out, while lingering slightly in the rough surface of weathered brick. Though his sleeper's clothes were crumpled and sweaty with anxiety and sleep, his body had tautened inside them. It was the cold coming. He got up. He put the book away in his pocket and began walking through this orange light to forestall anyone in search of him.

As to the orchard, the sound of summer was natural to the river.

He could not remember the river at 'Kudjeri' without its willows in leaf. Now (and reality is always present tense, whether for mad kings, or unemployed, ham actors) the cages were waiting. To be sure these communicated, but hints of steel nudged the fantasy of possible escape.

Inside a chosen cage there was no objection to his kneeling down on the petrified mud at the river's edge. As a boy he had stretched out to drink, and afterwards lain, regardless of discomfort, staring at his own reflection. This evening he knelt, and stirred the brown, rustling water, and splashed his face with enough of it to counteract the stickiness. As the water hurried over the stones beneath, he could see his face, when he dared look, at the other end of this tunnel of light. To be truthful, he had considered suicide once or twice in his life, but had not come at it: on each occasion the water was too shallow. In any case, he was not by temperament a suicide: theatrical gestures only convince when you can share them with an audience.

It made Sir Basil snigger at least; while realizing he was found out.

'Basil?'

She was coming towards him, sticks snapping as she trod on them; there was no escaping his big sister; and here on his knees he was at greater disadvantage than when she had caught him playing with that old car.

But she gave no sign of wishing to use her advantage. She approached shivering, it seemed. Perversely, and for the first time at 'Kudjeri', she had changed for dinner. It was intended to be simple and inoffensive, but the Princesse de Lascabanes had her gift for drawing attention to simplicity; how her little white would glare through the fug of the Macrory kitchen. He could not remember having seen her in white before: he had only known the perennial *veuve*, the discreetly expensive Frenchwoman.

She was holding her elbows to make her arrival appear as casual as possible. 'We had begun to wonder why you had deserted us.' Delivered gently enough, it had the measure of formality.

'We? Who?' He got to his feet, managing his bad knee with care. She avoided a direct reply. 'Anne's afraid the dinner will spoil.' 'What's she giving us?' 'Can't you guess?'

It was a somewhat half-hearted joke.

Then she laid her cheek against his. Her skin felt slightly greasy, which made the affection she was offering more intimate and spontaneous. Their relationship had grown dove-tailed, they were taking it so much for granted.

So the Hunter children held hands for the return. They leaned on each other in the climb up the river bank, before wading, almost luxuriously, through the sea of dry, winter tussock, to reach the house.

When she had seen the children to bed Anne Macrory came back to the kitchen where her guests and her husband were still sitting over the rejected fragments of their spotted dog.

'Didn't you like it?' she felt it her duty to ask.

Because they were listening to Anne's husband, Dorothy avoided committal; Basil did that thing with his crow's-feet, which served as reply, and had been known to win sympathy. As for Anne Macrory, she had fulfilled her obligations by putting food in front of people: whether they liked it or not was of less importance; perhaps life, or her Scottish ancestry, had persuaded her that what one eats is necessary rather than enjoyable.

And Rory was holding forth, she only saw at first, because she was so used to him.

'Anne will tell me I'm drunk,' Macrory said; 'but a man — even a passionate one — needs to keep his fire stoked.' Several private drinks were glittering in his eyes, though he had not offered his guests so much as the sight of a bottle.

Anne said, 'I wouldn't presume to tell you a blooming thing — at any rate, not a thing that matters.'

She plonked down at the tableful of remains. Elbows dug in, she slid her hands under the cap of her matted, dust-coloured hair. Her speech was that bit too precise: she looked as though she had been drinking too, but she hadn't; she would have made a sad, sulky drunk as opposed to his fiery one.

'Particular when the frost sets in,' Macrory said, 'a man needs to put heart into himself.'

'What if it's summertime?' asked his wife.

'By summertime it's second nature.' Macrory laughed for his own encouragement.

The Hunters smiled the contained smiles of overhearing, disbelieving guests. Their mouths were growing cavernous besides, with mutton fat and yawns.

Running his tongue over the roof of his mouth Basil could not have felt more desolated: he might have been standing under the carbonized girders of a London railway station, waiting for the train to carry him back to an unsuccessful tour of the Midlands. He closed his eyes to blot it out, and found himself instead, still running his tongue around the structure the mutton fat had emphasized, in the belly of a spiritual whale: unlike Jonah's, his would not spew him out till she died, and perhaps not even then.

The Macrorys were still at it, he heard from his depths.

'Our son Robert—our eldest—who you haven't met,' Macrory flashed his teeth at his guests to make amends for what they had missed, 'a clean, methodical lad—and cold—he'll succeed where his parents failed.'

Anne tensed her nostrils and closed her eyes. 'Robert is pure Robertson.'

'Isn't yourself a bit too much of a Robertson?' her husband gnashed. 'Of "Kirkcaldy"!' He leaned across the table to take his trick.

Anne only smiled as she answered, still from behind lowered lids, 'Once I was!' Then opened her eyes to look, still smiling, at her friend Dorothy Hunter, and again at her husband after digging her elbows deeper into the kitchen table. 'Do you suppose I'm complaining, Rory, that my awful pride was extinguished?'

Rory squirmed; he showed her the crown of his head as he

stirred his hair: it made almost the sound of broken glass as you sweep it up. 'Robert 'ull come good,' he did not exactly groan, but burped; and once or twice he scratched an armpit.

Anne was rocking on the points of her elbows. 'I'd like to think parents don't imagine their children.'

Driven by embarrassment, the Princesse de Lascabanes had risen from the table. She might have wanted to efface herself completely. Unable to, she looked for her handbag, which she had stowed away somewhere and forgotten. If she could find her bag, she would have that at least to hold.

While Macrory continued whipping his obsession round the prison of his skull. 'He can't help but succeed, from inheritun his grandfather's cold blood—and knowun his bloody messes of parents.'

Dorothy had found her bag.

'Robert's loaded. Like the French princess and the actor knight.' Whether he had aimed it in humility or bitterness, the superb Hunters were reduced to a crocodile handbag and a pair of cornelian and filigree cuff links.

Dorothy's throat felt so dry and choked she would have withdrawn from the success stakes regardless of whether Basil still considered himself a contender: as an actor he might decide to act it out; when she realized the Macrorys were training on her neither envy nor resentment, but their admiration, and, in Anne's case, love.

There was nothing in the inventory of her character or features which could possibly explain it; or was it her white dress? unpretentious enough, she had thought, and like most of her clothes, just outclevering shabbiness. But Anne was lapping it up; Macrory's eyes seemed to be having a love affair, not with the dress, nor her body inside it (she was pretty sure) but with what she stood for.

When Anne explained, 'Dorothy, we only saw your mother once. She drove up not long after she and Father agreed on the deal. I'll never forget her. She was wearing white.'

Dorothy's voice grated. 'Even as an old woman, white was one of her affectations.'

Basil was moved to defend their mother. 'She could never resist her sense of theatre.'

'I'd say Mrs Hunter was a flirt.' Macrory lolled remembering. 'She asked me hadn't we met before. Or perhaps we hadn't, she decided. Anyhow, she hoped we would meet again.' His eyes, his lips were licking at prospects he might still be considering.

Anne was unperturbed. 'Yes, she liked to flirt. With either sex. And although you knew what she was up to, it didn't matter. You let her seduce you with her eyes. What great persuaders her hands were! And her lovely voice.'

'She was all right,' Macrory agreed.

'I loved your mother,' Anne said.

While it was Dorothy her daughter they were looking at. Basil too, was beginning to take notice. He had raised his head. Surely to God Basil was not in love with Elizabeth Hunter? With her arms Dorothy de Lascabanes tried to cover as much of herself as she was able; though she probably only succeeded in suggesting that she was suffering from a stomach ache.

Basil had continued looking past or into her, when the telephone shattered the whole house. Anne went slommacking to answer; she was wearing a man's felt slippers tonight. Dorothy opened her bag and took out the mirror, then was afraid to look in it. Nor did she dare look at her brother.

Anne was not gone for long. 'That was Mrs Emmett again, to tell me nobody understands her, and couldn't I help.'

'You can't 'uv thrown 'er much of a lifeline to be back so quick.'

'I told her she'd better ring another number. We're out of business.'

'Bankrupted!' Macrory beat so hard with the spoon on one side of his plate, a bit flew out.

'Ah, dear!' Anne laughed; she pressed against her husband before stooping to gather up the piece; she said she was going to bed.

Basil too, left the kitchen: the telephone's false alarm had unnerved him; and Macrory lounged out, his slow gross manner emphasizing that neither his wife's silent invitation nor his guests' presence would influence his true, his secret life.

Ashamed for expecting deliverance by telephone, and for wearing her innocent white dress, Dorothy directed her anger at the ostentatiously unconscious Macrory long after he had left the room. Alcohol had intensified his insolence; it had glazed his eyes more brutally, and brought out the snakes of veins in the whites. His muscular attitudes were odious; she disliked his smell; body hair revolted her.

Her own sober breath was finally rasping.

Not only was she allergic to Macrory physically, she resented his memories of Mother: of Elizabeth Hunter revealing possibilities (to Macrory of all people) as she stepped from the car. (How much had Basil realized at the telling?) In a white dress. Had the glass been conscious of it when you put it on in Mother's room? Macrory had sat palming off those suggestions of Mother's nymphomania to mask his actual thoughts. Were you the Second Nymphomaniac? The one who hadn't found her feet? When God knew, everything in your experience of *that*, disgusted. Thoughts even. (What had Basil been looking at?) Thin arms are incapable of shielding anything vital.

Looking down, Dorothy found her dress exaggerated a nakedness which had never occurred to her before. (But Basil, a preoccupied, cultivated man—Shakespeare in his pocket, could not have noticed.)

Macrory would have.

The hall was not so dark that an oval rosewood mirror failed to reflect a steely light. The ugly mirror must have been one of the few bits of Robertson loot brought with them from 'Kirkcaldy' to 'Kudjeri'. It should have mocked a Hunter, but seemed instead to cajole: hips still impeccable; faintly mauve gloves of skin ending at the elbows; face wavering behind glass dissolving into water.

She was not drunk. It was most likely this glimpse of herself in

Mother's white which inspired Dorothy de Lascabanes to prove to Elizabeth Hunter she could play the game of generosity, or self-aggrandizement. She groped in her bag for the notecase. She could not remember its ever having been so fat: it was money from Mummy's gift cheque. It both thrilled and hurt Dorothy to take hold of so much ready money. She decided against counting. She would make a grand gesture. But after crumpling the notes in a careless handful, she could not resist confirming the extent of her generosity, and found that nobody would be able to accuse her of stinginess after this.

Though she could hear a crackling from the fire he had lit in the study, there was no sign that Macrory was still inside the room. She paused at the door, to listen; more irrevocably, she pushed it, however gently, from ajar to open.

He was lying on the hearth, his offside knee drawn up, so that his shoulders, his head were forced back, to help the other tensed leg balance his body. Though his eyes were closed, he was hardly relaxed: his Adam's-apple, which moved once after she entered, looked too self-conscious. She found herself glancing, by accident, at what she supposed they call the 'crutch' of this repellent man, to whom she was in any case only about to discharge a debt.

'Mr Macrory,' she began, when once or twice during their stay she had addressed him by his first name (not without ironic overtones) 'I'm afraid my brother and I have been imposing on you far too long;' only a lethargy descending on her prevented her adding, *sponging on you in fact.*

As she spoke she stood squeezing the handful of notes; they should have dripped sweat, but were so dry, they could very easily have emitted sparks, or caught fire.

Macrory opened his eyes and looked in her direction. Did he notice the nakedness which the dress had revealed for the first time tonight in the kitchen? Or was he, rather, listening for echoes of Elizabeth Hunter as she stepped radiant out of the car?

Madame de Lascabanes blundered on. 'I'd like you to accept this — from both of us — in appreciation of all you've done. Your wife too,

523

of course.' Macrory cocked an eyebrow, as though sceptical of Anne and Basil's part in it.

'Please!' The princess heard herself trumpeting.

Macrory turned on what was, for him, an exceptionally agreeable look. 'I never thought of friendship as something you pay for, Dorothy. Not like love.'

If he had left it at that, but he didn't: he carried on smiling at her, for an improbable proposition she had made, or worse, a professional service she demanded and he could only half-heartedly perform.

The Princesse de Lascabanes had never experienced a similar situation, except in her imagination. 'I'm sorry to have explained myself, apparently, so crudely. I also realize I misinterpreted a metaphor you used at dinner.'

It was humiliating to have chosen a word the fellow might find laughable for never having come across it. Her double gaffe produced in her a *frisson* as though somebody had drawn a wire brush across her slackening skin.

Then she remembered to drop the handful of notes back into the darkness of her bag. It was in one sense a relief.

'Such full lives,' the princess murmured, 'and your children — you must find the children most rewarding.'

He was still looking at her; so she went.

Passing through the house she did not hear the sound of her own movements: it was Elizabeth Hunter in pursuit. *Whatever the name — Hubert Edvard Rory — didn't you know Dorothy it's the same man one chases?* With Mother forcing you to look back it was impossible to escape shame. The *frisson* revived on Dorothy's arms, along the passages, and up the stairs. Stairs are worse: the sounds made by comparatively modest garments will swell voluptuously when thoughts are attuned to them. *Nobody — least of all you Dorothy — likes to admit to all the names Arnold isn't one is it would be too ridiculous but what about ... ?*

Dorothy shut out the voice; her ears whammed. If Basil had been there, they might have held hands, felt the warmth flow between them as reassurance of affection. She longed for this affection: its label carried the only convincing guarantee against a cold old age.

It was splitting cold tonight in the upper storey of this damned house. After leaving the fugbound kitchen and mounting the stairs, Basil could practically feel the chilblains opening in the backs of his hands. He had suffered from them as a little boy. They painted his watery sores with balsam of Peru, and gave him mittens to wear. Tonight on the stairs and in Alfred Hunter's dressing-room he was trailing this wintry scent of chilblains. Put the mat on the bed, on top of the blankets; the weight might help keep the shivers down. Supposing his bladder, victimized by age and the climate, returned him to little-boyhood, would the Macrory woman scold to find a map on the floor? Yes, she was a scold. His almoner-daughter Imogen was the only one who might offer comfort. But she wasn't his. If she were, by blood, there could be a Goneril lurking in her; Cordelias are too hard to get.

Where the hell was Dorothy? He often wondered what women do in bathrooms, to spend so much time locked up in them.

He went into their parents' room. 'What are you doing, Dorothy?' Whether she was there or not, he had to hear the sound of his own voice.

She was in fact standing in the middle of the room beneath a shadeless bulb, which still appeared to be streaming strings of crystal beads from Elizabeth Hunter's reign. Arms round her ribs, Dorothy herself stood streaming and glittering with misery, her bony nose clogged and swollen.

At first he would only allow himself to admire her virtuosity; but as a pro, he could not avoid taking his cue. 'What's worrying you, darling?' His cavernous, his ballooning, his deflating voice was horribly, sincerely convincing.

They were grappling shivering with each other in what might become the performance of their lives.

'Oh, Basil!' She was deafening him; and smelt—they both

probably did—of mutton fat. 'What have we got unless each other? Aren't we, otherwise—bankrupt?'

'Are we?' He was pretty sure she had come up with a wrong line; or else his memory was letting him down.

More important the discoveries they were making, which were not quite grief, passion, despair, horror, but something of them all, under the threadbare Macrory blankets, in the great bed. Elizabeth Hunter had specialized in spacious beds: so much of her life was spent in them, and still not spent; her children might go before her, bones broken by their convulsions on this shuddering rack.

If, instead of passing from one room to the other, he had thought of saying his prayers. But to whom, after all this time? Himself?

Now there was nothing to be done about it. Perhaps the grater instinctively loves the cheese. Wives don't love: they swallow you. And most mistresses are in it for calculated reasons.

But Dorothy! 'Dorothy?' He might have suspected the reality of this rather thin human substance he was—embracing? If he had been drunk at least; but Macrory had seen to it that each of them was sober.

'What is it, darling?' Sobriety can become more obsessed than drunkenness; she was too absorbed to more than mumble.

It seemed to her that if she had been fond of, instead of trying to love Hubert, he might have responded. Love can freeze the limbs; affection thaws the instincts.

So she and Basil were comforting each other.

Somewhere in the night he rejected their drowsy nakedness. 'Do you realize, Dorothy, they probably got us in this bed?' Such thoughtless candour poured them back into their separate skins: to turn to ice.

Till she felt she must tear open a darkness which was at the same time stifling her.

This stick-woman was staggering, tripping, lashed, he could just see, before she reached the curtains and started snatching by handfuls, at last wrenching the window up.

The moon was at its highest and fullest above the ring of mineral hills. Her exertion, and the icy draught from the opening window, flung her back. She might have fallen if he had not been there behind her to support and comfort her nakedness with his own.

'You've got to admit it's beautiful.' It was her brother looking over her shoulder at the landscape at 'Kudjeri'.

'Oh God, yes, we know that!' she had to agree; 'beautiful — but sterile.'

'That's what it isn't, in other circumstances.'

'Other circumstances aren't ours.'

It rent him to touch with his hand the hair his sister had screwed up in a knob for the night.

She let him lead her back to the bed. It had become an island of frozen ridges and inky craters. They lay huddled together, and he tried to conjure their former illusion of warmth, under a reality of wretched blankets.

Eleven

'Is it cold, Sister?'

'Yes, dear, it's cold,' Sister Manhood replied, 'or cold for here.'

At the sandier end of the park, people were tramping, exerting their bodies in the kind of makeshift clothes worn for a cold snap in a climate which is officially warm. Clothes and sand were making the going heavy for the walkers; every one of them looked middle-aged; when probably the majority, without clothes and exposed to summer, would have turned out young and aggressively athletic.

Sister Manhood was glad of her woolly. Pink and fluffy, it made her look bulky. It couldn't be helped: she ought to be thickening.

'The bed's cold,' Mrs Hunter complained.

'You *feel* warm. You've got the hot-water bottle. And your jacket and socks. Your feet are warm.' The nurse was unscrewing her dried prawn of a patient from the position a nap had left her in.

'Oh, it isn't the body! I had a dream.'

'Wasn't it a nice one?'

'No. It wasn't. I was in my bed. I don't know where my husband was. Perhaps he had died. No. It was worse than that. He had gone off leaving me alone at "Kudjeri"—with my children Basil and Dorothy—before they were born. Were they twins, though?'

Sister Manhood could hardly stick it. (What if it was twins inside herself?)

'In the dream, yes,' Mrs Hunter said. 'But in life, I can't remember. Were they, Sister?'

'You're the one who ought to know. You had them.' For God's sake!

'In the dream they *wanted* to be twins. I could hear them calling from inside me—blaming me because I prevented them loving each other.'

Sister Manhood shoved a chair aside so hard she overturned it: she had just about had this old sod.

'That isn't uncommon,' Mrs Hunter remembered. 'People who aren't capable of loving often blame someone else. I did from time to time. I blamed Alfred. That's why he must have gone away and left me with my hateful children. They weren't his, you know.'

'I never heard that before.'

'Oh, I got them from him. But I made them into mine. That is what the children resent—already—why they are protesting inside me.'

'At that rate, by your own argument, Mrs Hunter, you are the one to blame.'

'Who knows?'

Mrs Hunter must have sensed she had started something in her nurse: her hand began soothing, and she asked in a voice the nurses used, 'Are you well, Sister? You *seem* well.'

'I'm well enough.' A baby isn't an illness.

'We'll both feel the better for my visitor.'

'Oh? Are you sure you're expecting a visit? Nobody told me.'

'Didn't they? Some of the women in this house are so full of their own thoughts it doesn't occur to them that anything happens outside their heads.'

Sister Manhood could have fetched up, but was inquisitive enough to ask, 'Is your visitor somebody I know?'

'It's Mrs Wyburd, and her own idea to call. I shouldn't have thought of it.' Mrs Hunter sounded quite definite.

The nurse perked up: she had never set eyes on Mrs Wyburd and was curious to see what the solicitor had fancied; she even went so far as suggesting, 'Better let me do your face so that your visitor will catch you at your best.'

'No,' Mrs Hunter said, 'Mrs Wyburd is an honest woman.'

Sister Manhood was all the more curious to see. So when the doorbell rang, she went along the landing, and leaned over the banisters, as though hoping to surprise a secret or two before honesty closed down on them.

Mrs Lippmann was opening the door to a person dressed in what the fashion reporters of some years ago would have written up as 'donkey brown'. Mrs Wyburd was one of those women who go so far and no farther with clothes, Sister Manhood recognized. Clothes are to clothe, Mrs Wyburd's garments seemed to claim; not that she hadn't given them thought: they were in what is called 'the best of taste', and the materials, though unobtrusive, must have made a hole in her allowance. Above all, Mrs Wyburd's general appearance suggested that she was a 'lady': another and independent mystery. That the mysterious 'honesty' referred to by Mrs Hunter in no way depended on Mrs Wyburd's ladyhood was obvious enough, because Mrs Hunter herself was a lady, and Mrs Hunter's honesty was of an intermittent, womanly persuasion. Better than nothing, Sister Manhood supposed. To solve the mystery of Mrs Wyburd she would have to get a better look at her. The solicitor's wife, standing in the hall with the housekeeper, had probably never been so closely stared at, except by the inevitable doctors and dentists, and the ruthless eyes of children. But Sister Manhood's inquiry got her nowhere: it was like as if she had been told to admire some brown, crumby vase because it was a valuable antique, and all she could see was its plain shape and ordinary dull old brown. She ended up a bit miserable: the imperviousness of this brown figure made her feel a liar, cheat, unmarried mother, and nympho into the bargain.

Down below Mrs Lippmann was saying, 'You must know to find your way, Mrs Wyburd, from being here before.'

The angle at which Mrs Wyburd held her head conveyed surprise, amusement, perhaps also cynicism. 'I know it of course. But from long ago. Yes, I know my way,' she admitted; it was what she could see the housekeeper had been hoping for.

It might have suited Mrs Wyburd well enough to be left to her own devices in a house she had known long ago. After the housekeeper retired, the nurse watching from the top of the stairs could see the solicitor's wife was hesitating over what to open and where to enter; her time was short. But obviously the mysterious honesty referred to by Mrs Hunter got the better of Mrs Wyburd, and she began trying out the stairs with her unfashionable, but good, probably custom-made shoes.

Feeling herself at an advantage, if only a very slight one, the nurse revealed her presence. 'Oh, Mrs Wyburd,' she called, while descending just enough of the stairs, 'I'll show you the way in case you've forgotten.' She was smiling down at the mildly startled face below. 'I am Sister Manhood. You won't have heard of me,' Flora knew she was being insincere; wasn't it the sort of thing you do? 'But you hardly count as a stranger — not as Mr Wyburd's wife.' At the same time she raised a hand in trying to control an express giggle propelled upward through the shaft of her throat.

'I don't know you, but have heard about you from my husband,' Mrs Wyburd replied in a voice probably caused by her walking upstairs.

Just how much she had heard, Sister Manhood wondered; a couple might be colourless but it didn't prevent them enjoying purple talk. So she stared the harder, while smiling her formal kindliest, as the solicitor's wife continued mounting.

Though the face was guarded for most of the ascent by the brim of a velour hat, to one side of which was clamped an inverted cockade in stiff, grey, mushroom silk, Sister Manhood caught glimpses of powdered skin during Mrs Wyburd's prudent approach. There was nothing you could criticize, finally. If the mouth was doctored it had not been treated in the unnaturally natural style of today, nor had it been dealt the bloody wounds of a Hunter past. Mrs Wyburd's mouth was what you would call natural natural. For that matter, you mightn't have dropped to the powder if nervousness or haste hadn't smudged it. Then when the visitor reached the top, Sister Manhood noticed what looked like a single deep pockmark where powder had lodged, beside the nose, on one cheek, and freckles (red ones) to which the powder clung. Flora Manhood was fascinated by Mrs Wyburd's pock: there was nothing you could have done about that; as for the freckles, in trying to disguise them, the sufferer disclosed perhaps a faint crack in her honesty. It made Sister Manhood warm towards her: she hoped Mrs Wyburd, in spite of the badly camouflaged freckles, would be a match for Betty Hunter, who had chosen to remain undisguised.

'A stiff climb!' the thin trim lady murmured to fill the silence.

For a moment she was staring back at the face of the glowing, pretty young nurse as though into a nostalgic morning of her own youth. Then as there was nothing else for either of them to say or do, Mrs Wyburd followed Sister Manhood down the passage.

Mrs Hunter cleared her throat, an operation in which more than a hint of phlegm was involved, and raised her voice from where it was sunk amongst the pillows. 'It was a charming idea,' she said, 'Lal—to pay me a visit.' For all that, the old thing was looking in an opposite direction.

'It was more than an idea, Mrs Hunter,' said Mrs Wyburd with a jerk of her head which produced from the wing-shaped silk cockade a sound as of pin feathers, 'I wanted to thank you for your present.' She blushed, perhaps because she wasn't wearing it. 'Letters are unsatisfactory, and often get lost in the post.' She lowered her glance. 'A voice is more personal, don't you think?'

Mrs Hunter turned on her eyes. 'Oh, I can see very well at times. Today for instance. But close up. Over there you look like something under water. Come here and sit beside me on this little chair.'

As the visitor went to obey, the nurse fussed at pulling the chair closer to the bed. Though left out of things, it did not occur to her to sulk: the situation was too absorbing for an observer.

Mrs Hunter was making a gentle noise of eiderdowns; she was stroking the back of one of Mrs Wyburd's by now gloveless hands. 'The freckles, Lal—you still have them. Are they all right? One used to hear that, with age, freckles can become dangerous.'

'I've never thought about it,' Mrs Wyburd confessed.

Sister Manhood watched the renewed blush gathering under the visitor's skin; the increase in colour left the single pockmark with its drift of powder more exposed than ever.

'Why not, Lal?' Mrs Hunter asked. 'I insist that you see a doctor. Have him examine the freckles. That's reasonable, isn't it?'

'Reasonable—yes. But I don't think I'd like to be told what I don't want to hear. Or be the cause of distress in others.'

'Pfooh! What good will it do the other ostriches—to have you walking amongst them—a living cancer?'

Vehemence gave Mrs Hunter a fit of coughing. Sister Manhood offered water.

'What—are you still here, Nurse? when I want to talk confidentially with my friend. Ask my housekeeper to make the tea. Only tea. I don't think we'll bother about anything to eat. Mrs Wyburd was never interested in food.'

Mrs Wyburd had folded her hands in her lap. She sat smiling straight ahead. She did look honest.

'I'm sure Mrs Lippmann won't forget the tea. But isn't it early, Mrs Hunter?'

Mrs Hunter stared at her nurse, who left the room.

'I have another nurse who brings me roses. She must have forgotten today. I can't smell them.'

'This isn't the season for roses.'

'No. There aren't any.'

'I remember how you loved roses. I should have brought you some if they had been in season.'

'She is the one who is. The pretty one. Permanently. She thinks I can't smell it, but I can.'

Mrs Wyburd was not liking it at all. She glanced at one of the mirrors. Though she was in fact alone with this unpleasant old woman, other people might have been present.

'Wasn't his name "Arnold"?' Mrs Hunter went on hammering.

'Who?'

'The solicitor.'

Mrs Wyburd uttered too hoarsely, 'Yes.'

'Do you remember the goatsbeard?'

'The what?'

'Astilbe.'

'I can't think what you mean, Mrs Hunter.'

Mrs Hunter laughed. 'You were the one for botanical names.'

'My memory isn't what it was.'

'My mimulus of Double Bay!' Mrs Hunter was mimicking somebody's voice.

Mrs Wyburd sat looking at her knotted hands. 'How are the children?' she asked of her protectress. 'I was hoping they might find time to pay me a visit.'

'They have their own affairs. Oh, yes!' Mrs Hunter sighed. 'Be thankful for your garden, Lal.'

Mrs Wyburd was glad she had her reflection for company, even if an ugly one, its (cancerous) freckles masking the record of so many bungled attempts to console those she loved.

'Does my husband love you?' Mrs Hunter pursued.

'I hardly think he did,' Mrs Wyburd answered; 'in fact you know he didn't.'

'Yes. I am the one.' Mrs Hunter stirred.

Mrs Wyburd was relieved when the nurse brought in the tea.

'It's the jasmine you're so fond of,' Sister Manhood informed. 'Can't you smell the scent from it?'

Everything, as ever, was in honour of Elizabeth Hunter, but she who had been all for scents, turned her head and would barely breathe.

Mrs Wyburd swallowed what she was not prepared to admit: her true feelings for Elizabeth Hunter.

While Sister Manhood poured the tea and handed the cups, she was trying to crook a finger, but that seemed to have thickened, like her body. 'Let me prop you up, Mrs Hunter. Shall I help you with your tea?'

'Of course not.' Then, 'Leave it – thank you.'

Sister Manhood left altogether, and Mrs Wyburd sat sipping too soon: her palate was scalded; the pouches under her eyes were running; her (cancerous) freckles must have looked, she guessed, like drops of rust. She no longer dared face herself in the glass.

Mrs Hunter would not touch her tea, such was the crisis towards which they were heading. 'Where is my husband?' she asked.

'I should have thought,' gasped Mrs Wyburd, 'buried.'

'You needn't remind me,' Mrs Hunter said, 'of what we know. What I meant was: Arnold – does he treat you kindly?'

534

'He's an honourable man, and I'm married to him.'

'Oh, Lal! Does he *love* you?'

Mrs Wyburd managed, 'Yes.' Why should this creature be allowed to explore your nakedness, first with her claws and now with her vindictive mind? 'He loves me,' she asserted, though it was like jumping into darkness.

She felt completely naked, with Mrs Hunter always looking closer.

'Arnold was hairless,' Mrs Wyburd's torturer seemed to remember.

'How do you mean? He isn't bald even now.' Mrs Wyburd was shocked by her own laughter.

'But does his beard?'

'I couldn't tell. Every morning he shaves it off;' with the electric razor the girls persuaded him to adopt several birthdays ago.

'No astilbe,' Mrs Hunter only mumbled because she was already thinking of other things.

Mrs Wyburd could feel that her eyes were controlled and dry, but she failed to prevent a perspired tear from plopping into the dregs of her tea. The roof of her mouth was cauterized.

Mrs Hunter said, 'Now I remember, Lal, why I was persuaded to send you that chain. I don't know why I should say "persuaded" when I was *compelled*—isn't that the word? If we care to admit, most of life is compulsion or coincidence. So I gave this chain. Which I was wearing in the storm—on Brumby Island. And survived. You are the one I wanted to have it.'

Was it generosity, or humbug? Lal Wyburd could not tell; she might have cried if she had not been trained by Arnold.

Then Mrs Hunter decided, 'I must ask you to go. I'm tired. Not as tired as Gladys Radford. They had to give her oxygen. Do you remember Gladys?'

'No,' said Mrs Wyburd; her cup almost shot out of its saucer. 'You're the one who has the memory.'

'Thank you,' Mrs Hunter said. 'I have nothing else.'

Mrs Wyburd was putting on her gloves. Mrs Hunter must have heard it, but she did not look relieved.

'Will you kiss me, Lal?' she asked.

Mrs Wyburd laughed. 'Why, yes! Did you think I wasn't going to?' She knew she was blushing for her lie: she preferred to kiss even Arnold in the dark.

Mrs Hunter was raising her blind head on the end of its ringed neck: the effect was ancient and reptilian. Lal Wyburd felt herself contained in what might have been an envelope of vapour, or sentimental pity, inside which, again, her mind was reared in horror, not for the decayed humanity she had at her mercy, but beyond the mask, still the legend of Elizabeth Hunter's beauty.

By grace of desperation she recalled an incident of years ago when she and the girls were on their European tour. Dawdling with appropriate Protestant incredulity and disapproval through the town of Lourdes, they found themselves automatically taking their places in a queue. Too late Marjorie at the head of their party realized they had been roped in to pay their respects in the grotto of the miraculous vision. There was no way out. Marjorie, one saw, bend and actually kiss the rock in front of her like any Roman. Heather turned for a moment, crimson with scorn, if not panic, before they were jostled forward from behind. Heather marched past, her head held high. What, oh, what to do? Then Lal Wyburd ducked and, in no way disrespectfully, kissed the air several inches above the surface of the slimy rock. She walked on dazed but thankful she had managed to avoid hygienic and spiritual contamination without vulgarly demonstrating.

And now here below her Mrs Hunter's lips were probing trembling around at nothing.

Quickly Mrs Wyburd stooped: she kissed the air just short of the older woman's face.

Elizabeth Hunter must have heard it. She sank back on her pillows looking fairly well satisfied. 'Love me!' she murmured, scarcely for her caller.

It might have been another conquest, not so much of an individual as of the abstract: in any case, she would chalk it up along with the others.

Mrs Wyburd left. She was glad neither the housekeeper nor the nurse was anywhere in sight: they might have asked questions, or worse, complimented her in some way. She walked downstairs looking at her feet, holding her handkerchief to her mouth, to stop up an emptiness where that kiss should have been. Still, she had her husband, whom beauty had failed to destroy. Nor would death if she could prevent it.

Mrs Wyburd cried, though.

After being dismissed from her employer's room Sister Manhood had gone outside and was walking around in the garden, sort of doodling, with her body for pencil and her mind as lead. She had only ever bothered about what is called landscape while she was a kid, when you have the time to take notice of a leaf or insect (perhaps amuse yourself killing the insect) or cowpat (pick up the dry ones and bowl them along) later there is always yourself standing in the way of trees and things to prevent you seeing them except as dim and superfluous.

Walking in Mrs Hunter's garden she tore off a leaf, or two, sucked one, dropped the other, before taking refuge in the sleeves of her fluffy cardigan. She hid her hands. She wondered how much longer she would be able to hide the shape of her body from practised eyes, or whether the solicitor's wife had already got the message.

The nurse watched old Mrs Wyburd leave the house and pass through the garden on her way to the street, so busy with her own thoughts she was not noticing anything around her. Even so, Flora Manhood slightly smoothed the skirt over her stomach. Then she folded her fluffy pink arms above her fallen breasts.

The gate squeaked. Mrs Wyburd had gone.

Over the indistinct garden the sky was clear and watery with one torn-out cotton wool cloud piled high above the racecourse and the convents. Flora Manhood touched her face; that too, had swollen: its white, turnip skin. She would have allowed a mere stranger (not quite true) to kiss away her independence if that had been possible.

Then the tingle tinkle of the little bell: it was the relic summoning you to a duty, of which Mary de Santis would have made a devotion.

Sister Manhood walked very firmly up the swirling, not to say dangerous path (Mrs Hunter liked to tell how two people had broken their legs) towards her non-devotional duty. Her arms were hanging perfectly indifferent inside the cardy. When that wasn't her at all. If only she could have felt cold and indifferent Col Pardoe might never have happened; Sir Basil bloody Hunter would not have entered into it.

The garden at dusk encouraged in Flora Manhood's mind too much that was distinctly irretrievable: speckles on birds' eggs *wotcher do with the muck Snow when you've sucked it out? why you spit it* dogs with dots above their eyes freckles on an old woman's lids moles in the angle of a man's arm *teeth Flo what's got into you? you don't understand only books and* MAHLER *not that what you love you want to eat oh Coll-urnn.*

Lottie Lippmann was standing in the darkening hall looking like a small rat come out of a creek bank.

'What is it, Floradora? Are you sick?'

Flora Manhood said, 'I got a bit of a bellyache.' Though Lottie was solid gold, and had been around, she was too pure to confide in.

'She's been ringing for you,' Mrs Lippmann said.

'You're telling *me*! Couldn't you have answered – Lot?'

'I am preparing myself. She expects me later,' Mrs Lippmann said.

The nurse realized that the housekeeper, who at first sight in the dusk, and through the shutter of her own disturbed thoughts, had suggested some small wary animal, was excessively calm and in some way resplendent. Though still wearing an old woollen kitchen-stained shift and her comfortable felt slippers, she had dressed her hair smoother than ever before; the roots were visibly straining at the straight white parting even by that light, the eyes more luminous for the dim hall and state of anticipation.

'Later I shall come to her,' Mrs Lippmann repeated through

naturally dark lips, lowering oiled eyelids on a confidence she was not at liberty to share, though the nurse probably guessed.

It was too spooky for Flora Manhood. She went upstairs. In passing the bathroom she felt a nausea rise in her, and went in to give way to it. She stood looking into the lavatory bowl in an attitude of penitence; but nothing came. Nothing would be made easy. Except that the nausea passed. And Lottie must have taken the tea things she was glad to see on going into the patient's room.

The remains of a voice succeeded at last in detaching itself from where it was stuck. 'I want you to make up my face, Sister Manhood.'

Her own name sounded repellent to the nurse, who snapped back, 'That's just what you wouldn't have when there was some reason for doing it.'

'Mrs Wyburd mightn't have understood.'

If there were any implication that Flora Manhood might be included in the hierarchy of those who understood, it was wasted on her: she was too distressed by her own condition. She was plain cranky in fact, and in no mood for games.

She jerked at the cord of the bedside lamp, and when the light flew out, Mrs Hunter did not preach her usual sermon about who pays the bills. This evening the old thing meekly waited, already holding her face to receive.

Because of the mood she was in, Sister Manhood slammed around a bit before bringing the vanity case and dumping it hard on the bedside table. Mrs Hunter did not comment. Though the gristle was taut in her throat, her face smiled for grace about to descend.

Tonight as she smeared and moulded the cheeks with cream Flora Manhood did not even ask what her client was going for. Nor did Mrs Hunter suggest; she submitted. It could not have occurred to her, in her trance, that an apostasy might have taken place.

Certainly the custodian of the sacred image had never felt less religiously inclined. What if she did a real hatchet job for once? So she dusted, and pasted on, the shimmering greens of all fiends; the idol's brutal mouth would scarcely overflow after she had contained its crimson with a thick wall of black; if steely lids sharpened the swords those eyes could flash in their most vindictive moments, at least their victims would go down laughing.

Flora Manhood was laughing for her own art.

'Is it all right?' Mrs Hunter inquired. 'She is going to dance for me presently.'

'It would send you if you could see!' Sister Manhood grinned. 'You'll both give a performance tonight.'

When she had wrapped the body in what used to be a robe of rose brocade, and seated it in the chrome chair, Sister Manhood shivered, as though the lift were rising, and the masks waiting for more than the patient at the end of the aseptic corridor.

To remember and fetch the wig was some distraction. She found herself bringing the green one, which Mrs Hunter had worn only once, and never asked for again. (*Though I can't see it Sister I don't feel it comes off — as an idea*. Tonight it did.)

When she had arranged the lifeless hair, Sister Manhood patted it as nonchalantly as she could. 'Flowing free!'

Acceptant in every department, Mrs Hunter smiled and said, 'That is what I visualized;' then remembered, 'But my jewels, Nurse! Have you forgotten?' Anxiety almost produced a hiccup.

Whether she had or not, the girl brought the case. As the jewels were loaded on her, Mrs Hunter appeared to appreciate their shuddering collisions. 'How we enjoyed suffering!' she giggled at one point.

The two great emeralds Sister Manhood had screwed to her ears were clubbing her cheeks before settling down. If it had not been for support from the chrome chair-back, an emerald stomacher might have dragged her down into a horizontal position, or lethal pin pierced her to the heart.

Sister Manhood had, in fact, pricked the skin in bridging the eroded cleavage; but as you saw it, the old biddy was too far gone with vanity and age to feel.

The nurse lightly wiped away a drop of blood from a superficial wound; even when she dabbed the place with alcohol, neither fumes nor pain seemed to reach the actual Elizabeth Hunter.

Instead her breath gathered to ask, 'Have you given me my star? My sapphire?'

'But your fingers must be just about paralysed with rings. And the sapphire won't go. Not with what I've already put.' The artist in Flora Manhood was offended.

'It must!' Mrs Hunter insisted.

They both began scrabbling through the velvet trays. When it came to jewels, Mrs Hunter's fingers were more agile than her nurse's.

'It isn't here!' Sister Manhood shouted louder than her patient's deafness required.

'My star! Could it have fallen on the floor? I gave you one, didn't I? the pink – but only the pink, Dorothy.'

Sister Manhood was crawling groping round the chair. 'Yes, the pink – the pink's in writing. You don't imagine *I* took your other sapphire? I didn't want either of them.'

Mrs Hunter smiled and said, 'No.'

Dusty and breathless, Sister Manhood was also snivelling by the time she righted herself. '*Anybody* could have stolen the thing.'

'Yes.' Mrs Hunter smiled. 'Or I might have given it as a present. Kate had so many dolls she was always giving them away and often couldn't remember. It doesn't matter – in the end – does it?' She did not exactly settle the rose brocade but let it slither around her shoulders into a more natural line. 'Now will you call her?' The lips had grown tremulous with unusually controlled impatience. 'Tell her I am ready.'

From the doorway Flora Manhood looked back, afraid of what she might have created. Old Betty Hunter's green and silver mask glittered and glimmered in the depths of the room. Nobody could accuse you of malice when you had only emphasized the truth. As for Mrs Hunter, she looked for the moment conscious of her own fiend, and was resigned to accepting responsibility for it.

You, on the other hand, would never know for sure how much of the evil in you was of your own making, and how much had been forced on you by others, by Col Pardoe, Mrs Hunter, people you simply brush up against – or God, if there was one; only there

541

wasn't: there was no scientific evidence. Not like this child, playing on your nerves, threatening to split your head and make you throw up. The child was real enough: your own deliberate creation, whether for good or evil; nobody, least of all Sir Basil Hunter, could be blamed for that.

Flinging back the door, not so much to summon the housekeeper as to dash for the bathroom, Flora Manhood almost collided with what she did not at first recognize as Mrs Lippmann.

She was wearing this grotty dress she claimed Mrs Hunter had promised her, and which in theory anyone of right mind would have considered a ghastly joke. But in practice the dress worked. For in the days when Elizabeth Hunter of audacious legs had glided out through the dusty light in the opening steps of the next foxtrot, the chiffon frothing and lapping in waves from beneath the spangled surface of what must have given an impression of liquid metal, or restless water, the skirt would barely have reached her knees; so now this stumpy Jewess was able to wear it, certainly not with dash, rather with a reverence suited to the austere tunic the dress had become.

Gravely the Jewess inclined her large head with its coil of hair as she passed the nurse. Eyes already fixed on the heights to which she aspired, Lotte Lippmann must have forgotten the pains in her feet. If she was conscious of garishness in the seated figure, she chose to ignore it: she was too devoted, or entranced. And Mrs Hunter smiled. She held out a hand so tremulous with jewels it appeared to be establishing a beat. Lotte Lippmann accepted the hand together with any other conventions.

Flora Manhood had never taken part in a mystery: almost with Col Pardoe, if she had not resisted; almost, if she had been equal to it (less clumsy, ignorant, frightened) with Elizabeth Hunter at moments when the old woman had been willing to share her experience of life. Now the nurse's lips were muttering and jumbling as she stood in the doorway holding her belly and watching for what was about to happen.

On advancing into the centre of the room, Lotte Lippmann smartly clicked her heels twice, and bent a knee in a girlish curtsey, or obeisance. That much Flora Manhood understood. What she saw was only the dancer's back: all those vertebrae like beads where Elizabeth Hunter's nakedness had been, now ending in the coil of hair gathered tight at the nape of Lotte Lippmann's neck.

Lulled by the heavy devotional air which filled the room (ought to slip round and open the window to ventilate) Flora from her distance began telling the vertebrae. Though she wasn't a mick. And Lot a Jew.

Oh but you felt sick get away and vomit it up or get rid of the whole packet (would somebody find it in the lavatory bowl and accuse you of it?)

None of this deterred the immediate participants, Elizabeth Hunter conducting a rite with one green hand, or Lotte Lippmann, who had turned, and begun interpreting their dance.

The dancer at first moved haltingly: the stumpy arms hesitated to fling an impulse skyward. This was a dance she had never performed before: every twig on which she trod, alarmed; leaves turning to metal tore at her sleeked hair. So she ducked her head. While her 'public' was reaching out to snatch her back into their midst: paws fringed with reddish hair, or alternately, the white lollipop imitations of fingers, were preparing to tweak her nipples and evaluate her undersized breasts, her conic-sectional hips.

Because this was what the dancer had experienced of life she was tempted to continue clodhopping amongst familiar swine though it might not be what her mentor expected of her.

The metronome was growing erratic. 'Is this what we're paying for? There's too much of yourself tonight.' The emeralds glared.

Lotte Lippmann might have looked more desolated if she had not grown used to carrying a cross of proportions such as no Christian could conceive.

'Give it time, Mrs Hunter. I must feel my way, mustn't I?' she called back in her only slightly desolated voice.

Balancing on one deformed foot, she stretched a leg, with its knots and ladders of blue veins ending in a scarred pump. If it had not been for the dress she might have flopped down in a heap amongst her own physical shortcomings. But the dress hinted at a poetry which her innermost being might help her convey; it reflected a faith in love and joy to which she tentatively subscribed.

'All the old cabaret stuff,' Mrs Hunter continued nagging because her housekeeper liked to suffer; 'I got that out of my system a hundred years ago.'

But know about it too well the *ein zwei drei* men poking their snouts against an ear lobe as they push you past the saxophones oh yes bestiality is familiar didn't you choose to rut with that that politician Athol Thingummy you know it down to the last bristle the final spurt of lust and renounce men anyway for tonight.

Now surely, at the end of your life, you can expect to be shown the inconceivable something you have always, it seems, been looking for. Though why you should expect it through the person of a steamy, devoted, often tiresome Jewess standing on one leg the other side of a veil of water (which is all that human vision amounts to) you could not have explained. Unless because you are both human, and consequently, flawed.

To encourage her housekeeper Mrs Hunter called, 'I expect your arabesque will be exquisite, darling, when it has firmed up a bit.'

Lotte Lippmann got such exasperated giggles she almost toppled over. Then they were both contentedly snorting.

'A couple of crazy bitches!' Sister Manhood stamped across the room to let in some air, and left them to it: she could not stand any more; she could not see what was funny; she belonged nowhere tonight; she shut herself in the bathroom.

Nor did Lotte Lippmann, a serious person and satirist, know why she was laughing. But her ribs were aching, for some adolescent sacrilege she might have committed. At least she was liberated. She was free to unite in pure joy with the source of it (not this travesty Floradora had been cruel enough to introduce). So Lotte did a little dance she might have remembered from earlier in time, down the street, twitching her apron, pigtails gambolling behind her.

Mrs Hunter was appeased. 'Now I can tell you are entering into the spirit of it.' She could feel the air moving around her; a skirt caught for an instant in the rings in brushing past her hand.

Lotte Lippmann was certainly dancing, but with eyes closed, nostrils pinched, as though the risen dead might stand before her, still trailing the stench of burning.

Mrs Hunter's brocaded knees were slightly moving as they pursued a course of their own through mornings full of the smell of cow manure and frost, and linseed cake and steaming milk. *If you dance Kate you'll dance the chilblains out of your blood.* That old plaid skirt with the burn below the pocket ballooning as you twirl. What became of Kate Nutley? Probably still waiting outside the dairy. Kate wet her pants because the cold. *If they were mine I'd dance till they dried and nobody know I'm going to be a professional dancer.* You had spoken the truth, in a sense. How the sky used to whirl on frosty mornings. The past is so much clearer than the purblind present. Every pore of it.

Lotte Lippmann had embraced her dance at last, or was embraced by it. She was dancing caressing her own arms, her shoulders, with hands which could not press close enough, fingers which could not dig deep enough into her dark, blenching flesh. She opened her fearful eyes, parted her lips, to receive an approbation she might not be strong enough to bear.

Nor might Elizabeth Hunter. Her wired limbs were creaking as she sank lower in her steel chair; the bones of her knees stuck out through the brocaded gown; the flannel nightie, the lamb's wool bootees, were no comfort. She moaned for what the dancers had coming to them. All around her she could hear the sound of the woman's breathing as she fought the dance by which she was possessed. You don't at first re-live the tenderness: it's the lashing, the slashes, and near murder. So Elizabeth Hunter moaned. Like a stricken cow lying on its side.

IT yes it is a dying a *beige* cow its ribs showing white through the hide (they couldn't surely have showed up white but perhaps they did). The eyes. There was nothing you could do for the cow—any more than for yourself. Gently touch the ribs with your toe (in actual fact if you want to be honest you kicked that cow because of the immensity of dying and ran to look for Kate to tell her about this one scraggy paralysed cow not about the immensity she would not have understood it but Kate was never to be found when wanted). They were calling from the back door. *Elizabeth? Where have you been? Don't you realize we worry about you?* You danced to show you were not in the wrong that you didn't belong to them except as the child they 'loved' you 'loved' them in return everybody doing what is expected. *I found a half-dead cow. Pooh! Putrid! It couldn't get up. An old cow.* They said *the poor thing can't because it is the drought don't you know Elizabeth Salkeld haven't you any pity in you?* You danced because you knew more than the people who loved you more than the stones of the walls of houses. (Pity is such a private matter something between yourself and the object you must hide it from.)

Elizabeth Hunter was trying to plant her bungling lips on the wind the dancer was creating round her. She tried to grasp hold of something. She couldn't. She was the prisoner of her chair. Her attempts were as needless as ineffectual as drunkenness. She subsided.

Now that her other self had been released from their lover's attempts to express tenderness in terms of flesh (no less touching, tragic even, for being clumsy and impotent) their movements became more fluid. They were dancing amongst what must have been trees the light at first audibly flickering between the trunks or was it trains roaring rushing you towards incurable illness old age death corruption no it was the dying away you must be hearing through moss-padded doors a bird's glistening call then the gulls scraping colour out of the sky. (What was that sooty one got pierced?)

Lotte Lippmann's hair had come undone. Though still part of her, it was leading a separate life. Flinging itself in opposite directions. A tail of coarse hair lashed Mrs Hunter across the mouth.

It stung. It was bitter-tasting, as might have been expected from the pace at which both were galloping.

As she closed in towards the climax of her dance, Lotte Lippmann was shedding her sequins; though the structure of the moonlit dress held.

Mrs Hunter was dribbling: to hear the waves open and close at this hour of morning in nacred shallows carrying the shells back and forth whole Chinaman's fingernails and the fragments the fragments becoming sand.

It was sand which Mrs Hunter could feel grating. Ask the night nurse for Optrex. A cold eyeball in blue glass. Or was it That Girl still? Maids used to fly off the handle and mope in such a way on discovering they were pregnant.

A woman was still dancing *dancing* for no apparent reason.

When Mrs Lippmann suddenly flopped. 'What more do you expect of me?' she panted into Mrs Hunter's knees.

'Nothing. Go! You're hurting. I don't feel like being touched.'

It caused the housekeeper pain: she was not yet wholly released from the ceremony of exorcism.

But Mrs Hunter was relentless. 'Send my nurse to me,' she ordered. 'I want to relieve myself.'

She had a hollow tooth she was not prepared to spend on till she had paid off the lay-by on the caffee o'lay caftan.

Standing at the bathroom glass Sister Manhood probed her tooth with the quill pick she kept for that purpose. The pain she sent shooting up the tooth was almost ready to shriek (Would the quill, perhaps, do? ... *I always ever used the bark but Mavis she swears by a hairpin* ... Ugh, not a pin!)

Coot crying round the lake in the park poured the darkness thicker on. They found the body floating in the lake: it was a man, though. Lottie galumphing in the old girl's bedroom is enough to bring the plaster down. Dancing. Join the witches and dance it out— ha-ha! Or go up to the Cross when you had handed over to St Mary, hang around a street corner, or a more likely lurk, do the motel foyers and get yourself murdered. (*Investigation has revealed that the 25-year-old trained nurse found strangled with her own scarf on the floor of a Pacific Towers bedroom was two months pregnant. Sister Flora Manhood lived alone in rooms at Randwick. Her landlord Mr Fred Vidler 63 was thunderstruck. 'Can't understand,' Mr Vidler said, 'what* motive anyone would have in taking the life of such a fine girl.' Mrs Vidler 57 was too upset to give an opinion. 'Almost my own daughter,' she whispered from under sedation. The nurse's most recent case, 86-year-old wealthy socialite and grazier's widow Mrs Elizabeth Hunter of Moreton Drive informed the police, 'Yes, I expect she was honest. Who's to say what "honest" is? She was engaged to my son, or the chemist, I forget which. I gave her my pink sapphire to clinch the deal. Not the blue as well, mind you. Personally I always thought her a twit, nothing more than a breeder, as she proved by starting too soon. But I suppose you would have called her honest. Can you claim the same for yourself—what are you? Sergeant?')

Sister Manhood was getting a certain amount of enjoyment out of her own post-mortem. If she had been less pregnant the stolen sapphire might have swelled into a large boil on her inflamed mind. Now it only intermittently throbbed. Though of course it must burst sooner or later, when the accusations began.

That her legs were already trickling she did not at first realize what with the tooth the coot the thumping dance the sapphire and the sensation in her lower abdomen.

When it was trickling oozing not actually flooding.

She was wet, however.

Her lovely blessed BLOOD oh God o Lord who she didn't believe in but would give her closer attention to as soon as she had the time and as far as she was capable.

When she had made herself decent Flora Manhood might have shed a tear or two if she hadn't felt so angry: kidding herself into a two months pregnancy. A nurse!

A banging on the door. 'Yes. What is it? Lot?'

'Mrs Hunter wishes for you, Floradora.'

'Wishes?' Shriek shriek. 'Aren't you comical!' It was not all that funny, but Flora Manhood was so free she would have liked to take out her joy on someone, tell them the joke against herself.

While Lotte here might have crawled up out of the depths, hair hanging, that grotty dress in the worst tatters; only the eyes were human.

Their expression was so apprehensive Sister Manhood thought to ask, 'The star sapphire — did she tell you? The blue one — somebody snitched it!' In spite of the wound you could see opening in Lottie's mind, Flora Manhood had to laugh for her own acquittal.

The housekeeper groaned and shifted her spongy feet. 'I am the one they will accuse. *Ach, yoy!*' She hobbled thumping in the direction of the dividing door.

The little bell had begun its tinkling. Years ago for the devil of it Flora Manhood and Snow Tunks had pushed against another, blacker door, padded and studded. They stood beside the basin of urky water just as the bell was rung to signify nothing can become something, if you let yourself believe if you had the power to look far enough deep enough not get the creeps the gooseflesh the giggles craning to see above the heads or around all those red Irish necks.

When here along the passage this same bell, except it had an angrier, more desperate ring.

'What is it, Mrs Hunter?' Flora Manhood was bouncing like the rubber ball she felt: tell her about the Baby that Isn't; have a laugh together; the old thing would soon forget. 'What can I do for you?' the nurse asked.

'I am the one who must do. I want you to help me on to the throne.'

Help, indeed; Sister Manhood was so strong she gathered up the bundle of trussed flannel scratching jewellery baby powder stained brocade and ratty sables in one armful.

She dumped it on the seat. 'There, dear. Hold tight!' Seeing the claws still groping for the mahogany rails, 'Got your balance, have you?'

Mrs Hunter murmured, 'Yes.' Balance is always a matter of chance.

Again Sister Manhood thought she could feel the trickling of her joyous blood. 'Now if you are happy — comfy — there are one or two things I must attend to. I'll leave the door open so as you can call out if you want me. Or here's your little bell.' She fetched a stool and stood it with the bell beside the commode.

It tickled her to think that all but the same tinkle which brought

Flora Manhood might summon the Holy Ghost (not that she intended blasphemy: she could perhaps in time sort of believe; what would Col have thought, though?).

Mrs Hunter had no complaints to make. Her nose was brooding: she was so deep in concentration she was glad to hear her nurse go. Nobody could help her now: only herself, and grace.

If she strained periodically on the commode it was as a formality to please her nurses and her doctor. Now the real business in hand was not to withdraw her will, as she had once foreseen, but to will enough strength into her body to put her feet on the ground and walk steadily towards the water. There was the question of how much time she would have before the eye must concentrate on other, greater contingencies, leaving her to chaos. That this was threatening, she could tell from the way the muslin was lifted at the edges, till what had been a benison of sea, sky, and land, was becoming torn by animal passions, those of a deformed octopod with blue-suckered tentacles and a glare of lightning or poached eggs.

Alfred my dearest dearest you are the one to whom I look for help however I failed.

And know that I alone must perform whatever the eye is contemplating for me.

To move the feet by some miraculous dispensation to feel sand benign and soft between the toes the importance of the decision makes the going heavy at first the same wind stirring the balconies of cloud as blows between the ribs it would explain the howling of what must be the soul not for fear that it will blow away in any case it will but in anticipation of its first experience of precious water as it filters in through the cracks the cavities of the body blue pyramidal waves with swans waiting by appointment each a suppressed black explosion the crimson beaks savaging only those born to a different legend to end in legend is what frightens most people more than cold water climbing mercifully towards the overrated but necessary heart a fleshy fist to love and fight with not to survive except as a kindness or gift of a jewel.

The seven swans are perhaps massed after all to destroy a human will once the equal of their own weapons its thwack as crimson painful its wings as violently abrasive don't oh DON'T my dark birds of light let us rather—enfold.

Till I am no longer filling the void with mock substance: myself is this endlessness.

From the bathroom window Sister Manhood could see the moon had risen: it was full, or almost (the moon is always less than perfect the moment after catching sight of it).

Her breasts gathered on the sill, Flora Manhood was humming very slightly, down her nose, against her teeth. She would have offered her love if it had been asked for—not sensual love: no *men*, for God's *sake*! but in support of some objective, or idea. Unfortunately she was short on ideas, as Col had hinted on and off, except the one she had refused to entertain, and which Col had insisted he would nourish in her. She laughed lazily (not sensually) from between relaxed lips. Shriven by her menstrual blood, she was reconciled, she believed, to what had been a shaky vocation, and was anxious for Mary de Santis to arrive, so that she might impress her, not with crude zeal, but with what St Mary would surely recognize as altered vision.

In a minute she would return to her patient and together they would celebrate this change. She would wipe the old thing's bottom with a tenderness it had never before experienced, and surely Elizabeth Hunter, with her gift for scenting weakness in others, was not such a cynical bitch that she would laugh in your face and tear your intentions to shreds. She could, though.

Was it the bell? Not the tinkled ascent of silver notes but thin tin crumpling and a tongue abruptly flattened out into silence.

Sister Manhood left the window so quickly the sash shuddered, the panes rattled.

When she reached the bedroom the muslin curtain was waving from its rod as it did whenever a wind rose behind your back. The swollen curtain was filling the room. It could have upset the little bell, now lying on the carpet.

For that matter, it could have upset Mrs Hunter.

The nurse rushed to shut the window. 'It's the climate!' she cried. 'You don't stand a chance!' (Actually Flora Manhood had never given the climate a thought till Princess Dorothy had started drawing everybody's attention to it; otherwise a climate is what you are born to, and accept because you can't avoid it.) 'The draught wasn't too much for you, was it?'

Mrs Hunter had slipped sideways on her throne while still hooked to the mahogany rails. One buttock, though withered, was made to shine like ivory where the rose brocade was rucked up. The eyes were mooning out through the mask which was the apex of her acolyte's creative skill.

'Mrs Hunter?'

Never had the nurse felt so powerless, so awkward, as in slewing this totem into its orthodox position.

In spite of the several corpses she had dealt with, it was Flora Manhood's first death, and for this reason she walked backwards and forwards awhile, hissing and gulping, and trying to remember where to go from here.

She knew of course. The books tell you. The lectures. And Sister: *remove any jewellery Nurse it may fall into the wrong hands.* And practice: block every hole so that nothing *nothing* escapes.

Though the mind can become as functional as the digestive tract after your feelings have been minced up fine, it did not prevent her touching the body several times when she had laid it on the bed, not expecting evidence of life (she was too experienced for that) but illumination? that her emptiness, she ventured to hope, might be filled with understanding.

As for knowing what to *do*, the nurse was already turning back her sleeves in preparation for the unpleasanter duties she had been trained to perform. Her arms were strong rather than shapely. The carpeted landing was creaking and thundering around her as she advanced on the telephone, to report to the doctor that their patient was dead, that he should pay his last visit and confirm that her responsibility was ended.

Twelve

AT HIS LAST dozing Basil had willed himself to wake early, to avoid any possible Macrory invasion, but on opening his eyes next, he was in some way conscious of having failed. It was early enough: in fact the sheets of spent moonlight still showed their random inkblots. Then why this shock of cold terror? He covered parts of himself as though his parents were standing at the bedside.

And Dorothy waking, crumpled, crushed. Hadn't she been supporting a weight? But smiling for Basil.

While prolonging the smile, Dorothy closed her eyes again. Less pressed for time in that the bed was officially hers, she could afford the extra snooze.

Till she too fully awoke to the same reverberating terror. The sheet hissed as she snatched up an armful of it to hide her breasts.

'The telephone!' Whichever of them had uttered the word, it echoed the other's fears: ringing and ringing through a cold house; and ringing.

When the ringing stopped it was impossible to tell whether the telephone had given up, or whether somebody had intervened.

To escape from the clinging bed Basil tore himself out with such violence his balls tangled painfully. He was nothing less than skedaddling into the room beyond, resentful of a wind which was streaming past his nakedness. Nobody was exclusively to blame; though instinctively, he might have liked to hold Dorothy responsible.

Either exhausted or appeased she was slower to react. She could have been lingering amongst some of her more disreputable thoughts before clothing them for ever in convention. She lay nursing the bundle of grey, early-morning sheets and ailing blankets. The terror with which she had been flooded by the telephone had almost ebbed before she threw them off. She glanced along her nose at her own distantly exposed limbs, which became, more distantly still, in Hubert's voice, *ton corps qui se réfuse aussi passionément que d'autres se donnent.*

The Princesse de Lascabanes shot out of bed and put on her mouth before anything else. There was nothing she could have done to hide from that cold increasing light the cruel slashes in her cheeks. Her general gooseflesh, her flapping sinews, she was able to clothe effectively before the sound of slippers reached her door.

'*Entrez donc!*' the princess called in a rational voice, ducking at the glass to know the worst about her hair; her heart would become visible, she felt, beating inside the gown she had swathed too tightly.

Mrs Macrory should have made the perfect messenger for tragedy: manner direct; speech precise (Scottish at one remove); of moral integrity to ensure a respectful relationship with the audience she was about to shock as well as console. But this messenger could not rid herself of the mouthfuls of ugly words; emotions which she should have curbed with objective tact, left her eyes goitrous.

'They telephoned,' she began, and was cut off immediately.

Not to improve matters, Sir Basil Hunter made an entrance from the dressing-room, adjusting the cord of a robe he had thrown on in a hurry, tamping with the palms of his hands the hair which sleep had tousled. In spite of these side activities the great actor did not withhold his generous attention: he would not be accused of trying to steal someone else's scene.

'They rang,' the messenger began afresh. 'Mr Wyburd rang,' she corrected herself.

'*Qu'est-ce que vous voulez nous dire, chère Anne?*' If she had not steeled herself with her second language Madame de Lascabanes might have imitated the lamentable mouthing of her friend, whose hands she took out of charity to chafe and comfort. '*Allons, voyons, n'ayez pas peur.*' The princess half looked to Sir Basil to interpret, but saw him refuse; it would not have mattered greatly to any of them if he had accepted.

To Anne Macrory it mattered least of all: she was too high on disaster. 'Mrs Hunter, your mother—died,' she said, 'yesterday evening.' It was so perfectly clumsily final the messenger sprayed the princess with the end of her line.

Incredulity rather than grief had moistened Sir Basil's eyes. (Dorothy thought her brother's expression made him look foolish.) 'How did she die?' he was also foolish enough to ask.

'I don't know,' Mrs Macrory sobbed.

The Princesse de Lascabanes pleated her brows and lowered her eyelids to accuse her brother's tactlessness and advertise her own formal grief. 'She would have died peacefully, I expect, in her sleep. That is how it takes old people.'

She failed to prevent a whinge rising, which she tried to pass off as a wheeze; either way, it fanned her friend's distress.

'How sad for you!' blubbered Mrs Macrory.

To disguise her shame for her hand in Mother's death and to celebrate an innocence which exists, if only in others, Dorothy embraced this poor woman. 'So tenderhearted! I do appreciate your sympathy.' In fact Anne Macrory's innocence justified one's bursting into tears.

Scorn for Dorothy's hypocrisy might have blazed up in Basil. (Or does a woman desperate for self-respect, reach a point where she can Christian Science dishonesty?) In any case, he had his own, more important part to play: that of the son.

So Sir Basil tensed his calves; he began striding, stamping (excusable on a freezing morning) digging always deeper into the pockets of his robe, which, since their visit to 'Kudjeri', he realized incidentally, equalled in sleaziness the garment decent Anne Macrory herself was wearing. It didn't deter him: with the twitch of an eyebrow, he raised his profile against the window (it faced east, and the sun was rising from behind the hills) to deliver his awaited speech.

'I imagine everybody would agree that Mother had from life all she could have wished for: beauty, wealth, worldly success, devoted friends, and—friends. We would do wrong, surely? in mourning her. Nor can I feel that, after living her life to the full, she would have regretted dying,' (appalling if he had been weak enough to settle for 'passing away'; he might have fallen if it hadn't been for Dorothy) 'if she was conscious of death at the time. It could happen, I suppose, that one who has led a materialistic life does become afraid at the last moment. I *hope* Mother was not afraid.' He glanced at Dorothy, who had been frozen into listening regardless of whether she wanted it.

Her grief had dried: perhaps Madame de Lascabanes anticipated an item of which she might disapprove, or it could have been because Mrs Macrory was doing the crying for all of them.

Anne appeared genuinely moved. 'Whatever else, it's so terrible for the children!' Most of her own six had crept up by dribs and drabs and were standing behind her in a loose queue.

It made Dorothy realize that bereavement could become a luxury; she squeezed her friend for showing her what she personally would never enjoy.

Sir Basil frowned; he hadn't finished. 'Well, nobody, not even her greatest admirers, can deny that Mother was materialistic. And vain. Shall I ever forget—the night of my arrival—the Lilac Fairy!' Laughter revived the golden timbre for which his voice was famous; it conveyed a bounty rather than bitterness, as he heard it.

'Poor darling,' Dorothy began to twitter in short sharp laughs, or coughs, 'alone in that house with all those women! How they imposed on her! Luckily she was able to see the comic side. Mother had a certain superficial streak which is probably what kept her going. But her *aloneness* was pitiful.'

Mrs Macrory blew her nose on a crumpled mauve tissue she found in her pocket. 'I didn't know her,' she remarked: she might have preferred to keep her vision of a dazzling figure descending from a car at the steps of 'Kudjeri'.

Sir Basil was composing his last words. 'For all her faults, she was an enchantress.' He would not look at Dorothy. 'I'm fortunate to be her son.'

Dorothy would not look at Basil. The paddocks were coldly steaming by now. She chafed the backs of her own hands, and glanced at her travelling-clock. 'We must pack our things,' she announced to the room in general. 'It wouldn't be fair to Mr Wyburd to delay getting there. I can imagine his distress: my parents were his close friends, and only incidentally, clients.'

Her excluding him from the relationship may have piqued Basil. 'To any solicitor over a certain age, death must become just another formality. I shouldn't worry about the Wyburd: he's drawn up far too many wills.'

The abrupt descent to reality reminded Mrs Macrory, 'I ought to be getting your breakfast.'

Sir Basil lowered his voice, 'Nothing elaborate,' he begged, 'on such a morning;' and contracted his crow's-feet at her.

Though a person of serious intentions, Anne Macrory was already enjoying the pleasures of melancholy retrospect. 'I don't know what the girls will do without you! The sewing lessons!'

Dorothy had begun the meticulous organization of her crocodile dressing-case: a present from Mummy and Dad. 'At least we've fitted everybody out for the summer. And shan't we write to one another?' she suggested vaguely as Anne left, trailing after her the string of children.

The topics they should choose, time would decide, or dispose of, along with other superfluities.

Quenched by anticlimax Sir Basil had gone into the dressing-room, and was throwing his things into his case. 'Don't you think, Dorothy, you ought to eat a chop for the journey?'

It was too frivolous for her to answer. She must concentrate in future on those practical virtues her friends saw in her, some of which she had found she actually possessed. In any case, she would not accept to share the blame for any of her brother's dirty work.

Till Mog, that rather disgusting, *au fond* frightening, fat child, appeared beside her. 'What's a kermode, Dorothy?' she asked while chewing on a doorstep of bread-and-dripping.

Deprived of her title and her privacy, the princess snapped. 'Really, I haven't the faintest idea.' But shivered.

'He said she died on the kermode.'

'Who said? And how do you know?'

'I was listening when Mr—the solicitor—was telling Mother.' Mog continued chewing and looking.

One could hardly protest, *Go! Go! Leave me to my wretchedness!* Instead the princess offered a smile to outdazzle the frost. 'Don't you think you should lend a hand with the breakfast?'

Mog said no, it wasn't necessary; but drifted off soon after, of her own free will, having seen as much as she wanted.

'Poor old Arnold Wyburd,' Dorothy called to the adjoining room, 'he must be upset—for his famous discretion to let him down: to babble about a commode—to a stranger—on the telephone!'

Basil had come to the doorway. 'I don't understand.' She could not believe in him: he was holding his head at too humbly suppliant an angle.

'Didn't you hear? Mother died on the commode!' She would have liked him to join her in a private laugh, herself already racketing in that direction.

But Basil remained serious, she saw. 'Dorothy,' he was advancing on her, 'nobody will ever know what we know. That makes us dependent, doesn't it? on each other. For kindness.'

She fended him off. 'There are plenty of others, I should have thought, who'll dispense kindness more professionally.'

'Yes,' he said, 'only because they don't know me as we know each other.'

He waited for a change of heart, which did not occur, or no more than by a flicker of horror.

'I don't understand what you're getting at, Basil.'

'It seemed understandable enough last night.'

'Don't bring it up! Ever! I want—ohhh, to forget about it!' If only she could lock a door, lose the key, and never again open.

He had, in fact, heard her locking him out.

So they continued their separate preparations, the dividing wall safely between them.

Her husband had put petrol enough in the car to see them as far as Gogong, Mrs Macrory mentioned at breakfast; Rory was sorry:

he had left to repair a broken gate he had come across the evening before on the far side of the property.

They would not be faced with Macrory. Like animals, like children, he shied away from association with death. The Macrory children, with the exception of fat Mog and the baby, lowered their eyes in the presence of the bereaved Hunters.

Mog giggled softly into her tea. 'On a *kermode!*'

After their release from table, Sir Basil remembered to distribute coins.

The children brightened; while the mother grew tearful. 'It's been so wonderful getting to know you both. It's been like—almost —one's first experience of the world.'

Thinking of the risks simple people may never be called upon to run, and the deceits they will not recognize, the eyes of the Princesse de Lascabanes moistened.

She looked for her handbag, but seeing it out of reach, consoled herself instead by giving her brother advice. 'Are you sure, Basil, you've forgotten nothing? Your pyjamas, for instance. Hubert always used to leave', it was too late to prevent its escaping, 'his pyjamas under the pillow.'

Basil mumbled, 'No longer wear 'em.'

Mog burst: a mouthful of milky tea flew back into the cup she couldn't stop fiddling with.

After the kisses and the promises, everyone else stood shivering in the yard as the Hunters were leaving. Tactfully, with the tip of her tongue, Madame de Lascabanes tried to feel whether any of the porridge on the baby's cheek had come off on her restored lips.

Sir Basil and the princess sat looking out through the car window. By leaning forward and pressing himself against his sister's shoulder, and by her withdrawing into a more rigid, oblique version of Dorothy, it was possible for him to be seen to advantage. While they all persuaded themselves it had happened. In spite of their dreamy, lingering smiles, the Hunters were probably the most disbelieving of any.

Sir Basil trod on the accelerator, and they jumped forward too jerkily for dignity. Then the princess put out her arm and gave a single long wave. A sword of light from the risen sun clashed with the rings she had not been wearing while at 'Kudjeri'.

They were driving away.

She couldn't stop moving around turning over from on her side knees practically up to her chin to on her back the legs stretched unnaturally straight stiff pointing into darkness. For the rest of the night. She was prepared. Began counting how many times she had changed from one side to the other but started her count too late. At a stage when she must have been not sleeping, lying (never sleeping is what She goes on about) she had hurt the cartilage (like Mrs Hunter) in one ear crushed it felt it would stay bent. (*Shall I massage it for you dear? No thank you Sister it will pass.*)

HUNTER, *Elizabeth, widow of* ... Mr Wyburd will put it in the *Herald*. Not tomorrow it is too late but the day after. Amongst the names. Some of those real ones are good for a breakfast laugh when you've the time. Death is only something to believe when it has happened in the DEATHS to people you don't know it has to happen to some to parents who again you hardly you never knew. Or patients a certain percent. Patients in the end though real you also luckily don't know. Till HUNTER, *Elizabeth* ... *at her home* ... *peacefully* ...

She reached for the lamp to switch the light on. Topheavy thing knock it over wouldn't be worth it. She gave up. Turned.

Ought to properly swab the mouthpiece from Badgery calling taxis after scrambled egg *peugh* might infect the lot of you *oh yes Doctor Doctor Gidley is it?* (Who else but fat silky smarmy Gidley?) *This is Sister Manhood speaking Doctor I have to report my patient— Mrs Hunter—has died.*

Said he would come right over. (Gidley favoured the American language, except in Mrs Hunter's presence, when he became more sort of English.) Sounded excited. So he might be over the death of a wealthy senile woman.

Ow-eugh—this ruined ear! Fully awake, Flora Manhood massaged her cartilage. There was nobody else to do.

She had flung off the pillows from under the body laid on the bed. She stretched the limbs as straight as they allowed. She closed what had been Mrs Hunter's eyes. As she went for the cotton wool the furniture was wobbling, toppling, almost meeting overhead, before righting itself. She arranged the wool pledgets, dampened so that they would sit steady on the lids. (Betty Hunter in other days might have turned cranky and thrown off 'a lot of unnecessary rubbish'.) Would all be neat enough for St Mary who must surely come?

Flora longed for Sister de Santis. What she desired more than anything was a feeling of continuity which, in Mrs Hunter's absence, de Santis might restore. Turning those cowey eyes on you: to forgive. Elizabeth Hunter never forgives: she lines you up for more of the same; which can amount to the same thing.

Between looking at her watch, expecting Gidley or de Santis, Sister Manhood remembered Mrs Lippmann ought to be told. Though unpleasant in some respects, it would be a mission of sorts. She went along the passage to what had been the maids' quarters, where an illuminated crack outlined the housekeeper's door.

'Mrs Lippmann?' She knocked formally, twice; the doors in the servants' quarters were a thinner, cheaper timber as opposed to the owners' indestructible cedar.

After a pause, Mrs Lippmann answered, 'I cannot see you, Flora.'

'But I have something important to tell you.' She opened.

'You need not tell me. The whole house already knows.' Lotte Lippmann was sitting on the floor of her narrow room, against the chest, directly opposite the doorway. '*Unser Alles ist uns genommen worden.*'

Dishevelled by her dance, Mrs Lippmann's hair was still hanging in loose tails, her face the colour of damp ashes, except for the eyelids and the lips, by nature darker, like brown figs, and down the cheeks, yellow weals scored with scarlet.

'If you know, then,' Sister Manhood's intention petered out; surprise had at least tidied up her nerves and poised her on the balls of her feet in the doorway.

Over the mirror on the rickety chest the housekeeper had hung a towel, which stirred as she rocked the chest with her head, in turning first one cheek, then the other, to press against the drawers behind, and retreat farther, if possible, from an intrusion on her nakedness. The handles on the drawers were shuddering.

It was all foreign enough to bring out the bossy nurse in Flora, when she had meant to be kind. 'Tt-tt, you've torn your dress!' she had to remark on noticing what was so obvious.

A wonder the dress had survived at all. Time and the more recent frenzy of the dance had certainly reduced it to a state of final tatters; but this did not account for a wilful, passionate rending, downwards from the yoke. Mrs Lippmann's breast had been laid bare by the destruction of her inherited dress.

All the while she kept her cheek turned, but the sounds she made were like as if you heard the cattle trucking through the night to market, up the coast.

In different circumstances it could have tickled Flora; or again, you might have given way to something deeper in yourself, that you preferred to hide; but were now too pressed and responsible, already the front-door bell ringing. If this was Gidley, he had got here so quick he must have been sitting waiting for Mrs Hunter to die.

So she too made it brisk. 'I advise you to get up off the floor. You'll regret it, Lot, if your joints set.' Fairly pleased with herself for upholding a tradition, she added, 'Later on I'll give you something for your face;' but stopped.

The contusions of the grey skin, with its open pores, had a look of pumice, but a pumice which was breathing and choking, while the head stirred the tinny handles on the drawers, against which the Jewess continued to press and rock. You might have got the creeps if it hadn't been for running down to the hall, to open and let Gidley in.

Because here was this creep of a doctor: no amount of Badgery salestalk would ever disguise the fact, or that Jessie herself, in falsies and interlock combs, was a sucker for doctors, and teaplanters, and actors' voices.

Since that first telescoping instant when she discovered that it had happened, Sister Manhood had salvaged something which looked like dependability. Her reflection in the hall glass was convincing: pretty, too. She bashed a shade more hair from under the veil to hang above her forehead: not for Gidley, for God's sake! for her own morale, and it could have been what She would expect.

The fat slob of a doctor was standing in the porch under the light she had switched on before opening the door. He was carrying his medical bag as usual. He appeared no different, except that his eyes were shining. Probably an attempt to assume reverence for what was a sad as well as an important occasion had given him the guilty air.

Dr Gidley said in his fat-manly voice, 'Lucky you caught me. My wife and I were out at one of those silly cocktail parties. We'd just got home.'

('My wife' must be something of a pressed flower.)

'She died quietly—behind my back.' Sister Manhood was glad to find it coming so easy.

'I don't expect she'll regret it.' He sounded a bit thick and awkward till realizing the drink inside him helped. 'Eighty-four, wasn't it?'

' -six.' It gave the nurse greater confidence, not to say power over the doctor, to be able to correct him. 'She was in her best form tonight. All for make-up and jokes. The housekeeper danced for her.' The doctor's lower lip was unable to accept that part. 'Then she asked to relieve herself.' The nurse was leading the way upstairs. 'She was dead when I went to take her off.'

'Caught napping for the first time in her life!' The nurse didn't seem to appreciate it.

The *idea* of Mrs Hunter, more than the old woman herself, made her feel superior.

They went in to what was, incredibly, a body laid out on Mrs Hunter's bed. The damp pledgets prevented you seeing what was underneath, whether human eyelids, or slits cut out of a painted mask. The green shadows on the cheeks had been emphasized by the nurse's tying up the jaw with a bandage and removing the teeth. A thick black line surrounding the lips had melted and overflowed into the cracked crimson, making the mouth look like a stitched seam, and increasing the mask effect.

The doctor laughed low. 'Kinky games the pair of you got up to!' He took hold of what had been a wrist, lifted what proved to be eyelids, flourished a nonchalant stethoscope; then he flicked once or twice at the object on the bed by catapulting a forefinger off a thumb. 'Elizabeth Hunter's bought it all right.'

Sister Manhood was suitably disgusted. No, she *was!* Hadn't she loved, not Mrs Hunter herself, but something she stood for? Life, perhaps. She whipped you on. Like when the menstrual blood had begun to flow again, and you felt it warm and sticky on your legs, something of love and life was restored. So Flora Manhood hated Dr Gidley, because it now appeared he had hated Mrs Hunter.

While he sat in the easiest chair to write out his certificate, she began busying herself. She must wash the body, and hoped to do so privately. But when she had fetched the basin, the doctor seemed prepared to continue sitting.

'I have to wash my patient, Doctor,' she reminded.

'Why not, Sister?' Didn't he know by heart every inch of Elizabeth Hunter's body?

She would screen the bed with her back.

'Expect you'll come out of it pretty well—isn't your name "Flora"?'

'I don't expect a thing.' If this dirty man forced her into talking virtuous, for once she needn't feel a hypocrite.

'The meanest of the rich remember their nurses in the will. If they don't, the solicitor reminds them. To remind them of the doctor too, would be logical, wouldn't it? But they almost never get round to that. Sometimes, of course, the patient's in love with the doctor. That's different.' He laughed his thickest.

Dr Gidley ('Graham') always on the up and up, with his young (monied) wife, his two little boys at the right school, his practice desirably situated, subscriber to the opera and orchestral concerts, and member of the A.J.C., called out Flora Manhood's bile.

When faced with her first, real death, she should have been capable of tenderness. She would learn, though. Washing these terrible withered limbs, and the little shabby, shammy leather pouches of breasts, a kind of love began to jerk rather than flow along her straining arms. Because Elizabeth Hunter herself was apt to ward off tenderness if ever you tried it out on her, anything of that nature had always been rather clumsily implied. At least the physical strain of washing her body now helped you endure the doctor.

'A very passionate woman, so they say. Well, you could tell.'

Flora Manhood at work leaned farther over: she had to protect Her; before anything, she must sponge away the signs of her own vicious handiwork. The mask did seem to be taking on the expression of original purity, and in assuming, to assure. Elizabeth Hunter's beauty, anyway as idea, hovered on the face of a skull to which a reality had been restored.

She had given the mouth its last wipe with the flannel when she realized from the breathing that Dr Gidley was close behind her, or closer still: he was rubbing himself, blubbery man, against her buttocks.

'Flora, eh?' At the same time making his obscene thrust.

'Dr Gidley,' she said into his face, because now that she had turned she could not avoid any part of him: neither blond bristles sprouting from the chin, nor belly threatening to pin her against or bludgeon her over the end of the bed, 'if you've forgotten your wife, I haven't forgotten my patient. I'd like to treat her respectfully.'

The doctor let out a sharp, whiskey sigh, and recovered a balance the nurse had almost upset. 'All the right sentiments! Like in the textbook. But don't you know a textbook is never for real?'

By now he was more wind than piss. She could have thrown him out if Sister de Santis hadn't appeared. In her street clothes. And her eyes.

The presence of such a professional figure as the night nurse called for a return to business. 'You'll see, Sister,' the doctor said, 'we've had a death in the family.' Then he laughed, perhaps for himself and little Manhood.

Sister de Santis advanced to the bed and touched the feet. She went to change into her uniform.

So Dr Gidley was free to leave. He winked, and cocked his head, whether at the pretty nurse, the corpse of his late patient, or a reflection of himself in the glass, it was difficult to tell; though the reflection was most likely: with its moist lips, swelling torso, and dandiacal tufts of hair frizzed out on either cheek, his was the image his mind's eye could most agreeably entertain. While Sister Manhood was left with the vision of a pair of naked calves, or immense blond bulbs grown to bursting, before they uprooted themselves from the carpet.

She had finished washing the dead by the time Mary de Santis returned. It was de Santis who dried the body, who plugged it (thank God) and tied the knees.

The two nurses exchanged remarks, both practical and comforting, in subdued voices. Sister Manhood brought a fresh sheet to cover the body. After they had spread it, and smoothed it over the major peaks and ridges, Manhood trimmed the nails. But it was de Santis who laid the handkerchief over the face. As their hands touched during their work, or they bumped against each other, or rubbed shoulders in passing, Flora Manhood came closest to expressing the love she might have been too abashed to feel for Elizabeth Hunter.

Finally Sister de Santis said, 'Don't you realize it's long past your time?'

'Yes, I'll go. And never come back. Not even for the bloody uniform.' She explained she intended to give up nursing: she had just realized.

'I expect you'll think better of it, Flora.'

'Not on your life!'

Her decision might have given her greater cause for rejoicing if St Mary had not used her Christian name. Instead she went out

566

soberly, to guard against possible damage to a fragility she had not suspected was in her. She changed, and did not return to the bedroom. She would write to Sister de Santis, if she could summon up the spelling and the grammar, to thank her for her moral support. As for Mrs Hunter, she did not want to look at her again: not with the handkerchief over her face.

And now turning in this narrow dark a coffin can't be narrower than insomnia in a hard bed well you ought to be able to replace what more or less belongs to you or anyway suggest it Lottie is the only one who will want to lie and suffer to feel those tinny handles pressing cutting into her flesh the night Elizabeth Hunter. It is still this same night. O Lord.

Again Flora Manhood almost switched the light on. But did not dare face up to the present in all its varnish and sharp corners and clutter of unwashed crockery. Better the past, however dark and humiliating some of the details.

So you are still running down the reeling path this night of Elizabeth Hunter's death feel the branch not cutting whipping the cheek it is still with you like the unnecessary lint a love offering for a scratch snuff the collodion right up and be grateful yes you are.

Flora Manhood drew breath when she had pulled the gate to: it is never fixed because old Betty is too dotty, Arnold Wyburd almost gaga, and nurses enjoy bellyaching. Those furnaces refineries whatever along the Botany skyline look real scary sometimes specially the one which turns into a fiery cross if you look at it through a fly screen. Well, you need never look at it again, not through the screen at Moreton Drive.

F-L-O-R-A spelt out makes you feel more real hard to believe you're free at last to roam around lie on the park grass if you want not at night when they murder people who are on their own but under the sun the weight of the sun as much as the warmth is what you crave for.

In the sun's absence, she began walking smartly down the street. She didn't depend on the sun, no more than on any man. And Mrs

Hunter dead. You would never go back. Not for the uniform. Not for the plastic bag either. Or the box of tissues opened only this afternoon.

She walked faster, to throw off the thought of her pretty bag. Through her dress, the air was playing on, if not between, her ribs. She shivered. She had forgotten it was winter.

Till she was simply walking. For the sake of it. Down Anzac towards Kingsford. Within sight of the neon sign she loitered on the kerb before turning into Gladys Street, but doubled back along the opposite pavement on reaching Vidlers' front divide; she could not have faced giving Vid and Viddie an account. She shot down streets she had never ever heard of Hardcastle Trent Dahlia Corella Cumberlong Dobbs re-crossing the Parade nearly at a run then shied off just short of Snow's the blue light still spitting on its pole pointing up the tuck pointing. Received again into the Parade, she was panting for all that is hectic, to match her own hectically flickering condition.

If you had been wise to yourself at the time you might have joined in Lottie's dance for Mrs Hunter.

Outside the Bellevue in a patch of light shed by a couple of milky globes a human object had been planted: a third globe, or turnip, or face of a woman who has reached the hazed phase, of coloured memories and dribbled resentments, was occupied in staring up.

'Doncher know me, Florrie?' The voice struggling to get out through the rubber hole of a mouth sloshed the self-pity around. 'One thing nobody can ever say's I never took the trouble to know a person who was down on ut.'

Here the weight attached to her was too great for this person: wrists flopping over a bulge of knees, head tumbling on the end of a telescoped fibrous neck, the body almost rolled sideways into the gutter. But saved itself, as a headlight flashing past washed the eyelids whiter, the mouth a wetter, more slippery rubber.

'Why—Snow!' It could be the night of worst moments. 'Is anything wrong with you?'

'Chrise, Florrie, thought you was the big wake-up. Carntcher see I'm stoned blue?'

'But in the gutter!'

'If you can't get yerself out of ut.' Snow was in fact lolling worse.

Bent over her only living relative so that the draught from behind shot up her mini, Flora Manhood could not have felt more foolish or less competent. By rights she should have got down on her knees, but she did not want to spoil her hose. The hose was no real excuse: instead of inventing pet-names ('Butchikins' 'Snowlo' 'Pore Youse') she could have grabbed hold of the hands from where she was, and yanked her cousin into the upright. She didn't.

'Are you on your own, Snowy?'

'I'm on me own.'

'What about your friend?'

'Which friend? Carla?'

'The one I met. Wasn't it Alix?'

'That one. Alix left.'

'Carla, then?'

'Not Carla. Carla went the way. Kay's the one. Walked out on me this evenun. That's why I got me load up.'

Snow Tunks began, not to cry, to trickle or dribble, gin or tears. With one hand she made a swipe at the silver sickle swinging from her mouth. Or nose.

'Wait on, Snowy. I'll fetch someone,' nurses have wrecked their backs hoisting the patient, 'somebody to help you up.'

'I can get up—if I wanter.'

'Call a taxi, then—to take you to your home.'

'I don't wanter. Not alone. Florrie?' Snow Tunks put out a hand, but only caught hold of the dark: Flora Manhood had stepped back.

The truth was: you could not bear her to touch you; Snow might stick for ever.

'The taxi's the best shot, love. There'll be a phone I can use in the pub. Call the Red de Luxe.' Too high, too bright, heels too busy across the pavement.

From where she was sitting on the kerb Snow heaved round to holler, 'Only if you'll come, Floie. You're the one it should have been. I reckon I sorter realized as far back as Banana Town you an' me couldn't do better than shack up.'

'Okay, Snow. Wait, Snowy.'

The bar door took some opening: the fug inside must have gummed it up. Snatches of men's beery laughter seemed to make the frosted glass balloon outward against the cheek of anyone, specially a woman, pushing in.

'Won't let me down, will yer, Florrie?' Snow was still calling from the kerb. 'It's you an' me an' bugger the rest.'

'Yairs yairs.'

Florrie (Sister Manhood!) managed to force the door open. On the other side men were standing watching an infringement of their rights. Whether pursy, beery-eyed blokes, of the type which crooks a finger at its schooner to establish this delicate relationship, or lean smoothies who show they know better by nursing a glass of pallid spirits, all were of the superior sex. Nobody ever said you can do without a woman; who can even become a permanent asset: to throw the steak on the grill, iron the shirts and keep the home nice and neat. Wives are economic like; that's a different matter. As for this girl, showing too much of herself in the doorway, she didn't rate much above a back-seat fuck.

Lucky for Flora Manhood's pride that the Bellevue stood on a corner. She could cut across this corner, jibbering apologies for the mistake she had made, and was already out the opposite door, in the other street, wiping her hands on such skirt as she could muster, to dry her embarrassment, not to say shame: for blokey men, for her drunken dyke cousin, and worst of all, HERSELF.

She was again faced with this delirious neon nightscape her life had become since Mrs Hunter's death. *Won't let me down will yer Florrie?* Like hell. If Snow herself had more or less put the idea in your head she couldn't complain. Any more than you explain.

Farther up, a police car was slowing down to take a squint. No hope of explaining to the Great Dane police boy you were only running away from your shickered cousin you were not the pross he would have liked you to be you were not even any longer identifiable as a nurse you were nothing but a woman of no fixed intention recognized capabilities or positive hopes.

But the car cruised on.

It was not till the sidestreets, up to your ankles in sand, that you started running back, out of this dead end. The sand was what handicapped: all the streets on this side were deep in it. As you squelched and lumbered you were sandpapered.

It seemed to Flora Manhood she would never get there: the paling fences, the shifting sands of the cross streets, were against it. Once she had lost a shoe running to catch a bus. She would lose a shoe now for sure, and the police car pick up Snow. You would have let down practically everybody you could think of.

Lying in this narrow bed knowing every spring and non-spring like you know the bumps the boobs the grain the tufts the funnels and tunnels the whinges of your own body what would you have done if you found the car pulled up door open alongside the Bellevue it wasn't but could have come and gone Snow had gone like everybody you are the one who is left and Elizabeth Hunter she has leaked out in a brown stream from under the handkerchief the sheet to mingle with the dark around you are a twit because E. Hunter is well and truly laid not a loophole left the cotton wool won't allow it.

Crossing the Parade, probably for the fifteenth time, Flora Manhood heard the traffic screech. Elizabeth Hunter herself, determined that nothing should prevent her having her way, could not have stalled it more effectively. Flora tripped, lurched against the plate glass, which at first buckled, but settled down by tremors against her flattened nose. Mrs Hunter's fingers always trembled if she won; if she didn't, they stiffened into claws. Considering the dead woman was not present even in a spirit nightie, only a nut would believe there was any question of influence.

Tonight the pharmacy window was divided between proprietary skin foods and OUR NATIONAL CAMPAIGN AGAINST THE HOUSE

571

FLY. His window dressing had never been bang on; he hadn't the time to give it thought, but left it to Bev Sills who was a doll, though he didn't seem to notice. Now it was late and of course the dispensary shut. So she went along the side and up the stairs to the residence. The same yellow asparagus fern was drooping out of a slit in the brown surrounds. The smell of gas was still there, and of burning chops when he opened the door.

He said, 'I've got some chops going.'

She went in, past him, into the kitchen, pulled out the grill to take a look. The fat flared up. The smoke started her eyes smarting.

'They're just about done,' he said, as though everything he had ever intended was coming to pass.

There was nothing much you could do about the chops. She turned off the gas.

She was sitting at the kitchen table. She had never wanted so much to sit down and stay sitting.

Col said, 'What do I owe the honour to?'

'Mrs Hunter's dead. She went this evening. I reckon that's my last case.'

'Don't tell me! What had this Mrs Hunter got?'

'I don't know. She'd lived it up, I suppose. You felt that if you zombied around long enough you might find out what you can expect.'

'And did she let you in on it?' Col had twitched back one corner of his mouth which made him look as though that side had never recovered from an accident; it was an expression she had never liked to see, because soon after, they usually started exchanging abuse.

'No,' she said. 'I don't know,' she modified it; but felt incurably ignorant.

Amongst the dishes on the table, bacon rind set in waves of fat, lettuce leaves wilted by vinegar dregs, one of Col's books was lying: *Thus Spake Zarathustra*, whoever he was to sound so certain. She who was plumb ignorant would probably remain so for ever.

'If you come expecting answers here, you know the only one you'll get.'

'I don't expect anything,' she said.

The smoke from the burnt chops was making her eyes worse than smart; they were running.

The other side of the fluctuations Col was still hammering away. 'From what you told me, you always hated that old woman.'

'Yes!' she cried. 'No—I didn't *hate*! She understood me better than anybody ever. I only always didn't like what she dug up out of me.'

'I understand you, Flo.' He had got down beside her. 'What you are. And you are it.'

'I'm nothing.'

He was kissing her thighs. He kissed between them, and she, the awkward bleeding goof, was holding his head against her belly. It would embarrass her to tell him she had the painters in and there was nothing doing.

He saved her the trouble by going to fetch something which would make her sleep, and a dressing for what he called her 'wound', where the branch had scratched her cheek.

She would have liked to share with him the joy she had felt when the blood had begun to run between her legs. But would not tell what nobody but herself knew. Unless Mrs Hunter had guessed. Sir Basil Hunter's misconceived, miscarried child would remain a secret: the dishonest touch is sometimes also necessary and harmless.

As sleeplessness can become a virtue of sorts or stocktaking in the bed he hadn't made since when he was all around you though sleeping on the lounge in the other room never properly heard him before sleeping too close in this narrow marriage bed She is knocking on the wood with her sapphire the pink it is yours isn't it the coffin Nurse is where one sows one's last seed I can see it germinating inside you like a lot of little skinned rabbits oh Mrs Hunter how can you be so *unkind* (giggle) always hated obstets but your own flesh is different my children are human we hope Mrs Hunter if the blessed sapphire works.

Miss Haygarth stood the tea beside his blotter. 'I got them to make it early. Later on, you mightn't have time to enjoy it.'

She had taken to creeping round him on her errands to his desk, standing too close, irritating him by her thoughtfulness, and more than anything by an only recent tendency to mumble.

'What are you saying?' he had to ask.

'... enjoy it before they come.' Miss Haygarth explained; even then half of it was lost.

At the door she turned, and the importance of her question lent her an adequate voice. 'Should I provide tea for the princess and Sir Basil?'

Mr Wyburd manœuvred his glance to the level required by his bi-focals. 'By the time they arrive you might try offering them lunch.'

Though the corrugations in which her employer's forehead was set implied seriousness, Miss Haygarth knew a joke was intended. She laughed for Mr Wyburd's joke; her round, rimless spectacles and the gums of her denture appeared unduly grateful for it.

Arnold Wyburd did not laugh. The cold had got into his right side, his right leg, from hanging about at the funeral.

Mrs Hunter had made a point of not knowing the inhabitants of the Northern Suburbs, but like everybody one knew, she was disposed of by the Northern Suburbs Crematorium, of which she had been a shareholder. The mourners from across the water were brought there in long black hire cars which slowed up on entering the precincts, and rolled the rest of the way on what seemed like supernatural impetus, past the perfect shrubs. Overhead a pennant of smoke streamed from the chimney. Not inappropriately, one of Sydney's black winds was blowing.

Even before the ceremony, as he stood about acknowledging smiles which went so far and no farther, Arnold Wyburd suspected the wind had marked him down: he could almost feel the twinges in his lumbar regions. There were few mourners. Since age and her condition had compelled Mrs Hunter to withdraw from the world, most of her friends had dropped off—or died; in any case funerals, like shipboard farewells, tend to attract recent acquaintances rather than friends. Though several of those present for the funeral could not have been other than friends: elderly people stuffed into long-lasting tweed or fur held together by moulted buttons, they limped or shuffled out of the past, peering through a brandy haze with an air of humorous incredulity.

The solicitor waited outside till the last possible moment, then walked in past the sparsely filled benches till reaching a row where his relationship with the deceased dictated he should sit. Not far behind him he was aware of Mrs Hunter's cleaning woman, and what must have been the daughter and perhaps son-in-law. (The tribe of Cush, he had found, are amongst the most dedicated mourners.) Sister Badgery, always at her most professional when out of uniform, gave him a therapeutic smile.

Arnold Wyburd was glad of the intimations of physical pain which came and went between himself and a mentally distressing situation. From time to time he moved in his seat to discover whether he could produce a twinge when he needed one. There was a smell of mothballs somewhere near, and the racket of a bronchial cough. Hands the plumper for a pair of black kid gloves were straining to get at the lozenges inside a difficult tin.

Mrs Hunter had not encouraged the clergy (*all the handsome ones are dead*) but the man in the dog collar who gave the address had done his homework pretty conscientiously. He spoke with consoling warmth of the dead woman's kindness, her beauty, intelligence, benefactor-husband, distinguished children, and managed to introduce discreet reference to her wealth. For an instant Elizabeth Hunter's image radiated all the human virtues in an unmistakably celestial aura. But Arnold Wyburd's vision was a blur: he could have been partially blinded by the vitriol she had flung at him over a lifetime.

He looked round quickly, either to produce that twinge from above his right buttock, or persuade himself he could see clearly, or accuse some of those who were absent. In any case, he frowned, and through his frown noticed Sister de Santis arriving late, dressed in what he thought he recognized as her usual navy coat, and in addition a shocking hat: nothing less than a Caliph's turban in orange silk.

De Santis took a seat in the back row on the aisle. She must have had an uninterrupted view of the coffin. But she was not looking at it, or at anything, as far as you could tell from her eyelids. The great onion of a hat would have disguised nothing if her face had not been closed. He admired her prudence in matters other than the hat. He must offer her a lift back. They would talk about Mrs Hunter, which in itself would be consoling, because a return to habit, and Sister de Santis might mention, he did not know what, nothing he had ever expected of any human being, certainly not his good Lal, not even the late Elizabeth Hunter; he was positively trembling for the arcane wisdom Sister Mary de Santis might reveal on opening the locked cupboard of her face after the funeral.

Arnold Wyburd was suddenly so ashamed he wrenched himself round to face the parson, the coffin, the pleated curtains still intact before the fiery furnace. What would have been a reckless action at the best of times, now produced an authentic twinge all the way down his right side. (Lal would be upset; he would keep it from her; though his behaviour must give him away in the end.)

The service was as short and decontaminated as a busy day at the crematorium demands. There were no spectacular outbreaks of grief, only the hint of a soggy patch here and there in the broken rows. Elizabeth Hunter's own sense of style would not have encouraged emotional excess.

Then, as they waited for the mechanism to release the coffin, there was the sound of tin buckling, clattering, and a rain of lozenges on the tiles. At once the glaring varnished box came to life: it began to jerk, to stagger down the ramp towards the parted curtains. The least military of men, the solicitor decided to square his shoulders: it might be what those behind expected of him. Nobody would see that he was not watching. Hearing was what he could not avoid: above his deafness and the bumping of his heart in his creaking body, he was forced to hear; in fact he ended by listening to it.

When he looked again the curtains had closed; he might have experienced anti-climax if it had not been for recalling the clause in what must be something like her eleventh will: '... that my solicitor and friend Arnold Wyburd take my ashes on a day when it is convenient and scatter them over the lake in the park opposite the house where I have lived ...' In the circumstances he was glad the twinge came in his side without assistance.

And again in the open, he was all spontaneous twinge, exchanging condolences with other controlled faces, some of which he could not identify; while those who had done their duty by the dead strolled amongst the wreaths, to look for the inscriptions on the cards attached, and perhaps discover somebody had been as stingy or as tasteless as one would have imagined.

Arnold Wyburd tried to think what it was he had to remember: oh, yes! to offer Sister de Santis a lift. He looked round for the Caliph's hat, and searched along a couple of the paths which led away from the holocaust between memorial plaques and the unnaturally perfect shrubs. In no direction was there any sign of an orange beacon, and he felt relieved at last. Would they have found enough to say to each other on the long drive back? and how would he have explained to Lal why he had chosen to give a lift to Sister de Santis of all people?

He told his wife on his return, 'You did well not to come.'

'You know I would have if you had wanted. But you gave me no indication.' She added, '*She* mightn't have wanted it.'

He noticed Lal was wearing a chain Mrs Hunter had given him for her. Her neck looked red and shrivelled, its freckles fretted by the turquoise clusters dividing the ceremonial chain.

'Was it a success?' Immediately she blushed for what must seem a gaffe. 'Well, you know how furious she got if any of her entertainments fell flat. I can't think how she would feel if she knew her funeral had been a failure.'

The pain in Arnold Wyburd's thigh became so inescapably violent she must have seen it reflected in his face.

'Oh, darling, what is it?'

'Nothing,' he said. 'A touch of my sciatica.'

'Ohhh!' she moaned.

He rather enjoyed her sympathy.

'Why don't I slip round to the chemist for a plaster?' She did so hope to be allowed.

'It's nothing,' he grimaced.

He was not a masochist, but wanted to bear this superficial pain without Lal's well-intentioned interference. At the same time he gave her a wry smile in appreciation of her sympathy, while tapping on her hand in the code they had used over practically half a century to communicate their love.

Out of prudence, Mrs Wyburd waited till his second helping of salmon loaf before inquiring, 'Was there anybody I know?'

'Nurses. Cleaners. Otherwise, the kind of face one half knows: the reason why one has never joined a club.' Arnold continued masticating his salmon.

Lal drank a draught of water. 'The children?'

Arnold began shaking his head, swallowing; he looked quite ratty. 'I told you. Or didn't I? Dorothy developed a migraine.' As he returned them to the plate the knife and fork escaped from his fingers and landed loudly in the pink slush and two or three white vertebrae.

Lal rounded her eyes and breathed under pressure for a treachery she would have expected.

'Basil was coming,' he was forced to tell, because his wife would surely prise it out, 'but didn't show up. I don't doubt they'll put in an appearance at the office—as agreed—to investigate the will.'

In fact the Princesse de Lascabanes appeared before the solicitor had touched his earlier than usual tea.

'You can't begin to imagine the effect these headaches have on me, but I assure you, to experience one of them is—*ghastly*!'

Suffering, whether of a particular or a general kind, had enlarged her eyes and filled them almost to the brim. Dorothy Hunter was a handsomer woman than Arnold Wyburd remembered.

The princess could see this, and she saddened her smile accordingly. She had forgotten how easy success feels. She knew already from her dressing-table glass that she looked appealing:

exhaustion had combined with relief to make her so. She was always at her most effective in garments which had reached the stage where the shabby has not too obviously taken over from the sumptuous, like her old Persian lamb, in the sable collar of which she had pinned a brooch: an enormous blister pearl in its targe of diamonds, one of the few fruits of her unfortunate marriage. Now if she was exhausted by the discomforts, not to say the shocks, of 'Kudjeri', she was sustained by knowing that Mother had chosen for herself the only reasonable way out of their impasse, and that the years of her own genteel and, yes, gallant poverty, were thereby ended. (No doubt there were lots of malevolent little souls who had seen the past situation in a different light, and who would begrudge her the ease she was about to enjoy. The attitude of the professional poor to the privations of the theoretically rich had always incensed Dorothy de Lascabanes; it was so *wrong*: a brooch, for instance, is more often than not the symbol of a substance which barely exists.)

The princess roused herself to pay attention to this decent old man conscientiously telling her about the weather while secretly admiring her looks. She must compose some specially amiable remark as a reward for a creature so simple he would never guess at the actual reason for her absence from Mother's funeral.

So she picked at the leather arm of the chair, tilting her cheek against her sable collar, and told him, 'You, of course, are the one I feel for. Anyone of a sensibility such as yours must have suffered most cruelly. I'm thankful you had my brother with you—to take some of the strain—on the day. As for Basil—a funeral is a gift to any actor.'

Arnold Wyburd decided not to reveal that her brother had let them down: she might have profited by it too inordinately.

While Dorothy wondered whether she would have squeezed Mr Wyburd's hand if she had been closer to it. As it was, the distance between them would have made such a gesture look theatrical, or even athletic. In any case, she had no desire. It was strange how Mother's death seemed to have cut most of her desires: before any, her hankering after a father. She was again appalled, very briefly, by that dream in which the solicitor had trailed his silky testicles across her thighs.

She glanced at her watch and said, 'I expect my brother will be late as usual;' and laughed for a remark which did not require it.

It immediately brought Sir Basil Hunter.

He was looking puffy, she thought, under a little tweed hat cocked forward over one eye. Either he was an actor playing a vulgar part, or else a vulgarity in himself had come to the surface since she saw him last.

In spite of the flash hat and an expression of glittering biliousness Basil had evidently decided to play it sober. 'Morning, Dorothy—Wyburd.' He sat down on the nearest uncomfortable chair, arranging his fists knuckle to knuckle against his chest as though one were to believe he didn't know what to do with them.

Thus disposed he looked from one to the other of his companions before delivering his line, 'There are heights of grief to which weaker mortals fail to attain.'

Dorothy was instinctively impressed by what she suspected of being Shakespeare, then irritated by Basil's pretentiousness.

But Wyburd murmured, 'Quite,' smiled in a sort of way, and looked down at the papers on his desk.

Basil accepted the solicitor's forgiveness as sentiment due to him; but could he be sure of Dorothy's charity as well? She gave no sign; she refused to look at him, as though she would trust the floor rather than an affectionate reality they had discovered in their relationship.

'As we know,' the solicitor was saying, 'there is the question of Mrs Hunter's will.'

Dorothy looked pained. She could tell from the angle at which Basil was holding his head that he must have plumped for wistfulness. 'Yes,' he said rather breathily, 'the will.'

She remembered the sound of eyelashes opening and closing. Or can you hear them? Isn't it, rather, the touch?

Since leaving 'Kudjeri' there were certain thoughts she had

succeeded in driving out of her mind. She could not afford to let such thoughts return.

Madame de Lascabanes opened her bag. She took out her handkerchief. She held it firmly against her lips.

Determined to prevent an outbreak of grief in his office, the solicitor hurried on. 'Of course we're all acquainted with the terms of your *father*'s will: the estate to his widow for life, to be divided equally between his children on her death.'

Basil at least was genuinely moved; it was the word 'children', applicable even at the end of the piece. He shivered slightly.

Dorothy had recovered her balance: money has great stabilizing powers. She was only surprised—she always had been—at Father's decision to divide his fortune 'equally'. As a woman she might have expected to be badly done by.

'So,' the solicitor continued, 'you will now receive your equal portions. It is more specifically your mother's will we have to consider. I think you'll find it straightforward enough;' he distributed copies to the children. 'But then Mrs Hunter was straightforward in almost everything she did.'

Somebody laughed.

'Don't you agree, Dorothy?'

'Oh, I suppose so—up to a point.' She buttoned her mouth and closed her eyes on anything beyond that point.

Arnold Wyburd blushed. 'At least I hope you'll find her will straightforward. Apart from one or two minor legacies, again it's the equal division of a fortune between yourselves.'

Basil and Dorothy looked appropriately grave.

'There are the bequests to servants, some of them now dead—and this gift,' he coughed, 'the sum of five thousand dollars to my wife—surprisingly—movingly—generous.'

Basil said, 'I'm only too happy Mother should have appreciated Mrs Wyburd. As I remember, she was an exceptionally likeable character.' He was so relieved at his own good fortune he could forgive Mrs Wyburd her five thousand; though admittedly, it came as a surprise.

Dorothy summoned nostalgia in a vision of freckles and the scent of summer. 'Charming—motherly. I always loved her.' She was fairly pleased with her own magnanimity.

'Where I fear Mrs Hunter erred is in failing to recognize what she owed to her latter-day dependents. I suggested more than once that she remember her nurses and her housekeeper Mrs Lippmann in her will, but by then she was so old, she couldn't believe she was destructible. I didn't continue bothering her because I thought it a matter we could easily settle, between ourselves, after her death.'

'By all means a little something to the nurses,' Sir Basil Hunter agreed. 'Isn't it one of the conventions?'

Dorothy settled for a long slow stare which she aimed at the toe of one of her shoes: some decisions she preferred to leave to the men, or anyway, till she saw them led astray by innocence or ignorance.

'How much would you suggest, Arnold?' Basil might have been projecting his voice into the darkness of the stalls, asking advice of a director during rehearsal; he was not afraid of, he respected, his leading lady, except when objective judgment was called for.

Arnold Wyburd screwed up his face till it disappeared. 'I believe Sisters de Santis, Badgery, and Manhood would consider five hundred an acceptable token,' he said when he opened out again.

'Five hundred each? Fair enough!' Sir Basil looked quite jaunty, and without assistance from a tweed hat.

Dorothy's dreamy smile was not for Basil. Then she tossed her head and coughed to let the solicitor know she accepted.

'And the housekeeper Mrs Lippmann?'

'Good God, yes!' Sir Basil was amazed they had forgotten the little Jewess.

'Five hundred?' Mr Wyburd asked. 'Your mother thought a lot of Mrs Lippmann, though she wouldn't always let her see it.'

'An excellent cook,' Sir Basil remembered, 'if you like that Central European stuff.'

Both the men were looking at the Princesse de Lascabanes, who at last produced a smile to go with her postponed reply. 'I expect Frau Lippmann has her virtues.'

'Five hundred, then?'

'Oh, I am not *mean!*' the princess radiantly protested.

'I should also like to submit,' the solicitor looked down as though addressing his signet ring, 'to—to *suggest*—a small gratuity for the cleaning lady—Mrs Cush.'

'Five hundred for Mrs Cush!' Sir Basil clapped his hands: boredom was fast consuming his store of prudence.

'The cleaning woman?' The princess raised a startled head. 'The one who was brought by *hire-car*—from *Red*-fern?'

'Mrs Cush does live in Redfern,' the solicitor confirmed, 'with an epileptic husband.'

'And varicose veins.' The princess sank her chin. 'We must all three of us resist becoming sentimental about epilepsy and varicose veins. I fail to see why the cleaner—a most inefficient one, my eyes immediately told me—should receive more than a hundred.'

The silence might have shamed Dorothy Hunter if it had not been for the Princesse de Lascabanes: only a woman of rational mind can save men from their impulses.

'If that is what you sincerely feel,' Mr Wyburd murmured.

'Why drag in sincerity? A sense of reality is what is called for!' The princess spoke so vehemently she had to hang on to the handbag sitting on her lap.

'One hundred for the cleaner,' Basil breathed; it was a matter of little importance, and his coming over could help shorten the session.

Dorothy was appeased, while making it clear that paltry concessions would not seduce her into relaxing her moral vigilance.

'Finally,' the solicitor said; but did he mean it? 'there is the question of Mrs Hunter's belongings—her furniture—her house.'

Basil hooted; Dorothy sighed.

'If there's nothing you want to keep,' the solicitor gravely advised, 'better dispose of everything by auction. Naturally there will be—

articles of sentimental value – the jewels, for instance,' he turned to Dorothy.

'Are there any jewels left?' Madame de Lascabanes broodily exploded. 'After the nurses have taken their pick?'

'And the electrician, and the man who mends the refrigerator?' The Hunter children were united in a good laugh.

Till suddenly glancing at this old man Dorothy realized how often she had been hurt by life. 'Perhaps I'll keep the jewels.' She relented with a cultivated sulkiness to show she was not too eager: in any case, Mother's jewels were bizarre rather than beautiful.

Mr Wyburd bowed his head. 'That leaves the house.'

'Oh, auction. Auction, Dorothy?'

She would have preferred not to agree with her brother, but submitted because it was practical. She opened her bag. The disagreeable stresses of the morning had left her with a touch of heartburn.

'One more point,' the solicitor offered.

Oh Lord! Sir Basil had risen: he was dusting imaginary crumbs off his flies.

'While the estate is being wound up, we can't run the risk of thieves and vandals at Moreton Drive. I have sounded out Sister de Santis and Mrs Lippmann, and gather they might be prepared to stay on, as caretakers, out of affection for Mrs Hunter.'

It was an arrangement neither of the Hunter children saw any reason for objecting to; though the caretakers would probably eat their heads off, Basil foresaw. Dorothy observed that, on the contrary, women in their position become depressed and develop frugal habits.

'I'm sorry if it's been in some ways a painful discussion.' While apologizing to his clients, it was the solicitor rather, who was looking ravaged.

Dorothy smiled at him. 'It's over,' she said softly; she could afford to be soft, at least in her attitude to someone who in no way threatened her equanimity. 'Or it is for me. You are the one who will have to endure the auction.'

'You're not planning to leave us, are you?'

'I have my reservation. I'm taking off tomorrow night for Paris.'

Basil forced her to look at him at last: he was making such ugly, unorthodox sounds. 'Isn't that a pretty swift one? Dirty—anyway, crafty. But typical.' The face which had appeared puffy on arrival was drained of a complacency probably induced by alcohol: the leaner, lined Basil was standing on the brink of something; or was it nothing?

'Is there any reason for staying?' She hurried on in case he should produce one. 'In this country to which I don't belong, and where I shouldn't choose to live longer than is absolutely necessary.'

'You're right. It's time. I only thought we might have slunk off more cosily together.'

'I can't remember our depending on each other—to any extent—at any point.'

She looked away on making her thrust; she could not see whether she had drawn blood, but was conscious of a wound opening in herself.

Arnold Wyburd took them to the lift. Very properly, the solicitor volunteered to drive the princess to catch her plane the following evening. She was inclined to think his presence, so unemotional and banal, might soothe her airport nerves. The lift arrived, and soon after, was sinking with the Hunter children in it. Their fellow passengers huddled together to give them room. Unaccountably, a frightened look had settled on the anonymous faces.

It was Dorothy who was frightened: what if she couldn't shake Basil off? If he trailed her from one hemisphere to another like some filthy dream she wanted to forget? They were stalking along this street together, in step, and silent. Equal in height, their eyes were at the same level when Basil closed in on her, forcing their progress to a standstill.

'Your strength, Dorothy, is probably your greatest weakness.'

Her strength? Her swaying, timorous, ugly, helpless self! (If only the towers would crash, grind you into the gritty pavement, Basil too, with his cocky hat, parted lips, that split in the cushion of the lower one—buried beneath steel and concrete; but together.)

'This is where I turn off.' The voice of Madame de Lascabanes described its arc as gracefully as casually.

He switched on his professional charmer's smile. 'Faithful to Air France, I expect?'

'Need you ask? I join them at Bangkok.'

Their laughter almost visibly splintered around them along with the other directionless refractions of a busy street.

Then Dorothy swooped down on the bundle of snakes he imagined he had seen writhing inside her. Not 'imagined'. They were there. He knew. Hadn't he unknotted and charmed them? He could feel them slithering still against his skin.

But Dorothy had ducked into the street she had chosen for her exit.

Sir Basil Hunter cocked his hat farther forward. (Never, in any circumstances, let plate glass windows fool you into taking a look.) He squelched on: it was his arches, his age. He would order a double Scotch, or two—or a whole bottle as on the day of the funeral. The *funeral*. (Remember you have inherited a fortune, and can buy yourself back into life, into art, into the affections of—almost—anybody.)

A revolving door propelled Sir Basil into the next scene. Un-usually dim lighting or the unexpected laughter of several couples seated in black glass alcoves upset his timing: he stood too long mumbling his smile; when a partition of the door still in motion whammed against an ear and sent his hat spinning. The alcoves showered laughter on this unknown comic (or did they recognize the leading man wrongly cast?). At least a waiter ran forward to present the actor with a hat which might have looked a mistake in whatever circumstances.

Sir Basil strolled to the bar. He ordered a double Scotch. And a double Scotch. He had his ghosts to lay. (VOICE FROM LIMBO: Don't look. The other one at the bar lifting her elbow so en-thusiastically is Shiela Sturges the actress. She's Basil Hunter's wife. They say he drove her to it.)

*

586

At Bangkok Madame de Lascabanes re-entered her world.

'*Vous désirez, madame?*'

'*Rien, merci.*' It was actually true.

The Air France hostess had inquired so impersonally that some (Australians for example, with their manic insistence on 'warmth') might have judged her contemptuous. Exchanging the ritual sliver of a smile, the princess and the air hostess knew better.

Then Dorothy de Lascabanes sank back and closed her eyes. For the first time in weeks, months, perhaps in a whole lifetime, she had achieved a state where nobody could force her to behave as a character of their own conceiving, quite unlike the one she recognized as hers. She even thought she might have reached that point of impersonality she had liked to believe attainable: protected against disorder, directed towards a logical destination, saved from desire (oh God yes—beyond reach of importunate bodies, clutching hands).

She whimpered once or twice with relief, and rubbed her head against the antimacassar before remembering her coiffure. At once she started rearranging herself more practically. It composed her mind as well, to sit obliquely, calves pressed against the case in which she carried her jewels.

When she had laid hands on those inherited from Mother, she must see about having them re-set; though it was doubtful whether many of them would be wearable. She would keep them as sentimental tokens: because the worst mothers in the flesh do not necessarily destroy the touching concept of motherhood. (What sort of mother would you have made if fate had dispensed a child? Madame de Lascabanes was thankful her new impersonality would not be required to work out an answer to that one.)

How she would occupy herself in her state of spiritual (and economic) emancipation was more to the point. For a start, she thought, she would go through her cupboards and drawers, but ruthlessly. She would make inventories. She would restock only with the very best quality, *necessary* clothes, preferably in black; though she looked well in green: *amande ou tilleul, plutôt qu'un vert*

587

trop criard. And shoes: she might indulge, not in an orgy, but give way to her weakness for what can be an elegant means of disguising the ugliest member. She saw her shoes, of the style she had always worn, and which outlast ephemeral trends in fashion, tilted in methodical rows on the brass rails at the bottom of her *armoires.* Before any, she cherished a shoe in matured leather, of a patina she had created herself by long and devoted polishing.

Dorothy de Lascabanes was filled with such an exaltation she glanced round to see whether anyone else had noticed. But the light dictated by those stern angels watching over their welfare had forced her fellow passengers into varying stages of dormancy. In the seat next to her, a Pakistani was turning yellow. The princess edged closer to the aisle.

And books. In the library more than anywhere an inventory is essential: that volume of Pascal the Cousine Marie-Ange, *personne d'autre,* had carried off, more for the binding, one suspected, than the argument. The princess nursed her reverence for the French classics and the years of pleasure she promised herself in their company. (Weed out the books: Bourget, Bataille — all one's mistakes; Maurois? *on attend.*)

And men. Because all that was finished, it did not mean that some elderly, distinguished connoisseur might not occasionally offer to share the subtleties: of Stendhal, Odilon Redon, *poularde demi-deuil,* a bottle of Chassagne-Montrachet *en tête à tête.*

In reassessing worldly pleasures, it occurred to the princess she might also change her spiritual preceptor. She visualized an un-known hand, sensitive though masculine, writing on the fresh white sheet it was in her power to become. Enraptured by her own pious ambitions, she flung back her head regardless of the grubby antimaccassar. *Aidez-moi, mon Dieu,* she insisted, *je recommence ma vie.* Then in the name of prudence, *Sainte Marie, mère de Dieu, priez pour nous pauvres pécheurs, maintenant et à l'heure de notre mort.*

For the plane had started to shudder and roll. From inside the rug with which he had shrouded his head, the Pakistani moaned. Rejecting as far as possible this evidence of human frailty, Dorothy regretted her Dutchman who had experienced the eye of the storm, as he insufficiently told during her flight to Mother's bedside.

The weather which had just struck them hardly amounted to a storm, little more than a disagreeably personal nudge. Supposing the hostile forces rubbing against these fragile walls ordained disaster, death would be the least part of it. What she dreaded was the moment when the soul tears free, no bland Catholic balloon automatically patted on its way, but a kind of shrivelled leather satchel, as she saw her original Protestant soul, stuffed with doubts, self-esteem, bloodymindedness, which Catholic hands, however skilled, might not have succeeded in detaching from her.

If her Dutchman had been seated beside her instead of this bilious black, she felt sure she would have found the courage to clutch his knee, and demand the impartial view of one who has passed through the eye of the storm. If it does not remain in the eye of the beholder.

And Mother: what could Mother have told of her experience on Brumby Island? She was senile by the time you might have asked. But could anything of a transcendental nature have illuminated a mind so sensual, mendacious, materialistic, superficial as Elizabeth Hunter's? (Poor Mummy! it is wicked to malign the dead: *Sainte Marie, mère de Dieu, priez pour nous pauvres pécheurs, maintenant et à l'heure de notre mort. Amen.*)

It is to some extent calmer the nameless street you are walking down these are yours the hopefully lustrous shoes the new Balenciaga habit this the church you have been searching for bundles of pale-green spaghetti as columns dark water in the leaden stoup never touch the syphilitic water sign yourself with air my knees are old and cold offering 15-deniers in the name of faith how frightfully hard religion is on stockings the priest the surely no this Protestant expression which refuses to distinguish sheep from goats these Dutch-coloured fingers offering not the nice hygienic wafer but a chalice of *qu'est-ce que vous me faites mon père* spilling the stain will never come out rubbing spreading the unspeakable oh OH

Head lolling, the Princesse de Lascabanes mingled her moans with those of the Pakistani.

rub and run escape the Dutch anathema can't you see *c'est moi
mon père* MOI God will understand I am real my soul is no Catholic
balloon Protestant satchel I am this flying shoebox the prayers
rattling inside *grâce à Dieu on atterrira à Orly à 07h 05*

Sir Basil Hunter refused his plastic dinner; if they had offered him a
real one he might not have had the appetite for it. Instead, he told
the hostess, he would like a second little bottle of Scotch: he held
his fingers just so far apart to make it look tinier.

She was a sonsy piece: if it had been the sort of thing you were
looking for. He wasn't. No return flight had ever caught him
feeling older: just the part for which the lavatory mirror had
cast him.

Could it be that when Mummy dies, the age hidden in her little
boy floats to the surface? Balls of course. He was all whimsy
tonight: the Scotch was bringing it out. And in any case he had
never really cared for — well, he had been fond of her, on and off —
as a safe exercise, from another hemisphere. She had been *there*:
always as an abstraction, sometimes as a positive enjoiner.

Or flesh: at a distance she was still visible, palpable, out of respect
for sensuality perhaps, or the acting profession, hesitating, it seemed
deliberately, at the head of the stairs (all beautiful women stage-
manage their entrances, either intuitively, or more likely after endless rehearsal on feeling the first tremors of power in their green
girlhood) then this woman is descending, not yet revealing her full
radiance, keeping it veiled in false modesty, at least as far as the tip
of her nose, because her lips are already faintly faintly smiling to
herself as she glances at her feet (that shortsightedness which is neither
confessed nor denied) till about the fourth stair the light breaks from
inside around her, it is the moment you never catch in a flower however determined you are to witness the miracle of exploding petals,
that is exactly what happens as this being descends, in a burst of
sensuous joy she needs to share with those standing in comparative
darkness below, controlling their breath, their blood, their amateurish
attitudes. while her sun beats down on them, the rustle of her skirt,

her fall of jewels promises relief from their drought of waiting, from their *yes Mrs Hunter no Mrs Hunter how well you're looking* at their last gasp they are not relieved they are made drunk.

Her smile is a perfume. *Basil! Aren't you in bed?* This is my 'mother'.

Sir Basil Hunter looked at his fellow passengers, to dare them. Nobody had noticed; nor that the face he had brought back with him from the lavatory mirror was in a sweat: this slightly rotten fruit — her son.

He would perhaps feel better if he loosened his tie and unbuttoned his collar. It might be less painful in the end if one never allowed oneself to forget that flesh and tuberoses are only a disguise: death is the reality. Or that old doll leering up, out of a lot of greasy lipstick and a purple wig. *Why have you kept me waiting darling?* On the contrary, everything hurtles at you with diabolical speed.

That letter from Mitty Jacka (*don't bother forwarding mail to Gogong; this is to be a complete rest*) he found waiting at the Onslow after returning from their weeks of exploration ha-ha! at 'Kudjeri'. He still took out the Jacka's letter, misshapen from pockets and soggy with sweat, to re-read bits of it, often aloud,

'... since then, Basil Hunter, never a word. Your feet haven't gone cold, have they? ... my total involvement with your interests ... my ideas crystallizing ... had hoped for yours. Isn't it to be a marriage of ideas? Not only ours, but finally, that of an entire audience. This is what theatre is about!' (Surely, Mitty: not only in the gang bangs of now, but away back at the moralities.) 'My antennae tell me that what I have longed for — for you — which is *us* — has actually happened, and that you will soon be sending me details which will make our plan viable. I have warmed up Aaronson; more, he is downright hot. Says we can have the Slaughterhouse. At his price, I need not tell you ... most anxious, as you can imagine, to hear ... No room left, unless for me to quote Aaronson: *It will be the finest thing for living theatre if a man of Sir Basil's calibre can face the public with his very own version of the naked truth ...* ' (Oh yeah? Show them your cock and balls no matter what the cock-and-bull.)

Sir Basil Hunter laughed; it sounded fatty, he thought. But what the hell! He had the money, and money cannot let you down.

He ordered himself another teenzy bottle of Scotch, and sat waiting, hands plaited over his paunch (always lose it before the production, just as you can throw off the grog if you have the willpower).

Oh he would confound them all, the Jackas and Aaronsons, along with the legions of contemptuous youth, by having another go at Lear, and fully clothed. Before it had completely left him, he would dredge up enough of that sensibility which sees, and smells, and knows by instinct. There is a moment, he liked to think, when you can look back and catch the light off the vanishing dew, before the soul has been irrevocably seared. Was that a bit too much? But he had suffered, hadn't he? his poor forked animal; not least at the hands of his old dying mother and his sister Dorothy Cahoots. And could now look forward to the years of his maturity.

He tried himself out sotto voce in this unappreciative aeroplane, projecting his voice forward into the cavern of his mouth, rolling the words around to extract the utmost in timbre. The results pleased him. Yes, he had matured.

What the smell it is a sealed attic the russet scent of leftover apples the live ones rolling bumping if you touch them off the shelf the rotten splurge brown obscene making a graveyard of the boards *these apples are Mummy's darling I've put them here for a purpose* what purpose you don't ask because half the time a person doesn't know *my fruit my darling you have your play haven't you I shouldn't dream of interfering with the play* like hell she will save it up she will drag out her voice it had got buried under the wrinkles the sheets *what is its title* in turn her little boy doesn't want to tell least of all his mum it is I think because this is a collaboration with everyone including what are called my privates my or 'our' *Year by Year with Lear* by

Bas Hunter Mitty Jacka Sol P. Aaronson and A. Perv Audience the old is only laughing she is holding something in reserve under her lilac wig it is your call to get into the drag the wig the crown they have made it of Plasticine not to be conformist and Plasticine will suffer more on the road to Dover the ugly daughters can dong it better Histryl and Moan *we have engaged Enid and Shiela to give it greater significance* hope you know best Mitty I am the actor king who can't be bothered except with the psyche before the performance limber it up to expose on that tree with only a fool audience to grovel for the bits which fall putrescent lucky for theatre I'm not the soundest fish last call Sir Basil wet the whistle twice for luck and a third before you go on you may never taste another time Sir Bazill that would be Enid she was all *ills* and *isses* and a sharp elbow recognize it anywhere Sir Basil's entrance only project project whoever said *attend the lords of France and Burgundy Gloster meantime we shall express our darker purpose* COURTIERS laugh the bang-on boys without their jockstraps the jiggle-joggle Bangkok mares everybody's in the cast a real benefit performance knock you down too soon if they don't take care Gloster's a baby that's how they want it today renewed fanfares of juvenile laughter with a pizzicato on the testicles shake all you maracas audience laughs THIRD ATTENDANT hits herself in the eye with an independent nork it isn't any laughing matter then DOROTHY CORNWALL *aren't I the legitimate sister?* JACKA cracks her whip *yes yes everybody's in it and everyone is everyone that is the absurd point doesn't life outpanto panto* but DOROTHY insists *this is my real panto-brother-sister* oh shit my beard is full of birds the audience is loving it the young trolls are lining up together with their liquescent warlocks to build this tunnel thing bet it wasn't improvised ENTER A BEARDLESS KING in real crown (stuff the panto) in lilac wig in ghastly gash BODIES make stairs for REAL KING to descend begad it's Esmé Berenger or Judith Somesuch come to bury a leading man little Shiely Albanesi moans there's too much earth on her hands too many sister-daughters but don't you see this is total knockabout LILAC KING opens her legs go on Bas on all fours natch it's the womb stint you've got to expect in living theatre well it happens doesn't it they pull you through beneath the lilac pubics ATTENDANTS writhing and lithing some of them jolly appetizing fruit if you had the time if somebody's heel hadn't put out your eye if you hadn't choked on somebody's parts at least you are born at last MITTY blacktights JACKA *He is born our King of Kings* (crack) forward Basssll *well folks here I am this is my real role your fool* (jingle bells little soft shoe here) the audience is loving it as for the OLD KING she yawns she is above it she wants to get out from under and into her coffin SISTER-DAUGHTERS simmer as FOOL hogs the scene their bearded king of a crypto brother *how now where's that mongrel?* anyone Dorothy is at liberty at a pinch to pinch a line she takes a fancy to and FOOL has all the plums *I'll go to bed at noonlight with my sister* Dorothy will kill you for this to say nothing of Enid Histryl Shiely Moan and all the others only Cordelia the almoner the one who matters who might care is absent she always was whoever played the part ought to cut it Mitty

oh the intervals of time the oiled oceans patent leather jungles glass mountains white airports streamlined nembutal the audience is coming back too soon as always the sweat doesn't dry discovering motives don't you realize he is as he is because he's arterio-sclerotic I've worked it out everybody is clever today

CURTAIN UP or would be if there was

so why not cut Cordelia Mitty yes we'll cut her at future performances LILAC KING (yawning smiling) *all these daughters bore the pants their lives are one long menopause it's my fool-son I'll choose to lie with in my coffin* as if DOROTHY CORNWALL will allow *I am the one must kill our fool-brother-son-king* silence in the total audience then FOOL *oh Dorothy yours is the kindness which exchanges cap for crown and incidentally pray you undo this button* a great roaring of participation DOROTHY CORNWALL *oh oh buttons are obscene* (silence ALL as she uproots penis) PLASTICINE KING *then I am free if only you take my tongue too and perhaps uvula for good measure no more an actor* AUDIENCE surges down aisles meeting WHOLE CAST halfway to become involved with one another when finished return C. to stamp KING into coffin.

The LILAC OTHER has evaporated in the sun which burns too bright.

'Sir Basil Hunter!'

'Yairs. *Yes?*'

'We're landing in fifteen minutes.'

'For God's sake, where?'

'Amsterdam.' Like all air hostesses she is smiling for an invalid, in this case, an unsavoury old man.

'Well, wasn't it a short hop!' Still the FOOL.

He must tie his tie, button his collar. If he hadn't more than undone it: he had torn the damn button off.

Compose a wire then, to the Jacka, if he could get his tongue round the significant word. (FOOL: You can't throw a stroke at my age, can you? FOOL'S RATIONAL SISTER: Don't be silly! Young children are known to have had them.)

If dreams were reality you mightn't have done a murder, slept with your sister, or contemplated what amounts to professional suicide. (MITTY JACKA: You ought to realize by now — if you are in any way creative — that the creative act remains the great suicide risk.)

The dreams oh the wet between the legs.

Persuade this vivandière to remember charity and bring out another little bottle of Scotch.

Arnold Wyburd almost never left his office later than five-thirty p.m. Unless the traffic was exceptionally hostile to the Wyburd schedule he could expect to open his front door at six o'clock. After hanging his bound Homburg on the topheavy mahogany stand he would check his time with the grandfather clock at the end of the hall. The grandfather, Bill Hunter's carriage clock at the office, and his own gold repeater with blue-enamelled figures and hands, were synchronized. It gave him a sense of security, not only to keep in step with time, but to keep time in step. Tonight he saw on consulting with the grandfather that somebody was five minutes out.

He had developed the habit of making a slight pfiffing noise when faced with irritations or shortcomings. He made it now.

Lal called from the living-room, 'Is that you, Arnold?' as she always did, and it was never anybody else.

She had on her glasses. They looked too big and heavy for her face. The girls brought the children's socks for her to mend, and she was peering at a sock she was darning.

'You'll ruin your eyesight,' he warned, though both had realized long ago it was impossible to improve each other.

He switched the light on. She was vain about her darning: doesn't it remind you of *petit point*? she liked to ask and offer it as proof. Now the light showed she was smiling at the darning egg.

He bent and kissed her on the bony structure of the forehead, avoiding the finely quilted cheek; to kiss her on the cheek at that hour would have been going too far.

'I think I shall retire,' he told her.

'Oh dear, have you a cold?'

'No. From the office.'

She did not answer. She sighed. She had heard it before.

He poured himself his evening whiskey, rather more than usual, and swamped it in case Lal should notice. Not that she would have disapproved: he was his own sternest judge, and this was a day when recurring thoughts made him the object of his deepest disapproval. To make matters worse, he could tell from her frown and the pleating of her lips, above and below, Lal would have liked to comfort him.

'On Thursday next,' he informed her, 'the auctioneers will take care of the furniture at Moreton Drive. The house itself can be offered for sale.'

'Is it so long?' Long or short, Mrs Wyburd could not have reckoned; she only knew their life was no longer disrupted by commands and tempests. ('She did bully you, you've got to admit!' she had once dared remark, and as soon wished she had not.)

The solicitor went upstairs to what they called his study. At least he kept some of his law books there, and on a Sunday afternoon, would sit down to answer any letters his wife could not be expected to tackle. Otherwise the room was not much used, though he liked to shut himself up in it briefly on returning from the office: so as not to be disturbed, was the explanation he might have given if he had been asked for one; there was a clock too, which required his attention.

Tonight after checking the clock against his gold repeater Arnold Wyburd went to the bookcase and took out Halsbury Vol XV. His bearing was so stiff (he could almost hear his bones cracking) his manner so deliberate, anybody watching might have suspected a long contemplated, dishonest move.

It was, in fact, dishonest: one of his two memorable dishonesties.

When he had found what he wanted by exploring the space behind the books, he sat awhile at his desk, beside the lamp with the green porcelain shade inherited from a great-uncle on his mother's side. He did not feel less guilty, but more resigned to dishonesty, when at last he began to chafe, to revive, the jewel he was holding in his hand.

Finally he looked at his sapphire. He invoked the star hidden in it.

He fitted the live sapphire on to the little finger of his left hand, above the flat blue, formal signet he had worn since his twenty-first. The sapphire glowed painfully.

His eyes, normally pale and reserved, snapped and glittered. Caged in the ribs from which he had only once escaped, his breathing had become a torment: more so, the eye of the sapphire, with its bars, or cross, of recurring light.

He could hardly bear to look at it. He closed his eyes, preferring to experience through memory the invitation to drunkenness the nipples tasting unexpectedly of rubber the drops of moisture as flesh was translated into light air nothing all. Perhaps this was what others know as 'poetry' and which, he would have had to confess, he was unable to recognize on the page.

He was shocked to hear footsteps on the stairs. He dropped the ring, which rolled where? under the desk? some-where.

'Arnold?'

His dear wife; temporarily blinded, he would not be able to face her.

'You're not brooding?' she asked.

'*Yes!*'

She withdrew as though she had been burnt.

When he had got on his knees and found it, he returned the sapphire to the bookcase, ramming Halsbury Vol XV into the void where his jewel would continue smouldering.

Sister Badgery had come, and Mrs Lippmann was giving them lunch in the breakfast room.

Badgery said, when she could get a word past her chicken, 'Quite like old times, isn't it? Except for Her.' She swallowed. 'And Flora Manhood.'

For some reason the others were unwilling to chat. 'What's become of little Flora?' It would have been unnatural not to inquire.

Sister de Santis professed ignorance. Mrs Lippmann made no attempt to answer; she had never looked so livery: some Jewesses are near as anything black.

Sister Badgery said, 'Perhaps she's decided he's Mr Right after all. Well, good luck to her!' She sighed, laughed, and popped another forkful of chicken into her mouth, all at the same time. (She would pay for it: creamy foreign sauce, smelling, she would not have admitted to her thought, of some women's stale underwear.)

'Will you attend the auction?' Sister Badgery asked; they were so down in the mouth she only wanted to cheer them up.

Neither Sister de Santis nor Mrs Lippmann could whip up enthusiasm for auctions.

Sister Badgery might look in. 'Buy myself a keepsake. If everything isn't beyond my means — as it well might be.' She showed her gums, and a morsel of chicken fell back on her plate. 'Perhaps find a present to take my friend Sister Huxtable.'

'Sister Who?' Mrs Lippmann asked.

'Winifred Huxtable of Auckland, New Zealand. Don't you remember — she and I — went with a group — year before last — to Lord Howe Island?'

Her audience seemed peculiarly apathetic. Sister Badgery tilted her

598

head, dropped one shoulder, and began mopping up her sauce with a gobbet of bread. They would both know she knew what you don't do; but weren't we among friends?

'Surely *you* must remember, Sister?' A corner of Sister Badgery's mouth failed to contain a drop of that grey, stale-smelling sauce. 'Win Huxtable – a large girl with a flushed complexion. Well, she's a woman now. And more flushed, if anything. Didn't we all do obstets together?'

Sister de Santis had to confess she couldn't remember doing obstets with the flushed Winifred Huxtable.

'There are those who *say* – malicious people,' Sister Badgery crooked a finger to flick a speck of sauce off her front, 'and a great many people are malicious, aren't they? they say that Win Huxtable in her middle age is red as a beetroot. If she is, nothing can be done about it. I know. She and I never refer to her affliction. Those same malicious, hurtful people imply it's caused by alcohol. It isn't. I could assure them. Not that Win doesn't enjoy her brandy dry – socially. She never goes too far, though.'

Sister Badgery might have enjoyed another mopping of sauce if Mrs Lippmann had not begun clearing the plates; there was nothing you could do about that either, short of forgetting yourself.

'Sister Huxtable and I have planned a coach tour of New Zealand – both islands,' she informed them after controlling her wind: that sauce again.

Sister de Santis held up her throat and smiled encouragingly at the wall.

Mary de Santis is putting on weight. 'It's thanks to Mrs Hunter – her gift,' Sister Badgery said rather loudly. 'The five hundred dollars.' She crooked her finger above the still unused pudding spoon. 'Do you – I ask you in confidence, Sister – do you think it all above board? I would have expected more of Mrs Hunter, such a generous woman – and lovely lady. What I mean to say is, she mightn't have had her own way. Others may have dictated, so to speak.'

Sister de Santis might have been listening; she might not.

'Don't think I'm not grateful,' Sister Badgery insisted. 'It's thanks to Mrs Hunter that I'm doing this little tour of New Zealand with Win Huxtable. Only if the legacy had been slightly larger — Win has had quite a windfall — we might have got as far as Japan.'

The silence was awful in the breakfast room where they still had to finish what Mrs Hunter had always, and now Sister Badgery herself, referred to as 'luncheon'.

Sister Badgery suddenly snorted down her nose. 'It looks as if I have a lust for travel!' The confession made her giggle. 'You will understand that, Mrs Lippmann.' She turned to the housekeeper who had brought this 'tort'.

'Oh, I have travelled. But have no lust.'

The Germans are a heavy lot.

As the housekeeper dished up the pudding, Sister Badgery noticed a bandage.

'Damaged yourself, have you, dear?'

'It is nothing. I have cut my finger. It is my new little vegetable knife, which is sharper than I have thought.'

Sister Badgery sucked her teeth. 'There's nothing like a superficial cut for incapacitating a person.' She had done her duty, and might be allowed to return to graver issues. 'This will,' she said, 'if you won't think I'm harping on it. Mr Wyburd, though a good soul, was always too soft. Sir Basil Hunter is the perfect gentleman — you can tell. I know nothing about actors, but can recognize a gentleman.' Something forced Sister Badgery to pause. 'It's Princess Dorothy — I feel — would not be above manipulating.'

Sister de Santis looked down at her plate; Mrs Lippmann was too far off: perhaps on her travels.

'And the sapphire. Did they ever find it?'

'Not as far as I know,' Sister de Santis replied. 'It may come to light when the furniture is gone and the carpets have been taken up.'

'It may. But I think I know it won't.'

'Possibly.'

'I have my — *intuitions*.' Sister Badgery was proud of that. 'In fact, if I wasn't a nurse — but I wouldn't give up nursing, not for worlds — I often think I might offer my services to the police. I am always right.' Laughter exposed almost the whole of the pale gums before the mouth closed abruptly; she might have overdone it, owning to psychic powers in front of a colleague.

'Will you take a little trip yourself, Sister?'

'Oh, no! I couldn't! After sitting here all these months.' Thought of her recent inactivity seemed to agitate Sister de Santis; she shifted heavily in her chair.

Though she wasn't one to criticize, Sister Badgery had always considered de Santis rather on the stout side. At the same time she had admired her colleague for a certain stateliness of manner. Today and out of uniform, she had shed the stateliness. Tactful is tactful, but in the course of luncheon, de Santis had not expressed a single opinion, not even with her face. You could not say she looked unhappy, not like the Jewess. Sister de Santis was more sort of calm: she had the smooth, washed look of some of the more simple-minded nuns.

Sister de Santis raised her voice; the tablecloth in front of her subsided. 'As a matter of fact I've accepted a case. I'm expected tomorrow. It was the obvious thing—since the auctioneers are taking over.'

'We have our professional duty of course.' Sister Badgery was very firm on that score. 'Is it a difficult case, Sister?'

'A young girl paralysed in both legs.'

Sister Badgery shook her head, sympathy straying between her vision of this young girl and the slice of *Torte* the housekeeper had put before her. 'Win Huxtable had a private case—a boy in an iron lung; it got her down in the end.' By which time Sister Badgery considered she might decently help herself to cream.

'Cream, Mrs Lippmann? I must say the tort looks scrumptious. Your puddings were always lovely.'

Neither Mrs Lippmann nor Sister de Santis was prepared to touch the *Torte*.

Sister de Santis might have removed herself already. Though she was faintly smiling, the smile was an impersonal one, stranded on her lips as she withdrew behind her eyes, amongst her thoughts.

She was, in fact, again seated at the bedside of this young girl, where she had been ushered and left.

'What is your name?' she heard herself asking to break the silence.

'Irene.'

'You're lucky to have such a beautiful name.'

'Is it?'

'To me it is.'

'I loathe it!'

Although it was around eleven o'clock Irene was lying stretched on her bed pricking a card with a pin. Her rather lifeless hair was laid along the sides of her cheeks and over her shoulders almost as far as the small, but aggressively mature breasts. The long gown, printed with a yellowish green design, must have been carefully arranged in those folds where the skirt covered the legs: the folds were too formal, like stone. Sister de Santis was reminded of a figure she had seen on a tomb.

The girl continued pricking at the card.

'Wouldn't you be better sitting in your chair?' the nurse asked.

'Oh, I'll sit in my chair! I'll sit in my chair all right! Today and tomorrow. And tomorrow.' She drove the pin savagely into the card.

'Do you enjoy reading?'

The girl shook off the whole idea. 'I watch the box – if ever there's anything of interest.'

'What interests you most?'

The girl dropped the card. 'I like to watch brutes exerting themselves. Specially killing one another.' She laughed to herself, then looked sideways at this stodgy nurse. 'Do you think you'll like me?'

'Perhaps I shall if I get to know you as you really are.'

'Oh, I'm worse – worse than you could possibly imagine!' A convulsion of the hand on the long green skirt dragged at it and rucked it above the little-girl's feet and useless legs.

The nurse got up to arrange the skirt in its original folds. The girl's hostility appeared to have increased now that the stranger was introduced to the unmentionable.

Sister de Santis noticed a bowl of anemones standing on the sill of a bow window. The garden beyond was a labyrinth, not without glimmers of fruitfulness.

'Did these anemones come from your garden?' she asked for the sake of saying something.

'I don't know. Yes, I suppose they did.' The girl seemed unwilling to consider anything beyond the fringe of her inturned thoughts.

'My last case loved flowers. She was blind, but she enjoyed their scent, and she liked to touch them. Roses were her particular flower. I used to cut the roses early in the morning and stand them in her room with the dew still on them.'

You could almost hear the girl listening: her eyelashes. 'Sick people must be disgusting,' she said. 'To have to handle them! I'd always rather be surrounded by beautiful, perfect people. Even if they're cold and cruel. I don't want anyone I have to pity. To offer pity – that's the most disgusting act of all.'

'Mrs Hunter wasn't sick,' Sister de Santis said. 'She was old. She had been a great beauty in her day – a success. She was also cold and cruel when it suited her to be.'

'Was she happy?' Irene asked.

'Not altogether. She was human. In the end I feel age forced her to realize she had experienced more than she thought she had at the time.'

Using her elbows and ugly handfuls of the bed, Irene was raising herself higher on the pillows; she had developed unusual power in her arms and shoulders, the nurse noticed, and decided not to help.

'That's all very well, but what shall *I* experience?' the girl asked.

'I'd say you have the will – haven't you? to find out.'

She didn't reply. She had resumed her original occupation of pricking a card with a pin.

'What's this?' Sister de Santis asked. 'Are you making a pattern?'

'A pattern? NOTHING.' Suddenly Irene leaned over and stabbed the outstretched hand with the pin.

When she had recovered from the pain and her surprise, Sister de Santis – they were both staring at the bead of blood which had risen to the surface of the skin.

The nurse asked, 'Why did you do that, Irene?'

The girl's lips, her eyelids, had thickened. 'You won't come,' she mumbled.

'If you want me I shall.'

The girl had slipped back to a lower position on the bed. The nurse was again reminded of the figure on the tomb, except that blotches had appeared on the cheeks, their human ugliness emphasized, if not illuminated, by tears which had oozed from under struggling lids.

When it seemed that Irene would not commit herself further, Sister de Santis left.

The mother was waiting to waylay the nurse. 'Now you know what to expect,' Mrs Fletcher began in a high voice which the tiled hall made sound more chittery. 'I didn't want to come in with you because Irene holds me responsible for everything she considers bad.' The mother's wrinkled prettiness tried to turn the situation into an amusing one; if her daughter had not been her cross, the pursuit of pleasure might have taken its place.

'I shall come on Thursday,' Sister de Santis told her, 'if that is convenient.'

'Thank God!' Mrs Fletcher used the term with professional ease, and such vehemence that a scent of gin hovered around them as they stood discussing hours and the inevitable money.

'I could live in if you wanted,' Sister de Santis thought.

'If you haven't a life of your own!' Mrs Fletcher jittered worse than ever with gratitude and amusement; then she said, 'It wouldn't be fair if I didn't warn you she literally tortured the last nurse into leaving. She is so warped, she is only convinced by what is evil.' The mother laughed.

The nurse repeated they could expect her on the Thursday.

Now as she watched Sister Badgery devouring the *Torte*, Mary de Santis wondered how she would have answered Mrs Fletcher if pressed to explain what constituted her own life. Memory of her parents had faded since Mrs Hunter's death: if they recurred in physical form they had the wooden faces of the figures in time-darkened icons. Her own clothes were a habit. She sat with books

more often than she read them. (Dante had died with the forgotten
cadences of her father's voice.) And desire. Incredulously she watched
Sir Basil Hunter's silken ankle as his foot beat time to boredom in the
garden of the Onslow Hotel. Of all her personal life it was perhaps
physical desire which had died the most painful, because the most
shamefully grotesque, death. Would she have admitted wearing that
hat to the funeral if she had been accounting for herself to her future
employer? Her betrayal of Mrs Hunter that second time was only
outdone by Sir Basil's absence.

Sister Badgery had spooned up the last of the lovely cream, the last
fleck of apricot.

Sister de Santis had thrown that orange hat away. She could have
confessed truthfully to Irene's mother that she was entirely free.

'What is the name of this family?' For Sister Badgery names were
of considerable importance.

'Fletcher.'

'Which ones, I wonder?'

Sister de Santis did not know.

'Well, there's the flour Fletchers. Isn't there jewellers too? Cheap
jewellers, but the cheap ones often come off best. I expect you've
fallen on your feet, Sister.'

Now that she had eaten her meal, Sister Badgery had to go: to a
former patient become a friend. 'Say goodbye to Mrs Lippmann,
dear. I can see it's one of her moody days.'

The day itself was moody. Sister Badgery was thankful she had
brought her brolly. Already as she opened it, big cold drops were
falling out of purple clouds.

'Oops!' she called as she went clicketing down the path. 'Shall I
make it?'

She would not have stayed on though, not for anything, in that
ownerless house. Spooky too. She thought of the cosy chats she would
have with her friend Win Huxtable inside the coach as the New
Zealand scenery went whizzing past: scenery, like silence, depressed
Sister Badgery.

Sister de Santis lingered a moment on the path to watch the

lightning: the enormous drops of cold rain flattened themselves on her face as though it were their chosen target; the white lightning was directed at her, though without malevolence.

About five, when the storm had cleared, Mrs Lippmann made them a cup of coffee. After watching Sister Badgery eat a meal in the middle of the day, the two women could not have raised an appetite between them.

Sitting quietly sipping their coffee in the kitchen, the nurse was humiliated to realize that, in her state of excited anticipation, and in spite of the affection she felt for the housekeeper, she had forgotten to ask Mrs Lippmann's plans for tomorrow.

'What do you think you will do?' Sister de Santis asked with what she hoped would convey intensified interest and rekindled warmth.

'I shall be with friends,' Mrs Lippmann answered in her normal, grave, low voice; then raised it to the raucous pitch she had used in her performances for Mrs Hunter, 'or,' she grimaced, 'I may take my things to Central Railway waiting room, to sit a while, and assemble my thoughts.' As she closed one eye, the other glittered with irony.

They laughed together, and Sister de Santis caught a glimpse of the top hat, the wilted bow, and the little cane with dented knob quivering under Lotte Lippmann's armpit.

Presently the nurse left to start her packing. The housekeeper, though she had finished hers, went to the room in which her belongings had always only waited to be packed: it had served, in fact, as the barest waiting-room. Except that on the dressing-table, propped against the glass, on the lace runner which might have been worked by one of Mrs Hunter's dead maids, the lovers continued holding each other in front of the empty bandstand, in spite of the faded sepia, and fingerprints eating into them.

When she had undressed, Mrs Lippmann went in to take her bath. The heater, with its permanent smell of gas and flames roaring inside the copper cylinder, had terrified her in the beginning, but she had grown used to all such minor effects. Outside the window of the maids' bathroom the sky was more convincingly on fire, the blaze smudged by fingers of smoke from the chimneys of Alexandria and Waterloo. It was suffocating in the narrow room, but it did not occur to her to open the window.

Lying in the steaming bath, Mrs Lippmann watched the hair, more like ferns or the roots of water-plants, floating around the shoulders, straggling towards the breasts of this still curiously solid body. Then she reached up and felt along the ledge behind her head for her most practical, recently purchased vegetable knife. The pulses in her wrists were winking at her: all this time her fate had been knotted in her wrists. She cut each knot of veins with care.

Closing her eyes she floated with the dead maids, the entwined lovers. Or if she cared to look, she was faced with a flush of roses, of increasing crimson. Opening and closing her eyelids growing drier brittler. Her eyes afloat, so it seemed. If she smiled, or sank, she would drink the roses she was offering to those others pressed always more suffocatingly close around her.

After a long attempt at sleeping, Sister de Santis realized she would not succeed. She got up. Her veins, her heart, were throbbing with life as she went from room to room throwing open the windows. Furniture groaned and cracked; some of it seemed preparing to topple. At moments she became aware of her own creaking, her thumping clumsiness, and went more softly so as not to disturb the housekeeper.

The light in Mrs Hunter's room was at this hour neither moon nor day. Here and there stood the empty vases: columns of crystal and trumpets of silver. The great empty bed fluctuated like a sheet of dreaming water. What she knew to be a silver sun let into the rose-wood bedhead had more the appearance of a stationary crab suspicious of an intrusion on its shallows.

Mooning around a room shortly to be emptied of its associations and emotions along with the furniture, Sister de Santis wondered how she would convey to this entombed girl, her future patient, the beauty she herself had witnessed, and love as she had come to understand it. She felt herself again the bungling novice. Perhaps she was ageing. But she continued throbbing, flickering, inside her clumsy flesh.

Seeing the dark was beginning to thin, she went down presently.

She put a coat over her nightdress. She took the rusted can which she kept filled with seed. In the garden the first birds were still only audible shadows, herself an ambulant tree.

The hem of her nightdress soon became saturated, heavy as her own flesh, as she filled the birds' dishes. Reaching up, her arms were rounded by increasing light.

In the street an early worker stared as he passed, but looked away on recognizing a ceremony.

A solitary rose, tight crimson, emerged in the lower garden; it would probably open later in the day.

Light was strewing the park as she performed her rites. Birds followed her, battering the air, settling on the grass whenever her hand, trembling in the last instant, spilt an excess of seed.

Her throat swelled as the light climbed, as she trudged back, trailing her sodden nightdress along the path where 'at least two people have broken their legs'. The little scoop clattered against the rusty can.

At the topmost step it occurred to her that she must take this first and last rose to her patient Irene Fletcher. She would return and cut it before leaving: perfect as it should become by then.

She poured the remainder of the seed into the dish on the upper terrace. The birds already clutching the terracotta rim, scattered as she blundered amongst them, then wheeled back, clashing, curving, descending and ascending, shaking the tassels of light or seed suspended from the dish. She could feel claws snatching for a hold in her hair.

She ducked, to escape from this prism of dew and light, this tumult of wings and her own unmanageable joy. Once she raised an arm to brush aside a blue wedge of pigeon's feathers. The light she could not ward off: it was by now too solid, too possessive; herself possessed.

Shortly after she went inside the house. In the hall she bowed her head, amazed and not a little frightened by what she saw in Elizabeth Hunter's looking glass.